RADICAL LOVE

RADICAL LOVE

FANNY HOWE

Nightboat Books
New York

Printed in the United States

The five novels in *Radical Love* were previously published as *Nod*
(Sun and Moon Press, 1998), *The Deep North* (Sun and Moon Press,
1990), *Famous Questions* (Ballantine, 1989), *Saving History* (Sun and
Moon Press, 1993), and *Indivisible* (Semiotexte/MIT Press, Native
Agents Series, 2000).

The author offers thanks to her friends at UCSD;
to Robert Grenier; to Glenstal Abbey;
and to the John Simon Guggenheim Foundation.

ISBN: 978-0-97671-853-6

Typset in Caslon
Text and cover design by
Brian Hochberger

Cover photograph of Fanny Howe by George Hamilton Montgomery.
Used with permission.

Cataloging-in-Publication Data is available from the
Library of Congress

Nightboat Books
New York

CONTENTS

AUTHOR'S NOTE

The novels were written between 1985 and 2000, four of them when I lived in Southern California. They are together in this volume because they cover the span of my own generation. I was born in America at the start of the Second World War. I lived in a politically conscious household in Massachusetts, my mother was a theater person and writer from Ireland and we visited her family there beginning in 1947.

These stories take place by and large in Boston, Ireland and California, all places I know well. While each one is a coherent whole, the five are interlinked by their time in history and by the presence of children and the effort to hold childhood high. Each page can be in most cases glanced over as if it were a prose poem, a complete unit.

I hope this collection will contribute to a literary tradition that resists distinctions between poetry and fiction as one way to save history from the doom of duality; and accordingly I want to thank the editors who

have encouraged me to pursue this hope by publishing the books—
Douglas Messerli, Robert Wyatt, Chris Kraus and now Kazim Ali and
the editors of Nightboat.

Fanny Howe
2006

RADICAL
LOVE

Nod

Between a children's progress from a heavenly world to a world that is a likeness of heaven and then to a world which is delivered and upheld by a dream of heaven, there is only the world.

It's like the slope she can finally see when she closes her eyes and the leaves on a wet seaside pavement. Behind these and to the right, the pink stone house. And sometimes it comes as a pattern of weather or a bitter smell whisking through a berried hedge or gas spilled on a sidewalk.

In a dream she might see a girl or woman moving around some empty rooms realizing that this is no longer where she lives because she herself made the choice to leave. But the vision is still elusive and she can catch hold of nothing hard and believe in it.

Nod

She thinks that even then she guessed that people lived two lives. One was physical, frantic, random or lost. The other was airy, transparent, hopeful. But she couldn't put the two together, not when she was young. Now this is the task. To melt the edges between the two lives. To return to that problem and turn it into a progress—that is, the story of a story—the not-quite, the almost, the allegory of a maybe, the too-late, don't know, the no-more.

But even as she sits here contemplating the memories, and some of the facts, it is actually the words that are writing the story, so that a sequence of signals rises up from the paper to meet her mind, just as buildings at the end of a park come forward to welcome the approaching pedestrian. And once again she is only being given what she is also making.

She is coming to meet herself who has no sure knowledge of who she is or was.

x

This is in fact a spirit-story like many stories people have heard before. And it begins with one poor woman who had a daughter named Irene (after the mother's Greek grandmother). The child was willful and focused. Her father was as gentle with her as her mother was doting.
The three were at ease together because the young husband was at work, in a lab, until all hours every day, and the woman also worked, but at night, teaching other women to sing at the Conservatory of Music. So when the two met, they were interested in what the other had been doing, and when the daughter was asleep, they joined each other in the dark as hot-blooded friends.

Their existence was—in those first years—like bands of sound moving in clusters—or wave packlets—across a uniform or neutral spectrum. The time might for each have been hummed like a piano string stretched taut inside wood casing. They were in harmony, bound and determined. Yet the laws of objects are mysterious and not the same as common sense or natural reasoning. Things that work in accord often move imperceptibly towards failure. And the husband said: "No matter how intently a human mind studies a phenomenon, it will elude cognition."

His wife was a woman for whom one man was not enough. In those same congenial years she managed to have a prolonged, if sporadic, affair with a translator from Norway, whose subject was Icelandic poetry. This lover was like a smooth journey down a perilous hill of ice. Choice made him nervous and he felt guilty about sleeping with a married woman even as he was exploring her. They met in her studio on a small street in the village for several months of extended and voracious sex.

Paradoxically this affair made the mother turn her full attention on her husband and child. It was as if a problem in her nature had been solved by rushing between two men. She was not a beautiful woman—in fact she despised her own face for its pale and weak mold—long front teeth resting on a red lower lip, a soft underchin, a singer's soft bosom. However she made other people feel safe in her presence because she was so confident in her judgments.

During this time she began treating Irene as a small muse because she showed signs of radiant beauty and a love of song. She began to teach the tiny child to breathe and project her nursery rhymes. Robert Louis Stevenson was her favorite.

All by myself I have to go, | With none to tell me what to do. | All alone beside the streams | And up the mountain-side of dreams.

And for that season the mother and father came together in bed for several weeks running, each one stinging throughout their limbs and groins with a just-tolerable lust. The Norwegian lover generated more desire than ever in the woman and she fell on her husband as if he were an exotic treat. At night the little girl heard the howls of her mother's yearnings—not quite operatic sobs—echo down the thin hall of their brick flat—while the father pounded and groaned.

In the morning the mother explained that she had been having nightmares and told the poor child to calm down, she had nothing to fear, and then she smiled in a lopsided way at the father who stood at once with his face to the sink or left the room.

The strangest things are there for me, | Both things to eat and things to see, | And many frightening sights abroad | Till morning in the land of Nod.

Meanwhile the father thought his wife was seeing through him. The fact is, he had for many years been subject to depression and his only way of surmounting this was to seduce with intense, focused stares, certain women whom he then agonizingly embraced, pawing at their inner thighs and breasts, begging them to massage his sex, and then withdrawing before penetration or coitus. This activity turned him into a walking sorrow and only the sanctuary of his wife's body allowed him to let loose his seed and his grief. She gave him the consolation he had to have in order to surmount what he called "Doubting-Castle, the owner whereof is Giant Despair."

So while he secretly conjured up these wanting women, the mother never stopped thinking of her Norwegian lover—even after he had returned home to marry a woman of his own—and she imagined her husband as a swim in a glacial lake that turns into a steamy vent only when she paddled into the right area.

(She was at the same time beginning a career as a performer whose singing and talking in unpredictable surges had put her in major roles in avant garde opera.)

Under the influence of a socialist realist musical she got pregnant again for a second time and gave birth to a second daughter, one who was weak at birth and whom she kept alive only by hating her. The irreversibility of the infant's presence was awful to the mother. An unwanted and unending interruption of her career and her sexual hopes. She rarely touched her. The female child seemed to reek of her sex's pathetic weakness to such an extent that the mother paradoxically transmitted to the dying baby a sense of its own unrelenting power. It survived alone in a crib—a doll bathed in the salt of her own tears. And the little girl was named Cloda after the father's Irish grandmother Clodagh.

x

The mother for the first four years of Cloda's life either neglected or tortured her. At first she justified it by saying that the child was stupid, impossible to train, and then she said the child, like a dog, responded best to the sound of anger and the feel of pain. Finally the little punishments ran on their own steam, habits that had staked a claim in the mother's spirit. No one (but Irene) noticed the way her nails dug into Cloda's wrist on the street, or the way she twisted at her neck in stores, or the many times she hissed, I'll kill you, into her ear when Cloda whined or expressed a desire. This child brought out a fury the mother never knew she possessed, made her skin flush and twinkle, made her eyes misty gray, made the streets sway under her and turned her sadistic. Sometimes she even ran her hand hard over the little girl's organs when she was bathing her, and pushed the soap up too high inside her.
When Cloda cried in public places, people around murmured, "Brat!" and pitied the mother who looked so harassed and uncomfortable. Only Irene witnessed the sharp kick or twisted wrist and at first she protested and protected her sister, but then she retreated and kept her distance from the two of them. Sometimes she did the same as her mother and tormented her little sister. But more often she vowed to kill them both some day for being so loud, unruly, and embarrassing.

The mother could be seen walking swiftly along the pavement, head erect, a nobility in her attention to dress and make-up, while the small child dragged back from her clutch sobbing and saying I hate you!

And passersby would hope that the child was punished severely as soon as she got home.

And she was. She might be locked in a bathroom with the light off, or shaken by the shoulders over the toilet bowl until she threw up. Sometimes her mother scraped her bare bottom with the bristles of a hairbrush and threatened to make her eat her own feces, and once she tied her to a bed post with a belt, stark naked, and left her there screaming for three hours. The mother never slapped her face or spanked her in a normal, rushed way. Her punishments were oddly inventive, and produced a look of moist delirium on her face, as if she were alone with a pornographic study. But then her fury ebbed and was replaced by contrition and Cloda was sent to her room with cookies and milk before the father had returned from work.

By the time Cloda was old enough to choose her own clothes in the morning, dress herself, and generally care for her own needs, the mother had found ways to convert her rage into a passionate attention to her own career.

And at the same time the mother and father discovered that they had one thing in common besides their children and that was the quest for a perfect place to live. Both launched into the tribulations of travel and uprootedness with the belief of pilgrims en route to the Holy Land. Sooner or later they believed that they would find a house with a year-long garden, a distant view, a respectfully reserved community, a mild four-season year, a lively city nearby and someone to rent the place whenever they wanted to leave again. The children, subjects of these pilgrims, were dragged along and forced into new schools almost annually.

The family traveled while the father changed the course of his career and wrote biographies of scientists for a living. Many essentially moneyless families travel, even if only from house to house in the same neighborhood.

Nod

This family—with just enough earned by the father to get by—and by the mother—and with all of them at night playing musical beds—moved from London to Ireland, all over Ireland, back to London, then to Amsterdam, Venice, and Ireland again. They were neo-nomads.

x

Cloda would have the same appearance at thirty-nine as she had at nine. An exceptionally smooth and rosy complexion, full red lips with a sensuous twist in the smile buried there, blue up-from-under eyes fringed by long black lashes and very thick black eyebrows and a loose mop of black curls that fell over almost every feature, a husky difficult voice that emerged rarely, head tipped down and to the left as if a dog had trained her how to listen, a body neither thick nor thin but athletic, and a generally disheveled under-dressed style. She laughed more than most people, and often for no reason that anyone else could understand, with her right hand covering her mouth. She conveyed a love of secrets as well as a wild side that became the political version of her sister's personal lack of self-control. Later she would tell herself:

I hardly remember the time we spent in Ireland. I don't remember how our mother treated me. I don't remember having a dog. I don't remember a house by the sea. I don't remember anything much at all about that time.

Try as I like to find the way, | I never can get back by day, | Nor can remember plain and clear | The curious music that I hear.

For years, instead of trying to remember or re-imagine that time, she tried to discover what time is. Unable, as a child, to make much sense of mathematics, she was often wrong about everything involving calculation. Therefore she became obsessed with measurements. And would think: "If time is the rate at which one object changes in relation to another object, then the space between them is also consequential in relation to

7

these objects, but this must mean that space has to have another relation-ship to an emptiness beyond numbers, a negative first, outside time."

Or she went over the words of Saint Augustine: "If we conceive of some point of time which cannot be divided even into the minutest parts of moments, that is the only point that can be called present; and that point flees at such lightning speed from being future to being past, that it has no extent of duration at all. For if it were so extended, it would be divis-ible into past and future; the present has no length."

It was years later, when she went mad, that she circled certain buildings in bare feet in order to test the issue of time.

Her feet grew so blue and wrinkled they looked like prunes, but she continued to thank God for her blisters and her sores.

Her doctor could not change her attitude which he termed "masochis-tic." Nor could he change her mind about the subject of past and pres-ent, which she insisted were twin illusions.

She said that all spirits were equal because they dwelled in the same moment. Then she became convinced that she was the Virgin Mother, Queen Maeve and Clodagh all at the same time. Readers today, steeped in Freud, will insist that it was her unconscious talking. But her refer-ences were so outmoded, they seemed to pre-date the interior terrain of both Freud and his readers. Outside, America was reconstituting itself: corporations, computers, electric cars, airports, and traffic like sheep of steel following the proverbial sleeper's accounting.

Even her doctor began to use terms like "totemism" and "projection," surprising himself, because he treated her as pre-logical in order to communicate with her at all. Sometimes she said she had "immaterial bones" but that they were protected by God, and that's why they didn't shatter when she kneeled at the communion rail. Her accounts held his gaze fixed on her lips. She would never change a lick of her story, though she could see that he was lip-reading rather than really listening. Usually the moral of her story was that "being lost" was a desirable condition.

She seemed to know everything about fairy tales, pagan Europe and witches burned at the stake, but there was no trace of a hallucinogen or any other experience with drugs in her blood or in her conversation.

Really mad people like her are not content to narrate their experiences, they have to act them out. But she told stories before she went out walking.

In one of her psychotic fantasies she said Mary and Joseph came floating to her on a cardboard cut-out of Bethlehem painted with twinkling stars and snowdrops. Mary was sucking her thumb and Joseph carried her down the hills in his arms. A little donkey brayed like a barn door and now there was an image of cornucopia covered with mathematical symbols. She said the Jesus baby took her own nipple into his mouth then, and with her face buried in her red hood, she nursed him.

"When I am nursing, my organs contract as if they were playing Bach, and I am seized by pleasure that causes me to squeeze myself into a vanishing point."
The doctor noticed that flies buzzed away from her and landed on other patients instead, when she was in this particular psychosis. She gagged on warm milk. In the 15th century she would be burned at the stake. Witches used to hold fire in their two hands and showed a wonderful ease with animals. Depending on history's mood, dogs or wolves were the animals portrayed in their heroism. But her particular form of psychosis was modest. And she seemed uninterested in pain therapy.

"Priests would never approve of you," he told her, "so why do you stick with Catholicism?" Even if all religious ethics were extinguished, my own belief would continue, she replied. Once he massaged her feet which were sore from all her walking, and for this time he thought perhaps she did love to suffer. But when she groaned with pleasure at the touch of his fingers, he felt wheels rolling up his vertebrae like a dozen tiny bicycles.

The doctor began to believe that her interest in religious studies—old fashioned as they were—was her only hope of a cure (and this was one doctor who actually wanted to cure his patients and send them on their way.) So he began to share reading with her—from Joan of Arc to Celtic mythology. And finally he entered the world of mystical writing and read about the practice of "samadhi" where an Indian guru presses his penis against his patient's genitals, but never penetrates her, while she soars into ecstasy and the doctor asked if she wanted him to try that method of therapy, since she liked ecstasy so much. She only replied with the comment: "You have the wrong word for that state of mind."

She was incarcerated with a mob of fatigued women, who lounged around all day. The doctor called them his "pajama girls." They annoyed him profoundly and he assigned a new doctor, whenever possible, to cope with their exhaustion. But he didn't want any other doctor to deal with her, and so next he put her in solitary often where she could lie flat on her back and tell him stories. Sometimes it seemed as if she were the parent and he the child, despite their physical positions. He listened, nodding, swallowing yawns, but with an expression of weak pleasure on his face.

One day she begged to tell him the rest of the story of The Fairy Year, as she called it, though he could see that it produced a fever of anxiety in her. In the past she had said she wasn't sure who told it first—her sister or herself—but that he would recognize the characters—and now she was ready to be the one to tell it. A few false starts—

"I'm telling you this because . . . The Danes occupied the east coast of Ireland for 300 years. But they left no trace of Odin or the Frost Giants. What is true will always be true. And superstitions will always belong to their particular land. Draw a red thread tight across the door to prevent a fairy from coming in to get me tonight. By the way, the children of fairies and mortal women are very musical, but have horrible tempers. They are usually beautiful . . . They emigrated from Iran to Erin on foot. Get it? Iran to Erin? That's why they retain Persian influences in their dances and songs. Did you know that? And while they are generally jolly, they can turn dangerous in a flash—murder even, and kidnap—and they believe in the sacrifice of human girls for the preservation of their race. They're not alone in that . . . As I walked through the wilderness of this world," she continued softly and then when she saw the doctor twist on his pillow, afraid she was boring him, she hurriedly began the story that she titled "The Fairy Year."

X

It was after many years of traveling that the nomadic family settled in Dublin. That is, when Cloda was thirteen they arrived in a house with a ponderous crash of boxes and bags, as if this was it, they were here to stay. The parents remembered Dublin as a place that almost approximated their dream situation. It was close enough to the continent for the father to continue his research on—now—the military, minerals and oil; and for the mother to perform when called upon.
So they lived a little south of Dublin close to the icy Irish sea and mounds of sloppy rocks. A stone house—two blocks away from Sandymount Green and right near the sea.

Black-haired and boyish Cloda learned how to skip stones fifteen times on the surface of the water, while inside Irene sang with her face lifted like a looking-glass to the ceiling. When people saw Irene they were grateful to the biological world for its busywork. And everyone, even her sister, wanted to reward her for being such a pleasure to see.

Cloda rode her fat-wheeled bike up and down the winding streets, and never played competitive games because she was a sore loser. Or she sat outside in the garden trying to make birds land on her outstretched hands; they never did. Many evergreens had been planted in their Irish garden, and red roses that didn't smell crawled against the stone walls. Cloda wrote a poem: *Rose, red rose clinging to the old stone wall mankind also clings to what little he knows.*

This was the first poem written in their household, and in her excitement over its existence, she kept saying, I don't know where it came from! I don't know how I did it! The father criticized the last line. The mother asked which Chinese poet she stole it from. And Irene, who was under great pressure over an assignment, begged to bring it to school, under her own name, for a contest, which she then won. After this, Cloda's voice changed. It was strange. Like a pubescent boy, her voice cracked when she spoke more than ten words in a line. She developed an annoying habit of clearing her throat at the end of every sentence. Or else she chose silence.

The father, who had begun to drink a good deal in the evenings, noticed her silence and told her this story seated by her bed, his chest steaming asthmatically as he seethed out his words:

"St. Columcille—dove of the church—learned poetry from Gemman, the Bard of Leinster. He went on to found the first monastery in Derry, performed many miracles, had the gift of prophecy, and was particularly appalled by the competitive nature of poets. They were revered and supported by the rich, but if someone failed to treat them with sufficient generosity, they composed mean verses about that person and other poets. They were so egocentric and vicious, the craft was actually abolished for a time. St. Columcille intervened unfortunately. Poets can be pretty awful. Artists in general are sons of bitches."

He lay back against the wall with his wine tipped against his chin and raked his memory for another story.

"I may be of German extraction, my dear," he said, "but my grand-mother for whom you are named was the one from whom I got my brains. Those 'sauer Krauts' have brains too, but not the speedy and poetic Irish kind. I think you may have inherited that kind. Ah, the gaps in time, and the way one generation leaps sideways into another! . . . I'm a failure, a mediocre scholar, as you by now must have figured out, but my brains are—if I do say so myself—the intuitive and imaginative sort that don't give out easily.

"Guess what? I have a wonderful story for you. In 1882 a British steam-ship came across a floating mass of seaweed and gurry as dense as a float-ing island south of the Azores, and when the sailors climbed on top of it to look, they found spears, bows, and other weapons encrusted with periwinkle, scallop, barnacles, and other mollusks, like pebbly filth in the strings of a mop. It was a land-mass tossed up from the ocean floor—after a storm—a puckered tapestry—part of Atlantis perhaps—an earth-work. So the things of the world do not get passed by time, but continue to develop, once invented . . . Bored?"

She shook her black hair, her head turned towards her chest, and now, emanating disappointment, he rose from her bed, then paused at the door. Both of them listened to the mother singing her scales down the hall. It was a typical evening in their house. He would roam around for another hour cross-examining the girls, quizzing them about their homework in history, geography, science, and shouting "You aren't even wrong!"—his greatest expression of outrage—when one of them made a mistake. His words slurred, his eyes reddened and watered, before he slumped off to bed. However, each night he made it patently clear that he was most fond of Cloda who read dog and horse stories and hated facts; it took the form of tender verbal condescension.

"My dear Clod," he might say, "you are excessively identified with animals."

And he was deeply irritated by the excesses and vanity of Irene. He referred, frequently, to a night in Holland, when she was ten, when, for the first time, he let her look through his microscope. As soon as she saw the cells moving on an otherwise still wing of a dry bee, she became obsessed with the microscope, and began putting everything she could find—crumbs, spit, paper—onto the glass plate to examine it. And then she smashed the whole operation when he tried to drag her away without touching her skin. Screaming, stamping, clawing, she even bit him, as he pulled her by the neck of her sweater back into her room.

The way he referred to this night was with this dour statement: "The first truly human utterance is the Cartesian insistence on the ego cogito."

Each night before bed he called Cloda to him, and asked her to unbuckle his briefcase for him and remove his papers and sort them out on his desk. "For work in the morning." The smell inside his briefcase she associated with power, it was almost as strong as the smell of newly poured tar. The smell covered her flesh. The father never touched either of his daughters—not since they were toddlers—but jumped away from them as if their auras were flames.

Sometimes he told Cloda to push her hair back from her brow, begging her to show more of her face and insisting that she was very pretty. But it was like a dare she couldn't take. Other dares she was famous for: jumping off of rooftops and high branches, making her bicycle leap through the air, lying on the center line while cars drove by, picking the pockets of people on buses. But she did not have the courage to show her face.

The poor father was a gourmand, it was the last active remnant of his time in a lab. He even, each October, made jams in huge pots and the windows of whatever house they were in steamed (with strawberries, raspberries, tomatoes, plums, apricots) pastel winnowings up from the boil. Not only did the steam from the pots heal his asthmatic attacks, it also excited him, the gooey dyes filled him with desire for his wife and other women, when he canned the jams by hand and cooled them on shelves all over the house to the joy of his youngest daughter. He also collected bottles of all shapes and sizes and placed the special ones in sunny parts of the house, where they stood proud-shouldered like glass soldiers.

That year in Ireland, Irene—until now protective of her sister in their first-day-at-school situations—showed she was bored by her task, and abandoned the younger one to her fate, while pretending at home that she had not. Cloda didn't dare expose the lie, and so she found herself protecting her sister who had not protected her, and feeling contemptuous of all teachers and parents who believed that she was telling the truth whenever she lied. It wasn't long before she felt most at home with the worst-behaved children in school.

Cloda had always played outdoors every day in every city until the darkness had firmly settled over the trees and rooftops. Irene, meantime, stayed inside studying or practicing her voice. Despite the division of activities they enjoyed, however, there was an area between them that was shared. Paradoxically this shared area was non-existent. A gap that defied description, because it had MINE written in one place and YOURS in the same place. So the site was a demonstration of a physical problem.
Irene became a performer (her voice liberated her from her imagination) singing in professional theaters when a young girl was called for. Cloda was not allowed to hum in her sister's presence. It caused such rage in Irene, who wanted always to be the only one to do anything well. In her enforced silence she developed a hunger for the speech of others—especially her mother's—whom she experienced as a series of erroneous gestures, mis-heard statements, a kind of inoperative robot who wouldn't give her what she wanted. While the gnostics had terrified themselves over their intimacy with the "wrong father," she did the same over the "wrong mother." She longed for a manifestation of the one who would put things right.

x

In all their travels, the family spent most of their time at home. They had little money and spent most of it on food. They ate the same breakfast cooked by the father: egg, fried tomato, bacon, homemade jam on homemade bread (toasted), tea with milk and brown sugar. Irene always made her own lunch, being fussy about food at school—bread lathered with a thick layer of gooseberry jam . . . Kennedy's bread, with its parade of happy children painted on its paper cover. She wrapped it in tin foil and carried it among her books inside her green schoolbag.

Cloda nibbled at the school lunch with her chosen gang, but after school they went together to a candy store and sucked Lemon's arctic mints while reading comic books on the shelves.

At night the family ate at eight, their father's dinners, and washed up with their mother afterwards. He was tipsy by the time they sat down but continued to sop up the wine, purchased with much fuss every Saturday. He dozed in his study while the females cleaned up. It was during those occasions that the girls grew to know their mother most intimately. When she wasn't working, she was unbalanced, dramatizing her actions and her facial expressions in ways designed to prove that the body and face are costumes, pure material slipped over the slippery frame of a spirit. In order to prove that she was too good for a drain, a handful of garbage tossed in a bag, or the smell of sud and rag on her long fingers, she wore huge pink rubber gloves and a silk slip while she cleaned. She ripped off her dress and threw it on a kitchen chair, each night after dinner, and set to work on the dishes with such a vengeance she was often drenched down the front of her slip. One night she might pretend she was Medea, the next night Lady MacBeth, or else she memorized lines from the Lake Poets. She called dishwashing hour her "rehearsal time" and practiced the scales or sang The Road to Manderlay so that she would not be wasting time.

Nod

Sometimes the mother ordered Irene to stand on a chair and sing, instead of drying dishes. And then she would run the palms of her hands up and down her slip and watch with acute—even misty-eyed—pleasure. Sometimes her face, watching Irene's face, assumed a look of desire. Without fail her black hair was done in a neat braided bun raised with a comb to reveal a neck soft brown and long like a Flamencan dancer. But her mouth remained triangular, her teeth very long, and her chin weak, no matter how concentrated her gaze on her daughter was. There was no way her daughter's face would turn into her mirror's face. Nonetheless she looked at Irene as if she were seeing herself as a pretty girl.

"My God, I love it," she murmured to Irene. She massaged her creme brulee bosoms with the flat of her hand, and sighed painfully. "I want you to do everything I never did!" "If only you had known your grandmother—you would see. You are exactly like that side of the family. You could be a second Garbo. But God, my poor mother—doomed to marry a man she didn't love, to raise children on nothing, and never, never to get a chance to develop her singing voice. Dragged from Athens to America by a brutish husband shouting from his bed, and still my poor mother went everywhere singing. Like Edith Piaf. House-cleaning and dress-making in the rich areas of Chicago. She always sang, or whistled. Never forget this. If you want to be a star, you have to sacrifice everything for it. Don't let anyone get in your way. Be an outright diva. Power is the only way to have a dignified life. I'm only thankful my poor mother has a second chance in you."

Who am I like? Cloda would invariably ask. Ask Daddy, was always the answer.

And Cloda would observe that her mother had a Picasso-esque face— one that seemed to include a profile even as it stared directly into your eyes. So much—too much—seemed to be contained in her mobile features that she sensed that there were always two of her.

So she went to her father and asked, Who am I like? And he always said, Beats me.

x

As Irene grew, she developed her voice and her temper at an equal rate. Her mother's half-truths and night howls formed an incomplete world for her, zones of unknowing. The child was an hysteric, terrified of her own imagination that rambled, dragging her along, into spectacular undergrowth. She had to slash her way out with shouts and curses directed at passersby. While lost and struggling in that weedy territory, she was filled with fears that took the form of rages. If the family had been religious, she would have been a fanatic or the patron saint of dread. She mistrusted almost everyone.

Few knew this because she was a star pupil, a voracious reader who did all her assignments on time, expressed lots of curiosity about world history and sang angelically. She was wholehearted, and the diligence with which she approached a subject was her great virtue.

One part of God is said to love those who are wholehearted better than the dabblers, debaters and do-gooders who are weak in spirit. And this part of God seemed to love Irene indeed. She had a face that seemed more created than inherited, given strong bones, but delicate contours. Despite her bloodline, she looked Scandinavian.

She was excessively (not lovingly) attached to her mother—to the point that she displaced her father on many nights, making him sleep in the room with Cloda so she could sleep with her mother. Maybe her fears were born from those sexual arias that terrified her as a child, her mother's howls, suggesting more violence than pleasure. Maybe they were born from the hours watching her little sister's fits and punishments.

In any case for a few years the apartment at night—beginning with dinners doused in music and evasion—was a house of contradiction. An unlighted tunnel of rooms with the figures of parent and child switching beds or listening to cries approaching melodies.

X

Like many, if not all people, Cloda began to defend her beliefs in her sleep. In her dreams her sense of error was so profound and luminous it suggested an equally—if not greater—way that was right. Yet the right way was the hidden way. And in her dreams she encountered instead the wrong door, the wrong street, the wrong direction, the wrong room. And these encounters horrified her, confused her, kept her lost. To be in error is to feel oneself to be far from the source of happiness. It is to be far from or late to . . . and distance and time become then one thing, in the dream a torment of misdirected moves and inefficient machinery. To be in error is not to be wrong so much as to be separate from the source of a peaceful conscience, and the windy gap is cold and deep, like a portion of sea that seems to run right through the earth and meet its opposite ocean. She couldn't get home because she didn't know where home was!

Hope became her home instead. (Unhoping hours are the same as refugees from a cruel government.)
The emotional climate of their household held them in thrall, no matter what the outer landscape was like, it was a palpable veil. The mother over time and travel had turned her anger at Cloda into indifference and her indifference into benign neglect, but she never altered her idolatrous feeling for Irene; it was as much a fixation as a faith. She expected Irene to devote herself—without an inch of slack—to a singing career and to become even more fanatically hard working than she herself. Irene's beauty was to the mother a kind of miracle, something she didn't know she had it in her power to create. While she treated Irene as a possession, therefore, and her ultimate responsibility, she also feared her as an irrational event, a performance she had not directed. Irene seemed to fly ahead of her like something both precious and reckless and she chased after her, crying instructions and warnings. And sometimes curses.

Nod

In one opera based on the abduction of Persephone, the mother sang as Ceres: "If the earth is ever again to see any verdure, it must first grow along the path which my daughter will tread in coming back to me . . . Until then my hate will reign!"

And these words made her whole family turn in circles, wondering which one of them she was addressing. And the way she moved on stage—her movements were her signature and what made her unique as a performer—was like a wooden puppet, with jerking joints and her head thrown back, her eyes upturned and her mouth a hole. The father observed all of this with a look of bewildered pity. No matter how bossy and absurd his wife could be; no matter how plain he knew her face to be, he found her sexy, he was moved by her, he felt her to be a suffering soul and a comforting body.

Finally, one night she received a call from her cousin's husband in Dijon—an Algerian Jew who directed socialist opera in small cities west of the Alps. He wanted her to play the role of a revolutionary heroine who is ultimately hanged—wrongly—by her own comrades. She strode around the house, stiff-legged and singing her ecstasy at the top of her lungs: Yes, yes, yes!

x

And so that was how—in the fall of their second year in Ireland, the parents left the children, now 14 and 17, in the care of a middle-aged woman named Catharine while they traveled to the continent for several weeks. Before they left, they fought like siblings—in vicious, unedited bouts that were both competitive and discarding. This was not their usual approach to separation. But now they slammed doors and fists on tables and slid bowls to the ground to shatter and shouted about rights and responsibilities, about Hitler and children, about Poland and Scapa Flow. The mother marched up and down stairs with her hands blocking her ears, as he stood at the bottom shouting up at her. "Bitch! Bitch!" It was almost as if the on-going defeat, occupation and partition of nearby countries had put war into the air they all breathed. They sucked on rage and exhaled the poisons from the pages of *The Irish Times* and *The Herald Tribune*. Like two people ultra-sensitive to the rocking of an enormous tanker, they felt the catastrophic waves underneath their feet, but took them personally. Each tremor was interpreted as a weakness in the relations between them.

And even though the father knew that the water that makes a wave doesn't travel across the sea with it; and each particle whirls in a circle with the passage of each wave, and then returns to its original position; even though he knew how storms develop in irregular gusts, and rain under wind responds to shifting pressures, and it is this wind that manipulates the surface of the water, twisting it into higher and higher points, and that a wave will fall into foam when it is a seventh as high from trough to crest as its distance is to the next crest, and that a bad wind can blow off the tops of waves; somehow, perhaps because he was raised on cozy Victorian novels, he felt safe crossing the English channel where many were mobilizing for war. The parents thought only of adventure. Like eternal tourists who would find hell "interesting" they felt the boat tilt, heard the dishes slide, staggered against the sway of enormous waves and shouted interpretations at each other. Never before would they have left their children. But now, something in the impending doom made that necessary. Furious at each other, they separated— but promised to return and start again.

Before departing the mother had told the girls to be good and obedient, to do everything just the same as they would if she were still there, and then she added: "Since you will not have your father around to neglect you, this is your chance to experiment with independence. Be glad and rejoice that he's gone, the son of a bitch. But don't, Irene, veer from your work, sing and sing, because nothing but work can keep you sane and safe in this world. Don't get distracted!"

To Cloda, "You beware of your older sister," said the father into the mirror where he was looping his tie. "By this I mean when she begins to act conceited and imperious like her mother, just walk away from her. It's not her fault. It's inherited."

Cloda and Irene were confused and frightened by their parents' messages and their moods when they left. Their parents were generally formal and even affectionate with each other. So now Irene dreamed of her freedom from her family, from school—only months away—and that year she became a full-time worker in her field of choice, a martyr to music. There was for her no more world. Nature and society gradually receded from her reality and she lived happily among inventions, secondary sources, and music, where she labored to be an immortal and a mother-killer. There was no outside for her. Only a single relationship: between audience and artist.

x

While the father was off researching the history of petroleum for the US government, the mother was singing socialist songs:

On winter nights the stars in the country sparkle like sharp projections of icicles from our earth's own ones . . . The diamond fingers of ill will develop in abysmal caverns when prurient fingers dip in . . . A people whose quills are money-green will shoot away the workers of the land, the nobodies, who know nothing can be owned . . . Return the lambs to their origins after wearing them like clothes! See the shift of juniper and dewdrops sprayed over the last roses of the year!

In Geneva the father told people, with a laugh, that he had come there to get a break from his wife and to find out first-hand what Germany was up to—and also of course to contribute to the history of the world—not taking sides—with his work on oil. He didn't expect to stay long, he said, a month at the most, and he believed himself to be immune from danger, because he was an American citizen working for the Government and under its constant protection.

N o d

"What is evil?" Nietzsche had asked. "Whatever springs from weakness." As soon as he left Geneva and moved on to Paris, he began to feel uneasy, even frightened in a deep, barely palpable part of himself. The news, the names in the news—Goebbels, Hitler, Churchill, Chamberlain—overshadowed all the old ones: Black Forest, Alsace-Lorraine, Rhine, Marseilles—and a sense of imminent horror made objects sharper, just as the shadows in December are sharper than in April and the snow that falls at night is never brighter.

The grime, the unemployed, the children playing hopscotch on the roads, the broken tennis-nets, the bands in public parks—seedy old men in red uniforms—the wet-walled slums and statues like trout stopped mid-flight, the thick riverwater and the black fences dug into stone . . . He was daily met with an emotion that seemed to adhere to people's skins, coats, to the cut of buildings, to the words for those buildings. The browny green military presence didn't help his fantasies. And the scrawny metallic parks, with their deciduous leaves cracked and browning on frosty grass—the benches were too cold to sit on. Masculine plaster busts in these parks were ghastly reminders of civilization's ability to make heroes in hell.
Europe, he went so far as to say, was once again about to be the most destructive geographic space on earth. And frantically he looked around for a woman to fondle.

x

In Ireland the girls interpreted their parents' leaving as an abandonment. They were scared, especially while the radio was churning out reports of war. Irene had already sublimated many of her childhood terrors into a desire to out-do her mother as a performer and used this desire as a way of overcoming her fear. However, despite the admiration she was evoking here and there, hate—disembodied as a sigh—engineered its way from the sky and the sea into the household rooms, contaminating everything from cupboard to cake. Hate sat in corners watching, hate hung over the dinner table, hate floated in the dark rooms at night, and hate sat on the stairs waiting. Hate must have dropped down from the skies and from the minds of those people cooking up atrocities. Or it might have risen up from the ground where new slaughters fertilized the snow. Or it might have arrived through dreams and taken form on its own. "I am a hater, you are a hater, she is a hater, this is the world." This hate was not the opposite of love it didn't cancel or erase the possibility of love; this hate was the opposite of courage. It took root wherever self-knowledge didn't dare go. Hate came from the east and traveled west, it came in news reports and papers, on ships, and in images of soldiers fallen, it came in the smokes burning through the clouds, it was everywhere, and welcomed by haters everywhere. Wet little Ireland seemed to want to weep it out of its eyes. The low sky rained endlessly.

x

In September the rose is in its second bloom, and on the bog both orchid and bell-heather are in flower; plum blue whortleberries and red barberries grow in the woods, and now the symmetrical black turf-ricks begin to burn against the cold. Their household—shabby with flotsam from other people's lives—once sparkled into a sensuous paradise in the kitchen only—when the father was home. Now, with him gone, rows of half-eaten jams dried on shelves, and bread greened, and milk curdled. Colored bottles grayed inside sleeves of dust. Outside the dirty glass panes leaves developed into rusty and leathery flakes that shivered in rain. And the smell of the turf-ricks burning filtered into the streets. The girls were always cold from the damp stone floors in their basement flat. A ghost banged around a closed room, once a root cellar, and the girls in their twin beds at night heard it and converted its chaos into a theory about men and the cries of women.

Irene, emotionally very childish, gave in to sadistic urges sometimes and told her even more childish sister stories about graveyard visitors, ghouls, werewolves, vampires, rats and male rapists. She described penises as rootlike protrusions that knocked against the inner thighs, and expanded like sausage shaped balloons. Her father's condoms were her proof. When penises entered a woman with the wooden weight of a broomstick, they moved the lungs aside to get into the throat. Like digging a hole to China, the stick could reach from one open end of a woman to the next.

Irene told her sister that she had hidden in a large clothes hamper in Amsterdam and watched their father pee and could swear on a stack of Bibles that his penis hung halfway to his knees. Cloda believed this and dreaded ever seeing her father again. But then Irene told her that you could tell which men had big ones by the length of their noses. And because their father's nose was relatively small, Cloda began to grow skeptical. But she didn't want to ruin Irene's fun, so she said nothing.

And one night Irene told Cloda a story she had made up: Once upon a time in Europe there lived a man and a woman at the edge of a piney forest. They were poor. The woman was wild as if she had no defenses against nature, and the man was as numb as their primitive culture. They had two daughters whom they could not feed and so one morning they crept off into the forest to fend for themselves.
On their way through the thickets they passed an oven that was cold; broken railroad ties; a crashed warplane; and a coven of witches munching on stew and laughing. The woman was starving by then and so she felt no need to hesitate before going up to the witches and begging for some food. They said in secret to the woman, Go right ahead. This pot is never empty. It's full of humans, like you.

The woman sat down cheerfully to eat. The man followed but didn't realize what he was eating and he kept saying How good! It must be my appetite! And they rolled up some brains in flatbread and said, Eat, eat. This comes in different shapes. He guzzled and then the man and woman fell asleep.

Meanwhile their two daughters awakened and followed their footprints into the woods, believing that their parents were looking for sticks, or food, to feed them. Instead at every step they took they smelled meat cooking. It was so disgusting the oldest girl kept gagging and stopping to throw up. The youngest went down on her knees and crawled because the smell floated above her shoulders.

Before long they passed the oven, but now it was full of potatoes cooking. Naturally they stuffed as many as they could in their pockets. And then they heard the laughter of fairies in the woods—lovely musical laughter, and singing, and relieved, they ran along the railroad ties that joined together, magically, with each step they took.

And then they hid inside the broken airplane, in its cockpit, while the witches walked by them, carrying the bodies of their parents on their shoulders, covered with American flags! After the witches passed, the fairies came out of the woods, and demanded that one of the girls sacrifice herself immediately for the sake of a sick fairy child.

What did the fairies look like? Men, but little. They had big sad starry eyes. And black beards! And you know how it is with fairies: they want the prettiest of mortals for their own breeding. So they took the oldest daughter for their sacrifice, and left the ugliest one behind. This was one time it was definitely better to be plain.

What happened to the ugly girl left alone in the plane? asked Cloda. She figured out how to make it fly, said Irene. And bumped along into the sky. *And what happened to her sister?* Raped—then burned. Sacrificed. *I hate that story. It makes me sick.* I just made it up. For you. Bitch.

Irene's temper was unpredictable, so no one ever dared disturb a moment of her happiness. Let it last as long as possible. Irene was magnetic due to the above-normal force of her self-interest. But most people thought they had met Cloda somewhere before, she was so difficult to place. She was always hiding, clearing her throat and looking away. She had a morbid fear of adults that surfaced during this time when her parents had gone, especially on one of those nights after Irene had whispered stories to her. The ratio between sister and sister was one to zero. Irene was the singer and Cloda the empty vessel into which her sounds poured. Yet Cloda's gullible personality was helpful to Irene, keeping her sane, the way goats calm highly bred horses. Always bordering on suicidal feelings, Irene was comforted by Cloda's animal and criminal behavior. Cloda actually believed in the existence of fairies, it seemed, and this made her venture into dangerous places, as if on a quest.

x

Soon after their parents left they learned from Catharine that the fighting in Europe had already left 91,000 people killed, more than 1000 planes and 1400 tanks lost, and 750,000 people imprisoned. The girls had shared visions, in the dark at night, of each parent's body hurtling towards the stars, still in one piece, but sending out showers of sparks. Their father sent them thin little notes on paper with an unreadable gray watermark in the middle. He quoted the words of a dictator: "In war there are no winners, just a heap of graves." Then he assured them he'd be home.
But the voice of Hitler on the radio seemed to make all the firmaments and all their hosts and legions tremble. His voice made all adult pronouncements seem connected to those curses on earth that are said to cause reverberations in the heavens.

Even children hundreds of miles away could feel an unpleasant tincture to the air they breathed as when a storm is coming the leaves turn inside out and the birds look perplexed as if to question,

Why, why, why?

x

That fall turned into a winter where leaden clouds impacted over the stone houses and dark evergreen dripped rain in the mornings dark until noon. Like the time they lived at Hampstead Heath, the cold was in everything homey, there was a wetness to the way it got inside. Not like their white soft winters in Amsterdam, when they were always enclosed in clean rooms, this was solemnly cold and dirty. The traveling people, called Tinkers, huddled on bridges and in doorways with their boxes and hats laid out for change. Cloda stole for a family of them, went into small shops and came out with Cadbury chocolates that she gave to the kids. For the first time she was blessed for stealing.

She sometimes after school sat for warmth in the Carmelite church near Switzer's on Grafton Street, hunched near the candles to keep warm, and watched the people come and go with a devotion to dolly images that she wished she could share. All her worship was securely focused on things that moved—either by their own volition or by the force of wind or water.

She had been called, by her father, "kleine Pantheistin." Sadness painted sundress blue and gold onto the walls did, however, excite some of her senses. Cloda began a secret after-school life, when she pulled her father's forbidden camera off the shelf, stole some film, and taught herself how to regulate the light and distance in the frame. After school she squatted in parks and on bridges taking pictures of leaves close up, interiors of flowers, and of people doing things they thought they were doing alone. On these days much in this world appeared to Cloda as a costume show designed to cause confusion. This began with her earliest impression of a natural world worn by an invisible inhabitant, the "God" no one but Catharine mentioned; it increased with the activities of her theatrical family; and it was confirmed daily by the inconsistencies in human statements.

The low Irish clouds cantered overhead, frolicking on the blue, like packs of sunny ghosts liberated from boxes underground. She took pix of them too. She began to think with her camera, through her camera, its black properties, its needs, and how these regulated outcomes: the surprises she found after developing the film, the rude ones as well as the good, and the anonymous faces capturing myriad feelings, all these gave her a politics and a poetics simultaneously. And after she saw her first movie—A Free Soul—to become a filmmaker was her plan, after years of practicing secretly, in a way which insured her triumph.

In this late fall of that year some people were importing iron ore from Norway for making weapons. For some reason the radio went on and on about this, and about turning Narvik into a sort of military base, where it would be easy to force the iron ore ships into the open sea. No one knew much about Norway at that time, but many in Ireland identified with its neutrality, since Ireland was neutral too.

"In fact Norway has a socialist government and a weak army," said Cloda's teacher. "The King is a naval man and beloved of Norwegians. No one is going to believe that anything evil is coming out of that country. Those who are good at air war are not so good at sea. This is our best hope over here. England stands between us and the rest of Europe. Let's pray that the oceans serve as barricades."
The name NORWAY was floating close to their house. And meanwhile the mother in Lyons was rehearsing an aria in a very cold theater.

When will people stop and ask, Who owns the money? Then and only then will war end. Oh where is the thump of apples and where the smell of nuts and plums being gathered up from under the trees for the harvest! Oh who is withholding these things? And if a benevolent manual labor were created, then the entire mass of people, the seconds, would be winners, and storm the administrators! But then they would lose their tenderness and turn into their oppressors!

After a slow descent from the sound of her own voice, she let the accompanying instruments zing and twist their way to the end, then stood, her long teeth resting on her lower lip, listening acutely to the echoes and coughs. She was wrapped in many sweaters, her hair had tumbled and was wild. Andre, her director and her cousin's husband, was distractedly talking to the stage manager, and at the edge of the stage stood the Norwegian translator she had loved so many years before. When she saw him, she felt weak, as if she might faint, but slowly approached him with a heroic smile. He brushed her lips with his. That night she stayed with him in a small hotel outside Verona. There was a blackout and searchlights flashed on the wet streets outside. They didn't sleep all night, but made love and discussed the situation in Europe, agreeing that it was almost impossible to care about art or music or books anymore, under the circumstance of an approaching war. And they kept returning to "food and love-making" as the only two acts that continued to have meaning. In the morning, both exhausted and enervated, they had coffee and rolls and said goodbye—for a short time. He was—for work reasons—on his way to Ireland.

x

Cloda's Irish gang was a pair of sisters she met by a field, where they were camped with their family caravan. It was the reverse of the time of year when hope of light and green returns. But despite the cold the traveling (Tinker) sisters cared for their little brother all day every day, pushing him up and down O'Connell Street in his carriage, while he held a bottle to his lips, or sobbed, his fingers iced lolly red. They gulped down C & C Indian Tonic and stared in the windows of Brown Thomas ("the loveliest store in Ireland"). On weekends they sometimes took the train to Killiney and climbed the hill, hanging their legs over sheer cliffs to spy on others, or to walk beside the cold sea. Shards of broken china gleamed in the grey rocks—broken mugs and platters from the teashop on the beach, but also from other lands—England, Spain, they imagined, collecting bits of sea glass together.

Cloda one day took six of her father's eight bottles down to the beach. The water at dusk had rolled away like a scroll, leaving only the gulping sand and glowing pebbles. She, with her friends, walked out across this mush as fast they could go, and then she scribbled a note and corked it inside the garnet red bottle, and hurled it into the approaching tide. The other bottles she left standing upright like bowling pins. The note gave Cloda's name and citizenship and address, and under these she wrote:

I'm being held hostage! S.O.S!

Then the group of them turned tail and ran back to the stone wall, where they could climb up and watch the sea engulf the little line of colors and sweep them away.

Cloda's new friends spoke in an accent so thick she often couldn't decipher their meaning, and sometimes they spoke in Gammon and she didn't often bother trying to understand that. They were younger than her and communicated physically and with facial expressions that she had no trouble interpreting. She only went to school often enough to stay out of trouble, and most of her time was spent walking around Dublin with the girls and their baby brother. Always the sea, like a mountain of jelly, jiggled off to the east, and in the late afternoons it was pure liquid gold, too bright for eyes to see.

x

There are many sisters affected by this story. The Catharine who cared for Irene and Cloda at home needed the money to help her own daughters as they struggled through college. She was a widow with a swollen red face, leathery from the raw weather and the drink to recover, and a gap between her front teeth, a pleasant smile, and intelligent eyes. She said "Now" in a firm voice when any gesture was complete. Her interest in her own daughters was so intense, she barely had any left for Cloda and Irene. She was not, however, unkind, just neutral and occasionally curious. Where had the parents gone for so long? Did they do this often? Letters and phone calls arrived, but the parents kept postponing the date of their return, although Catharine begged for freedom.

"There is no doubt the war is spreading. No one is safe! Oh if only I could go home to my girls!" she cried to the two sisters. Sometimes Catharine spoke Irish or, like a schoolteacher, explained to Cloda and Irene that Gaelic and Welsh were part of a larger Celtic language.

"You can trace it through names—of tribes, chieftains and places like rivers even, or settlements. The Celts were terrible barbarians," she said.

And then she told them about banshees—how they were little girl women, as big as sightings of the Virgin Mary, weeping by water, and you always knew when a banshee had passed because a comb was left behind. Usually on a stone, she added. What do banshees do? asked Cloda. They are heralds of the dying, Catharine replied and planted a glass of lemon barley beside Cloda and added, Now.

x

One November afternoon there was a knock on the door while Irene was studying a part in a Yeats play where songs had been written especially for her by a local folksinger. She was in the middle of the line: *She sleeps high up on wintry Knock-na-rea* when there was a second, louder knock. Cloda was as usual roaming the outdoors. Catharine was marketing. And Irene went to the door cursing and nervous.

The man outside was tall with an oblong face and smooth wide lips, bright blue eyes and a hooked nose. His blond hair fell across his high brow, and he pushed it back when he saw Irene, then gave her a cavalier but seeking smile.

"You must be Irene? I'm an old friend of your mother's. Hal," he said and held out a hand.

Irene recoiled, but took the hand and squeezed it. The moment was uncanny—as if she had expected this man, had been awaiting him like the day of a violent event. A cab hummed behind him, the door ajar, and the sea flailed in the beyond. They occupied the pink one in a row of houses that led to the beach on Dublin Bay. A bitter scent of boxwood floated around her and the man inhaled through two wide nostrils like an athlete finishing a race. He smiled and lines cheered the severity of his face. Your mother sent me. I have a letter from her, he said. Here.

Trembling she read her mother's handwriting. "Hal is a very old friend and needs a place to stay near Dublin. He's doing some work on Celtic poetry. Put him in the ghost room, please, and be polite. I'll be back in a minute. Love ever, Mum."

So Hal was given the ghost room where there was a narrow bed and wooden locker, a desk and a window that had loose rattling glass. He fixed it up in a day, so it was transformed from an evil and landlocked space, sealed away from the household, into an airy square smelling of Old Spice and wool, where the girls could pause and catch the sun shaped as a large cruciform. Outside the train to Dublin banged down the back of the garden.

He was an easy-going man, easy to take in because of the almost catlike way he moved, and his soft formal speech. But there was no escaping his being a male in a house filled with females and this fact—as palpable as the smell of meat cooking—seemed to cast a kind of spell around his person. Whenever he entered a room, the atmosphere changed, softened, grew obedient.

He told Irene he had known her mother first when he was very young, not even ten years older than Irene was then, and her mother was in her early thirties, and the Depression was about to begin. We had a little romance, he said with the wide smile that smashed his features into many lines. Was I even born? she wanted to know.

Of course! Don't you remember meeting me—you must have been about—nearly seven—no, you wouldn't remember, would you. You threw up on my neck.

Why? she asked. Because you were jealous of your mother paying attention to me. Why else?

Where were we? Going on a picnic—in New England. Where was Daddy? At a conference somewhere, Hal said and jumped to his feet. He joined Catharine at the sink. She asked, Is Hal your real name? No. It's Hallstatt, which was an iron-using prehistoric culture. I'm named after that. In their tombs men were buried with a sword, pottery and pork, he said.

"I could see burying you with poetry far more than with pork," she remarked with a joyful laugh.

Catharine was noticeably relieved by his arrival. She kept remarking on his good looks, and even flirting with him in the kitchen. "You almost look Irish," she said. Well, in stature and dimensions of the head and face the composite Irishman might well be considered one of the same type I come from. Eastern Norway. But the Irish are believed to be part Mediterranean.

"Is red hair Mediterranean?" Hair of the rufous variety is very rare, he said with a teasing grin because she made fun of his formal speech patterns. He had this formality instead of an accent.

Irene noticed the flirtation between them and also how his eyes continually traveled her way, measuring, musing, penetrating, and she hid her face with her hand while reading in the same room with him.

Catharine asked him what he knew about the whereabouts of the parents and Irene heard him answer:

Rather typical of being American. You mean spoiled? Well, in a way, but more naive perhaps than spoiled. American, yes. They don't really believe that War is getting serious, that the invasions are only the beginning. Western democracies are pathetic in their hesitation. But the U.S.

is the worst offender. A kind of sinful innocence. Weakness like this? Well, it gets what it deserves. You will see.

"I try to pay no attention," said Catharine. Well, you're a woman, so you don't need to pay attention.

Yes, she does, said Irene. She could die too. Only if it comes to a take-over of Ireland, which could happen, of course. And you should see the British soldiers—half-starved and neglected since 1918—they look like walking corpses next to the robust youth brigades. Not an attractive race, the Saxons in England.

"I don't know why the parents are over there," Catharine sighed. To pretend it isn't happening, said Hal. Paradoxically.

Well, I'm glad they're gone, said Irene from behind her book. Let them pretend as long as they want. Yes! Hal concurred enthusiastically. Hey, where did Daddy's bottles go? Irene asked. "Well, it's sure I don't know," Catharine said defensively.

Cloda? Everyone looked at Cloda who covered the smile on her lips with her hand and let her hair fall like the curtain on a last shameful act.

x

Hal told both girls about Scandinavian legends—how Freyja wept golden tears and slept with any god who would have her. And she also slept with four dwarves in order to get her hands on a beautiful gold necklace. He told the girls he had a son named Loki but he was separated from his wife and rarely saw the boy. How old is he? Cloda asked. About your age, I'd guess. What about his mother? They live in Stockholm. We're good friends.

Each morning he took the bus to the library at Trinity College and stayed all day. Sometimes he didn't return until after the girls were in

bed, but Irene lay awake listening until he returned. The ghost room—
now a guest room—seemed to emanate presence—his—through the
floorboards and up through the base of her bed and mattress.

She was physically disturbed by his ease around the house, as if she was
decoding, with unease, or rendering void, a danger. She speculated on
what he meant by "romance" with her mother which caused a breathless
response to the sound of his steps. Their pattern was a secret code, each
footfall a message from the rest of his body. She looked up the word
"romance" and learned that it had a chaste meaning.

Irene had been in love twice before, and both times with girls who
looked like her. One was Dutch and the other was Dutch, and she met
them both in Amsterdam. She didn't know that her passion was the same
as being in love with a man, but assumed it was unique and sexless; she
didn't know that they looked like her, either. She just found each one
of them terrifyingly beautiful and was unable to take her eyes off of
them. She was fourteen the first time and sixteen the second. With the
first one she "practiced" romance with long languid kisses and explor-
atory touches. With the second one she still called it practice, but was
frightened of it, and withdrew when the experiment began to feel like
experience. On her bike she had several times had to stop, gasp, swoon,
and put one leg over the other to deal with the emotions in her groin.

One night, while she was sleeping over the guest room, her whole body was
seized with that same kind of wounding pleasure, a sensation that tore up
through her navel and spread around her thighs and spine, with the sweep
of a shark passing neatly between rocks. And she awoke to her own thrashing, and ripped off her blankets with her legs, only envisioning the man
below her in his narrow bed, his face turned up to her back, his eyes closed,
and his large hands motionless as a corpse she wanted to kick back to life.

Mortified by this occasion, the next morning she nonetheless wanted
it to happen again, but nearer to him, where he could be called upon

to ease the pain. But she reckoned that this was insane, she was always afraid she was going insane, which was her analogy for turning into her mother, and her anxiety gave her a radiance that illuminated the objects around her body. He noticed it. He remarked, You look feverish, Irene. Should you go to school?

I'm fine, she whispered and banged out of the house without her books or jam sandwich. He came after her, carrying them against his chest, and tossed his forelock back and smiled his row of even teeth in a conspiratorial way.

They leaned against the soft rock seawall during the exchange which he prolonged with wonderings about her health. The seaweed slapped gold against black stones below them. Industrial Dublin was dimmed by early morning fog across the bay.
Are you sure you're okay? he asked as if he knew what was wrong.

Sort of, she demurred and a wave of nausea passed around the area inhabited by last night's pleasure.

He handed her the bag and the skin of their index fingers underneath the nails felt the contact so they snapped apart.

He offered to pick her up from school someday and said he wanted to go to her rehearsal with her—"to watch you sing"—grinning down, down to her upturned lips. She mouthed an o.k. and it was agreed, some day. She went on her way up the winding stone path to the main road, her spine rigid with awareness of his eyes. But when she turned he was gone.

x

One day Irene surprised Cloda by letting her ride her thin black bicycle, saying: You can ride it, if you do me a favor. Okay. What? Ask Hal about his romance with Mum, Irene whispered. Ask him soon! How? Just find a good way. You can even keep my bike if you do. Gosh, thanks! Great! I will! Cloda ran out to feel the bike, in case it had been twisted out of shape, had a flat tire, or a missing chain. She mistrusted every act of generosity coming from her sister, but this time she was not justified. The bike was fine.

So she took off at high speed in search of her friends with their caravan. Many years later, riding a bike through the country, she would repeat the feeling she had that day—again—without knowing why, or remembering why, it was so exciting.

But she would see the wheel-prints cut into the slough. Tough cold mud on stones, puddles saturated with decades of cowpads dark green, and other slime, shot by.
The deep dawn waters were level and undimpled by boat, fish, or wind, off to her left. A black cow drooled on a wall. The mountains declined like textiles on a shelf. Clouds unravelled ahead of her, and the way the parts of them moved around seemed to be designed as a lesson in math or physics and creation itself seemed to be a demonstration of higher principles, all matters of speed, energy, light, space, time and imagination enacted as Platonic proofs on the round globe.

It was the good kind of coldness she experienced then—the cold door into the true liberty of knowing why she was there—here—in this world. To feel the necessity of her own being. A deliverance from confusions and actions steeped in the poisons of personality—what a pleasure. Necessity was the word she would use, and, later, sufficiency. For such happiness.

Her admiration for the traveling people in their red wooden caravan was at first based in the imaginary, because the closer she drew to their real life, the more it repeated the cruelties of the rest of the world. That is, children smacking children, no one comforting them, and above all— for her: the baby unwiped and unclean and uncomfortable, his spinning carriage mud-caked wheels, bottle pressed to the circle of his red tongue, he didn't have any will of his own yet except by crying. Often she wanted to cry with him and felt her own temples throb and her sex pulse when she saw the torment inflicted on him by his older sisters.

But their red wagon and huge fat dray horse were still an emblem of another effort going on—she could see that—the image expressed an agreement with distance that included a rejection of time as physical, a set of wooden wheels, a weight, and wanted to accede to that wonderful agreement by constantly demonstrating it—on roads where others could see.

They were really pausers more than travelers. And she began to imagine the things that they saw, the paths that they took, the dreams that they dreamed, and to wonder: Was she herself an emigree from a distant land? Was she not the adopted child of her mortal parents, someone who really began in the maple rings? Was she still wanted in Fairyland as a bride for some chief? There is after all an ancient and potent charm that mortal girls have over fairies. She imagined the faces that they did have; not the starry orbs her sister described. And she felt sometimes that the wind that blasted on her cheeks was the breath of a fairy, and that the frost-prints on her windowpanes were fairy messages meant for her. When she had a cold and fever, she longed for a fairy doctor to work the cure. Are fairies grumpy? She had heard that they were and had read that they danced like aristocrats. If you were kind to them, they would protect you. If you were mean, they were mean right back. She could learn from fairy behavior, she decided, but only if she could actually see one. And how else could she do this except by running away from home. At least, in this case, it would be her decision to become invisible to those around her.

x

Cloda approached Hal that night after dinner, while Irene waited, hands folded and twisting, in her room. Cloda coughed, cleared her throat and asked: "What kind of romance did you have with my mother?" And as she asked him, she turned a little pink behind the black screen of her hair.

Whatever do you mean? he wondered with a teasing tone. I mean, did you kiss her or just wish you could, since she was already married. You weren't even aware, so what would you know? Well, I know what you said. You said "romance." I said "little romance," I think. But in any case, yes, I did kiss her, but I regretted it right away. Not the kiss—your mother, mind you, was beautiful and very kind to me—but the wish for more kisses—given that she was, as you say, married already, and so it stopped. Right there. I put a stop to it. I returned to Norway. Was my mother mad or sad when it stopped? Good question. She loved your father very much. So I think she felt just the way I did. We were in New York. She was part of a circle of artists, painters, poets, and I wanted to be part of that circle, and she was very encouraging. I am sure by now it was all a waste of time. Waste of time? Why? Well, I never panned up—is that the word?—as a poet.

Cloda studied him as if poised to take a snapshot with wasted time as its subject. His pensive profile was turned to look at the evening bay, where the tide was way out leaving a vast plain of rippled yellow sand between them and the city. She saw that his nose was long and his profile ship-like in some way. She worked at suspecting the worst of him, then realized she must report the results of this conversation to Irene, fast, and so she bolted inside, a messenger whose whole value was use-value.

When she reported the kiss to her sister, Irene rushed to the bathroom and threw up. She was often sick, violently heaving, spitting and splashing over toilets before performances and after—but Cloda had never seen her heave on the wings of a message like this.

Irene rushed towards the bathroom, hand to mouth, but managed to cry out, I hate that bitch mother. I'll kill her! Wait and see!

That night Catharine produced baked potatoes and lamb for supper and Hal slipped her some money, part of his board. She stuffed the money inside her bra and turned away as if embarrassed by the transaction. He, on the other hand, seemed easy in all ways.

Nod

Do you realize I'm twice your age, Irene? Hal asked. You're seventeen and I'm thirty four. I'm about to be eighteen, she corrected him. And that doesn't mean that you couldn't be her father, Hal, said Catharine with a little tight smile. Well, I could, but I'd have to have been very young. My age, Irene told him. Almost eighteen. Younger than when you knew Mum. What were you? Twenty two or something? Something like that, he said. I'm not very good at math. Well, she was too old for you anyway. Too old for him? What do you mean? asked Catharine.

He had an affair with my mother, said Irene and smiled at Catharine's stunned expression. He did! I swear! It wasn't an affair, Hal said and spat a lump of gristle onto the side of his plate.
Whatever it was, I don't want to hear about it, said Catharine. Stop right now. You Americans will never cease to shock me. The whole world is losing its mind. Look at it. We might as well teach Yiddish instead of Irish in our schools. So many Jews coming over and taking Irish names. Shh, said Hal. Better Yiddish than British.

Cloda watched them all closely and wondered about the power arrangements in the room and their effects on all of their behavior. Catharine was clearly the servant in the group, because she was being paid to be there. This meant that she didn't really want to be there. She had to be there only in order to collect some money. Hal was able to pay for his room and board and so he was a person with a good deal of choice. He could appear or not appear. As for herself and Irene, they were either the lowest common denominator, or the highest—because their existences accounted for the entire arrangement. They were the living obligations that made all the rest fall into place.

If she ran away, she could be sure that the obligations would be lesser. Irene could practically live alone—with Hal here now—and finish school, and that would leave Catharine free to return to her own life. Loving this thought, Cloda moved to the kitchen window to press her ear against the ice cold glass. Wishing only to hear fairy-music, instead she heard a far-dis-

tant thumping sound, the same kind she heard in America on the fourth of
July; it was rolling down from the Hebrides. Bombs?

At all times her senses were poised before the sounds of the outdoor
world; she would spend much of her life running away, leaving early,
finding excuses to disappear into the open air. But now she withdrew
from the glass with a shudder and turned to the artificial light.

x

Years later a medical nun tried to persuade her to seek a geographic cure
that would make her feel safe. This nun believed in the powers of nature's shapes and smells, and said that she herself would die happy in a
field of dung with the smell of cow manure floating in her hair. "Because
I grew up on a farm," she explained.

But for the poor mad woman there was no such comfort. A one-room
cold water flat seemed too luxurious to bear. Instead she would sleep
outside on the ground, or walk around the convent walls until the sisters let her in. Sometimes delinquency like this landed her in holding
cells. The officers naturally assumed that she was a prostitute. Or those
offences commonly associated with vagrancy—including swindling and
trespassing—were added to her record.

Once she asked a Sister: "What is a metaphorical forest? Probably a 20th
century city. Roads are rivers, cars are alligators, humans are birds of
prey, and buildings are those tangled areas of any wood that are impen-
etrable without a machete—or a bomb. I sound like my poor father."

"Maybe you are happiest when you sound like him," Sister suggested.

"No, I am happiest in a forest where I feel invisible. In a village, prison,
or hospital, one is not so free, but guarded and judged in every gesture. Interpreted. Even here the person is seen as a dragon stuffed with

meaning, dragging dangerous unconscious associations around with her. *Uber die Archetypen des Kollektiven Bewußtseins,* Jung would say."

Jung! This is the century of the AntiChrist in which he participated fully, the nun said to her.

Cloda referred to her own libido as an inverted worm, whirling like a screw into the source of her being. She couldn't want anything less, or little enough. The wolves in her forest were dressed in uniforms. Although she sported no yellow pigtails, no freckles, no lily green skin, and not even the dirndl or the kilt and safety pin, she still feared being an Aryan. Freud would say her anxiety began at birth, and then later with her step-like-mother, but existentialists would say it was "built in" to being in this world.

She said that she knew how it felt during the War, although she just missed the actual experience. She told the nun that during the War Europeans excused their anti-intellectual populism claiming that it was a natural response to poor schooling. But then, having blamed educational institutions for the evil that they did, they subtly justified the quality of their crimes by referring to their own superior intelligence.

"This is how I know that thought itself is hypocritical," she said.

If she had been in an occupied country, people would have pulled lace curtains aside and peeked at her passage when she was walking the streets. Her red hood would dip her skin with a rose tint and the black of her hair raise suspicions that she might be a gypsy. But this was America where cars sped by, seemingly empty.

Did she have hairy hands? How long was the shadow from her nose to her chin? Could you tell time by it? Does she pick up pennies from the mud or curb? Did she resemble a gorilla when she was a baby?

Nod

Holderlin wrote: *Hurtling down from the Alps She comes to us, A stranger, awakening, The voice that shapes humanity.*

Every face greeted her as a fleeting revelation of what it meant to be a foreigner, even to oneself. They seemed to be asking what it felt like to wear her face and shape through this world. From questioning to condemning there is not much distance. It's about the same distance between the poor who have no power and the powerful who once were poor. After all, how do you remember what is coming?

"If the city is a forest, this convent is my agricultural storage center, my farm," Sister remarked. "I know why you are suffering. From being watched too much. Remember Europeans liked to stare at Indians performing spiritual acrobatics. Buried underground in a catatonic state, locked into caskets, sleeping on beds of nails, shoving spikes through their cheeks, rolling their penises around a rod, pulling the eye out of its socket and putting it back in . . . And why, then, didn't their corpses smell putrid? Why in the end did they smell of jasmine and rose like our own little Therese of Lisieux. The European colonialists in the 19th century stood around and watched and smelled and wondered. They are doing the same thing, as psychologists now, with you. You are sweet, like honey. I tell you what. If your chest is golden, I will believe that you have been touched by something holy. If it is the color of your back, I will have to say you haven't."

And then Sister opened Cloda's shirt and stared at the flush racing between her breasts and buttoned her up again. Moses turned to fire and gold, and so do the chests of enlightened Yogis. Sissi, the Empress of Austria, was a hysteric who believed she was a mystic.

"I never heard about the color of her chest, but I have to grant to yours the rosy tint of dawn. The blush of modesty is holiness itself."

Now she was taken back to the hospital by the nun, who told the doctor that this patient was clearly "commissioned by God" to demonstrate the truculence of faith. He nodded obediently, watching all the while the patient herself, who affected a look of revelation and irony simultaneously.

She was seeing behind almost every object—the hub of a wheel, the curl of a leaf, the house with its mouth, the windows with their frowns, the trees with their arms—her mother's face!

x

While her parents were away, Irene practiced lines for her role in a Yeats play. Her voice warbled from bathroom to kitchen to bedroom and back again.

Look no more on the half-closed gates of Hell, But speak to me whose mind is smitten of God . . .

And often she asked Cloda to help her practice, or had strange tantrums as if the house itself were part of an obstacle course, and everything that happened there existed as a deliberate impediment to her reaching her goal. When things went her way she was nice to everyone—and she deposited kind words as she passed. But when she encountered disappointment, the whole house knew it. She clawed at her hair, she vomited, she threw things and pointed scissors at her wrists. And these were responses to things like a missed phone call, a broken zipper, a pimple, a line recited wrongly from memory.

One night after dinner Irene lay face down on her bed, tearing at her face, weeping. I want to die, I want to die, she sobbed as Cloda sat on the edge of the bed, biting her nails and asking what was wrong. That bitch mother of ours. Find out if they did anything more than kiss! Find out about his wife! Go on, Cloda! Quick. Or I'll kill myself, I swear! I told you already—they didn't—do more. Tell me again. In detail. Every word. He said "we only kissed once, just a peck on the cheek," and then they both agreed to stop seeing each other ever again. That was it.

Nothing. He said he thought she was ugly anyway and too old for him. He did? Stop clearing your throat! It's hideous! I swear. He told me that. That she was ugly? Irene asked, her face raised and smiling. I think it was mean, but yes. Good. That bitch witch is ugly. And now she jumped onto her feet, rosier and prettier than ever, with her streaked face, and said to Cloda, Now find out about his wife. Go on. I want to know. Why should I? Because I asked you—I'll pay you. What if I won't? I'll take back my bike from you. I never should've given it to you anyway. But it's mine now. You gave it to me! No, it's mine and you know it. I got it for my birthday. Then why did you give it to me? I shouldn't have. I was stupid. You never rode it. I did too. In the spring. I would, now too, if I had it. You don't know what an agony it is having to take the bus everywhere. In this dreary weather. I freeze. I feel sick. Today I almost threw up on the bus from the rattle of the engine and the fumes. The bike is mine. That's not fair. It is fair. I'll take it back if you don't ask Hal about his wife. I'm serious.

A stormy look settled on her face then, and her hands flew to her cheeks, and as she drew her fingers down them, she cried, Now! Cloda mimed her actions and her Now! and they both started laughing.

x

When frost or steam coats the inside of a window, the way it smooths and greys the exterior images has the effect of creating a non-specific nostalgia in an observer. Mist must have its correspondence in an emotion. The father, then in Zurich, wondered: Christmas? No, more Octoberish. He watched clouds chill on daintily disintegrating leaves. Rooftops grew wet. Looking at the blonde woman before him he felt a sharp stab in the heart of the world, and around him everything that could, seemed to turn gold.

He was bitterly explaining himself to this woman: "Voluntary nomadism, my dear, like voluntary poverty, takes many forms. "Those who

46

like to see a new view, make a little mess and move on, and these can
be artists, gypsies, salespeople or rich people. "They can't be parents
like us who leave their children for several weeks only because they
are restless. "Real nomads move as a group. Nobodies move separately. Look. Red roses burst from a dry stick and huge complex organs
are born from a cell. Get it? Even if you were to rip into these with
instruments of analysis and could this way begin to predict and even
reproduce the narrative of their becoming, the original question of motive cause would continue. I don't know why we left our home and
our children—especially given Europe's condition, but I suspect our
marriage was coming apart already and we hoped to restore it by being
alone and elsewhere."

The woman, whose head lay across his bare legs, blinked perplexedly.
Her yellow hair covering his genitals stirred. She asked him: Why are
you staying here?

"I'm obsessed by the question of evil . . . Psychology has somehow removed personal responsibility from destructive actions. We only see the
causes of crimes now, and produce a false forgiveness."

"What is a false forgiveness?"

"A prison sentence. . . . A sacrifice. War. These are, believe it or not,
forms of self-forgiveness for the action of evil. They justify it."

"Since you already know this, why then stay here?"

"Will I ever in my lifetime have this chance again? To see the formation of evil on a grand scale? The arrival and enactment of devastation?
Something in me, something masochistic maybe, wants to participate,
even more than to witness . . . Don't say it. I know it's a poor substitute
for helping people, the way you do. But I have never been at the heart
of history, I have always just missed—somehow—the great events—because of my birth date, my birth place—who's to say. But this is a sin-

gular opportunity. Just to sit here and watch it happening. A singular opportunity."

"Yes, it is," the woman agreed and tried to lift her head, but he held her pinned down with an expression of pained delirium. Into the grain of his leg, she whispered: "But as Einstein has said, War is low and despicable, and I had rather be smitten to shreds than participate in such doings."

Am I participating, he wondered.

"Mild interest is not exactly participation—but maybe something worse." She extracted herself from his grasp, she was fully clothed, and thanked him for his observations. Well, at least we haven't committed adultery, he added. Officially.

x

Cloda and Irene examined photos of their parents and agreed that their father was good looking. So why would their mother need anyone else? He might not be as tall as Hal or as sophisticated (and his shoulders were definitely narrower) but his hair was thick and he stood with his legs bowed and parted as if he were a hockey player.

They looked together at his photograph and forgot the negatives. All they saw in their father was positive, was good. Irene put the picture back on the shelf in the kitchen beside the one of her mother, posed at a piano, ironic and glamorous, and stared intently into Cloda's face.

Take a picture of Hal for me. Please? Okay. Good and now tell me. Did you get the information I wanted? How much will you give me for it? How much what? Money. God, you sound like a greedy pig. Come on. I did you a favor. I won't give you anything until I know what he said. I need money for film. First tell me what he said. That's not fair. Too bad. You're so mean! Stop that nervous cough. I hate you. Good. It helps me

to hate you more. You promise you'll pay me? Go on, tell me. He showed
me a picture of his wife. She was blond and pretty. His boy Loki too. He
said he also has a girlfriend and she lives in this house. What? Who! Me,
I guess, I mean he was obviously joking, said Cloda. You. That really
was a joke. Now pay me. No. What did he look like when he showed
you the picture? Did he look sad, like he still loves her? He just smiled
and that was that. Smiled? You know, nicely. Well, that's really pathetic.
Hardly anything. I won't give you anything for that. I might even take
back the bike, it's so pathetic. If you don't pay me, I'll give your clothes
to people who need them. I bet you would, too. First kiss my foot. Then
I'll pay you. No. Then kiss my wrist. Why? Because I'm—you're my
slave of course. Irene opened her palm and showed a pile of change.
Her blue-veined wrist caught the light as if the skin were nylon. Cloda
kissed and spat in one act, then grabbed the money, and ran.

x

That night they were all in the kitchen, washing and drying dishes,
when the mother called from Rome. First she talked to Irene in a perfunctory way, then to Catharine, saying she would return very soon, and
then to Cloda to whom she said: "I don't dare tell Irene, she'll have a fit,
but your father has fallen for another woman. A young blond American
do-gooder. We may never see him again. Now let me talk to Hal."

While Hal murmured into the receiver, Cloda told Irene what her
mother had said, but it was hard, because her mouth was so dry and a
pulse in her throat felt like a bird had been born there.

Chunks of black turf smoldered in the hearth and Cloda began to pump
violently on some bellows, only pulling up smoke. Irene stared at the
rows of half-eaten jams crumbling inside their glass jars as Hal set down
the receiver with an expression of inward gloom. Then Irene headed up
the stairs slowly towards the toilet. Hal wiped one plate for a long time
without saying anything.

The mother had said to him: "Everything is lost, everything. We can't perform. I can't perform. Not with this situation developing in the background. My voice just died. No spirit left. The others all feel the same. My poor cousin. The production closed down. I'm so glad you're there, darling, to welcome me when I return. It must have been a complete intervention by the gods that made you see my name on the poster. I'll be back soon! . . . Oh please take care of the girls. Especially Irene who is so eccentric. Cloda can survive anything, but poor Irene needs constant parental intervention."

He rubbed his closed lips with his index finger while Cloda watched this gesture with an anxious unease. There was something secretive in his fingering of his own mouth. He might wear an expression of concern in his eyes, but his mouth was filled with other intentions. He asked the mother questions about her safety and which route she would be travelling back to Ireland. And then he handed the phone on to Catharine, who agreed to stay on until the mother returned—"and then I'll be on my way," she noted happily. "Me too," Hal said.

When the kitchen was clean, Hal told Cloda that he was going to take Irene for a walk, and he went to the stairs and called her. Cloda eyed his movements and muttered, "See if I care what you do."

Hal and Irene left the house for the darkness, took off their shoes and laid them on the stone wall above the strand, then climbed over onto the rocks and down to the sand.

It glittered spoon-sized drops of moonlight for leagues across the ebb-tide and as their feet rounded each ripple, mollusks gurgled and drooled from their sand-holes. The city glittered ahead.

What if the tide comes in fast? asked Irene. Well, it probably will and we'll have to run like hell. Aren't you scared? No, he laughed. And you shouldn't be either. You've got me.

Nod

These three words passed through her ears and left a pain there. Her eyes burned, she stubbed her toe and screamed a curse, landing up against him. He straightened her, then squatted and looked at her foot. He rested it close to his body below his belt and recited a poem, as he pressed hard on her narrow bones and said:

Three sisters of lying: perhaps, maybe, guess! Three sisters of youth: desire, beauty, generosity! Three renewals of the world: a woman's belly, a cow's udder, a smith's furnace. Three of the highest spirits: a student having read his Psalms, a servant having laid down his load, a girl having been made a woman.

What was that? she asked A poem. Shall I say it in Irish? It was written a thousand years ago.

Yes, say it in Irish.

Teora seithir goa: bes, doig, toimte! Teora seither oited: tol, ailde, feile. Tri aithgin in domuin: bru mna, uth bo, ness gobann. Tri as mo menmnae bis: sco-loc iar legad a shalm, o cus gilla iar lecud a eiri uad, ocus ingen iar ndenum mna di.

That's so beautiful! Irene cried. Hal dropped her foot and jumped up asking, What did your mother tell you? I don't want to talk about it. Nothing. She told Cloda. About Daddy. He's gone off with another woman. You must be terribly upset. I'm revolted. But luckily I'll be leaving home soon. Won't you miss him if he doesn't come back? No. Well, then, that's lucky. It leaves room in your heart for a new love. Have you had your first love yet? No, well, I had a crush on an actor, but that's all, a year ago. Boys must chase you. No. I'm too funny as in peculiar. I think. Or something. Anyway, in Ireland boys don't seem to care that much about girls. It's fine with me. How could it be fine? Everyone wants to be loved. Boys here are really childish. Insecure.

Hal laughed and cast his arm across her narrow shoulders, then paused to look out at the blackness of sea meeting sky at the end of the puckered sand.

I was preparing to comfort you, he said, about your father's infidelity. I'm sure it will pass. Say another poem, said Irene.

Bitter is the wind tonight, it tosses the sea's white hair. I do not fear the wild warriors of Norway who course on a quiet sea . . . Do you fear me—this wild warrior from Norway—?

She shrugged and drew away from his arm. Retreating, she looked up at him and her huge, long-lidded eyes and sculpted lips had a marbled shine to them. Fear occupied every one of her features. We better go home, she said. Cloda doesn't like being alone.

I never noticed that, he said with a wan smile. Why not?

Well, it's because of, see, it's new, it's because of those war planes we see—flying out from up there—you know. And with Mummy and Daddy gone. These off-shore bars were made by an ice sheet retreating many eons ago. Did you know that? he asked. No, and I don't care, she said. Hal went silent, then trailed her for several yards before telling her to go on without him. She cast a glance over her shoulder, poised to continue, then asked Why?

Okay, come see, he said and held out his hand. She took it, curiously, hers was ice cold, and he lowered her palm down below his belt and told her to feel what she had done to him. Then he rubbed her palm across his thick, buried member, and dropped her hand saying See? Irene jumped back and Hal looking pained walked away, fast, towards the horizon. She called I'm sorry!

Then she ran back home with her hand pressed on her thigh, while she rubbed her skirt over the top of it as if to scour it with the cloth dipped in air. Her gestures were violent, her expression feverish. I'll kill her, I'll kill that bitch mother, if she comes home! she was hissing between her teeth.

When Irene returned to the house she was flushed to her roots and grasped hold of Cloda by the arm, dragging her up to their room. There she sat panting on the edge of the bed.

God, I'm glad you exist! she nearly sobbed. If you weren't here I wouldn't have had any excuse to come back! From where? why? asked Cloda. The water, the beach, the most important moment of my life. Can I go now? No! Well, what do you want? Go spy on him. See how he's acting.

Obediently Cloda left the room and slid on one hand down the bannister to the basement, where the kitchen was empty and quiet but for the ticking of a clock and the drip of a faucet. She sidled down the dark hall towards Hal's room, a beam of light shone its line along the doorjamb. She squatted and peeked, realizing as she did so that anyone must look guilty when they were being spied on. She had often thought of being a detective. Now she saw him in his room, sorting through papers in a relaxed way under his small lamp. She was thinking erratically: "Everyone loves the speed of light because it is stuck to gravity, but everyone loves the number three even more, and often people use three numbers to measure the position of a thing in space. I wonder if you could measure things even if there was no gravity and you were free-flying through space . . . "

She felt like her camera in the hands of an unknown photographer—that is, empty and attentive simultaneously. What was he doing that was sinister? Nothing. He was a bit restless, though, slapping the papers around and holding them up to read them, then walking a few paces between his bed and the desk.

She watched him stop and think and wondered if the reason older people began to forget things was that they already knew enough. He looked perplexed and began to rub his lip with his index finger in that particularly unpleasant way that she had noticed before. It made her feel the way she did when she watched a cat licking itself with amazing relish. He went to his dresser and took up a white whalebone comb she had noticed in his hand before, and he raked it through his forelock slowly. And now he seemed to consider the door as an option, so she slipped away quickly, back down the corridor and up the stairs, three at a time, to her sister's bedroom. Nothing, she announced. What do you mean? Nothing. Come on! He was just reading and stuff. In his room. Nothing. I don't understand! God, it's too insane! Can I go now? You're so naive, yes.

Cloda went into the bathroom with her camera and sat in the dark, unloading her last roll of film, which she would bring to be developed the following day. There were pictures of Hal on it, among other things. "Pride comes before a fall," she whispered without knowing why, or where she had ever heard that remark.

x

Cloda decided to run away from home on the same day that a violent anti-communist and Minister of Defense in Norway warned his King that the Russians and British were going to invade Norway. From inside that room to the outside, and up, the air seemed to move skeins of tension around, weaving light and bad thinking into knots and bombs.

Downstairs but in her ears Cloda heard Hal talking to Catharine about "Belgium" and "Holland" as well as Ireland being "compelled" by Britain to give up her "neutrality." Words like "luftwaffe" and "torpedo" batted at her ears. Hal had already told them that a "U-boat" had "torpedoed" a British aircraft carrier off the other side of Ireland—it was called "Courageous."

Nod

The names "Deutschland" and "Graf Spee" travelled from his mouth and her ear returned an echo of that word and halfway between his throat and her eardrum lay a place that captured horror. Oddly half the time it took for the whole event was equal to the distance traveled multiplied by the speed of light, and where she stood, poised at the door for escape, she believed that she could escape not just his voice but the situation that generated his voice—the war—by leaving. *m-sh-hiden-heah-d's vewden ach—owpen ooden iden koost-froon hide-veenka veezen cristal nacht-shahten-einzahden-goo-den-hime-lahnd-doy-chen-kitch-path-olodge-ik-stein . . .* These foreign sounds nonetheless trailed her from radios as she pushed her sister's bike alongside windowsills away from home.

Now Cloda had rolled up a blanket, and inside it a change of clothes, and she headed south to Killiney to where the traveling family had moved their caravan. It was December and a cold mist, nearly snow, clamped down on the coastline. The Vico Road was awash with pallors. The knife-pointed palms softened into nothings. Cloda clambered down the seawall staircase towards the stony beach, and saw the father of her friends fishing there. His dog—a short-haired hound named Pooch—was seated by his side. Pooch was a dog loyal only to one person, and indifferent to the rest of humanity. His tail curled into a spiral, revealing his tight little balls, and he wore an alert but abstract expression, and responded to no one but his master, the father. Pooch earned money for the family in the warmer months, by swimming out so far into the sea that his head seemed to be a fly zooming between the sky and water, and people screamed and called him back to no avail. The father then charged them for his whistle, which returned Pooch immediately to land. He made a lot of money this way.

The father always looked anguished and was rarely at home among the many women who inhabited the caravan. His gristled face made her think of handsome pirates drawn in stripes of ink. Whenever Cloda saw him he was fussing with an object that needed attention, and to her he was an object of sympathy. His obvious desire to escape, to be alone, to be outdoors—coincided with her own desire. Unlike her own father who drowned his furies in a domestic wine and creaked around in a state of guilt, this one was overtly everything. One day he showed Cloda the signs left by other travelers—a string on a tree, two bottle-caps hammered into tar, a red stripe of paint—that indicated the threats and possibilities in the immediate vicinity—like a mean dog or a generous neighbor—and he knew secrets about birds and fish that increased his image in Cloda's eyes as the first "real man" she had known.

He was pleasingly anti-social and spat black wads of tobacco juice onto the stones, but if he looked at Cloda even quickly, she swelled with the expectation that he would understand her. Cloda stood on the stones and dared herself to speak to the father fishing there. He seemed to sense her before seeing her and began to speak without turning. Watch the tackle, he remarked. As if it had been an instruction, she squatted to see the scattering of hooks and pebble gray balls in his tiny box. Lined up tidily. And an ugly bag of wiggling worms.

Why are you carrying a blanket around, he asked. I'm going to sleep out tonight. Why? I don't like my house. Your parents will worry. No, they're away. Just strangers are taking care of us. Us? My sister and me. Do they need work done around the house? Hal said he wants to fix the wall. What wall? Out back, where the train runs by. I can do walls. Tell him. Okay, she said proudly.

See that bird out there? That's a Blue Goose, a vagrant from Greenland. It looks lost. They haunt the great bogs of the midlands, those birds. You see at this time of year many birds flying down from Norway and Iceland—or storm-driven shags from Scotland. You can see the Gray Lag Goose in Wicklow, they leave in Spring, and the Greenland Whitefronted Goose, there are lots of them in Wexford on the slobs. They favor callow land, or grassy land by the loughs. I love to see a Shelduck returning to Ireland from Norway, and I'll be following them inland myself. If we can get there soon enough, we can catch the cliff-breeding birds on the west coast. Summer visitors. The birds who come to breed. You wouldn't believe how many vagrants and passage migrants come to Ireland. They love our turloughs and the ducks feed in the kettle-holes made from the melting ice in early spring. They're like comfortable dew-ponds, perfect for forming a sward, and rich grass to hide their nests in. When we move on, we'll head across the Bog of Allen and mind you, I can guarantee we'll be seeing geese, curlew, snipe, grouse, meadowpips, skylarks and stonechats. They come to live among the bog-cotton and heather. Where's the Bog of Allen? asked Cloda. It's the whole middle of Ireland from Dublin to Galway. Some people call it dull land. I call it beautiful and rich in bird life. Can I come with you? Don't be ridiculous. Go on home now.

She idled around him for awhile, waiting to see if he would pull in a fish, and then clambered back up the stone staircase and headed for the caravan. The girls—they were all redheads, except for the father, in that family—wanted her to play Gin Rummy with them. She tried to divert them by asking if they liked their father. No, said one. We hate him, said the other.

Cloda put down her hand and said she didn't want to play cards with them, since they were mean about their father. She had no way to confess that she couldn't bear losing and therefore she couldn't play games. As a result, huddling into her blanket, she received their furious blows with laughter and when the mist began to tighten and crystallize into snow, she had excuses to go home.

x

Soon the mother wired from Athens that she would be returning in a week's time, in order to see Irene perform and spend Christmas with them. Hal and Cloda read the telegram in the cold garden while a train tore by only feet away, shaking the artichoke tree and the wall, where the traveler's father was working. Boulders had rolled onto a flower bed from the force of the trains passing so close. The father said it would take him two afternoons to cement together the boulders back in position, and he told Hal what he would charge as if Hal was the owner of the house. Hal was agreeable and Cloda liked him that day because he was polite to the traveler man.

Irene was away doing technical rehearsals for the show, and she had said she wouldn't be home much at all that week. Now Hal announced to Cloda that he was going to watch Irene's rehearsal that night and make sure she got home safely.

When will you be leaving here? asked Cloda. You mean today, or for good? For good. It will be up to your mother. I still have much work to do on my subject.

The rehearsal took place at the school Irene attended near St. Stephen's Green in an auditorium that seated 100 people in stiff steel chairs. The programme included three of Yeats' plays—On Baile's Strand, A Singing Woman, and The Countess Cathleen—the latter set to music by a 17-year old boy who played the guitar sweetly backstage while Irene played the boy poet Aleel and sang in a dun brown outfit, ashen ever since she glimpsed Hal lounging by the exit door.

Technical rehearsals are always boring, she had told him, and this was no exception, with pause after pause to adjust the lights exactly for each figure according to position and color. Hal sat restlessly in a stiff chair, never speaking directly to Irene until one break when someone told her that her father was there. Hal protested with some urgency and embarrassment and told Irene he would meet her later at the Red Bank Restaurant.

And though she agreed and believed him gone, she nonetheless began to glow pink as neon and to sing better than ever with her small breasts rising unevenly, her nipples pricking the cloth. Her hair was cut in a Cleopatra style, thick hair that contained three different colors—auburn, brown, black—lending it a density that scattered at the lights. Hal hovered behind a wall watching the young musician watching her and her oblivion to this attention only made his own emotions more severe. Irene spoke with full concentration and charm:

A man, they say, loved Maeve the Queen of all the invisible host, And died of his love nine centuries ago. And now, when the moon's riding at the full, she leaves her dancers lonely and lies there upon that level place, and for three days stretches and sighs and wets her long pale cheeks.

She was in love—with herself! Hal noted with growing pleasure, because this meant that he had to be jealous only of her egoism, its pursuits, and no one else. If the boy were to pounce, she would recoil in surprise, but if the boy approached with a plan to make her famous, she might return his gaze and do anything he asked her. So Hal thought over his own actions of the night on the sand and—leaving the theater for the street—felt that he had, by chance, done the right thing. He had lured her towards her first sensation of her sensual self. This must be the way, he figured smiling but at the same time ripping a rock out of its place in the wall.

Later when Irene found him, she found him engaged in a highly charged talk with three large Irishmen. They were all leaning over a small table with two pots of tea between them, and papers. Hal jumped up, at her entrance, and hurried her out onto the street again, but not before she had time to realize that he had a life of his own, with other people, in Dublin. She asked him about this and what they were talking about since it sounded political; and he explained:

"No, no, it wasn't political at all. Those are scholars. *Labhraim le strainseiri.* We were talking about early Irish poetry . . . Irene . . . One of them was telling me about the Norman conquest when relations between the Welsh and the Irish were carried on with an easy exchange of cultural and aesthetic articles. The rhyming couplets in early Hiberno-Latin verse indicate an imitation of Cambro-Latin verse rather than native

Irish poetry. This is important for understanding the kinds of influence at the heart of the work. I mean, prose tales with verse highlights are a common Celtic form with Indo-European antecedents. Sanskrit stories even come in that form!"

x

Meantime Cloda—alone at home—Catharine was with her own children—again left. She was determined this time to sleep away from the house and maybe finally discover if fairies existed. Even the idea of them!

She went to the caravan on her sister's black bike through the dark and felt this way the happiness of being a hard sea animal that machines its way gracefully through the ecstatic interiors of the outside world. Her pink innards likewise had a life of their own, her body was neither hers nor her, but a vessel she rode as a visual being whose ideas and dreams and memories were floating outside her skin, sometimes all the way up to the sky, loose attachments to the machine that got her from A to B. Yet she really didn't plan her path between numbers but instead was driven by physical restlessness and just happened to wind up wherever she did. That night she rolled inside her blanket near the caravan and stared through clear air up into the starry sky. She could hear the murmurs of Gammon from inside the caravan, words sprinkled with occasional English she understood, and she pretended she was one of them.

But then the father arrived out of the wall of trees like a projection of their potential free will. It scared her, his coming like a thing that moved. And he growled out orders at her now, the way he did at his children, telling her to go home. She said, rudely, "I can do whatever I want!"

And he replied, It's not safe here. Cloda couldn't think of another fresh response so she just lay there, stubbornly, while he looked down at her.

He nudged her with his toe. Go on, girl, get home with you.

No. Now the father smiled slightly and said, All right. I'll have to take you then. Up!

She jumped up from her blanket, hauling it along with her, and now she trailed him down a slope to the bike he kept parked near the caravan. He ordered her on the bar in front of him, side-saddle. It was a rusty old bike with fat tires and she tried to keep from touching him, though his heat covered her side and neck. All the way along he talked about drunks and tramps, and then bumped the bike around some winding roads, until he pulled up beside a grove of trees as purple as grapes and ordered her down. She did what he said. She wondered if she was sup-posed to be scared, since she wasn't, as she went ahead and followed him around two very fat old trees, gnarled and rotten, towards a stone structure, which he pointed out to her. The moonlight illuminated its chair-like shape.

This is a Druid seat, the father told her. It still has bloodstains on the stones from ancient sacrifice. Go on. Get up. Get in. Now make a wish. You seem to be a troubled child in need of magic. Close your eyes now. Wish.

Shyly Cloda did as he said, fitting herself into the cold stone seat, closing her eyes and wildly searching her brain for a wish. Only one—for her father to come home!—came to her then, and it was so pathetic to her, she embarrassed herself, and tears stung her lashes, as she jumped out of the chair, saying, I did it.

He marched back through the trees with her rushing after him. Back on the bike the father said, "Across this world there are varieties of people who have no homes—some are running away from something and others are running to something. It's the latter category to which my people belong. We travel to each other, we are a family scattered but always reuniting. This is the only category to which a young girl should belong. You can't choose a new family. Stay with your own."

Now Cloda—tired—sort of absorbed what he was saying and remembered his daughters telling her about their relatives in County Clare and how they planned to be there by spring for a wedding. Sleepily she imagined caravans rattling all over Ireland with these families rushing up to greet and embrace each other, but this image seemed also to spill from a huge backdrop of the little red-faced baby brother, mouth ajar, howling, as if all the families were falling from his tonsils, across his tongue, blown on a storm of his tears, and unequalled, unanswered grief.

Then she realized (an electric shudder against the man's chest) that she had forgotten her sister's bike and she put her hand to her mouth, as if to contain her horror.

x

Many years later—on a bus in Central Turkey—she would wonder: "Are tinkers gypsies, or are they scrap-dealers who move to work? Were gypsies deported? Are fairies nomads? Are angels fairies? Are itinerants people who want to live in a new home every year? Are sedentarists the norm? Was the goal of the Nazis the conquest of Eastern Europe, or all of Europe? What was the bombing of Scapa Flow? What does it mean—"the road is my driver"?"

x

On his way with Irene to the train station that night Hal continued to explain his meeting with those men in the Red Bank Restaurant:

"One of those scholars back there, Irene, explained a fact to me. The Viking settlements in Ireland became containers for culture from the western islands to Norway and Iceland. Icelandic poetry contains the tightening and normalizing of the Irish verse line. Isn't that amazing?

Nod

No coincidence when you compare the intra-linear rhyme and consonance among 10th century Icelandic poets and 7th century Irish poets. After all, not only in the arts, but also in war, the Irish learned cruelty from the Norse, which helped them during the Norman Invasion. Now you see certain links continuing, between the Irish and the Germans, they have much in common, you'd be surprised."

Like what? asked Irene. A common enemy, said Hal.

As if from nowhere a sheet of rain blew across them, covering what had been a clear and star-spangled sky. Hal pulled out an umbrella and popped it open over them, and held her arm tight to keep her close from the wild downpour as they hurried over the bridge. Don't let me bore you any more, he said. What is your favorite line from the play?

She sang: Lift up the white knee, Hear what they sing, Those young dancers That in a ring Raved but now Of the hearts that broke So Long, long ago For their sake.

How sweet, said Hal. Why does a girl play the part of a boy though? It's traditional, with this play. It's very odd. To waste your beauty so. Don't I look okay on the stage? You were angelic. How nice it is that your mother will be back in time for your performance.

Nice for you, you mean, said Irene. Why? he asked, turned down to read the bitterness in her voice on her lips. Never mind, was her curt response. He drew her into the shelter of a doorway. No. Tell me. Why nice for me? Now that she's free, you two can start up again where you left off. You don't need to think about that, he said and pressed the print of his thumb on her lips. Or speak about it either. In any case I'm almost done with my research. I can leave here sooner than planned.

Good, she said and pushed past him into the rain.

He followed with the yellow umbrella extended and caught her arm again. If you were a few years older, he said.

Well, I'm not.

And you should be with a boy like that one—back there—on the guitar.

Well, I'm not.

I'm sure he'd like to. The way he looked at you. Aren't you glad your mother's coming back?

Anything would be better than this hell, she said and repeated, Anything.

Hell?
You know what I mean.

You're not being serious, are you? This sounds like a scene from a play!

Don't be condescending, said Irene and drew apart from him.

Well, then, tell me about the hell.

I can't, she whispered and pressed her knuckles on her teeth, biting down as tears gathered and fell.

Hal didn't notice this because he was too tall to see her face easily and because he was afraid they had missed the last train and would have to ride the bus home. So he began scanning bus routes posted on poles until he found one that would take them to Sandymount and by then she had drawn herself in again and wore her more usual questing and awestruck expression, staring at the lights in the windy puddles. They moved again into a storefront shelter on the deserted street, side by side, faces turned away from each other. He had the collar of his jacket turned up and seemed to have sunk inside it to contain the heat of his own body, while she stood with her blue cape wide open, dramatically available to wind and rain.

You look like Leslie Howard, said Irene and gave a huge smile to the rain, all teeth, and shook her shoulders, laughing alone.

Her hair shivered and shone, and Hal tugged a lock of it gently, asking, What's so funny?

Nothing! she screamed, convulsed, and held her belly tight.

Hal stepped back, perplexed. Her mood swings aged him. He was embarrassed by his inability to keep up with them, as if they were strenuous activities and he was limping along behind. Now he only wished the bus would hurry and get them home. But she stopped laughing as fast as she had begun and edged nearer to him as if to ask for forgiveness. She stood in front of him this time, boldly pressing her body back into his, her hair falling inside his collar where it opened at his throat. He put up his hands to part it. "Don't get caught in a button." And he slipped his hands then onto her waist and pressed her against him harder, his navel resting in the small of her back. Only their breathing stirred them until the bus arrived wheezing and empty down the street, and they boarded, with quick sharp breaths, and climbed up to the top floor and the front seats to look down and out at the driving rain, as the bus tipped around Trinity College, medieval gray and unlighted. They sat on separate seats up there, each of them red-cheeked and sweaty.

x

The next day was unaccountably sunny. Goldness gushed down between white clouds and into their wintery garden. Irene pulled a wooden fold-up chair out back, as if it were summer, and sat with her skirt whirled around her knees and her throat curved back, face up to the welcoming heat. Meantime the traveler father rolled boulders onto wet cement and packed and scraped them together so that a dry wall became a wet wall, and stones wouldn't fall.

Hal was in Dublin and Irene was wondering about the men with him the night before, they seemed suspect to her for some reason, not scholars contemplating the influence of Sanskrit on Irish verse, but something worldly, worse. Now Cloda ran out to show her her photographs and Irene scrutinized them greedily at first, then slowly and critically, and then with some questions that suggested a special interest in the art of photography. Cloda felt herself grow flush with pleasure and anxiety. A chance to show off!—both to Irene and the father hunched over the wall. But also a chance to lose control of the secrets of her camera. How hard is it to take these? asked Irene. Not hard. Well, I mean how much do you have to know? Not much. I bet you do. That's why you've got too much shadow in this one. And that picture of Hal is too light. Look at his face, it's almost empty. You need to really get the rules right. Typically, you're sloppy. But I like this picture of Hal alot. Can I have it, and where's the camera? In our room. Bring it down. I want to try it. Nervously Cloda ran upstairs and brought the camera to her sister whose serious—even professional—attention more than justified her own involvement in any activity, but simultaneously threatened it. With her hair all over her face Cloda leaned over to explain—with tremulous authority in her voice—how the camera worked. Irene listened and examined the dials, numbers and lenses intently.

Then she said, Great! I'm going to try it. Can you find me a book that will explain the dials? Somewhere upstairs. I'll look.

From the kitchen came the claws and barks of male voices and war news on the radio. Despite the sun, Irene sensed an environment polluted by human wickedness and pulled tight on the arms of the chair, rising. It folded like a fact confirming her suspicions—and crushed one of her fingers between the slats. She let out a scream. Pooch yelped and the father hurried over and broke the wood in his hands, freeing her flattened index finger. She was hissing her hurt at the pain while he walked her inside, and held her hand under the trickle of icy water into the soapstone sink. Cloda ran down from her room and saw the man looking at Irene closely as if her face offered the solution to some problem he had been having. His face contained repose and thoughtfulness, breathing beside the sobbing girl. Then he picked up a towel and mopped at her cheeks, before spotting Cloda at the door and stepping outside again, all in one move.

What happened, what happened? asked Cloda. And Irene explained, concluding: That hideous man—who is he?

If Cloda had been able to speak her feelings, she would have said to her sister: "Don't you see that all men are a variation on an Original Man and didn't emerge from sex and the bodies of women as women themselves did? Men simply reproduced spontaneously, as a million variations on one theme—aloneness—from their first moment on earth. Their hardness, their brash voices, their hair and muscle, these are only the variants. The basic man was always mean and when he wasn't violent, it was only self-control that explained it—a self-control equal to an actor's. A man's natural state is rage. I've always sensed that men were dangerous because women acted so nervous around them. A good man is therefore not a real man. A queer man is a free man, and a cheerful man is a man in a temporary state of liberty from his bondage to rage. But this is not "a hideous man"—if you just tried to talk to him!"

Cloda, coughing, approached him in the garden, where he was smearing a lash of cement across a dent. In the sun his face looked like a stone face carved into an abbey wall. She noticed that his hands were unlike the pale freckled and round-fingered shape of other white men. He had brown muscular fingers with oval nails like seashells, each one was precise and pink.

Um, Um, have you seen my bike? I mean the one out at your place. In the trees. I've got to get it. It's my sister's. No, he said, I haven't. Well, could you look or ask the girls to? We're going on. Tomorrow. On where? Last night the wind got in our way. Knocked the caravan off kilter. My brother's coming to get us going again. Then we're heading on to Bray Head and on down to Waterford.

You luckies! You have your family. Your sister, he said, and the change in his features made her step back. You'd better watch after the likes of her. What for? She's got too much beauty for her own good. That hasn't got anything to do with me. Don't you love her? What do you mean? I would, he said with a small grin.

Cloda backed away from him, grinding down on her teeth to the roots. From six feet away, with her limbs hot from an interior and hellish flaming, she had her first experience with a contorted emotion, one that twisted pleasure and pain in a knot, and pulled tight. She wildly wondered if an evil fairy had taken his form, making him say things he didn't really mean.

I know how you could see her more, she stammered. Is that so. Every night. She walks. Home. Here. Alone. At ten. Why's that? After her play. She's an actress. She'd love to—see you see her. He made no response to this, and Cloda went inside breathing heavily as if the air was medicinal, a potential cure to the fire interior. Inside their room, Irene bandaging her finger and still moaning miserably.

Fucking shit. Imagine having a goddamn accident on opening night, Irene said. I have the worst fucking luck. Where's my camera? I'm bringing it to rehearsal. Well, give it back when you're done. Where's my bike? Outside, obviously. Why do you look so wild? I do? You should grow your hair. You look better when it looks a little wild. Don't cut it again. Soon you'll have boys after you. Well, not here, but somewhere. I mean Ireland is not exactly romantic that way. But you've got to stop acting like a boy or you'll turn into a lesbian. It's embarrassing to have a sister who is so retarded. What's wrong with you anyway? I'm going out. Well, never let anyone see you smile. You don't have a good smile, Cloda. Cover your mouth. I'll see you in the play. Bye.

x

Opening night brought Irene all the kudos she could desire. She got three encores and most teachers' raves. Cloda and Catharine went together to see the plays that night and sent flowers backstage. But when Irene opened the card and read their names, instead of someone else's, she was downcast and tossed the flowers aside.

Outside, Catharine said to Cloda in low intimate tones, her head tipped sideways and down: "It's going to be hard on you, dear, having such a magnificent sister. Losing is hard. The worst of it is that you can become a monster, while the winner becomes kinder and ever more of a divinity. The winner's virtues increase while the loser becomes twisted and bitter. I've seen it too often not to know that it's true. You have a hard road ahead of you."

Cloda spat out a wet lop of her hair that she had been chewing and looked up at Catharine with horror, as if her words had been a prophecy. Hal didn't come to that performance but said he would wait and come with the mother on her return. He was studying all the time, as if on a mission to finish fast, and they only saw him in brief moments during those days.

Irene felt a disturbing hunger she had never known before. An appetite that couldn't be stopped by bread and butter or gooseberry fool. Still, she located it inside her stomach behind the navel and down to the top of her v-shaped, silky but childlike hairline—a hollow—as if it were food she wanted. She liked the yawning hope of it. The vacancy that she could ogle inwardly and call her own.

A pond, a mirror, a well with her own invisible eyesight, and insight, turned inward to it; and it was alive.

Like a pretty little insect something flashed around inside it.

At night returning alone from her performance, Irene rounded the bend at the bottom of the hill, and saw a man in shadows by a tree. She crossed the street to move away, but paused then, too, believing it was Hal, waiting for her, and so there was a prolonged set of seconds, when she was scrutinizing a form that was motionless. Her hunger ate a larger hole in her belly, her bowels went weak, and she felt a moistening in her loins as the man lifted his hands and adjusted his pants. He was too thick and too small to be Hal, so she ran home, cramping at the letdown that was greater than her fear. Later that night, exhausted and having to go to school in the morning, Irene could hardly sleep for the thought of Hal working underneath her bed. She lay on her stomach with her face in her pillow, wishing that she could have one more night alone with him before her mother returned. She whispered at her sister, Did you see him? Did he say anything? Is he leaving soon? Do you think he's avoiding me? Do you know what he wears to bed? Cloda crossly told her to go ask him herself. But Irene couldn't imagine releasing such over-active and overbright queries into the air. Her own time on stage gave her a feeling of hiddenness, despite the bright lights and the audience. The stage was a mirror image of audience and world, or the thing seen from the other end. To see the stage was to witness the vulgarity of fake order. To be on stage was to participate in veils and mysteries. She pre-ferred being seen to seeing.

Now she told Cloda about the figure in shadows outside. And Cloda, ever curious, went to the window to look out. And sure enough she saw the person, like a variation on the stones and the sea and shadows around him, but with a will and freedom from gravity that led him to lean into the light. It was a man on the long slope. It was a familiar man on wet pavement, leaves around his feet. It was the traveler father, staring up at the very window where she stood. Cloda sank back to the side, in the curtains, her temples pulsing up portions of pain, but she said nothing to Irene who lay on her bed like an analysand seeking a revelation.

x

The next morning, hidden under some vines in the front garden, Cloda saw her sister's bike. There was no note explaining its appearance. There was no need for a note. Cloda wheeled it around to the back of the house and put it safely in the little conservatory filled with dried earth and rotten plants. She was panting with happiness. First because her sister had not found out that she had left the bike in a field miles away; second because the travelling man had been outside their house for her sake and not for the sake of her sister.

Now the clouds labored with their piece of space, pushing it this way and that and their own bulging shapes often looked tough as a chew. Sometimes a message would be scripted on twilight's wall: a lace-like tree erupted into a language she might miss by squinting towards the pink air behind it. Yellow sometimes. Or a cloud fell in the night and grayed like gas everything now not in sight. Coastal fog. Antidote to blitzkriegs. Why were the Christians saying "donner and blitzen" as if its evil context had no relation to the reindeer playing in air? Was every Cathedral constructed in order to be a temptation to bombers?

For so many years she wished she could literally rebuild her days in the way the world stood then. A tree up there, a cloud over to the west, a colorful wind floating in the kitchen window . . . She believed if she could re-enter the actual architecture of those days she could locate the start of her earthly terrors. This is when she would open St. Augustine and find directives:

"Circular movement, which guarantees the unchanged preservation of things through their repetition and continual return, is the most direct and most perfect expression (and therefore the closest to the divine) of the zenith of the hierarchy: absolute immobility."

x

The mother's return home was dramatic because of her changed appearance and affect. She might have been Medea crying "O women's love so full of trouble, how many evils have you caused already?" It was hard to judge whether she arrived in this condition or assumed it, shortly after she arrived home. The first night, she curled around Hal's arm and he shook her off, explaining:

"It happens, when one goes away from home for a long time, that one loses one's attachments to one's family, and then he has to relearn them. It makes him feel estranged, guilty. Many men returning from war have had such an experience."

Men? she asked wonderingly. You're talking to me, Hal. A woman. I have returned from a war. You were there. You saw. A political problem, not yet a war, he corrected her. No. You're wrong . . . Why can't I touch you? He said, But you can! Here's my hand . . .

They were all crouched around a turf fire over the kitchen, and Hal raised his hand to her while his eyes slid to the left where Irene sat with the concentrated stare of a feline trapping a rodent. He winked. The mother caught it, took note, stood and went to lock herself in her room for twenty four hours, until it was as if she had gone away again.

When she came out, her black hair had thin white streaks; her neck was loose; her eyes were ringed. She was either apathetic or enraged, moving among the three of them like a mental patient allowed home for a day visit.

Irene cringed and questioned: What's her problem? She's just tired from traveling, Catharine explained. Well, she doesn't have to take it out on us!

Nod

This was on a Monday when the theater was dark and Irene could stay home. She and Hal went to the little grocer in Sandymount to buy fish, green beans and potatoes, and after supper Irene followed him into his room and shut the door behind her. She wore an anxiously searching expression as she settled on the edge of his bed with books pressing into her backside.

Recite more poetry to me, she said. I need some poetry. Why? What's troubling you? he asked from the corner. My mother. Please say a poem. Don't be mean to your mother. She's insane, I hate her. She's suffering, she's seen terrible things. Like what. Her own face? I don't know yet. She won't talk about it. Well, I wish she'd just leave again. Now that's unkind. I want to be alone. Again. With just you. And the others.

Hal lurched away from the wall and sat on the floor beside her legs, knees up, head down on them. He addressed the floor: All right, I'll recite a poem.

Sea-horses shine in summer as far as Bran's eye can see. Flowers—streams of honey—gush forth in the land of Manannan, son of Ler. The glittering of the sea on which you sail, the brightness of the sea on which you row, has poured forth yellow and blue—it's like solid land—

I don't remember the rest, he concluded. You should have been a poet yourself, she said. I bet you'd be good at it. No, I wasn't. I was pretentious and awkward. I had no sense of music. It was a fabrication. Luckily I knew when to stop. Some of us are born to translate the genius of others. Actors are like translators, said Irene. No, not really. Please don't contradict me all the time, she said and rested her leg against his, leaning down.

Okay, he agreed and stroked the bone of her ankle. He removed her black walking shoe and placed her blue socked foot between his legs with a sigh. What she felt there in the instep of her foot made her curl over to conceal her emotions in the aura of his body.

He said, "You're way too young, I can't, this is wrong," and drew her down to him so that she was resting between his legs and he could raise her skirt as if it were his. Which he did. And pressed his two thumbs on her cotton-covered groin as if it were his too. And kissed her neck, saying, "We can't, it's not right, I'm too old for you, please go . . . Your mother."

You'd rather be with my mother? she asked. Don't be ridiculous, child. Child? All right, I'll go.

She made a move which made him move and say, "Don't!" And again she relaxed back into him, but instead of embracing her, he circled her neck with his hands, saying, "How easy it would be for someone to hurt you," and then he leaned over whispering into her ear, dropping his hands onto her breasts, and she jumped as if electrified and wrestled herself around to a different position, this time with her face facing his and her whole body up against his, and her knees up on either side of his chest.

"Don't, Irene," he said again, "it's asking too much."

And he nudged her backwards, away, and lifted her to her feet as he also stood unsteadily up and then seeing the expression on her face, he held her against him, planting the impressions of his body into her belly and telling her he desired her but he had to leave her alone, and go.

Why? she asked.

Because it would end badly. I'm old enough to know that much. You'd get tired, want someone younger, in a matter of weeks. No.

But now the door winged ajar and the mother stood there, wild-haired, in her slip, and just as fast as she appeared, she was gone, with a slamming of doors behind her. Irene literally wiped the smile off of her own face before Hal could see it, and sat down on his bed. Well, he said, now the worst has happened. We might as well go on.

He removed the books from his bed systematically, locked his door, and pushed her down on the bed, under him, rushing to his climax on the center of her bare stomach.

She didn't leave his room. Outside at five a.m. the milk wagon clopped and clanked along the pavement. She heard the hooves and they sounded like the lap of waves underneath a dock. Clop clop. The glass milk bottles, left out empty the night before, were now exhanged for new full bottles, and a third of each was topped off with a yellowy cream that the sun would warm if the milk stayed out too long. They made their own butter from that cream and laced it with lard. But the bread was delivered too—thick brown moist bread—that they ate with the last dashes of their father's jam. Like this many horses clopped through the background of each day—not just horses, but ponies and donkeys, going this way and that, along the stones.

She listened to all these sounds, that morning, with an acute awareness of their transience, of a winged violence that would end the sweetness of those deliveries. When, afterwards, Hal and Irene lay together, he promised that next time all the pleasure would be hers and he added that he felt he would kill rather than let anyone hurt her. Irene didn't speak through the weight of feeling she had on her. It had to do with the gasps he uttered, his collapsing power as a form of pleasure that she had engineered. She had never felt such delight in making someone sound as if they were suffering. But the imprint of his pain, a milky smear on her skin, he wiped away expertly, saying,

"Don't worry, you're still a virgin," now without a trace of agony in his voice.

So she said, crisply, "I'm not worried, but I better go clean up." And she rolled to the north and stood looking down at him for the first time ever.

His smile crossed his white teeth exactly when a donkey brayed outside in the dawn.

x

If American was an ism then the mother would be one of its strongest, but most unconscious, proponents. There was an aspect of excess to each of her emotions, and the girls, who had grown used to the muted pastels and grays of Dublin, were jarred by their mother's colorful clothes, by her face that seemed to be exploding with an ego approximating nationalism, and the assumptions of muchness that trailed and preceded all her words and gestures. They had to reassess their own Americanisms in the light of her presence, and to see where they, too, were verging always on excess.

On this one night however the mother seemed to shrink thirty years into her future—into a grey, dry and elfin body. In her room alone, she sat on her knees speechless though utterances winged and beat at the interior of her cheeks. But at 3 a.m. she left her room and entered Cloda's bedroom where she was in a deep sleep, her black hair finally spread back from her face and looped around the pillow. The mother hovered over her. Then she went to the little desk in the room and took a pair of scissors in her hand and went to the bedside. Her face was the consistency and color of wet clay, she chomped down hard on her teeth, until her jaw trembled, and with concentrated skill she began to snip off all of Cloda's curls, stuffing them into her dressing gown pocket as she did so. All around the skull she cut, even lifting the back of the girl's head to reach the hair behind, cutting close to the skull, so that there would be no way on earth she could hide her face.

The operation was performed in a very mild light that shone from outside, and it was complete within a matter of minutes. Now we can see you, she whispered.

Then the mother flew back to her room and tossed the hair into the fire that burned and hissed around lumps of turf. She cleaned it all off of herself, batting at her body with her hands, and pulling last strands out of her pockets to watch them float and crackle in the short flames. Why was she laughing to herself? And talking in whispers? As if she were two? Or three? When she climbed into bed she lay for a long time listening to the tick and tock of the fire as it nibbled up whatever was there. Since winter mornings were dark until nearly nine she slept finally for five hours before being awakened by Cloda's voice.

Ma, Ma, look what happened to me! the girl was sobbing and clutching her face in her own two hands. Red and swollen from howling, fear. Why did you cut your hair? asked the mother. I didn't! It just happened! I woke up! God, darling, calm down. It will grow back. But look! I look awful! Here, I'll fix it. Go to my dresser and sit down. Cloda did as she was told still holding her face and keeping her eyes averted from her own image. She was wearing her school uniform, but the shirt was hanging out and her long socks hung around her ankles. Behind her the dwarfed mother crouched, her hands on her daughter's shoulders, and she couldn't stop shaking with laughter, or some kind of excitement, as she confronted the face before her. At last we can see who you are, she giggled. It's not funny! What happened? Who did it and why? Did Irene do it? Tell me!

No, Irene was locked downstairs all night. With her legs unlocked. It must have been—it must have been—what? Fairies maybe? Quick. Fix it! Cloda screamed. The mother combed at the short, chopped hair, and saw that she would have to cut it very close in order to make it uniform.

In the end Cloda would look like someone who had mites, or was being quarantined, with her black hair cut so close to her scalp and the terror on her face fully exposed. She refused to go to school. Her mother was kind and let her stay home. She even let her hide in bed for the day and pampered her with cups of tea and toast. And Catharine went to town and bought her a pinkish gray wool hat to wear, and she told Cloda stories about great saints who dressed like men in order to do daring things and about nuns whose heads were shaved because they were holy.

But why did the fairies do this to me? Cloda kept asking. What does it mean?

Catharine pondered the question, then started a story with the words: "One night many years ago—from under a dry rose bush—in a rough garden near the Irish Sea, came a band of insects walking in soldierly formation—imitating men—their wings pointing to the moon . . . "
But then she decided not to tell that tale and said instead, We don't know it was fairies, now, do we? You might have even cut it yourself in your sleep, for all we know. I didn't. Well, it might have been an intoxicated fairy then, though you never hear of them being drunk. They only like to have a little of everything. Did you leave some water at the bottom of your glass before retiring? Maybe they came to drink some and saw you sleeping . . . Oh, I don't know what I'm saying. I think there is a perfectly good reason for it.

Later that day Catharine found long strands of black hair in the grating of the mother's room and accused her of cutting her daughter's hair.

You must tell her you did it, she said fiercely. You'll make the child feel she's losing her mind. Never play with belief like this! Belief? It's idiocy, the mother answered and clasped her neck. What is she to think then? Please let's drop the subject. It's hardly worth a discussion, let alone an argument. I can't drop it. She doesn't know what happened, she is bewildered, frightened. I tell you, you can't play with belief. It's a sin! God, how I hate those terms. How I hate the infantilism of the Irish. Belief? What the hell do you mean by that? Belief in what? I'll tell you what I believe in. Self-interest.

Your own cynicism and cruelty to your child—how could you? What is she to think? She's odd enough already without you making her think she's mad. I pray to God she'll survive you and find her way somewhere else, I pray to the Mother of God that she gets away from you. Catharine, we don't really need you here anymore. I had meant to tell you this. It's just not necessary and I can't afford it anyway. My husband is using up all our savings on his sex life. I hardly made a sou in Italy.

Is it because of my words about the hair? You can't take a word of admonishment? Is that it?

No. I don't see it as admonishment. I see it as superstition. One more piece of Catholic madness. To think she will be that upset about a little shift in her appearance. She looks much better now. You can go home to your family now, thank you very much.

Catharine packed and left, but only after telling Cloda (who was wearing the gray hat in bed) where she could find her if she wanted to visit.

x

Irene tried very hard to play down one teacher's remark about her performance: "Why is an American girl playing an Irish boy?" but she was embarrassed by the question and became paranoid enough to imagine all the other actors were asking it too. Not the guitarist, Aidan, who played off-stage while she sang, because it was he who had refused to act in the play, being shy, and who had urged the director to try Irene; but all the others. She was ashamed of being an American and even began to soften her consonants, add a small lilt to her sentences, and speak through clenched teeth. Indeed the night her mother came to the show, with Hal, Irene refused to go home with them, but said Aidan would walk her to the train. Hal asked, And how many more nights is it playing? Only next weekend, she said. And will he walk you to the train every night?

The mother, hearing this exchange at the door, grabbed Hal's arm and shoved him out to the sidewalk. Monster! she said. Leave her alone. Why should I? Only because you're jealous? he replied. And as he turned to walk towards a pub, she whirled her yellow cloak around her and headed off into the night, talking furiously to herself.

Hal hovered in the darkness uncertainly and then hid in a doorway behind a large sign painted with two ice cold penguins having a conversation.

One said: "Without a shadow of a doubt, you cannot eat a better sweet." He felt his temples and throat pulsing as if he had eaten something bitter and was having a severe allergic reaction. He could hardly swallow. When he saw Irene exit with the boy at her side, the two of them shyly and slowly walking a foot apart, he retreated further into the dark, then rushed off after the mother.

Meantime she was dashing towards a cab. In hot pursuit, Hal hit a man by chance, a beggar, with his raised arm, then whirled and slugged the man by choice this time across the face, uttering a Norwegian curse, as he also witnessed the mother climbing into a cab and taking off. The beggar was bleeding from the nose and uttering sobs as Hal tore into the misty streets, forgiving himself as he ran.

The American mother by this time was cruising past the General Post Office smoking with the gusto of someone drinking thirstily. The driver wore a gray hat and a pleasant smile.

To calm herself—her hands were shaking—she asked him what he thought about the situation in Europe.

He said, Soon they'll be rationing our sugar, tea and fuel. It's bad. The emergency. I mean, I don't trust the fellows in Vichy, do you? I happen to be pro-communist myself. I went to Spain. We had Father Flanagan on our side then, but the rest of the clerics were rotten. I tell you, the priest's pig gets the most porridge. I don't know what poor Jesus would say.

He was a Jew. He'd be heading for the wilderness.

Nod

Now is it true? That's what they say is happening. The Jews is being maligned.

I was just there. Much of what you hear is exaggerated, and much of what you don't hear is outrageous. You have to keep human paranoia in mind at all times. What do you know about that? the driver asked. I have two cousins—children—in Provence. I have to get them out of there. Their father's a Jew. And their mother, my cousin, is utterly hysterical. She thinks they'll be kidnapped and taken forever. I think she's lost her mind but the fact is, Hitler is extremely dangerous and there is another major war brewing.

Our Government might help you get the children out. We've got ins with the French. I don't know political people. I mean, personally.

No, of course not. But you might approach someone in the range of them. You Americans have power, he said.

Not the women. Ah, I think I have to do this on my own.

Have you got children yourself? Two girls, but they've grown away from me. This is the way with them. Most teens are as lazy as a piper's little finger. One of them is truly beautiful. It has ruined her. She thinks she's entitled to any man's love and attention. And of course they leap on her, thanks to her looks. What about the other one? She's innocent and fortunately ordinary. It's a bad time for girls. They're loose and careless like the leg on a pot. The young one is strangely moody. Are you sure about that? She might just be sad that her sister is so fair and she's still in her boots. I don't know. Their problems are nothing compared to people their age in Europe. My duty is to get those two little boys out of Southern France to pacify their parents. I mean, how could I not do that? Besides, it would be a good way to commit suicide, she added in a whisper.

Now they began to speak simultaneously, the one not listening to the other: He said: Then you better do it soon, I tell you, before this turns to all-out war. We want to keep neutral and that's fine, but there's no staying clean in wartime. Everyone gets dirt on their hands, no matter where they stand. All good things have the status of dreams . . . And she said: It's supreme selfishness to think of romance at a time like this. In history. I mean my daughter—incredible selfishness. I really wish the worst for her—I wish- well, I wish she'd know what it is to be plain—to be ordinary—even fat—a potato—slut. I would put a curse on her if I weren't her mother! I do put a curse on her!
And she slammed the door on the astonished driver.

x

When Irene, later that night, returned, the house was dark, her sister asleep, and Hal not yet back. She was feeling chilled and cast off from normal warmths, having left the sanctuary of theater for the walk with Aidan, whom she didn't really care to know very well, and having walked several streets alone.

She slipped into a pair of pink cotton pajamas, scrutinizing her sister's shorn head with a high degree of pity. Pathetic, she whispered under her breath, for written on the face of a sleeper is such vulnerability that even a condescender weakens at the sight of it. Irene had always seen Cloda as a born failure because she was younger. The weird loss of her hair made it even more obvious. She was a little crazy maybe, like their mother.

Sometimes Irene felt guilty in relation to Cloda, too, and wished that she could prove that she was herself not perfect after all, not deep down, even though her surface appearance suggested otherwise. Sometimes Irene complained about everything that happened to her so that she wouldn't be viewed as ruthless. After all, she always got everything she wanted and she realized early on that people preferred luck, or talent, to calculation. So while she engineered her desires with tremendous focus, she developed, simultaneously, a persona that seemed tragic. She gave an impression of someone who had suffered terribly and was therefore— like her mother—hypersensitive to insult and disappointment.

Irene was the living proof that being the chosen one is not always a blessing.

(One has to continually prove one's worth through work. Isn't that right, Doctor? After all by now everyone knows that the elect need worldly success in order to prove to everyone that they are, in fact, endowed with a special grace. Otherwise sacredness would seem to be equally distributed among all people!)

That night Irene concluded: "Obviously Cloda cut her hair in order to out-do me in the play. Because I'm playing a boy. I mean, it's so pathetically obvious . . . "

Then, without waking her sister, Irene went downstairs and no sooner had she left a mustache of milk on her upper lip than Hal entered the house and the kitchen, with beer on his breath. He walked directly to Irene and licked the milk off her lip, then pulled her down the hall into his room. He locked the door.

What if Mum wakes up and comes down? she asked, excited now by the rush of events, and growing warmer by the minute.

Too bad. She already knows enough.

He started unbuckling and unzipping and prying off his shoes all at once, while she wrung her hands, asking What are you doing?

Sleeping with you.

I don't dare.

Then pretend I'm your doctor. Let me examine you.

Now his pants clanked to the floor, his shoes toppled and his shirt tails parted to make room for that member of the human family she had never yet looked at close up.

Get under the covers, he told her and turned off the light. His knees were shaking like a man having a heart attack, when he joined her under the sheets, whispering, It won't hurt.

Are you sure? First say a poem, Irene insisted.

What though the seas look lone, What though the winds make moan, Round our isle's prison wall? Since love sails all the seas, Sings love in every breeze, Tis enough: oh, tis all.

Did you love my mother? Irene asked. Shh. Let's not bring her in on this. But—did you? If I had, I wouldn't be able to love you, would I. I don't know why not, but it's really disgusting to think about. Then don't. Don't.

She eyed him and was attracted to his near-indifference, his averted face, something in his coldness that was like a smooth journey down a perilous hill of ice.

x

Cloda awoke before anyone else. It seemed more like October than like the December day that it was. Whirling winds turned up compost heaps of leaves and sent them upwardly flying, and old still-red petals, long buried, shot to the surface of the earth, a palette of rhododendrum colors that might have been the fruit blossoms of spring. The ocean gleamed and leaped, each wave as individuated as a separate fish (salmon, trout, mackerel, carp, plaice, shark, tuna, minnow).

Nod

And the bellies of gulls were as white as canvas paint. If you stood by the stone walls looking out at Howth, you could see the silver spears of the Sugarloaf Mountains as clear as clouds and even the cliffs of Wales, it was that fresh, and imagine curraghs chopping back and forth carrying poetry and weapons from centuries earlier. Cloda put on her hat—comforted by the fact that Catharine had given it to her—and started walking alongside the sea wall. She was going to play hooky, that much she knew, and maybe, today, do something even more . . . The disappearance of her hair had done something to her emotions, making her scared of a world in which such things could happen—bitter at her family's indifference to her fear—and wholly drawn to water, wind, trees, light, birds, stones, mountains. She held her mouth up and open to drink the sun that was bright, if cold, and ran with determination south. That morning she took the train to Dun Laoghaire and lay on the grass in front of the Royal Marine Hotel.

But when the sky was like a yellow-tinted see-through candy-wrapper she walked back along the tracks towards Dublin. Dressed in blue jeans, sneakers, and a flannel shirt. She saw huge-winged birds landing on the water and war planes—khaki-colored—zooming in darkness from the north to the east. One of them she thought was a fairy, but then it turned out to be a lame seagull. She met a lost dog on the way and let him follow her. They trailed along ocean's edge on the beach, where she skipped flat stones and the dog went swimming to retrieve what couldn't be found. She walked and swung her arms in an attempt at a boyishness that her sore and blooming bosoms discouraged.

The harvest-like wind that rattled the stones around her encouraged a wildness and a desire to stay free, but she had nowhere to go but home.

Over and over again she tried to leave but always returned, as if the house was magnetized and she couldn't resist, couldn't break through the range of its power.

Nod

She returned with secret wishes, unacknowledged, every time, that she would be welcomed warmly by her sister, who would say "God, I missed you because you are so wonderful to have around," or her mother who would turn and recognize and understand her all in one move, or her father—just, simply, home again—for good—but none of these things seemed to happen.

Now she looked at the face looking at her and loved it too. The dog was doe-brown, a hound with blue eyes and good proportions, no collar, a neat penis, and a smooth pointed tail. She crashed to her knees to kiss his wet skin. All of Ireland seemed to be contained in his skin. She thanked God for the dog who licked her very precisely—not with excess relish—on the back of her hand, then bounded around, barking her forwards excitedly. She rose and ran.

At the familiar last stone staircase on the beach—a long difficult climb along a wall—the smell of piss was intense from men without toilets—and halfway up she could see one of them at a small distance—half hidden by boulders—fishing in boots to his thighs. It didn't surprise her to see this father there, but she sat on the steps for a while before venturing to speak to him. Then she went forward shyly and asked him if he had any rope for her dog who was sniffing around Pooch. He said he had seen some up in the rocks behind him. Cloda climbed and found a heavy noose-like lump of rope which she dragged down the boulders, bringing kelp and shells along with it, and a condom and somebody's wig. Industriously she tore these things away from the rope and asked the father for a knife to cut it with. He indicated the sackful of fishing gear at his feet and she got out a serrated knife and sawed at the rope. The father asked where her hair went and lifted her cap to look. She backed up, saying she didn't know. Then he asked where her sister got her good looks and Cloda again said she didn't know. He remarked that it must be hard for her having such a glory for a sister. He himself wouldn't mind the privilege of sharing a house—let alone a room—with her.

It'd make you bitter as thick milk having her for a sister, I'd say. Hey, what's more important, Cloda asked boldly, being pretty or being nice? In a girl it's better to be pretty. Men never care how nice a girl is. But the girl herself might prefer being nice. I tell you, a shrew gets her wish but suffers in the getting. I've seen this happen. Your sister is probably a shrew, she's probably suffering, but no one will care as long as she's got her looks. I don't enjoy telling you that. Anyway, you're a nice looking little thing, don't worry. Your time will come.

Cloda reddened with pleasure and backed away with her dog now tied to her rope. She called: "I told you when you can see her—after her show—at night—or on her way to school in the morning—or I could—arrange—something—"

x

Later when the brown dog was saltily walking at Cloda's side she felt a hunger that was nearly nausea, as if she was eating herself from the inside out. It was tied to her conversation with the traveler father—not even his words, so much as her own, her urging him on towards Irene as if he were a spirit sick with need, and a sacrifice was all that would suffice. The sacrifice of a siting. Of her sister.

Now with this hunger she remembered what the traveler children said when it was time to eat: "I'm corribed with the krolus." And she asked her dog, "Are you corribed with the krolus?" He wagged his tail and she stole a bun off an outdoor stall to feed him and herself.

Around them were little green gardens sealed off by walls and cold. In a park she used to put her face to the ground and smell the soil that made her feel safe in the world. Now she could just smell her dog and feel the same way. This was a luxury. Was she crazy? She edged along ecstasy night and day, an almost unbearable excitement made her jump at a whisper and flinch from a shade. Was this Americanism or something biological? Sometimes she whispered with her lips moving, "Mommy,

Mommy," but it was never her real mother she had in mind, but someone unknown, an eternal un-human. It was the sound of the name that
smoothed her down, like the the sound of the Irish for woman is the
beautiful *man*. Longing was her motive cause, but longing for an un-
named being, a submersion of her hyperactive self with a slow melt.
Sometimes she buried her nose in her palm and covered her mouth, and
inhaled, saying "Mommy, Mommy," so no one could see that her safety
was complete by being self and sense contained.

Yet she burned without cease over her sister's successes and over the knowledge that Irene was the preferred child—not just by their parents, but by
the structures of the whole world. And she wondered if it was a problem
induced by measurement alone, and that if she lived on her own in another
place or family, would she finally rejoice in everything she herself possessed.

Irene's performance was only one in a series of examples of these false
measurings that later would amaze her by its lack of proportion. Irene only
sang a few songs and said a few lines in the midst of others in a school auditorium where people wanted to experiment with Yeats' experiments in
objective drama. Big deal. Why did it have such importance at the time?

x

That night her mother surprised her by being in a rage at her for running
away. How was I supposed to know where you were? she screamed. But
then she didn't punish Cloda with a lecture or starvation. Instead her
mother wouldn't speak to her for two whole days, wouldn't respond, or
notice anything she did or said. She didn't ask where she was going or
what she was doing or anything at all. She turned her face away from
Cloda. And in this way she rendered Cloda just as invisible as she had
been when she was following the tracks alone.

Cloda heard her mother talking to everyone else about how she was going back to Europe again, but just for a short time, and how she was

taking some pills to relax her since she was so nervous about traveling back to France. And her mother talked about the father having an affair with another woman, and about how much she hated men, especially Hal, and she cried about it and went to bed and lay buried in bills, legal documents and Henry James.

Cloda, with her new invisibility, saw as if through a camera lens that her mother had a youngish face that would not last much longer. She wanted to kiss her and make her skin go smooth again, but she skulked, instead, by the curtains, where she could make sure the dog was safe in the garden, and continue watching the dramas.

I hate you. Why won't you talk to me? she queried, but her mother yawned and threw herself on her side, her shoulder lifted under the blankets, a drumlin.

Irene came and went, furiously, telling her mother to get up and stop acting like a teenager, and they quarreled about Hal, about sex, about each other's selfishness.

I really want to die. I hate the world. I hate Christmas. I hate men. I hate Hitler. I hate old age . . . was the mother's litany. And indeed Christmas had come and gone without anyone paying any attention to it. In fact it was a subdued event all over Ireland that year, given workers' strikes and threats of war.

But now the mother announced that when she returned from Europe, they would all go home.

Home where? asked Cloda, but she was ignored. Home where? asked Irene. Home, America. I'm not going, said Irene. I will, said Cloda. We'll go this time to my city. New York. What about Daddy? asked Irene. What about Daddy? I'll worry about him when I get back from France. Why are you going? asked Cloda. Why are you going? To rescue two cousins of yours—Jean and Pierre—and bring them back here and then with us, to America. And if I'm lucky, I'll die doing it.

How old are they?

Yeah, how old?

Six and nine. I've told you about them. They're the only children of my first cousin whom you have never met. She was raised in Provence and lived there all her life. She is worried about the war and her children and she doesn't want to leave her husband. I promised her I would return and get the boys and bring them back to America with us, if necessary. Anyway, I have nothing to live for.

Saying this, the mother threw back the blankets and planted her bare feet on the floor. Her ankles were by now streaked with small veins and her feet showed that they had supported her body for forty years. Irene backed away from her mother and stood in the half-open doorway. Cloda was breathing fog for writing on the glass windowpane.

Cloda, darling, come help me pack, the mother now said, breaking her silence for no reason at all. Pull down my bag from the shelf up there.

I have to go to the theater, said Irene. It's the last night, and we're having a party.

Well, don't sleep with everyone there.

Irene swung at the air beside her mother's cheek and walked with long strides from the room, pounded down the stairs to get her cape off the chair and told Hal she'd be home late.

Meantime upstairs Cloda set to work helping her mother prepare for her crossing—first by boat over the Irish Sea, then by train over England, and then by boat again to Calais, and then by train down to Marseille. It would take two nights of travel and as usual she packed heaps of clothes, far too much for a trip that was intended to involve an immediate return.

She began to preen and clarify her features in front of her mirror, and Cloda sat and watched her attentively.

Can I bring my dog back to America with us? she asked.
I don't give a damn.

Good. But maybe we should wait here for Daddy.

No, not after what he has done. I'm not waiting for him. He can follow us. Please tell that swine Hal to come see me, she said when her face was fully coated with base, her eyes lined, and her lipstick pressed between her two lips.

Cloda placed herself, as if hiding, between the curtains and the window, while they talked.

I'm returning tonight, she told Hal who stayed at the door. I have to. Something strange and terrible is happening there. I'm terrified myself. My cousin married a Jew. Believe me, she's never read anything more Jewish than "The Merchant of Venice." Neither has her husband. No Torah, nothing. But they seem to be very good at manufacturing paranoia. I don't understand any of it. But something in my gut tells me I have to do this. I just have a feeling . . . What is racial purity? What can it be? It ended with Adam and Eve.

No, said Hal. You're right. It's very late in the world's history for racial purity, though I suppose certain Nordic types—and deep Africans—could try. I have noticed that the further north you go, the smarter people get. Haven't you?

No, I haven't, unless you mean by "smart" cruel.

He turned his profile to her, saying: I want to tell you that I realize you are doing something very courageous. It's dangerous.

Good.

But it's the American in you. You always think you are protected by some magic investment authority of your government.

I don't think that now. I think we're on the edge of disaster. All of us. But don't tell the girls how dangerous it is, unless you want to be more sadistic than you already have been. In fact the children should be safe till I return. You've obviously way over-stepped every decent boundary already, but now that it's done, I ask you to stay here with them till I return. Then I'm taking them to America. If there's a snag, we'll be safe enough here, where it's neutral.

Not neutral enough, said Hal. Here you have your fascists too. The Irish sent men to fight on both sides in the Spanish Civil War. Don't forget. You have your IRA working with the Nazis in order to get the British out of Northern Ireland. Neutral! The Irish have only one issue: Ireland. About that they are never neutral. I don't trust the Irish or their idea of neutrality.

Stop hating everything! Cloda screamed. Or go back to Norway if you don't like it here!

I forgot she was here. If for some reason I don't return—the mother said.

Stop being an actress! Cloda called out.

If for some reason I don't return, please make sure the girls are safe. They should await their father's return and if he doesn't come back, then I don't know what.

Nod

I'll take them to Norway with me. Obviously. But this is ridiculous. You'll be back in a week. Then I'll go home on my own . . . I'm sorry for all that's happened here, since it has caused you pain and you've always been good to me, a friend.

You have absolutely ended our friendship. I don't want to talk about it. Cloda?
What.

Do my top button please.

Cloda gave Hal a scornful look and he left the room at once. She then clipped the button at the nape of her mother's neck and in the looking glass they met each other's eyes. The mother suddenly let out a cry:

"Oh, oh! I don't want to go back! Don't make me go, Cloda! For godsake, it's not my problem just because I'm a goddamn American. Why doesn't my cousin bring them here herself? Her hysteria is appalling. Whine, whine. Just like the Irish about Ireland. Why am I going? They're her children, not mine. As if I don't have enough already. Two here—one sleeping with someone under my own roof—you running away daily—why? Why do I have to go back to France? I'm scared. I need to take care of my own problems, not hers! The last thing I want is two nasty little boys! But then the poor little things, I keep seeing their eyes!"

She stood up and Cloda was aghast at the transformation that had occurred between the gray heap in the bed and the perfumed and jewelled woman in high black heels shouting. This transformation had often seemed like witchery, a kind of horror show to Cloda, but just for that hour she admired her mother's energy in making sure she looked "of a piece," as she would say, even as her hysteria grew.

When her mother departed Cloda lay on her face in the cold garden until darkness covered her completely. Then she took off her hat and felt the tufty hair on her head. Catharine had said: "Fairies are fallen angels. They all fell like frost—forked and white on a windowpane—on the same day. They can turn evil in a flash—murder and kidnap—according to legend. They believe in the sacrifice of human girls for the preservation of their race. Oh, I tell you, they are full of surprises. Jolly one minute and mean as snakes the next . . . But you're way too old to believe in these things!" I am, said Cloda aloud. Way too old. "These are stories for little children, not for the age you are."

I know. I'm sorry, said Cloda softly. Yet she couldn't stop wondering what she had done to deserve the wrath of the fairies—how had they made her believe in them?

x

Hal paced around outside the theater while a bang-about wind tossed up leaves, papers and grit. His eyes burned. Irene had made it clear that she didn't want him to come that night, since there was a cast party to which he was not invited, but he was unable to concentrate on anything useful while she was out having fun. In the process of his emptying himself into and around her (three nights in a row) she had become almost cavalier and he more intense. Yet she was, in his arms, like a cold winter branch with buds like spears only beginning to appear. He might have rushed them towards an earlier bloom, but not by much. She was a tight one.

When the audience moved into the wind, buffeted by it and by their own exclamations, he started to leave, wanted to leave. So he stood at a greater distance until she and the other actors came outside. She was laughing with a small group in that hysterically clubby way actors often do after a show. The wind only made them laugh harder and draw closer. Hal stepped after them, calling her name, and saw irritation break out all over her face when she whirled back to meet him.

Nod

What! I told you I'd be late. There's a party. No, I know, I'm sorry, but your mother wanted me to make sure you got home safely every night. She could care less. No, it's true. I don't believe it. Well, Irene, I'm only staying till she returns, then I'll be gone back home. What?

Hal was pleased to see that an expression of distress settled on her face with this news. Her head turned, she looked cornered, desperate, and her friends called and waved for her to come. So she moved backwards away from Hal towards her friends, now including the boy with the guitar.

Will you come pick me up at the party? she asked him. No, it's now, or else you're on your own. Can't we meet somewhere—at the train station—later? No, my dear, we can't. I'm not your father. Well, I can't! It's the last night! she screeched angrily. All right. Good night.

Hal left her with a returning sense of his own power. Her panic, her obvious attachment to him—and her absurd shrieks and awkward moves that contradicted the grace of her appearance—made his posture lift to its usual height. He didn't desire her as strongly as he wanted her to desire him.

x

Cloda slept in an armchair that night, with the hat on her head, the dog at her feet and the light on. The windows banged and twigs scratched the glass itchily, and leaves grated over the cement. She dreamed that she was lying in a field when a pack of doll-sized humans rushed at her, bearing white spears that they pressed into her temples while they pulled at her hair. And into this dream came the sound of this song: *Take time to thrive, my Rose of Hope, in the garden of Dromore; take heed, young Eagle, till your wings are weathered fit to soar; a little time and then our land is full of things to do . . .*

Nod

Cloda twitched nervously awake when the song stopped—Irene's voice coming from Hal's room—and the dog was now barking outside—and the sun was shining on her lap. Out the window she could see low white clouds under a solid grey band whipping past at high speed. She climbed the stairs, and slipped into her mother's room where the bed still lay ajar and disordered. Cloda straightened the covers and tucked in the sheets, then went to her own room, not surprised to find no sign of Irene having been in that bed. It was Sunday. And Cloda changed her clothes quickly, wanting only to avoid any contact with Hal and Irene. Hal had told a story once:

"In a Scandinavian settlement in the 10th century a female slave who belonged to a chief agreed to be strangled and stabbed—in other words, sacrificed—and laid beside the chief because it would bring her honor in the next world. She was feasted and feted ahead of time and in this ritual joined myriads of other celebrated female corpses laid out in sacrifice beside the bodies of powerful men, in order to have a happier time on the Other Side. It was typical of the cult of Odin."

Cloda began to lift the camera from inside Irene's schoolbag but it felt heavy, alive in her hands. She set it back inside the bag and stepped away as if it had acquired a diabolic power since entering her sister's territory. This was a moment she would never remember though she had evidence—old photos from that year—to prove that she had once been interested in photography.

Cloda stopped outside the door to Hal's room and squatted down to peek through the keyhole. Verboten, her father would say. Her legs wobbled supporting her behind and her breathing was irregular, spasmodic. The keyhole was no larger than her eyelid but she could see much of the room and its occupants.

Hal was seated on the floor and Irene was wearing his shirt and leaning at the dusty windowglass, her profile in a deliberate mask of weltschmerz that he was ignoring. He was, instead, occupied with polishing his enormous shoes, while his socks hung on the thin radiator drying. Then he stood and pulled his fingers through his straight yellow hair. Cloda, transfixed as if by a miracle, felt faint inside the evil being generated by her own glands. A strange paralysis gripped her, while her thoughts flew towards escape, towards travel across the Bog of Allen. By demeaning herself on her knees, she was voluntarily casting a spell over herself. Her tongue dried on its root, her eyes teared, her eardrums pulsed, and she slipped with difficulty onto her feet feeling she had joined the belly-moving beasts. Then she slipped down the hall to the lavatory. To a long chain and a cracked wooden seat where she sat and built a ladder in her mind out of her wickedness.

x

Outside she headed hard and fast into town. A gust of rain drove her running into the church where only a couple of people were praying. It was the given place for shame and she couldn't resist kissing with a little lick of her tongue the stone hem of Mary's gown that resembled a salt flow. She did. And it had a stone taste, also a resemblance to paper, but she could swear there was a trace of salt in it, and when she looked up she saw that the feet of the Infant Jesus were peeping out from under a stone blanket and they were as pink as laughter's hidden lips, and she reached up and pinched one, just to see if it would curl, but it was smooth like plastic. The baby had a crown on his head, his arms were open, and under the whole sculpture was written: REGENA DE COR CARMEL. Then she saw an older version of Jesus dying on the other side of the church and she scooted nervously over there, but was too short to do what she really wanted to do. Lick his stone chest. See if it tasted of salt, or wore a little bead of sweat, a tear. But everything was dry about him and his tilted face—his face tilted exactly as Mary's had been when looking down at him as a baby, but now he was the mother, looking down at the person looking up at him, who happened for that moment to be her.

Nod

The rain stopped as quickly as it had begun and Cloda left Grafton Street with the dog, stole a Cadbury's chocolate bar near Clery's Department Store ("41 stores in 1") and headed back towards Sandymount, thinking she would take the dog down to the beach in front of their house and look for some new friends, now that the travelers were gone. She had noticed two new girls on the beach recently and wondered if they would be nice. Often Irish girls were fascinated by her American clothes and accent and this made it easier for her to become friends with them. Down by the shore the waves were horse-tailed and white, and she wandered up in the direction of the tower where a police car was parked with blinking lights. Two gardai were out on the rocks, squatting over an abnormal shape. It's strange how you can always recognize a human even when it is crumpled or otherwise distorted. Cloda's recognition was instant. She didn't want to approach any further but found herself surrounded by the two girls she had seen and some other neighbors. Everyone was holding onto their faces, clawing a cheek or lip, with eyes terrified. "It must be a body washed in," one said. "No, it was stuck on the rocks," said another. "How would you know?" asked a third. "It was my Michael found him." "Him? Who?" "We think it's one of the travelers, who's been hanging around. People have seen him digging for worms . . . "

Cloda pulled the dog's rope and ran home, saying Mommy, Mommy into the palm of her hand. Hal was in the kitchen and she pulled him outside, begging him to go look, to find out, though he said, angrily, he didn't know what she was talking about and didn't really want to.

She insisted, so Hal walked slowly towards the crowd as an ambulance pulled in, and given his height, he was able to see clearly what was happening. Black hair, arms dangling, grey blue face, huge black water-logged boots being slapped onto a stretcher. It was the traveler father. Cloda took off the other way now, bolting down to the rocky beach with the dog galloping cheerfully at her side. She scrambled along the slippery rocks, cut her hands, and finally curled inside a watery cave. She let the salt soak her shoes and pant legs up to her knees, shivering violently, but gagging at the taste of the spray on her mouth and the way her body thrashed inside her spirit like a fish spastic for air. She closed her eyes tight and even in that darkness she saw the lights of the universe twinkling. In the sea itself she felt the spirit of the dying man, and the tongue of his one-time kindness to her lapping at her ankles. She tasted his words on her mouth—"Mommy, Mommy"—and smelled his love of birds as a gull's call passed through her ears onto her tongue and up her nostrils. His body had floated on water, and sent its energies into the waves, and now they splatted against her bones in the little black rock cave smeared with green moss where a white whale-bone comb tossed. She pulled it free and stuck it in her pocket, then squinting she saw clouds, dazzle, sun-lines, and a horizon speckled with birds and aircraft. A vague smell of gas rose up from the sea. Her tongue sought a loop of her hair to suck. None there. Was it her fault? Her tongue sought a loop of her hair to suck, but found only air.

x

The night before this morning Irene's cast party took place in the director's floor-through flat on Pembroke Road. The ceilings were very high, the windows took up most of the wall space on the east and west sides. A palatial staircase led to the flat past a stainglass window shining under a chandelier. The furniture inside was stuff that might have been lugged along alleys and beaches—half of it was broken, missing a leg or a back, or springs. But people made themselves comfortable anyway. Outside the wind bammed on the huge windows. On a table were bottles of beer and stout and dirty glasses. There was an upright piano that one of the actors played and soft talk slipped around smoke and glass. Irene sat side by side with Aidan in a state of profound uncertainty.

She was listening to a woman speculate, wrapped in a thick sweater and hunched over, chain-smoking, whiskey stirring in the wrap of her hand. Her voice was nasal, nearly British, lyrical.

"The body is like a hospital with an entrance for out-patients only, lovers who come in to be healed, then leave. Not a mental hospital, where sense and sensibility dissolve, but a hospital where the stories cohere, case histories lead to discoveries. I think, having been mad, that I take coherence very seriously and I am offended by those who make a game of disruption and call it chance when the results are "interesting." The avant garde? Not really. The sign of their comfort and consolidation with the ruling power is their very ability to spoof it. They have no fear, only fun. They are the ones who don't uproot the systems that they mock. It is enraged people, who have experienced the indifference of authority—it's they who are the ones who change its form, and are themselves destroyed. In this sense, it is up to the losers to save the souls of the winners while losing their own souls twice over . . . As for Yeats, he was fundamentally soft."

Everybody roared in horror at her cynicism, but Irene leaned in closer, longing to hear more. Aidan held her back with his white, lightly freckled fingers. At first Irene only showed him her profile as she watched the party because she didn't want to lead him on. His hand on hers might have been a lamb chop as far as she was concerned since it didn't belong to Hal. But she wanted to be fully present in the moment and the place, and not to yearn so foolishly for a much-too-old man. She pressured happiness to rise in her and finally only urged it on by looking at Aidan fully and seeing his admiration for her written all over his face. The face of the other as mirror—this never failed to reassure her of her own importance. Once again it didn't fail her, but it also didn't fully inform her of her powers. Only Hal seemed able to give her that feeling.

She didn't drink, having been revolted by alcohol's effect on her father, so the level of party hysteria rose without her in it. Aidan wandered off to find whiskey, quickly tipsy, and she went to gaze out the window and the trees and bushes tossing up and down. She felt she must get home and she asked the stage manager the best way to do so, and everyone crowded around her, begging her to stay, giving advice on buses, and saying goodbye all at the same time. She made a dramatic exit with her blue cape flying and her face turned up in a mask of tragedy as she uttered her final goodbye. The play was over but eight words kept grinding through her mind: "The Shadow of shadows on the deed alone."

x

Only a quarter of a mile away Hal was walking through the dark streets on his way home. He had been drinking, so his thinking had the buzz that sets off quick insights, as if the cognac had literally burned a new path through his memory chambers. Even if he could have—and he couldn't—remembered the usual path from A to B, now he found that there was another swifter path and the distance between them was all but invisible. Scientists might call a place where this path is found "random" or "unpredictable" but Hal felt that the path was in fact earned. It had to do with his work. Early Celtic intralinear rhyme contained a principle that underlay early Celtic-Germanic alliteration. So the line "*ben zi bena, bluot zi bluoda*" came through his ears as a precursor of rhyme! In other words alliteration preceded rhymed line endings. Oral languages, often taught in secret, must have carried with them the alliterative grammar of liturgy! So he must look more deeply into druidic lore and religious ritual to see if a code was transcribed in sound between lines. (Hal was a code-breaker and maker.)

And this meant that he might need to stay on in Dublin for a number of reasons. He realized that he could simply move into the city, when the mother returned, and continue his studies, while Irene came to visit him. And now as he meandered drunkenly along the seafront, he thought of her post-pubescent breasts with a surge of lust. She was as close to being a child as anyone he had ever slept with. (Both sisters were abnormally naive, he thought several times.) The buoyancy of her breasts was also a matter of her youth and therefore vulnerable to change. And his heart, for a flash, pounded furiously in the panic that she would let someone else see and touch them to the point that they would droop. He had far preferred the hot-blooded and spicy feel of her mother. What he felt for Irene now was nearly abstract by comparison, but nonetheless potent.

He was a man who deep down believed that a woman without beauty was disposable. He had also violently shaken and smacked women whose beauty drew other men to them; but then he had also learned to go ice cold with some of them, and just leave, the minute he sensed that they might leave him. This had happened between him and his wife. Now he wondered what he would do (as if he didn't belong to himself!) if he found Irene was fond of another man.

In fact at that moment Aidan had rushed out into the night to join Irene at the bus stop, still carrying his drink, and he insisted on riding with her all the way to her home stop. She said she was sort of glad, because the solitariness of the streets made her uneasy. So they sat on the upper deck with one other man—a priest sharing a seat at the front—and it was when they were approaching her stop that she saw Hal walking outside and he looked up and saw her inside the bus with Aidan leaning over her. He stopped on the street and she was too surprised to wave. When she got off the bus and Aidan went on, the wind covered her face with her hair as she looked this way and that for Hal.

He had disappeared, and instead all she saw was a darker smaller shape with a black spade slipping and sliding on the rocks that led up to the seawall where she stood. She was sure it was that same man she had seen before (not Rumpelstilskin, not an ogre) and decided to wave in a friendly way as if to dispel the possibility of evil with this gesture. And the gesture made him stop, in fact, and stand absolutely still, his face raised like a little gold shield reflecting the moon. She gave another tentative and gentle wave, then turned and ran back home with her head pushed forward. She fled then into Hal's room to hide inside his bed.

Only minutes later Hal himself walked the same path, but he lurched to a halt when he saw the man pressing his face on the kitchen window of their house. Then he threw his arm around the man's throat and dragged him down the damp street and around the bend to the sea. Hal was cursing like a madman but his gestures were as efficient as an animal trainer.

x

Years after he had passed away Cloda's memory of her father was troubled by a glut of confused statements. While he said that light is composed of waves, he also said it was impossible to know if there was such a thing as light-waves.

He was annoyed by the way scientists would repeat the same theory of waves and troughs instead of inviting poets along to conjure up figures of speech. "Scientists think metaphorically," he said. "But they can't articulate new ones." However he just as frequently berated poets and writers for their ignorance about science, and said that nothing would progress in the human intellect until the two disciplines—art and science—merged their insights and their ways of describing those insights.

What is the length of time required for three clouds a half a mile long to cross the moon at twenty miles an hour?

The answer to the situation described could only be a description of an answer, he concluded. For instance, poets say things like: "A patch is better than a hole. Thinness is better than stoutness. A bad person is better than nobody. And that's all there is to that."

And Cloda would stare at him as he uttered these statements and hope that he was using an oblique method to guide her back to a progress as straight and direct as railroad tracks and this way she might wend her way back to a childhood that gave her the attributes by which she was known and judged by others as an adult. But she was invariably let down. His abstractions led only to the mind that he now called Disappointment.

x

That night Hal entered his room half-naked, tearing the remaining clothes from his skin as if they were burning when in fact they were damp. He balled them up and shoved them under the bed on which Irene rested. His hands were almost blue with cold and trembled when he lay them on her two breasts, making her scream and recoil. But he said, Let me warm them between your thighs, and she did, squeezing tight and laughing. He held her from behind hard, his breath was heaving, he felt rather ill.

Your feet feel wet they're so cold, she said. It was a long walk home, he explained. But you disappeared! I went down to look at the water. I was a little drunk. Were you mad at me for being on the bus with Aidan? Should I be? he inquired and gagged. No! I was racing home to you. He just wanted to be sure I was safe. Did he need to? Did anything bad happen? Someone try to rape you? Are you kidding? I mean, here I am, with you, where I want to be. She turned around to him and put her hand between his legs, taking cold of his limp and tiny penis and tugging on it roughly. What's wrong? It's just the cold. Wait till I warm up. How long will that take? It could take days, I'm so cold. Stop joking. Does it take a long time? Not if you handle it right, not so harshly. Like what? What do I do? Nothing. Just leave it alone. Let's sleep for a while. Sleep? Just for a bit. Then it will all work out. This chill will disappear forever and we can start again. Say a poem. I haven't got one in me. Not tonight.

Instead Hal began to ramble: "God, I hate this country. Cold, cold, and people so proud of their stupidity. Mythologizing madness. Tinkers and egos the size of—of—cannonballs! Animals at heart, them all. Guess what? Do you know about gypsies? Like the man who fixed our stone wall outside? They are not so romantic as you think. The Romanies—the same blood root as Irish Tinkers—emigrated from India into Persia and Europe between the 5th and 13th centuries. In Western Europe many Romanies are nomads still. What are their particular names? The

Manouche, Finnish Gypsies, the Kalderach, the Sinti, Jenisch and the Barenegre in France, the mercheros of Spain. In Norway there are two groups of travellers—the Taterne and the Fantene, and in Holland—yes—the Woonwagenbewoners. Each of these groups has a cultural—even ethnic—identity of its own and they are mainly linked by the fact that their main economic base is their extended family. Also they all believe in the right to travel which is damn lucky since nobody wants them around.

I should have stayed at the party, said Irene.

x

Two days went by and the general opinion on the cause of the Traveler's drowning—without autopsy or inquest—was both "accidental" and "unknown." Then one afternoon two gardai were visiting the houses in Sandymount and inquired of Cloda, the only one home, if she had any knowledge of the man who had drowned or if anyone in her household had heard unusual sounds that night. She gazed up at the two rosy-cheeked, white-lipped faces and took a deep breath. Her voice was all but a whisper when she said, "I found a comb in the water there." A what? they asked with lips twitching indulgences. "A comb. It might have belonged to the man who killed him," she said. Well, where is it then? She ran down the hall and twisted the comb out of the back pocket of her jacket and showed it to them. Ah, I'd say it's nothing, one of them said. But we'll take it along anyway, the other one added. "Maybe a banshee . . . " Cloda whispered.

And off they went, leaving her weak-kneed and dry-mouthed at the door. She didn't hear anything more. Indeed the case then fell into an area of uncertainty encircled by the kind of apathy that comes with certain crimes. The crimes against the very poor. He was a man whom no one would even bother to murder—this was the basic conclusion—let alone seek reparation for. Indeed the dog's viciousness to the gar-

dai elicited more passion from them than anything else about the matter. Pooch would let no one come near the body, but danced around
with fangs bared and foamy teeth, and they finally had to shoot the
dog and let him float out to sea—all this before Cloda happened on
the scene that day. The night after the gardai's visit Hal came to Cloda
in her bedroom and asked her if she had seen his comb. He had been
looking everywhere, he said, with no luck. "What's so great about it?"
she asked him from her desk and without looking up. Well, you know,
it's a kind of antique—you've seen it—"I gave it to the police," she
told him. Oh good! he laughed. The police! That's how important it
is. She watched his chin clamping on mirth and smiled herself. No,
seriously, Cloda, have you?

She looked at the windowpane across her desk where dry leaves on a
falling vine would scratch all night. "The police have it," she said and
focused on the whistle of the train off to the left, south of where she
sat. "You can go get it from them." But—why? He strode up behind
her and slapped the palm of his hand on her brow, pulling back her
head in a way that was both rough and familial. Her head now rested
against his belt buckle and she couldn't twist to the side. Her asked
her why again and it was their reflections on the black window glass
that now addressed each of their living faces, reflections interrupted
by frilled leaf-shapes, the veins drooping and dry from cold. "I found
it in the water," she told the glass. The water? What water. "Outside,
the sea, the night the man—you know—died. The next morning, I
mean." Well, that was a terrible thing. The drowned man. It had nothing to do with me. You were the one who knew him after all. Get. The
comb. She twisted now, but he held on. "Okay," she said with tears
arriving. "Okay!"

You won't, he muttered, releasing her in a way that let his hand sweep
over her neck. Because you are involved, he added, and you want me to
pick up the pieces.

Nod

That night Cloda put on her jacket and began to walk south with her dog down the center of the train tracks, only leaving them to lie in the bushes when a train racketed by. She followed the parallel lines into the dawn, out the north side of Dublin, then abandoned them to wander across a field, away from the sea—east—she assumed the Bog of Allen was a space somewhere out there... But the name "Bog of Allen" was unlocatable as a terrain. The dog trotted cheerfully forward over brown grass, frosted stones and a dumb grey sky hung over the two of them. No fairies for her but an increasing transparency occurring with each footfall, a sensation of buoyancy on pebbles and humps close to flying.

There is a rabbit called a brown hound. There is a moth called the hound of fur. There is an otter called the dog of the water. There is a German word Schweinehund.

But when her hound took off after a bird and disappeared, she called and called (Here, puppy, puppy, puppy!) and searched to no avail, her breath diminished to something the size of a bee and just as erratic.

When by five it was dark, she realized that she had not lost the dog any more than the dog had lost her, and this mysterious equality thrust itself on her like a vista that tipped straight up. The separation between dog and person was a physical reality made of emotion. She could feel his fear across the night as something absolutely similar to her own. Stars were so numerous, they filled the surface of the sky with as many lights as a city harbor. Puppy! Puppy!

While she fell towards sleep against a wall her stomach churned nervously. She didn't know what to do. Repeating puppy, puppy in a soft litany she trailed her hand along the edge of the stone wall and saw how the moon was smothering in clouds and then when the moon was clearing aside the clouds. She paused to measure and muse on these motions. Anything to make time pass!

Black dots and lines were silhouetted on the sky, and when the wind blew, they seemed to slide on a rink of ice. She wanted to die right there. Hang her neck from an acer in a fairy grove, twist her spine into a gnarled elm tree, be trampled and buried by a Frost Giant. Maybe now, at last, an army of fairies would troop through the grass carrying spears of ice and lance her cheeks and eyes and ears. Maybe she herself could kill someone else. To die, or to kill? What was worse? To kill probably. But still she uttered a curse on Hal and called up all the spirits of wronged fairies, elves and humans to do him in. She didn't have a clue as to which root or flower worked on curses, but she tore at the bark of a maple tree and held a strip of it— shaped like the head and body of a lamb—and muttered curses on Hal.

To be devoured by a wolf! To be pecked at by crows! Drowned by fairies! Squashed by a bear!

The night wore on with astonishing indifference. She scrutinized the shapes of all things as they emerged into sight, then realized that she was absolutely lost, at least until dawn when she could follow the direction of the sun. She sat, then, listening acutely, hopefully, for that dog's particular high-pitched bark, but heard only some nightbirds sending signals through the branches and crickets.

Puppy! Puppy! When a drop of light fell on the far horizion, she dozed and dreamed until she felt as if she were pressed like a rose leaf inside the covers of a collection of fairy tales, covers that had the mulch and wood smell that surrounded her now. Compressed to near transparency, where pink is the color of everlasting love, she could die happy. She would be part of a story that was wise and finished.

But even in the sun she had to struggle blindly to find her way home, and she was crying for her dog and herself until she caught sight of a road and some shops, and then she hurried, clear-eyed, to get directions. As soon as she heard her voice in the air, and saw the face responding with words, she was depressed.

Glancing back across the repetitive terrain, she seemed to glimpse herself still there batting her hands at the intractable blackness.

x

I had my chance to give myself over to nature forever and lost it. Now I have to die as a human in the hands of other humans, and I don't want to.

If all evil has its source in me, no wonder I live in the fear of God. You say that the proof of sanity is the return to normalcy after a bout of wild behavior. You say the success of a cure comes when the patient is freed from ecstasy as much as from despair. But what if these are canals to a black source where silence is the depth of hearing?

You, Doctor, tell me to please get well and leave, but then you want me to suffer for you by demonstrating my ecstasies for your notebook. You are the incarnation of benevolence in this hospital. Where would we women go otherwise—with our ennui, our inabilities, our fits? The whole outside psychic terrain has been sprayed and sterilized against us. You take care of us and keep us safe. You are our Solomon but you live in a dry land. I know the warning: "Do not arouse, do not stir up love before its own time." But where will you be when the flowers appear on the earth and the time of pruning the vines has come, and the fig tree puts forth its figs? Inside, at your desk? Staring at lazy women through a crack in the door? You read the world physically but at a distance. Sometimes you behave as if you are being persecuted by us your patients. I am treated as a "noble savage" because you sense that I am well educated, and there might be some male power behind me. I love Bach, I read librettos, I play chess, I love poetry, yet you resist hearing my interpretations of my own problems because I don't use your jargon. The Catholic Church gives as much significance to each act as any doctor does. Traumatized by one day in history, generations have sat transfixed by the Cross, unable to get to the other side of it, the resurrection, to forget what happened and move on. It's a mass trauma that has lasted two thousand years, the crucifixion, and the children of this church are of course riddled with psychoses and interpretations. I understand Catholicism. It's the only science I do understand. The combination of thorough study with leaps of faith—well, this is the most reliable approach to the truth that I know. So what you diagnose as narcissism is really just happiness. I am happy as a daughter of Jerusalem. It is my happiness that frightens everyone.

Sometimes in the midst of her story to the doctor, she would doodle, drawing diabolical penis-figures on paper bags. The doctor looked at these pictures of little penis people living on the side of things, not on top, and assumed that it showed her vision of the world to be a wall, not a circle on which one stood, head up, but a vertical plane on which these creatures paraded like insects up and down.

She told him, from her point of view, that each figure was like a revolutionary who is just a common criminal who has concocted an ideology in order to justify a day's anti-social act. She used as an example the way that the doctor had arranged an entire hospital around his anxieties about evil women.

"Pathological thinking is overloaded with meaning. So who is the pathological one in this case? The patient or the doctor?"

She added the obvious: "The absolute referent in the Western world is a white male adult intellect." She said her neck was like a bottleneck, she would choke on her own words, and even quote Heidegger or someone, saying stuff about the excruciating experience of completeing actions inside a vacuum. Then she thrashed around the bed, legs spread, calling for Daddy or Catharine to come and take her home. He told her to cover herself and show some modesty.

N o d

Sometimes she would drop to her knees, rigid arms extended, and remain unmovable for hours. If he pushed down her arms, they sprang back into position again. Her knees grew red and sore on the floor, but she wore a serene expression.

For some reason the doctor couldn't even bite into his sandwich when she had spoken of her sex life. His appetite was worse than nil. He felt revulsion for the whole world. A thick exhaustion would follow and he would shove everything on his desk to the side. She would penetrate him with her eyes, later, asking if he felt all right. They faced each other through the window the size of an index card. She was often unwilling to see the whole of him. He didn't indicate any interest in her question, but she always seemed to know anyway why he had failed to eat.

He was developing a theory from his "work" with her that the forgotten parts of a life are the very parts that give that life meaning, so that remembering them would actually cause harm.

Nonetheless he tried to get her to remember her childhood, but she always said: I can't think of anything wrong. Only God knows what happened to make me like this. My sister is famous for her films about crazy people like me. My life is her material.

But one day she recounted an experience that she had had when she was very little. Her mother had taken her into a store to choose the sweater she wanted for Christmas. The store was like the interior of a lighted chandelier and smelled of sweet perfumes. In the children's department she saw her sweater: it was navy blue with a parade of happy monkeys knitted across the chest. On Christmas morning, when she undid the package, she found the wrong sweater inside. It was red. It had white diamonds knitted around the waist. She didn't say anything but actually developed a fever and hid inside her bed, because in that one moment she realized that she would never get what she wanted in life. Not ever.

From her reference to The War he guessed she was in her late to mid-thirties. She let him know that being herself was very painful as if she "were a mummy wrapped in painted canvas, and where the canvas meets the numb skin of my inner body, there is a terrible rubbing, a constant erasure of all possibility of remembrance."

He asked her why she walked in circles and she said she wanted to cast a spell on the ground, so that nothing could move forward in time. "Only a ray of hope can thrive in this space."

He didn't give her electro-shock therapy or strap her down on a bed in a strait jacket (the way he did with the other pajama girls) but put her tenderly in lock-up.

And again and again he tried to release her into the city, where she could either land in jail, or be returned to him, or die.

Since she could hold her breath without a gasp for well over a minute, and remain immobile for even longer, and since she could go without food, and did, for days, he believed that she could survive outside. He suggested a religious life but she smelled his condescension, pinched her nostrils and waved at the air. Then in order to encourage her, he pretended he believed in God and Nirvana—that they were the same—and because it was a time in American history when gurus abounded, he could refer to a system outside the psychiatric one as a possible method for curing her. She was grateful for his shift in vocabulary—from "psychiatrist" to "divine organ"—from "mania" to "ecstasy"—but wasn't fooled by his pretence at having faith in salvation.

It was nearly Christmas again, and she paced around the locked ward where she had been placed after stealing meds from a nun who wrote JESUS on windows with her own feces.

She promised the doctor she would depart before the first of the year. And on that eve she said she had a taste of blood in her mouth and it was the same as the bite of foil, or iron, making her teeth into shafts of pain. On a chunk of wet apple strudel she saw whole cities as if through a metaphysical microscope. She compared these cities to France on the eve of the Revolution, where blood-lust and madness consumed a whole population, and drove people to commit abnormal acts of torture in the name of an idea. She identified the time she was witnessing as The Night of the Long Knives. But the Berlin wall was already up and dripping into the apples.

And she told the doctor that one of the Grimm brothers hoped that his fairy tales would simulate "the desire to wield a big knife, one that can cut through all barriers with complete freedom—at last."

The doctor pointed out that she was juxtaposing historical events, and complained that he didn't understand the recurrent metaphor of a knife, as if he were a critic and she a poet.

Oblivious to his complaint she saw in the pastry the logical conclusion of all fairy tales: fat-cheeked girls plucking eggs from the inside of living hens, flying knives cutting off children's sucking thumbs, serpents with apples stuck in their length, cooks with rolling pins slamming the heads of geese, while ashes fell from the skies.

"Certain cultures love images of steam and snow sliced with shining ice, and veils of fog shrouding islands on steel-gray seas. They love gloom. They send others into exile in such places with a perverse belief that it is a utopia the prisoners are riding to—the utopia of absolute cold. They justify their plans with this faith that they have in the absolution of misery, and that silver light that sheets the winterlands . . . "

She read all this on the sugary surface of the sopping strudel and reported it to the doctor who assured her that the worst had happened already. Not to worry. "There is no future-laden world outside, then?" she asked. You'll know about the future soon enough, he replied and dodged her as she passed.

The doctor had a good generous face, bright honest eyes and a black beard. Being extremely short, he bought his clothes in the boy's department and exhuded the power of a man who must compensate hourly for his missing inches. These lazy women who surrounded his days helped him stay sane. He would muse: "They are the last heretics against a work-addicted world. In a post-industrial modern society, these mad women lounging around hospitals are the true defenders of a time on earth when work did not prove worth."

How can you just loll around all day, doing nothing? he asked her once. She replied: How can you just walk around all day, idly watching us?

Both of them were forest-dwellers, after all, preferring the company of the wild to the tame. But it was a long time before the doctor figured out a way to get her to function rationally, above all consistently outside the hospital ward.

One day he offered her the job of gardener on the grounds around the hospital and told her he would set her up in a little cottage near the front gates and on a four-lane highway. And as if trying to make her feel useful and intelligent, he asked her advice about his patients. She generalized: "The wholly wounded have to be wholly healed." He thought she had said "holy" and his mind wandered nervously away. Always he feared the return of her manias. Now she grabbed his hands in hers and examined them with tears on her lashes, saying, "Your pink nails are like seashells, your knuckles are so brown . . . Why do they make me cry for joy?"

Backing away, he replied, "Calm down, it's nothing. My dear friend, since most of the world is absent, air should be your model of heaven. Not physical details."

And later that day he gave her a little excerpt from Kafka's notebooks that she pinned over her bed. He supposed that he played the part of God in her life, or maybe she even fantasized about loving him.

"Strange how the legacy of cynicism is belief," he reflected, thinking
how her parents must have treated her.

And a week later he heard her begin her story where she always began:
"One night many years ago—from under a dry rose bush—in a rough
garden near the Irish Sea . . . "

As soon as I was halfway through the story, I heard him breathing in low
regular patterns and discovered to my amazement that I had put my
doctor to sleep. It was wonderful to gaze on his closed face, to see his
hands folded on his chest mid-twiddle, thumbs upright, and his mouth
ajar. His soft eyelids were flat against their orbs, he didn't seem to be
dreaming. His will and his intellect had fled. His notebook dangled like
a children's storybook from his parted knees.

And looking at him I remembered the face of a boy who had shared a
cabin with me many years before on a sea voyage. When the little boy
was asleep, his expression was like the steam that dreams its way from
the surface of salt water in early morning and seeps into invisibility under the heat of the day. His expression was without malice, mistrust or
sorrow. It was a look of repose that marked the true border between this
world and the unseen one.

But unlike the boy, the Doctor snored. And that was the moment I tiptoed (sick of fiction) past him out of the brick building and set off to
exercise my happiness in foreign lands.

x

On her return home Cloda went to the docks to watch the ferry arrive with
her mother, but daily she was disappointed. She feared her mother was
lost. She was for that time aching in her joints and abdomen, nearly crippled by somatic reactions to the traveller dying and her mother's delay in
returning. She went to Catharine's house in Irishtown and stayed there
with her for a few nights, just to be close to a functioning female in a house

that was cluttered with things accumulated over years. Catharine on her own territory was kinder to Cloda than she had been before and took her to evening mass with her after the ferry had emptied and no mother appeared. Catharine taught her some Latin words and how to pray the rosary.

And in order to reassure her about the ease of ocean travel, she told her the story of Brendan the Navigator, who left Ireland in the 5th century and travelled to Iceland where he met a colony of Irish monks already settled there. Apparently he then headed west in a massive oak vessel made of a single woven sail. The boat carried grain, plants, pigs, fish, sea-holly for the scurvy, wooden casks full of water, and three trained raven to look for land. They steered by the sun and the North Star and on their way west passed the Aran Islands, fog, and the icebergs of Newfoundland. His crew was made up of sixty men, including several priests and a jester. But the thing about Brendan that Catharine liked the best was that he loved his sister Briga, a nun in Galway. They did everything together but travel the seas. And when Brendan was dying, it was in Briga's company. She could see he was afraid and asked him why. And he replied: "I fear going alone for the way is dark. I fear the unknown, the presence of the king, and the sentence of the judge."

This story frightened and haunted Cloda, who kept asking Catharine about the judgment of God on people who caused evil inadvertently. Catharine told her about The Chastisement Day and how on that day everyone would be known inside and out, and it would be themselves that knew themselves and that would be even worse than a judgment coming down from above.

"Just keep saying O Christ without stain, never leave me! she advised Cloda warmly.

What do you mean by "Christ"? Cloda asked.

It's not the same as Jesus, Catharine explained. I mean, I don't eat Jesus in the wafer. I eat the Christ. The Christ is like a—well—a chemical.

It goes into your system. Oh never mind. Your own mother or father should have taught you these things. Stick with the fairies."

How can I if I don't believe in them anymore? I like Briga and Brendan better.

x

The New Year came and went and finally one day Cloda let herself in to the darkened house and saw her father's famous suitcase gleaming by the stairs. There he was, seated at the kitchen table with his hands warming around a cup of tea. He was alone. As if coming upon him for the first time in her life—he was somehow changed—she didn't just see him: she beheld, discerned, perceived, made out, recognized, glimpsed, watched, scanned, noticed, stared, peered, peeped, viewed, scrutinized, inspected, surveyed and observed him.

Her father had a receding hairline that gave a kind of Roman edge to his regular anglo features. It also accentuated a dreamy, nearly mystical expression that he wore at all times, speaking softly and between his teeth, suggesting a withheld sorrow. Cloda remembered that he was athletic, a powerful swimmer who joined the polar bear clubs in all climes and swam in salt seas throughout winter. But she also remembered that he had had an affair while he was gone, and so she didn't want to speak to him at all.

(He would never talk about it to any of them anyway. The blonde woman had left him to return to America. She worked for a Catholic Relief organization and was determined to help people escape Europe before it was too late for them. Planning for others to escape she was also planning for her own liberation from the gathering violence.

(Before she left, she said to him with her face in her hands:

("The madness of this world is that it worships brains and people don't even know what they are. Nobody knows what intelligence really is, or how it differs from instinct. I can't live in such a world. Where am I? Don't you see what is happening? Intelligence can invent right and wrong reasons for absolutely anything. I can't live in this world, I really can't . . . It's going to be awful!"

(And then she did leave Switzerland and him—their affair happily un-consummated. And the father awoke to the fact that it was time for him to go home—not just to Ireland, but all the way home.) When her father finally came upon Cloda, he was on his way to his room to unpack. He saw her shape in the bed and berated her for not saying hello to him. Then he embraced her with unusual strength and said, "I'm terribly worried about your mother. This man, Hal, who is he? And why is he here? He said your mother was meant to return two weeks ago! I don't like a man living in a house alone with my daughters. God, but I deserve it, for leaving you! Where is your sister?"

Probably at the library, said Cloda pulling back from his tweed and sweat. I don't know.

Well, I'm back now, so things have to get under control again. Do you hear me? I told that man he could leave right now. He gave me the creeps.

I wish he would die, said Cloda.

Well, that's a bit strong. Now tell me what you've been up to. Are you worried about your mother?

Sort of. But have you ever heard of Saint Brendan the Navigator, Daddy? Did you know that the Irish were in America before Columbus? People were able to cross oceans on practically rafts. So it's not that dangerous out on the sea.

"Oh, it's an old rumor. Well, I shouldn't say that. Maybe it's true! The Shawnee Indians apparently talked about an Irish missionary in Florida—propelled there by wings over the sea—a kind of god to them. Can you imagine anyone being able to cross the Atlantic ocean on a raft? Just take a look at the sea outside this house, how rough it is."

I don't want to. She had not wanted to imagine her mother tossing on the sea and went back under her blanket still traced with dog and her own hair.

The father continued: There's also a legend that in the very far north, you can see distant lands painted on the sky on certain rare nights. In Iceland you suddenly see Ireland, its whole and intricate shape floating overhead, and he went on to say, and who cares if it's true or not?

X

From that night on he cooked charcoal blackened fish, pots of rice, peas, and took charge of the butter-churning in the morning. He baked bread but had to buy their gooseberry jam, instead of making it himself. He sipped Irish whiskey while he cooked and talked to Cloda who listened to his anecdotes with complete attention for the first time in her life perhaps because she was almost always alone with him.

Together they listened to War-talk on the short-wave radio, and they heard Italian, German and American voices. But they always listened to the radio low, because the phone might ring down the hall and the mother be calling to let them know when she would return. Irene was hardly ever there, though she always came home to sleep at night, in order to hide from her father the true nature of her relations with Hal.

Those relations continued now on a narrow bed in his basement flat in Dublin. The gloom against the window panes was colored yellowy gray, as if bilious solution were being poured over Dublin, or splashed up from the sea, and the rain dripped silver lines from wood over glass to wooden sill. An electric wall-heater was used only rarely, so they wrapped their bones around each other, and hung on. Irene went on going to school, and pretended she was in the library late into the night, although her father seemed indifferent to her activities, he was completely focused on an absence far greater than hers. Whether it was the absent mother or lover, neither daughter could guess. But he was distracted, wildly cooking as if the only necessity he understood was the one that had to do with food. Otherwise he was sloppy, unwashed and indiscriminate in his interests.

x

Hal was gone during the days, and sometimes Irene heard him talking to men outside on the sidewalk before he joined her in the dark basement room. Sometimes he would spend a long time in the bathroom before joining her, and then he was already erect, arrived just so, and set to work applying himself to her body with full almost anxious attention. Other times he lay limp and distracted, staring at the glass panes as if they were extensions of his own eyes near tears. When he was inside her, he kept at it for a long time and she engulfed the physical contact, feeling it as basic as love itself, although she never felt more than the pleasure of an internal massage. There was no great and glorious rush as she experienced on her bike, or in her sleep. She wanted him in her nonetheless, as much as possible, and was hurt or cross when he couldn't be aroused. He didn't love her or her touch but he felt morally obligated to continue with her. Sometimes he regretted the whole occasion and plotted how to escape Ireland without her or any memory of his time there. But then he felt guilty because of her youth, her trust, and focused on her muscular and upright breasts. Otherwise he experienced her body as a tight, dry thing and had to fantasize his way to an erection before entering her at all. When had it changed?

Nod

On the night of Irene's cast party when he had wandered home alone. Ever since then he had wanted to go home and never see Ireland or the people in it again.

But Hal was not what he seemed to be, the mother would say much later. "I mean, he might have been working for the fascists—it certainly looked like that—supposedly, but maybe not. And we think he might have been a Communist, working with the IRA, on the side of the fascists against the Allies. Or he might have been a spy for Norway's right wing anti-Communist group. He kept returning to Ireland mysteriously, during the War, and apparently he dreaded it every time."

Whatever his involvement in Ireland was, it occupied him fully. Still, he had a sort of prolonged hate-affair with that country after that night when he returned home wet and impotent. He couldn't plan his exit soon enough. It was as if the country itself was his personal enemy, a vituperative body of land that would one day successfully down him, which it did.

One April day—deep into the War—the enemy unloaded about 100 tons of bombs over Belfast, killing 745 people. They also, by mistake, dropped a bomb on Dublin killing 71 people. Hal was one of them.

x

Irene went with him to Norway, despite her father's furious efforts at stopping her. It was only years later, when the war was over, and her career was launched that she wrote home and explained:

"I'm sorry I left in such a rush, but Hal was desperate to escape Ireland. Believe me, I never found out exactly what his politics were and I didn't care. As he would say himself, It was a man's war. All I can say is that I returned to Norway with him, where he took good care of me throughout a year and a half, despite constant trips back to Ireland. I lived as far north as you can get in Norway and experienced the deep snow as a kind of erasure of all that was going on in the rest of the world."

In Norway Irene, isolated in a farmhouse with a pair of paleskin relatives of Hal's, stopped throwing up and started getting fat instead. She ate salted fish, brown bread, slathers of butter, cakes, raisins, chocolate and cheese. She drank beer and grew soft from whipped cream.

Hal bought her a little movie camera for a present and she drilled away at films of snow and shadows, then edited them (screaming fuck and shit) in front of a lamp with a razor, scotch tape and clothes pins, then ran the attached strips through a small projector. The images dancing on the wall made her groan or sing for excitement, and the relatives said she should record her own sounds as voice-overs on her films, they were so strange. She did.

She read voraciously from books in English in the house—Dickens, Hardy, the Russians, Austen, the Brontes, mysteries—and was occupied every minute of her day, even as she guzzled.

At first she believed that a gain in weight and flesh would excite Hal, who complained of her lack of contours and juice. But then he said he missed her firm little breasts and her flesh and her appetite took on a will of their own. It was as if her new fat helped her feel terrible about something real instead of something she couldn't grasp, like her endlessly producing hate. She hated the relatives. She often hated Hal. She hated not knowing about her family or if her mother had forgiven her. Her guilt was great. Hal's aunt suggested she take a clearing oath by finding a silver plate in a stone that contained the eyes of Christ and Mary's bones. "Shake the dish, while you tell the truth and you will be cleared of your guilt."

But Irene didn't believe in magic or religion. And she continued to complain constantly—about her neck, hair, back, about the snow, the dark, the loneliness. Sometimes tears poured down her round cheeks as she sat at the white windowpane and pushed food into her mouth, salting whatever it was from the mill of her grief. She assumed that everyone was watching her. And so she made the drama of her fat a subject for anyone and everyone around. She promised people (as if they cared) that she would lose weight as soon as the war was over. But she didn't. Instead she swelled into a form that must have been held in reserve, her adult form, and just like a mourning dove she cooed new sound-forms as backgrounds to her very far-out films. Over the years people remarked that she would be beautiful if she only were thin. She knew that people said or thought this and that the excess flesh was a way of withholding her virtue, of her remaining permanently potential, an ideal. Being fat was, in other words, a way of being thin because every person who saw her thought of the buried slender Irene—and in this way the vision of her thin self was imprinted on her frame like an x-ray. Being fat was also a way of proving that she was not "all right" even though she got everything on earth she ever wanted. Prizes, honors, employment, fame.

There were plenty of times she hoped that Hal would die or disappear for good. And then he did.

"Now I know, in retrospect, that although Hal was cold to me, this very coldness brought the heat to my surface and as a result I never have been without a bedmate. He never hurt a fly in all his life, and so he disproves the theory that you die as you live. For me, anyway. When I return to America I will immediately begin to work seriously as a filmmaker. But first I want to have more fun over here. Because you know what? Even if I'm fat and grumpy, I still eat man at night."

People can forgive a funny person almost anything, and the one fact about Irene that many people forgot to mention was that she was very funny. People tossed around laughing in her presence. And she watched this phenomenon with a small twist to her lips and an expression of controlled content in her eyes.

Nod

x

Cloda waited at the ferry for the thirteenth time, hanging her legs over the dock and feeling a damp breeze against her cheeks as a beneficent emotion from the skies. She thought of tossing bottle after bottle into the water with a wide variety of messages inscribed and sealed inside, but then this seemed to indicate a lack of faith in the original bottle she had once pushed into the water, a lack of faith that could throw the whole world off its axis.

She closed her eyes, listening to hoots from the boat and the mad splashing of water in chaos under the wooden dock, and finding a music in it. From a distance you would witness her as an obscure girl in her early teens, dressed drably, the type who always wears her sleeves draped over her hands, so only the fingertips show. Her posture suggested defeat and her surprisingly sensuous mouth hung open as if she couldn't breathe through her nose. She would probably be chewing gum. She wore a woollen cap pulled low down on her brow and her black electrified hair stuck up on end inside it. A strange dog usually sat at her side (its owner somewhere nearby) and seemed to operate as an extra sense-receiver for her. She watched a dog's reactions to sounds as if they were signals showing her how to react. Sometimes she curled up her hand and looked through the hole with one eye, the other one squinting. And sometimes she leaned forward recklessly as if she were preparing to fall into the bashing sea. She was restless, like someone at the start of a race.

Now the passengers poured off the boat, many of them foreigners, and people struggled to meet and embrace, but Cloda moved back near the street as if to distance herself from disappointment.

However, this was the time her mother did return, with the two boys at her side and Cloda ran to meet them, making lots of other people mad at their American pushiness.

Nod

The mother wore an abstract—if not deranged—look as they took a taxi to their house, but the two little boys were upright watching everything out the window, alert, terrified.

At the house, the mother and father circled each other nervously. She babbled about Hitler and going home, while the father stirred a giant pot full of watery potatoes and dried peas for a soup. Meanwhile Cloda tended to the two boys, one of whom threw up on the kitchen floor while the other one cried. After cleaning up the mess the mother and father retired to their bedroom, leaving the soup to simmer on low, and they stayed there, locked away, for several hours. When they emerged, they reminded Cloda of the people they used to be.

The miserable boys trailed Cloda from room to room and ended up sleeping in Irene's bed and whispering in broken English to Cloda at night, telling her about their mother, father, friends and village. And in the process she taught them new words and then in the morning she bathed and dressed them. She took them to school and introduced them and hovered around, making sure that no one was mean to them. And very naturally she became their permanent provider since the mother had no interest in them and the father returned to his work. She loved the two boys and worried over them and for awhile her posture straightened and she grew stronger in character and confidence as she continued to forget almost every detail of that year in Ireland.

(It was twenty five years before she would begin to remember that year, and only because of a haphazard confluence of sensual impressions: a pink stone house on a wet salty street and the bittersweet scent of boxwood in the air. She was flooded. She felt into a trance. She took off her shoes, left her job, and began to walk. People thought she was hearing an imaginary voice from the attention on her face, but she was following another sound in every town: the bark of a dog.)

Nod

When the five of them returned to New York on a boat filled with emigres from all over Europe, Cloda continued to mother these boys and to care for them, until their own mother finally returned to them.

x

And that happened in the same year and the same month—October—that a boy was hurled from a boat by a blast and found himself floating off the coast of Brighton. Flotsam was orange and hot amidst the cries of the drowning others, his friends, and now the waspy buzz of planes was swallowed in the rise and fall of salt water at his ears. He was soaked as if he was all holes from his nostrils to his arms and ripped at his boots to loose their weight. Then freed—he was a good swimmer off the Carolinas as a boy—he started hauling his arms through the sea toward the gray lump of shore that was southern England.

He was by nature a slow-moving and optimistic person, and so he didn't panic or fear that he wouldn't survive. Instead he took his time rolling and floating and humming and imagining happy times ahead, on land, and even a return home, to America, and the war won. But soon he began to notice that time was slower than usual in the water, and light was heavier, space scarcer. He tried to maintain his buoyancy, both of body and spirit, but having nothing but his tiny head and its enormous weight-draining capacity, he began to flag. The optimist in him gave way to the slacker. He lost interest. Nothing matters that much, after all. Why not take a nap and sink?

The sky's mistiness made the land hard to articulate or believe in. But something glittered now just ahead, pricking his curiosity and he reached out and slapped at the surface of the sea. But the glitter kept sinking and rising again at a further distance. He batted at it repeatedly until it finally fit into his hand. A red bottle, corked, no label, a paper inside. So the boy put both his hands on the bottle and used it as a float, though anyone, including himself, would know that a bottle could not hold up an 18-year old boy in Army gear. But in this case it did. And with its reassuring measure in his hands, he thrashed his path to the first rock outcropping, where he rested for the remainder of his swim. He took the bottle with him. In fact he took it with him into his real life at home again in America at the end of the war. And often he held it up to the light, luxuriantly, happily, to check that the print was intact on the piece of paper inside. He was convinced that the words inside would lead him to only one more miracle. But because he was a slow-moving person, he savored his hopes and set the bottle on the windowsill while he took his time. And while he did, the salt in the cork evaporated into the bottle under the rays of the sun and the words turned as white as the salt they came from.

The
Deep
North

At first it wasn't clear. No truth. No belongings. There was snow on the trees, rooftops, streets and that gray light you see in old movies set at sea, where ice floes break the boat apart. This to me is the image of the knowable. Ropes and stripes, black and white, and what you look at, looks back. If it's a dream, or if it's what is actually seen, then it comes to the same thing: broken language, foreign syntax, the incomprehensible nature of the world. Anyway I didn't even want an answer, that's a fact. All answers are hells. I just wanted to locate the process that underlay the surface image, to put my hand under the top without looking at what I let out. Whatever it was, it didn't belong to me. That is the nature of the truth.

One night two small children roamed the woods alone. Their mother, who was fondling some man, and their father, who was self-absorbed, didn't notice. A highwway of moonlight cut through the spruce and scrub of the Cape woods and they heard the distant crush of waves on sand. No one, for that time, really cared where they were. The effect of alcohol, which children learn to dread, made them fly into the warm night air. Their pajamas damp around the hems, they trotted hand in hand, into the thickets, silent of birdsong, though fog horn called *forlorn to* fog horn.

The boy was the guide. The girl let him lead her because he was four years older. Pretend, he said, we are slaves escaping. You're the slave and I'm the master's son. You said I want to go to the North with you, so I took you with me late one night. You were actually the illegitimate daughter of the master, too, by a slave woman who had very pale skin. I was incredibly brave, so I agreed to take you, like this, to the river where a canoe would meet us. Okay?

His story raced down the tracklines laid by the moonshine and trees and watercolor shadows danced on the gray trunks, as they passed. Her eyes were teary with excitement, it was so late, and her real parents so far behind. Her conviction that they would notice she was gone, and get mad, made her stomach stir round and round, and she held tight to her brother's hand, so the lines on their palms pressed.

When we get to the end of the river, the boy continued, we will be met by a party of escaped slaves and Indians. I will leave you with them, and they will raise you in the wilderness, as one of them, while I roam the country, alone. . . .

That night they lay on the sand dunes huddled in a knot. She was unable to sleep for thinking about her freedom and staring at the night sky and its illuminating stars. Only the black sky, with the sea smoking nearby, could inform her of her position as God's agent on earth. Her brother was twelve, she was eight. She was sure this escape was connected to her proximity to a Divine Being, even though she lived in a family of committed atheists. The weight of her little head on her brother's arm numbed him to sleep while her eyes gained access to those showers of stars. At last she was free from the blank eyes of her mother, and her father's vocal competence. As her brother's little sister in American history, she felt she was also freed of a future where grown-ups never changed. That intransigence, when finally believed and accepted, was more horrible than the thought of eternity. Like the appetite of the ocean, going back and forth and nowhere special, it was character itself.

In the dark the water seemed to pour out of the sky, and at dusk it came in gray, a form of air denser and wetter by weight alone. At the murky horizon, she saw how the water poured from space. But what, then, were the red rose balls, the nettles, the clover, lace and golden-rod, the spruce and shrubbery which together murmured as if a spirit was locked inside? A little boxwood smell filled the dewy air. Crows quarreled and small birds sang. Gulls bit at the tops of the caving water, white to white.

When she finally slept, the boy woke up to watch and listen to the sun unveiling the world. Landscape is all that greets the most enormous desires, even if only the landscape of a face. He looked at his sister's untroubled sleep, placid and closed like a law, and seeing that she was no longer a brown-skinned and brave slave, but the familiar sister he saw at home, he pulled away his arm and ran back up the beach on his own.

One August day the mother, father and daughter were driving together through Boston. They were going to visit the brother where he was bedded in a single hospital room. He was sixteen and suffering from asthma. They were running tests on him to find out if he might have an allergy to something at home, which he said he did.

It was 1952. The daughter, G, had returned from summer camp, brown from sun, her black hair streaked gold and still in her camp clothes, she smelled of pine and oil. The vacancy of her green-eyed stare—she was now twelve—expressed the shock in visual juxtaposition between this hot and steamy street and the valleyed green of Vermont.

Her parents were quiet, which was not normal. Usually, if one was quiet, the other was not. The mother's classy New York accent gave to her voice a complacent tone, which the father, a New Englander, had absorbed and integrated into his own nasal twang. This influence of her on him was perhaps the only one any outsider might notice.

G wanted them to talk, as if their words, like shells tossed up from the ocean, were reassuringly refined and enduring. "Look," she said, "Look at that man!"

He was lying on the curb, his face pressed into the concrete, red and scraped.

"If you look closely, Dear," the mother responded, "you'll see he's lying outside a bar. That means he's drunk, nothing to worry about."

They stopped at a set of lights, and she could see almost the length of the street running under the el to Forest Hills station. As a place that never sees light, it looked like the inside of an unhappy life. Its density of object and shadow, of billboards, neon, trash and dark-skinned humanity, put a reflection into G's eyes, like reminiscence transplanted into the present. "An added look," as they say. Her parents began talking when the light changed. The mother started:

"I don't care what Dr. Simon says. Tonio was born high-strung. Asthma at this age? No. He's putting on an act."

"Well, it may be an act and it may not be. But Dr. Simon is in charge now, and we have to take him seriously. He says it's asthma."

"He says it's asthma, Tonio says it's an allergy. I say it's nerves. Maybe it's all three," the father suggested.

The mother then breathed high in her throat, almost a hiss. G heard these sighs of her mother's as the background music to her own emotions and experiences, as if her mother's voice was her private soundtrack. She sighed herself, a minimal puff, and her stomach made a motion on its own. She was often afraid of each member of her family, though she had no idea why.

She knew her brother was up to something; he didn't want to come home unless it was conditional. On what, she couldn't guess. G always felt, within feet of her brother, a change in the air's content. A tunnel has a similar effect, especially when you have to turn on the headlights entering it from daylight.

Remembering his black hair and olive skin, his green eyes and wide red mouth—a composition not unlike her own features, but paler and more aquiline—she put him, now, in some lofty frame. His moods, which frightened her at home, seemed connected to the streets around, their aura of tragedy and injustice.

Outside, the air was wobbling around hot traffic and people, while the car circled a concrete grid supporting the el. The heat made watery ribbons across the surfaces of things, as if it lived inside those things and didn't ignite from above. G leaned out her window to watch the activity, to smell the air and hear the voices. Inside she contained the traces of that black lake water with its iron qualities, its reflections of pine and stone; but she pulled herself away voluntarily. She wanted to know where her brother was placed, and was reassured by the way the people outside were taking the heated streets for granted.

"How can people live like that," said the mother with a trace of disgust.

"Dunno," he replied and went on to speculate about lowered expectations among the poor. "I think they just get used to it," he concluded. "Besides, this isn't real poverty. They should go to India to see what real poverty is."

The hospital was down a small side street, empty of activity. "Is this the way you came when you brought him?" G asked.

"Yes . . . Now Anna, you take Gemma and go on in. I'll park."

This was the way they usually did it. The mother was left at the door while the father parked, even if only a few feet away. Now A, small and tanned, approached the entrance to the hospital as if it were her possession. This was always her way of dealing with the world. In her late forties, she was buoyant, thirtyish and vain. Her face was straight-lined in structure, except for a small indentation in her chin. She had the green eyes, brownish complexion and black hair of her children because of her Italian mother—an "aristocrat' according to A.

Now G, in the wake of the mother's perfume, drifted after her, to the elevator. The familiar click-click of the high heels ahead of her made her believe, for a spell, that the world was composed of efficiencies.

"Hey," called the father, rushing up behind them. "Here I am."

"So you are!"

The two of them drew together automatically, the image of lucky-in-love and lucky-in-money, though not, at a glance, suited to each other. His small sandy features—mouth and chin measured in trim proportions—were those of a thoughtful, well-bred boy. Pleasures of youth were preserved by his loosened tie, scuffed shoes, and frayed seersucker jacket, but his brow was furrowed, as if to remind the world that he was in fact thoughtful and grown-up. His hair, worn in an overlong crewcut, spiked a couple of inches above his skull, and his lips were frequently pursed. He had a habit of pulling his horn-rimmed glasses up and down the length of his nose, suggesting that the world was a book and he was constantly dipping into it.

"Tonio is expecting us, isn't he?" asked G.

"Of course he is," the father said, and he put his hand on G's shoulder, steering her into the elevator. (She wore, by the way, a look of terror which she hoped someone would notice; they didn't.)

They found T in his bed, under the covers. The sun lay heavy on the thin white sheets. He was curled up, his eyes shut with his long black lashes deepening the blue shadows under the lids. G, seeing him so reduced, looked away and blushed.

"Darling," said his mother.

He lurched upright, all in one move, then stayed on his elbows, propped up and frowning.

"Why did you bring Gemma here?"

"She wanted to see you. She's just back from camp."

It was not an affectionate family. No kisses accompanied this explanation. Instead G stepped back and looked around the room for something she might like. Leaf shadows danced on a white wall; she slipped to the window to find their source.

"How are you today, Dear? Sleepy? What's the doctor saying to you about coming home?"

"Nothing."

"It's bound to be soon. Tomorrow maybe?" the father noted.

"I hope not. . . . If I do, I'll just get sick again. Besides, the two of you do just fine without me there."

"No, we don't. Don't be silly."

"Oh Mother, don't lie."

"Mother? You mean Mummy," she corrected him.

"Did you learn any songs at camp, Gemma?" the father suddenly asked. This was a familiar signal and G whirled around from the window, obediently. Her face was rounder for his question and her eyes brighter.

"Do I have to?" she inquired. The father nodded and smiled at the other members of his family, as if to say that at last he had found the key to their happiness. G opened her mouth and closed her eyes and sang in a high but strong voice. She was trying not to giggle, and clutched her hands in fists. *"By the Green Mountain water With the moon in the trees I laid down my rug and paddle And knew I was free. Yodel-ay-whoo-whoo! Yodel-ay-hay-hay! I was free!"*

"Are you going to Italy?" the boy asked his parents. His interruption was his judgment on his sister's performance.

"I don't think so," said the mother.

"Too bad. I hoped you'd all be away for a while."

"Well, sorry to disappoint you," said the father who had often expressed his conviction that T was spoiled and not nervous, or sick, ever. It was obvious to everyone in the room that he was now about to say just that, because he looked down at his son with his lips locked into a dangerous knot, and his glasses up across his eyes for a hard reading.

G stared out the window, but her face was blazing. She heard her brother's voice crack as he began to react.

"Gemma, take yourself for a walk down the hall," said the father in a falsely good-humored tone.

Hurriedly, the girl did as she was told and walked the hall the way they had come. Her hands were gluey and her stomach churned. The smells she brushed against made her feel ill, and she was torn between the desire to stare at the patients and to pretend they didn't exist. Wasn't disease catching; so why put all the sick people near each other where they'd get sicker? She stared at the floor, and gasped a quick breath, stopped at the elevator, held her nose and guided her shadow back again.

Then she stood outside the door to T's room, listening. A nurse was in there now. She had an accent and a voice that reminded G of the smell of vanilla.

"You don't want to get him upset now," she was saying to the parents. "That can set off another attack, you know."

"He's faking," the mother was saying. "Believe me. I know him."

"I don't think you can fake an asthma attack," the nurse replied.

"You'd be surprised," said the mother. "It's time for him to come home."

"I don't want to go home, Mother," said T.

"But why not?"

"I'm allergic to it."

"Oh come on. That's so childish. You're just like my mother's family—high strung. It comes with the breeding. But in this country it's too hard to survive with that kind of sensibility. That's what's wrong with you. Inherited sensitivity—"

"You two are acting like idiots," said the father. "Fight, fight, fight is all you ever do. Now what are you after, Tonio? Just say what you want and let's get on with it."

"If I go home, I want my freedom. That's all. Not much."

"Freedom? Yes. I'm suffocating. That's the meaning of asthma. I don't even have a car."

"A car? Is that what you want?" asked the mother. Then she said to the nurse, as if to a maid: "You can leave now."

And now the nurse walked by G, shaking her head the way people do all over the world. G wanted to follow her, but didn't dare leave the door.

"By the way, Pa," she heard T say in a loud voice. "Speaking of meaning. What's the meaning of life?"

"Dunno. But when you figure it out, don't tell me."

Now his family left T; they used the stairs this time, in single file and speechless. When they stepped out onto the street, they were met by the bright hot sun, and it was as shocking as if they had been inside at a midday movie. The father looked perplexed, as he often did, while the mother caressed her upper arms with her fingers. Inside the car no one spoke, but passing back again under the rattling tracks of the el, G stared into the slums of Boston and perceived them as a form of x-ray, a study of the inside of the self, which she could not interpret.

In a matter of hours, her brother was released from there, never to return. In the months to come, with a car at his disposal, he was hardly ever home; he was off in the mountains, skiing, when he wasn't at school. The mysterious attack of asthma never recurred.

At the end of one August, when G was small, a woman was hired by the family to be their maid. Her name was Darlene; she was originally from the Deep South. She was a petite, pretty woman with coffee-colored skin and a long neck. She seemed to see speech rather than to hear it. Her eyes flew up and down and around catching the words, then let them settle, before she would respond with an expression of intense visual focus on her face. She read voraciously in hours snatched between cooking and cleaning. She read the Russian novelists, and books on European and American history, and sometimes she was annoyed with G for hanging around. She called G "the dark little white girl" and so did Ron, her fiancé, whom she had followed to Boston. G often sat in the kitchen after school and talked alone to Darlene or listened to her and Ron speaking across the table, stove, sink. G sometimes sat on top of the refrigerator with her legs hanging over the pictures she had drawn, which her father had hung there. She watched Darlene read in the same tidy way she did everything else. She sat erect on the edge of the kitchen chair and turned the pages slowly, pensively, occasionally gazing off into space.

As she grew older G was aware that her parents' world was in turmoil over issues related to Russia and Communism. At dinner these were the topics. Names like Welch, McCarthy, Hiss and Chambers were like titles of books on espionage. The names were code-words in war and conjured up images of tall grass, safaris, guns and gas. The adult world was a system of concealment and hidden decisions, tremendous ambition and attention to surface. G's father was an administrator in an arts and scholarship foundation. Feeling himself to be on the side of the enemy (money), he went out of his way to stay close to professors and artists and to sustain a political position that would allow him to live twice: once as a manager of time and money, second as a thinker and liberal. It was a difficult balance. As if he had two eyes looking in separate directions, he was often heard to say, "I see what you mean, but on the other hand . . . "

The family lived in a wooden frame house on a rural street. Crabapple and Japanese cherry trees, bleeding hearts, tiger lilies, lily of the valley, violets, myrtle and wild columbine lathered the garden as well as the August and autumn flowers, orange and red like the leaves. The mother raised a little vegetable garden in boxes; beans and peas climbed up strings. Inside the house the wallpaper was flowered. The downstairs rooms were furnished by the eighteenth-century Europeans; but the rugs were Persian. These rooms sat in an eerily expectant state like stage sets.

There was an upright piano in the study, and this was for G to play while her father read at his desk. He had insisted that she have lessons in music, singing, dancing, and he hung her drawings all over the house. He called her his girl wonder and liked to have her perform for him and others, though she squirmed, writhed and hated it. When he watched her singing, or dancing, his eyes acquired a dreamy expression, his tense features softened and his became the face he was gazing on. He saw a great future for her, and participated in its planning as if she were a little spirit he had unleashed from inside himself and he could steer it forward, a part of himself, into a victorious future. His own sense of failure was prodigious.

While the father reveled in G's accomplishments and always begged for more, he never seemed to see her in the hours between them. So she was surprised, and even hesitant, when he took her for a walk in the woods soon after T returned home from the hospital. He told her what the names of trees were (a maple he identified as an elm and a birch as a beech) and kept his hand on the back of her neck which she held rigid. He told her how she was like his side of the family and he said that he and she shared a certain view of the world which would always help them understand each other. She was proud to the point of blushing and her mind filed through ways to please him. But something, at the same time, held her tongue. She was afraid, she realized, to say or do anything clever because he would at once forget her and make an event out of the act. He would make her take singing lessons if she sang in the car, or art lessons if doodled while she talked on the phone, or if she told him she could identify a scarlet tanager, she was taken to the museum to look at taxidermy. So now she didn't dare do anything at all but walk stiffly by his side, inhaling his attentions.

His hand played at the nape of her neck, his thumb trailing in and out of the soft groove there, and they gazed into the varying depths of shadow and light, greens so hard they were nearly black, and he told her what she was and who she was and where she would be in twenty years, till the sun was like a spill of liquid, ferns were like ironed Christmas trees and mushrooms were like penises, and nothing was exactly what it was, but like something else. She smelled skunk cabbage and its odor clung inside her nostrils, merging with her feelings about herself. She scooted, then, out from inside his hand and went to tug up a stalk of grass to wear between her teeth. It arced out in front of her as she walked an arm's length away from him. She saw from the corner of her eye that his hand was still raised to receive the back of her neck again, but she pretended she didn't see, until it went down.

A white bird leaves the snow.

Gradual disentanglement from cars and chickenish seagulls.

I'm unearthly too without my cream toner, moisturizer, shampoo or conditioner; but my wings have shriveled.

Madness is a loss of moral sense. You know this when you have a mad person in the house and wonder where their brain screws into the divine scheme. If only you could find it for him!

Nobody knows where I've been—its emergencies, its gustiness, its huddled beggary in welfare offices—no one knows the people in trouble I've been and seen. Fists racing at my face, stacked in an alcove where I escaped into politics and bottles. No one but those who are there all the time knows the underworld close up in this town.

Where flashlights are like watch-fires, the torsos are removed from incinerators and elevator shafts. In the area of low forms, my anguish is an echo, the story of a story. That's not good enough when your cry is too big for your body.

Many years later, on a train to New York, G forgot who she was. She was gazing out the window at apartment buildings—some hammered shut and some occupied—against a floral pink sky. She had a pair of seats to herself and she rocked uneasily with the motion of the train. Her hands were folded on her lap, her left still wearing the garnet engagement ring and gold band of her early marriage. The train, then, entered the tunnel approaching Penn Station. As if she were turning to gold, a numbness came down her skull, moved through her neck, shoulders, chest, arms and on, all the way to her feet until she was a shell with not even the hiss of the wind inside.

The experience, as she knew at the time, was called a massive anxiety attack. The name didn't produce relief, but the opposite. The terror increased. Like desire going backwards, and backwards, obliterating all hope and imagination. G, then, for the first time ever, forgot her name, where she was coming from and where she was going, and viewed herself as an alien among aliens, a particle supported only by the density of an indifferent eternity. Around her, people were getting restless, pulling down their bags, putting on their coats. She didn't move, even when someone dropped down close beside her. It was a woman darker than herself, with an overnight bag on her knees.

G was black-haired, green-eyed, and brown-toned like her mother, but her feelings about this likeness disgusted her. Sitting in the train that day, doused in sweat, she tried to restore herself by turning to the woman beside her. That placid dark face she read as a sign of kindness and wisdom.

"I'm sick of traveling. It makes me feel unhealthy," she said.

"That's too bad," was the low reply.

"Do you like to travel?"

"I don't know. I just do it."

"Are you from Boston?"

The woman did not answer but tipped out to the side and looked down the aisle as if she had suddenly remembered a runaway child. G ran her wet hand across her wet brow. Then she pulled her sketchbook out of her bag and flipped it open to a page where she had drawn pictures of old men in a park. Black webbed lines, spidery, incomplete. Her father would have loved them.

The woman glanced at the picture and asked, "Why did you make those people so ugly? That's unkind."

"Ugly?"

"Look at his nose."

"It's an exaggeration."

"Hm. Not in my eyes."

G closed the sketchbook back in her bag. She said aloud but to herself, "I have to take the world as it is. I have to accept reality. I have no choice". The woman looked at her knowingly, then rose to her feet and departed down the aisle.

The train lurched, stopped and the platform was dim but deserted outside the window. G, glancing at her own face mirrored over that image, was taken aback by the glitter of her eyes and the ferocity of her own expression. She wondered, aimlessly, who she was and where she was going. Someone so fierce should know these facts. The figures swimming beyond her face were like fish in a deep pond, a trail of souls moving through murky light, everybody lost.

She hauled out her bag from under her seat and headed outside, knowing she would take the first train back the way she came. Anxiety ("depression," her mother would say) curled back inside her like a creature that fears the motion of its nest, her body. It went in, and as it did, more than the mere statistics of her person returned. As she climbed the stairs with the crowd, her eyes fixed on the concrete floor, she remembered pleasure, as hard and for as long as she could.

She had hoped to leave her husband, Adam, and to make a new life in New York. The way they talked to each other was frightening to her—he in the language of Freud, of Wilhelm Reich, of others who saw the psychological subject as being the whole person. This was his field, and he was young in it and couldn't resist explaining herself to herself in those terms. "You are functioning with a diminished libido and a fear of separation bordering on psychosis," he might say. Or: "You suffer from an enlarged super-ego which dominates the infantile aspects of your personality. This keeps you at a level of suspended and unfulfilled genital fixation" He told her that the Civil Rights movement was a misplaced rebellion against the father on the part of adolescents. If she said she believed in something, he said she really meant that she was "interested" in that something.

At the same time Adam was hot-blooded and could hardly get enough of her sexually. This pleasure bound them to each other long after the mental wounds they inflicted on each other had become permanent. G had many talents: dramatic, artistic, musical, scholarly, but they were like distractions compared to the quest that drove her forward. His irony was the opposite of her whole-heartedness, it was a poison that she recognized too well.

Why do women live? So much is against us. We give birth to flesh and metal is waiting. We train our children to be just and they are swallowed by injustice.

The military is on standby, not really but yes. Why all this technology then? Rehearsing the murder of the world? Coming events can affect present experience. For instance, I'm approaching someone who doesn't even know it. Unfulfilled volition doesn't die, but lives until its chance comes again.

What's the difference between being alive and being a machine?

The stone feels nothing, not its atoms or time. Metal colors layer the water, leathery leaves cover the ground. But children feel.

To be fully human is my greatest desire. A system of mystical ethics should follow and make sense of things.

An S of benches and prickly fruit trees shows me, as I approach, that my action and my time are one and the same.

Am I moving now toward the future or am I the steady consciousness that sees through my body traveling through space?

In 1950 the family spent the month of August with their uncle at Lago di Garda in the North of Italy. They had been there once before, right after the war when the first civilian air flights were just back in operation. The plane bumped across the Atlantic while people threw up and had ear aches of epic proportions. The mother was eager to see her uncle with whom she had lost contact for the better part of her youth and marriage. This man, and Italy itself, were territories she considered her own in some deep mythic sense. They freed her to be more than a mere American, in the eyes of other Americans.

The uncle met them at the train. He was a tall balding man, with a big bouquet of flowers for each member of the family and a hired limousine to take them to his mountain home. G was still clutching at her agonized ears, while her brother wore a savage mask of nausea. But none of them was too uncomfortable to notice the landscape and the architecture, spare and pastoral. They passed through light, empty streets and on to the lake, where pink flowers dashed out of the stones and the blue water was painted with mountains. Boats buzzed, and scooters sped by their car, but no machine could undermine the grace of that misty air.

That August the uncle sat in a wicker chair on the lawn, under a straw hat, his silences profound. He gave no indication that he was glad any one of them was visiting.

"Don't take it personally," A told her husband and children again and again. "He's always been moody."

The children didn't mind his quiet, though G sometimes tried to win him over by doing little acts and skits in front of his chair. In the evenings they ate pastas, salads, fruit, cheeses and breads; then the children would sit and listen to adult conversation which, in this context, contained an urgency and intelligence otherwise missing. There was a lot of war talk, politics, subjects P and A rarely mentioned when alone together, but often in company. P had been in Germany at the end of the war, Britain in the beginning and never in active combat. It was just desk work, he said.

The uncle didn't like to talk much about where he had been, and only gave the most minute details about hiding in the mountains and, finally, in Switzerland. T, who had read a lot about strategy, the Napoleonic wars, torture and Aryan superiority, insisted on interrupting and asking questions. His love of drama made him bloodthirsty and his love of his mother made him want to appear as intelligent as his father. That was hard. P was a man who alternated between bewilderment and authority. He talked at length, aimlessly but eloquently, giving the impression that he knew a great deal about most every subject. Indeed, he often told experts in one field or another all about their subjects. He was known to be exactly wrong on every topic. He almost had the facts, but not quite, and he was so nice, no one ever corrected him. Not even his wife.

While the men talked, on those evenings, she got drunk and roamed through the perfumed gardens, restless and depressed. Her doll-like face became slack and flushed; her eyes looked inward; and all her senses were awash in emotion. T, furiously, watched her through the screening darkness, and when she flung herself over the father's back, twisting her fingers through his belt, T leaped up and retreated with great sighs. G, figuring he knew something she didn't, followed making gagging noises. It was all an act on her part; she was not yet aware of adult sensuality. Her parents didn't interest her nearly as much as T himself did.

That summer his self-interest was total. And G, flashing around the edges of his smudged looking-glass eyes, was about as interesting to him as a passing bird. He lived in books, and emerged with a passion for himself as the reader. By the act of reading, he made all that happen. War, redemption, romance. He affected a limp and believed he was the replica of Andre in *War and Peace*, learning his speeches by heart. Sometimes he stood with his hand on his breast, like Napoleon, and sometimes he kept his hands in his pockets and looked up from under, moodily, like Leslie Howard in *Gone with the Wind*. G, his enraptured audience, still kept him from going too far.

She developed a series of routines in Italy. Most of them were imitations of T himself: one showed him lying on the grass tossing and gasping and complaining about the terrible heat of the sun and equally terrible chill of swimming; another showed him yawning sequentially and insisting he wasn't tired at all. Then she had one of her mother mincing around on very high heels, and stumbling over the gravel, with her fingers extended as if for drying nails, and asking if someone would please shake her up a martini. G had the hardest time doing an imitation of her father. While she tried acting him out as an absent-minded professor, T called directions at her which contradicted her plan. Then her father himself appeared, and not realizing whom she was imitating, became involved in giving her acting lessons and made her recite "To be or not to be" in a monotone. If she protested, he looked pained, and this action of his later became the one by which she imitated him.

The old uncle had a small yellow airplane with four wings, which he flew twice a week, taking no one with him. He went up alone, and sometimes flew right over the house while the family waved up at him. When he was gone on these excursions, the tempo of the household picked up, and spirits lightened, and each person realized how strong an effect one person's character can have on a group. The mother painted her toes and fingers; the father drew from his briefcase a folded copy of the New York Times crossword puzzle. It was a sign, always, that he was ready to relax and retreat pleasurably. If you can get the upper left-hand corner of a puzzle, you can get the whole thing, he always said. And indeed he would complete the upper left-hand corner with words and definitions that fit, but were wrong. And then he'd go on to the rest of the puzzle, which became more and more frayed and complex as time went by. Finally he'd stuff the puzzle in a wastebasket and wait for the next Sunday's.

One day the uncle emerged from the house in a leather aviator's jacket and cap, and boots too. The father looked perplexed, as if he was not sure whether a laugh was expected. He got no help from the mother who looked, for once, equally surprised. After all, that outfit was dated by decades and evoked unhappy memories of war. The uncle was not a joker, though. Everyone clung to that one biographical fact as he strode past the borders of tall flowers, pink and yellow, to the car. No one even smiled. He turned and said, "Go down to the beach and watch me fly."

"What fun! Of course we will!" cried the mother and got to her feet.

"In about an hour," he said sternly and continued his departure.

When he was gone, the parents shrugged and murmured, and T went on and on about the priceless beauty of the leather uniform and how he wished he had one just like it. The father then went into a lengthy explanation about the history of aviation and war, and G stood like a stork, one bare foot lifted to rest on the other knee, staring off into space. The sky that day was whitish blue, with a suffusing silence that seemed to take everything in: buzzes, splashes, whistles, talk.

Later the family trooped down to the lakeside, where dinghies of all colors were laid upside down, and they sat with their feet hanging off the dock, looking nonchalant or cynical. Finally the toy-like buzz of the yellow plane was heard over the mountains, and they watched it emerge from the whiteness. Nobody spoke. The plane, releasing a plume of white smoke, pointed its nose upwards and rose in an arc, directly over the center of the lake. Then the silence took over, like shock; the engine stopped; slowly, gracefully, the plane dropped straight down, turning in circles, the smoke left high up behind. It fell right to the top of the lake, and bounced and sank, while the family watched. It happened very fast. A motorboat shot out across the water to where it fell.

"Take Gemma to the house," the father told T.

"But what happened, Pa, what happened?" the boy asked.

His voice quivered and cracked as it had when it was changing. His sister was crying. He dragged her up the rough, stony lane, between banks of vines and wildflowers with a tender and bitter smell. The two of them looked back and up, stumbling, like those witnesses to an apparition of Mary which appears only to children.

If your government lies to you, then you are living in an unjust society, you are supporting nihilism. I steer my body north, salt in my eyes, humming as the dog leaps the cones of snow. White covers where the spring hides carnations plumper than fluff.

I think sensuality suppressed causes pain and elicits a sense of tragedy which is all biological. Blocked lust is a torment tighter than a throat. In the context of repressed desire, a blush either means shame or pleasure. I understand the sign of a wagging tail better than a human laugh.

In one Boston bar vodka is forbidden as being too "soviet". I love white wine, the way my tongue can wash away its daily cursing. Then reflections on a car's windshield make me remember danger and only music circling my thighs lets me pulse again.

The Deep North

One Saturday G went to the school she hated, a brick building at the crest of a green hill, and she climbed the fire escape, slid up a window she had unbolted the day before, and climbed inside. It was raining outside. She was fourteen when she stood with the curtains twisted in her hands and wrists and looked at her own colorful image on the glass, like the face of a young saint in a church. Then she cracked open a little box of matches and lit the curtains, watched the fire surround her face, and climbed out the window and down the escape, ran and rang the fire alarm in the red box at the side of the street, and walked home, dragging her hot sneakers through puddles.

In 1959, August, G received a letter from T who was in the Army:

Gemma, I seem to get no farther than your name across the page. An hour ago I sat down in this tent, thinking to write before dark. Now the lantern is lighted and still I have nothing written.

Your letter came today. It was strange. I do not understand the parts about love and happiness, but the solitude I do. Rilke (I think) says of solitude: "Thou art as rich and clean and wide as an awakening garden." Sometimes I think of this, and how solitude is the price of freedom. I know you always wanted freedom more than anything else.

Gemma, your letter is very serious for you. Are you very much in love with this man? I guess you must be. The trouble is, what you say is hard for me to translate from where I sit. I really can't understand my past, our past, or why I'm here, but here I am! The pine needles are still warm from the sun, and wind waves like a sea through the trees and it's cold under my field jacket. My hands smell of oil and canvas, wood smoke and sun. My head is heavy and my jaw rough from shaving in cold water. Under the little writing table, near my feet, are my helmet and pistol belt. Shadows move on the tent walls and soon it will be my turn at guard.

Why I like it, I couldn't tell you. I conjure up enemies like yellow men, black men whom I chase through the tall pines. At night I creep silently, with the other men, bathed in cool stinking sweat and mud from the swamps and wanting cigarettes so bad, I could scream. We eat mostly out of tins because fires are illegal on maneuvers. As long as I can pretend I hate someone out there in the dark, I find I can turn with love to my fellow soldiers and continue to wage this hot and bloody mock war. I think a person needs to invent an enemy if one isn't provided naturally.

Please keep in touch with me. I worry about you and your attitudes. You must not try to outdo your liberal background with anarchic politics. Just because your environment is one way, it doesn't mean you have to be another. I hate to think of you married. And to a Jew! I have to say that. You're too young and all men are shits.

Save yourself for

T

I can't live without reality even when my head is aching. The lies I've been told to survive! Think: everyone was avoiding a direct statement. Do I get a break, a reward for this? When I meet the hypocrisy inculcated in me since childhood, it is discharged in action, a surprise to me. Everything living into the present has an effect on the future. Unnoticed horizons exist, I think.

I dreamed I was a boy sailing on the sea and at last a man would lie down and hold me normally.

Home, I want to leave you. But the move is too long, the weather too cold for you to take yourself out today or ever. Fish in an aquarium can't be moved either.

If you don't want prediction, take risks. In this way the small change of ordinary thought can be discarded for something more poetic. Like a boy bathing in a river with electric wires, changing the environment is one way to opt for an authentic experience.

During one winter the tremors set off by surrounding politics became more personal than usual. The parents' voices murmured and snapped in dark corners after the lights were lit elsewhere. They disagreed about things going on outside, and even about their own histories. The nut-brown mother walked around with a glass in her hand; she smoked and sat with her skirt raised far above her knee, her eyes bored or yearn-

ing. Always dressed in expensive and fashionable clothes, with her curls
bobbed around her ears, in a dim light she looked very pretty and young.
Habitually she studied her calves, the slope of her ankle down to her
foot and her hands, at a distance, and at length. She liked having money
and wearing it too.

Money was a political issue. How she handled their checkbook was
a major subject of interest. She had inherited all of her uncle's money
after his sky suicide, and the house in Italy as well, but P wanted none
of it. Uncle Joe had, as it turned out, been a Nazi collaborator during the
war and the property in Italy and his acquired wealth were, to P, tainted
by this association. But A said, If you had been in Italy during the war,
you would have been a collaborator too.

She loved having the Italian house, her own income and the independence they gave her. Where before she had been under P's rule, now
she defied and talked back at him.

Like her daughter and Darlene, A also giggled about her husband's
friends, but right in front of him. She couldn't, she said, stand either
ideas or ideology. For two decades she had a lover, one of P's painter
friends, and A was the first, in public, to joke about the man's being "a
fairy." Meantime A and he met once a week, every Thursday, in his studio in the Back Bay and joyfully made a joke of the reputation she had
begun for him. Since she inherited the house in Italy, she developed a
slight Italian accent and wore only the clothes she purchased over there;
P drove a battered old Ford to work and fussed about the high cost of
educating his children in private schools.

"If you don't want any of the Italian money, that's fine with me," A
told her husband. "I'll keep it for myself while you play poor."

He didn't argue with her, but rubbed his head and made a joke about
the high cost of loving.

"You old fraud," she teased. "You old goose. Do geese see God? Can
you say that backwards?"

"Do . . . gee . . . see . . . odd, go . . . dog?"

"Try again! It's a palindrome!"

She had learned it from her lover, among other word games she ran around her bewildered spouse. He had a new style himself. It was modeled on certain European professors he admired, and was meant to supply the aging process with dignity. He wore his hair longish, tossed gray to the side, and his face acquired a melancholy cast, the handsome weakness there was shrouded now in a sort of fashionable gloom. His work was completely administrative, but he passed for a great scholar now with his tweeds and long gray hair.

The premises are now sealed and sold. Tenants gone.

It's on the other side of the tracks I want to be when the snow spills creamily down a set of stone lips.

I see the halfway girl, whose baby was taken away, balance on the cushion stuffing. Bags are stacked in the hall, and around the basement burner.

Damp places hold in the ruin and never the fun.

The boy now a man on a bed is dreaming of fishing. Give him your net, fisherman of heaven, and multiply the glitter of his illusions before he changes his mind and blows up the world.

In time it must all make sense, the suffering sent forth from one body into many.

At eighteen G was a Communist sympathizer, who also drank too much . . . . Sweetened alcohols of any source or color, and like her mother, she smoked and preened her hands and feet. She was set to graduate from college a year early, and her friends were activists and beatniks with reputations, like hers, based on intellectual brilliance and wild behavior. Her figure was dark and skittish and her tangled curls and blazing green eyes won her the nickname Haywire-and-Gemstone.

"Where are you from?" people would ask her. "Here," she would say and wince. "I'll be leaving soon though, and I won't come back. I hate Boston. It's a hypocrite's jungle."

Once in a darkened bar, she was giving a detailed account of the class structure in Boston, when she was noticed by her husband-to-be, Adam, where he sat with his friends nearby.

"How can they serve her alcohol? She looks fourteen," he said.

"Haven't you ever seen her?" his friend inquired.

"I don't think I have, or I'd remember."

The friend went on to tell Adam all he knew about G, and where she could be seen, and when. Adam filed away the information. He was boyish, with wire-rimmed glasses and a full pink mouth which contradicted the serious frown marking his brow. He was, in style, a youthful version of G's father. The difference was etched in his mouth only, its sensuous weakness.

"I'm going to marry that girl," he told his friend. "Wait and see."

"I certainly will," was the bemused reply.

Adam snatched at his chance on a windy afternoon in Boston. She was passing over the Mass. Ave. Bridge with her skirt flying all around while she modestly poked it down. *If middle class life is so grotesque,* said Adam in her hair, *why do you want the poor to aspire to it? Why?* Who are you? she wondered. *Someone who has been listening to you and disagrees.* So leave me alone. *But I'm interested in what else you have to say about this.* Too bad. You'll never hear it. *You're not very polite.*

They were stopped by a red light, side by side, backs to the river. She glanced through her blowing hair at him. Everyone should have the right to a decent life, she said. That's all I'm interested in. *That sounds realistic,* he stated. *Why don't you let me buy you a drink and you can explain it more?* I don't want to. That's why not. *I'm harmless.* No, you're not. You're an enlightened skeptic.

Though bored by his seeming equanimity, by his smile as smug to her as a stuffed animal, she found something attractive in him too. It drove her at him. She felt she could say anything to him, and dodged cars to cross the street, eager to escape such liberties. He followed, talking softly and persuasively over her shoulder, and when they reached the other side of the street, she looked into his face and recognized the cold charm of his personal history. It resembled her own. For a long time she had been without the ability to love a stranger, and since you are barely alive without such an ability, she was enfeebled emotionally, all mouth and vocabulary. She strained towards the invitation he was making, and said "Okay, I'll have a drink. Later."

"Now," he said, and his lips beamed insistently; taking a step closer and her arm, he added, "I hear you're a genius. And I know you're planning to graduate Summa a year ahead."

"That's why I'm so tired," she sighed and let him steer her.

"You don't look it. You look as fresh as the proverbial rose."

"I'd rather be as fresh as the rose itself. Not the proverbial one."

The slope of her soft cheek and transparent green of her eye, and a smatter of freckles was all he could see through the net of her hair. She looked as if she were pushing through cobwebs in a dim room and needed guidance. He eyed her thin body with its unexpectedly high round bottom and said, "I think you're the most beautiful girl I ever saw in my life. I love you."

She laughed.

"Do that again."

"Ha—'

"Can you also cry at will?"

"I used to, when I did skits," she said. "But now acting scares me."

"Do you love me?"

"I hate your type."

"That's good. We've got something strong going already. I love you and you hate me. Great."

"Forget the drink," she told him and took off down another street.

He didn't follow her, and she began to keep an eye out for him after that. Working mornings in a bookstore, then going to classes and studying until deep into the night, she still kept a half-hearted watch for him, being generally uninterested in the love of boys and men. She was, at the time, obsessed with a desire to leave Boston, and her rush through college was only a way to get out fast.

When you love, run for your life, or suffer.

Remember a person in an elevator passes out when the doors take too long to open. Hesitation can kill.

And when a truck is on fire, the people jump over a bridge to put out the flames.

Run, run. Or grow tin. Each subject yearns for the safety of artifice. Humans aspire to be robots.

The Deep North

When I am near one particular man, a third party made only of heat energy is created between us.

Put us twenty feet apart and that is the exact size of this third party. I can't explain the feeling, because it might be hate, though it feels like sex. No, I don't want to admit it, but I wouldn't want to live if I didn't hate.

Dear T—

Freedom is all I want. I know that now. Not to be tied down by love, family or school. To be alone and away and moving. I'll visit you en route, I promise.

Love,

G

And this was how Adam persuaded her, finally, to get close to him. "I'm driving around the country in September," he lied. "You can get a free lift with me."

Adam had come up from behind, where she was complaining to a girlfriend about her lack of travel money. They were outside the bookstore as she was leaving work for the day. She whipped her head around; her hair trailed over his lips, he was so close. The sensuous mouth opened and smiled, but the gray eyes behind the glasses were still and fixed on hers. He lifted his hand into her hair, pushing it back.

"See you," said the girlfriend and left.

"I can promise you a free ride," he repeated. "But you'll obviously have to give up the hate you feel for me. You'll have to turn it around. Are you a virgin?"

"Both," she replied.

"Come on, I'll buy you lunch."

His hand stayed weighed in her hair. She let it lie there, as heavy as a collar. Even as they walked to the sandwich shop, she in black and he in pink, she felt a yearning for him and it was tied, frantically, with her feeling that she could verbally abuse him and get away with it. He was familiar in his clean and pressed clothes and boyish manner; he was strikingly like the father whose heat was as soft as the heat of a rose.

A relationship is fixed and frozen from the moment of impact.

Breeze and sun will melt the diamond chunks of ice, but nothing can dissolve the fit of two characters.

Oars creak under ice. It's been fifty days below zero. Clandestine amounts are paid to the homeless and crazy, the way the ring of water on a barroom table is wiped away in a flash.

An emptying carafe, a laugh across the room, talking about spice, hobbies, anguish over money, while others suffer and starve.

Hospital beds seem to be waiting for me.

By the time they were married and had necked, frenziedly, their way to bed, she found she could not be satisfied. There was no resolution to her anger at him or her desire for him. Each was projected into infinity and after a while, all she wanted was his approval, but it was not forthcoming, could not be. He could not forgive her for the error which neither of them could identify. They quipped and snapped with their tongues, and craved with their bodies.

They never did leave Boston to go west, because of his work on his doctorate. Her parents rarely came to see them. They disapproved of Adam whom they called The Semitic Phase, but not to G's face. Nonetheless, she, noting their emotion, felt herself orphaned into a sore form of the freedom she had sought. The spaces between all people expanded. Finally, Adam left her for a woman he could understand, and they parted with miserable, wondering expressions.

When G got on the train that time, her appearance was ravaged, fortyish, and she had lost the connection between labor and returns, necessity and words. Some leftover energy kept her going forward, as if for a day when she would arrive at the start again, and be restored to youth. Every day felt like the last day of her life, the one day in which all the others reach fulfillment. Simple pleasure (sex or alcohol) was an important thing to remember then.

I'm not sure I'm saying the right thing. But it is at the level of race (physical appearance) that hypocrisy begins. My country is constructed with its beginning at that same level. This hypocrisy is revealed every time there is a tremor or a rupture in daily life.

A steel table glows in the dark. A whale comes up for air. I have glimpsed what is lying there under all the manners.

Once I had universal appeal. All people would confide in me because I was sweet and a hypocrite. Love was no stranger then. Now if I had the comic sense, I would try to play that part again.

Do you know how it feels to be a cartoon character? I don't think so. Not fun.

A man who looked like Abe Lincoln often wore a tall silk hat around the house. When he got drunk, he said, "Me free them? Never!"

That's what it feels like.

One summer, A took the children to Verona, and Darlene too. It was the tail end of summer, and a rushed spontaneous trip. A had to get the house fixed up for some new tenants who would be renting it for months to come, and the enterprise gave her a sense of purpose which she often lacked.

She hated aging, the cruelty of the body's fattening conclusion. Her waistline thickened, even if she fasted; and menopause and dying represented her whole predictable future. Her green eyes, once illuminated by all that passed before them, now looked inwards, as if a shade were half-drawn on a sunny room.

Want to come swimming? Go for a walk with me? Get some gelato? Need some help with those beans? G asked Darlene again and again, because her mother seemed to want only solitude in which she could brood, like one moving into the shade on a hot day. No one could get her out to do anything. Not even T could seduce her away from the cool house and its trivial problems, which she tended to, half-heartedly, but with a pretense at their importance. She sent Darlene away with G every day, and for several hours they would roam the roads and beaches, hand in hand, mouths agape.

One day A saw the garbage man, a golden god-like Northern Italian. She watched him steadily through the curtains as he hurled trash from the end of the path into his truck, his long muscular torso bare and burning. In the midday sun, his spine was a damp shadow running between golden beams.

The next time he came back, she was out there waiting in short shorts and a little white cotton blouse tied under her fulsome breasts. She got his attention by holding up a bag of fish and laughing and saying "Can you get rid of this? It stinks." In Italian.

Now A returned from a prolonged exchange with the garbage man, and her face was fiery and she had the familiar moisture in her green eyes. She said, "He's very funny, and intelligent. Imagine!"

"What did he say that was so impressive?" asked T.

"Nothing, really. It was just the way he said it."

"I'm sure he has a wife and six children."

"Oh probably. So what?"

"You were flirting with him."

"For God's sake Tonio. He's practically your age."

"Not quite."

"Why don't you go find yourself a girlfriend, instead of spying on me? I'm old and I'm married," she added.

"Oh yes, I forgot," said T, coldly.

"Well, you're not. Why don't you enjoy your freedom? Go and pick up some girl."

"And then what?" he asked and folded shut the book he was reading.

"I won't say in front of Gemma. But you know perfectly well."

"How do you know I haven't already?"

She laughed, walking away. "You sound like the person who said he didn't need to read a book, because he had already read one."

T, watching from a chair on the lawn, let out a great sigh of disgust, and G, scared, chewed her nails. She hated being caught between her mother and brother who were like emotions put into physical bodies, bodies without control, and emotions as wild as any mistral. They hissed, sighed, groaned and mused around her, always loud, always in a state of excitement, whether it was gloomy or delighted. They were drawn to each other like kitten and dog. With her father, or Darlene, G could be and see clear. But how confusing it was to be stuck between her mother and brother! She bit her nails and was always sure she must be making a mistake of some kind, when she noted falsehoods behind their deeds.

The Deep North

T watched her go, his eyes narrowed, and his lips. G spat her bitten nails into the grass and tried to think up a wisecrack or a soft word to settle the situation. But he was up and gone, down the path to the beach, before she had fixed on the statement: *I hate grown-ups, except for Darlene.*

A few days later T was taken away by some friends, to visit Florence and Rome, and immediately A was taken away, too, by the garbage man. At night. On the back of his Lambretta, she sped away, saying to G, "Don't mention this to your father or Tonio, okay? They might misunderstand."

The word *misunderstand* then came to G as the essence of all that was fearful in the world. She wanted to misunderstand her own thoughts about her mother, as much as her mother wanted to be misunderstood; yet both of them, at the same time, wanted to be loved. If you could only love what was presented as superficially true, then you were always attached to a set of lies, and the realities played amoral games in a chasm. This image of the human person was also the image of the universe.

One night G decided, bravely, to challenge that image, and she lay awake to see her mother returning with the garbage man. If they kissed, it would mean that what looked to be true was, in fact, true. She left her window open beside the bed, and the cicadas shook the air with their singing; a scent of lemon and flowers floated in. And when the lights of the scooter crossed the ceiling, she sat up and peeked out. Her throat was tight as the light went out and she saw and heard nothing but shapes in shadow. She knew if she stayed seated she would burn through the dark in her eyes and see what she felt she ought to see. But if she saw them kissing and couldn't tell anyone, what good would it do?

Her indecision for that time made her hate herself as much as she had ever hated grown-ups. Who could she hate more, the one or the other? The sound of her mother's voice settled that, and she fell back hard onto her bed, scared to trembling, because, in the end, she didn't dare know what was really so, and forgot instead.

In the morning she saw that her mother wore a puffy, satisfied look and she sensed what it meant. They were leaving in a few days for home. "Will you be glad to leave?" G asked her mother. "Of course," was the response. The mother then eyed her daughter over the rim of her sea-blue cup and said, "Paolo, the garbage man, was just a friend, as you know. Can you believe it? He's a communist!"

So? wondered G because her mother usually saved her confidences for her son.

"It's so interesting. Everyone, Dear, in this country seems to be either socialist or communist. I can't wait to tell Tonio. He'll be very interested. You couldn't possibly understand yet, but it's about time the working classes took some power away from the rich."

Her eyes glittered with the excitement of the newly informed and her long manicured fingers were lifted for morning inspection. They gave her permission, it would seem, to withdraw into her own private thoughts.

"Wasn't Uncle Joe rich?" asked G.

"I guess so," said the mother without attention; then asked, "What?"

"Nothing, never mind."

G lay her head down on her folded arms, on the table, and squinted until the shapes around the window vanished. Like a miniature screen, the window shimmered images: figures, faces, places. They were scattered and broken, though, by a hand on her neck. A soft warm squeeze and she leaned into Darlene's palm and rested there. They both looked at the mother as if she was an image cast by electricity, paint, or light on a wall beside them.

Then A became dimensional, shot forward, a sharp look at Darlene, and a sigh preceded her words, "Don't mention any of this please, Darlene."

"Any of what?"

This question forced A back into her usual posture. She couldn't stand to be known by anyone.

"My private life. Here," she said, "is none of your, or anyone else's business." Darlene gave a short laugh and moved away and G felt the currents change. Her mother was watching Darlene with the eyes of a hater.

After they returned from Italy, Darlene and Ron took G to his mother's place. It was a cold fall day and they drove over the river and out through the brick and gray of the Fenway and its nettled attempt at being pastoral. G chattered away in the back seat, excited by what seemed to her to be an enormous event; for years she had wanted to see where Ron and Darlene really lived.

When they left the trees and river, they entered into the city and passed under the el. Shadows criss-crossed the cold cement and a wintery wind blew up papers. G had the sense of familiarity which belongs more to dreams than to waking time. A psychic dread of large shapes enveloped her head and throat like a little hood worn by falcons. Ron's dark brown hand was dropped over the back of the seat and she reached out to hold onto his long fingers. He gave her hand a squeeze and she leaned forward on the seat to be closer to their voices, which were subdued precisely so she wouldn't hear them.

"The woman hates me," whispered Darlene. "Ever since that sex scene in Italy."

"Don't worry about it."

"I have to, baby. But he's okay, you know."

"Uh uh. What passes in him for charm and goodness are something else."

"Like what?"

"Confidence, indifference."

"There's not a mean bone in his body."

"Maybe not an active mean bone. But he'd let you sink before he'd reach out to stop you from drowning. Wouldn't want to get his hand wet. I tell you."

"Come on. He's not so bad. He's not prejudiced."

"Ha. He's the type who believes that only white men are allowed to be integrationist. Watch and see. He'd never express it, of course. Too polite. But I know. None of those liberals are what they seem to be. They have no non-white friends, not a one of them. They seem to think it's in such poor taste to notice a person's race that you're better off not noticing him at all. It's like that. I tell you."

"Who are you talking about?" asked G, as if she didn't know.

Ron's mother lived in a little blue house pressed between some red brick projects and apartments. It looked across an avenue onto Franklin Park, which held the city zoo. The house, like many in New England, was very old with low ceilings and windows with small panes. The day being Sunday, the mother had prepared a large dinner for them. Several bowls of food, rice, yams, greens, ham, beef, muffins, and butter were set on a round table in the small dining room adjoining the kitchen. Ron's four brothers and sisters and various small children lounged around the house, eating, talking, playing cards, listening to the radio, while their mother, a slow-moving woman with quick examining eyes, served the food. No one paid special attention to G, but she heard herself referred to as the little white girl more than once, and she knew that they knew she was there, seated on the edge of a red leather chair.

The children went off to play, and G stayed, listening to a discussion rising between Ron, Darlene and the older members of the family. It was all about politics and religion, about race and money. The feeling was tense; Ron was in danger and making a mistake. The mother and a sister were on the side of Jesus, and things taking time. Two of Ron's brothers were on the side of the Army and getting an education. Another sister, Darlene and Ron were on the dangerous side together, a place where their family didn't want them to be. Ron did most of the talking, trying to convince his mother, in particular, that segregation was unnatural, that "the problem in this country is economic, and if you can eliminate class, you can eliminate racism." His mother disagreed, vehemently, and spoke of the need for complete spiritual renewal. The sister who was on the same side as Ron—a tall slim woman with a serious face—tried to persuade her mother, in soft tones, that the spirit would just have to wait till the body was fed. And the two other brothers (one was in uniform) spoke of getting a foothold "in the ranks" and of hanging on hard to the system until you can claim it and call it your own.

Young as she was G sensed that she was at the heart of the world outside. The words flying around her came from a center of experience unlike any she had encountered before. The city outside was their target, but was also their arsenal. All that brick and steel, stone and speed became an image in G's mind, an image of actual emotion, the result of conflict and desire. A wall was not just a wall; it stood for a feeling. In the room she occupied for those hours was an expression of emotion intimately tied to the physical products around the people. G felt herself turn into one of those products who had no value, as far as she could judge, or feel.

The discussion grew hot, then soft. No one wanted to injure the mother, and Ron, constantly insisting on the last word, was finally told to shut up and sit down. He did, pulling the Sunday paper with him. Passing a section across G, to his sister, he sighed deeply. G crawled out of the chair, to sit beside him. A slight shift in his position acknowledged her presence. This undramatic move was enough to reassure her that she did after all have some value, the value of being alive.

At home the mother was waiting in the kitchen. The father was out at some meeting. And as she had been at home all day, A wore a flushed expression, her hair uncurling in places. Tension hid her lips. How was it, she asked, but didn't wait for an answer. Go upstairs, she told G who passed, obediently, through the swinging door but there paused to listen.

"You've got to leave tomorrow, Darlene," said the mother.

"What? Why?"

"Because of Ron."

"But why?"

"You know why."

"I don't."

"You do. And just take my word for it. You have to go."

Branches creaked beside the pantry window, and old leaves, stuck around from the fall, crackled in the window frame. G stood still among the shelves and dishes.

"The FBI spoke with my husband last night."

"Oh, it's because- !" cried Darlene.

"Yes."

"And he told them his name, his address?"

"They know everything. He had to tell them. It's the law. Darlene, you can't take risks like this. You're a Negro, and as if that's not bad enough, Ron is a party member. You're associating with a Communist."

"Associating," Darlene responded: "Associating!"

"At least you can't while you work for me."

"Well, I don't anymore. That's for sure."

"Don't speak to me like that. Remember your place," said the mother, and as her clipping heels approached the door, G fled.

She ran up to her room and her bed, and hid there alone. Though she tried, she couldn't make complete sense of that scene, but she knew there was no one around to comfort anyone in it. No one inside the house, or outside the house. No one in the world because it was the world that had entered the house. The cold finality of the operation gave her her first contact with politics.

In one hour her idle and contented gaze turned into a look of scrutiny, sometimes suspicion, and even though she forgot that experience, in its specifics, she watched her parents differently afterwards—with the eyes of a guard one day, the eyes of a prisoner the next.

Darlene was gone before the sun was up, and G would never locate her or Ron again, though looking often in passing faces for theirs. This search, even as it became unconscious over the years, let her see beyond the attributes of race into the particularities of a face. The search in this way was subversive.

There are animated bodies other than my own, but I can't really know them without love.

This is the horror. All I guess is, by the time I've touched someone, we've both moved on, and loneliness puts us each into perpetual motion.

The city is all one color because snow is on the way.

It has an appearance of absolute stone. Houses look rejecting, clubby, with their windows and their smoke. Being rejected is actually freeing. You can love in peace.

In 1962 G drove to the Committee on Racial Equality in Roxbury where she was working voluntarily, interviewing, chasing down slumlords. The sun was blazing through the windows of the car. As she passed up Columbus Avenue under the el on Washington Street, her eyes took in the sights: trembling heat waves emerging from concrete and steel; shadows bearing down like enormous claws from above; children playing with rocks, bottles on the sidewalk, their clothes shabby both from oversoiling and overwashing.

At a set of lights, she lurched into gear, feeling her own solitude unfold like the opening leaves in a camera lens, one after the other, leading nowhere. Shit, she whispered, sensing the imminence of an anxiety attack. She kept driving, hunched over, with the awareness of annihilation coming closer, a literal natural force, rolling down those ruined streets.

The judgment of God, like a lion's paw, seems to get its weight from its other parts resting firmly on the ground, elsewhere. She stopped the car in the sharp shadows under the el. A train broke through the silence overhead. *Divorce, divorce*, was the word in her head. *Divorce*, and worse, *mortal, torn, divide, unborn.* . . . And she leaned down her head, the engine rumbling against her feet, and her mind was led by words, one after another, away from the safety of its own control, but spilling forth, as if pressed upon to bursting. Little flashes of resistance, which she held up like shields before them, were flattened at once. The words became nasty, contemporary and cruel (*schizoid, paranoid, autistic, catatonic, psychotic*), the opposite of *flowery* or *dowry*.

She turned off the engine. She was now on Blue Hill Avenue, a ravaged strip of commerce running straight from downtown Boston toward the suburban hills. Dark faces glittered from the heat moisture. She stared at them all, deep breathing, and tossing back those words with an attempt at wit, at nonchalance. Psychosis, depression: terrible cold terms by which humanity described itself. And she couldn't laugh.

The white sky blanketed the curvature of earth, and the jutting hardline buildings. The solid people all seemed to have been shaken down out of that blanket, cast down from its soft center. The images in her eyes, these, came from miles away. What does it mean? Why have we all been spilled down on the ground, for this?

Ruined buildings, fallen flesh and the litter of a civilization strewn out in long term decay: nothing good flickered on the screen in her vision, but behind them was an emanation, a memory of emotion, of a time when the word and the thing were one and the same. To be saved by a word! To be healed by a word: would be to be uplifted, from under that weighted paw. Fear was her disease, expecting a word like *love* or *charity* to cure her.

But the first word was *despair* and it sailed into her vocabulary, like a tall ship from some haunted other time, tilting over a cold ocean. Despair, she realized, is what I'm feeling. It's an ancient feeling, and is born in each person. Despair, the word, came like a sweet-dropping medicine, a coat of taste for her fear. Never had a word had such reverberating power for her. Never had one word been so strong it could humiliate all the little psychological bits and pieces, those labels that peeled off like slogans in a long rain.

She huddled on the sticky plastic seat of her father's old Ford, her hands squeezing the steering wheel, her whole mind and mouth centered on the word that had saved her.

I was so far North by then, I had to duck under the moon to find my way home.

Everyone only wants to get home to bed, where things begin and end. If you shut your eyes and stretch out your arms, even then you can't get rid of your body. The affiliation is morally binding. The body has more sides than the moon. Is it really my own?

Bubbling springs force water onto a dry and distant tongue. So do feathery cream cakes and sweet black nibs of chocolate. But whoa. Hold the pleasure. I forgot the world had seductive offerings to make. I forgot that love was pleasure.

In the apocalyptic but inconclusive book that P was planning to write, there was nothing ahead for Western civilization but plague and trouble. When he first imagined the book he set out to prove that self-interest, the perverse child of Emerson's self-reliance, was responsible for social problems. But as his eyes widened on the issues of poverty and decay, and his conservatism increased, and his need to keep his liberal associations remained stable, he grew confused, and lost sight of an argument. "Absolute pragmatism is our only hope," he would state one day; the next he would say, "Absolute pessimism is the only perspective on civilization's ills."

"Come on," his wife would groan. "Don't be such a poop. The world isn't going to end. Not while we're around anyway."

"Maybe not, but soon after," he said glumly.

"Then what will we care?" she asked.

"All this work? For nothing?"

"What work?"

"Michelangelo, Shakespeare, Einstein . . . That work."

"That work!" she screamed from her place in her nightgown. "Why always the famous people? Why always the big guns? Why always the people who have it all? Why always the men? That work! Einstein? What about a garbage man's work, what about a ditch digger's work, what about the work of the people who built the Globe theater, what about the women who gave birth to them? You ass! I hate you! Michelangelo, Einstein, Shakespeare! What about their wives and their children? What about the people who nobody ever notices! I'm so sick of it, so sick of all of you, pompous sons of bitches, I want out, I want to get out, I've got to get out, let me OUT!"

The father sat on the edge of the bed, in striped pajamas, speechless. She had never had an outburst before, so he sensed it was somehow critical, and he should be afraid. But he could only turn up his palms on his knees.

And indeed, within days, she was gone—to Italy, to her new home.

There is no longer any class outside the class of character and no history to admire. You can actually live as if you have no culture, no perspective particular to a date in time. You are an individual whose prime and solitary property is your own body. Dying becomes a hell beyond all reason or justice in this ahistorical context.

I don't know where I came from or how I ended up in jail. Did that old body belong to me? Am I the same one—frail, unsheltered? This, an offering to the world?

When A left him, the father's somber face was justified. He lost his appetite, he cried, alone, at night. His ability to perform helped him to continue, superficially the same, through the days, playing tennis, talking about budgets, searching for new funds, rattling off pleasantries and platitudes that amused the secretaries who loved him. He assured everyone it was not a divorce, or even a separation, but a long-needed change for his wife. They both loved Italy, and he would join her there in the summer. And these statements were true enough so that even he could learn to live with them, and with her gone, after his suffering was exhausted. But one form of hope had left him permanently with her departure. It was the hope that he would, one day, understand human nature.

I try to remember the house of my origins, but water leaks through snapped plaster. Lathing shows lines that are really black air. The tiles are dust around the fireplace. The outside walls, wooden, brown, have settled at the edges of the ground and curl up from it.

Society demands expression from us, even in jail. Distinguishing facts from each other is meant to turn justice into meaning. But there seems to be only a comic law left, emanating from each act and fact.

My body is sunk in sensation on my bunk, and the geometry of its hope is found in opposites.

I want each part of my body to be united with another, unlike it, and to find rest like this. But I lost my chance.

G's virginity had gone to Adam, and after she left him a couple of times she tried to see if sexuality's proximity to love might cure her terrible sieges of depression. But they didn't heal her at all. Once, after sleeping with someone, she asked herself, How can I be happy if there is no divine scheme?

In a while she became very close to someone at the newspaper where she worked on copy. He was a father of three and already the proposed husband-to-be of another woman, since his recent divorce. G didn't know about the other woman and he certainly didn't tell her. He was a person who lived in the future, fussing and making plans, in order to allay a fundamental anxiety about the uncertain nature of his own character moving through the world. Since he couldn't predict himself, he would predict the world. He was robust, heavy-drinking, a poet and journalist who called himself a Marxist, too, and who wrote a column in that weekly paper. His friends were like hers: vehement rebels, some with red bandannas and Van Gogh beards who seemed unable to remember or experience pleasure. Unlike G and her man.

The first time he sat beside her, in a parked car, she was aware of a supernatural heat arising around them and merging somewhere between. Cliches like "I'm on fire," or "It's bigger than both of us' captioned her responses. When his sleeve brushed her hand, she "melted." It was like coming upon great art after browsing in mediocre galleries; the recognition of what was extreme annihilated all in-betweens. She looked at him as if he were personal destiny embodied in the flesh, and as if she must say, "I give up."

In actual expression it took the form of sex. They spent two thirds of their time engrossed in each other's bodies in bed, and the other third of the time figuring out how to get there. She was horrified by the wideness of his sex appeal, but he swore to her that she, of them all, was the best, the special. Reassuring her did not require much work on his part, the inevitability of their physical attachment was so undeniable. She was happy almost all the time, and felt her self was true at last, not an invention.

His friends discussed anarchy, socialism, violence and smoked grass, which made them passive. Some took LSD and ended up in mental hospitals. They were all penniless and enraged by the forces of law and hypocrisy which surrounded them. Jazz and poetry were their cultural passions. The women were quiet and cat-like, moving around edges in tatters and sandals. The centerpieces on many tables were fat heaps of candlewax.

G's man was naturally happy and he exuded paternal warmth which she sank into. She was attracted to his size, smell, humor and weakness for alcohol. They drank together, had sneaky sex in his foul apartment, talked politics and poetry until he had to make a choice and chose the other woman. Lying to G, he said he was returning to his wife because of the children.

She didn't fight to keep him but cried aloud and long. He said he wished she'd get mad instead of just sad like that, and he accused her of acting like a victim instead of a consenting adult. She threw a dish that held a burning candle and old wax—red, yellow and thick, at his face; it missed and he left, shaking his head at her violence. Later she had terrible cramps and something resembling a miscarriage, or maybe it was one. She would never know.

My generation had a problem with hypocrisy. We couldn't stand it.

I was always wondering, How did this happen? I felt there was a secret embedded in every sorrow.

"It sickens and terrifies me not to know." If you haven't understood something by the time it's over, you probably won't. Why didn't I notice I was doing something wrong?

I did, but instantly swallowed each insight with further misunderstanding.

How long can I stay here, where I don't know how to be happy?

When will my number be up and will I see it flash in the walls around me?

Success is an attribute belonging to someone else, not to me. Often when I say something intelligent, a man will say No, and then restate what I just said, in his own words! I hate this too.

Boston in these years is a red brick fortress where the smell of the sea gives a tantalizing but false impression of a city at liberty. Among dripping spigots and gargoyles several stories high over the Common, people are judged according to class, race and beauty. There are many cliques, and few spill into the next at the edges. Success is both despised and revered in this city. You have a better chance of surviving it if you get it elsewhere and arrive in Boston already launched as a winner. If you get it here, the enemy factor can be overwhelming. Hate is right near the surface and the old institutions are immovable. Failure is the best show in town and pleasure comes only when you can hide with it. Boston rejects its own offspring, vomits each child out onto the pavement and watches him or her crawl through the shadows toward some poor sort of survival. No helping hands are offered. The most prejudiced body of people are the most powerful, though that body switches nationality once every couple of generations.

Because she was poor at making a living and pitied her father too, G lived in his house. Every day going to work from there, she crossed boundaries that were switched by vehicles of construction and de-construction, none of which concealed the divisions being erected. Streets were torn up and buildings were torn down. One day a store was there, the next week it was gone. Whole areas of business were obliterated, leaving a racetrack for cars to speed and smash up along, coming in and out of downtown Boston. In the winter these areas filled up with heaps of white and gray snow; in summer they trembled with trash.

At home G pretended to be necessary to her father who hardly no-ticed her at all. They only spoke to argue about politics. No, he replied to every suggestion of an idea coming from her. No, he said. Not so. The failure of Russia to live up to the revolution is the biggest failure of this century. Not capitalism. No. Russia has single-handedly poisoned every possibility of international understanding.

"But you can't deny that capitalism is inefficient at the very least," she said.

"No. Capitalism doesn't work, no, but it's not because it's inefficient."

"Why then?"

"Because certain valuable parts of society are not being used."

She stared at him, then, with her eyes darkened by a frown of confu-sion. Isn't that what she had said?

Once a smooth and charming talker, P now rambled on and on. G noted, in him, a rising to the surface of the submerged patrician and it made her uneasy as if she, too, might have such a person hidden inside. He was asked out to dinner endlessly, now that he served the function of being an extra man; but his pre-sleep actions and sighs gave his loneliness away. While G and he slipped past each other, night and day, four former African colonies became free nations, voter registration among blacks in the South increased by the thousands, and schools were integrated.

"The powerful only talk to the powerful," Ron had said more than once. "So we must only talk to the powerless."

The Deep North

At an early age, I quaffed too much cheap wine with my friends and hired myself out to a circus of sorts. Academia: a house of illusions.

Like a provincial violin playing in a noisy gallery, my thoughts were utterly unoriginal and driven by the desire to impress quickly.

My ancestors had left no net with which to catch a person falling away from the will to power. And without that will, you are a problem for everyone, uprooted and undemocratic. . . . And then of course without property, all that's left is the hard wooden world of the poor.

One day P woke up and P was for Poet. He said he knew it all along. It was just a matter of time. P wrote poetry suddenly; seated at his desk visions of candelabra and cards and stars all came together in a stream of logic belonging only to him. He called it Verse. It was very formal metrically. Puzzling; but suggested an intelligence caught in a garden net; a bit of a struggle, the mind thrashing among raspberries and lettuces, but made cozy by context. He had never been so happy nor felt so justified. His verse was published, too, by people who owed him favors and who genuinely enjoyed his harmless words. The lateness of his muse's arrival made him an original. He was, indeed, like one in love—humming, whistling, walking quickly. And he swore his previous life had been a preparation for these days. He saw one personal pattern where before he saw a mess. He told G, All the events which seemed beyond my control were acts of Destiny leading me, blindfolded, to my muse's door. It's extraordinary! There is an order, after all! I don't know what to name it, or where it comes from, but isn't it wonderful?

Soon after losing the bearded Marxist, G entered the subway station which blasted up heat, as from the mouth of a dog. It was late July and early evening, and a Sunday. G's face wore the preoccupied and lively look it got when she was thinking about two things at once and in opposition. One was funny, the other was a nightmare. Most of her spoken jokes were self-deprecating and could easily lead into the closet of comedy.

The platform was empty but for her and four young white men, circling around a youngish black man. It looked like a game, because the white ones were laughing and jumping around like kids, but there was no mistaking the serious fear on the black man's face. He was not dressed shabbily, but in a gray business suit; he had no defense. Two of the whites held up half-empty bottles of beer. She could hear in the distant tunnel the sound of the train, and with a feverish sensation covering her skin, she shouted out, Leave him alone!

She might as well have been a ghost or a gust of wind, because they went on shouting epithets at the man, and trying to grab a hold of his shoulders. He was quick. His fear made him fast, and vicious, and he struck out successfully three times, but then he lost all vitality as they went in on him as a pack.

G seemed to leap through light years, to melt into a hard thing, propelled without thought, forward. She was enraged, and fearless for those few seconds, throwing herself into the group of men, who were distracted by her clumsy force. They were trying to pick up the man as a group and to heave him, with shouts of one, two, three, onto the tracks beside the platform. Each could hear the train in the tunnel and the sound of its roar was all-engulfing within those stony walls.

G's anger took her over, and she kicked and used her fists on the bare flesh, their arms lifted, their faces, laughing, until it was too late for them to do as they wanted, and they threw the man in the grey suit on the ground, kicked him, and ran back out of the station . . . just as the train pulled in.

G was shaking from her knees to the top of her head. She watched a handful of people pass, pausing to look at the man getting to his feet, to brush himself off, and straighten his tie. Someone asked her if she was all right. She nodded, and as those others retreated, and the train pulled out, she became terrified, all the anger departed, and she started after the small group of commuters quickly, only wanting human company, in case those four should return. Her breathing was not automatic, too high in her chest.

At the top of the stairs the night air was mild, and black trees blew silhouettes against a yellow-grey city skyline. The Boston Common was there, few people around, and few stores lighted. Still frightened, she headed for a row of taxis when a hand on her shoulder made her lurch forward and start to run.

He said *Wait* with an accent, and she turned to see the smallish man in the grey suit, his lips cut, his cheek scraped, and one eye puffy, trying to smile. Thank you, he said several times, and asked to know what he could do to repay her. Nothing, nothing, it's okay . . . But you're shaking . . . . So are you . . . . Not like you. Your knees! . . . Forget it . . . . I can't . . . . I just want to go home. Really . . . Let me take you. In a cab. Please . . . . Around them headlights beamed and passed, and they kept a distance of several feet between them. She could tell he was African, but that was all. *All right*, she relented, walking forward with him after.

"My name's Augustine," he said. "I was just on my way to Harvard Square, you know? Then these men came out of nowhere and jumped me. I never had an experience like that, not even at home. And I owe my life to you."

Together they climbed into the back seat of a yellow cab, and she told the driver to take them to Harvard Square. She didn't want to talk. And not, even, to listen, she was still so shaken by what had happened. All along the streets she scanned the faces for the four white men, and even into the passing cars, afraid they might find her, and enact some vengeance.

The man was quiet now, himself, and dabbing at his wounds with a handkerchief. He, too, stared out the car windows as: they glided around the corners of the Common toward Beacon Street and Storrow Drive, along the river. Both their faces shone in the sweat of the night, and hers was dark with a summer tan. She unrolled the window and her black curls blew up and away from her neck.

He suddenly gasped, laughed and said loudly, I'm alive! "Yes, you are," she agreed.

"What is your name? I owe my life to you, I do."

"You already said that, but you don't," said G.

"Then what do I owe it to? Luck, the subway coming at the right moment, I don't know."

She didn't look in his direction the better to analyze the mystery of the event, and its loneliness. What stunned her was the sensation of having been there at all, of having nothing to do with it, of blacking out, in a sense, for those seconds of violence rebounding from her. The intelligent and restrained self, her self, with whom she identified night and day, was simply not present during that time. To be praised, then, for taking action made no sense at all. No rational decision had been made; she had physically reacted in a way she was utterly unprepared for.

"If I had been in one of my nervous moods," she told him, "I would have run the other way. Luckily, for you, I was feeling good."

"Yes, indeed."

"What happened anyway?"

"Don't ask me. I don't know, you know? As I say, I was just waiting for the train, when they came up behind me. That's all."

She noted he was smiling, now, with his voice as well as his face, and she smiled back. He tipped back his head and laughed, and she laughed, too, their faces to the windows and wind blowing in.

On the streets, in Harvard Square, they stood around, then headed for a brightly lighted cafeteria, where the few faces turned to watch them as they passed. Inside they got tea, slopped onto a plastic tray, and sat at the plateglass window.

"I come from southern Africa," he told her, "from Durban, to be exact. I don't know if you know anything about Africa."

"Not much. Only about Lumumba."

"Well, I was schooled by Episcopalians, which is why I speak English, you know?"

"Yes, I wondered."

"Here I'm studying international law, actually."

"Really," she murmured, hanging over the heat of her cup.

"Do you want to give me your name?" G went ahead and gave it to him, her whole name, finding nothing to fear in someone who came from so far away and with whom she could laugh so easily.

He, meantime, thought she was a person of color, meeting her that night with her August tan high on her arms, legs and face, and her kinky hair flying.

"You must be West Indian. Or Cape Verdean maybe?"

"Why do you say that?"

"Well, your skin tone, you know. You must be of mixed blood?"

G looked down at her arm lying on the formica table top. It was café au lait, the same to the tips of her fingers, and she wondered at this fact, saw it as a surprise, and looking up at his smile, she couldn't resist the lie: a small reward, or gift, to herself, from her future.

"My mother is West Indian," she said with a big joking smile. "She lives in-um-Barbados."

"And your father?"

"Here! I live with him."

"He must be of English extraction?"

"That's right."

"Can I walk you home, Gemma," he asked then.

"No, no, it's nearby, don't bother."

"Well, I'd like to see you again, to take you somewhere a bit nicer than this, you know?"

"Oh you don't have to do that."

"No. I want to."

"I don't know," she murmured vaguely and gaped at the window, trying to think up an excuse.

"I'll tell you what. I'll be outside here on Saturday night, at six. If you want to join me for dinner, do. If not, I'll understand.

"That's nice of you. Okay!"

They beamed at each other, and she took account of his face now, and his frame: compact, with neat, rounded features, pursed lips and hands both elegant and able. She was not much smaller than he, which contributed to a sense of ease for her. They parted outside the restaurant with him tactfully refraining from asking which way she was walking, or where she lived, and she walked aimlessly by the rough bricks of Brattle Street, under heavy perfumed leaves, talking to herself and smiling.

Time is adjusting my accounts. I wish I could re-ship all the injuries I sent out and could see them travel twice as fast by return and blow up in my hands. I would deserve it.

The Deep North

Relationships constantly reach crisis points, but inside these walls everyone has "seen it all before." Biblical parables are rarely used by revolutionaries, but in prison, as in hospitals, personal memories serve as illustrations.

Mental torment is hidden in the underground. Let me, then, slip into the absolute night, with faith pinned bright as starlight on my heart. If I could only find my first childhood! Why is it so hard to locate?

They went, that Saturday night, to a French restaurant on Beacon Hill. There was a small courtyard for outside eating, with white wrought-iron tables and birch trees studded with Christmas lights. For a while they talked the usual, about Cuba, Kennedy, Communism, poverty in Boston, slumlords, the Welfare system and the domino theory; and meantime G was being affected by the lie she had told him. Deception made her pity Augustine as a victim, hers, and the pity in turn made her feel more at ease with him than she did with most people. Pity made her empathize with him, wholeheartedly, while being herself—if only at surface—a person of color made her distant from but likable to herself. When the subject turned to race, she was almost ready for it.

"Did your mother and father have difficulty, as a mixed couple, in this country?" asked Augustine.

"Uh, yes, of course! They lived a pretty isolated existence without many friends between them. His family wouldn't speak to him again after he married her. They were horrified."

"His family? What about hers?" asked Augustine, as if surprised that she would only register the reaction of the white family.

"Oh well, I don't really know. They were off in the West Indies, what was left of them."

"I see. And for you? The child, or children?"

"Children. My brother and I. We were proud of it, our heritage."

"No one teased or was cruel to you?"

"Only sometimes," she said quickly and sought to change the subject. "It's hard to talk about."

She looked into the Christmas bulbs with a kind of restless twist to her shoulders.

He asked if she had ever been in love.

"Once, yes," she admitted and her eyes flashed at the thought of the man.

"What happened?"

"He went back to his wife and children."

"Ah. That's bad. Loving someone married, I mean. Especially if you're not married too. I always heard a married man should only have affairs with married women, and vice versa. This way each person has love to return to, when that one ends."

"That's very cynical," she said.

"I don't think so at all. . . . Ideally, however, one should not have any affairs, with or without a married person."

"All I know is, I was happy when we were together, and I can't imagine it would ever repeat with anyone else."

"Was he black or white?"

She told him white and now he paid particular attention to the shape of his fork. He turned it up and around in the light, examining the notches and grooves in its flat fake silver.

"You know what I think constitutes happiness," he asked; she shook her head. "When you can lie down in the night, knowing you told the truth, you did your work and you're able to love. . . . And you know what I think constitutes pleasure?" Again she shook her head, but this time it was a flinch. "Ha! Lying; not having to work; and only riding on the tops of people, using them, you know? It's very simple. Why then do people confuse happiness with pleasure?"

"The circuits. Get crossed."

"True," he agreed, "they do. It's all physics."

He could become serious and distant unexpectedly. Augustine was the first man she had met who believed in God and the divinity of Jesus. She questioned him, a lot, and with hunger, about that, and this attention from her increased their bond, so that this particular evening was one she remembered in detail. She remembered the date, the hour and the weather of that night as if the facts contributed, at last, to the meaning of the occasion.

The Deep North

After dinner, they walked for several lonely blocks, in the warm summer air, to the combat zone where there was a nightclub called Slade's Paradise. It was a sleazy spot with a long bar down one side, and tables and a stage on the other. Primarily a black club, frequented by the occasional white sailor or student out on a lark, it was not unsafe for whites to go there, in 1962, because the division was too complete to cross with even the contact of violence.

G and Augustine danced in the style of the times, not touching, but circling close, bending at the knees and lifting up again; and then they watched a female group sing and gesticulate in gold lamé dresses, hair straightened and bobbed. The club was hot and filled with those foresexual smells of alcohol, sweat and smoke. G observed Augustine less intelligently now, and more with the desire of a twentyish woman who is ready to be filled with love and children, a little desperate at the nerve ends, but still selective, cautious. His small, tense frame in a herringbone suit and slow-moving hands made her eyes spark and moisten, like her mother's years before, so she leaned in close to this man waiting for him to touch her. He didn't. Not there, not on the streets and not even when she dropped him at his building, before driving back to hers. He just thanked her for the evening and promised to call. When she went inside, she breathed the air as if it were a liquor that could pass into her body, and give it a rush of emotion. For something, in her, was missing, only to be replaced by something lesser and lighter.

It was a few weeks before Augustine phoned G again. He had moved into Boston, and she went to see him, crossing a border between red brick townhouses and waves of newly poured tar to a strip of stores—hair stylist, coffee shop, wholesale meat, bargain outlet, Tae Kwon Do studio, flophouse and liquors over which he lived. She would cross this border, back and forth, many times, in her visits to see him, whose apartment windows rattled from the nearby elevated trains. His white curtains, white as sails in the sun when she first saw them, soon grew grey, blowing in and out of the screenless windows.

The first time she went to his apartment it was with the flushed anticipation of physical love. Sex with him would affirm the lie that she was a person of color, and would then set her on a fresh course, a liberation she longed for. She had no doubt of his desire for her, and her internal organs felt as red and fresh as roses shaking in drops of rain and sun. Warmth traveled the stem of her spine. She breathed from her abdomen, knocking on his scraped and cracked door. When she saw him, she was both hot and shy. Immediately she sank onto his sofa, waiting for the rest to follow. He handed her a cup of tea on a saucer.

"It's wonderful to see you," he told her.

"You too."

She imagined herself with her soft brown skin and black curls pulled into a pony tail like someone from some old Southern novel. She smiled in a way that would be called demure, and tilted in his direction. He wore his shirt sleeves rolled above his elbows, and smoked a small cigarillo. He talked about his home and said:

"I'm engaged to a woman who is now living in Geneva. We will be married as soon as I've finished school."

He leaned out and took a book off the side table. In it was pressed a photo of his fiancée, a smiling African woman, who looked, to G, like a student, too, with a sweater and blouse neatly buttoned and a bookshelf behind her. He looked at this image as if it were alive; he was smiling into it.

"What's her name? Tell me about her," said G and he told her while her temples and throat throbbed less with disappointment than with embarrassment. After this day she entered the rest of the season with his friendship central to the system of her time, her work, her new image. Her lie about her race made her see the world fresh the way you do on the first October day which is clear and blue. Each green leaf sustained the shadow of another green leaf - a black cut-out. The pavement glittered with mica unnoticed before, and squirrels ate nuts with focused relish. Grains of sugar seemed larger than ever; cream was sweeter; and the smell of the air anywhere was human and familiar. It was like being in love with the new person that she now was.

The Deep North

G, liberated from the sense of being on the killer-victor side of history, let her freedom carry her into territories where she forgot who she was. She cross-examined Augustine and others on African colonialism and literature, in the effects of oppression and racism on the Third World, and so on. Her ignorance accompanied her to parties with Augustine, where foreign and Afro-American students got together around midnight to eat and dance and talk. She questioned people left and right, unaware that her curiosity was making many turn away from her, wondering, suspiciously, what her background was. Into that winter she often worked with Augustine in his small but immaculate studio with the gray curtains hanging over smudged glass. He was a person fixated on one goal—to leave the United States with a degree in law, expertise he would use closer to home. He was not very interested in gossip—about G, in particular, towards whom he was instead protective.

In January she left her father's house and moved into the same building as Augustine. She took a studio apartment two floors below him and supported herself writing articles for the local papers, working on housing violations for the Congress of Racial Equality and typing for people, mostly students she met with Augustine. She was living, now, within walking distance of the hospital where T was treated for asthma; and she was also within walking distance of Ron's mother's house. She passed under the shadows of the el daily and climbed its iron stairs to go to work, and to look across the rooftops of brick flophouses toward a bunched-up downtown Boston. In the fertility of a powerless life, she was happy.

A failure of faith is at the heart of a failure of nerve.

On Primary Day I wore heavy tweeds in the still-warm weather. Political placards swung to and fro as I ran down the center of the main street, stopped traffic.

My mother wanted to give the physician information about me, and my economic situation and the sadness I felt. I told her it was unfulfilled sexual desire being transferred into grief, and this stopped her from taking that drastic and embarrassing step.

The Deep North

*Those who have suffered severe displacement and separation really have no
need for more suffering. They have, instead, a fear of all new events and only
crave an end to drama and change. For this they are called lazy and irrelevant.*

*Many people who are professional believe that in the end you have no stan-
dard of value available to you but theirs and since they have power, you must do
as they say. The process is called axiology.*

G only recognized the danger she was in when her brother came to see
her, unexpectedly. He laid his back against the wall and sprawled on her
single bed, frowning. He patted the bed. She sat beside him and prayed
that none of her friends would call on her now. If they saw T, they would
know at once that she wasn't what she said she was. Even with his healthy
tan, he was unmistakably the product of a privileged white family.

"Mother wants you to go to Italy," he told her, "and to spend some
time there alone, or with her, in the house. I think it's a good idea. You
can't live like this. We don't live like this."

"Like what?" she asked, genuinely curious.

He waved toward the window, where frost was bulging inside the
glass, and toward the ceiling, cratered and stained.

"Come on, Gemma, you know what I mean."

"No. You don't understand," she told him, "how happy I am. I'm on
my own, but I have lots of friends."

"What friends?"

"Never mind, let's go out," she said, threatened by the vision of her
friends entering with the lie she had given them. But he stayed solidly still.

"You've always had friends. You had a higher IQ than me. What
about a man?"

"Not right now, no."

"You should get married, settle down, if you're not going to practice
your genius."

"I will, but I'm still young."

"Don't marry someone poor, please."

She examined his handsome face, now narrower and tighter like his
father's, but with the full lips and brown skin they shared. He spent so

much time, these days, in snow and sun, he was very dark. To her his face was so familiar it was like some famous impressionist print you see in every bookstore. It was fixed in time like that, outside of possible injury.

"Just because you married someone rich and glamorous, it doesn't mean I have to, too."

"I'm just telling you what Mother asked me to tell you."

"As if I'd listen."

"Well, I told her I'd say it. Anyway, at least come out and have dinner with me. Come on. I'll pay for everything."

They went to an Italian restaurant in the North End. She wore a ratty fur coat, purchased in a junk shop, and galoshes with buckles. Her frizzy hair was pinned down with barrettes, making her face, over its wide bones, show every shift in expression, more than she knew. She ate like a pig and guzzled wine cheerfully, while T told her about his sexual and other adventures. He worked as a ski instructor in Italy most of the time, was married to a Swiss woman, was bisexual and constantly pushing himself to extremes, physically. He didn't read much any more, but loved the opera and the ballet. His red mouth, greased against chapping, twisted often into a bemused expression, suggesting he was ready for anything. He talked about their mother, intimating that she was silly and beneath contempt.

"I haven't seen her for ages," said G. "I don't know what she's up to anymore, and I don't much care."

"You can't be that callous. It doesn't suit you."

"Well, I have nothing in common with her, or Father. I feel I was born into the wrong family, though not in relation to you."

"That's right. I look into your eyes and you're still my little sister. Why have you chosen such a dreary life though, why? Here you have money and this glorious Italian house at your disposal. Loosen up! Be more Mediterranean and not such a Puritan."

As she used to, G felt a slight waver of excitement in her, just at the force of his presence, and she almost confided in him, about her false identity, about her lie she was calling her life. The words hovered in front of her lips, and emanated a kind of gravity that she wanted to resist. She put food in her mouth and drank to keep herself from speaking, and as she did so, she was aware of the enormity of the lie and also of its absurdity. It even occurred to her that maybe everyone knew she was white, and that the lie was being reversed back onto her. Like looking in two mirrors: one behind, and one in front; excessive perspectives wheeled in the air around her. If she clapped shut one of the mirrors, the image would vanish, but not what it had showed. That would stay, attached to the actual physical body she occupied, the one she labeled "colored" when it should have read "white."

"I see you still love your wine," said T. "More? Why don't you live with me, or someone like me?"

"My God," said G.

"Shocked? I'll let you do anything you want."

G had changed color, seeing the bearded journalist—his name was Dieter (said like "Peter")—enter the restaurant with a woman. His beard, graying, and his streaked blond hair, smoothed back from a high white forehead, made him look older than she remembered. He wore a black three-quarter-length overcoat she would know by its smell.

"Who's that?" asked T.

"A man I hate."

"Looks more like love to me."

Dieter pushed the woman aside toward the cloak room then, and came to G's side.

"Where are you living now?" he asked.

"In Boston."

"I'll find you," he said. "Don't worry." And he walked, confident and smiling, to another table.

"What an awful man," T remarked. "How did he know I wasn't your lover? What is he—sexy?"

"I guess."

"You don't need that kind of man. He looks like he stepped out of a Swedish movie about the Black Plague. Come home and sleep with me instead. Wouldn't that be the fulfillment of our most secret desires?"

"No, it wouldn't," she told him. "You really are disgusting."

"Not in bed. I can show you how to do things that will please that man there."

He was as serious as he could ever be, and she was too. When he got her home, she ran in alone and slammed the door as if he was chasing her. Then she grabbed a bottle of cheap burgundy and listened down the hall to hear if anyone was home. Off at a distance she heard music and laughter, and she hesitated. She was in a high state of excitement. Part of it came from the fear of being discovered as a fake in the presence of her brother, and in his wake; the other part came from seeing the man she loved and hearing his promise to find her. If he did as he said, however, he might expose her lie to those friends down the hall (all under thirty and none of them rich, or white), just by being with her.

She ventured into the hall and, bottle in hand, passed one open door, where there was no music but voices, past another, where there was music and no voices. She climbed the stairs to where two students shared one small apartment exactly like hers, and the door was open, and a crowd was assembled inside. Smoke veiled the door. She paused, feet away from the entrance, overcome with consciousness not of the lie, but of the truth. She had no right of access into black society; she was not really close to anyone but Augustine; she was a reverse subversive and as homeless as she deserved to be. She returned, then, to her apartment, alone with her embarrassment.

Nature's intention sometimes seems to be that all should be forgotten, that there should be no trace of a human event. Sometimes it seems that the pulse of all living creatures comes from a voluntary rebellion against that supreme intention, which longs for emptiness or only the rub of wind against wind. Sometimes all the varieties of wildflower, fern, pool and sea seem to spring from subversion, the genius of the spirit in disguise, as it struggles against that omnivore, nature herself. In this way the spirit becomes the enemy of nature, but fits itself to her forms, and hides there, inside her, holding her together.

The minute Dieter entered her rooms, G took him back. She fell into his arms when he held them out, overwhelmed by the kindness of a destiny that returned him to her. It was a chilly afternoon, and he told her he was free for her alone, he was free for good. In his briefcase he carried a bottle of scotch and a bar of chocolate-covered caramel she particularly liked. He was writing, on commission for a respectable publisher, a book about charity in America, he told her, as they drank their way toward her bed.

"I hate the way I feel so outside my subject," he said. "As soon as you move into big-time publishing, you lose that visceral contact—the kind I can see you have—with the underdog."

"Why do you want it," she inquired.

"For the book. So it will ring true."

He laid her back, then, and set to removing her clothing with the authority of one who has been there before.

In spite of G's efforts to spend more time with Dieter in his renovated townhouse, and to avoid this way a possible confrontation between him and her friends, they spent more time at her house than at his. He loved her better in a context of poverty. While she was moving among the down-and-out, he lavished her with attentions. He let her use his car any time; he bought her clothes and dinner out; he put up bookshelves, curtains, lightbulbs in her apartment; he pampered and praised her. She hid from Augustine and her black friends and slipped in and out of a kind of slangy street talk that she identified with blackness. He liked it. She told him the secrets she had learned about life lived on the margins, and about the effects of segregation on the imagination. She never, though, told him about the lie she was living. She was terrified of his finding out, and in her longing to stay with him for years and years, she imagined leaving Boston with him, and that way leaving the lie behind, buried and gone.

There was a late spring snow that made May blossoms all the more profuse that year. Along Commonwealth Avenue the magnolia and dogwood spread handfuls of pinks and whites; cherry and apple blossom puffed along the sidewalks of Boston and Cambridge. G bolted from job to job, and imagined each one was a rung on an invisible ladder, which climbed through the fluffy trees to a point where there was a vista displayed. That vista was really a map of the world. Many of her friends now were Freedom Riders, heading south to join the Movement. Wanting to follow, but held back by a dread of her own secret exposing her, she worked all the harder at bringing cases against slumlords in Boston.

Her parents wondered what had happened to their brilliant daughter, the one who graduated early, Summa, who should have been, as they saw it, married at best, and a law student or writer at the very least. But the mother lived almost always in Italy now, and could forget from there, and the father had learned to turn his tolerance for disappointment into verse. The world was, daily, confirming the worst. He liked that. Neither parent nor lover knew how she was straining to see her way free of their traps.

Dieter continued to be fascinated by her friendships, especially those with Africans, West Indians and Afro-Americans. As she breezed back and forth across boundaries usually impassable for whites, he marveled at her character which gave her such access. At the same time her unwillingness to let him follow her there, and to let him share in these friendships, troubled him.

"I think your attraction to those people must have a sexual basis," he teased her. "You can't convince me otherwise, so don't try! I bet you feel that white men have failed you, or you did until we got back together, and so you moved in the direction of black men. Don't worry. I'm not mad, not jealous, but I know I'm right."

"You're not right, you're wrong," she said, reddening with the confusion that his argument produced in her. "'Those people' are my friends, my best friends, and nothing else."

"Well, why do you hide me away then?"

"You are jealous," she said with a delighted smile.

"No. It's my fault for leaving you before. You were alone for too long—I mean, for a hot-blooded girl like you."

"I didn't have any affairs," she insisted. "I swear!"

"Well, you moved out of your house. You basically changed class, and you seem to want to change races. Where do I fit in?"

"You know where," she said, climbing onto his comfortable knees.

"I still say - "

"Well, don't -"

And both of their expressions glazed over, as eyes do when their owner decides to dream instead of see.

My bed's window looks into the cosmos, and offers as many optical delights as Mount Palomar with its relay satellite and dish antenna.

Comedy is the ceiling of society's self-understanding.

All those laughing galaxies are like sperm heading for the black hole, or The Womb of Being, and if you want my opinion, this similarity should lead a scientist to a profound truth. But men finally committed the ultimate sin when they stepped on the moon before a woman could. She would have seen the whole panorama differently.

I'm a modern spiritualist even when I stare out at a flat blue roof of snow.

I have a different point of view from those who need instruments.

Love, which excitedly insists that one individual is an exception to all the others, can be exhausted by this very excitement. Dieter drank too much, and G did too, and every time they were together, they became drunk, and consequently they suffered the following day. Dieter dealt with the suffering by working all the more intensely on his book, locked up in his home with six-packs of beer, while G, who couldn't afford the cure of alcohol, became tremulous, fearful and subject to those harsh waves of anxiety that once lifted her up and over like efforts on the part of pure spirit, locked into substance, efforts that seemed liberating in intention.

It was late fall when Dieter's book was nearly complete that he got in the mood for change, again. He felt stultified by Boston and figured he should move to New York to ensure the success of his manuscript. He was not happy with himself, or the habits that had sustained him over those months. And he decided to switch from cigarettes to a pipe, from scotch to wine, and from his relationship to G to some X, Y, or Z who would not be time-consuming. He set a date, February first, for the delivery of his manuscript and himself.

Meanwhile he feared telling G of his new program. He didn't want her to cause a scene and tried, frantically, to think up a way of leaving her which would make her believe that she had brought it on herself. He lavished her with the loving kindness of one who is leaving. He pitied her for not knowing what was coming. He dropped hints of his restlessness, and of his obsession with success.

"Before I'm forty I want to have an international reputation," he announced. "I don't know if I can get that, starting from Boston." She agreed that this might be a problem.

Everyone but G suspected Dieter of planning to depart. Augustine, among others, felt that Dieter was unable to commit himself to her because of her racial background. Others felt, on those rare occasions when they ran into him in the hall or her apartment, that he was a man who feared black men, that he was a coward in dove's clothing. While he was jovial and courteous, fear danced in the sparkle of his eyes. During one encounter on the dark stairs, he and Augustine agreed to meet on their own; each one wanted to scrutinize the intentions of the other in relation to G.

It's essential to stay right up next to God. A disembodied ego can inhale too much oxygen and go mad, and receive from healers the kind of investigation applied by scientists to their experiments.

Complete objectivity, when applied to another person, is impossible. Empathy affects the information and the objectivity becomes a form of psychological torture, within minutes, hours.

Law: a weak people cannot become strong and still remain committed to the ideology of weakness.

You are on the side of the rich or of the poor, and no change of fortune should influence which side you choose.

Making symbols out of particulars is the job of terrorists, who express contemporary despair more concretely than almost anyone.

A light snow was falling outside. Inside a vent blasted a faint smell of fish onto Dieter's face, his hair blew back as if he was on board ship. Smoke rose to the ceiling and hung there while he and Augustine sipped on beers.

"Are you bothered by Gemma's background?" Augustine asked after a while.

"Why would I be? You couldn't get much better," said Dieter with a conspiratorial smile. "Blue blood is supposed to be the clearest in this country."

"Blue blood?" Augustine asked, curious. "I never heard that expression."

"I can't believe you lived in Boston this long, and haven't heard it."

"Ah well. You know this city is as bad as the Deep South in many ways. I never met her father, but Gemma's mother must have left because it was intolerable here."

"I suppose he was intolerable. He's pompous," said Dieter.

"And racist too?"

"I don't know about that. I think he's a moderate conservative type."

"Well, he'd have to be somewhat liberal to marry her in the first place," Augustine noted. "That's very rare in his generation. Interracial marriage occurred in Europe during the last war, I heard, but not here, on home ground."

"What are you talking about?" Dieter asked, straightening, and his bright eyes sparked as if viewing a far horizon across the sea. "Who had an interracial marriage?"

"Gemma's parents, of course. That's what we're talking about."

Dieter's was a quick mind, and his thoughts now raced up and down every possible avenue, before finding the one that gave him the widest access. He shrugged and smiled.

"Sorry, Augustine," he said, "I was just drifting, getting distracted. Please go on with what you were saying. I agree that interracial marriage was rare here, is."

"Yes. And that's the first question: does her race bother you?"

"No. Live and let live. You know that's my attitude."

"I know, but I mean would you be able to marry someone black, like Gemma?"

"I wouldn't marry anyone at this point in my life, man," he replied. "Not even a rich white girl with a brain."

Augustine scrutinized Dieter carefully, seeing how deftly he was avoiding a direct response to his question. The avoidance in this case was the response he expected, but something more was troubling too. He waited for Dieter this time to speak.

"Does Gemma talk to you about her family background?" Dieter asked.

"Sometimes, but not much."

"How would you describe her racial type?"

"Well, mulatto, I guess. And you?"

"I don't know the word for it, I guess."

Now they both stared off into a distant space and forgot each other and the necessity for conversation. Dieter knew at that moment he could utterly humiliate G by giving away her lie. But he drew back because it was more strange than he ever could imagine.

The next evening he went directly to G's apartment, after completing his quota of work for the day. The twilight lay blue on the rocky streets, and from down there, the light in her window, coming through bamboo and chintz, looked as innocent as a child's hair. Dieter went through the usual moves of opening drinks and smokes before confronting her directly with the knowledge he now had.

"What do you think you're doing about this race issue?" he asked, his voice all outrage. "You aren't any more black than I am!"

"I can't explain it. Just leave it alone!"

"I've met your brother, I've seen pictures of your parents. I even met your father. I know what you are. Your mother is Italian American." She was frightened and her legs trembled. She sat on the edge of her bed, afraid that he would strike, or, worse yet, leave. She found she had no words of defense or explanation. It was like a dream of teeth falling out. No hard little words pressed over her tongue, her lips.

"I could have told Augustine, then and there. I should have. He should know. I'm really shocked at you—overwhelmed. I always thought of you as completely honest." He moved, paced and pointed, stressing her deception's effect on his trust. And his trust's importance in a love relationship. He wanted to know how she got away with it for so long, how she felt while she was getting away with it, and how she felt about herself.

She couldn't speak. Mute, she sat with her hands clenched on her lap, in a sweater, skirt and long socks, like a schoolgirl. He paused and looked at her as if seeing her anew. In his eyes her skin tone and kinky hair took on a new appearance because of her lie. She was not, as it turned out, what she said she was to anyone but him, not black or white, but a mystery, which rhymed with history. Down the hall came the sounds of a Miles Davis melody, played over and over by one of her friends. She sat attentive and her eyes were fixed on the dark window. He moved over and stood near, where he imagined her being black, being truly her lie and so sexually tied to the black men in the building. Still accusing her verbally he fell, then, onto her, and while she believed that he was making love to her, in his mind he was raping her.

Later she would understand what she barely could at the time. He knew. But not she who was the recipient of the motivated action. Not knowing in advance made it possible for her to have the experience and she wanted it.

Now she misses his body in bed, the salt of the human beside her, even though he mistreated her. No one would give her credit for kindness and forgiveness under these conditions. They would only admire her rage which never erupted.

Perpetual dinner smells and lowered postures instead began to sicken her.

Rain on the river, ducks that land on waste, a sky dense and low, blackbirds yelling Let's go, let's turn off the sun and find our true colors.

"I'm tired. Pull me along with you, will you?"

She sat down.

It was clear to everyone who knew her that, when Dieter left her, G was effectively destroyed. That she came from some privileged and educated background, black or white, was obvious to her friends, but it was now irrelevant in the face of her excessive drinking and her attraction to anonymity to the point of self-annihilation. She scraped bits of money together, just managing to pay her rent and eat meager food and drink chemically infected wines. She became and remained pale. Friends watched over her by taking advantage of her weakness in a way designed, also, to keep her from harm. Someone was always staying with her; someone always needed a place to stay. And that person then made sure that he or she and G had something to eat, that electric and fuel bills were paid, that the machines kept functioning for their survival.

In the following summer, Augustine left to return to South Africa and then to move to Geneva and his fiancée, permanently. Before his departure, he and others agreed that G was not black at all. They wondered if she had ties to the CIA, if she had, for all that time, been spying on them. It was not so much her lie that made them suspicious as her tie to Dieter, who seemed, in retrospect and with his growing success in New York, to be suspect. Augustine left without saying any of this to G, and her other friends left too, heading south, or to New York, away from Boston, which they said was hell for any person of color, and none of them said anything to her either. It was a way of forgetting her.

G's apartment windows stayed open night and day to let the hot air circle around the room. Some changes occurred in the neighborhood and young whites moved in and became her friends. At all hours were the classic sounds of breaking glass, raised voices, music and cars. Assassination mushroomed, its cloud like a male organ disseminating smoke, and folk songs suggested that America's innocence lay before Columbus. Some of the white people in the building headed west, and told G to join them in Utah where they were going underground to manufacture weapons. After they left G was usually found seated on the stoop with a drink, a cigarette and an eager, questing expression that called people over to talk about things like student riots, the Kennedys and God.

It was months before any member of her family came near her.

However, one day A came looking for G. Perfumed and neatly coiffed, she rapped on the door of G's studio, then stood, with her nostrils compressed against the smells she associated with illness and poverty. She gave no indication that she was suffering from nervous cramps, a violent headache, symptoms of dread. The night before she dreamed she had won the Nobel Prize for Despair. Music fell down the stairs like a slinky going bang, zip, bang, all the way to her feet. When G opened the door, it was four on a rainy afternoon.

"Why," said G instead of Hi.

"To see you. If you're all right."

"See? I am."

"Can't I come in?"

"Sure."

A entered, tentatively. The single room contained a single bed, a table, two chairs, bookshelves containing books and clothes, a radio, a couch covered with sheets and pillows, and a wine bottle with a dripped-out candle stuck inside it.

A sat and then stood at the window, facing out at the rain.

"Now. If you can tell me," she said to her daughter, "someone or something that you want, I will get it for you. Or we will know, at least, what it is that you really want. Can you think of something?" G thought about Dieter intensely for several minutes, and then she thought of alcohol. Both were things she wanted. But she joined her mother at the window looking out.

"I don't know, Mother. Outside there is a whole world, and I can't think of something I really want."

"That means you're depressed," said A with finality.

"It could mean I'm happy."

"I wish I believed that but I don't. No, if you don't come with me, which you should, to Italy, then I think you should enter a hospital and get some treatment. Before you do something permanently harmful. I really do."

G was rocked by a violent shudder at the words hospital and treatment. It traveled the length of her spine, just as if she had one hand in water and one in light.

"What's wrong?" asked her mother.

"A chill," she replied.

The rain clattered on the glass, cutting into the dust, forming runny lines.

"Well, no wonder. Living here, you must be sick all the time. . . . Please listen to me. I want you to get well, to be happy. Come with me—or—if you could just see a psychiatrist for this depression, whatever has brought you here."

"I'll think about it," said G obediently.

"I'll call to find out what you decide," said her mother.

"All right, do," was G's passive response.

"Gemma," her mother said, "do you think a mentally ill person should be held responsible for their crimes? Are you capable of crime? Are you mentally ill? My uncle Joe was, of course, and my mother was, too. Do you think you inherited something? Or are you making decisions?"

G gave her mother a radiant smile and opened her empty hands.

"Mother, that's the question of my generation. Someone else will have to answer it."

Then A left and G watched her from her window as she exited the building, briskly, and hurried to her car with the pretense of ease and even pleasure built into the snap of her heels. It was August, 1963, and the March on Washington was no longer in progress. The rain in Boston fell as scattered showers.

If I see through myself, what am I seeing through?

When my sight goes way out, I don't hate anything. Even when the rain never came. When it finally did, I lost laughs under umbrellas of greens and little lambs stood woolly in the wuthering storm, pages from THIS WONDERFUL WORLD fluttering up pinafores and ribbons and the wind in them all.

I was so glad to be a child again, I slipped out of the glass where my treasured dreams were all the more precious for the night in which they were stored. And the tiny limbs on which those raindrops spattered beat off the lie that there could be a greater love than this—the love for what is.

I remember a desert where the sun fills my cells and I can rake in the sand and this way begin to build a new kind of city.

You see, I let many facts fail and also their names and stood, three fingers up, with my pulse buried in cloth.

I saw Saint Joan holding in her arms a little fruit and the words, It's here—Charity! And the Communist Manifesto was a work of poetry.

*The rain cleaned the glass until I stained where it had, and now there was
nothing but fiery light which also made a stain I couldn't polish by hand.*

*I covered my face and didn't peek and this way kept hope safe in the way of
all concealed mercies. And when daylight again illuminated my stains I rubbed
the glass between the Testaments with a cloth and fists.*

*Divinity flamed the names in which a new vocabulary would be born, one
which would truly save me. But my tongue was stuck to the roof of my mouth.*

That night G lay in the semi-darkness on her bed, her knees folded up to
her belly, her eyes open. The raining was done and water alone dripped
from the gutters. The occasional car greased by with a splashing sound.
There was a party somewhere in the building (those who had not gone to
Utah to build bombs were having fun) and G was alone in her place, preferring for this time to hear the music from a distance and to drink alone.

She remembered the school she had burned a hole in, a matter of
miles away, and saw herself in the same hospital room T had once occupied, with the same nurse and fears. As if nothing had changed, she
remembered her brother as a boy saying, I'll give you a reward if you do
me a favor. And the reward and favor were just the same: that she should
lean down and kiss, first his feet and then his stiff white organ in the
woods where they lay. He laughed at her for her humiliation, he called
her his little slave, since he was the master's son. And he said there was
no such virtue as shame.

Now you can't start over, she said to herself. Her own shadow she
envisioned as a little hunched figure, growing larger and larger, a proportion on a wall. The end.

She woke up as a child in a patch of warm sunshine, soaked by it, and
realized at once her brother had abandoned her. She got up, brushed
the sand off her face and pajamas, collected a deep breath of air, and
looked for a path to the house they were visiting. A part of her still slept
as she walked barefoot along the sand, looking into the hobbled spruce
forest. Her mouth was a black 0 through which she breathed short quick
gasps. She turned circles, seeking help which wasn't there. Active shadows flicked at the edges of the sand. Now she came to the end of the

beach where stones were piled, and she walked back again, scanning the woods. The look of the lost: the pupils grow small, the eyelids hooded. She walked this way and that, but never fully awoke.

There was after all no path but flames of sand weaving between shrubs. She turned around three times and felt as if she were hanging by a thin thread from the round sun overhead, and was twirling in an immense and rejecting system. She tried to be confident and sang a little song, but it was fragile in the wake of the tidal sounds. She gulped and sat down, whimpering, and made an oval basin in the sand, where she could curl up under the sun. There she lay, glinting at sand, for one hour, two, three, while the tide rolled up close to the rim of her basin. And finally at nearly noon, she heard her name. There, way inside the woods she saw a dark-skinned woman with a well-known smile, carrying a bucket and shovel, calling her name.

Then she was thrown forward in her bed, as if knocked from behind and under, and tossed into a wholly new place. It was that kind of shock, but a speeded-up attack of despair, too, a lash of physical horror shot from inside. She threw herself forward, upright. I have to wake up. The hour was only around ten. She got up and stuffed her whiskey in her purse with the little money she had, plus toothbrush, comb and a change of underwear. I've got to wake up. She was shaking up and down.

G rushed through the damp warm summer night to Back Bay Station. There she wrote out a check, which would bounce, for a ticket to Ogden, Utah. The last train to New York left near midnight, and she took it. She was dressed in beatnik black and a pair of leather sandals molded to the shape of her feet. From New York she went on to Chicago, where she arrived the next day with $4.35, some of which she spent on a half pint of cheap scotch.

Next she took the train out of Chicago, west again, seated in the dome car through hours and hours of flat land, of lonely houses shooting out light in the night, until she stepped into the streets of Ogden, Utah, wide awake.

The air was as sweet as lake water. Relaxing wholly, she let herself be carried forward, step by step. East by south she walked with the thick sky lifting light from under its rim, as if the sun was its secret and clouds were playing in it.

With no more money and no more alcohol, in a dry state she washed herself in the air, gave herself a new name and aim and disappeared.

Famous Questions

Their vehicle idled while the couple studied the woman. She wore the expression of astonishment and sorrow seen in fifteenth-century Italian paintings of the Blessed Mother. She wore a pale blue dress, sleeveless, and no shoes. A straw bag on her lap. Brown arms and legs. A brownish chest and throat. Straight, thin shoulders. A halo of reddish gold hair, frizzy and wild, and a freckled brown face. This face was soft-featured and deflected the light.

—Is she okay? The man asked.
—Or insane, his partner remarked. Maybe drunk?
—Drugged?

The street sign read Ave Mañana. A nearby mall was sealed up like a shelter from fall-out. Palm trees were bright and orderly; on the flan-colored stucco were pasted anti-Vatican notices which the couple pulled over to read. Their van had a Massachusetts license plate, though they were in southern California.

Famous Questions

Both the man and the woman were dark-haired and tanned. He had a thick brown mustache that curled around the corners of his lips. She had a scar on one cheek and Asian eyes.

—Should we offer her a ride? asked the woman.
—To where? Sure, go ahead.
She rolled down the window as he pulled the van to the curb. She leaned out and spoke.
—You look lost. Can we help?
The young woman smiled eagerly, with a hint of adventure.
—I'm not exactly lost, she said in a low, melodious voice, but I don't really know where I am, either.
—Well, then, where did you come from? the man called out.
—Nowhere. I mean, I'm just traveling. I have a purpose, is what I really mean, even if I am lost now.
—Which is?
—To bring people together, to make people see that suffering isn't necessary.
—Oh, God, a nut, the man muttered.
—Wait a minute, said the woman inside the van. Whatever your purpose is, you look like you need a meal and a bath. Want to come home with us?
—Lord, have mercy, the man muttered and climbed out of the van.
—Sure, I'll come with you. I trust your voice, your faces.
She stood up while the man unlocked and swung open the back door for her.
—Don't think we're rich when you see our house, the woman inside told her.

The house was up in the hills overlooking the tops of others just like it. They all had orange, striped roofs. Theirs was a six-bedroom ranch with a pool and wider view to the Pacific. Gophers were their main problem except for the smog, which distilled in the valley. The couple told the woman that their opulence was not the result of a drug deal, not from inherited wealth or a clever move in real estate. It was not, however, from hard work, either.

—We discovered one day that I was wearing a piece of jewelry worth ten grand, the woman explained. We sold it and gave an eighth to the church. Then we rented out our crumbling apartment in Boston and headed west. We'll stay here until the asbestos has settled.

The younger woman said her name was Echo. If she was a hippie, a leftover flower child, a bag lady, a psychotic, a druggie, a white witch, a cult queen, a slum goddess, a rich girl from Westchester County—it would all make sense. No label did not fit her. She went upstairs to the guest room. The woman showed her the bathroom and gave her a dress to wear.

Downstairs the man was half-naked, eating a pear. Thirty-five, several pounds overweight but muscular, he moved the fruit around in his mouth with relish. Juice dripped from his mustache. He was barefoot and stood with his groin thrust forward in a way that was both erotic and feminine.
—Aren't you going to cover your chest? the woman asked. I don't want Echo seeing you like that.
He looked down at himself, surprised as she approached him and stuck her hands in his pockets.
—After we swim, let's go upstairs, she said, and went to their room to change. He called after her,
—You better put a move on it before everyone gets home.

She was the first in the pool, and the man came out next with Echo beside him. She was wearing a white cotton dress and eating fruit. She was the color of peaches. She smiled in a strained but friendly way, watching the man join the woman in the pool.
—What are your names? she called.
—Mine is Kosta, it's Greek, he answered. She's Roisin—Rosheen—Irish
—What strange names we all have, Echo remarked.

Famous Questions

—Have you ever noticed, Roisin wondered from the water, that immigrants assume Anglo names, and those of us who have been here for generations take on the names of our lost ancestors?

Echo did not respond but sauntered up and down the edge of the pool and out to the patio, where she gazed with some rapture into the sweltering haze. Brown hills. The flowers had to be watered every night so they could drink in the dark, the way the people did. Echo cupped an iris in her hand, examining its form and purple color as if it were a silk scarf for sale in a boutique. Then she released it casually and came to the poolside to look at the couple playing in the water. Kosta had hold of Roisin's feet and was pushing her through it, gently.

—It's wonderful to see people with no negative feelings, Echo said in a sharp voice.

—Don't worry, we have them, Kosta protested from the water.

—But I can tell you aren't afraid to be happy. That's great, she said, now in that low, melodious voice that made her sound wise and middle-aged. If you don't mind, I'd really like to spend the day here resting up.

—No, that's okay, Roisin called.

—But I want you to ignore me. Go upstairs and hide away, whatever, while you have the chance. It's the Sabbath and you shouldn't work, said Echo.

—Don't worry, Kosta told her with an amused smile. We know what to do.

Up in their large master bedroom with its wall-to-wall carpeting inches deep and low lighting and pool-blue curtains drawn, the couple lay in bed, she over him, while they talked.

—Her accent is from the East Coast, she said. But she's mentally West Coast. Do you think she's beautiful?

—Getting there, I guess. But no sense of humor.

—She's mysterious, I think.

—Yes, I guess she is, and pitiable, said Kosta.

—That's what made me ask her back. I felt sorry for her. And we're so lucky, right?

—Right, he said with his eyes closed and a smile.

Their hands locked and unlocked against the pillow; he raised his knees.

—We should do this more often, he whispered, in the middle of the day. Are you safe?

—Don't make me answer that.

She moved away from him and turned her body toward the window. He sat up fast.

—Hey! Do you think she's down there robbing us blind? My new camera!

—I'll go look, said the woman. Calm down.

She wrapped a towel around herself and went to the door, where she could hear music playing from down the hall. She tiptoed in its direction and looked into the guest room, where Echo was asleep, the radio playing beside her. She had her face covered. But the bottoms of her feet were exposed, as worn and blistered as an old woman's. Her straw bag drooped open, revealing a book, a wallet, a toothbrush, a hairbrush, a wooden box. Roisin covered her with a quilt, then walked down the hall to where Kosta stood, his body dyed light blue by the sun in the curtains.

—I'm up, he said.

x

Roisin believed that to live is to suffer, but acts of mercy can relieve some of that suffering. She believed that people only live once—and that it is a scandal, therefore, that some people are oppressed, tormented and restrained from enjoying what society offers. She had, since childhood wanted to help others gain access to those benefits; social service seemed to be her vocation. She liked to make other people happy, to keep the peace, and felt most powerful in the process of emptying herself for others. She had had a disrupted childhood and told Echo, when she asked her in the kitchen, a little bit about it:

"My grandmother was the one who raised me. She never hit me or punished me at all, but an atmosphere of hysteria surrounding her terrified

203

me. She was always screaming her responses—to the news, to gossip, to a dropped pot. She worked in a hat-stitching factory and had a lot of girl-friends, as she called them, from work. At home, rain or shine, she wore a trench coat around the house and bedroom slippers. Her meals were disgusting—scrambled eggs with Jimmy Dean' pork sausages and Tater Tots, or a boiled potato dripping water onto the plate where a black ham-burger sat like a turd. She shrieked at my father especially. His whole life was structured around animating women to rage. I don't know if you know that type. He closed his eyes and listened with pleasure to the women in his life screaming at him. Most of the time he was driving a truck. My mother disappeared when I was very small. Dad always told me I was in the wrong place at the wrong time from the moment of my conception. My grandmother called me the poor thing. That's where I come from.

—God, said Echo. Wow . . . But what happened when you left home?

"Granny gave me her Ford and set me free at sixteen. The real problem was that I had a brain. No one knew where I got it. It was treated like a mutation. Get it out of the house. Take it where there are others like it. That was their attitude. I got a full scholarship to college and went for it. But I was really fucked up emotionally and didn't last too long at a stretch. I dropped out after two semesters and earned enough money to go to Ireland. That's what students did in those days. Bummed around. I was an insatiable reader, and my bag bulged with books. I knew a lot of Yeats by heart. Ever heard of Yeats?
—Of course. Echo looked insulted. I love poetry, too.
—Well, that was really where my best life began. In Dublin.
—What do you mean? What happened?
—Another time, said Roisin.

By noon the heat was overwhelming. A citric haze hung over the land-scape like lemon juice squeezed into water. The brown hills slept un-der blankets—knees, elbows, necks, and shoulders. Roisin felt that the Holy Spirit had recently crossed them, leaving a body shuddering under the covers. So much of the plant life seemed to try to follow the sky. Noon bells rang from some church below. Stocky, frowning, dark, she floated face up on the water, her arms extended to the side. When Echo came out she was wearing Roisin's one-piece suit. She had the figure of a runner—tight, muscular, flat-bellied. Sun had left freckles all over her arms and legs. Some strands of hair curled out from her crotch around the cloth, and they were red gold like the hair on her head. Under her arms it was the same. She stretched, smiled into the water, and took the plunge. They swam together up and down the length of the pool when Roisin drew her underwater and showed her the two glassy portholes that were cut into Kosta's underground studio; they, were thick and nautical and seemed to be underwater lights but weren't.

Above, in the air, Echo asked if Kosta could see out.
—Yes, but he shrouds himself in darkness, said Roisin.
—Then he's missing the whole point of California!
—Not for him. He's working.
—He seems like someone who would be a good father.
—So far he has been.
—And what do you feel about being a mother?
—I want more because God, I still haven't recovered from the miracle of giving birth to Liam. I'm not kidding. I'm still in shock. Either I'm amazed at his existence—that he's here at all—or else I'm in dread of his disappearance. The world seems hostile when you have a child.
—But your child is the world. So if you love him, then you have to accept and love everything that has made him what he is.
—That's probably true.
—Sometimes I think we should go back to polygamy. I mean, then everyone could have what they want. There aren't enough men to go around as it is. And this way a woman could choose to have a child or just to be a mother to children. See what I mean? It's tragic really to be deprived of certain things.
—My mother-in-law says that failing to get what you want does not constitute tragedy, in spite of what most Americans believe, said Roisin.

—I think she's wrong. It does constitute tragedy.

—Well, it's good you have opinions, Echo.

They smiled at each other across the lip of blue water, and Echo took off, doing the breaststroke up and down, gracefully. Roisin climbed out into the sun and watched her until she, too, left the pool. She climbed onto the hot dry stones, threw down a towel, and told Roisin to lie on it, face down. Roisin did as she was told, and Echo squatted beside her tense body and began to prod, with her hands, at the soft parts of her skin.

—I feel fat and plain, said Roisin.

—You're not. You just need to tone up. Exercise more than you do. You have beautiful smooth skin. It feels like silk.

—How old are you? Roisin asked.

—Twenty-nine.

—You look nineteen.

—That's from being free. The minute people settle down, their bodies settle, too. You must always keep moving if you want to stay young.

—What about friendship, love, work?

—They're really illusions. I mean, I have friends, but I always move on. This way—you know what?

—What.

—They love me longer. Better.

Now she leaned over Roisin and wrapped her hands around her back and into the top of her bathing suit. They closed on her breasts. Her breath was quick and close near her neck as she leaned there.

—What are you looking for? asked Roisin.

— To see what your glands are like, if they're healthy.

—It's like playing dead. I want to laugh. I'm not used to this.

—Relax, said Echo. You want to get pregnant, don't you?

—Are you trained in massage, medicine?

—Of course. I trained in Finland and Mexico. Turn over.

Echo lifted up her hands, and obediently Roisin rolled over and closed her eyes, a big smile on her face.

—Don't tickle me.

—Don't worry. And I won't hurt you, either.

—I'm modest, always was.

—I can tell. You mustn't be modest with me. I'm like your physician now. Think of it that way. I want you to have a baby, that's all. You've been very kind to me. If I can pay you back, I will.

—Are you sure you can accomplish that?

—Yes I'm sure, but don't be upset by what I do. It won't hurt.

I'll try, said Roisin, but she was shocked when Echo pried her fingers around the tight band of her bathing suit and began to insert them inside of her. She jumped.

—Do you really have to do this?

—Yes. It will show what kind of herb you need to use as a suppository before you can conceive.

—But are you sure?

—It'll take one second. Relax. How did you get your scar?

—What scar? Roisin asked.

—The one on your face.

—Ha. I thought you found something I didn't know about.

Echo didn't laugh or smile as her shadow crossed over Roisin. Instead her eyes were closed, her expression was both serene and attentive like someone listening to music. A bee was buzzing in the flowers close by. Her fingers fluttered inside of Roisin, and she sighed, Hmm.

—What? asked Roisin.

—The scar, how did you get the scar? she asked.

—I don't remember, Roisin replied. Are you done?

—Yes, said Echo, and slipped out her hand. She put the tips of her fingers to her nose and inhaled. Her eyes were still closed when she said, I know exactly what you need. Tomorrow we'll go to a health store and start the treatments.

She moved, pulling her shadow away with her and Roisin watched as she dived back into the water and swam a few laps rapidly. At one point she lifted her head and gasped a smile at Roisin, which suggested secrecy. But it caused Roisin to cover the scar on her face with her hand, as if it were a deformity.

x

Seoul-Soul-Sole-Solo
On a Sunday in June of 1950 the North Korean Communist artillery crossed the 38th parallel into South Korea. The United Nations was given the power to restore peace, and Truman ordered the United States to give air and sea support to a Korean government headed by Syngman Rhee.

Three months later General MacArthur put seventy thousand U.S. troops—the X Corps, plus the First and Fifth U.S. Marines Divisions—ashore at Inchon, just west of Seoul. North Koreans retreated beyond the 38th parallel to their "privileged sanctuary." On October 24 MacArthur ordered Generals Almond and Walker "to drive forward with all speed and full utilization of their forces." They made their way across the Yalu River, and these forces were devastated by more than half a million Chinese Communist troops hiding in the countryside. It was the worst American military disaster in this century.

General Ridgway, army chief of staff under Eisenhower, insisted that the calamity in Korea proved that we should stay out of Indochina. The Chinese revolution had, after all, produced a liberated Afro-Asian community. (Third World: from tiers monde in French, referred to those nations who gained independence after World War II.) Chou Enlai and Nehru drafted and endorsed the Panch Sheela, a five-point plan pledging their own and other Third World countries to nonaggression in each other's affairs. To think of Asia as a country of the Western nations was no longer possible.

Between 1955 and 1965 the Chinese Communists made great progress in that part of the world (though the bodies of severed heads of both

Chinese and Communist people clogged the rivers of Indochina). More than once Eisenhower pulled the United States troops back from the brink of war in Asia, warning the country of the danger of the military-industrial complex as he did so. He also propounded the domino theory, which would lead Dulles and Nixon to assume obligations to the nationalist leader of South Vietnam, Diem, and thereby lead the United States into a land war in Asia, the very error MacArthur would warn against. Americans remained stationed in South Korea for decades after the war there was over. "Westward the star of empire takes its way," said John Quincy Adams in 1801.

One serviceman—a survivor at the Yalu River—out on a night on the town in Seoul, got drunk at a bar with an eighteen-year-old girl named In Jae who had been kicked out of her own home. She had recently tried to drown herself by putting her head into a fish tank in a hotel lobby but soon turned to prostitution instead. She was tiny in her bones, brown-skinned, with a strong small chin and a set of prominent white teeth. She was clever and proficient at languages, learning to speak English as soon as she needed it. She wanted to get to America.

The soldier, like someone who has swum out of his depth, was lonely and desperate. Because she was both of these, too, but at home in the streets of Seoul, he felt strong and safe when he was beside her. He claimed her. He married her. He renamed her Rose. He got her pregnant and brought her home to Boston. Then he was ashamed of her (not of himself) and didn't want her anymore and told everyone he only married her in order to get her the hell out of Korea. The marriage was annulled by the Church, though the baby—Roisin—was baptized and raised Catholic.

The story of this serviceman and this woman was enacted again and again and again, with slight variations, in the years following World War II when the balance of powers was re-forming itself in astonishing ways. It was almost as if these small personal events were atomic particles attached to a system so powerful it was indivisible from each of its parts, and these events involved no natural choice or will by the participants. Indeed, this same serviceman would say, simply, "It happened," and accept no praise or blame for the union of two that produced a third, a child.

x

Later in the day Kosta and Roisin picked up the boy, Liam, and Kosta's mother who lived with them. She attended a Greek Orthodox church in a town several miles from theirs. Ma she was called, a scrawny woman with straight white hair and brown eyes and the hunched posture of many chain-smokers. She had a Bronx accent and an intense manner. Her husband had been shot in a cross-fire between two drug dealers on his way to the store one evening when Kosta was twelve. She went on teaching elementary school as she had for years, then retired and moved to Boston to live with Kosta when he settled down with Roisin. Now she dangled her cigarette out the window while they sped by some orchards.
—Stop the car, said Roisin.
—What for?
—I've got to look at those oranges close up.
Kosta pulled the van over and she jumped out; they watched Roisin go down the rows of orange trees, with her face up, like one transfixed. At one point she dropped down on her knees to look at the bright globes of fruit, nested in green leaves, pressed on the blue sky. Her family said nothing. Often she made everything stop while she examined wild geraniums, mariposa, or a line of tall palm trees. Sprays of color and shape that never seemed to shake, fail, or fall the way they did in the East got her full attention. She jumped up and down, she made the sign of the cross, she laughed. In the distance the still mountains rested like long, laborly human hands. She came back to the car, head bent, somber as if beauty depressed her.

Ma was talking to Liam where they sat together on the back seat, holding hands. He was twelve with reddish-brown hair and freckles. When she asked him, Did you have a good time, he shrugged.

—That's all? she cried like one who loves a good story.

—No. It was great, said the boy.

—Great. What does that mean? What did you do? Eat?

—We watched a couple of movies. Played ball.

—In this heat you played ball?

—Well, when it was dark we did. They had lights outside. They're rich.

—Like us! shouted Kosta with a laugh.

—And don't forget it, Ma whispered at Liam. Because it won't last long.

—I know, murmured the boy.

—What were the parents like?

—The father is in business, the mother does real estate, I think, but she wasn't there much. They're Mexican.

—Do they speak Spanish at home?

—No, they're like third-generation American, he said with authority.

—Then they're not Mexican, Roisin called back. They're American.

—How many kids? asked Ma.

—Just one.

—Is the father nice? Handsome? Mean? Ugly?

—Come on, Ma, I don't know. Handsome, I guess, and nice. He does something with cameras at his work.

—Sounds promising, said Kosta.

—You might want to meet him, Liam told him.

—I'm glad you've got a friend, but I am fine as I am. This trip is about work, for me, said Kosta. The women groaned to show their disapproval of his attitude; he smiled at the sound.

Kosta was a man who wanted to be good. Like a boy troubled by the inconsistent judgments of adults, he was never quite certain which way to measure the standards for himself. It was only in his work, alone, that he was sure. He began filming when he was fifteen. His mother bought a home movie camera for herself and gave it to him, as she did with most of her purchases. At first his aspirations as a filmmaker were stereotypical, involving visions of Hollywood and exotic locations. He started by making very simple documentaries on a super-8 camera. This was how he ended up, too, in a sense. He said he never "wanted to be famous, only to be good." His mother, with smoke billowing ahead of her and a cough, wished he wanted more.

His films—each one lasting no more than thirty minutes—were delicate and luminous. He could spend three years, and did, on a twenty-minute film. In general he went around everywhere with his camera, and when asked he explained his aesthetic like this:

"There's an object, and its shadow—its twin. Each is equal, as each visual frame is equal to the next. I aim for the elimination of excess and get it by balancing light, color, and dimension in such a way that the action appears both imprisoned and freed by its surroundings. Each scene is framed in exact proportion to the next—short sequences with a dark area between, a blink of an eye. They are mosaics. I have learned a great deal from my Greek heritage. To me my work is religious, like the making of icons."

When he came to California he was stunned by the quality of light there, so much softer than that in the East; and he heard symphonies in ordinary sounds. He was learning to record those sounds—drips, splashes, rustles, engines—and to give each one a place in his harmonic system.

"Do you think he's a failure?" his mother wondered.
Roisin shouted, No.
Jobs bored him. He only wanted to watch or make films. Sometimes he drove a cab, sometimes he coached basketball, sometimes he worked for a friend who was a gardener with a truck full of rakes, hoes, and bags of lime. That was in Boston, where he had two women to take care of him, Roisin and his mother.

When he wanted an audience for his films, he'd have a private screening—very private—in the gym of the school where his mother taught.

He would invite his cabdriver friends, a couple of gardeners, a sax player,
a cop he liked, a young priest named Tom who Roisin liked, and some
of her women friends who usually just came to check out the guys. This
made an audience of twenty and the same audience almost every time.
A few people realized how fine the films were (the gardeners, the sax
player, a nurse, and the priest), but most of them were bewildered by
the lack of a conventional structure and a conventional vision of beauty.

When people asked Roisin why Kosta didn't try to get a bigger audience
and more recognition, she would say, It would ruin his work. It's his ability to work without praise and attention that gives the films their force.
  "But doesn't he drive you insane? I mean, he just lets you go to work
while he tinkers in a dark room," they would continue.
—This is how I like it. Believe me, she replied with conviction. I love
what I do. And besides, he does the cooking and the housework and
picks Liam up from school. Liam—and his films—are my priorities.
The van approached the house slowly, and Ma said, "Welcome to the
mortuary," because she disliked the house and California and didn't
want them to forget it. Kosta pressed the door-opening device from sev-
eral yards away, and the garage yawned open.
—If you want to go back to Boston, you can, he said to his mother.
—I'll wait till you've run through all the money here.
—Maybe I won't. Maybe I'll figure out how to invest it.
—No way, said Liam. I don't want to live here forever.
—You want to get back to that dark little hole, the snow, the rain, and
the ruins of Boston? Really?
—Yes, said the boy. It's home.
—Come on, let's go in. I'm taking you to the track today, so go put on
your gear.

The garage door slid back down again, and they stumbled through the
dark to the back door. No mention was made of Echo inside the house.
And she was nowhere to be seen when they entered. Roisin didn't call
her name but went from room to room, looking. Kosta slipped down

to the basement to make sure none of his equipment was missing, and then when it wasn't, he explained to Ma their encounter at the bus stop.

—She just looked burned out, lost, so we brought her back. Don't worry, he said, she'll be gone as soon as she's rested.

—You look guilty, his mother replied. I know that expression.

They were standing in the downstairs hall, and Echo's voice emerged from the bathroom there. "If you want me to leave, I will!" she called, and then she emerged in Roisin's dress, with her hair pulled back in a ponytail and her feet still bare. She placed her hand on Ma's arm, smiled benignly, and said, "You can just drop me back at the bus stop where you found me."

—No, no, stay awhile, said Kosta.

—We've got a guest room, Liam added, his eyes admiring.

—I know, she told him. I already took a nap there.

—Liam, get your BMX gear and let's go, said Kosta.

Ma found Roisin upstairs in her room. What do you think of Echo? Roisin asked.

—I'm not sure. She looks like two things at once, said Ma.

—What do you mean?

—She looks God crazy on the one hand and sex crazy on the other.

—Ma . . . what do you mean? Roisin repeated.

—Like one of those Hindu boxes with figures copulating on the outside and inside there are holy writings. That kind. I've met them before. They're always skinny.

—Oh, come on. She's harmless, desperate, I feel sorry for her.

—Mark my words. No one can be both harmless and desperate.

—I've marked them.

Roisin went to the kitchen, the only bright room downstairs; the others were gloomily shaded by long heavy curtains that folded down to a thick dark red carpet. The owners of the house were spending six months in a foreign country, leaving everything—including liquor in a small glassy bar—behind. The kitchen was sunny with a window facing the distant hills. Tall flowers and short fruit trees stood motionless in the haze.

Echo joined her, and the two of them began to construct sandwiches from cold cuts, cheeses, greens. Echo's hands were trembling, and Roisin made her sit down and eat before the others. She wolfed down her food in silence while Ma stared at her. The stare was questing rather than judging. Outside, bees, butterflies, a hummingbird, bobbed in space and light. Roisin gazed abstractly through the glass at them until the images were reflected on the surfaces of her eyes.

—You better take Echo to the mall, Ma said, and buy her some shoes. It's open on Sunday.

—Is there a health store there, too? Echo asked.

—There's a health store frequented mostly by alcoholics looking for vitamin B. That's California for you.

Echo did not smile but focused on the appearance of Kosta in the door. He was buckling his belt and moving with a swagger particular to men who like to enter a room full of women. He clapped his hands together and rubbed them and smiled enthusiastically at the faces turned toward him.

—Here's your sandwich, his mother told him.

—And there's a beer on ice, if you want it, said Roisin.

—Do you want my chair? asked Echo.

—No, no, I'm fine, he said, and ate at the counter.

—You and Liam will be late for the race, Roisin said.

—It's okay, relax.

—Are you going to film him? She asked.

—I'll give it a shot, so to speak.

—You're really a filmmaker? asked Echo in awe.

—I am.

—But nobody's ever heard of him, said Ma. It's a miracle, he's a magician, he produces work and no one sees it.

—I'm sure they will someday, Echo assured her.

—All my film is going to rot anyway, said Kosta, because I have no way to preserve it.

—Poetic justice, his mother commented.

—They're teasing you and each other, Roisin explained to Echo. Echo studied Kosta's face as he chewed quickly and greedily, gulping down beer between bites.

—I hope you're teasing, she said, because such pessimism is terrible.

—It's not pessimism, it's realism, said the old woman. The film will rot.

—Don't be so serious, Kosta told Echo. Don't you know how to smile?

—No. It isn't funny.

—Well then? Kosta wondered.

—I just think we should constantly look for cures to suffering and never give in to negative feelings, be they physical or mental.

Kosta groaned. He disliked optimism and apocalyptic talk; he hated it more when he was in one of his periods of religious fervor than when he was, as he was today, skeptical. The greater his faith, the greater his mistrust of the faith of others. Now he gulped down his milk and sandwich, and only when Echo wasn't looking at him did he steal a look at her. Roisin did, too. Echo ate her sandwich, even when it was with greed, with refinement. The way her hands moved, and her jaw, suggested some power and pride. And when she was finished eating, she didn't pick or look for more but, with a kind of pristine finality, wiped her lips. Kosta saw Roisin watching him watching Echo and winked.

—Think Echo would look good in film? he asked.

—Gorgeous, a knockout, she has class, said Ma.

—Class my ass, said Roisin. I hate that word, Ma.

—What kind of film did you have in mind? the old woman asked.

—One of mine.

—What a great idea.

—Can you stay a few days, Echo?

—Sure!

—What's this film about? asked Roisin.

—When has anything I ever did been "about" something?

—Excuse me. You know what I mean.

—It's about what it always is about. Time, motion. Color, color, color.

—Is it okay with you, Roisin, if I stay? asked Echo.

—Fine. I won't be here much anyway.

Raisin walked into the hall and halfway up the stairs, listening. Some-

times she heard a baby's voice; it was half creak and half cry; it was nothing. But she moved slowly, her head cocked. When Liam came out of
his room, in his biking uniform, she held up her arms and walked against
him. He hugged her, then passed on down. Raisin went into her room
and shut the door; she lay face down on the rug and talked to God.

At midnight Kosta, Roisin, and Echo sat on the patio by the pool with
glasses of wine. They had watched two movies on the large-screened television inside by the bar, and Kosta was answering questions from Echo.

—I'm not interested in beauty, he was telling her. The surface of a thing
is not necessarily beautiful. It just is. Beauty, embellishment, decoration, they bore me as much as memories do. Or dreams.

—I don't understand that, she protested. To me beauty is the solace we
are offered by our Creator.

—Can you define it?

She hesitated, then said, No, not really. But I know it when I see it.
That pool, the blue lights moving inside it, you, the flowers, and the
ocean . . . It's just obvious when it's there.

—Me? He laughed.

—Yes, because you're full of life. Happy.

—I am?

—He is?

—Yes. I can tell he's basically good-spirited.

—And what about Roisin? Kosta asked.

—No, not so much. She's somewhere else most of the time. Not in the
moment.

—True, said Kosta, still grinning.

—How long have you been married?

—We've been together just about twelve years, said Roisin.

—God, that's great. Your son is lucky to have both parents.

—Well, said Kosta, he doesn't, exactly speaking.

—What do you mean?

—I'm not his biological father.

—No? Who is?

—His biological father, said Roisin.

—But who's that?

—He lives miles away, she said, and plunged into the water, breaking apart the still surface and sending lights flying.

—She doesn't like to talk about it? Echo asked Kosta.

—It's an old story. Not very important. I've raised Liam as if he is my own son.

—That's very good and generous of you.

Echo eyed Kosta through the shadows and sipped at her wine or rested the glass on her thigh. He was smiling pleasantly, having covered his thick waist with a towel. A silver and turquoise crucifix glittered through the hairs on his chest. One foot prodded the other one at the end of the chaise longue where he half lay. Echo queried him about the problems of being a step-parent, and he shared them with her, though they were minor. Then, when Roisin climbed out of the pool, Echo met her, like a champion from a ring, with a towel she threw across the smaller woman's shoulders. Roisin, grateful, rubbed herself dry and sat on Kosta's lap. Smog veiled a cluster of stars.

—Where did you get the name Roisin? asked Echo.

—My father liked it from a song he heard. My mother, who was Korean—they met over there—couldn't pronounce it. Apparently she called me Low Thing.

—You look Mexican, Echo observed.

—That's because of the mix.

—Where are your parents now?

—My father's in Boston. My mother disappeared years ago.

—Tell us about you, said Kosta.

—It's boring. Some other time. Okay? Echo quivered a smile at him and stretched her muscles. Beside her chair was the pair of white sneakers Roisin bought for her at the mall. She had also purchased herbs for her pregnancy plan. Now she wore a wide-eyed stare, benevolent with wine. Roisin felt Kosta under her damp suit, he was growing hard. The hair on his legs prickled hers when she moved. His stomach, hairless, rose and fell against her side. Their eyes met, and his wide mouth turned down

at the corners, his teeth shone between, and he parted his lips wide and
ran his tongue across his upper lip, now gazing by Roisin at Echo again.
—Want your wine? Roisin asked him. She leaned over him and reached
to get his glass from the ground, then sank back onto him.
—Sorry, he whispered, but maybe you should move?
She got up and threw her towel over his lap, then sat on the hard ground
between their two chairs.
—I think I'm tired, she said, and I'm signed up to work tomorrow.
She was staring at the surface of the pool where a bug was making waves.
Water still dripped from the spigot in the ivy, where the sprinkler ran
each evening after sunset. Echo, who had been still, moved restlessly on
her chair and then jumped up, sighing.
—I'm beat, too, she said. Thanks again for everything.
Kosta muttered a response, then threw the towel off his knees. While he
turned off the lights and locked the doors, Roisin padded up the stairs to
their room. She was full of wondering—if Kosta and Echo were in love,
and she was only in the way, if they had sent signals one to the other, if
she was only waiting now to make her move and he was waiting, too. She
wondered if they had a plan around the film he would make of her and
if he already had stopped loving her, Roisin, because she was sallow and
stocky. As she hung up her bathing suit in the bathroom, she asked herself
how she could have let Echo into the house: a stranger, perhaps dangerous. Listening for him to come down the hall, she wondered if he would
stop at the door of the guest room, with Echo there looking out, and if
they would exchange a look of tension and promise. The heavy carpeting
hid all footfalls. She stood at the bedroom door, trying to hear if he paused
or spoke to her, but there was no sound. She climbed into a nightgown
and into bed, and the covers met her chin as he entered. He was serious
and soft, a towel loosely wrapped around his naked hips like a skirt.
—What's wrong? he asked her.
—Nothing.
—Well. Here I am.
He switched off the light, and she welcomed him into the sheets. He
kissed her cheek and rolled away, yawning, "Too much wine."

The following morning Echo made a paste out of the powdered herbs and vitamins she had bought in the mall. She made it in the kitchen beside Roisin while everyone else still slept. It was seven, and Roisin had an hour before she had to wake Liam for school and go to work. Echo only wore a sheet wrapped around her breasts and buttocks.

—You need clothes, Roisin told her. I'll have to lend you more.

—I have a little money, don't worry, and one dress is plenty.

—Where did you get the money?

—Picking fruit east of San Diego.

—And you saved?

—Well, people have been good to me. I've been fed by strangers like you.

—Tell me.

—Things just happen. I wait at a bus stop or sit in a park, and people come over. Or they let me know where to find other people who will take me in—it's like an underground railroad, for one.

—It's amazing to hear such a thing.

—Yes. The world, when you let yourself be at its mercy, offers quite a lot. It's like being a bird, an animal.

—But it can be cruel, too, yeah? Roisin asked.

—Well, yes. I had to ward off a few predatory men. But I don't let myself dwell on the down side of things.

—I know. Have you ever been married?

—Never, no, never will.

Echo's fingers squeezed and ground the paste rapidly and efficiently. They worked without her attention. She looked out the window at the gathering smog as she worked and talked.

—Why not?

—Oh that's for another time . . . Go put this stuff up you and then lie down somewhere—by the pool, whatever—while it gets absorbed.

—Then what?

—Nothing.

—Don't I have to run upstairs and seduce Kosta?

—Not yet. In three days, after nine treatments, you will.

—Are you sure it's safe?

Famous Questions

—Absolutely.

Roisin took the cup of mocha-colored paste and did what she was told, then lay by the pool, covered by her towel. Around her was the click of eucalyptus leaves, the hum of insects. A dragonfly zapped over the water like a helicopter. There was a smog alert already. No asthmatics or emphysema victims should step outside. Roisin breathed deeply, testing the air, and her eyes stung more than her lungs. Echo sat on a chair nearby.

—Please tell me more about you, Roisin said.

—A life with nothing to tell.

—Do you at least have a boyfriend somewhere?

—No.

—A girlfriend, maybe?

—No.

—How have you avoided it?

—On purpose.

—I guess so.

—I like to keep my life quiet and solitary in order to do my work.

—Where are you heading now, specifically? asked Roisin.

—There are some people near Seattle I know. They have a workshop in healing I want to attend and perhaps give some classes myself.

—Religious people?

—No, not in the sense you mean. You go to mass.

—That's true, sometimes, said Roisin.

—Well, I—we—are creating an alternative system. We hate laws. Dogma.

—I can understand that. How long do I need to lie here?

—Another few minutes. You don't want it to all slip out.

—Don't you get lonely?

—No. I'm in love. With the world. How can I get lonely when I'm in the natural world, my mother?

—But nature doesn't like people. It runs away from us.

—I'm hoping to change that, said Echo, and reached out to kiss a leaf.

—That's quite a task.

—Someone might as well try.

—Saint Francis did, if that's what you mean. Do you want to be a saint?

—Oh, no! I just want to work on myself, to feel good.

—What do you think of Kosta?

—He's tenderhearted, deep, said Echo quickly.

—Wait till you see his films. They're very good.

—Too bad no one ever sees them.

—I don't know, said Roisin. Things that grow in the light don't last as long as hidden things. Babies, say. I mean, darkness is where the heart is and where action is. Where works develop in their own time. I believe this.

—Your husband has a darkness to him, said Echo. But his work should be brought to light and shared with others.

Then she sank down beside Roisin, and her shadow crossed over that closed face. Her warmth, the whisper of her breath, and she lifted the edge of the towel and felt between Roisin's legs, making her jump.

—Does it feel absorbed now? Echo asked.

—Just about.

—Don't swim for a while.

—No, I'll go get ready for work.

Echo stood up and jumped into the water, naked. Roisin sat up and scanned all the windows and doors for male faces, her expression appalled. For a second she watched Echo plow up and down the water, still cold from the night, and she started to call, to request that she put on some clothes. But then she didn't and went inside instead. Ma and the smell of coffee awaited her in the kitchen.

—Echo's swimming, said Roisin. Naked.

—What a princess she is.

—What do you mean?

—I bet she has a trust fund. I know her type. They're all the same. They drift around, talking about freedom, but really they are well off and ambitious. What do you bet she was into drugs, will sleep with anything in pants, and is too proud to be part of any institution that she, herself, did not create? What do you want to bet?

—Ma, that's so bitchy. She's just a sort of an aging flower child.

—Go upstairs and get ready for work.

Roisin did as she was told but paused on the stairs to watch Echo, naked, wet, stretching her limbs by the pool's edge.

x

Roisin, a social worker for many years, was volunteering at a clinic where babies and young children awaited foster parents or their own parents to come and get them. They were there because of a profound flaw in their childhood home—weapons lying around, or drugs, or foul diapers and garbage, or they had been physically abused. Roisin had to pass through security and three doors before she was admitted to a nursery where kind women cleaned, fed and played with the children. She was happy there, sitting in a little closed pen where the toddlers wandered around with blocks and balls. But she felt at the same time that her own defenses were being eroded, her heart was losing strength, that she would scream and tear down the walls if she thought too hard on the fates of the children. She admired and wanted to emulate the calm solicitude of the regular paid workers there. She was trying to learn from them and sang while she was teaching the children to play patty-cake and composing their case histories.

x

The days following Echo's arrival Roisin arrived home after six. Kosta, Ma, and Echo took care of Liam and all the shopping and housework, and for that time Roisin was not essential in her own home. Echo had stirred things up by the novelty of her presence, and an enthusiastic response kept everyone busy. She did all kinds of exotic cooking and took Liam horseback riding three times that week. Ma went along with them and sat in the van reading Solzhenitsyn. She revised her opinions on Echo, and though she still called her the Princess, she did so with some affection and right to Echo's face. Kosta took frame after frame of Echo's body parts as they performed routine motions. He was "after something new," he told Roisin, "to do with motion and surface." He rented videos of old films, and at night they all watched them.

Echo gave him two hours of her time daily. She was, they soon learned, very practical. Under her serene and serious exterior, there was a wizard that took note of all incoming and outgoing money and time. She knew the workings of Wall Street as if she had played the market, and she did not balk at capitalist ventures that involved usury. Meditation, she said, helped her to keep her life under control. "I could be a financial whiz, I just know it, as a result of good kundalini." When Roisin asked her why she didn't just go into business, Echo replied, "I am trying to hear the clang of the universe. It's all I desire at this stage in my life."

—What do you mean "clang"? asked Liam.

—Well, it's like breaking the sound barrier with your spirit. You go out very far and enter this area where hearing and sounding are the same. And you experience an enormous clang.

—Neat!

—Try it sometime, she told him.

—I don't see how it can be connected with making money, said Roisin.

—The more distance you get, through an expanded consciousness, on the workings of the world, the better you can predict and control them, was Echo's reply.

—But why would you want to make a lot of money, then?

—Why not?

—I mean, wouldn't such an experience liberate you from those desires?

—Not at all. They aren't desires anymore. They're something else. They're just pleasures, like toys. Having money and success is a pleasure. This is what God wants for us.

—How do you know?

—When you are God-realized, you know these things.

—Are you? asked Roisin with a frown.

—No, but I've talked to people who are, and that's what they say.

They were eating a vegetarian meal prepared by Echo, who was eating hungrily.

—How do you stay so thin? Ma asked her. And eat so much?

—I exercise two hours a day without fail.

—That explains it.

Famous Questions

—Two hours is a lot of time! cried Roisin.

—It keeps me sane.

—So that's what you do locked up in your room, said Kosta. She just smiled faintly in response.

That night in the dark of their room, Roisin said she didn't believe in God after talking to Echo. "Give me an atheist any day," she continued. "Don't you have the same reaction?"

Kosta murmured, "Not really. She's on a genuine quest. You've got to respect that. It doesn't affect my feelings at all."

—Aren't you annoyed by how she acts like she knows what God wants?

—She really doesn't bring it up with me.

—Smart of her, Roisin muttered.

—I thought you liked her, he remarked.

—Why do you think that?

—The two of you keep sneaking off together.

Roisin smiled in the dark and rolled across him. He had his hands clamped together behind his head, and he lay, impassive, with his eyes closed. She moved his legs and elbows around, but they just snapped back, listlessly, into place. She poked and pulled, at him and felt his mouth to see if he was smiling. He wasn't.

—I'm tired, he said.

—Well? I feel like a ghost in this house.

—Lots of times you've been tired, too. Lots and lots of times.

—True.

—So don't worry about it. Go to sleep.

—Only if you promise tomorrow. Mañana.

—Okay. I promise.

—Early, to bed, though. Remember.

The next night, Friday, after drinking lots of wine with one of Echo's best dinners—a chicken and peanut stew—Kosta took her down to his dark-room to show her some clips from the films he had developed that day. They descended, carrying their glasses, he in his usual spotless khaki pants and white T-shirt and she in short shorts and a pink see-through blouse.

225

—Where did she get the money to buy those clothes? Roisin asked Ma.

—Kosta gave her some.

—He did? How much?

—I don't know. She needed them. What the hell.

—I don't understand her. She just told me she didn't need anything more than she already had. I guess Kosta persuaded her she did.

They were washing the dishes and cleaning the counters and stove top, while Liam sat at the table reading a comic. Roisin, whose skin was an Asian gold splashed with pink, had a wine flush on her cheeks and neck. She was pouting and gritting her teeth at the same time. She threw things around, and Ma finally whacked her with the damp dishtowel.

—Hey! What's your problem? the older woman asked.

—I don't like her.

—Then ask her to leave. You're jealous, right?

—Of what?

—Of her and Kosta. She's seeing him as a genius and a hero, and you aren't, and you know that's dangerous.

—So what should I do? Kick her out. I don't care.

—I do. Don't, said Liam, still focused on his comic.

—Why not? his mother asked him.

—Because she's really nice. Kosta would never do anything anyway.

—Right, said Ma. He wouldn't. He's too passive. You know that.

—I just wish he would let me get pregnant, said Roisin with a heated glance at each person.

—He can't afford a baby. He'd never support you. Be realistic.

—Great, said Roisin.

Ma never kissed anyone hello or good-bye. She stayed tied up with herself, her arms often clutched tight against her thin chest, a sweater cast over her shoulders, the only arms she would accept. Smoking was another way of keeping people at a distance; she shrouded herself in fumes. Now her cigarette got wet on the edge of the counter, and she lit another, her long fingers trembling. Roisin watched her inhale as if she enjoyed the sight of the old woman holding the smoke in way deep and watching it trail from her nostrils, as if she envied her.

Ma said, "I wanted more children, too. I worked like a dog, I was a terrific teacher, but I still always felt I failed in some way. Was it because I didn't have more children? Or was it because of my bad character? I'll never know."

—You and I should have a child together, said Roisin unsmiling.

—We could adopt one when we get back to Boston.

—Yeah, but he wouldn't help support it.

—But if it wasn't a baby, we could do it together.

—That's a thought.

—Come on, Mom, said Liam. I've got to go.

—Okay, okay. But keep an eye on those two, Ma.

—Don't worry. Kosta is not the unfaithful kind.

Roisin and Liam went into the garage, then, and she drove him to his friend's house for the night.

x

When Roisin returned, Ma had already gone to bed. She circled the downstairs rooms, then slipped down the basement stairs and stood outside the dark room door with a debased expression, eavesdropping. Straining to hear what their low murmurs signified, she wore the look of one who wants to control the conditions of her own humiliation. She squeezed her hands together and hunched her shoulders and leaned to the side.

—There's so much more that I need still in the way of equipment, Kosta was saying.

—Well, can't you afford it now?

—Not really. It would be a luxury.

—What is it you need?

—A better sound system, for synchronizing, see, and even a new camera.

—So get them. It should be your top priority.

—The editing is definitely the exciting part of it all. But not when your equipment is crappy.

—I have a feeling that you're not trying hard enough.

—That may be true.

—Why not?

—It takes too much time—hustling, for money.

—You need a benefactor, she told him.

—Yeah, we all do.

—I love those shots of my feet walking by the wall.

—You have beautiful feet-bones.

—I thought you didn't care about beauty, she teased.

—You got me there.

—Does that make you a hypocrite or what?

—I hope not.

There was laughter and a long silence while Roisin drew in a deep breath and turned to the stairs. As she padded up, the voices resumed behind her, and she stopped, listening again, now with the same expression she wore when she heard the baby crying. She seemed to be wondering if the sound was an invention of her own or had an external reality, and she really didn't know.

When Kosta and Echo came upstairs a little later, their conversation preceded them into the kitchen, where Roisin was sitting alone. They were still talking about film, now about surface.

—Film is ultimately an exercise in disappointment, he was saying. The surface is bound to offer no clues to anything inside. Surface is only evidence of an intention which we can never know.

—That's really interesting, said Echo.

—I keep thinking the surface is going to tell me its secret, but it never happens.

—I never even thought about film that way, she said with awe.

—I doubt if he did either, said Roisin.

—Hey! Kosta protested, pouring them each new wine.

—Roisin and your mother love to be hard on you, Echo said.

—Shouldn't we go to bed? asked Roisin.

—I'm not really tired yet, he replied.

—I must say, I'm beat, after riding and stuff. Look at this. Echo lifted the edge of her shorts at her crotch to reveal a redness from the saddle she sat in that day. Then she said, "Pain. I'm going to hit the hay. It's Saturday tomorrow and I've almost been here a whole week. Am I overstaying my welcome? Please tell me."

—No, not at all, said Kosta.

She expressed her gratitude and tugged down the back of her shorts as she turned to go upstairs. The creases under her buttocks were exposed to both Kosta and Roisin, who whistled after she was gone. "You've got her all wrong," Kosta said. "I think she feels good about herself, yes, but she has no seductive ideas. None."

—Don't you think she's sexy?

—I haven't thought about it, he said. She seems completely chaste to me.

Roisin grimaced, since "chaste" was Kosta's highest term of praise for a woman. Next came "modest" and after that "hardworking."

Her body, which had been primed for pregnancy for a few days now, sank onto a chair. She lit and puffed on one of Ma's cigarette butts, made a loud sound of disgust, and spat the juice and taste into an ashtray.

—I'm going to bed, she said, and jumped to her feet.

He didn't seem to be aware of any of her moves or statements but gazed at his reflection on the night window. A three-quarter profile and a slight smile gave him the image he most admired after moving his head this way and that. By the time he was settled with that image, Roisin had gone upstairs.

x

She watched a helicopter buzz low to the world. Close by, closer than she liked, were military and naval bases. Sometimes on the freeway a convoy of military vehicles drove down the right lane. There were long stretches of forbidden territories, with high wire fences and "Top Security" signs. Inside there were barracks and machinery like the type seen in industrial parks, bug-shaped equipment and rows of cars that had been allowed into the area. If she averted her face, she saw an orchard, a hill, a pelican, a seal.

"When I was learning about photosynthesis, this little girlfriend and I decided that humans were created to feed flowers with their shit and bones. We went to Catholic school and we came to the conclusion that God wanted the garden and people to squat in it. We thought that was really funny. Hysterical," she laughed out.

Echo was massaging Roisin in the early morning; it had come about without conversation or effort. The sprinklers were whirling rainbows around the flower beds, and striped petals—runways for bees—cut colors against the cardboard-brown background. Roisin squinted at them and sighed as Echo's hands kneaded at her back.

"When will you ever tell me about yourself?" Roisin asked. Echo leaned her face down.

—Hm? What?

Roisin repeated the question lazily.

—You sound like you don't trust me—just as I am, said Echo.

—It would just be good to know something about you, that's all, like were you ever in love, what your parents were like, etcetera.

Echo inhaled deeply and sighed out the air, her hands pausing over Roisin's shoulders. Sometime we can talk, she said, when both you and Kosta have time. I don't want to overstay my welcome, that's the main thing.

—Kosta wants you to stay—for the film.

—I know, but still, there's you, too. Any progress with pregnancy?

—He's been sort of cold. Nothing, said Roisin.

—That's surprising. He seems like a hot-blooded sort of man. He's always asking me about my love life, as if I have one! Does he think a woman can't live without a man?

—Probably. I don't know.

—Well, I think the treatments will lose their impact if you don't act soon. I'm not kidding. What's he doing now?

—He's asleep.

—Maybe you should go up now and see if you can get him going. I mean, you're more relaxed than usual. Okay?

—Okay, but somehow you got out of talking about yourself.

—I really like being taken at face value best, Roisin.

—Without a history?

—Correct . . . Now go on upstairs. Quick. I have a feeling this is the right moment.

She sat back and Roisin stood up, creaking at the knees, stretched, and entered the house. Echo was smiling after her from her knees, her hair red in the early sun. She looked like a garden statue of a nymph, triumphantly posed beside a fountain. Roisin went up the stairs, two at a time, and found Kosta half-dressed in the bathroom.

—Oh, no! she cried. Don't go so soon. Can't we be together?

—But we have to drive Ma to church, he said.

—Not for an hour, please?

He smiled and placed his hands on her face. "What's got into you?"

—I just got the order from Echo.

—Ah. Well. In that case.

He drew down the straps of her bathing suit and led her to the bed, his expression growing serious. The flush of sunshine on the sheets had warmed them, and from where she lay, pressed down by him, and inside his arms, she could see out the window the top of a palm tree. It was the very symbol of "vacation." She heard Echo swimming as his ten fingers pressed against her spine, and she closed her eyes from the luxury of the scene. Kosta moved very quickly, spoke in her ear, then twisted back and away, as his hand dropped down on her navel, and she followed him over, asking him to remember their home in Boston . . . the smells of street life, of restaurants, the lumps in the mattress, braking and shouting outside. She kissed his chest and stomach with the expression of one who has swallowed something sweet. He came back over her again and again was quick, but quiet. He seemed to be transferring his power to her when he dropped aside for the second time and she leaped up in a rush.

—You forgot to ask if I was safe!

x

That afternoon Roisin drove alone to pick up Liam at his friend's house. She was talking to St. Clare the whole way over, asking her to make sure that she was pregnant since she felt sure she was. Her face raced from one expression to the next, the way a baby's does, concluding with a morose look and a sigh, "Forgive me."

The van wound up a serpentine hill to a nearly flat house made of glass. Spiky plants grew around it. The pool was as abstract and opaque as jelly. The father of Liam's friend was weeding the garden when she drove up along the curb. He stood up and presented himself—Ray Vargas, a golden-brown man with smooth Mexican features.

—You must be Liam's mother. We really like that boy, all of us.

—Hi, yes, good.

—Come on in, sweetheart. I like to get my hands dirty, he explained, and rinsed them off under an outdoor tap, then wiped them dry on his jeans. I figure, he continued, if I forget how to pull up weeds, I might as well admit I've forgotten how to live.

He was good-natured with the creases and crinkles of dollar bills—soft and extinguishable. The way he carried his affluence was easy with an underlying grasp on earthiness. It was as if he was struggling not to be weakened by wealth and wanted to be sure he lost nothing when he gained everything. Roisin, a sucker for anyone who called her by an endearment, followed him inside, where the light spilled over blond wood and white upholstery. He had said, "Come on in, sweetheart."

Inside he called the boys, and Roisin heard the distant zing! of video games and saw through a half-open door a picture of John F. Kennedy. Under it was a photo of Robert Kennedy. She stared at them like one who is spotting land after months at sea.

—Liam! she called with eyes watery with recollections of Camelot.

—Want some coffee, tea? Ray asked her.

—Tea would be great.

—You're new around here, right?

—That's right.

—Tell me how you got here while I put on the brew. Sit down. Make yourself comfortable. I'll give the boys fifteen minutes. How's that, sweetheart?

—Fine, good. She sat waiting, and when she heard the murmur of Liam's voice in another room, she relaxed and brushed the small tear from her inner eyelid—the Kennedy tear—and beamed at her returning host.

—Liam says you do something with cameras.

—Oh, I'm marketing some of these new video camcorders.

—What are they?

—They're great little toys. I hear your husband makes films. I'd like to meet him. We're always looking for talent.

He then explained in some detail about synchronicity of sound and image and about its logical connection to the video revolution and how much more efficient it was, economically and aesthetically, than an 8-mm camera. As he spoke he emulated virility and well-being, seated on a chair that looked like a curled-up sheep. Steam rose from his cup around his lips and teeth.

—There's big money in this camera, he said. Your husband really should take a look at one."

—So you're a businessman?

—Sort of. Into investment and marketing. I'm a jack-of-all-trades.

—Are you a Kennedy Democrat?

—That's right. I'm a sheep among wolves out here.

He curled deeper into the white wool. She told him she was a social worker in her real life and she did some political work on the side. But, she said politely, I don't know if you are at all interested in politics.

—Not as much as I used to be back home. It's not my state, see, California, and I find it hard to get involved. I can't figure out the people, she said.

—I know what you mean.

—Moving kills the voting instinct. That's why we have such a low voter turnout in this country. It's too much a transient population.

—True.

—It's great to hear that little Boston twang, it sure does make me think of the old days. I was really into politics in the sixties, but I've been out here too long. My wife loves it, but I have to go to New Mexico every few weeks or so.

The picture-glass window showed the same panorama Roisin saw in her house, except browner and emptier. She could imagine cowboys cantering between the frames, dust rising, guns flashing. It seemed that they had reached the end of their communication because she called Liam sharply. Ray went off to stir him up while she stared heatedly at the landscape.

—Here's your boy, he said. We'll all have to get together some time, a cook-out.

She agreed, and they all said abrupt good-byes. For a while Roisin cruised around the neighborhood wondering how many more Democrats might be hidden behind the shrubs and palms. Her expression was tense.

—I was surprised, she told Liam, to find out that Mr. Vargas is a Democrat. They're so rich.

—So are we, according to you.

—Ours is an accident and will be over soon. He worked for his.

—He's not a bad guy, Mom, said Liam, though I know you think he is because of his style. He's really generous and fun. He took us out to miniature golf and to dinner and the movies. He always does stuff like that. And he always insists that I should eat a lot, have dessert and popcorn.

—That is nice. Just as nice as Kosta.

—Different. Kosta is always thinking about something else. When we're at the track, he's reading the paper . . . Is Echo at home?

—Yup. Why?

—She's nice.

—You think so? Look at that house. Yuck.

They paused in front of a colonial mansion with white columns and a white fountain and a white wrought-iron gate locked for security. You had to buzz at the outside gate to be admitted. An American flag hung in the center of the front lawn, as if to advertise the owner's victory over the world at large.

—What's so nice about Echo? asked Roisin, driving on.

—She pays attention. I can't explain it.

—Hm. I guess I understand.

—Jealous?

—Of course.

—Don't worry, Mom. You're my favorite. She's a little weird, anyway.

Roisin eyed his soft profile, the slope of his nose, cheek, and chin, and his green eyes under long lashes. He was staring out the window with a thoughtful expression. Then he began to turn the dial on the radio until he stopped at some Irish music. "She Moves Through the Fair" was being sung by traditional singers.

—Do you know this song? he asked his mother.

—Yeah. It's old, everybody knows it.

—Tell me, just a little, about him.

—Who him?

—My father, come on, you know what I mean.

—I've told you everything.

—No, you haven't. Please?

—Why? It's not as if he matters to us.

—Please?

—I'll buy you a Whopper if you drop the subject.

—Mom, come on.

—What would you do if I had a baby?

—You're always asking me that. Nothing ever happens. Why don't you adopt one? Paul Vargas is adopted.

—He is?

—He told me last night.

—Is that so?

—Yeah, they can't have kids for some reason.

—Were you talking about your father, too, to Paul?

—A little.

—What did you say?

—Nothing. Just that he's Irish and I never knew him.

—Can't we leave it at that?

—Please, Mom.

She turned the car out onto the freeway and raced forward, silent, while the boy curled into himself.

—Paul says he plans to find out who his real parents were, he said.
—That's sort of mean to the people who raised him. They're his real
parents, the rest is just biology.
—Just?
—Shh.

Roisin scanned the gleaming hoods and fenders ahead. Brilliant as
foil, they all seemed to be scanning and searching, too. "God, we
might as well be flying in the winds of Genesis," she said to him. "I
mean, I wonder if the whole world was set on its course then, and we
are just tearing forward in a directed path, as a result. I mean, I really
wonder. That would mean that we have no choice, but just a destination. And then what about our mistakes? Would there be such a thing?
I think everybody wants freedom more than anything. I don't know
how to tell you about your father or anything else. That's the problem. I just remember you—and the feeling of holding you away from
eternity, which seems to be closing down all the time, like an eyelid.
I always held you close, or lots of times, as if I could protect you from
that—big yawn!"

—Come on, Mom, don't give me a lecture. All I want is a few facts.
—I can't talk about it, Liam, it's not that I don't want to.
—Why not?
—I don't know why. It's like a dream. If I talk about it, it becomes some-
thing other, something deformed. Once again the boy curled into himself,
this time raising the volume on the radio around Irish music to a blast.
—Please, Mom, he whined again. Why not?
—I can only tell you a few things about Myles. You know most of them
already. The guitar. The poetry. He got sick and went home. What else
do you want to know?

A couple of nights before, she had dreamed she was with Myles at the
end of a dark road. It dropped into a cliff, yet she still sensed she had
a choice to make, whether to go forward or return. The subject of the

dream was fear. And the cliff was a hideous organ, carved into an earth which was its cathedral. Pipes of many colors climbed the side of the rocks, and as she stood there, wondering, they turned into body parts, internal veins and bones, and she felt that the human body was the cathedral then with no one making music inside. She turned to look at Myles and saw Liam.

—I mean, do I look like him? the boy asked.

—Actually you do, the older you get. He had your hair color, your teeth and hands and ears. Your eyes are a mix of his and mine, and of course we all know you have my mouth.

—Was he nice?

—Not particularly. He had charm. A queer sense of humor because he was bitter, like a teenager. He couldn't get over how mean the world is. Sometimes his bitterness got the better of his humor, and he was a little reckless. But he was the type to help people in trouble. Of course Kosta does that, too.

—So I'm sort of like him?

—Sort of, but you're much better. Not bitter. And you've obviously inherited his musical gift.

—If I met him, would he recognize me?

—Good question, she replied.

—Okay. So now tell me please? You always tell me the most when we're driving.

—Some of his friends were purists, some were commercial, but Myles was called by them all "the Pure Boy of the Western World."

—I don't get it, Liam murmured. What did they mean?

—Just that he was very sensitive to corruption.

She turned on the engine and started to move at a snail's pace up the road toward their house. Now she looked depressed, her lips downturned at the edges and her eyes watery. Liam stared out the side window, expressionless, as they cruised toward the driveway and in.

—I really want to hear the rest, he said.

—Well, come on upstairs. We'll visit Ma and then talk some more.

—You promise?

—I swear. If not today—soon. Before I die.

Back inside the house Roisin did not inquire about the filming sessions between Echo and Kosta.

Ma did. "What's going on down there? What do you think they're up to? They go off together for hours at a time . . . I wouldn't stand for it, if I were you. Why don't you say something?"

—I don't know, Roisin replied with her hands raised.

—You're acting like you want something to happen.

—That would be insane.

—People who are not insane are imperfect.

—Come on, Ma, I think it's innocent. Besides, it makes him so happy. I haven't seen him like this for ages. He came out here for something just like this. It's great. Let him enjoy it! He's free! I'm not his keeper! Neither are you.

—I still say the problem is with you. You are acting like you don't care.

x

Roisin told herself she was pregnant. As a result she walked around in a restless and disoriented state or lay on her back in her room as soon as she came home from work. She stared into the blue shadows with a fixity that suggested that the room was her inner life and her body an object within it. One evening Echo entered the room wearing Liam's terry-cloth robe; she sat on the end of Roisin's bed, where papers were scattered from work that day.

—Can I talk to you for a minute, Roisin?

—About?

—Kosta wants me to stay longer.

—And?

—I thought it might bother you.

—In what sense?

—You might not like me staying any longer. You might not like me spending so much time with him.

—Why not?

—Honestly, Roisin, if you weren't so . . . well, outspoken, I wouldn't talk this way. But you never mince your words.

—What's the problem?

—I just want you to know, you have nothing to worry about. I'm a virgin.

—Are you sure? asked Roisin.

—What a question.

—Well, you could be very naïve, though I doubt it. Why are you? That's really great.

—Are you making fun of me?

—No. I swear, I think it's great. After all, you're not married yet.

—That's not why.

—Then why not?

—Because of reasons. I mean, I'll tell you sometime. But I just wanted you to know.

Now they both stared into the blue shadows, Roisin flat on her back and Echo poised on a seat of papers.

—What's the Holy Spirit? asked Echo.

—It's the spirit—you could say, atmosphere—Jesus left behind. It attaches us to heaven, it goes from here to there, it's everywhere. I think it's the same as time.

—Kosta mentioned it, but I didn't dare ask him what it meant. I'd sound so stupid!

—See, Jesus said, I am the Way. And that means that there's a path from earth to heaven, which also means we are already part of heaven.

—Explain that?

—I can't do any better than that.

—Do you feel sick?

—But don't tell Kosta. I think I am. Pregnant.

—Why not tell him? Echo cried out: It's so exciting!

—I'm not sure. I want to wait.

—You must be happy. You ought to at least tell Ma.

Echo looked down at Roisin's face in a swarm of questions. They gathered around her eyes and lips and tangled in her reddish hair. "You're sure you don't mind if I stay?"

—Go on, said Roisin.

—Won't you ever say something about what you're feeling? What do you want?

—Everyone's happiness, Roisin answered.

—Everyone else's but yours, Echo suggested.

—No!

—Well, I think we agree on more than you think we do. We are, after all, both women, and that means something. The world will have to be saved by women, don't you agree? Men have made a mess of it.

—I think the issue is probably power rather than sex. The ability to live without notoriety, inside a community. If everyone could learn to do that, it wouldn't matter who they were.

—I don't know about that. Sounds communist, idealist. I think everyone has a right to some power, I really do, especially over their own bodies. When the new age comes, people will understand that their bodies are like cars, driven by their consciousness, and then they will begin to take care of themselves, and to be detached. But even then each person will want to feel important.

—Probably. Do you feel the poor deserve their fate?

—They earned it, I think, in an earlier life, Echo said.

—This is where we disagree. But does it matter? You seem to be harmless and even kind, so why should I fight about ideas with you? I don't want to. I know a lot of people are very cynical, and the reason they fear and oppress others is because they really believe that weak people are just like themselves, but bad at it. So they don't want to help them. I doubt if you're like that.

—How did you and Kosta invent such an egalitarian relationship? Echo asked.

—Ha! Roisin let out a laugh and ran to her desk drawer and pulled out a paper. See this? We wrote up a manifesto!

—Let me see.

Roisin handed her the ragged piece of paper, tea-stained in one spot, and ripped in another. It read:

WE AGREE to sustain the strengths of female history, which include anonymity, community, nurturance, subversion, and resistance.

WE REFUSE to join in any war games, to participate in those systems that injure children and other dependents.

WE WILL RESIST institutions that encourage hunger, thirst, oppression, imprisonment, slavery, mental illness, military weapons, excess speed, and fame.

WE DECLARE our ideology to be called REALISM because we want to see the world as it is, free of illusion. (But where ideology is a substitute for action, we dissent.)

PRACTICAL TECHNIQUES for resistance will include equal household and professional labor for both (or all) parties involved. Garden, cook, clean, feed others, nap and dream, do work that brings no reward, work for ones you love, not for those you fear, make love, go to the theater, movies, ballet, clubs, listen to music, play with children, and participate in any community action that supports and sustains those activities for all.

Echo murmured: I don't believe you wrote this up.
—It's pathetic but we did. I took it very seriously for a long time.
—And Kosta?
—He did, too, in the beginning. But little by little it ended up with me and Ma taking it to heart, as if we were married to each other.
—Oh, well. I mean, men. You know.
—Do you have many women friends, Echo?
—Not really. I tend to get along better with men, Echo said. Do you?
—Yes, I've left them all behind, though, in Boston. I miss them.
—Well, at least you've got Kosta.
—Yes.
—And I really hope we can become good, close friends.

—You and I? I don't see why not, said Roisin, returning the manifesto to the drawer. She turned as Echo was rising and papers sliding.
—That makes me so happy, Echo called with her child-smile. I feel the world is good.

x

In the following days a high-class prostitute with connections to the president was bludgeoned into oblivion by a homosexual transient. A fearful terrorist threw a baby out of a high window and Ma came home from a trip to town with Echo and told her family she had cancer in her lungs and pancreas.

"Don't give me any lectures about smoking," she screeched at Kosta. "It's too late and I don't give a damn. I'm not going to the hospital. I'm not going to have chemotherapy. I'm going to do it the way they do it in the old country. I'm going to go on drinking my tea and smoking my cigarettes, and that's that."

She stared at them expectantly, her hair wild and windy, with her prominent bones and blazing brown eyes thrust forward. Kosta put his head in his hands and sobbed, and Roisin stared out the window at the smog drugging the open air.

"Let's go for a drive," Ma said, and knocked the back of Kosta's head with her hand. "Come on. Straighten up. Everyone dies. No big deal. When will Liam be home, an hour? I'm never happy without him. Let's pick him up at school, go out of the city, and find a gorgeous place to eat tonight, okay?"

—Okay, Ma, said Kosta, who could hardly stand up. He made his way to the basement, wiping his eyes on his sleeve.

Roisin and Ma stood together over the sink, staring out the window.

—Sometimes, Ma said, I can suddenly taste the Bread of God on my tongue. Right out of the blue. This is one of those times.

—Want to call a priest?

—No. I think tragedy always brings the divine into the head. I wonder why. Not that this is tragedy. Much worse I should be bludgeoned by a mad man. Right? I mean, think of it. One candidate is corrupt, and so

242

is the other one. Nuclear power plants. Up there in the sky, there are satellites we can't see. Under the ground they're testing atomic bombs. Right at this moment boys and girls are being tortured just south of the border, and here we stand. It's a horrible situation, being alive, or maybe it's just a place to visit. I hate the word God. It sounds like a bearded leftover from Mount Olympus, or a big aging clown. Fog. Paper. I hate it. I know my God, and that's not Its name. Don't bring Echo with us on this drive. It's just family, okay?

Roisin sat on the backseat of the van holding Liam's knee while music poured up from the component behind them. Outside there were miles and miles of gleaming shields on the freeway heading north at rush hour. It was slow until they turned west toward the coast. No one was talking. As they curved between the brown hills, a smell of jasmine swam through the open car windows. It was dusk and a golden hour over the water. "Think—in the East the leaves are beginning to dry up and turn yellow," said Ma.

Kosta's hands were squeezed tight on the steering wheel when they pulled into a space near the Laguna Hotel. His bones were whitening his skin. Once parked, he slumped a little as if someone had dropped a wrap across his shoulders. He helped his mother up the hotel stairs.

—What's wrong with Kosta? Liam asked.

—I'll tell you, said Roisin, and called to the others to go ahead. She and Liam walked slowly along the sidewalk, arms locked, heads bent, while she told him the news. He smiled for a flash, then shrugged, pulled away, and got mad at his mother. She put her hand on her forehead, seemed dizzy, and leaned on a parking meter. He stamped his foot and walked around a few times before returning to her side. Then they went after Kosta and Ma and found them on the balcony overlooking the sea. It was gold and green when they arrived and orange by the time they were leaving. Below them, some people surfed and swam. Along the coast the cliffs were spattered with flowers. Ma smoked and coughed and stared at it all without making any comments on waiters and other patrons, even though Roisin did, halfheartedly, trying to be funny. No one laughed.

Kosta gave her a dirty look and turned to his mother. "What's the situation with your medical coverage?" he asked.

—Echo helped me check all that today. I'm fine.

—No matter what, we'll take care of you.

—Don't worry. It won't be long.

—It was good of Echo to help you like that, said Kosta.

Like a colored shade, orange flooded his face: imitation consummation, at the mention of her name. Water covered the ridge of the fiery sun, and they all stood up to go. Roisin put her arm around Liam, who put his arm around Ma. She leaned out and hissed at Roisin: "Two evils have befallen us already—your job, my illness. A third is inevitable. I think it's lust."

x

Two days later, "Echo was making love to herself," Kosta told Roisin. "When I came into her room looking for some Scotch tape in the desk there. I just stood by the door, watching. I didn't really believe what I was seeing. Her right hand was cupped over her—you know, her left hand held a white—I guess, an object. Her fingers were buried there, and her knees were raised. Her breasts lay flat. They're very small. Her eyes were shut, her mouth open like a sleeper. When I moved to the end of the bed—don't ask me why I did—I saw the . . . her—hidden lips, and I put my hand on her knees. To stop her. From hurting herself? I don't know. From moving? From living? I'm sorry. She stopped, obviously surprised. She . . . I . . . we—looked. She dropped apart her legs. I lay down there. On her. It was all sudden—unplanned. I was fully clothed. It meant nothing?"

He told Roisin this story in order to explain the condition of his briefs, stuffed in the hamper, which she discovered beside the washer. He was shaking when he told her. The hour was nearly noon, and the sun was spread kindly across his back and shoulders. They were alone in their room. She was also shaking.

"The whole experience was over almost before it happened. Maybe it never did happen. I wasn't even there. I don't know about her, she's mysterious. She's trying, you know, to cordon off, in herself, an area of chastity, of goodness, from the world. It's pathetic. Touching she wants to fight history like that, alone, with her sex. It's a kind of hidden resistance. I mean, she's never been penetrated by a man! Yet she obviously has sexual feelings. Right?"

By now Roisin was lying on her back on the thick shag rug, in order to prevent her knees from buckling under her spastic gestures. A spider's web swung from the chandelier overhead. He sat on the end of the bed, his bare feet near her back. He pushed at her with one of them.

"It didn't mean anything, Roisin. Isn't that what counts? I left immediately."

"Should I—will, I will, will I—tell her to leave?" asked Roisin.

"No!"

"You want to do it again?"

"Of course not."

"Then what?"

"I'm not finished with the film."

She jumped up and slammed him across the chest, neck, ear, and cheek. Then she left the house with the car keys and the car, Liam calling after her, "Buy me some Life Savers at the store, Ma?" And she took off in the blast of a Saturday sun.

She was a danger on the road as she watched her own private X-rated video. Across her eyes played the film of their pornographic encounter. While the hole in the ozone layer over Antarctica widened, she saw fountains of semen shoot out of a vibrator. White flesh was stuck to brown, red hair was caught in red lips, and belts and zippers and buckles functioned as weapons. The room: blond tones, a soporific pullout bed, a toilet shaped and colored like a valentine. Each was a confirmation of the miracle of color: where what sifts down from the sun, lifts up from each curve on earth. Green light, orange, blue: here the humans responded to light, too, like underwater fronds, weeds, fish so inert they lay still until pulled by a force they couldn't perceive and so the lowest forms of life lie prone until disturbed

She talked aloud:

"This automatism proves that history is where the wicked profit. No will, no hope. Primatology compares apes to humans. There are feminist apes; they are training the little apes how to forage while the fathers are smoking hookahs rolled in a banana leaf. All creatures are marching toward extinction with joy, thinking it's a game as the cruel pursue them through the liana and meadows and city streets. White fields of flowering potatoes hum with bees, and as one part drops, the other part lifts. How do I transport my consciousness from one place to another when it's everywhere already? Am I just moving my body through it?

"Children go out into the day and take their place's there, dots on a chain, and all their body parts are under and inside the eye of the heavens, but unprotected. How can I love what will take the children away? Loneliness belongs to the Creator, who takes it back to Itself, having parceled it out, I don't know why. On those roads leading out of Los Angeles there were dry mountains and a facility for criminal offenders who are young. The body was sent forth, alone, with its allotted portion, and as it grew older all it asked for was a little cold wine under the setting sun and a good sleep. All pain is lodged in the fact that the body is a machine.

"I call down heaven over and over until its loneliness merges with mine. Hell is rising with the shapes of insects; it's all mechanism and technology. It likes d—th. It is insane and loves no one. It lives for itself like labia and prick. It is response and disturbance. It lacks interpretation. It tortures the machines by knowing them. Once I saw blue water in winter under a flashy sun. Patches of white snow floated on this water, it was in the city, and I stopped the car and put my feet in. It was an irresistible attraction. It was not a decision. A decision is only a recognition of the inevitable.

"You mustn't run after the thing that despises you and turns away. If you love a man who doesn't love you, never see him again. If you love a woman who won't marry, give up and walk away, she will never marry, or if she does, it will be a mistake. If you love a fool, know it's a fool whom you love. What is meant to happen is immediately recognizable and will not turn away from you. This is why giving false hope is a sin. Giving someone reason to believe when there is none is a sin. Say no; that's your freedom. "If I was pregnant, the clarity of it is now ruined. These are my questions: Can you marry twice, if one husband is still alive? Isn't the concept of a second marriage like an equation that can't be proved? Isn't it like saying you can be in two places at the same time?"

X

It was pitch dark when Roisin climbed into bed beside Kosta. He was still, but she was still moving, her physical self driving across the desert and back. Her pulse raced, and her mouth was dry.

She thought she was alone when Kosta suddenly spoke, saying, "I'm sure it happened because of what Ma told us. The shock. Besides, you never should have brought Echo home here. I can't live in a harem."
"You're trying to blame it on me and your mother?" whispered Roisin. She lifted her fist and smashed it down on him, without noting where it landed, but she felt his nose crack; he gasped, and she leaped up and turned on the light. Blood, black as ink, suffused his mouth around his nose and teeth. He had his eyes covered with his arms. Then he rolled away off the bed and went toward the bathroom, holding his face, blood pouring between his fingers. She looked for a weapon to kill herself with and ran after him into the bathroom with her arms outstretched.
"Just shut up and go get some ice," he said.
She ran through the house, touching her nose and teeth, into the kitchen, where she tied ice up in a towel and carried it back to him. Now he was on the bed with his head back, his eyes shut. He put out his hand and took the pack and held it on his face.
"We better go to the hospital," she said.
"Forget it. It's broken. There's nothing they can do."
—Aspirin?

—And cognac.

She got him what he wanted, quickly, and water and climbed under the blankets beside him. It was four in the morning, and a bird sang too soon out in the dark.

"Don't ever do that again," he said. "Or I might do worse to you." His eyes were bleary over the ice pack, rolled to the side to look at Roisin. She cried and pulled at her skin, but he pulled her hands down and told her to stop. He looked at her for a long time with an expression of pity.

x

Echo ministered to him, believing their story: They were just out for a drive, they said, when they had a small car accident. Ma said, "If it was Roisin's nose that was broken, I wouldn't believe a word of it. But since it's a male nose, I'll buy it. Why isn't the van damaged?"

—Because we didn't really hit anything, said Kosta. She just put on the brakes too hard. That's all.

Echo dashed around, getting him new ice packs and cups of tea while he reclined like a sultan by the pool. His eyes were growing swollen and blue by midafternoon. Roisin would not look at him but followed Echo's every move with the eyes of an enemy. When Echo stood at the end of his chair and asked him what he would like for lunch, Roisin snorted rudely. In the kitchen she asked Echo when she thought the film would be finished.

—I don't know. He says soon, but with his nose—

—Oh, he'll be back at work tomorrow, Roisin assured her. What will you do then, when it's time to go?

—Head north, the way I was always going.

—With your virginity intact?

—What do you mean by that? Of course.

—What does it mean to you?

—A choice. That's all.

—And what set it off?

—A trauma. I mean, a serious trauma.

—What kind?

—When you don't hate me, I'll tell you.

Echo played over the stove, where she was fixing a grilled cheese sandwich for Kosta; her back was turned to Roisin.

—Do you still think you're pregnant?

—No.

—Well, you may be wrong

—I'll have one of those sandwiches, too, said Roisin, and left.

She went out to the pool and lay across Kosta. "I can still feel the crack of your nose in my hand," she said. "Forgive me!" He said he already had. "Then why won't you touch me? You're in love with her?" He didn't respond.

—I wish I could wear the water, he said instead.

—You can, can't you? Swim.

—I don't have the energy, feel like shit.

—Oh, God. I'm like a man now.

—A lot of it has to do with Ma, you know, it really does.

—I'm sure, but I don't want to talk about it, Roisin said.

—It? Which it?

—The worst one. The one that can't be reversed.

Everywhere Ma went now, so did the shovel, the skeleton, the stone, and the worm, since she announced her cancer. Grim images seemed to follow her on her rounds from room to room, cleaning. They might have been sewed into her dress, though she didn't mention the cancer again or the pain. Only once, when Kosta said she should go lie down, she said, "I'll be lying down long enough soon."

Kosta looked at his nails, which were cleaner than Roisin's. He was a man who took two showers a day and never a bath because he couldn't imagine steeping in his own dirt. He was clipped and immaculate and displeased by the spread of his waist in recent years. He had been lean throughout his youth with the long-boned face and long-lidded eyes of a Goya. He looked sensitive and haunted and like one who has just entered the last day of his life. Thick now, with a mustache and yellowing teeth, he was still fussy about his appearance and worried about growing old. His attachment to his mother was his primary one.

—Remember the first words you ever said to me, Roisin announced quietly.

—What were they?

—Who's taking who for a walk?

—Oh, yeah, you and the dog were tearing along.

—And you were leaning against a pole, waiting for the bus on Third Avenue. I sped by with the dog, the baby, and the carriage. And I ignored you, she said.

—Wasn't that the day you sold the guitar?

—Right. I had money and was planning to get the hell out of New York.

—You passed me again later, and I called out, "Where's the dog?" and you ignored me again.

—I had just heard a child in the laundry place saying to his mother, I want a pet ghost, and was cracking up—in both senses.

—God. You looked wild.

—I never told you this. That night I telephoned my father. I can't go on, I told him. His television blared, then reduced its volume, and the darkness in my ears cleared, and I could see into the cavern of his mouth, into the source of his speech, where his true image stood erect like a survivor of a storm. My ear listened to that image and the waves. Where are you? he called. You got yourself a baby, right? That's right, asshole, I basically said. What's its name? he wanted to know. I told him William, and he asked what happened to the father. I told him he had gone back to Ireland, and the bastard said, "I knew he would. From day one." I could see him in miniature form inside my head, a man-shaped voice with a lopsided face. I swallowed violently, almost choking, and bammed down the phone. That was the night I almost killed me. But then there was the baby, and the dog.

—Was it the next day you fell and we met?

—Right. Splat on the pavement. And there you were, lifting me and the baby up, dragging us in the door. My knee was bleeding, I was so sore! But you and the baby were laughing as if everything was right with the world. You were so nice to me. Why? Was it my scar? Did you feel sorry for me?

Echo's shadow came over Kosta's knees then, and Roisin raised herself up to look at her.
—How did you two get together anyway? she asked, and the point of her pink tongue moistened her lower lip.

"He was doing penance in those days," said Roisin. "Mothering came easily to him anyway, since he was his mother's darling. Besides, he was in love with a boy, Nando, a drug addict, who had small hopes but the compensation of tremendous desires. You probably never meet people like this. But there are lots of them. He wanted to please. Kosta was always attracted to people both lost and passive. He always has been. Nando was a major involvement of his—the last before me. We both hid away together, where he could pity me in peace and learn to forget Nando."
—Well, anyway, here's your sandwich, Echo said in a cheerful voice. I hope you like it.
Kosta called to Roisin as she went inside: Thanks for telling everyone my life story.
—Everyone? wondered Echo.

While Kosta and Echo were swimming in the pool, Roisin snuck down into his darkroom and looked through the porthole window at them. She had no interest in the images on those strips of film dangling off little wires around her. Her head was pounding and her eyes throbbed. The blue water before her rippled in ribbons. And then their legs, white and lighted, danced into her view, followed by their hands; they kicked at each other, must have been talking, heads like meat on glass plates from above, their hands grasped, and she pulled his down to inside her thighs, pressed him there, or else it was his will, he pulled away, swimming, his knees going up and down through drillions of bubbles, while Echo treaded water and her knees pointed down, then he circled and paused behind her, and she turned, her legs swiveling around. The brilliance of the little balls bouncing against the circle of her view made what Roisin saw look happy. Echo arced back, doing a backward somersault, and her face, eyes open and mouth, swooped by, her hair floated down, his hands followed, hers, his, theirs.

Upstairs Ma answered Roisin's questions about angels: "In the sky there are transparent creatures, part of an invisible hierarchy belonging to the divine realms. These creatures," she continued, "run before and after living matter, outside of time. They are often jealous of the way the human being is compressed into solid measures and senses. But they have a job, also, to protect that very solidity. So you see, the distance between a human being and the Blessed One is vast, but thickly settled. Like between Boston and New York. Actual time is an expression of God's intimacy with us creatures. He is participating in our senses. That's what makes the angels jealous."

They both stared up at the sky through her bedroom window. It was thickened by smoke and fog from invisible sources.

In this room the light was lozenge orange. The double bed was covered by a quilt with a jungle design, and there Roisin curled. Ma was under one sheet, one leg dangling off the side of the bed. She was smoking in the dark, and the spark on the tip of her cigarette rose and fell rhythmically, while her lungs crackled inside. Splashes and voices came from the pool.

—If the bed had wheels, Ma, I could tell you a story, a good one.

—You can only tell those stories when you're moving? asked Ma. I never noticed.

—Just about. Or at sunrise and sunset. Don't ask me why.

—Well, pretend the bed's a car and we're on a long highway. Or pretend it's five A.M.

—I can't. I know it's night and I'm here, said Roisin.

—Can you recite a poem, then? What's his name, Gerard Hopkins?

—I can, but I don't want to.

—You should've been an actress, but you don't have the temperament . . .

Why did you go away that time a few years back? Ma asked.
—What are you asking me for now?
—I always wondered.
—I went to Ireland. Why?
—A search for roots? That's not like you.
—No. I went to look for Liam's father.
—Is that so. Were you mad at Kosta or something? Ma wondered.
—No, I just felt lost, I guess.
—You still do, don't you. Secular to the core.
—No. Or.
—Did you find him?
—Don't tell Liam, Roisin said.
—I won't. But this is what happens when there's a child. You're tied to the person for life. That's why I wish to God you'd have a baby with Kosta. But anyway, tell me. I won't say a word to anyone.
—Kosta knows it all.
—Do you still love him?
—Of course.
—So that's all that matters. You don't need to say more.
—Why did you like me, Roisin asked Kosta, in the first place? Was it only because I was lying flat on my face in the street?
—No. When you stood up, I liked your mean look and your scar.
—What a contrast to Echo! she called from flat on her back on their floor. You're madly in love with her, aren't you?
—I don't know what I am.
—Then tell her to go.
—I can't. Not yet. I've got to see it through.
—What through?
—Whatever it is. I've got to.
—Great. How am I supposed to feel?
—Mad. At me. I know!
—I want to hit you again.
—What can I say? Better you should feel mad at me than just sad and broken, the way you did after Myles. But please don't hit me again.

—If I marry you? Will that help? she asked.
—What for, marry? We aren't going to have children.
—How do you know?
—I don't want any. We've been through this.

He wore an expression of misery so honest, she couldn't continue her anger. Instead she watched his attention turn toward Echo as a weather vane turns on the roof of a barn. There was no volition behind this form of attention; he didn't even seem to enjoy it.

"I remember," she told him, "what it was like to be in love. I do remember, and I feel sorry for your sick self, you shit head. I hate you and hope you get squashed by a Mack truck after getting VD from her, the kind that blinds you for life so you can't make any more films. Bastard. I really hate you more than anything on the face of this earth. You pig. I've got a secret from you. Ha ha ha ha."

x

That night, driving to pick up Liam from the Vargas house, she watched how the evening was cushioned, not yet black, in the hills. Palm trees like paintbrushes in murky water dotted the hills. Her sighs were nearly sobs. Ahead of her on the freeway she seemed to see speechless wraiths, but they were angels, jealous of the baby inside of her. They couldn't, she thought, ever bear the compactness of flesh and juiciness of mortality, but they believed they could, they thought it was a privilege, and they flew this way and that, speechless, mute.

The glassy house was well lit, but only one car was parked inside the open garage. Roisin rang the bell and listened to crickets in the dusty bushes from the retreat of her car. She didn't want anyone to see the red-eyed face she wore that night.
But he came out—Hi there!—Ray, in bare feet, white pants, no shirt, grinning, and leaned in the open window. Don't you want to come inside?
—No, thanks. Not tonight. I'm in kind of a hurry.

—There's a slight problem.

—No, what?

—The boys aren't back yet. She's gone to get them. They went to the movies. So come on in, have a drink.

—Don't mind my face. I'm tired.

—Your face?

He stopped his grin as she plunged into the open air beside him; he examined her features as a physician might do.

—I don't see anything wrong; was his comment.

—Good.

—Sure. What'll you have to drink?

Inside she saw his half-full glass on a table. She told him she would have whatever he was having, and he asked her if she liked Bob Dylan. She told him of course, yes, Dylan seemed to sing for her. Ray sat beside her on the white love seat while she gulped at her drink. Dylan began singing.

—So Liam is your only child? he inquired.

—I hear you have only one, too, she said, nodding.

—Yes, unfortunately. I wish I had four or five.

—I hear you're a good father—that's what I'm told.

—And I hear you're an idealist.

—From Liam? I hoped I was a realist, she said.

—Realists don't quit easily.

—What do they do—compromise?

—Stick with the goal.

Dylan's voice began to give Roisin a melancholy run around her youth at folk festivals until she was swallowed by her own nostalgia. The drink was tickling the cells in her brain as she tried, instead, to focus on Ray, big and sprawled beside her. It was a moment marked by its falsehood because neither one of them was aware of the other's true mood. Then Roisin made an effort to stay alert.

—How's the camera work? she asked.

—Great, but I still want to meet your husband.

—Come over, let's see when, next weekend?

—Sure. I doubt if the wife will be able to come, though.

—Why not? I've hardly laid eyes on her.

—She goes to Vegas lots, with her girlfriends. They play the tables, have fun. What a drag, he added, and Dylan's voice became an affectless background as Ray rambled and referred to his wife as pagan.

—Pagan? Roisin mused. I wonder what that really means.

—Well, let's consult the dictionary.

And off he went to the bookshelves while she tagged along, wanting to sustain her intoxication. They rocked side by side over the definition of pagan, in his red study.

—Polytheistic and hedonistic, he quoted. See? That's her all over.

—What about you? You pagan, too?

—You East Coast folks are too caught up in suffering, he said.

—You sound like our house guest!

—Who's that? he asked, and looked about a foot and a half down to her face.

—A girl named Echo, a woman.

—Echo? She must be some leftover flower child.

—Exactly.

—What does she say about you, your attitudes?

—Same as you. She believes in healing, happiness, and the body.

—You don't like her, do you, Ray said.

Roisin peered around the corner into the kitchen—an arctic circle if she ever saw one—wishing he would offer her a new drink.

—Why don't you like her? She's fine. My husband likes her.

—Uh-oh. No hanky panky, I hope. Is that why you look sad?

—No. I always do.

—And that scar. Did he do that to you?

—No, never, he didn't, I swear.

—Okay. Just checking. Can't stand child abuse, wife abuse, not even self-abuse. Can't stand any of it. If a man has to prove his masculinity with his fist, then something's missing with his dick, if you don't mind my language.

She blushed and he laughed, and now they stood staring out the picture window at the twinkling landscape. Stars above, lights below. The al-

cohol gave her sea-legs and a sense of passage, rocking. Ray poured her and himself another drink and they continued to stare outside.
—How did you get that scar? He asked and laid his thumb along it. She tilted towards him for support.

"One day—pushing the baby, with the dog tied to the carriage—I went on my day off to a pawn shop to sell my husband's guitar. It was a clear and sunny day, but the pigeons in Cooper Union and the derelicts had a blank quality that alarmed me. The world had no sound. Or it didn't reach me. I stopped, straining to listen, with my legs wobbly and unmuscled and the guitar heavy on my shoulder. The dog sat and scratched. My rosy-cheeked toddler Liam bounced. My mouth was parched. I felt I was in a desert watching mirages. And I heard only the voice of my mother, who once said, The world is too big. I squatted down and peered into the baby's face. But now I couldn't see what was in front of me. Instead I was flooded with the sight of my mother, leaning down to me, where I bounced joyfully with my pet dog on a floor. And her burnished face, Asian eyes and strong chin, were compressed to bursting. But it wasn't a floor I was on, it was wet cement, pavement. We had been walking for hours through the rain, she pushing me and the chain of the dog's leash banging like a flagpole rope by my ear. While I laughed from the cold, she rolled me onto the ground, spilled me out beside the dog, and took his chain and raised it up and struck it across my face. The dog leaped up. Barks, screams, I couldn't see. Now I sat on the ground, the guitar thumped and strummed inside the case, the baby cooed, and the dog licked my face. I put my hand on my cheek; it wasn't bleeding but soft and dry. The dog licked my face again, the baby cooed and kicked. Beside me was a length of chain-link fencing. It was where she left me, the chains between nowhere and cold to the touch."
—Who came to comfort you? asked Ray, as if the scene were being acted out in front of his eyes. Wasn't anyone there?
"That part I don't remember. Anyway, I never saw her again. She was on the lam—she bolted—hit the trail—removed herself—disappeared. But

the weird thing is, I can still love her. That's how I learned to love God.
Don't laugh. It was because I learned, early to love without any returns."

When she heard the crunch of tires on gravel, Roisin sobered and sprang
toward the door like a guilty guest.
—Here they are, he said, home-again-home-again-jiggety-jig.
—Good-bye, she told him. See you Saturday.
And she hurried out into the dark to catch Liam before he went in. The
wife—white as a carnation under kitchen lights—waved cheerfully at
her as the garage door slid down to the ground.

x

At home that night she sequestered herself in Liam's room, giving him
some help with his guitar. She taught him old tricks she remembered
from Myles, resurrected by the sound of Dylan singing, her drinks
and inspired by her anger at Kosta. She told the boy about his father's
lyric gifts and about the way he held the instrument lower on the body
than most people, and how he believed in a voice from the back of
the throat rather than from the lungs. He liked a plaintive tone, she
explained, one that was sort of raw and suited to wildness, to poverty.
He hated anything extra or fake. So the trick was to capture something
in yourself, in your own voice, which was free of pretensions . . . Liam
listened attentively and remarked, "He sounds sort of like Kosta. Kosta
hates fake stuff, too. Ma says that's why he's frustrated, it's impossible
to be that idealistic."
—I didn't know Kosta was so frustrated, said Roisin.
—Was I a cute baby? Liam asked.
—No. Hideous. No. I'm joking. No. You were beautiful.
—Did my father like me?
—He hardly ever saw you, that's the truth.
—Did he leave because of me?
—No. He left mentally, way before you were born, even, maybe, before
you were conceived. It had nothing to do with you.

Famous Questions

—Tell me, said Liam, still hunched like a question mark over his guitar and idly picking at the strings. When did you know he wanted to leave?

"Okay, so it was the winter I started taking classes for my master's degree in social work. We spent Christmas in Vermont at the house of a record producer and her young lover. There was a large group of us assembled in the yellow farmhouse set in the woods. Snow covered nearby meadows and trees, the rooftops of the house and barn, and the sky hung low and gray, delivering feathery drops which swept the windowpanes like ghosts of leaves. I went for long walks with the dog, venturing into the pine woods to listen to the swish of wind and needle and flake, and my own boots crunching on the varieties of ground. Sometimes it creaked, sometimes it sank soft as water or cracked like a board. Small paw prints dappled the surface, and birds chipped at snow-impacted berries. I wondered why we didn't live in the country and posed the question later to Myles. Our eyes watered, our cheeks were pink, and the steam from our lungs merged in the air between us. Our mittened hands were curled together. Well, maybe we will someday, he said. Why not now, soon? I questioned."

—I've got too much to do, Myles told me. They've asked me to go on tour, singing "Old Mother MacRee" and shit like that. There's lots of money in it.

—Who would go?

—The usual boys—Conor, McCool, you know. They're excited. They want to do it.

—I'm not surprised. Who'd play and who'd sing?

—We'd alternate.

—You want to?

—They say if I don't, that's it. They'll ask Paddy to go instead of me. I can't blame them.

—But what harm would it do you to go?

—I don't know. I'm tempted. With the money we could get a little flat of our own, at last, and you could finish school.

—That sounds good to me.

—Yes, but then it would mean singing revolting songs about the old sod to old sots on Saint Patrick's Day. Stirring up the boys in Boston over the IRA. I don't know if I can manage it.

—But that will mean the end, if you don't.

—Sounds like that, doesn't it?

—Are they all waiting for your decision?

—You could say so.

—It's just a job.

—Not really. I know it sounds stubborn and stupid, but I can't help it. I think of music and poetry as somehow sacred. I do, and that's the truth. I don't think anything else is sacred, but them I do.

—After the tour, you could go back to your real music, I suggested.

—I don't believe so. I believe I'm being destroyed.

These words were said with such conviction, I looked up at him and worried. His icy cheeks were streaked with water.

—I want to go home, he said.

—Getting cold?

—No, I mean real home. I mean Ireland.

—What?

—Just for a short trip.

—And leave me here? I whined.

—We can't afford us both.

—How long?

—Just two or three weeks. It will help me clear my head.

So we trudged back across our tracks in the field of snow as the sky reddened and blued for the fall of the winter day. Light from the house lay in yellow squares on the snow, and an evening wind spun across our feet, sending up showers, sparks. We didn't know it, but we were walking toward the conception of you—the love of my life—that night in the house, though we were children ourselves.

—Did he go to Ireland then? asked Liam.

—Not then, no.

—When?

—Later. Ma's calling. I've got to go.

She left the boy seated with the guitar across his knees, his eyes round, wondering.

On Saturday Ray Vargas came over alone and lounged in white linens on the patio chaise longue, while the dimpling water sent up lights to his smiling face. Echo darted around like a servant, passing hors d'oeuvres from person to person. She was dressed in a buttercup yellow dress that she had bought with money from Kosta. Avoiding his gaze, which trailed her like leaves drifting at an angle, she also avoided Roisin's. Ma was watching baseball with Liam, and the food was in the oven. The two men brought out instant competition in each other, until they were hollering about cameras and computers and equipment, neither one listening to the other. Kosta behaved as if he were covering up a crime he had committed that very afternoon. His bravado did not come naturally to him. Ray was more comfortable with it, and it was something like a threat when he offered Kosta the use of some of his new camera equipment.

—Okay, okay, Kosta agreed with his hands raised, but thanks, believe me, I'm happy with what I've got. I've made some amazing pictures with my humble camera. Right now I'm working on a series of scenes with Echo there—starring, so to speak. Even in dim light it's coming out just great.

—Well, just wait till you see my Betacam, Ray roared, and held up his empty glass to the hovering Echo. So you're the star of his flick?

—I guess you could say so.

—I hope I get to see some of it before the night's over.

—It's up to Kosta.

—And how about your wife, guy? You don't take shots of her?

—Roisin? No, I know her too well, said Kosta.

—I think I'd take a hell of a lot of pictures of her, said Ray. She's got a face full of mystery. What are you half of—Chinese? Japanese?

—Half Korean and half Irish, said Roisin.

—What a combo! I was in Korea.

—What for?

—Stationed. For two years right after Nam. Hated it.

—Why? Tell me, Roisin pleaded.

—It was dirty, they treated the women like slaves, and they were racist on top of it all. They beat up my best buddy, a black guy from Atlanta, wouldn't let him into clubs, stuff like that. The buildings are real pretty, though, some of them. Sometimes, even now, when I get into Chinatown, I get nauseous, I remember Seoul. I think I'm going to be served dog bones or rat meat. Seriously, that's what Korea means to me.

—That's more than it means to me, Roisin told him.

—However, I did meet a couple of great women. That's my experience. I love women. To me they are the truly superior gender. I mean, hell, they know how to love, how to treat things right. I wouldn't mind if they ran the world, not one bit. How about you, Kosta?

—Sure.

—So I can understand why you shoot pictures of Echo. But I wouldn't neglect your wife. With those eyes and that scar—wow!

Roisin stood up and followed Echo into the house. Both had blush-red faces. Echo leaned over to put the casserole into the oven to warm, and Roisin hovered behind her, seeming ready to push her in. Then, instead, she traveled upstairs to check on Ma and Liam. The smell of popcorn preceded her into the room, where they were positioned in front of the television, eating. Ma was in a rage that Mets were destroying the Red Sox—but her emotions seemed to empty rather than to fill her. She was blanketed against pillows on her bed. Liam, with his head back and mouth ajar for incoming handfuls of popcorn, wore the soft country look of his father. This look only emerged in certain angles, Roisin noted, and only when she happened to be seeking it out. Tears tickled her eyes as if from pepper, coke, or onion, and she left the room, fundamentally unnoticed.

Going directly into Echo's room, she surveyed her narrow cluster of clothes hanging in the closet and then opened the drawer in her bureau. Reckless but with the clarity of the sea wave when it's up and breaking, she leaned over the stack of panties (scented with lavender sachet) and saw there an object she had never seen in her life. (A rubber penis like a mummified relic of castration.) It scared her, and she slammed shut the drawer and ran back to her room, where Liam and Ma sat shouting at the television. Climbing into bed beside Ma, who had warmed an area near her body, Roisin succumbed to a devouring fatigue. Hideous images followed and found her in her sleep, including the one she had just witnessed in Echo's room.

It was Liam who gently woke her.

—Kosta is upset you're not downstairs, he said.

—Too much wine? Ma asked.

She swam up from dreams and hauled herself onto her feet, fitting together the parts of the household scene she was reentering. Somehow it seemed to her that Echo had impregnated her with that thing, that Ray was Liam's father, and Ma and Kosta were married. A line in the dream went, "Beware what you wish for, it might come true." Passing down the stairs, Roisin sorted out the parts of the dream that were false from those that were true. She found Echo alone in the kitchen.

—Where are the guys?

—Down in the basement. Looking at the film. I'm so excited!

—Any food left?

—I've kept a plate warm for you.

—Why are you so excited?

—Because I'm just sure Ray will love Kosta's work. And you know he has connection with film people? He was already talking about his company's need for someone to make short commercials—to sell the product.

—So they hit it off.

—They talked nonstop.

Roisin leaned on the counter, heavily. Echo stood back, reading the meaning of such a posture.

—You're too negative, Roisin, in your attitude, she said.

—It's a strange world we live in, Roisin replied. People declare themselves pure—even virginal in some way—and they are actually nothing of the sort. It's all artifice. I'm sure you don't like my attitude. But I don't like your assault on Kosta's art. And I feel sorry for him that he is getting seduced.

—Those are such sixtyish things to say, Roisin, I can't believe it. I mean words like "art," "corrupt," "pure"—no one uses them anymore. Wake up. This is not just the age of Aquarius—it is the age of technology. You can't keep him caged up in the basement like some wolf-child or something, while everybody else is progressing with the equipment. You just can't.

—You're the one who talks about your virginity, said Roisin, as if it were an artifact carried through generations of one family. Technology? I thought you were in favor of natural living and herbal massages, etcetera.

—I'm in favor of a blend. Between technology and nature. I love Kosta's work, and I think he's suffering from neglect. You think he's happy with being anonymous. I don't. I think he has a lot of bitterness stashed away about that. And some of it can be attributed to you—your attitude, which is so negative.

—I don't think you know very much about art, or about how it's made, or about how the world can intervene and ruin a thing.

—Here's some food. It might make you understand me better, Roisin, if I told you something about myself.

—I'm sure Kosta can tell me for you. You have told him everything about yourself, haven't you?

—No, I haven't, not by a long shot.

—Go on, if it's so important.

Echo sat down across from Roisin, both at the kitchen table with a jar of fresh-cut flowers between them and a bottle of wine. Echo wore an expression of unease, and her forehead creased, as did the corners of her lips. Her fingers continuously squeezed the petals of a rose while she spoke.

"My father was a banker, we grew up outside New York. He took the train to Wall Street every morning at seven and was home at seven every night. A little drunk already. My mother was a woman who volunteers. As my brother Frank used to say, she was never called, she volunteered. She was never required, or even needed, actually, made unnecessary by money. Piles of it. We had cleaning ladies and gardeners. My mother sat and stared out the window. At fourteen I left home, ran away, and bounced back, then ran away again. This was the late fifties, early sixties. It lasted through high school.

My brother Frank was a far bigger influence on me than either of my parents. He was three years older, very handsome, and good at everything—music, sports, academics. He was my idol, really, and he was likewise very involved with me. His best friend was a boy, or man, called Philo. Can you believe it? Philo came from Texas. Went to college with Frank. Philo was a huge guy with lots of hair. He was brilliant, with his slow Texas accent, and a wild quality to him? Philo was like me in those days—into dope, trying LSD, living on the fringes of things. He always went around in a big army jacket, even in the summer, and sometimes he slept in parks. He said he missed the wide-open spaces and the Chisholm Trail. That was a joke, of course, because he was embarrassed at being a kind of cowboy in an Ivy League school.

"Philo was the one who did the job on me, no matter what you want to call it, good or bad. See, I was hiding out in this commune in Vermont, it was Indian summer, and these people were really good I was living with. They were into self-subsistence. We farmed, we built our own shacks, we cut wood. I was sixteen and never been kissed? Believe it or not. With all that dope and stuff, I was as tight as a drum with my body. Frank was the love of my life, and he had told me I could do whatever I want, but not that. I always did what Frank said. Anyway, so there I was with this community of idealists, just like me, perfectly happy, and my father sends Philo, of all people, to come get me. Philo, the wild man. I guess he thought I would hear reason from a rebel like myself. Philo drives up in a white Triumph convertible and orders me to pack up my stuff and come home. He tells me Frank wants me back.

"I was worried, thinking something might have happened to my brother. But Philo wouldn't tell me what he meant, or why Frank wanted me back, and so I packed up my few belongings and did what he said.

Driving away with him, I had a feeling of importance, you know? Philo wheeled around these back country roads, through meadows and woods, and I was begging him to tell me why he had come to get me. He started talking about his theory of shapes. That's what he called it. As far as I can remember, he said that shapes were the equivalent of emotions, they were emotions. He pointed at mountains, trees, the pink edge of my blanket sticking up, at the cuff of my jeans, and said, See? That shape is an emotion. That one's joy, that one's disgust, that one's pity.

"At first I laughed and went along with this theory. I humored him and asked him to tell me what the shape of the car meant, what the shape of his beard meant, and the bow and arrow lying on the backseat; that kind of thing. He answered each time, seriously, and then he said that where there is no shape, there is spiritual freedom. I was kind of surprised at the word spiritual crossing his lips. Talk about cynical. He was a complete existentialist. If he talked about kabala or witches, it was with total cynicism. And he would always retort to my expressions of joy or faith, "If you wish it." With a smirk on his face.

"But he was a hero of mine. So when he pulled the car over, removing the bow and arrows, and said we must go for a walk across the meadow that spread out by the side of the road, I was pleased. The day was blazing with autumn colors orange, red, yellow—set up in heaps against a royal-blue sky. He was talking and talking about shapes and freedom, and I was still proud to be the receptacle for all this genius. But as we got farther and farther across the field and toward the colorful woods, a chill came out of the trees and over the grass, and his mood changed abruptly. Until he was sitting on the ground with his face in his hands—weeping. I was scared. I offered him a joint, I offered to drive him home, he just sobbed and looked up at me with his beard wet with snot and tears and his eyes all red. He told me to go stand in front of an elm—the leaves were red as blood—and I did what he said. I remember noting a few tiny cobweb nets on the grass around my feet, undisturbed white veils with dew on them, still from the night before, and then I looked up and saw him, with his bow and arrows a few feet away from me. His eyes were as cold as cat's-eye marbles. I remember losing all respect for him in a rush and thinking he looked like a huge insect, a machine that runs without any meaning to it.

"He lifted the bow and the arrow and aimed them at me. The wind was like a cold hand on my face, a mother's hand, and I closed my eyes to feel it cover me and to feel my way through it up to the sky. He shot one arrow right into the trunk above my head, and two more flew by my left shoulder. They made a terrible windy sound, heavier than you would imagine. And he called out, "If I hit you on target, you're mine!" Two more arrows shot past my left side, he only had five, and so he stopped and approached me where I was standing as rigid as the tree. He pulled out the arrow above my head and leaned his whole weight against me, his arms going around the tree. He rubbed up and down on me, panting like a dog or something."

Kosta called: Echo!
Roisin screamed: Shut up!

"Okay, so he pushed me down and straddled me, saying more about shapes than I can remember. And I was wondering if there was a God and who would rescue me and wanting to shit and vomit at the same time. He said, "This is where I want your second life to begin. Right here. At point S for Suffering. This is it. Here. November 22nd. Now. Today. Your next life has just begun." And then he jumped up with a laugh and went to collect the other arrows in the grass beyond the tree. I began running, back to the car as fast as I could, but he followed and even shot a couple of arrows after me, but they missed. It was a miracle. I ran and ran, down the road, then, hearing the engine rev up behind. Another car came—a pickup truck—and I jumped up and down, signaling, and the people stopped to let me in. It was a family of farmers. They put me in the back. I lay down and through a crack in the wall saw Philo's car following, then passing by. In the back of that truck I vowed

I would never be part of any violence in the world—never!—and walked all the way from Manhattan to Washington D.C., as the first stretch of my journey; He was right. That day was the beginning."

—But wait, called Roisin, what were the last words he said?

He was crouched in the grass, retrieving an arrow, and he said, as I began to run—it must have been the start of a story—"Once I slept under a bridge." Those were his last words.

—What were you wearing that day?

—A pair of jeans, a flannel shirt, sneakers, a sweater.

—Didn't your parents try to find you?

—I don't know and I don't care.

—What about your brother?

—He's still in New York where he works. I never contact him.

—Same last name as yours?

—Yes, but my real name wasn't Echo then.

—What was it?

—Never mind, it's horrible.

—Do you always think of sex now as a terrifying thing?

—Not always, said Echo with her face averted.

—Haven't you had physical contact even with anyone?

—I don't want to talk about that.

—Why not?

Now she looked both vague and petulant, unlike the fierce narrator telling her story. The rose petals were scattered around her hand on the table. She had dug a cross in the wood with a thorn.

She said, Because you're jealous of me, and I don't want to nurture that.

—Oh, that's all?

—Yes.

Then she went on to describe a journey, empty-handed, across the continent where she found people who believed, as, she did, in the healing power of pleasure. "If you dread pleasure and happiness, you will get sick and die way before your time," she concluded. "Look what happened to the Jews during World War Two."

—What? What are you talking about? The children too? asked Roisin, then raised her hand to stop the answer from coming.

"My mother," she said instead, "ate a bowl of rice, cucumbers, and soy sauce every meal of the day. Not out of choice."

—But it sounds like a very healthy diet!

—Have you ever been violent yourself? asked Roisin. Or felt it?

—I have felt anger, rage, hate, of course. But I have ways of dealing with those feelings, privately.

—What do you want to accomplish in my house?

—I want to leave you all happier. You pregnant, for one thing.

—And Kosta?

—Happier, too. Especially about his work and his need for recognition.

—And my mother-in-law?

—Tomorrow I will give her massage and herb treatments to make her feel better. I do believe the cancer is self-induced. But now do you trust me more? Do you understand me better? Doesn't that experience with Philo explain me to you? If only people can understand each other!

—Have you ever taken drugs?

—Yes, she admitted. For several years I smoked marijuana day and night and took some hash, coke, but not much, and other stuff. Now of course I'm clean, except for wine. That's my pleasure.

Roisin turned away, and her mind traveled across the continent, over all its rivers, mountains, deserts, fields, and cities to the meadow in Vermont. She wondered where Philo was now and what he meant then.

—Do you think he really meant to rape you? she asked Echo.

—Of course.

—Why didn't he?

—Because he loved my brother more. I was a substitute, nothing else.

—I wish I understood what he meant about shapes, said Roisin.

—I don't know. He also said, "The world is broken into parts."

Kosta's face suddenly broke into the light of the kitchen as he rose from the basement with Ray behind him. His brow was clear and sunny, the creases in his cheeks deep, and he was smiling. The light closed around his blue clothing, filling each fold with more light.

Famous Questions

Ray said, He's a find, he's great!
Echo smiled with the pleasure of one who has successfully engineered
a historic meeting. Roisin covered her eyes with the palms of her hands
and rubbed the darkness in.

x

While the two men shouted their messages to each other, Roisin retreated to the basement to rewind and watch one of the films, alone.
It was her favorite—a kind of speed ride along the streets of Boston's
urban edge where they had lived. A flattened and whitened ground was
striped with doe-brown blades of grass. Dots of dirt speckled the rims of
the roads, and slush flushed up from under the cars. Past the hospitals
and the Home for Little Wanderers, past the Greek convent where Ma
spent three months as a pseudo-nun, past the large and luminous pond,
and past the silk-white arboretum, the lace of the snowed landscape flew
away and turned into wooden three-deckers, bars, garages, and closed-
down brick schools. Past the furniture store where her father worked—it
had aged without anyone attempting restitution and stood, a pale green
building, with the word Sale permanently scrawled across its windows.

(The last time she had seen her father she went into the darkness of the
showroom, unannounced. Crushed velvet, fake Scandinavian, laminated
wood, and two men in the far back with the mattresses, smoking and
watching TV. One of them was her father. He stood up first to inspect
the customer, Roisin, then raised his hands in astonishment. He was
wearing a shiny blue suit and pink shirt and was the image of an American failure. Cologne as stenchy as insecticide, as repellent as afflatus,
accompanied his stride to her side. His face, now a cluster of knots and
gnarls, contorted with a false grin. They exchanged information about
himself, herself, his wife, his mother, her mother-in-law, her son, while
she backed, inch by inch, to the door. Outside sleet was falling and she
wanted only to be in it, to walk in sneakers down those cement streets.
As he talked her mind was racing, O failure, there is your white man,

America, a veteran, now a creature of minimal ambition, a worker too exhausted for mobility, a man who leans on women, a man of tasteless jokes, of ignorant opinions, of cowardice and cruelty. He asked her as she opened the door: "How does a Kerryman find household help?" She shook her head and gaped at the street. "He marries her!" he roared, and slapped the air. He would never let her forget her Irish husband.

Past the stony streets, bar-lined, bleak, the camera moved, past the apartment where they had lived, and pausing in front of the Victorian house, where Roisin had cared for teenage girls—runaways, mothers. In the falling snow, tucked behind willows and pudding stone, it looked as cozy as a children's illustration. Inside you would imagine teas and fires crackling, old dogs moving slowly from Oriental rug to rug, and loved children lolling on large chairs. The dots of wet snow zipping and flashing across the camera formed a cold screen between Roisin and that house which she had left for this, California.

Now a flash of light admitted another figure into the tiny room, and the door closed behind Ray. He stood at the side of Roisin, watching. The camera panned in on a swirl of lighted flakes around a streetlight, and the film ended. Where is that place? asked Ray in the dark. It looks like a moonscape.

—That's my territory, said Roisin. It's a house I worked in. Not far away are the dreariest malls in the world—graveyards galore—and nurseries that sell stunted little pines—lots of franchises chained around the side of the city. I could walk through complete darkness and find my way to those places by heart. I'm never lost there.
—I know what you mean, he said.
—Yeah, because there I know what to do and who with, and my arms can stretch out, even if I'm blind, and trust that not pleasure will be there, no, but trust that grief will be dripping all around me. Isn't it wild? That's my America—my United States—my republic—the outer sphere, the wasteland that supports the ladder for climbing to riches.

—Well, Kosta certainly captures that social landscape. He must have made it for you.

—I think he did, in some way.

—Did he ever do anything to make you happy, plain and simple? Ray asked.

—Yes! He whistled for me. It would come from the kitchen first— tweets and trills, so cheerful—He did the whippoorwill, bobwhite, blue jay, mockingbird, loon, sparrow, and cardinal. I called and he stood at the end of my bed, like Pavarotti at the Met, doing those bird songs until I felt all better. This was the old days, the first days. The baby was laughing his head off, too. Kosta was great to us.

That same night at dawn Kosta snuck out of their bed and went down the hall to Echo's room. Roisin, secretly awake, couldn't keep from wondering what he did to keep her in pleasure with her virginity intact. Outside, clouds like tutus under stage lights floated in the blue. She envisioned herself up there sitting in air, flying east over light-spattered meadows, and her mind turned to Philo, the shape man, half dream, half shadow, a tall hairy man whose interior thorns prickled and pointed at his heart. The pain was unbearable but caused his vision to wobble in such a way that the objects in the abstract world around him deepened into new dimensions. Once he was very tired after walking long dirt roads for many miles, and he lay down under the arc of a stony bridge to rest. The bridge was gray and patterned with stones lugged to that place by anarchists. (They lived like elves in the hills of Vermont.) Philo: I love! was the echo that lived in those stones and ran through them like whistles. Philo, I love. The water, long and black, flashed beside him where he lay listening. For a while he felt the pressure of the thorns release, and his heart felt renewed, like the whole dark rose, compacted of sweet petals. He dozed and dreamed his own life story. He dreamed he had strayed off the trail intended for him (Chisholm, it was called) and had found himself, after that, permanently lost. His life, this way, began again—its second beginning was in a state of suffering. This was the true way, letting him understand that all of life began in suffering and happiness was only a temporary release from it and we all had things backward. This was how he read his story anyway and how he experienced his life. Interior pain and a consciousness of fragments, shapes, the bits and pieces of a once whole and palpable creation hurled into space . . . When Philo awoke from this troubled dream, he saw he was under the bridge still and filling, again, with pain. The world's bits and pieces fluttered and swelled and hopped around him, making sounds as alien as any he had ever heard. He understood there was only one way to relieve the pain—by passing it on to another!

x

In the blue water laced with gold beams, Kosta and Echo swam in circles, entwined. While she pulsed, he expanded. They rubbed, tugged, undulated, and stuck their hands inside each other. Pleasure itself stung, buzzed, hummed, and trumpeted from their genitals into their throats, where it stuck, was swallowed, and swelled in their chests. Hair afloat on the surface of the pool, they watched each other through half-closed eyes and their mouths thickened.

This is how Roisin found them that evening, while Ma lay coughing in her room. For some time she stood inside the sliding glass door and observed their actions with a curiosity that included the emotion: I understand everything they are feeling. Echo parted her legs to let him rest in that circle, tightly bound, and her face was turned up to the stars as if sunny with intense joy. Then he pushed her down under the water, where she did the next thing, but by then Roisin had turned away. She went to unpack her backpack in the laundry room and then climbed the stairs and fell asleep on the rug at the end of Liam's bed.

During those days Ma spent most of her time on her feet, doing the wash, cooking, and even reading the newspaper standing up at the kitchen counter. She said she wanted to die on her feet like Emily Brontë. The disease had covered her lungs and some other parts, according to the doctor, who also said no hospital would admit her at this stage. He gave her morphine to take whenever she wanted. And he suggested getting a visiting nurse when the pain got even worse. Meantime Echo took the role of healer, including lighting up joints and showing her how to get high on weed. When Ma needed doses of oxygen, Echo administered them, humming and kindly rubbing the legs and arms of her patient. Roisin stood at a distance, hands lifted, empty.

Kosta said that his mother needed Echo now. He wouldn't look at Roisin when he spoke to her but averted his face, speaking off to the side. This was the sign, Roisin told him, of a cleft heart.

—In love, she said, one looks and the other looks away. You used to look at me.

—Stop these generalities, he said. I don't know what I'm looking at or why. I don't know what I'm doing or why. My mother is dying in front of me. Someone is helping her. That's all I can see. The issue of love doesn't interest me right now. I only want to see my mother's pain relieved. And I don't want her to die.

—When a person is free, she is several degrees more gullible, more trusting and impulsive, than a person who is under the protection of the law—that is, owned. When a person is free, she feels that her actions have the shadowy quality of a crime. But when a person is married, a person is choosy, cautious, and critical. She stays out of trouble. Marriage is a covenant and ordinance entwined in court and conscience. The married person is safe and sanctified by ownership. We are not, either of us, single, but we are both free.

—Which is to say? asked Kosta.

—You can do what you want.

—I don't know what I want.

—I bet you do. You want everything you can get and keep.

—Isn't that normal? It's normal to want it, but not to expect to have it.

—I agree with what you say about freedom, I really do. Take Echo, for instance. She's incredibly vulnerable. And an original. She's trying to stake out a space for herself in the world, one that's free of the shit of society. She needs protection of some kind, though. And you want to give it to her.

—Yes. I do, he confessed.

Kosta and Roisin were driving down the freeway, having picked up more morphine for Ma. Strapped upright on their seats, they didn't look to the left or to the right but talked out at the coming view. If they were moving forward into the traffic or if the whole scene was driving at them, it didn't matter. Both wore the stoic expressions of completed works.

—The fact is, said Kosta, there's not much passion left between us, is there. I mean, you would never marry me, and I would never give you a child—and so there we are. Here. Impotent. Nothing. Friends—yes. The best—always were—but life has to have a sting to it. Doesn't it? I've lost my faith—completely—somewhere—in here. I'll be underground soon enough, forever!—so why should I live underground, too? Can you tell me? I want to be appreciated—I want my work to shine, be known. Is that wrong? It's become painful to me—to be—down there— in the dark—always alone. She wants me to show my stuff around— she encourages me—gives me hope—what can I say? It's not that you don't. Since we've been together, I've become what I am and my work is what it is, partially because of us, you. No, completely because of you . . . But she's the first—and it's very chaste—so chaste it might as well be . . . well, transcendent. I would never complain about you—but what can I say, do? I don't want to go on sneaking around! Help me.

That night Ma threw all her shoes and pillows at Kosta. A book followed and then two bottles of pills. She was in her room, and he was at the door. She was shouting, "Get that slut out of this house!" and he was protesting, murmuring to himself, "But she gave you massages . . . she made you feel better . . . She was kind to you . . . You're being old-fashioned."

Roisin sobered up quickly and ran up and down the hall, with Liam following her, both doubled over and clutching themselves. Echo tore past them in a peach slip, crying. Kosta closed himself in his room with his mother, but they, outside the door, heard every word. He berated her for spying, for snooping in his business, for listening in on him and Echo. He said it was wicked that a woman her age should submit to such tactics. He tried, in various ways like these, to make her feel guilty for discovering his attachment to Echo, but it didn't work. She litanized: "Pig, slut, cheeky fool, rotten, degraded, weak, sinful," and so on. Then she started coughing and stopped talking, and Kosta was silent, too.

Liam grasped his mother's shoulder and wondered aloud, "What's going on?" And Echo screamed from below, as if in reply, "We love each other!" Liam and Roisin moved back and forth, talking, in his room. She said, "Where's that lap harp I brought you from Ireland? Oh there . . . It's like an animal, a pet, isn't it? Its ruined wood and thick strings, its primitive shape (neither round nor square), and the sounds it makes are," she told him, "strangely similar to your father. Intimate, humanly generative, a kind of creature. Caress it, talk to it, take it out for exercise, and it will love you back."

Liam held it on his knees and said, "When I've really learned how to play it, I'm going to go to Ireland and meet him."

Roisin then entered Ma's room, shut the door, and listened to Kosta speak to her while she lay under a quilt staring at a miniature of Christ from the cathedral of Ravenna. He was saying: "Look, I promise it doesn't mean anything. Where there's no penetration—I hate that word—the whole experience is oddly free of . . . well, guilt. It's like being with an angel or something, I'm not being blasphemous, but where there's no possibility of pregnancy, somehow the act of love is changed into something almost . . . well—pure."

Ma replied: "It sounds as if you're saying that consummation—a better word than penetration—is associated with impurity. How could you say this? It's the only way to have a child, after all."
"I never wanted a child, and I'm only saying that it doesn't feel like

adultery if conception isn't possible."

"That means," she continued, "that birth control will have eliminated one of the Ten Commandments. You are sinful by making sex sound tainted. If you would just have a baby, you'd be a man—and I'd be happy."

—Happy? Bringing more suffering into this world? Echo doesn't want to do that any more than I do.

—I thought she believed that suffering could be eliminated through her kind ministrations.

—Don't be so hateful, Ma, Kosta pleaded.

—Hateful? I'm only being logical. You don't want to bring suffering into the world, but you are obviously experiencing a good deal of pleasure these days.

—Lots of suffering. Ultimate suffering. I mean, look at you! Your pain.

—This conversation is making me suffer. And words like those. Does it mean that God has abandoned me just because I'm sick? No, it doesn't, and don't make that mistake. It's an evil thought. I'll never forget the basilica St. Martin and the mosaics there. You should have seen them. The life of Christ was shown on the left—the miracles and parables— and scenes from the Passion were depicted on the right. Near an apse, the Virgin and Christ were enthroned. Fabulous candle holders, a sense of rotation, two concentric rings, and I think it was there, on the ceiling, an arbor of lilies, animals, angels—those eyes! Those circles! I think, when all is known about galaxies and stars, an image will emerge from them, in the heavens, of the face of Christ.

Kosta left the room and Roisin stayed behind, seating herself at the window, where she could be shadowed and watchful. She and Ma spoke back and forth through most of the night while the pain swelled up in the room and like a stinging fly landed wherever her voice did. Roisin sent Kosta out at dawn to see if there was some relief available through an emergency ward at a hospital, then watched the sky fill up with blue.

Ma said: "When I lie here I am now either in such intolerable pain, I want to press my face into its imprint, all mud—of God—or else I am so stupidly drugged I can leave my body like a child sneaking off from school and travel . . . I know there's nothing to fear . . . Mud is my new name for God . . . My name is Mud. Have you heard it? Take me for a drive, dear, I want to see things pass by, I want to be outside . . . Bring me to a place where everything is brown; hand me the newspaper under the bed, there's a story in it . . . Tell that witch Echo to leave, get her out of here. I want to look at Liam. All my schoolchildren are in his face . . . Open the paper to somewhere in the middle on the left upper side . . . It's about Mercury. Where is Kosta? I want to go for a drive."

Roisin scanned the newspaper, page by page, and found the story on Mercury, a town in Nevada, sixty miles northwest of Las Vegas; it was a nuclear test site.
—I found it, she told Ma.
—Read it. We've set off twenty-two bombs in one year there. Can you believe it?
—Underground, and the earth is probably thrown off its axis.

Roisin read it, and Ma dropped asleep. It was like a disappearing act: her mouth fell open, her eyes were sealed, Roisin could see her fillings and her tongue. Outside, small clouds scudded across the early skies. Roisin woke Liam up for school and went to make him breakfast in the kitchen. When he came down she was at the table with her hands around the edge of a blue cup of tea, and his toast and eggs were hot on the other side of the white table.
—You look well rested. Did you sleep okay? she asked.
—Yeah, but I dreamed about a ghost. It was wearing a long shirt—I mean, it was a long shirt, floating around this room, empty. I said it was a ghost, and you said it was an angel. It was hanging in the air, with its sleeves out. I think it's because I did my wash before bed last night. Then hung up my blue shirt out on the line.
—That must be it, Roisin agreed. She watched him slurp down the toast and syrup, and she sipped her tea.
—Actually, said Liam, I think it was the ghost of Myles, my father.

—Why do you say that?

—You once said he wore blue shirts all the time.

—This is true.

—And it was big shirt—a man's shirt. See what I mean?

—I do.

—Let's go.

He got his books and they climbed in the van to drive him to school. On the way down the winding roads, Liam asked her how soon after he was born his father left them.

—Almost immediately, said Roisin. He got hepatitis and left America. That was the last time.

—What did you do to make money?

—I worked in a Chinese laundry in New York. They let me keep you in a playpen beside me. All day there was steam—from the iron—from the streets—from the trains—but it was warm and cozy in the back of the laundry, with you, watching you roll around and play.

—What did Myles do when I was born?

—He came to the hospital room—a ward—where I was. They let me keep you and nurse you a few hours a day. He came in, having missed the actual delivery, and looked at you as if you were some kind of explosive. Then typically he said, Poor creature, and nervously pushed you back at me, "What will you name him?" he asked me, and I told him William, after his father. I also told him not to call you "poor thing," no matter what. Then he gave me some money and started for the door. Came back. Looked long and hard at me and said, "Now you'll never be lonely again." That was the way he was. Both crude and sensitive.

—But it sounds like you never saw him again. Is that right? asked Liam.

—No. Not yet. He was at home when you came home from the hospital, but soon after that, he got sick. I had to make a choice—to take care of you or him. I chose you.

—Then no wonder he left.

—No, he didn't leave because of that. He left because he wanted to be in

Ireland, and because I didn't fight to keep him here.
—Why didn't you?
Because I could—because he could—because it was easier because, in the end, it's easier—for some people—to love alone.
—You?
—Here's school. Go on now.
They pulled up behind a yellow school bus from which his friends emerged. He climbed out with his sneakers untied and ran awkwardly to join the others, entering the asphalt playground behind the chain-link fence. The shadows were engraved as if in coal, though the sun was drawing up colors around them.

There in the kitchen, Roisin washed her cup and said to Echo, "We are going for a long drive, with Ma, into the mountains, probably overnight. Would you please take care of Liam till we get back?"
—Sure, of course, but why? Are you going, I mean.
—Ma wants to see the world.
—And then what do you want me to do?
—Well, you know she's upset about you and Kosta. I think you might want to move out for a while.
—Alone?

Roisin pulled a towel around the inside of the cup and imagined the face of an infant, clean inside and out. (A tea-brown face with pursed lips and long black lashes.) Meantime she stared dreamily at Echo, who wore the anxious expression of a child awaiting the departure of a bee from the top of her head.
—I don't know if I can handle that, said Echo.
—You have to. There's no choice. This is one-life-to-live time, not a game.
—What? You're whispering, Echo urged, and leaned forward.
—I don't want to be mean. I want you to be happy, and Kosta, too, I really do. But Ma is the important one right now. Okay?
—Okay, said Echo obediently, turning to gaze out of the window: as long as you want everyone to be happy. Then they will be?

Now they heard the van engine and garage door sliding down. The kitchen floor trembled, and all the sounds were like rain. When Kosta entered the room, it was with the confident step of a small emperor. He asked Roisin if she wanted some gum and placed a stick between his teeth, drew it in, chewed, and smiled at both women. Roisin said no and left the room, but Echo said yes and opened her mouth wide.

Kosta told Ma he had found her a hospital where she could be comfortable and they would administer drugs more efficiently than she could do on her own. She was standing in the kitchen with Roisin, both were ready to travel, and Ma said to him: "Forget it. I don't want to be comfortable." She wore baggy pants and a big sweater and sneakers, her bag hanging off her thin shoulder. Her face was brownish. She said she wanted to see the mud. "No hospitals, not for me. Take me for a drive instead."
—Do what she says, Roisin told Kosta.
—What about Liam?
—Echo will take care of him. I've worked it all out.
—You're so fucking organized. Women.

They waited for him to pack. Roisin lay on the floor with her head on her bag and saw mud flying across the camel-brown surface of the earth, dipping and rising where the valleys and hills were carved like unfinished sculptures. Her arms were spread wide, and she turned over and over, sometimes facing the deep sky and sometimes the solid face of the mud. When she pointed her arms straight ahead, she went faster; when she extended one and bent in its direction, she tipped down. Logic and gravity were the same. From where she whirled, speeding across the mud, she could only see the things that weren't actually there: shapes of humans and animals and their faces. The more she was aware of them not being there in the mud, the more she wanted to cry, land, or rest.

—She keeps falling asleep in the strangest places, Kosta said.
—It's a sign of perfect obedience, it happens to women when they're pregnant, said Ma. Too bad she's not.

—I was just dozing, Roisin remarked, and stood up. Let's go.
The sky grew wet and rushing with clouds as they headed east on the freeway. Roisin pretended there was a baby swimming inside of her and stole several looks at the distant and irritable Kosta. Ma slept, on and off, in back. When she was awake, her expression was almost rapturous facing the rain on the glass pane.

Then in the mountains there was snow laced across the surface of grass and stacked in the arms of green fir trees, and the winding of the mountain roads was a little sickening to Roisin, who rolled down the window to feel the cold wind on her face. No air felt so clear before, so close to being water, she said, and Ma began to talk to them from behind.
—I want to go to Mercury, she announced, and be left there in the morning. This is serious. I want you to drop me there and let me protest what they're doing. All my life I wanted to protest and only now do I have the guts to do it. I'm risking nothing. I'll be gone in a matter of days, no matter what I do. You must obey my wishes. I'm going to sit on that test site, and that's where I want to die and how. That's where I will be happy to die. Don't you dare deny me this wish. Now look at the blue jay in the pine tree there. Kosta, do your blue jay for me.

He grimaced but pursed his lips, whistled badly, then whistled well.
—Do the whole routine, she told him.
He did. Sparrows, mockingbirds, seagulls, whippoorwills, bobwhites, robins, cardinals, and starlings came out of his mouth. He ended by warbling the loon, and Ma applauded from the back. Evening dropped down blue and hard in the mountains, they stayed in the Dottie Dimple Motel, Ma in a room beside theirs. Kosta didn't talk, wouldn't, but sat staring vacantly into his hands while Roisin got them all food and drinks. They lay awake in the dark and heard Ma coughing through the thin wall.
Kosta said: Don't leave me now, Roisin. With Ma gone, I don't know. You can't, please. I'll get rid of Echo.

Roisin put her hand on his face, found it wet, and she drew his head down next to hers. His cheek experienced the same salt and wet on her face, and she asked him how he could have made love to her all those years, if what he really desired was something else. Something virginal, say, she continued. An act free of consequence. No children.
—I don't know, he said, it's horrible, I suppose, but I thought we agreed.
—You did?
—Didn't we?
—Do we agree about Echo?

Steely morning light fell on the snow, and the sun was a sulfurous ball as it is when reflected off water. They drove down through the mountains at dawn—down toward the brown of Nevada. Like paper bags tossed across a flat surface, the hills seemed discarded, hollow, and unclaimed. Ma was hunched in back and plucking at the lint on her coat. There was no changing her mind, though Kosta tried. As the land softened from hard, iced-over stuff to a muddy surface, she prayed just under her breath, in Greek, then she crossed herself when they entered the Mercury town limits. A white line ran down the center of the black road. Tumbleweed was caught in an iron fence.

—Pull over, she said. I want to get out here. It's empty, just what I wanted, I can find my way.
Kosta pulled over obediently. She opened the car door and climbed out, leaving her bags inside. She slammed herself out, and they followed. Kosta fell on his knees, hanging on to her, crying. She put her hands in his hair and told him to stand up like a man.
"I just hope they see me protesting," she said. "Pray that they will. And Roisin, take care of Liam. Now go on, the two of you, drive off . . . Please go on."

All around her there was brown land extending on either side of a single fence. A radio tower was like an insect. It ran into the gray sky, and the air now seemed charged and charted with government surveillance, as

if they had arrived, by chance, at a place where humans regulate nature.
—Go on! Ma ordered them, waving her hand around and now crawling
through a rip in the wire fence. They climbed into the van and watched
her stagger to her feet and walk, her coat blowing around in the ocean
of air.

Once I knew the shape, it was the law and I could live inside it. Before
I was looking always for a hole, a view of sky. I knew that this exit was
unavoidable anyway, seeing that the air was the biggest, and I fell on my
face in the dark, returning to the shadows for help. If the world maker
wanted shadows, it then made substance; if it wanted those shadows to
move all the time, it made the substance seem to move in relation to its
own static darkness.

x

Many hours later they arrived home. It was deep after midnight and
Roisin went directly to Liam's room to check on him and he was there
asleep, but Echo's room was empty. Kosta moved through the house,
unsmiling but full of will. He wore the look of a messenger and the pos-
ture of a winner. But he couldn't find her on the first or second floors,
though her clothes were still in place and the drawers held her things.
And his eyes widened and his shoulders stiffened while Roisin stopped
him from calling the police.
—Why would she leave Liam alone? he wondered.
—Maybe she decided to split altogether, and this was her chance.
—No, no, I am sure not. He looked panicked.
—I never trusted her.
—No wonder. She's a complete zero, weird, empty-brained, bitch.

Be a shadow, you will be close to God. Next best be a mud person with
a mud soul. Make the shifting of families forbidden. Be slow to make
promises, you know why. Major changes occur unnoticed to even the
hunting eye, and you should never be the architect of violent change.

Kosta did not sleep that night. While Roisin and Liam slept into the morning, he wandered around the dawn-pale town looking for Echo. Then he took the van and cruised around the streets striped with sun and shadow and even went past the bus stop—deserted—where they first encountered Echo. Shielding his eyes from the rising orange sun he drove back home. Roisin was still tossed into parts around the large bed and Liam too.

Mother, I have reached an impasse in my thought. It's you! No. It's the end of a he, the end of a they, it is a one.

The shape was the impasse against the dream trying to get out of it. So the shape is the evil, and cause of suffering. Ma? How do they justify their cruelty to others, those men we know and don't? Can't we raise them to a lighter sentence on each other? Why can't our children be safe?

Kosta, breathless, descended to the basement, now praying that a note of explanation from Echo might be there. Instead he found chaos: all his film shredded, in tatters. Scissors had neatly cut each reel right up the middle, severing every image; then other snips of the same shears had taken off sides and parts which lay like negative confetti all over the floor. Even his earliest films, packed in a metal box, had been manicured, maimed. The note was there, though.
It simply read: FAILURE.

Kosta fell onto his knees, curved over, his hands clamping the back of his neck, saying Jesus Christ again and again. He writhed, he rolled, he clawed at the pieces of film, he threw them down, he got up and stepped all over them, and then he shoveled them into a bin with his hands, as if he was a gardener disposing of thistles and leaves.

At seven am, he climbed the stairs and told Roisin that he was leaving her. She lay on her side with the edge of the quilt on her ear, believed he meant that it was all over between him and Echo, but then she heard him say: "I have to go and find her. She is my soul-mate, my own and only, the real thing. She was right to ruin all my work. She was right, Roisin. She understands me. She knows it's the only way for me to go forward. I have to go to her, Roisin. I love her. I love her. She is my reason to go on living. I'm sorry. If Ma comes back, don't tell her. I can't help it. I've got to go find her. I adore her. I want her. She was right, she was right, it took guts, she has courage, I can't live without her."

She heard him gather his things together. She couldn't lift her head from its own leadenness; it weighed the same as a baby she had held in the clinic and that weight seemed to be the cause of her bleeding, the end of a pregnancy that never began.

x

A few years later, alone and home in Boston, Roisin told Liam the story of his father because she was ill and thought she was dying.

Do you remember me telling you that I went to Ireland when I was in college—just took off with a sleeping bag and a few clothes—the way kids did in those days. I was in love with Irish literature, and I was fearless and questing after something new. In Dublin I trudged the streets daily, plunging into the darkest church basements to look at bones and remains of saints, and taking a tour of Kilmainham jail where men had been tortured and cold breezes blew out of dark cells; I visited dolmens and waterfalls, haunted castles and fixed-up castles, I walked around the rhododendrons on Howth and barefoot on flat rocks, reading Joyce, and sucking in the gray salt air. I don't know what I thought I would find, but I felt I was looking for something. Lonely, I only felt myself to be in company when I was walking; walking I discovered multiplies the self into selves. It was good that the dark came late in those weeks because I dreaded having to return to the little bed-and-breakfast I inhabited on the Stillorgan Road.

The family there was very gentle and quiet. Children and parents who had black curls and pink freckled cheeks. I had a little flowery room with a sloping ceiling, where I lay on my back and read. Then in the morning I had a bowl of Rice Krispies with the family. One morning they asked me to go with them to mass and then to a lunch party afterward. In all the drama of castles, prisons, dolmens, and tinkers, I envisioned this occasion as dreary but an obligation. I felt myself to be one of their children and giggled throughout mass with the youngest one. It never occurred to me that the day might become important.

There was a group of people in this house we visited on the Stillorgan Road. It was a house filled with antiques and portraits. There were three very old women and one old man, all of them chain smoking and drinking. The women didn't look a person in the eye but conveyed intimacy by leaning close to speak, while addressing the floor or some distant object. I had begun to notice this was an Irish characteristic. They sat in the garden on white wrought-iron chairs, with plates of foods before them. An earlier rainfall had left a silver glitter on all the vegetation as if it were dawn. They gazed, we all did, on an array of flowers and herbs. These included tied and tidy rose bushes, strawberries, sweet peas in gentle pastels, climbing rods, fuchsia, thyme, tarragon, and lavender. The garden was hidden by high walls; on the other side you could see the tops of trees with apples on them, hard red brown objects like dollhouse fruit. The children stared greedily up at them and clutched a sack of stuffed animals between them. I sat with the grown-ups and guzzled the tea and cakes—little lumps of sugared dough with pink icing, the brown bread, butter, and strawberry jam. A bitter smell of bayberry mingled with the warm sweet flowers. Then a large boy appeared, or was it a man? He was in tweeds, but scruffy, and I could tell they all knew him well.
—How are you, Myles, and how's your music coming?
The hostess was like a very old elf, of no particular sex, who seemed weighted down by the cardigan she wore over her back and shoulders. Myles murmured his response in a voice so low, she had to tilt to hear him.
—What's the difference between a saint and a martyr? the old gentleman asked no one in particular.
—I don't know, Billy, said the old elf.

—A martyr is married to a saint, dear, he roared.

The fellow, Myles, smiled, and I smiled, too. We all watched the children from my family, like formal twins of different sizes, boss two other children into a game involving fallen apples and stuffed animals.

—Don't worry, the lady from my family said to the grandmother of the other children. My children bully, but it never goes too far.

Then Myles began to talk rapidly and audibly about politics. The old people looked up at the restless sky as he rattled on about South Africa and the Middle East, about the civil rights movement in the United States, and about student protest. He lit a cigarette and glared at me.

—Are you an activist in the U.S.? he asked.

—She's just a child, darling, said the elf.

—I am, I told him, nodding earnestly.

—I personally, said another old lady, this one with an enormous head, I personally believe that war is for the middle-aged. And I also believe that no one can be a peacenik without being a protector of the status quo. That's what I think. It's a terrible world.

I felt excited, and nervous, as if I were a green blade of grass shimmering between sun and water. The third old woman looked like a witch. Her chin almost touched her nose. She said, everything that has to do with numbers is evil, everything. And that includes money. Money is evil.

The gathering had been billed as a lunch party, but there was no lunch. My family seemed content enough. The man went in to get refills for everyone, and the woman trailed the quarreling children, with a cake in her hand. At one point Myles went inside. The old women began to whisper.

—He's just like his father.

—I wouldn't be surprised if he's a card-carrying member.

—Ach, no, not Myles. He's an artist.

—I wish more people knew it.

—They will, the witch said with assurance.

And when he returned, two of the old women beamed, and the third one murmured. Ah, virility.

—Are you really from Boston? he asked me.

—Yes.

—Well, I should take you out and show you around.

—That would be great.

—I don't have a lot of money, but still.

—Americans never admit how much money they have, the witch announced then. I think it's because of the Puritan ethic. They're ashamed of any sort of padding, really. They want to seem independent . . . Am I wrong?

—No, I think you're right, the old man replied. I once knew a businessman from San Francisco. He came here to fish every summer for years. The story about him goes that he once spent a week trying to catch a salmon. On the seventh day he did, but by then he was in a rage, of course, at all the time he'd lost and the money . . . On the way to the hotel he growled at his fishing guide, "For God's sake, one salmon has cost me six hundred pounds!" . . . And the fisherman, unperturbed, replied, "It must be very good salmon, then, to cost so much."

They all laughed, especially Myles, who then told me he would like to take me to hear some traditional music that very night.

—Do you like traditional music? he asked.

—Yes, but I can't find anywhere here to listen to it.

—I'll bring you to a singing pub, how's that?

He had, he said later, never expected me to know anything about music, but I was already on the side of things where folk songs were coming from, and would continue to come. I knew Woody Guthrie, Pete Seeger, Odetta, Merle Haggard, John Jacob Niles and Johnny Cash and had their records as well as their social attitudes. He had, he told me later, asked me as a joke, to make a bit of a fool of me, and was surprised when I knew something about literature and music.

He arranged when he would get me and left as the old man was telling a joke about a priest asking an unwed pregnant woman, "Are you sure you're the mother?" I sat on, facing the garden, while the children moved animals among themselves and spoke in strange voices. Beside me the old people were laughing with my family and exchanging stories. I remember feeling a safety in the world I had not experienced before. It didn't have anything to do with Myles, but with the garden and the old people in it.

It turned out that his meeting me was as fateful as any he had had. He was desperate to leave the country and get to the folk music scene in New York. He played guitar and sang Irish songs, but he wanted to take up flute and fiddle and write his own music.

—I've got to get out of Dublin, he told me. Here if it's not the church that poisons your ambitions here, it's the people. Vicious, gossiping, provincial.

It was our third meeting, and we had taken the train to Dalkey. We walked the narrow winding streets there, beside walled gardens draped in fuchsia bushes. A convent's bells pealed continuously. We made our way down to the beach in Killiney, where we bought a tray of tea and carried it across the flat rocks and broken crockery and sat in the cold, talking.

—I know a couple of people in New York, and this woman who wants to bring me over, he told me. She thinks she can help me get started. Any ideas?

—None. I don't know anything about that.

—You're just a child, aren't you? Sixteen?

—Seventeen.

—That's not so young. We only have two years' difference between us. We blew the steam off our tea and. sipped, eyeing each other over the rims. I was at ease with him because there was no intimacy. For ten days we expressed our passions in a competition of quotes. If he didn't sing to me as we walked, he quoted Yeats, Keats, the Romantics. I countered with the verse I knew and counted my stars that I knew it at all. It was a way to talk across our cultures, deeply.

One night we drank some beer in a pub and got tipsy enough so that afterward we sat in Stephen's Green on a damp bench and exchanged a soft kiss, then more and more. He at once wanted to marry me, and in a rush spoke of our future together.

—But I have to leave soon, I told him. I'm running out of money.
—For God's sake, I'll follow you.
—Good! I cried.
—It may take a year. Can you wait?
—Of course. What else do I have to do?
—Then it's all set.
And we fell to kissing some more. I was too young to be suspicious of his enthusiasm, and he was too young to fake it. My entire experience with men was limited to my father. Limited is putting it mildly. Myles had a mother, who lived somewhere in Wicklow, while he lived in town with friends. Our lives were reduced to a positive poverty: a self alone in the world. It never occurred to me to struggle to stay with him, there. Now that I trusted he would follow, I actually desired my solitude again. I knew what to do with it.

He gave me instructions on how to keep up with the music scene. It was already lively in Boston as well as New York. And we spent our last days together plotting and clutching at each other. Then he took me to Shannon Airport on the bus. On the way he asked me for the third time about my scar, where I got it, and I told him again I didn't remember. He begged.
—It had to do with a dog and a baby, I said.
—The dog bit the baby? You?
—No, I replied, and inhaled the smell of his skin and his jacket to carry away with me.

With my last bit of money I bought my grandmother a cloth leprechaun at the airport, then said good-bye to Myles, and we both were weeping. As I watched, through the porthole, the rough green nest of the island receding into the sea, I remember feeling (a rare feeling) allied with my mother, who once said, "I can't leave this room. The world is too big."

Several months later he arrived and came to see me, where I was then settled, successfully, in a dormitory in Boston. The confidence his existence had given me had resulted in good grades, a flourishing social life, and active engagement in political activity. When he arrived I showed him off like a pet, crudely, pridefully, and didn't understand his responses to the speed and brutality of the nation he was now in.

I was unnerved by his long silences and murmured remarks. In this new context, his tweedy and shabby country look was anachronistic. Blasting the radio and snapping my gum, I drove him to New York to meet the agent, Lyn, who was going to get him set on his career. My bravado was a vapor, but a poisonous one nonetheless. I suppose he only stayed with me then because there was no one else he knew.

—You can't be gentle here, can you, he remarked in those first days. I thought he meant the general "you," the American You, but he meant me.

Manhattan, the whale, chewed and swallowed us at the Triboro Bridge: the bridge of its palate over a brown tongue of water. Once inside, careening down the concrete highway, we assented to the life lived there, and even liked it. We went to the Village where the folk-singing scene was in full swing and drifted around, night and day, through those streets wafting up odors of subway, bread, fruit, and perfume. Sleeping on Perry Street, in a two-room sixth-floor walkup occupied by an Irish fiddler who worked in a restaurant during the day, we lay side by side on a spread-out sleeping bag under blankets, and we whispered our hopes and plans as if we could predict the world.

In New York I dropped my cocky act, and my posture sloped, as did his, under the weight of rocky shadows. In the Village there were the Clancy brothers, Bob Dylan, Mary O'Hara, Bob Gibson, Carolyn and Richard Farina, and assorted singers and players who hung out together in saloons and each other's flats. At first everyone was engaged whole-heartedly in each other's work. Music was all that anyone talked about, except, occasionally, for the theater, and record companies for traditional music were opening up around. In the fall the city was at it's best—not too cold, but clear-aired and colorful. Produce out on the streets at dawn was more dazzling and tempting than in summer or winter, and after hours when the city was quiet and wet, you could walk for blocks without feeling the temperature as a hostile pressure.

When Myles got settled into a loft with some singers, and found a job as a busboy, he was welcomed into a circle of Irishmen who like him wanted to stay in New York. I drove back to Boston. Soon his letters came, beginning "Me love," and followed by a litany of grievances. Even as he described jovial drinking bouts and singing with friends in the White Horse and Chinatown and at clubs and apartments late into the night, of reminiscing with other Irishmen and talk of politics here and there, he suffered. A few times I visited him. He wanted me to come settle in, to marry him.

One night Myles and I drove from opposite directions to meet somewhere exactly halfway between the places each of us lived. This was before we were married. We found ourselves basically pinned under a pile of concrete abutments in a bar that had such greasy tables they were like the bottoms of old unclean pans. The glasses were stained horribly, too. Every time the door swung open in came a smell of ocean. We were madly in love that night, the waiter called us Bill and Coo.
Now I remember that Myles was rather pale and flat-featured, with eyes as green as sand jewelry, reddish-brown hair, those rotten teeth, some freckles—it was a boyish face. His lips were soft, the hands long but square-tipped—like yours—and his ears small and close to the skull. He always wore blue workshirts and jeans. His guitar always lay at his feet like a dog.

God, imagine in the grit of concrete, of steel underground tracks and cars studded with people shooting around in the dark—his neck smelled of smoke and turf. Like him I was filled with famous questions and quotations and loved the aphorism and the virgin quality of a lapidary literature. We shared our love of poetry and drama, too. But I remember when we went outside that night we cut our fingertips in the rain as sharp as glass and mixed our blood!

Shit, I was a wild person in those days, who felt nowhere so at home as in his arms. Physical heat made me feel that I was in a safe place. I was terrible and reckless—don't ever be that way and it was he who had to push me back from going too far. I felt safe with him, but then I would immediately feel suffocated by my happiness and want to get away from it.

I think I must have been compelled to lose everything then. I think I was engaged in some quest that meant that I had to suffer the uprootedness, which then made me yearn for the safety I couldn't stand. Insane?

I can tell you now that driving back to Boston that night I knew everything I would ever know up to this very moment. Nothing more would be added to the understanding I had of search and loss that I had with him. I was only seventeen and had experienced the essential paradox of my life; the rest has just been renditions on it.

It was Granny who forced my hand; she was enthralled at the drama of such an event. "The poor thing doesn't know what to do," I heard her saying to a friend. "I'll have to get Father to speak to her." So Father Lally was called in. Granny's idea was that I should get the Irishman to marry me before he bolted. The priest was not so hysterical, or cynical. I went to see him, dutifully, and hoped he might, in fact, tell me if I should marry or not.

The church and rectory were made of an ochre-colored stone, almost yellow, and were fronted by a chain-link fence. Jesus fell from the wall, forward, like Prometheus bound and yearning. The stained-glass windows inside the church looked like crossword puzzles for six-year-olds. Father Lally, a small dark man with an anguished look on his face, was in his mid-sixties, though he seemed much younger. He lit up around children. I remembered how good he was to me when I was small and how cool he became as I grew into adolescence, until he hardly spoke to me at all. His office contained images of the Virgin that were childlike and one photograph of Pope John XXIII. As we sat in there, I felt him searching my face and instinctively knew what he was looking for. Traces of the child I had been; only then, when he found them, would we be able to talk to each other. I smiled and made jokes, I looked shy and gentle. He slowly warmed, his body untensed, he lit a cigarette, he gained a charming smile, and we reminisced about the school (no longer open) and the nuns who taught there.

Outside, the trees were dripping with lumps of slush. I saw the edge of the chain-link fence, and I could feel the cold twist of its iron curls in my fingers. It stood in space; there was no "right side" to be on.

Now, my dear, he said, and I warmed, remembering how he said "Dearly Beloved" or "My Dear Brothers and Sisters" when he gave the homily and how much the endearment meant to me.
—Yes? Father?
—Your grandmother says you plan to get married to a young Irishman. I think that's wonderful, but you're awfully young.
—Well, I'll be nineteen in a year.
—You mean you're eighteen.
—He's over twenty. He's a folk singer, a very good one. He's very nice and good to me.
—You're not pregnant, are you?
—No, I'm fine, Father.
—It's not a disease, you know, he said with a smile.
Roisin hunched up and laughed, Father Lally did, too and said he would marry us.

We had to wait a month. I remember March passed in a comic parade of gales, clouds, rain, and sleet. Everyone laughed at the weather. Clouds especially pillowed up in the evenings, streaked in gold and purple. The trees like black lace trembled at the horizon. A fluff storm—wet flakes and round, the size of feathers—splattered into April. Only a few cro- cuses were chewing their way into the light when Myles arrived to pre- pare for our nuptials. He carried instruments—flutes, fiddle, and guitar.

He was, in his harsh tweeds, the consummate country boy, and Granny did all but somersault around the house, she was so excited.

We had an apartment in a three-story wooden tenement. It was always cold. Hunched around her coat and bones, Granny stood by the stove, stirring horrible foods we had to eat and singing. Weeks-old chicken bones were turned into soup where turnip and parts of used potatoes floated. Hot Spam and ketchup, minced beef from a can on toast. Myles and she swilled down whiskey to digest it all. Our wedding dinner consisted of a canned ham, canned yams, and canned baby peas (the baby part was the treat). Ice cream served from a sagging carton on a plate was our dessert.

Myles dealt with this well, singing the songs she commanded, while moaning along with him. His two friends, McCool and Conor, arrived for the ceremony, too, and stayed in the apartment. They all roamed around with bottles of stout and stashes of pretzels, singing and plucking the guitar strings. She followed them. She swept behind their feet and sang. They were good to her, being used to old people, not shunting her aside. I remember after we had our blood tests. Outside the clinic I got depressed because ice and decay were clustered together—leaves with discarded cups and bottles, a crushed bird with old snow in its feathers. He walked beside me, fast, and talked about the priest. He said, "My desire to believe is my belief, and that's as strong as it will ever get. But I didn't tell Father that."
 "No, don't hurt Father's feelings," I said, staring up at Myles.
"Do you really believe in God?" he asked.
"I want to, so badly, it's what you say, it's . . . well, a kind of faith. I want to, I want to!"
He threw his arm over my shoulder, hard, and laughed: Don't get so upset.
My father came to the wedding with his new wife and the other children, who were perfectly nice. My grandmother was there. Some neighborhood people. And Conor and McCool, who played some Irish music before and

after the short ceremony. I felt as if I was on my knees the whole time. Or as small as a small child. I couldn't see any faces, but only shirts and belts. There was no joy, no confidence, but a terrible awareness of my promise: *I will*. It put me into history the way marching and demonstrating put me into history. My promise put me into life. I took it seriously. I read it in his lips, too, that he took the promise to his heart, too. You have the most freedom when you are writing your own history.

My joy found release in the car, driving back to New York, with Conor and McCool and Myles. I realized I officially belonged to another human being, I now was safe; he belonged to me. We sang for hours and passed the stout around the dark car. This was our real wedding party: speed and wheels across a black landscape.

In New York we lived in a loft on lower Broadway. It was not a large one, but it accommodated a bunch of us—ourselves, an actress, and four Irish musicians. We all had menial jobs; I was the only one who attended classes. Five hours a day I worked in a shipping office filling out bills of lading and writing up invoices, keeping the accounts and filing. The wood-and-paper odor of old desks and file cabinets gave me a sense of security similar to that of a library. On either side of those five hours, I attended classes leading to social work.

At home I was often alone with my studies while the others sang, rehearsed, got drunk, and wheeled and dealed. I would curl into our mattress on the floor, covered by frayed wool blankets, and read. Occasionally Myles checked to make sure I was there. Outside women often waited for him with no regard for my status as his wife. They were more substantial than I, but not by much. Shadowy, dressed in limp shirts and skirts, long-haired and pallid, in those days we hid our lamps under our baskets except to peek out competitively at each other.

The roar of male voices, like the traffic down below on Broadway, kept us down and under. We learned to block it out, to avoid thinking about what it meant. The man was the world. Therefore, our interpretation of reality, social, psychological, spiritual, aesthetic, was determined by the shape and manner of the man closest to us. Our choice of the man indicated our choice of a landscape, property, and neighborhood. The male body was an indicator of how brutal or how fair the world could be. If the man loved with affection, the world was an affectionate place; if he was cold, the whole of reality was determined to be rejecting. First there was the man, then there was the city. To have a man was to have access and a right to the city.

I might have suffered at the presence of women better looking and livelier than I, who were attracted to Myles, but he gave me no reason to fear. He was a man who wanted a wife so he wouldn't have to think about women anymore. This made him safe. However, my sense of something coming between myself and the city—a shape, a bravado—made me uncomfortable. So when he wasn't there, I wasn't safe. I bought a dog, who was my favorite link to the physical world. The dog was the representative of my power, being all animal and silent. The dog went everywhere with me. Whenever we went to the country—Connecticut or Vermont—the dog and I trembled for joy at the smell of leaves and soft earth coming through the car windows. Myles relaxed, the three of us grew quiet, and in the country we walked over fields, fantasizing about the time when we would live on a farm, as farmers, and farm.

Myles didn't adapt to New York, not the way his friends did. His father had been an IRA man, and he had politics in his bones. He couldn't be light-hearted when it was called for, or serious in the appropriate ways. He was a persistent and expert musician, but he always got in a fight with someone on the way to a performance. Not a physical fight, not even a drunken fight, but a quarrel over something trite that had, for him, enormous political consequences. He couldn't stand agents or producers, and he was hostile to audiences who talked while they played in a bar or coffee shop. His grudges took on aspects of class war. It was never clear whether he hated the rich because he wanted to be rich, too, or because he felt that money automatically canceled humility and generosity from its owner. At least it was never clear to his friends, who railed at him about it.

To me he was not a hypocrite, but I felt his suffering and confusion too well. Through him I watched the enormous city expand, buildings stretched all the way to the clouds, tunnels dove into infinity, bridges arced with the height of rainbows, city blocks were obstacle courses, and through them all teemed a fallen humanity. If his only access to a platform for his music (one where the audience didn't talk) was through salesmen and dealers, then his desire wavered and drooped.

Whenever we left the city and entered green shadows, and color once again radiated from living matter, I felt better, so did he. There were gatherings in people's houses, and we went, with his instruments and the dog, happily. Surges of joy carried us out into the woods and around meadows, but as soon as he was inside, with people, he was angry again.

"I don't want to be a professional Irishman," was one of his themes. "It's like being one of those buffoons in the Middle Ages," he said. "Playing the fool to the rich."
It would not, could not be long before he became physically ill and had to go into the hospital to recover his health. I was pregnant already. But we didn't know it. He lay with his back to me and he pressed a pillow over his feverish head. He said he wanted to go home the minute he was well. And that was the last thing I remembered about him and me together. A strange blackness folded over the months or weeks that followed.

I had a baby, I worked, was nervous and I met Kosta. I became a social worker, we moved to Boston. We were together with you and Ma and life went on. But suddenly I had to know what had happened to Myles and me. Ma asked me why, she wanted to know if I no longer loved her son. I assured her that my desire was independent of her and everything else, even you, the boy of seven then. I had to know what happened. So

I took a backpack and a sleeping bag and one other thing and began a two week trip away from home.

The stars were the first thing that excited me, viewed from where I lay in a bag on the West Coast of Ireland, they were as solid as sparks from a pyrotechnical show. A fountain, a spray, held still. The ground was hard and damp under my back where I rested beside Yeats's grave. Ben Bulben, a black humpbacked whale shape, was pressed on the gray sky. I couldn't believe what I was doing. Sleepless with excitement, I watched the arrival of day—silver and rose over the sea. By the bones of the poet I recited his verse in whispers and recognized my own face in a cloud of stars, low to the mud as I was.

I biked everywhere on my search for Myles. The first four days my legs ached, and after that they had muscles.

There was a Myles O'Donnell whom I traced to his farm in Connemara, where he lived with a wife and some children. He, they said in the town, played bones, spoons, and a harmonica, and he was a big sour man with an unknown background. I found him in his barn, among some smelly hay and goats, a toothless man with wild hair and one ear. He was the wrong one.
The next musical Myles O'Donnell was called "the singing monk" by the villagers who went to mass at the Franciscan monastery. That must be him. He had a lovely soft voice, eyes "as green as gooseberries," and played the organ while he sang the psalms. I went to mass and saw him. He was a big boy in a brown robe and sandals, with a rosy face and a large Adam's apple. Brother Myles sang very sweetly, but he was the wrong one.

As in all fairy tales I assumed the third Myles O'Donnell would be the right one. He was a waiter in a Dublin pub who had lived in America, sang, and drank too much. It was a rainy Saturday, and I had biked for three days. I spent the afternoon in movie theaters, then walked across the bridge to the green-and-gold-painted pub. Inside were crowds of wet people and umbrellas, loud talk, smoke, and Myles O'Donnell. He was a rotund fellow, not much taller than I, with little eyes and a crack for a mouth. I threw back a glass of Scotch and rode again, in the dusk and drizzle, to the house where I had boarded so many years before. I was told they had moved to Blackrock, and I rode down there and found them in a house facing the rocky, black sea.

They let me in, gave me a bed, and told me where I could find Myles's mother. And the next day, with the sun shining in and out, I rode the bike many kilometers to Wicklow, where she lived in a cottage hidden behind rotten flowers, raspberry nets, and half-broken apple trees. A smoking turf smell issued from every door and window. It made me swoon with pleasure. She was a wizened creature with huge horselike teeth that I took to be false; they were out of proportion to everything else. But she told me, through them, where her son could be found.
—On the west coast, near Donegal. I'll give you the house and number.
—So he actually has an address? I asked.
—It's a kind of an address. I've never seen the place myself.
—Is he married?
—Let's hope that's what it is.
In a scrawl, and smoking at the same time, she wrote the name of the town where he lived and where, she said, he fished for a living.
—Is he musical? I asked, and she replied, Indeed he is. Very musical.
And it was then she pulled out a picture of him, when he was about fifteen. He was holding a guitar, a boy who was the image of you.

Near Donegal days later it rained in great sheets, blowing this way and that, and water curled through the stony gutters, carrying wrappers to stuffed drains. I rode my bike all the same and in a billowing mackintosh headed for the harbor, where fishing boats in varying colors lay face down on a stone bank. The area was empty and all watery, and I found a little shed to stand inside, to wait for what I didn't know.

Hours later, things began to shine under a late afternoon sun, and I stepped out into the drips and gemstrung twigs with a solid sensation of protection. There are two kinds of places in the world that I know of—one where the safety comes by the law and one where the safety comes by the wilderness; I prefer the latter, though there you take your chances.

I moved up and down the water's edge, aware that hardly anyone knew or cared where I was, and this was good. Yet I also know that a sense of security comes from the knowledge of danger. All around me was water and stones. It dawned on me that a great momentum had begun at earth's genesis, and this was the speed at which we lived and moved, spun into a perfectly timed velocity, where control was minimal. A willful or weak jerk away from this momentum caused terrible suffering and loneliness. I believed it was not so much separation from the creator as from creation itself.

"Time is just reality slowed down, so it wouldn't all happen at once," said some writing on a wall. I believed that the importance of keeping a promise was simple: a mark of confidence in the laws of time.

Now I saw an old man like a thing dragging wings, his brown tattered coat, limping down the road. Then a car sped by. It was the usual sunny dusk I remembered in Ireland, with clouds hopping like lambs across a greenish sky. Across the water I heard a slapping sound— oars—from a lone fisherman rowing in from the sea, soaked, no doubt. His boat I could see was greener than the sky, and his oarlocks creaked and banged. Was it him, I wondered, since it was a broadbacked man with his color hair?

But it wasn't him. It was a friend of his instead. Glumly he told me to follow him up the winding hill to where I could finally see Myles O'Donnell. My heart skipped inside of me. The man walked stooped and fast, set in his jaw like one who hates to use his mouth for more than food or drink. His boots were wet and sloppy. I was much smaller than he, and dressed in sweaters, jeans, sneakers, a jacket, with my backpack pulling at me, and one other thing. This was Myles's guitar, which he had left, years before, with me.

(This guitar had a weirdly magical history. Because I went to a pawn shop to buy back the guitar, oh—years ago!—which I had sold when Myles left. Kosta, who even then did not like to work, had moved in with us, and I was feeling safe and even cheery at times. I had, on my way to work one day, noticed that the guitar was still in the window of the store; it was like something living where it leaned, all gold and lonely, in a cluster of radios and cutlery. I felt it lived for me and went to buy it back as soon as I had cashed my paycheck. While I was paying for it, I noticed under the glass counter a ring that dazzled me. Pretty good for fake, the man told me. I agreed and bought it. At home Kosta immediately dubbed the ring my engagement ring; it cost under five dollars. And I flashed it around for years to come. And that was the same ring that we sold to go to California.)

At the top of the knobby hill sat a couple of white cottages. The man waved his hand at one, saying that one, and left me there. I put down the guitar and pushed at my short hair, damp and prickly, and smoothed my jacket and dampened my lips. My heart and stomach tossed, for though his mother had hinted he was married, I didn't believe it.

The whitewashed cottage had an ill-kept garden in front and behind, and torn curtains covered the windows. The rich turfy smell of a fire slipped under the door and out to where I stood, stunned as Gretel before her father's house in the woods. How could he have left me, lost, in the enormous forest? Just to eat with another woman?

Wind parted and rejoined around my head, body, and the cottage. Its touch was softer than a comforter and as soft as water. It lifted me up by my feet and whirled me around in circles, so the clouds spun and the blue of the sky poured down like a force into my face. I blew up and up into the air, flaying and falling away from gravity, toward the cherubic patterns. Unleavened, heaven nonetheless captured the weight of my soul, and took it in.

Below I could see the west coast carved out of the liquid sea and the island, and the tiny cottages I had cycled by along the cliffs. My body stood wherever I left it, petrified as Pinocchio's wood, as the wind washed and whirled the real me into the blue. Sun-washed wings—a flapping and rushing, and the hairlike strips on quills, the bleached bones of birds, fell like sticks around me. Feathers instead of hairs, gills and fins instead of feathers or hair, and I, flying, heard a baby crying and fell, smack, down to earth. A dead fish lay on the ground before my feet.

A baby cried from inside the house and seemed to make the strings strum on their own. The wind sang down to the baby and also ran across the catgut, till the instrument sobbed and hummed all by itself where it lay on the front step of a cottage, like an abandoned infant. Lost in the universe, the baby cried from inside the house now, and its shape made the terms of its cries and needs. The guitar, meantime, also howled and sobbed on the steps of the cottage. Each strum was similar to the strands of gold braided through the clouds.

I stepped over the fish and hid behind a bush to watch. And soon the door did open, the baby's crying increased, and a man's arm reached out and took the guitar inside. The door remained ajar for several minutes. Then the darkness emitted the form of a man, who stood on the stoop, looking this way and that. Behind him was another shape, a woman, and the baby's cries quieted. I breathed with the wind and wondered at the bushes and brambles that held me.

—Roisin! he called.

A dark rose snapping free of its thorns, I took a deep breath, gulped, and stepped into the road. A car whipped by, making me slump and weak in the knees. Myles came down the path to greet me, and we met in the road there, with his wife hovering behind. I looked at his face: flat, not bony, soft and dreamy, and the taste of his mouth entered my senses from the air between us.

We called pleasantries out of ourselves, one to the other, and our new smiles were twisted uncomfortably on our old faces. The wife, a formless substance I couldn't focus on, went back inside, and Myles walked me down the road to where my bike was parked by the boats.
—What a surprise, he said more than once.
—I know, I know, I responded.
—How long are you visiting?
—Don't worry, hardly at all.
—On business, or what?
—On business, I said.
—And you thought you'd return the guitar?
—That's right.
—Well, well. And how is the boy, Liam? He must be seven.
—He's not here, he's great.
—Are you remarried?
—Yes, I told him. And how many children do you have?
—Just two, here, with her. You know.
—Yes, that's good. What happened to you, since?
—Well, he said, a great deal. I was involved, politically, and even went to jail for a while. When I got out, I began to concentrate on the old music again. Now that's all I do, when I'm not out in my boat. She's a singer, too, plays the harp.

We walked slowly but deliberately away from his house and exchanged grave glances now and then.
—And yourself? he asked.
—Nothing much, I told him. I just went on to meet the man I'm with now. I raised Liam with his help, got my degree, worked. Social work.

My bike had been knocked down by the wind. I set it up and hung on to the handlebars, scanning his face and the deep sky beyond.

—Have you seen any of the old boys, McCool, Conor? he asked.
—God, no.
—And are you happy?
—Fine . . . I only wish, sometimes, though, that your son could know you.
—She knows all about him. Send him over any time.
—I might do that, I said.
—Do you still live in New York?
—No, no. Did you have a church wedding?
—No, not at all. We're not exactly pious, either of us.
—Ah. Well. I guess I'll go. The guitar, you have it back, and that's the main thing. Everything in its place.
—And a place for everything. Isn't that the saying?
—I think so.
—You look about the same, he told me.
I studied his face. That transcendent gaze in his eyes gave me no cause for joy. Those were the eyes through which I once looked out on the hard world.

Myles, watching my moves as if they were clouds, was hesitant and stayed a few paces back while I wiped the rain off my bicycle seat. I tried to think of a towering line, one that would convey all that I had gone through. But my lips quipped, "All's well that ends well."

He didn't nod or sigh profoundly but continued to watch me from afar. Then as I tossed the last drops off the handlebars, he asked if I ever got the money.

—What money? I asked.
—The money I sent to McCool. Quite a lot, too.
—No.
—Didn't you call him, like I told you to?
—No.
—But I sent him several packets of money, for you, and letters, too.

—I never got them.

—Now I knew you were indifferent, but that's going too far. How did you ever take care of the baby, then? I was waiting for you here.

—Indifferent? I asked.

—Well, whatever you want to call it when someone doesn't stay on the team.

—I had strong feelings. Team?

—Us, marriage. Then why did you get the divorce?

—I adored you, I blurted out.

—Then why a divorce?

—You told me to.

—My God, the obedience! I was delirious, remember? Very sick. With the hepatitis.

—What happened to the money you sent to me supposedly?

—That bugger, McCool, must have run off with it. I wondered why I never heard from him again. I did send it, Roisin.

—I thought you wanted a divorce, you said you did.

—I did want to save you from the problems I had. Politics, business you were completely unaware of. That's true.

—Well, then. I think we misunderstood each other.

—I think we did, too.

—That's why I have no memory of it, I said. I never got your letters.

Now the sky was growing bruised and battered. Colors spread under its skin. I shivered and my eyes teared. He, in his brown knit sweater, was very large before me, taking up a good part of the horizon. I asked him why he married me in the first place.

—To get to the States, he said, was one reason. But the other reason was obvious, we both were in love. Why didn't you ever try to contact me here?

—I think I thought. I waited for. I don't remember. You, I imagined gone. You were.

—Ah, well, it's too late to worry over it.

—It certainly is, I agreed.

—But it's good to get it straight, he said.

I began to push the bike away then and hunched around the chill his words were giving me. It was the first time in my life I realized that a mistake could take you so far from home that you were, in a sense, permanently lost. Could your lost life be said, then, to be the end of, your original destiny?

As I rode away from Myles, he called my name, and I paused and looked back. Second thoughts softened his face now, and he strode after me, arms swinging. He asked me to come to his house and have some tea or stout, to meet his wife and children.
—I want to give something to you to bring to the boy. Is he at all musical?
—Oddly enough, yes.
Where we stood by the roadside I could see his house up the hill, and now I looked aside at Myles, as I had during our wedding vows.
—Well, I've got something for him. And you must have my address here, in case he ever wants to come over and see me.

—I'll come, but only for a minute, I said.
—Sorry I was gruff with you. The shock.
—It's okay, you weren't. You look almost the same. I know you.
—You too. Are you happy with your man?
—I guess. Though I'm having fun alone.
—You always liked to be alone. You just didn't want to admit it.
He took my bike by the hands and pushed it up the hill between us. The wind was slowing down the spokes.
—It's easier to be alone than to be left alone, I told him. How, did you ever get well again?
—I came home. The air, you know, is gentle here.
—And why did you make me divorce you, seriously?
—It's a long story. Besides, I didn't make you. You agreed to it quite fast, as I recall. You never fought for things you wanted.
—I didn't?
—Think about it. But whatever the case, you were my first love.
—Well, that's something.

—And the fact is, I couldn't get married to Liz in the church. That was a problem for her. It's not official, you know, in her mind, without the blessing.

—You want to get it annulled? You want my help?

—Well, that's a thought.

It was a thought he hadn't had before. I could tell by the way he stopped and looked up the hill. The wind blew back his curls easily, he was going bald, and I pressed my hands deep in my pockets, afraid to hear him.

—Ah, we won't bother, he said. Once is enough. One marriage like that. I mean, we had a child.

—I guess yes, I said.

—I mean, the rest is already in other hands, if there are any, which I strongly doubt. Funny she should care, though, being lapsed and anarchic as she is.

—I understand why she does, I told him.

—And do you still have your faith? Your belief in belief.

—Belief is something hardly anyone has. I have hope, despite everything.

—How can you?

—Because I have to.

—That's a good one. Come on.

His laugh I knew as well as the bark of a dog, or the slam of a car door, or the cough of a child. And I followed him up the rest of the hill in silence. His wife was wiry and dark—a little like me, in fact—she wanted me gone, though, so I took what he gave me for you—the lap harp—and I left without tea or stout. Then, walking alone down the hill with my bike, I realized what I had been looking for. Not him, not the reassurance he gave me, but truth, or whatever you want to call it—that is, the meeting of two people who share one story and agree on its meaning. That's what I had always been looking for.

Saving History

Unable to rest because unable to know.

If Christ doesn't rise in two hours, then God has forsaken us all. The whitening of the east spreads over the west. Mourning doves warble.

Morning men are raving on the beach, of alcohol and some mental derangement associated with loss.

Hugo told me all love doesn't end in tragedy. But he admitted that this was only HIS experience.

He had had, he told me, many happy love experiences. Of course they were all in the past tense.

He had painted his walls black and the windows were always sealed by green blinds. You could see nothing, except a small ring of light around votive candles. It was a building filled with young prostitutes, overlooking a miserable avenue in the south end of town. He had some political posters hung on walls, but only after your eyes grew accustomed to the light could you actually read the words: SOLEDAD, WATTS, UP THE IRA.

Saving History

x

Her skin did not respond to touches lacking in love. The first thing you really know is the touch of love. So why did she return again to his black bedclothes, to the pressure of his body on hers? She did not believe in choice, because she misapprehended facts. They had eluded her since childhood. Anything that had a weight, measurement and number—a correct answer—became blurry as the face of an enemy. She averted her gaze from facts. She lived impressionistically, with the kind of awe that makes you egalitarian. She didn't love him either, not at first, not until it was clear that they were stuck together in the tragedy of consequence.

x

In that city there was none of the convulsive unity you find in the great cities of this century: Paris, New York. There was none of that sense of the violent and the tender occurring simultaneously, as they might on a farm or a plantation. No, each element of expression was segregated from the other. It was a divided city, provincial and proud, dominated by the ethics of Protestants. In this city she developed her fear of institutions, a fear that was neurotic, if colorful. It led her to the usual ironies—a sentence of time spent enclosed in brick. But first she had to succumb to being fueled by this man who did not love her and never would. He would claim her, insult her, beat her, he would lie to himself and others about her, he would conjure her into alien forms—hostile and subversive after he had married her and made her pregnant more than once. And she would collaborate, for reasons unknown. Both did what they did for reasons unknown to them (the one liberating aspect to the arrangement), and both suffered equally though suffering can't be measured or numbered, and either you do, or you don't suffer.

x

Outside the sheep of snow lay down along the curbs. I have heard a book roar with a snowstorm inside it. People froze between the pages.

312

Beasts nuzzled their own teats.

I experience my abilities to think and imagine as actual geographies ruled by gravity and weather. I know that consciousness does not dwell in me, but I dwell in it.

Everyone's terror weighs the same. The critical issue is how to release it from its venue—to what we call Liberty: whether by standing on the ocean-swept deck obedient but in prayer. Or whether by setting off bombs. To liberate the terror. And vacate the premises where terror laps like an unwanted animal at a pool of water. Then to live with a little space in oneself, to brush it and sweep it and wash it with tears. And never to let terror enter again, never.

x

Hugo said Orpheus is everything because he made a religion of language, a paradise of words. A French nurse had named him Dumas when she found out he was "Hugo" and he was only a baby. He said this act of nominal determinism (although logically skewed) made him the poet he believed himself to be, and he was. How could he not be when he was so arbitrarily named? "I was named and so I name."

His voice was the voice of The End.

For reasons unknown, they fixed on each other, fascinated, and directed all discourse, one to the other, quarreling but unwilling to let go, whether by phone or by face or by mail. Hugo was the color of sanded cedar, he came from the Seychelles originally, then Tanzania (where he witnessed slaughter and was tortured) and Ibiza. His mother came from Punjab, his father was a priest. He was in the import business, but it continually failed him, and so he was a voracious reader of literature about struggle.

We don't care about her name yet because she has the advantage of the I.

x

I couldn't say it was love, but I don't think a woman can love a man unless it's her father or her son. I could say, though, that it was one interior life enclosing the other, and one intelligence devouring the other, and the way fate works when it wants to change society.

Fate eats. God announces itself as affliction, as a pain that is gruesome. God doesn't eat, but wounds. You have to know this in order to live.

When people decided to mix inventions into the real things—cement in water, steel pipes in earth, tiles under fields—they were only a few steps away from putting nails into hands, people into ovens, needles into arms.

I identify with the women standing back and watching the crucifixion drama, because I know how easy it is to become a participant in cruelty. And once that has happened, what's left for you?

x

He couldn't care for anyone but himself, because the givens of his personality were overwhelming. He was a person who only slept three hours out of every twenty-four. His mind was undisciplined. His reading was voracious, scattered, and he put all the information together from no matter what sources—into a unifying and credible theory. He was drawn to criminals and prostitutes. He didn't want to be one with them, but watched them with a dull pain in his temples. It was their social ignorance that plagued him, interested him, an absence of self-consciousness that was synonymous with no-law. He lacked a superego himself (or conscience) while he sometimes lay prone in prayer to Allah. It was his cowardice that finally acted in place of a conscience. He was really scared of being discovered and labeled.

x

I don't know this man but I suffer for him. How? I live out his drama, mentally, trying to imagine the way it felt to be him. I hope that in this imaginative action, some of his pain will revert to me. If I don't do this, who else will?

Saving History

It was her assignment for a few years to receive his blows and his cruel words. When it was no longer her assignment, and servitude was turning into slavery, she left, and he followed, making brutal and realizable threats on her life. They both, this way, entered a life of detachment, as in antisocial.

To kill and destroy in order to make room for business and technology is to have reached the conclusion that what a person makes has more value than the person.

We have only ourselves—compositional under misty givens—to blame. And only other human hands can transmit the tenderness we require. I can live without almost anything except love.

x

All women are prostitutes, he insisted. Wives are variations on that theme of utility. The wedding ring was a link in a human chain, hand to hand to hand, around the globe. The sign of the master-whore engagement was that gold band on a hand. He pointed out the flounciness of females on the streets, their pathetic embellishment of their bodies. Men embellish their egos, he said. Women embellish their flesh. They can't help being beautiful of course, he conceded. And together they scrutinized the females passing, experiencing the embarrassment on the faces they saw. But then he would accuse her of decadence, when she noted beauty on her own. It was hard to keep up with his varying judgments, always contradicting themselves from day to day. She was too sensitive to him, to all inflections of judgment in fact. Yet they agreed on books, movies, plays, politics; their opinions mirrored each other, no matter how wild and speculative they were. Something twinned in the way they both thought feelingly; their brains were receivers and purveyors of emotions, and they organized their thoughts into streams of near-ecstatic perceptions. While most people experienced their brains as dry factories of ideas, and memories, they did not.

The poetics of speech—especially angry speech—was their *folie à deux*.

He bought her a thick gold band encrusted with rhinestones. It had an antique look, she lost it, and he had to buy her two other rings before their day was over. I want to understand why a woman would try so hard to please a man who was cold and unkind. What's the deal? All people seek great difficulty, no doubt about that; they seek and even create the situation which will be insurmountably problematic. It would be a strange person who did not know that suffering is a way to stay alive.

x

Having learned the heavy stresses and the light—between subjugation and servitude—I will stand behind my actions, without a jot of remorse.

He smashed his fist into her face, as it lay on a pillow, and a geyser of warm blood rushed from her nostrils, she thought she was blind. At the hospital they diagnosed a broken nose, she had two black eyes for several days, and wore dark glasses. He was repentant, stunned, saddened by his unexpected bash. She forgave but couldn't forget what he had done. She flinched automatically when he leaned over her to turn off the light.

He anyway returned to his anger soon after, and directed it again at her. Words, words, poisoned words, about her background, her privilege (at being American, at not having been tortured as a child, at not losing her family to war), her inability to understand what it was like to be him. They lived under trees—swinging beech and elm trees—by then, in a rundown section on the margin of the city, a section that had once been elegant and summery. Rain ran lines down the dusty windowpanes. Her babies pressed their pink lips against her nipples and drank with their eyes raised to see her face. Their hands waved vaguely, they were "Irish twins" born within a year of each other, and sometimes by chance their fingers linked, as if they were members of the same body.

x

She was his mother, in the sense that she was the mother he owned. Mother? What, in fact, is a mother? It is the description of a person who has given birth. They say you only have one mother, but men who marry women who then give birth have two mothers. Equally, he was her second father, being the father whom she owned through the arrangement of their physical relations. Her father. So sex has astounding consequences, conferring confused titles on those involved. I love a singer who calls her lover "Daddy."

This was the center of both of their lives: the pit heart, the fall point, the cemetery at the center of all that is given. Sparrows had seeds, worms, and water, and they had food stamps, greens, and wine. Everything they had, though, was shoved to the side to accommodate the heavy presence of his past. Clock, phone, radio, rain.

x

His hand would lift like the word slide-rule, tilted, his lips narrowed, when he wanted to hit her but didn't. He was utterly lacking the tenderness of a person who has felt safe in the beginning (his beginnings were wretched and insulting, his belly and back a story of scars), but he was not innately violent. It was alcohol that incinerated the patience that was a good characteristic of his. Without that ability to stand in a line for a long time, or to sit in a waiting room quietly, reading, his essence was sunk. He was, with wine in him, restless, raging.

She lay in bed a lot, after work, with the babies on either side, sipping a can of Champale, watching TV. When she heard his tread, her mouth grew parched. Most times he would come in and only abuse her verbally. But once he pulled her roughly away from the babies, dragged her down the hall, and stabbed at her stiff torso with his phallus. He knew she only loved her children, he felt neglected and abandoned. She dreamed he murdered her double and buried the body in a baggie out in the yard, and she covered for him. By "dream" I mean she entered into her true story, sleeping.

He was verbally flashy, and mentally quick as anyone, he could have been a money-maker except he was so inconsistent, and so quick to hate. He said things like, "If you aren't a money-maker in one of the American states, you are as good as wastepaper. You have to fight to be multi-rich or lie down, dirt poor. There's nowhere to be comfortable between. Why do I have to feel so anxious about money? What is it? Numbers!"

x

The blueing of the east has begun. One bird shows frantic pleasure in this fact. Where are the bodies of fallen sparrows? There are so many of them lined up on wires, posted on rooftops, nestled in trees, you'd think their bodies would litter the streets.

x

The central question for Hugo: Was violence voluntary or a compulsion? In other words, did he make a choice to strike out or was it inevitable? And what might happen to him now?

As they grew, the kids (a girl and a girl) kept each other busy under tables and on jolly swings where they bounced side by side, hanging from the doorjamb facing both hall and kitchen. As toddlers, they both loved vanilla yogurt, flan, and Gerber's mixed fruits. Only one ate meat, which the littler one declined with a grimace.

Gray firmament, predawn, I am distanced from others and self, milking unending desire for union with the end of alone. The two stars that travel over the telephone wires. The placement of the moon above the chimney . . . Now I am conscious of such repetition and distance as being salves of the psyche.

x

Why do women let an old man dominate their fortunes? Why do the children vote for fathers instead of brothers? Why do men have this power over women and children? The erotic swelling . . . the necessity of birthing . . . must these cause such abject behavior that the earth itself is being shaken from its axis by the spill of weapons?

Saving History

x

One night he whammed and slammed her, knocking her right down the stone steps in front of their house. Then he launched off into the city, his face as twisted as a gargoyle on a cathedral wall. She made her way inside and stuffed clothes into a trash bag, dragged the children out into the cold, and lay them to sleep on the bag in the rear section of the car.

Snow spackled the windshield when she finally sped over the highway that night. She had a destination. It was Quebec, the very name of which elicits rapture from her each time she hears it. The roads were at first prone and sad and then leaping and dangerous. All French references were darkened by the hour. The girls snored on the backseat. Even that far north she glanced in the rearview mirror to see if he was following. Snow was the music to which she rhymed the lyrics of her thoughts under her fractured nose and blue cheeks.

x

Stood up, square lights, the children and I will enter monolithic cities together, but I will be too small to save them from the dangers there. O Carmelite poets, come to my rescue! Teresa, San Juan de la Cruz, Sor Juana! Dawn flooded the northern whites with a blue beam. It did strange things to the ice crossing lakes. Still the snow dreamed its way down to ground, and she had to move slowly, unsteadily, towards a plate of pancakes, maple syrup, and hot coffee.

x

Erotic thoughts kept her going. Nests give birth to birds, we don't know where they die. But the little blood-filled fist swells in a swaddling of twigs, hidden among the leaves, and finally splits its pink beak open to the sun. I am horrored by necessity: by the squeezing clam, the bubbles of suck in the sand, and by the automatism of the bird's motions. I am horrored by the bulge of violence, so built into all living systems. But

319

the milk that pricks and dribbles from my nipples is the same milk that nurtures the violent arts. And the milk of my groin is the same.

She knew he would find her. There is an intuitive map drawn on the wall of a compulsive person. This was the map he followed and which invariably led him to her. It always worked that way between them, that he would arrive just when she was beginning to work at a project of her own, that he would call, just when someone he hated had arrived, that he would find her talking to someone he considered an enemy. Now she knew he would trail through the most obscure woods of all (and later he will) and find her and the children. Sometimes she understood that this was not a conscious plan for him, and that he was surprised by what he stumbled on. It was as if he was receiving signals from somewhere else, ones so subtle that he himself lived unconscious of them even as he followed them. He would, she realized, want to locate her, but nonetheless he would experience his finding her as a semi-surprise. He would think he was just heading up to Quebec on a whim, or a business venture. And there she would be, walking the sweet streets of Quebec City! He would turn the corner and there she would be! Behind her in a plate glass window would be a display of rubber phalluses, which she didn't want the kids to see. And between them would be the icy wind of marriage. Breath-unifying. Tragic marriage!

Ecstasy reversed: where in ecstasy there is largeness, liquidity, joy, space, confidence and union—now in the case of such an encounter, there is a squeezed feeling, dryness, terror, confinement, loneliness and loss of hope. Yet there was something of one in the other. It was the sense of INEVITABILITY. They had that in common.

x

The wounded boy is the mean man. Trouble is he's got both muscles and mind. I get so flattened by harsh verbiage that I sometimes forget I'm lucky he's not hitting me. What did I do to deserve it? I must have done something that you don't do to men. But I can't remember what it was, and tiptoe into my future with my arm figuratively raised to ward

off the blows. Things hit me is my paranoid belief. Falling nuts. Fris-
bees from way across a meadow. A beach ball. A bike on a dark path.
A baseball bat. If I'm around and something's flying out of control, it
comes my way. Including of course fists, and babies' hard heads. I got
a split lip from one of the children's foreheads and everybody outside
thought it was Hugo who did it.

x

Sometimes the two words—Christmas Day—had a chilling effect on
her ears and eyes. Tinsel and pine awoke in her memory bank and
rattled like coins. The little streets of old Quebec City tinkled in the
same way—icicles from eaves, and down the steep cliff the rolling
river, touched by brutish blocks of ice and timber, reminded her of the
word RELENTLESS. They walked away from the plate glass window
stocked with dildos, each with a hand on the double pram, silver and
frosty. She felt the impression of pain like thumbs moving on her temples. He was wheezing asthmatically. A black three-quarter length coat
and soggy but shiny black shoes. He had his leather satchel.

He began talking reactionary—"We will send the children to the
nuns when the time comes. . . . They need to be trained early to be
chaste. . . . I like how tidy and clean it is up here, I like the feeling that
the government is liberal but the country is conservative. . . . I came up
here to try to make a new life, find a job. Why are you here? I knew you
might come this way, given your tendency to head north whenever you
run away from home, arrested adolescent that you are."

Bitch.

He batted her shoulder. She wore one of those long coats that stop
just above the ankles, it was navy blue, and some of her hair—coarse
black strands—shone against the fabric. She walked a little faster.

I want to stop this night-breaking misery we are in, he said.

You mean nightmarish?

Nightmarish. Don't you?

Well of course. Let's live separately, she suggested through parched lips.

We could share the same building but not the same rooms?
That's what I mean! You could have girlfriends, I wouldn't care.
But not get a divorce?
No, no divorce, she agreed.
I don't really believe in divorce.
Now that we've had the babies, what's the point?
They "brightened" and "conversed" now on their way to the car.
She was trying to keep the peace of course. She doted on her babies and
he was never mean to them, though he did not ever indicate a great deal
of interest. At least he wasn't one of those cruel fathers, the ones you see
everywhere, raging over their children in public places. He was indiffer-
ent to them, and only raged over her.

x

In the car heading south, they pretended they were able to control their
destinies. They spoke about their lives with benign smiles. They built
up a picture which made them both happy—of life in a duplex, him on
one side, alone, with the children only when he wanted them; her on the
other side, with the children most of the time and with her carpentry.
With this huge balloon between them, they were kind to each other,
considerate, and wished the best for themselves.

The children cooed happily in their car seats in back, three and four
years old now and the landscape whirred by like a winding sheet. Sad
hope! Dream of a new marriage! If only it had worked, she would cry
throughout the years. But the steady drip of grief, at these hopes' failure,
never left her after that day.

That night they slept in a bed-and-breakfast attic room, with heaps
of parti-colored quilts keeping out the chills, and the children between
them. And the next morning, they went over the border back into
Maine, and there she begged that he drive her to her little hometown by
the sea, so she could take snapshots of some of the houses she had forgotten. He agreed benevolently, without jealousy, without impatience.
He talked now about the social necessity of marriage, and contradicted

all his theories of women and prostitution in the blimp of his joy. Their silver car whirred down the highway from the outside.

And in the inside, she was also whirring with an inexplicable anxiety. Unlike him, she felt ruined. Stooped, plaintive, she lugged the girls over lumps of ice, and squatted with them beside her, while she snapped her pictures in the cold, quiet town. Like this she showed her true colors to the air—a mixed breed woman, squatting on the pavement, a native-born American alien in the Americas. One block of the town was being renovated by energetic hippies; their entrepreneurial tastes resulted in a wooden Indian restored on the steps of the general health food market. It was there that she offended him by something she said, and he got mad.

x

But this time it seemed to her, in her heart, that she was the one who had mapped their journey to this end. Not him. Because, as she cowered from his lifted hand, out of the store stepped a white man wearing a fur-collared suede winter jacket and big boots. When he saw her, he put down his bag and grinned. He said her name fondly. White smoke spun from his lips. His head nodded as if with approval as Hugo shoved her, and pulled a child away angrily. The white man pulled a knife from his inner hip and approached the husband. The husband then backed off, as if to receive a blow in private, out of sight of her, his face warped in a way she never saw before. She screamed and grappled for one daughter, the other one fell over on her side, beside the steps, and the white man slashed the coat of the husband. No blood was drawn. But she begged the white man to stop what he was doing; he ignored her. She ran into the store with the babies and squatted on the floor beside huge bags of cat food. People gathered at the window watching, and from them she learned what was happening. The husband was being hauled away by the cops, and the white man was explaining in what way he had been dangerous. She was shaking all over and crying too in dry heaves, the children were reaching for objects on shelves.

When the white man returned, he ushered her and them out of the store and into his car. It was obvious to everyone that she did not enjoy this rescue operation, but looked out the car window like a kidnapped child, seeking her father. What had happened wasn't fair. And she had led him there! Into a briar-patch of history's devising. No one really cared what her husband had done to her. He had been taken off by the police because he was a stranger and a shadow in that white town not because he had lifted his hand at her.

The white man brought her to the bus depot and bought her and the children one-way tickets home. As soon as they got there, she packed in a rush, full of errors, and ran away to another city. The father of her children put out a warrant for her arrest. She was wanted for kidnapping, then found. The idea was that he wanted to see and be with his children, and so she was put in place that was part prison for part crazy person, and the girls went to foster care to await a father who never came to claim them after all. In prison hospital she learned to make dollhouses, a trade she would pursue throughout the years. When she was freed, promising God that she would never marry again as long as she lived, she could not shake her fear that he would find her. Liberty and uncertainty were synonymous for her. She became a foot soldier and captain in her own solitary army, an army of three. With the children, now six and seven, on either side of her, she moved and moved again. And though she had to leave behind the dollhouses she made in prison, now she made much more elaborate ones, modeled on the houses in her childhood town. She sold them, reluctantly. They weren't really houses for dolls anyway, but spaces for her to live in.

x

She was Felicity Dumas, four feet eleven, with long black hair in braids, skin tone the pale brown of the inside of an owl's wing, nervous and birdish in gesture, with a thick ribcage and broad hips, with strong white teeth and strawberry pink lips. Unfortunately she had the IQ of a genius and only God knew it. She always seemed to be elsewhere mentally, lis-

tening too acutely to a far-off sound, or remembering something someone said who wasn't even there. People couldn't get her to concentrate
on them, it was maddening. If she saw a male configuration resembling
her husband, she stopped, squinting, her shoulders stiff, and ran to hide
wherever she could.

x

One day she really did see Hugo on the streets of Manhattan, near
SoHo, and he saw her. He was with another man, he looked happy, and
she was disarmed for a few seconds, believing him trustworthy—father!
But when he raised his hand to wave, she flinched, and hot-flashed. Now
she saw him running after her, gun or hand raised, and like a woman
having a seizure, she groped, stumbling, for the door of a cab, while her
brain palpitated and hallucinated for fear of catching his insanity again.

x

Her mind took over the rescue operation: she was walking down from
the Walhalla Plateau to Cape Final in Arizona, where she could view the
buttes, shrines and thrones of the Grand Canyon. What a basin of light
and time! Colors and all weathers lived in that stilly and holy zone: from
the most arid desert to the tip of Alpine peaks. Birds zoomed miles below her to their nests in the ruined pueblos dug into the walls. Reptiles,
spiders, wildflowers coexisted there. But the density of silence was like
a form of time she had never entered before, and it wouldn't let her stay
there alive. So she jolted back into her senses, as if she had just been
visiting the inside of her brain, its topology.

x

The cab rattled and banged up Sixth Avenue, and she looked in her
address book for the name of that white man who had helped her before.
It was a search and a gesture she repeated often. He was the same man

325

who had often rescued her. But now it was not enough for her to see his name, because she kept her finger closed up in the little book for such a long time, it grew red and numb.

Before long she left Manhattan, taking the children out of school, and went back to the town in Maine where she last saw the white man. All she wanted was for him to rid her of the problem. Make me safe from the father of my children! He had made her safe from one thing and the other before. He rescued her by ruining her life in the way that some people can do. His name was Temple, and since her teens he served the function of boss, seducer, never-lover, and owner of the world in which she was condemned to live.

—Between guilt and fear, there is this tie, Temple told her. Do you feel guilty for leaving him, or do you really fear him? Or do you maybe fear what you want to do to him?

—I really fear him, Felicity said. But I'm telling you this secret, too. I made a promise to God that I would never marry again, if the children and I could just be kept safe.

—I've heard it's dangerous to make deals with God, he observed, and now she had a glimpse of his old charm: he listened for the pulse behind the words being spoken to him, and measured it. Even if what he said was hurtful, at least it was DEEP.

They were in the reconstructed bar he owned. He told her to wait outside, where she could talk to a few old people from her past. She did, but dreamily. Sometimes the world's substance seems a watery reflection of something more solid existing in the mind. Nothing is really out there. As she waited for Temple to join her, she experienced this state of pictorial distance. Voices were like echoes, without a location in flesh. It was only a question of dreaming rather than being, though she still could just manage the etiquette of life. Temple in the past ascribed this quality to a genetic defect in her, then he realized that it was overdeveloped intelligence. But he only told people her oddness had to do with environment. Certain places and people seemed to bring it on. Himself being one of them. He looked at her now as if she was a parchment made of honey and he was hungry.

Then he lurched towards her and assured her he would remove her husband from her life, without harming him. She seemed not even to hear him, or care, but gazed at the glassy branches dripping with sun. Rivulets of snow rushed down the gutters. She listened to the sound as if gurgle was a language she could translate just by paying attention to it. He said he would have her husband deported and the marriage annulled, and now her face whitened to the same hue as his. She wrote her guilt on the roof of her mouth with the tip of her tongue: God forgive me! Meantime, her youngest child was shivering and coughing while her sister tried to keep her warm inside her coat and arms.

X

Two years later he made her pay. She was sent to Boston—by the same Temple—to stay with a friend of a friend of his. It was late winter. This friend—her host—was living with his dying father in order to take care of his mother. He was nearly young, a lawyer. He took Felicity in, with her two small children, because she was said to be homeless. And he was told that she would be a help with his sick father.

The apartment was a kind of infirmary—dingy and overstuffed and smelling of paint thinner for that time, and he was a kind of physician, a role he was not suited for, being nervous and private. She slept on a pullout couch with her children laid out on either side of her. By now her skin had the rough texture of a drunk or drug addict though it was living rough and homeless that made her that way. She carried pills and took them for her headaches—migraines, she said—and she managed each day to get the girls to the local elementary school—late—and pick them up late too.

She was very helpful in unexpected ways—cleaning up the kitchen and bathroom till they shone, then sitting at the window with a beer, just staring into the street. She helped his mother with his father—turning him over to change the soiled sheets, cleaning his pajamas, washing him in the most intimate ways. Her nostrils and lips tensed, but she otherwise showed no awkwardness or disgust in the face of disease.

327

One night, soon after her arrival, she told the lawyer that God would reward him some day for his hospitality to her.

He doubted that, and didn't say that she was herself repaying him with her actions.

Once she tried to describe to him the events which brought her to his door. He hardly heard her, he didn't want to hear her. All he could remember later was her description of a man who dominated her. She said, "Watch out for him, he's dangerous. He doesn't look it either. Not like a pimp or a pirate or anything. He looks good—blond, blue-eyed, well-dressed, like a politician! The only special thing you could notice about him is he can't keep his head still. Some nerve damage, I guess. It nods a little. Like one of those dolls. Like this."

Watching her head nod heavily from side to side, like someone who listens to a sad story and responds with the negative sway of the head, he felt sorry for the dangerous man. Abruptly, he wanted to hear the whole account of her recent past over again, and she told him, repeating it all without a sigh or lapse in intensity. Again, he didn't really listen. She was, he realized, the smallest American woman he had ever seen. And her story—about love, food stamps, children, lost husband—was so big it was impossible to imagine her supporting it all.

His father died around twilight on a Saturday. That day snow covered Boston and its environs. The son spent the afternoon sitting by the sickbed reading aloud Isaiah and watching his father's exceptionally long fingers pluck at the blanket as if pulling off lint. The father was white, at least his complexion was pale if brown in patches, the skin papery. At five, in the blue of the evening, when Boston's sky was lit with a gold sunset that illumined the snow, the son went out for a walk, and the father went into his final throes. The mother locked herself in the bathroom, covering her ears, like one who can't bear the screams of a birthing, and Felicity was left to help him cross over and out. She left her daughters watching television, and shut herself in the room with the old man, and held his head and shoulders over her knees, while he crackled and burned. She stared into his eyes and he into hers as he was dying, and when the immobility seized him, she felt a current pass into

328

her own bones. She sat for a long time, as this sensation (like a low-level electric appliance humming in her hands) ran through her.

When the son came in and found her like that, he stood at the end of the bed, wondering what her expression meant. She didn't say a word, though, but politely lay the father's shoulders and head down on the pillows, and left the room. Outside the city was hollowed by evening blue.

The next night the man left the house around six with Felicity and her two children. The two girls were obedient in the back seat. He took them to eat at a Mexican restaurant and then to a movie. Afterwards they all went to a motel to sleep. The man didn't want to be anywhere near his mother while she was in mourning. He had left her with old friends and had taken Felicity and her girls with him for no reason beyond gratitude. Even as it happened he couldn't explain, either, why they all ended up in a motel. But there they were, and the girls slept on the floor on pillows borrowed off of chairs, while Tom and she shared the same medium-sized bed, and watched television. She consumed a four-pack of peach wine coolers, and smoked cigarettes. She told him that the last time she had had sex was when she conceived the youngest girl, who looked sickly. That was several years before.

—How about you? she asked him.

—About three years.

—Wow. Do we qualify as virgins or not?

—No. It takes seven years to be re-virginated, said Tom.

—Who dropped that rule?

—My brother Dan. He's a connoisseur in that regard. He went eight years without.

—What is he, religious?

—No, well, in a sense. Let's just say we had the same mother, he said.

—She seemed harmless to me.

—You must be a poor judge of character.

—Why didn't your brother help out?

—Now? Well, he's my half-brother. My mother was married to another man, briefly. My father raised him, but Dan just stayed away as much as he could.

—But even when your father was dying?

—It's hard to explain.

The man looked at her in the light of the television. She gave off myriad emotions; he believed he would never understand a woman like her. The forceful chin, eyes heavily lidded, breasts round and firm on a boyish frame. And all that hair. And a baseball cap passed from child to child to her. He wouldn't dare touch her. Her unpredictability was frightening. He thought of her horrible life as he looked at her, then tried to assemble the parts for a life that was not horrible, and couldn't.

The night was memorable for its lack of completion. He lay awake watching television while she and the girls slept. This way he successfully avoided being present at his mother's first hours of grief, and at the same time avoided being present at his own.

x

Soon enough he was confronted with the difficulties of clearing out his father's possessions: clothes, shoes, papers. Each emptied article filled as he held it—with an immaculate presence, invisible and potent as a smell. The things that coated the skin, that served as protection from wind and sun, and kept the feet apart from the pavement—these were so pathetic as to make his eyes boil with tears of pity. A pair of bent and sloppy galoshes with rusty buckles made him twist with grief. Eyeglasses bent to fit the nose and skull. And then there were the papers.

He could not resist reading his father's notebooks, especially those dating back to the earliest years of his own childhood. And indeed here he discovered a piece of information which sent him into an ecstasy of curiosity. His father had written down the address of a federal prison where Dan's father was incarcerated. And he had done so more than twenty years before.

He was unable to speak to his mother about this news, because she was incapable of receiving negative information. Or so he had been taught. But he did mention it to Dan, on the phone, and Dan reacted by saying, "I don't want to know about it." So he was alone with a revelation which terrified him. If Dan's father was alive, in Southern California, and in prison, why was the story always told that he had disappeared "off the face of the earth?" The lawyer adored his own father, and thought of him as having an impeccable moral character—progressive, pacifist, honest. So next he called the federal penitentiary to discover if such a prisoner was there, still alive and well. Yes. Pedro was alive but very old in Southern California.

x

The lawyer began to fill up with dread now, and to wish he had not missed his father's dying hour, and to wish that he could ask him important questions. The silence of his absence horrified him. He couldn't accept the evaporation of a living body into empty space. He was scared he would forget his father's face. He began to wonder if Felicity Dumas, who had long since left with the friend who had brought her, could help him. He remembered her and the background comfort of her ministrations, and especially the moment she lifted a white wet cloth from his father's face and showed the impressions of two eyes, a nose and mouth intact there. He missed his father. He dreamed about Felicity holding the body at least three times, and she didn't seem as much a stranger as she should. He wanted to see her again—to fill in the empty space.

And he called their mutual friend who said, "Strange. I was going to call you. To see if you wanted a paid vacation to San Diego. In exchange for a favor. It has to do with Felicity Dumas."

"What about her?"

"She needs help finding a place to live, and get settled. It seems she is incapable of dealing with life's daily demands, and requires guidance. Male guidance. She's not my problem, believe me, but a mutual friend—He'll pay your way."

Tom the lawyer didn't ask why he had been selected for the job, but agreed to do it. The coincidental nature of the offer to see Felicity, and to go to San Diego, struck him with some suspicion, but it was the suspicion of superstition rather than paranoia. He couldn't believe how convenient the timing was. He thanked God.

"I wanted to go there anyway," he told Jay (an English emigré, and dealer by trade and nature). "Not because of her, but for a completely separate reason."

"Then good. Personally I'm surprised you'd agree to go at all," said Jay.

"Believe me, it's a piece of luck."

"Let's hope your luck lasts. Anyway, she could use a bit of help. I'll let you know more soon."

"There's nothing illegal involved, is there?" asked the lawyer.

"You'd be the last person we'd send if there were. A lawyer?"

x

For several days, after work in a small legal aid office on the margins of Boston, the lawyer spilled his way through more notebooks by his father. Most of them were jottings about weather, current events, art shows, ideas for paintings, with wrinkled clippings stuck into the pages, unattached and falling. He could easily throw them all away. But then he found the partial transcript of a trial, officially copied onto legal size white paper which was now yellowing, and the transcript was a kind of official statement—by Pedro Dominique—Dan's father—almost a confession. It read:

"At age nineteen I was a member of the Marine Cooks and Stewards Association—a Communist controlled union. Afterwards I enlisted in the US Army where I found out all I needed to know about race and class. When I was stationed in Texas I was given some Marxist literature to read. Most of it concerned class issues in Britain. I hate the English. In New York, during the Soviet-Nazi Nonaggression Pact, I went to rallies where the speakers were German Bundists and American Communists. I agreed with their conclusions. It was in San Francisco I got my Communist literature from the Party bookstore—the Maritime Bookshop. Later I was discharged from the Army and got seamen's papers in San Diego. This was where I got involved with the National Maritime

Union and became a card-carrying member of the Party. Do what you want about that. In 1944 I signed on the troop ship USS Brazil in Boston. Conditions on board those ships was sickening, with ten men sleeping in one badly ventilated fo'castle. One cold storage egg apiece every Sunday, it stank, the only fruit an orange once a week, moldy meat, mush full of weevils, no linen—for $25 a month. I never forget the odor from dirty sweaty clothes, or the stench of leaking oil. On that ship I was surrounded by militant pro-Communists for several months. I won't tell you who they were, so don't bother asking. They were great men. Then in Boston I met a woman and got her pregnant with my son Dan. Together we became acquainted with a printer who introduced me to some more fellow travellers, and I considered this man my first true friend. Under pressure from the government I changed unions and got a membership in the Marine Firemen, Boilers, Wipers and Watertenders Association and shipped out of Boston as an electrician. It was just about 1948 when the House Un-American Activities Committee began to hound me, as you obviously know already, and I was threatened with loss of citizenship and deportation. I went back to Boston to seek legal help, but my best friend by then was shacked up with my woman and my son and he wanted me out of town. I guess just about everybody did by then. So I went West. I changed my identity. And to this day I still believe—"

The transcript ended there.

x

In a matter of weeks the lawyer found the woman sitting on a curb with her two girls, in southeast San Diego. He drove by her once, did a U-turn, staring, drove by again, did another U-turn, and returned slowly, pulling up alongside her knees. He pretended to be amazed by this encounter.

She stood up and walked around to his window, squinting, and then her face shifted in relief and surprise.

—I don't believe it, she said. Fuck 'n shit.

—Neither do I.

—What the hell are you doing in these parts?

333

—Vacationing.

—You?

—Me too, he said. How are the girls? They look the same but bigger.

—Already? You came in the nick of time. Can we hitch a ride?

—Sure, get in.

The girls climbed, brown and smiling, into the back seat of the rental car. They remembered him with shy hellos. She was brown too now and her skin was smooth, clear. The only mark in her face was the kind of lining that comes with a lot of sun. As she gave him directions to her home, she examined him until he was ashamed and reddened.

—So? What are you looking at? he asked.

—You're paler than me.

—I guess I am.

—I used to be paler than you, she said.

She pressed her forearm against his to prove her point. Tom was dressed in shorts, a tee-shirt and sneakers. His skin was Mediterranean brown, and rough, as if he had fished daily on the high Atlantic for many years. But his mouth was soft, red, even delicate, and his expression distant and alarmed. He had a perpetual shadow of a beard, no matter how often he shaved. He was slender, his posture set back, tense and uncomfortable, as if he had been a fat child who never believed he was really thin. His arms and chest were hairy, but his hands were long, gentle and nervous. Felicity looked at him frequently, whenever they were together, as if to see which part of his person was in the foreground for that time.

They drove to the shack she inhabited. It was a small stucco building stuck behind suburban houses, and gardens gleaming with palm trees and bougainvillea. There was one bedroom and a tiny kitchen and bathroom. The girls slept on a pullout couch. But the place seemed barely occupied by anyone. A box of books lay unpacked on the floor, there was a small black and white TV and a few plastic dishes. The girls' toys were mostly of a boyish robot variety—bright-colored steel figures you could assemble in multiple forms. They lay scattered on the pullout bed. Tom stood at the door and asked her a question he had had in his mind since his father died.

334

—Did my father say anything before he died?

—Something about ferns, she said. Want a beer?

—No thanks. What about ferns?

—Something about keys and ferns being the same.

—They look alike?

—No, I don't think so. More like "the key to life is a fern." I don't remember exactly. That doesn't sound right. Sorry.

—No. That's good enough. Thanks.

—I still think it's strange, you showing up like this. You're sure nobody sent you to spy on me?

—Why would they?

—They just might. That man might. The one I guess I told you about.

—With the shaking head?

—Yeah, exactly.

—I don't know him, so you can relax, Tom told her.

—It's just so lucky, you know. I mean, today they're evicting us. I was out looking for a temporary shelter when you came along. If only you knew how hard it is to find a place if you're a single mother. Everyone hates us. We drive people nuts, just looking at us. They think my kids will rip the wallpaper off the walls, or something, just because there isn't a man in the house.

—Where do you want to go now? he asked her.

—You tell me.

—Money isn't your only problem. What else is going on? What does the shaking head man want?

—I can't tell you. You must be judging if you're a lawyer.

—I'm not, he insisted.

—You always look really tense and abashed at the same time. I can't imagine you up in front of a justice.

—You don't have to. I never will be.

—So what do you want to do with us?

—You can come along to my motel, and we'll figure it out. I owe you one.

—You gave us a place to stay already, she said.

—Big deal. You washed my father when he was dying.

She shrugged with her palms upraised and an expression of astonishment on her face.

x

Again they ended up in a motel, this time the one he was vacationing in, near Sea World. Outside a freeway was in constant use on one side; on the other was a view of Mission Bay, stiff jelly blue. Palm trees sprouted tall and thin as asparagus, or else sat squat as pineapples along the sand. Boats ripped up the water. The girls played in the wet sand and walked in the water until late at night and then they slept, again on the floor, while Tom and Felicity again watched television, side by side in a bed.

They talked. He told her his father had been haunting him.

—Wow, so tell me, she said.

—You won't laugh?

—Go on.

—Okay. Three times he's appeared in powerful dreams. Once emerging from a crowd outside. It was like a wedding party in the twilight of a strange hotel. Carrying his big hat. Then I saw gray shadows on a tree trunk in a town called John or Jude and they turned into him. Once, by Hell, where the air was like a dirty barge, he carried luggage. Each time he looked exhausted but astonished. He had been, he always said, away on a trip and never expected to stay away so long. He really just wanted to apologize and let us get on with our lives.

—Were you scared? Felicity asked, wide-eyed.

—I kept staring at the space he had physically occupied long after he was gone. Always I wondered what it felt like to be him dying. Was he terrified? Relieved? Obedient?

—Why are you here anyway? Tell the truth.

—To look for my brother's father. He's in prison out here, east of here. I have to see him. My brother won't.

—Here, give me some room, was her response.

—Move your legs then.

336

—There. Now? she asked.

—The pillow. I'm the one who cares about it.

—So take it. I'll sleep on my arm.

—I'm not going to lay a hand on you, Tom told her.

—Now the ashtray? Why not? she asked and flirted with her hair.

—I don't know you. You may be full of disease. Did you smoke when you were pregnant?

—Not as much. Tell me about your brother Dan.

—Did you drink?

—Just a couple of beers a day. Or Champale.

—You're lucky you didn't mess up your children. I mean, they seem fine though Matty still looks kind of weak. Is there anything seriously wrong with them? With her?

—As far as I'm concerned, they're perfect.

—Who was the father?

—I thought I told you all that. Before, she said.

—To be honest, I forget, forgot. I never thought I'd see you again after that weird night in the motel.

—And here we are again. I remember you always talked about your brother.

—That's right. My brother Dan. I did?

—So who's your girlfriend now?

—When you ask me that it makes me think you want to come on to me, and I really don't want you to, so let's not talk about things like romance.

—Fine, I'm going to sleep anyway.

She buried herself under the covers beside him, carefully avoiding contact under the sheet.

—I hate the smell of motels, she said, they smell like bones, but at least I'm safe, thank you.

—I thought you were going to smoke.

—No, I'm going to sleep instead, she said.

Tom lay awake for two hours in a state heightened by wild thoughts of home and future. Something in Felicity's spirited candor made his voice rise from his chest and an urge to articulation follow. He was usually quiet. But he had an invisible tongue in which he talked to himself. When he tried to voice his thoughts to others, he felt as if a long chute—a kind of upside-down cornucopia—led from his brain to his mouth. The words fell too fast, or got stuck. It was the descent from his mind to the vernacular which caused him greatest trouble.

x

In the morning she was sitting by the window, with a lighted match held up in the air, one after the other. She would light one and blow it out. She was crying inside the veils of her thick black hair. He watched her, again surprised by how small she was. With her legs exposed, he could guess she was about four feet eleven. He couldn't see her face.

—Are you trying to set the room on fire?

—I'm praying, she said.

—For what? And what have the matches got to do with prayer?

—I don't have any candles.

—What do you want me to do with you today? he asked her.

—I guess take us to a shelter. First tell me about your brother. Tell me a story.

—I don't have one ready.

—Shit. Typical. You can't just invent one. How come you're a lawyer?

—I'm interested in politics, in this country, you know, and the question of human freedom. Civil rights, civil liberties. I just wake up and smile when I think in those terms. Politics is my single passion. I inherited it from my parents, but I have a very different view from theirs. I don't care much about anything else.

—What did your parents believe in? I remember they were kind of poor which means they were probably Democrats which means you must be conservative which wouldn't surprise me.

—Believe me, you're way off the mark.

—Well, go on and tell me how your parents were, she prodded, lighting up a shoelace, and spitting on it.

338

Tom put his hand to his throat as if to dislodge his own breath; it was a gesture swift and accurate.

—Actually it was my brother Dan who opened my eyes to them. One night, in the winter, he and I were walking on the other side of the street from them in Boston. They were with their usual pack of friends, and Dan said they looked like Fellini characters, that they were all second-rate in what they did, or worse, they were losers. Look at them, look at them, he kept saying, and I never could look at them the same way again.

—That makes him sound kind of like a shit.

—No. Just realistic.

—But is Dan so great himself?

—That's not the point. He's uncluttered. They were cluttered, collectors of kitsch, they dragged their pasts around with them like bags of old newspapers. And they believed that they were brilliant and misunderstood. Only in Boston can you get such a combination of snobbery and ruin.

—Sometimes you sound like a snob yourself. Your father was really nice to me. Even when he was feeling so sick, he was polite. That counts for a lot. Tell me about him, and your mother. Go on. I like to listen.

—Are you sure? he asked.

—What else have I got to do? It comforts me.

—Well, you could see that we had no money. My father was a printer whose office was down near Chinatown and South Station. He printed flyers, pamphlets, one advertisement newsletter and a four-page leftist newspaper. At night and on weekends he painted in oils—dark images of urban life (red brick brownstones, stooped humans, the El, cars, that kind of thing) or delicate ferns, pastel-colored. He was fifteen years older than my mother. And Pedro. His life seemed to have no beginning, though he came from the South. There was a quality of timelessness to him because of his age. He was a kind and quiet man, as you could tell, whose favorite subject was liberty and how to pursue it.

—So how did he meet your mother?

—He served in the US Army during World War II, was stationed in North Africa for most of that time, and spoke often of playing baseball outside of Tripoli with an all-black unit. Apparently the three years in combat changed him from a New Dealer into something more internationalist, or radical. In any case, he met my mother in Boston, later, when she was working with the C.P. She was at the first meeting he attended, but she was with Pedro already, they were lovers, they never really married, and he felt sorry for them both and took them home to feed them. I don't think he and my mother fell in love until long after they were friends. He had just inherited his print shop from his father, and it became the center of political dialogue among anarchists, Trotskyites, Democrats and others. Deep down in Post Office Square he printed leaflets and pamphlets and a theater newspaper. He had many white friends at work, but he was always obsessed with race issues. Pedro was his best friend, Pedro, by the way, being black, and many years his junior. This fact and his political alliances kept lots of customers away, and he had a limited number of friends. But my father accepted this isolation with the same irony and good humor that drew other people to his shop. My mother was not so good-humored, and it was, after all, a really thick male environment. She must have felt excluded. My father was never up to her cynical wit. She had an Irish tongue, a kind of competitive conversation ruled her social contacts. Who could be the funniest and the meanest the fastest.

—But wait a minute. How did she switch from Pedro to your father? What happened?

—My parents really didn't talk about that. It was kind of a forbidden topic. Anything about Pedro was treated as unfit for human conversation. When I was born, and for a few years after, Pedro was still in the picture, but off to the side, and I don't really get the chronology or its meaning. But he would take Dan and me out with him. He was like an uncle—a poor one—who was humored, but rejected. My mother had been mentally ill as a teenager, and something in her nature made everyone bow and kowtow to her, as if we all feared she would go totally berserk if she was criticized, or if she received harsh facts. She ruled the house with this unarticulated dread. All I know is, my father became a pacifist, and my mother made him withdraw from political action, after Pedro disappeared, or just before, I'm not sure. She had a horror of the Friends

of Progress, Mankind United, the Ku Klux Klan, the Umberto Nobile
Fascio, the German-American Bund, and the group headed by Gerald
K. Smith. She thought these groups were dangerous to her personally!
She thought they would come and kidnap Dan. She even suggested that
Pedro was a counter-subversive. She said, when he disappeared, that he
was probably being sent abroad to work for the CIA. I tell you, she was
not harmless, and Dan moved away from home at age sixteen, just to get
away from her. Our whole house, all through my early childhood, was
sick with talk about the meaning of "un-American." My mother scrutinized every organization to classify it according to whether it was created and controlled by Communists, or infiltrated and controlled? Was
it Communist dominated, and infiltrated but not controlled? Or was it
Communist infiltrated only for purposes of espionage?. . . And behind it
all was the question of Pedro. Was he a spy, and a traitor, and would he
return to destroy them?

—I guess she felt guilty, said Felicity simply. I mean, after all, she
dumped Pedro for his best friend.

—At night as a child I lay awake, plagued with these images which
were like seeds, thrown forward into a field of air. I saw my mother's
fears bearing hideous future fruits.

—That's why you have that look in your eye.

The girls began to stir, and soon they took over. Straight black hair,
high cheekbones and wide pink lips, they could have been Arab, Latin,
Pakistani. They rolled all over their mother who kissed them passionately and listened attentively to whatever each one had to say, no matter how trivial. If one of them whined, however, she got screamed at
or smacked on the bottom as she flew by. A man who loved her would
have to make room for these girls too, and learn to spend a lot of time
outside that trio, without jealousy. He told her that. They watched television while Tom went downstairs and got them donuts and juice. On
his return he walked around them with an expression of pleasure that he
seemed unaware of feeling.

—Why do shoelaces taste salty? Felicity asked him.

—Lots of things do, he replied.

—The world of matter is made of tears, she said. We could make a banquet of all the things we tasted when we were kids. Towels . . . kneecaps . . . soles of shoes. . . . Were we really sucking out the grief?

—There were many salty things I remember, said Tom. Jump ropes. The skin of a football—and a baseball. They were salty, like shoelaces.

—Pencils are salty.

—So are some erasers.

—But paper has the blandest taste of all. Like rice.

—It would be good to make such a banquet, Tom said.

Felicity stared at his face, while he looked off into space somewhat self-consciously.

—How many times did your mother get married? she asked.

—Twice. Sort of. I mean, she never really married Pedro.

—Which of the men did she love the most?

—My father.

—Which son did she love the most?

—My brother.

—I thought so. Where did you live all your life? In that same place I met you?

—No. We lived in an even drearier place, way downtown.

—And Pedro?

—Pedro? He lived in a pit down in the South End. Near the project where my mother grew up. Near Holy Cross Cathedral. Do you know any of these places?

—Sort of. I spent a little time in Boston, here and there.

—Something like that. What about your people?

—I never thought you'd ask, she said. Anarchists.

—That might be an accurate word for my parents too.

She and the girls disappeared into the bathroom and the shower, and Tom stood at the window watching herds of cars thunder down the freeway. He rubbed the bristles on his cheeks and his eyes took on an opaque look, inward-turning. The hoods of cars evoked obsolescence even as they raced before his eyes in different shapes. What's modern about the past? Some things are finished at the moment of completion. Technology.

And even some relationships—they are done at the moment of consummation. . . . His mind was a swarm of word-sized figures and his face lapsed into an expression of deep familiarity with what passed behind his eyes, and how to get there.

x

TOO FAR would be his name for those long winters and the words in them, which stretched the margins of thinkable thoughts. Snow stuck to the bricks, whitening all that was red, and lined up on wires and ivy tendrils. Yellow daffodils and tulips drooped with their mouths ajar on their kitchen table. Books and oil paints smelled up the house. Dan shared a room with him. The parents in the only other bedroom. Pedro, in the earliest years, walked through the drifts under the tracks to visit. After he disappeared, the mother made Dan share the bedroom with her and the father, fearing that Dan would be stolen in the night.

When Dan left for New York, Tom was bereft. Each winter after, near Christmas, he would come home and they would all go to a Greek restaurant downtown for dinner. Dan wore a black overcoat, with the collar turned up and hunched over, like the mother, and looked cold, like her, in the speeding snow. Tom held onto the cloth on his sleeve and stayed close to him. His skin and black curls, long-fingered hands and slender wrists, his cologne and his subtle sidewinding smile, his garnet brown eyes under heavy lids and a tentative way of speaking—all these made him seem heroic and foreign to Tom.

I remember the streets were always glitzy for Christmas. The more vulgar the better, Dan liked to say, and together he and I exclaimed over the silver and gold tinsel drippings and the artificial trees in the department store windows.

But you should see New York, he kept telling me. This is all like an imitation of the real thing. You should get Mum to bring you to see FAO Schwartz, Rockefeller Plaza and all the windows down Fifth Avenue, if you really want to see Christmas. Boston is like a toy city after New York. It's a poor man's imitation of a city. When you're in New

343

York, you don't have to dream of being anywhere else in the world. Not Rome, not Paris even.

I dropped his sleeve and slowed away from his pace, walking alone between the lot of them. Always I knew that Dan was the real one and I was the fake, that he was the original and I was the print, that he was the winner and I had lost, that he was Manhattan and I was Boston, that he was wine and I was water, that he was coffee and I was tea, that he was art and I was business, that he was the soul of my mother and I was the body. But my eyes stung with salt in the white cold flakes because he had all but come out and said so.

He was sensitive and slowed to walk with me again, saying that he had a vision of my future. He said he could see me living in a one-room basement studio up near Harlem when I grew up. I would go to jazz concerts and otherwise live like a monk, or a hermit. I would be an artist of some kind, but he couldn't say which. "Every day will be like a package that you will wrap up and deliver to the world," he said. "You'll be the one everyone waits for at parties. And when you leave, which will always be early after arriving late, the party will disintegrate. You will be political and will be a leader of the poor."

In my childhood hard winters moved into town with great, driving storms and fields of white to cross on foot. There was a beauty to those days: warmth indoors with the harsh snow ticking on the windowpanes, glass vases with the flowers brought home from Haymarket, music on the record player, tea. My parents had good mad friends who stayed around, other women who had children, men who were misfits and artists, and sometimes there was actually a pervading joy in the house. The radio played constantly, news coming in brought shouts and dialogue.

And spring in the little park up the street—rose-colored crab apple, weeping cherry, flowering judas which is purple, blushing apple blossoms, white dogwood, early lilac, red and yellow tulips, bunches of violets and a meadow of soft dandelions. Around these, a black fence, cement, voices.

And now all I can pore over, inside the morning papers, is a statistic: one out of every twenty-one black males is murdered in this country.

Many of the remaining ones are in jail. And all I can feel, in a visceral way, is the sickness of facts. I don't understand how it came to this.

Where is justice, I keep asking. It doesn't do any good to lock anyone up. Longer and longer sentences are handed out, millions of dollars are spent to prosecute offenders who will be out on the streets again soon. Young dealers, boys and girls, are given terribly long sentences for their crimes—longer sentences than any of the rich will ever get. And what is it like in a detention home? Six feet by ten feet, furnished with a single bed, a desk bolted to the wall, a stool, a toilet, a barred window, outside an enclosed yard containing twenty identically dressed kids. If a kid is lucky he'll be in the care of the Youth Authority where they can eat chips, candy, and Cup o' Soup and buy cigarettes and smoke them. In Juvenile Hall you aren't even allowed a pencil. In both places they are so crowded they have to join a gang for self-preservation. I want to be happy but I can't with this information—the experience of it in my bloodstream.

x

Now Felicity and the girls emerged from the bathroom with rosy and moist faces. Felicity came and stood by Tom to look out the window. He pointed out a cloud in the sky which resembled a fishbone and asked her what it looked like to her.

—Snow, she said. I miss snow. Why do you look so mad?

—My mind. It's racing.

—Raging?

He shrugged.

—Actually you look sort of like a saint—Peregrine maybe, or, no, Saint Sebastian. Crazy mad. Way out there.

—Please, he protested.

—What I mean is I think I can trust you.

—Really? I wonder why.

—There's some stuff I want to talk about. My turn.

—Don't you have a lover?

—Nobody will ever love me again.

—You don't seem to need it anyway.

—You're not the first person to say that. Can I braid your hair? She asked with her fingers in his long loose hair.

—Okay but don't be seductive. I can't stand seduction.

—See, you are a candidate for canonization. I bet you cut your tangles out with scissors. I bet you hardly ever use a comb.

He sat on the edge of the unmade bed and she crouched, knees up, behind him. She was dressed in her jeans again and a checkered shirt, and her hands were rough and competent at the same time. He felt her breath on the back of his ear like a hair. She asked if she could hack off the end of his hair with a knife.

—It's a little rough along the edges, she explained.

—Come on, just braid it and be done with it. Am I really taking you to a shelter? Is this something you do often?

—No. I've only had to do it a couple of times.

—Why do you live down here?

—I heard there was good medical care.

—For who?

—No one. I just like to be near good doctors. I'm neurotic.

—The best hospitals are in New England. You could have stayed there.

—When I was first pregnant, she said, I stayed around New England. But then I had to run away from the father who was acting crazy. So I went to live on this island. Indian summer. I lived like a dog. When a woman turns into a dog, you can be sure she's near to God. My primary relationship then was with God. I still wish it was. The world destroyed me and my imagination.

—Where in New England? He asked. What island?

—Up in Maine. But it got too cold, and he found me. The good thing about here is you can sleep outdoors if you get desperate.

—That's a strange way to choose where you live. Especially when you have kids.

—I lack the will to make money.

—What do you have the will for?

—I make dollhouses, but they've all been sold.

—Do you believe society owes you a living?

—I don't think in big terms about society.

—So what are you going to do?

—It makes me cry to think about it. I don't know.

She gave a final efficient tug to his braid and let it fall with a thud at the nape of his neck. The girls stared into the television but moved their bodies restlessly. Tom said, Let's go.

In the rented car he began to take note of the littlest girl, who was one of those children who say wild and unexpected things. Her skin color was poor, as if she had rubbed buttercup juice into her cheeks, but her eyes were feverishly bright. Black as olives, and awestruck in their expression. She wiggled constantly, and whenever they walked, she hopped, skipped, jumped, then sank to the ground in a heap of thin bones, tired. Her hair started out neat and ended up messy in a matter of minutes. She chattered. If he listened, he could hear lines of surrealistic poetry coming from her, though she seemed to have no expectations of anyone listening to her at all. She didn't like to be touched much, but darted away from outstretched hands. This made her all the more tempting, and both her sister and mother were constantly reaching for a kiss, which she evaded.

The two girls sat in the back seat engaged in an intense battle using small plastic men. They had the air conditioning on, the windows rolled up. Outside: Plaza Boulevard—a dull yellow brick strip of commerce— and hot sun. The flat sandy terrain seemed to reject weight. The houses and shops were tacky, temporary shelters compared to the fortressed architecture of other cities. Taco and tortilla stands abounded; it was all but Mexico. Felicity wanted to cross over the border but he wouldn't go. She sulked and called him a drag, insisted on stopping to get some burritos and then slumped into talk about public education with her knees up on the dashboard. He was not listening, but cast critical glances at the beer can she held inside a styrofoam cup. They passed two shelters for the homeless and soup lines gathered outside dun-colored churches.

—In the fall the children will go to school, don't worry, she told him.

—I'm only worried about now, not then. You'll end up in a rehab center for alcoholics and your children in foster care if you don't watch your drinking.

—I know, you're right. But I'm only self-medicating, not drinking to be drunk.

—So let's drive up to the mountains.

—Yeah, let's go to Julian, she called over her shoulder.

The girls rejoiced at this mention of a town called Julian and she rearranged her posture to give directions. Driving, he rubbed the center of his forehead with the tips of his fingers as if he had a headache. He asked her to tell him the story of her life; his expression was cautious as he waited and she talked.

—I'm an Army brat, she said without hesitation. I lived everywhere. My Dad was a spy. We went to Trieste, Germany, the Guadalcanal, the Far East, Texas, Seattle, Oklahoma, Fort Dix, Florida, San Diego, D.C., back to Texas and back to Panama. I went to nineteen different schools, travelled all over Europe and the Middle East. We even went to Egypt and to Japan, Hawaii, Micronesia! But I always spent my summers in Maine, in our house by the sea there.

—Lies, said Tom. All lies.

—How did you know?

—You told me a completely different story before, he said.

—I thought you didn't hear a word I said . . . . All right, all right, that was the life story of the mean man, Temple, the one who's always after me.

—Why tell his story? Get yourselves confused?

—No, let's just say I was testing you. To see if you remembered anything I said before. You know about my childhood. Lee, tell him our life story!

Lee leaned forward, her face serious, even sad. She was the worrier in the group, the one who checked the time, and made sure none of them was being offensive to the outside world. She was as tender as a mother towards her mother and her sister, and showed little regard for herself. Her voice was measured, soft, insistent on getting facts correct:

—Our father lives far away, the little girl said. Where he was born. He's a mixture of Indian and Portuguese. He's very smart, probably a professor. Definitely a poet. But he was in the rug business when he was with us. Mama had to stay in a hospital for awhile.

—That's why I like the medical world so much, Felicity quickly interjected.

Lee continued: And Matty and I lived with a foster family. Then she went to college and almost got a degree in hotel management. But we didn't have enough money so she stopped. We've travelled a lot.

—Tons and tons! Matty called from behind. My father lives on the seashells. Pink ones and toenails.

—To Boston, New York, Canada, New Hampshire, Connecticut, Arizona, Mexico, California, and where else?

—Maine, said Matty. Where Mama was born.

—Maine. She likes borders, said Lee. So she likes being near the border of Canada and near the border of Mexico.

—She likes seashells too. She sells seashells by the seashore. She might meet our father on the beach someday.

—No, Matty, she will not, said Lee.

—Okay, that's enough, Felicity told her. Let's not get morbid.

The girls leaned back together and continued to play their war games with sounds hushed so they could tune in on the conversation in the front seat too.

—Well, I guess that gives me some idea, said Tom. But I remember before, you told me about the nodding head man, and how he used to break up all your relationships.

—Yeah, but let's not talk about that now, she whispered, indicating the children in the rear.

—You and I have one friend in common.

—Jay. He's no friend of mine, said Felicity. He's just what they call a contact. From what I hear he's one of these English types who comes over here and takes advantage of stupid Americans with his accent.

—That's right. They ask him to do commercials on the radio, so the product will have the royal stamp on it. And really he's a sleaze.

—No. We don't have any friends in common. That's what makes it really strange that you're here, she remarked.

—Well, I have my reasons. It's not really strange. I want to meet Pedro. In prison. And I have political interest.

—But why stick with me?

—It's better than being alone.

—What's the political interest?

—The same as everyone's. Law and order.

—I hate the law, she said.

—And I hate the order. I mean, the way things stand.

—But why isn't your brother looking for his father? Why you? Self-interest is generally at the heart of most matters, she added.

—I'll tell you why, said Tom, and nervously touched his throat. The two girls leaned up on the back of the seats then, their faces hanging over like donkeys in a barn. Matty put her hand around Tom's braid, and played with it while he talked. Outside they passed round brown hills, then rose up into the small mountains, greener from trees.

—Just before he disappeared, Pedro came to my school one day and took me for a long walk. We went to the Public Garden and watched the swanboats from the little bridge there. Everywhere I stepped his shadow covered me. His eyes were bloodshot, he had obviously been weeping, his whole face had that collapsed look, and he said that everyone would forget him—even his own son when he was gone, and if he died, he would be for-gotten, but even faster—and he said to me that I, of all of them, must never forget him, never let him 'rot in hell'—those were his words.

—Why you? Felicity asked.

—He said that I at least had a chance at getting power in this world. Something to that effect. And I should be sure to take responsibility for him when I got that power. What a laugh.

—When did you find out where he was? asked Felicity.

—Only recently, and by chance. When I was going through my fa-ther's papers. That's the horrible part. My father knew where Pedro was all that time.

—What's so horrible?

—Pedro was his best friend. He should've kept in touch at least.

—What for? Your father had run off with his wife and son. Why would he want to keep in touch with him? Self-interest rules, I tell you. It always does.

—God, Felicity. You sound so cynical.

x

But she was right, about self-interest, his, the way women are. They make these extravagant statements; you have to argue with them, you have to put them down; then, later, you realize they were right. At that point it's a matter of honor, whether you're going to steal their ideas or go back to them, apologize and congratulate them for being so smart. I didn't say anything to her, but my self-interest was obvious enough to me. I wanted to know the worst about my parents so I could finally be free of their influence.

x

We ate our way through Julian, preserved as a ghost town for tourists. Apples were the staple of the town's industry. The signs for pies were everywhere. With wooden porches and homey storefronts, the idea was to keep Julian as alive as a Hollywood stage set for a Western. The girls were happy. I left them all eating ice cream and pie and went for a walk down the side roads and into a grove of silvery blue eucalyptus trees. The sky was vague. I sat on a rock to smoke and think. It was soft and quiet there, the shadows a pale dapple of green, like those of houseplants on a white wall. I was glad to be among trees again. Southern California seemed barren to me, except for the comedy of palm trees. I missed the sudden heaps of green and shadow, armloads of dots dancing in the air. But now I felt another atmosphere —a thicker one behind me, and stood and turned. My father's ghost in broad daylight.

You came all this way for me? I marvelled.

He looked, as he had before, exhausted, and carried the gray bag. His posture was straight but his features were dusty and limp. He explained, again, that he had only been away on a trip, had never expected to stay so long. He was not mad that we had gone on with our lives in the meantime. He only wanted to apologize for the length of his stay and to make a few remarks.

Ferns repeat each other superficially, like keys. In reality, every fern is unique. The ground is a door, the ferns are locks. But why are we put here if only to die? Why not begin and end with space and leave earth out of the picture altogether?

He gazed at me vacantly, and I tried to speak to him before he could become a cloud or a shade, but he was gone before I stopped stammering. He left me hobbled with grief. Everything was the color of tears and rain-drained of variation. No green. Again and again I could not recover from that loss, but in each effort to replace his absence with an interest or object, he intervened reminding me of my duty to him. I didn't know who I was without my father.

Nothing about a fern resembles a lock, but a key can be imaged in the purfled edges, even though soft and green, not hard and gold. Even the fossil of a fern in a cowpad would not resemble the shape of a lock. Yet the fern reminds me of something relevant to a way in. It barely exists but seems, instead, to be inscribed: the replica of an original, something denser, darker, damper. Its liquid postures and invention of a tip, after an organized retreat in a cone's shape, makes it a metaphor for the spine and spirit endlessly aspiring. It is organized, more so than most forest greens which have a tendency to twist and crawl en masse around themselves, bark and stone. The fern is orderly and shy like a lock intended only for the one who holds the key. My father collected, pressed and painted ferns. I always wondered why.

x

They were ripping at red licorice ropes on the steps of a bakery when Tom returned. The sun was cooling and the shadows were darker. She squinted up at him and asked him what took so long. His eyes looked puffy. Had he fallen asleep? she asked. He said yes and asked what they would like to do next.

"The water, the kids want to see some water."

"Okay, guys, let's go," he agreed, steering them to the car. The littlest girl held onto his belt crossing the street. He held the hand of Lee, the older one, while Felicity scrambled around in her enormous bag for another can of beer.

They drove south and west to the coast. The Coronado Bridge was the turquoise of a swimming pool. From there they could see all the way to National City, to Mexico. The Hotel Del Mar was too expensive for them and they circled through the parking lot watching the tourists fumble with enormous cars. Then they got lost by Border Field State Park where helicopters were circling the sloughs, and egrets barked like small terriers.

Over some boulders the ocean lashed, panted, exhaled, inhaled all the way down to the border. They walked there by the Tijuana Slough Refuge and the sea. Surfers danced on the waves or lay like dolphins— black shiny dots in a splendor of passivity. The sand curled up like an unpressed hem, and the fencing, intended to keep out Mexicans, stopped before the beach began. Anyone could walk in and out of Mexico along the shore. The backyards of Tijuana were exposed, and above the beach was an American park filled with Mexicans eating lunch and listening to music. Farther along, the shoulder of Tijuana, scruffy as an old dog, tumbled into America, to stables for thoroughbred horses, black and brown and elegant horses, and into flat green farms of Instant Grass.

—The air is very sweet here, said Tom.

—It's Mexican air all the way from here to Oceanside. It's un-American air.

—Tell me what's really happening, Felicity.

—Now?

—Why not? I want to understand.

—It's so hard to trust you. I mean, if I hadn't loved my father, I wouldn't trust any men. Too bad I loved him then. It led to nothing but pain.

—Don't be so bitter. It doesn't suit you, he reproved her.

—If you knew.

—Then tell me.

—It has to do with Matty.

—What about her?

Felicity leaned over and whispered, She's dying, into his ear. He felt a line of cold follow the words down his spine. She said she would tell him later, when they were alone, the story.

x

That night Felicity told Tom that she had been traveling, for many months, from one city to another, looking for a hospital to care for her daughter. Matty needed a new liver to extend her life for a few years, during which time a cure might be found for her condition. Felicity had had no success in finding a transplant; they were hard to come by; and the poverty of the family did not make them prime candidates for a donor. She gave up hope about a year before.

Then Temple, who always had a sixth sense about her, found her in Boston, and called her down to where he was staying. He had heard about her daughter's illness; he thought he could help her.

Always he had known the exact moment when Felicity was about to go broke, and he wired her money; or he knew when she was about to be happy with someone else, and he stepped in and destroyed the relationship with lies, innuendoes, threats. Sometimes—as on her escape to Quebec—she called him out to rescue her. In earlier centuries whales and wolves and plague played the role that Temple played in her life; so did the gods. She had learned how to appease and how to avoid and how to exploit him. But after he had her husband deported, something changed, and she no longer knew which tricks to play to get her way. There was nobody left inside his body who made sense to her, in terms of a personal history. He still did everything on time, and kept his promises, but these seemed like deformities against the solid and cruel front he projected.

Saving History

X

With some dread she left the children in Boston and went to meet him in New York. They met outside a movie theater and the same illumination that was always circling his head was there, but now she felt the aura contained a substance as lethal as radiation. She kept a small distance between them, and they went inside the theater.

The lights to her seemed to dim and brighten again several times. Temple leaned against her. She drew a deep breath and decided to respond to him as she always had, in order to get from him what she wanted. He liked to talk about money. She tried to make him laugh by wisecracking about that subject he held so dear.

—A five dollar bill is my favorite, she said. I don't know why. And so is a nickel. There aren't too many of either of them. But that's not it. Five is friendly.

—In Australia they're making plastic money now. Can you imagine what that will do to our idea of money?

—Play money. I once had food stamps.

—Twice, he said.

—Twice, and they were like that. Monopoly.

—What's the value of an hour of your time?

—Something in plastic.

—It's all imaginary, anyway, said Temple. Always was. Now shh.

The lights thinned, the screen went white and music came out from the walls. Her anxiety was making her sick. She tried to control it. To be in the dark, with Temple in a movie theater nearly empty because of the hour—was making her cheeks stiff around her teeth. It was a distorted smile. She squeezed her cheeks so her lips bowed and looked to the right so he wouldn't see. You wouldn't begin to understand such a gesture if you've never made it yourself. There are landscapes in America, separated by hundreds of miles, which are all but identical. There are Main Streets you couldn't tell apart. Grain elevators, drive-ins, wooden houses with a dignity and simplicity which affirms function above decoration and a kind of humbling under the clouds. And a citizenry becoming more nomadic with each passing hour.

But they were on the backside of Manhattan, which had no one architect, no single state of mind, but which grew out of earth like an eruption from the unconscious of multitudes, or the final elevation of the Underworld to the top of things. Up near the Cloisters. The Hudson slugged along at the base of the Harlem River and she always imagined that river on her right, and the East River on her left, because that's the way she and he entered Manhattan—from the top down; everything about their habitat seemed to involve being behind, in back of, off to the side, just because they began north in Maine.

Temple never showed any signs of affection towards Felicity. Her anxiety came from her familiarity with his mix of obsession and indifference. He wouldn't let up on her, but he wouldn't comfort her with one moment of human attention, either. Machines express pain even if they don't know it (that's why they make those noises) and Felicity surmised that Temple felt that same kind of pain. She had known him from childhood. At least since she was a teen and he was a young man, but she had known all about him way before they met. He summered in Maine and she lived there, a townie, as he would say. From day one the relationship was established between them. She waited for him to express the pain he was in, and he showed her his cold profile. Like a radar machine, he kept track of her moves, remaining himself isolate and invisible. Yet she knew that he knew what she held within her as a potential.

The movie theater smelled of bathroom, public bathroom, or the way cheap bars smell in the afternoon. Green ammonia. Temple sat straight as a chair in the aisle, chewing gum solemnly, his eyes narrowed. They were watching Young At Heart and already it was one of Felicity's favorite movies. Frank Sinatra expressed his pain with every move he made. Felicity and Temple had been to the same movie and had the same kind of conversation about money when she was a late teen. But she was the only one of the two of them that day who remembered the original occasion and how similar it felt to this one. She knew very little about him—only that he had stopped dealing drugs and was now engaged in something like real estate, so he was still rich. She had come to him for help as a last resort. Meantime an aura of disappointment floated about him, one of those emotions so powerful it swelled and deflated in the air.

Tears tickled Felicity's smile as she watched the movie. The story was innocent and she reminiscent. Suddenly she felt Temple gazing at her, the way they do when they're thinking about taking you to bed, and her blood rushed up her legs like a run in a stocking. She was horribly dressed in jeans, a sweatshirt, a leather jacket, gray and stained under-wear, ripped socks, sneakers and a red baseball cap. But she still be-lieved that happiness was chasing her and she was only just missing it by inches. She wore that look they have when they're trying to trick happi-ness into getting caught. Now it took the form of her thinking Temple would break down at last, be kind, and rescue Matty. She pretended to be unaware of his gaze, but her fingers nearly broke among themselves, and all because he was looking at her.

She stood up first when the movie was over, and rubbed her eyes with her fists. The blood in her limbs was still inaccurately flowing too close to her navel and crotch, and she stretched to a child's height beside him. Temple, still seated, put his hands up on her hips and hauled himself to his feet, sighing. His hair was both yellow and white. The nod in his head continued. He was exceedingly handsome in an Anglo-Saxon way. For someone with a bullet still lodged in his bottom, he looked remark-ably sporty. Like a prep school teacher. He had the smile of a know-it-all, the kind that automatically lowers the self-esteem of its witness. Felicity looked at the gummy floor under her feet and followed him out to the sun.

—Let's go to the Cork House, he said. I'll buy you lunch.

She trailed him down the thickly shadowed street. Litter and stone. No animals. No birds. The stones smelled of lots of foods, beef, fish, bread, chocolate, those natural resources which the stony streets them-selves lacked. The Cork House had a plastic green shamrock hanging over its double doors. Felicity slipped ahead of him inside. It was a fam-ily restaurant and bar with four televisions, one in each corner, and a bathroom which was always out of toilet paper. She knew the place well and was reassured by its lack of progress.

He ordered the food but when he talked to her he seemed to talk to the television. He didn't look at anyone while he spoke, but always stared over their shoulder as if conjuring up another, imaginary, and better listener. He was, she realized, more sensitive about himself than usual, and lacking in a shared humor. When he laughed, it was his secret why. But she blocked out her anxiety, flirting over the lip of her beer, and telling him her terrible story with the eyes of a beggar. How many hospitals, clinics and doctors she had visited, trying to get help for her daughter, and how they all said the same thing. Since she had no health insurance, she would be at the bottom of a donor's list, and her daughter would probably not survive the wait.

—I can get you a liver, he said, but you realize it's illegal. You have to bring your kid to a clinic on the border—it's really a small hospital— where a surgeon will do it. You won't need to be there or have anything to do with the actual operation. Okay? He's perfectly qualified. He just can't get a license to practice here.

—I don't have a cent to my name.

—Well, I know that.

—So?

—I'll give you something to do, don't worry. I can use your help.

—How will I get her to the hospital?

—A friend will do all that.

—She'll be scared if I don't go too.

—I wouldn't look a gift horse in the mouth.

—Well, what do you want me to do?

—Deliver something to someone.

—Don't tell me what it is.

—Don't worry. Here's the food. Eat.

—As long as you swear the doctor isn't a quack.

—I swear.

—I'll do anything, she said.

He liked that comment and became almost seductive while she mopped up ketchup with her fries. He wiped a red drop from her lip with his napkin, then pressed the spot to his own mouth. He ordered her a Bloody Mary. He drank from it too, sipping from the wet area she had used. He put his hand on her leg, and they reminisced about the backside of Manhattan ten years before, when Temple chased a lover of hers out of her apartment on Avenue D with a can of mace.

—I'm glad to see you are learning to live alone, said Temple. You act like you've got a sign hanging on you reading GO AWAY. Why's that?

—I guess my willpower is on low. I can't do much more than worry about Matty, my daughter, the sick one. I really only care about my kids. These days.

—That's good. As it should be.

—Yeah?

—But I bet you drink too much.

—For what?

—For your health. And your attitude. You have lost your sweet wonder.

—Ugh, so?

—I bet you still like sex though, right?

—I don't think about it, I told you.

—I don't believe you.

—Well, it's the truth.

—Want to go to a motel for the rest of the day?

—What for?

—For fun. We can go to the Tower.

—Wow, that would be a laugh and a half.

The Tower Motel was a pink building that peeked at the Hudson through a lot of steel and concrete. It was set back blushing off the street, and was a notorious place for illicit sex, drug deals and gambling. The pink and green room smelled like the inside of a nose, Felicity said, holding her own between her fingers. The bedspread was frayed and dimpled, the sheets soft with age. He had brought her some ready-made Bloody Marys from a liquor store en route, and she swilled one down, hating herself the way she did every time she drank out of need and not out of pleasure. He said from his back on the bed, I never met a junkie or a drunk who liked themselves, or their habit.

—You really think I'm a drunk? she asked.

—Never mind what I think. Get over here.

—She climbed in beside him and buckled up her knees while she trembled.

—Are you safe? he asked.

—From you?

—You know what I mean.

—I take the pill.

—Did you want to get pregnant when you did?

—Uh huh. Being a mother was the best choice I ever made.

—Well, you sure didn't like the father much. You want to marry again?

—Never, ever, ever, not ever, NEVER.

—Why not?

—I already told you I promised God, when I was in that halfway place, that I would never marry again, if I could just survive the first one.

—And I told you that was a dangerous promise.

—Well, I meant it.

—And whatever the case, you got rid of Hugo.

—No, you did.

—You set it up.

—I was scared.

—Yeah, but you're fucked up. You give with one hand and take with the other. You send out mixed signals. It's all for attention, or so you can look good, or maybe you're just confused since your brains went. But I'm not dumb. I know that I serve the function of Bad Guy for you, so you can have a clear conscience.

—That's not a very nice thing to say. Besides, you seem to like doing these things.

—I do. It's true.

—But you don't even care about me.

—I must care if I like to see you suffer.

—Shit.

—Stop shaking and get out of bed. I don't want to sleep with you. You're too old, too used, too motherly for my taste.

She jumped from the bed and ran to the bathroom with her clothes in her arms. Awkwardly she dressed, her fingers fumbling with zippers and buttons. She even put her hat back on before she returned to the room where he lay. She stood over him, questioning.

—Why did we end up so much on the edge of society, Temple? Others, our neighbors, did okay.

—There's this theory I've got—of circles. Rings. Tracks. Whatever you want to call them. Everybody occupies space in one of these closed circuits. The Mafia and the Kennedys are together in one of them whether they like it or not, because they both have the same degree of power and money. Frank Sinatra's in that one too. Then there are little tight rings—where people are so rich they're free of all thoughts of money and power. Royalty, dictators, certain movie stars. However, the larger the rings, containing more and more people, the less power and money is involved, people become anonymous. Those were our neighbors, the middle class, or the middle circle. It's a circus, for Christ's sake. You could have been a star in the right ring. But you and I are in the waste dump—or not quite, the homeless and crazy are in that one, picking up garbage, the throwaways getting the throwaways. You and I are just on the edge of that one, no matter how much money we have. It's not a very big space where we are, but it's got a lot of people crammed into it—rejects, criminals, ones who didn't quite qualify for power or for anonymity. I should've qualified, but I didn't like the people in there, my people, my family's friends.

Felicity said, Sounds like circles of evil. Where do nuns and priests go?

—You mean the ones who keep their vows? You're right. They have their own little crystal ball.

—Is our circle totally debased? Felicity asked in a whisper.

—Totally, though I don't worship Satan or anything like that. I just maintain a position of secrecy while I do what I have to do. What I really turned away from was notoriety. You might recall that I used to have some measure of fame?

—Sure. I worked in your campaign. You gave those great speeches on civil rights and the Constitution.

—Good, you remember. I'm still a patriotic American, said Temple.

—Yeah, really. Are you happy now in this trap, track?

—No way. No one is content in the one they're in. That's the race. The sting. The bite. The kill. I want to be in the one above the Kennedys and they do too.

—Is it progress to move from one to the next?

—I don't believe in progress. Can't you see? That's the whole point of the picture. They're traps. They go nowhere. They're not hierarchies.

He tossed back the sheets then, exposing his hairy legs and polka-dotted shorts. His chest hair was silver. He looked as if he had never let his body see the sun. As he dressed, he spoke to her formally.

—Here's what you've got to do. Go to Boston for about a month. I have a friend who can find you a place to stay. Wait there till I contact you.

—But the kids?

—They can stay with you.

—They're already registered in a school there.

—I know. So continue to bring them.

—Then what?

—I'll set you up with a person down on the border. You'll switch your daughter with the package I mentioned. It'll all take place near a small private airstrip outside Calexico. You've probably never seen a landscape like that one. You'll stay in a motel that's located right next to the only ranch in the area. A gal will pick you up soon to take your kid to the clinic. She'll also give you the instructions. Her name is Mona. I hate that name. She's my slave. I call her Money instead.

—If she's your slave, I guess you can call her anything you want, said Felicity.

—Felicity, you are now my slave too.

—Sure, she laughed.

—Now here's some cash for your trip. And here's the name of the contact in Boston.

—I'm not too happy with this. It scares me.

—Why so? You've got a master now, said Temple with a tight smile and his head nodding as if he was riding the subway downtown. You always wanted a master. Many women do.

—Only when everything else has failed. The same goes for men.

—Are you sure?

—I am sure that slavery is available to all people, and masters too.

—Oh? I'll think about that. Hope I'll marry you someday? You used to.

—No.

—Why not? That hurts my feelings.

—Come on, Temple, don't play with me.

—Years ago I promised you I would always watch out for you. I keep those promises. I also told you that you will belong to me sooner or later, remember? You loved it. You thought it was romantic.

—Okay, but now I hate the thought. I told you I hate marriage. More than anything.

—Only because it brings slavery to the surface. Bondage.

—That's right, she said.

—But you're already in bondage. Why not get the benefits?

—I'm not in bondage. Why do you say that? I live alone.

—You yearn. You still yearn.

—And what about you, Temple? What happened to you? Why have you gotten so mean?

—I was always mean. Now do everything I said, he called. If you want to save your daughter's life.

—Can anyone be saved by someone evil? Tom asked.

x

She had no answer. He noted that she carried around a peculiar collection of books—Trotsky, Baudelaire, *Field Guide to Western Birds*, woodworking, *Wuthering Heights*. She never let her children out of her sight or mentioned their father. Her own father was part Eskimo, and drifted down into Maine where he worked as a logger and was tended by a small band of misfit women, all alcoholic and part Italian and Sachem Indian (offspring of the same anarchists who came to make marble gravestones in Vermont, and were chased into obscurity by the FBI and were the forefathers of Tom's people.) The anarchist tradition continued in this matriarchal tribe. She had a happy childhood, given gulps of Southern Comfort by loving women. Her father pushed her on timber downriver in the warm summer weather. The smell of lilacs in the spring and newly poured tar were sensations which sent her into maddened memories of early youth. Sometimes she longed for home, but feared to return since all but one of the adults (a cranky aunt) had been carried away by bad livers and heart attacks.

One summer she met Temple on the lake which lay near the river. He was lying back in a canoe, stripped down to the waist, his skin reddish brown from the sun and his hair bleached nearly white. She had heard about him—a rich teen, from a house on a hill, with no parents, both had died, and only an uncle to care for him. By mistake she saw him sucking his thumb, alone in the canoe, his face turned up to the sun. The gesture was both pathetic and arousing. She was embarrassed and turned her face to the water. She was sixteen years old, and fishing. She looked twelve, his favorite age for girls. He was said to be spoiled (even if orphaned), suspicious, ambitious and afraid of fully developed females. He paddled over to the riverbank where Felicity was nested on rocks among leaves and took her for a slow float around the lake. Her body was like a kid's and she wore a red cap with a visor to shade her eyes. He eyed her with adoration and desire, while she flopped around, rocking the boat and sticking her bare legs into the water. He imagined her as hairless as a baby, except where the black hair poured out from under her cap and her eyebrows and eyelashes were thick and expressive on her face. And he wrestled with her in the canoe, she was laughing hysterically because every touch felt like a tickle, until the canoe tipped over and they fell into the water. Then the way he grabbed her between her legs made her realize he wasn't just fooling around, and she pulled away and swam to shore, panicky and panting, while he swam after her, dragging the canoe along with him. She ran through the woods, home, but she was hooked on him, his hand had been like a hook in the privacy of her groin, and she spent the rest of that summer dragging around after him. He for his part had no desire for her, since he discovered, with his hand, that she was not prepubescent, but he savored her childlike appearance nonetheless, and admired her lack of education and security, and she became his sidekick, his Sancho Panza, his Tonto, his good luck charm for a couple of summers following.

Felicity for her part never wanted to lose her mind and understood that he didn't want her to, either. She understood it with her body and her psyche. His hand had let her know he was judging her as she judged herself. Smart! How could she not, therefore, be stuck on him?

x

One night at the ocean place when I was pregnant I trudged across shells and stones in the night with the water sloshing on my sneakers, and I looked up and saw the lights from a little saltbox, all yellow and gentle, and for a few minutes I wanted that kind of security. It looked so good! But I guess I'm just a hobo by nature. What can you do if you are what you are? I'm not like some of us who are thrown out like trash and don't want to be. They want the little yellow lights and what goes along with them. They want a roof and a root to correspond. So let them have it. They didn't ask to be born. We have to take care of each other's needs. I don't happen to have that need, but I do have some. For my kids mostly. Am I really the only one in the world who loves them?

—That's scary, Tom, I tell you, and why I've got to get settled. Later, I can walk for miles, get high, right? Getting high is getting free.

—Not really, said Tom. Then he felt ashamed and added: My job seems to be to shoot you down.

—My job, said Felicity, is to believe in everything.

They watched as an American spoke Spanish to a Mexican waiter who replied in English. There were lots of doors leading in. Geraniums grew along the edge of the gravel parking lot. They circled the doors, about twenty of them, and found themselves crossing a brick tile terrace where there were green chairs and tables and trellises spangled with Christmas lights. A little bar, a man. Delicate pink flowers fell from watery wine glasses. Calla lilies bloomed along a stone esplanade which faced the sea. There was a wrought iron balcony over each door and pink fans of linen stuffed in every glass on every table. A Mayan tin sun shone on the pink stucco wall. Felicity had put the children out on the sand to play and now she stood behind Tom on the other side of the wall. He asked her what it was like to be pregnant.

—Why, what for? she asked.

—It's a question I always wanted to ask someone.

—I'll tell you about the time I was pregnant with Lee, because then I was happy—alone—near the sea.

x

As with a great storm or onset, she could hear through the walls of her body, the hysteria of two whose voices hit a pitch neither male nor female. Getting pregnant only took those noises and an interior silence, a moment which she knew every time. Age-old urge, emergency among the whirlpools, the fragments and sweeping curves of her torso. A sudden squall, the flutter of a breeze in her ear, and she was done.

She began to harden with the first baby. A firm heel slid across the palm of her hand, under her navel, now like a moonsnail with a cat's eye at its apex. Her wastes, and the baby's, moved in opposite directions from the nutrients. Her breasts tightened to tips of pain. She entered her psyche daily on rising, and like Saint Clare who sucked the breast of Saint Francis, she frenziedly inhaled the Ave Maria. She dwelled inside, in fact. An expedition of several oar ships.

Perfumes of the senses met a collection of bones and springs, and in her genitals a language of body fluids and secretions, tracts and tissues, bone marrow, breast milk, joint fluids—she had to think of these. The creation could only read itself!

The embryo went to sleep early one night and in the liquidy darkness I stepped down the center of the road, by day bustling with cars

366

and tourists. I walked towards the point which circled back along a harbor into town. I took a westerly direction, knowing the sea would always have the last word.

This is the way to see a place—looking from darkness into lighted rooms. So the fetus derives nourishment from the light of oxygen. The white clapboard houses conformed like little teakettles or mausoleums, with a staircase down the center, a kitchen beyond, and on either side a living room and study. The walls were marked with pictures of schooners and portraits of seafaring men. Streamlined launches too, but no tramp steamers red with rust, no broad tugs, ropes, cables, or snakelike tubes winding from tanks; these were class ships. At twelve weeks the uterus is stretched like a canvas, larger than the pelvic cavity. It can be palpated above the symphysis pubis. But these rooms were white with polished wood. The furniture was stiff and economical. Like the ships themselves, they equated tidiness with worth. Old women dusted and drifted through the mannish spaces, giving to them the otherworldly sheen of sisters from the last century.

She was often sick, either hunched up or bent over, retching into a toilet bowl. Nature is extravagant. Her body was a difficulty in much the same spirit that a person's gender or income can be under certain conditions. Inside her eyes she saw placenta, membranes, amniotic fluids, cervical cul-de-sacs, a vulva and an interior like the gums of an infant. However, her mental dimensions tipped towards the metaphysical. God had been forced out of just such a world. She trudged up and down the island and daily visited beaches which were duneless but sided by slick streaks of beach grass. The shadows of seagulls spilled along water's edges. Silk pennants fluttered over the breakwater and sometimes rain glistened in the dark. Fishing boats and cutters had black-green barnacled bottoms. The ruin of the deck and upper structures of many ships looked like fruit picked by sharks. Every stay and handrail held a bird in the dawn. Sticky oil, belched from a tunnel, had birds stuck on their pin-like toes. The poop went down, the bow went up, it was her body walking and a teeny skeleton inside like a cabin.

On the strand the waves were disorganized, they champed and struck each other, currents tugging at a mash of pebbles. Few shells, and those were cracked scallops or an old horseshoe crab. A flotsam of styrofoam and plastic baggies. God's grave is blue and above. When you are living on the edge of your society are you closer to the center of the next era? If there was such a quality as human nature, she now had to assume it was grounded in the machine she inhabited and which, again, inhabited her. The vagina and cervix in pregnancy are blue to purple. She was sure drug therapy was the best cure for depression. Motion was liberation from the gross inertia of the body which held swellings small as berries and full of air. You could be healed by leaping in the sea which is why she gravitated towards water towns. There flowering seaweed cooled her sore fret. The surface oysters with pearls embedded in pink flesh made her feel like a link of woman, coral to red, nameless as a breast. Now a hint of autumn let her spirits rise, her mind race.

I don't want to be a king or captain or bishop or chair. A summer of record-breaking heat and humidity created a swimming pollution, humans gasped like fish. In the seas a scandal of unsanitary objects. While five thousand small herrings nested in the stomach of a sperm whale and each one of them contained crabs who in turn had eaten algae, night storms kept the beaches lined with silver wiggling krill and human feces. The air stayed dense and dirty as if the rain itself had been a form of excretion. Birth is a calamity. So I cling to my infant and it to me.

I have become unified with my materials. Thorns made the beard of Jesus what it was. No field of blue flowers. No matter what I touch or work on, it's only me touching or working. Conversion is not putting on something new but shedding something old.

In her first pregnancy she found herself finally focused on the presence of her body. Nothing was distracting from the fact that the mucus of the cervix is less viscid than sputum. She was conscious of how mechanistic and unnecessary a human life really was; every fact was an affirmation of perdition. Rich and poor women look stark but strong. Clapboard houses, low to the ground, with protuberant fans and television antennae nestled in shrubbery lusciously green and dotted with flowers.

Petunias, limp, with purple trumpets too, proliferated. Some gardens had salmon-pink borders of impatiens and on the roadsides the clover was ripe, a farm was for sale, fresh baked pies were lined up on planks beside beach plum jelly and apple cinnamon. Mopeds and bikes cruised the narrow roads where she crawled. Pastures humped under her back in the long grass, the sky was often misty or gray. She wondered, when she woke out there one day, if the objects she saw on the left in her dreams were emanating from that side of her brain.

Well, I said, you sweep people away like a dream. I'm glad when you call to me, Let's go. Seeking face. I WILL seek your face.

Is it human nature to crave the love of indifferent people? Does a displaced center become a periphery? She certainly did, even while she sustained bonds to distant friends. Past their shoulders she always seemed to glimpse the image of someone who had forgotten she was alive, and hardly cared to discover she was. One such person told her that the mirror for human nature was art and that the secret therefore of her essence could be found in the recognition that she would feel before certain words and works. Without such recognition she could only feel revulsion towards the experience of producing more body fluids, another epiglottis, endometrium, and so on.

Pregnancy created a tie to her own accidental source. To view the condition as a disease which she had caught was to reject the knowledge of a human for its own nature. A plant might look like it's growing a beard, but anyone knows that it isn't, since each form can only reproduce itself.

She didn't remain as static as a plumed worm—building its home in a papery tube. A trumpet worm constructs a permanent home from a golden cone in the sand.

She inhabited her inhabitant and kept on moving. The larvae of soft-shell clams do no less. In an environment that changes wildly, creation creates a lot of itself. In a fierce storm barnacles, worms, and mussels reproduce in droves. If she wondered who really owned her hand, writing with a pen, and where she could be located, she now knew one thing at least and for the time being: she was present at her own life.

The collar-like erection on the beach was made by a moonsnail to protect her eggs. So she was an organism which existed alongside the other particulars in the universe. She was really here where the egg cases of skates, called "mermaid purses," are dry and black with two spiny tendrils at either end.

By accepting the fact of her existence she had to accept the terms in which science generally spoke of such facts. Herring gulls eat horseshoe crabs, but she turned away from the temptation of brutalism. She, like some, tried to believe that the secret name of the power that is the fore-ginning of everything was HUMAN. While the integrity of her pregnancy was maintained by high levels of estrogen and progesterone, her personal integrity was maintained by identifying with eremites.

She had begun to feel close to the ground. The poverty line was dollars above her, she who had been one of the working poor. America ran through her sleep too fast. But beach heather with its yellow spring blossoms was not her bed either. Grasshoppers belong to beach grass.

One morning a cloud bank slipped over the island like a smoker trailing around a garden. Seaweed in the cracks of rock and bits of sponge and seaside goldenrod held her, lying in the sun. The trees were filmy, the national shades of noon still softened by immortal light. A caterpillar here, a snake there, by Labor Day most of the wildflowers were eliminated. Small baggy areas formed in the troughs between dunes, and she hid in them with a stolen apple pie. To be happy alone you don't need to be a martyr.

From some leaves thick as leather hung nuts, rocky brown ones with dimpled caps. Beach peas grew in the sand with wild cherry and beach plum. I'd eat kelp, sea lettuce, maybe even Irish moss. I didn't want to hitchhike at my age or in my condition; instead I scuffed my sneakers through the sandy soil and twitched with the pains in my calves. Pork of veal, pork of veal, someone called in a room through the trees. The light seemed painted on the surface of each oak leaf. So I remembered artifice, I a free woman who had neither home nor office, and then I saw my husband coming, and wept.

x

—Okay, okay, Tom muttered.

Tom shut Felicity down the minute he sensed that her story was on a down-curve. Don't get sentimental with me, he warned, but she promised she would stick to facts if he would just listen to her. "I'm in some kind of peril," she confessed. And in the hotel, when the children were sleeping, she hid behind the drapes, pressed up against the window and talked, while he stood, hands folded in front of his groin and head tipped down like one waiting in line for the Eucharist.

"Before I went to New York or met you, I traveled down here with the kids. Matty was really sick then. Between her illness and rejections from hospital officials, I could hardly get up in the morning. We moved back and forth along the border."

Crossed over. Squat palm trees with fanning leaves, a sandy soil, small adobe houses, wine red bougainvillea like paper, like velvet, graffiti of human faces on a cement wall, chickens nipping at nothing, and jacaranda trees as blue as lilac. There the people were thick, short and brown like her. They were like her brothers and sisters. When the earth trembled, there was an accompaniment of sound—rolling rocks, a thunder under the soil. She remembered Hades coming up from the Underworld near the red flowers with all that clatter. He pulled Persephone down but she held her daughter tighter to her. Pomegranates grew wild and red as peppers, and their seeds spilled from the pouches to feed the insects. They say that the songs of birds make fruits grow ripe. Honeysuckle thickened with fragrance outside a wall.

We slept outside. To our right was the sea; it always used to be at my left. I saw by the cactus that not only was all this land covered by water but that air itself is just a lighter form of water that we live in. Mountain lions are still being hunted down in the Sierras, it's late, but they survive. Like all of us they spend their lives on consumption, for time is food.

Felicity looked for a home in the papers:

WANTED—HOUSE DESPERATELY. Bank foreclosed homes. Free list of repossessed condos. Darling, immaculate, delinquent property. Government homes $ (you repair) By owner. FHA assumable. Mobile home, adult recreational park. Need a down payment? Carefree condo. If I can't find it, it doesn't exist!

My indecision about Matty was a plague. I didn't want to go near Temple for help again, I wanted to be free. But I was living on last dimes and her increasing illness. I went to lots of churches and prayed to Mary. But every time I started a novena, I would forget in the middle and ruin it. So no wonder they didn't work! I learned a lot from books, too, that we got from the public libraries. The kids and I would read about history and geography. We wanted to know where we were in the world.

Montezuma ruled like a divinity. Ancestral hierarchies were rampant. Many of them, even in the Americas, were derived from ties to Rome and the Church.

Matty broke my heart. I blamed myself for all the drink and smoke and went on drinking and smoking. Decisions are like climbing up a ladder into space. I didn't know how to make one. The only way to feel safe in space is by holding a baby. They take care of their mothers. Try it. Hold one someday. I hated my body in those days because I blamed it for her sickness, and then I felt nothing for anyone, not even myself. I was my own enemy. Hateful.

I felt no desire outside the desire for a miracle. If someone good would only save us.

The land had belonged to the Comanches and I was one of them. By 1830 Anglos outnumbered Mexicans along the border. Most were Catholic who despised Indians and Mexicans. Four to one. A serious problem for them was slavery, and why not? Mexico outlawed slavery in 1822. And they didn't want any more Americans coming in. Slavery meant disaster because slaves had so many children. Texas died for the freedom to keep slaves. Have slaves or die. Temple too might die for such freedom.

In 1840 Nuevo Leon and Coahuila tried to secede from Mexico.

A Republic of the Rio Grande was declared with Laredo as its capital. It produced one hero Antonio Zapata whose head was chopped off and pickled in brandy.

I don't want to be anything like a man.

The Taiwanese have set up offices in the US where they regulate business in the Maquiladoras. Vamanos, said the Mexican people and headed off to work, from onions to sugar beets to pickles to cherry trees to strawberry fields to peaches and the asparagus fields. The two borders—Cali and Mexi, Mexicali and Calexico. Sex confuses citizenship, and family trees take root in the river. Power to the people.

She ran out of money and hid in an orphanage, helping some nuns take care of abandoned children. There she learned how to organize large groups of people—how to build cubbies and line up the food—how to make shoes look neat in a row and how to put privacy and silence into practice. She learned how to be efficient under pressure, and how to live in a community. Matty however was getting sicker and the nuns urged Felicity to return to get help in America. In that sandy soil the flowers were sometimes brown, like orchids and irises and the streaks in pansies, and sometimes sexual in intent: desert flowers with rubbery ridges and frills gape up hungrily at the sky. They look like they were born to suck. Sometimes Felicity thought she saw them contract, curl in; they were colored yellow and salmon pink. She thought of all the orphans turned out onto the streets at age twelve when they lost the orange glow of health and grew ragged; she thought of the children north of the border who were in detention homes and gangs. She travelled to Children's Hospital in Boston, where again she was given small hope of an organ donor for Matty, especially when they were penniless, and she looked for Temple from there. He made the connections and she headed back to Boston and Tom, then South again with her daughters, according to his directions.

x

About a hundred miles east of San Diego, and a mile north of the border, she traveled under the influence of Mona, who liked to call herself Money, too. She was a transvestite who worked in a club on the Mexican side of the border "giving head," as she said, to the white college kids who came down for the weekends. She wore silk stockings and silk skirts and shirts and smoked cigarillos. In a pouch under her shirt she carried money and drugs. She met Felicity and the girls at the E-Z 8 Motel; she was carrying a box of candy in either hand. Red and gold lettering on both covers and crinkly chocolate cups inside. Except one—the left one—was not chocolate and Felicity was being sent to San Diego to deliver it to a man working for the border patrol. The other box she gave to Matty who began pinching each candy in search of caramel.

—The hard square ones are always the caramels, Money told Matty, then noted: She looks Mestiza.

—She is. We all are.

—Don't be nervous. I'll take care of her. Good care. Temple told me to. I do whatever he says and more.

—Is he your pimp or something?

—No way! Money laughed. He's my master. I'm his slavegirl. I do anything he wants. It makes me happier than it makes him.

—In what way?

—It keeps me alive.

She plucked at her elastic panties to show they were too tight and sauntered up to the oval mirror which was only as clear as wax paper. Leaning forward she scrutinized her lips, her teeth. She was smooth-skinned and pretty, with soft dark hair and large man-made breasts. Her features were Mexican, her expression melancholy.

—I'll see you back here in about twenty-four hours, she told Felicity. Just sit tight and see the sights. Your girl will come back. She just needs a checkup, no big deal.

Matty rested her face against her mother's leg, her eyelids seemed weighted down by her heavy black eyelashes. Her color was jaundiced. Felicity stirred up her hair.

—Why can't I go too? she demanded in a rude tone.

—Be serious, said Money. This is not exactly aboveboard. What we're doing.

—How so?

374

—No, you wouldn't want to know. The best thing is to just accept it as a gift from Temple and do your job for him, whatever it is. This way he'll be good to you and that'll be that.

—And what happens if I don't do it?

—He'll—I don't know, said Money with a shrug. You know him longer than I do. Come on, chica, let's go.

Matty buckled and cried, following Money into the heat, with her body twisted up like a question mark. Felicity grabbed Lee's hand and dragged her down the street, after them, but at a distance. She was crying. The yellow ground was hard as a rock, though there was no rock material in it that she could see. Felicity was talking to Jesus: "I thought you were the shepherd who left behind the ninety-nine sheep who were safe. You went out and searched for the one who was lost, remember? You were happy when you found it, since ninety-nine is a number that comes with the left hand, and you liked everything weighing in in the right hand. Remember?"

Crowds collected as she and the little girl progressed, and the streets began to thicken with commerce. Faces watched her weeping and walking and talking. Neon pagodas in the paved and pitted roads, lemonade and cigarettes, tacos in curbside braziers; she saw a guitar warped by grease drippings, and a man's hand on it. She smelled banana leaf tamales and bought herself a beer. She saw Money and Matty climb in a cab and she plunged forward after them. Hidalgo ceramics and Saltillo blankets lined the road, alongside toy violins, leather vests, chess sets made of malachite, pinatas and whips. Awnings, vending stalls, corrugated metal, tons of people. Some spoke English, some Spanish.

Felicity screamed Matty, and ran after the cab to pull her back out and take her away.

She got as far as the window and looked in as it moved away. Matty was looking down at her hands. Felicity could tell that Money had given her more of the goat's-milk caramels, and the child had chocolate dribbles on her chin, streaks of dust down the lines of her tears. Felicity's crying was by then a moan or a buzz in the back of her throat. Something ripped from the spirit is far more painful than something ripped from the skin, though I wouldn't want to test this hypothesis. At least I can swear an action does occur, and it makes me very sore. To say goodbye is sad enough when you can be sure the other will return. When that hope is fretted with uncertainty, the whole air is transformed and the strange thing is, you are the only one who knows it!

x

I don't own any of this. None of it belongs to me. Not the television or what's playing on it. Not the Gideon Bible. Not the road, the car, the dust or the movie playing down the road. I exist separate from all that, for the children of the Lord are like his fragrance, since they have fallen from the grace of the beginning, and still carry that grace and that fragrance in their mouths and ears and nostrils. They hold it in their hands. It lies in the light on their faces and in the darkness of their closed hands, and in their sleep.

x

The delivery of the chocolate box was unmemorable. I just handed it over to some big half-naked border cop at the door of a bungalow in Southeast San Diego, and then drove away. I sensed that this was only the beginning of my side of the bargain. Ficus and bougainvillea colored up the sunny alley alongside the bungalow and clashed with a to-mato-red Porsche parked there. Almost immediately I returned to the original motel with Lee. We lay in bed together watching TV and only went on the hot streets to get Zingers and Royal Crown Cola. The air was actually white. I didn't like being anywhere. I thought my guts would explode with the acid of my anxiety. If I hadn't had Lee to nuzzle up to, I would've collapsed. She played with her sister's toy soldiers. The room was like a battlefield rebuilt from World War II—cheap plas-tic khaki-colored soldiers hung off the bedspread, the plastic plant, the television wires. She went pow-pow and knocked them down, pretend-ing to be Matty, then climbed into my arms before returning to the kill.

I told her war was obsolete. I told her patriotism was an archaic concept. Once I explained what the words meant, and she understood, she asked, "Does that mean I can start playing with girl's stuff now?"

The day Matty was meant to come back, it rained and she didn't. The sky was murky, yellow, warm. I watched Lee's every move. Her smooth brown shoulders, the wings of her shoulder blades, her long shadowy spine, they made me smile proudly on the one hand and cry on the other. I didn't know which I loved better, her body or my love for her body. It takes years to come to trust the cars and curbs and sharp corners, to let your children move ahead of you, while your head is turned. Oh years. I had no idea, not one, of what was happening to my daughter whom I had watched over hour by hour, since her birth. It is impossible to describe the anxiety of those hours, now, spent with her out of sight. I stared into the television and then outside the window. Across the dirt road in a bar the putas sipped lemonade and leaned against their windows too.

In the evening a woman with man's legs brought me a letter from Temple, saying Matty was fine but needed another day to complete the tests. "We were unrealistic," he wrote, "about the time it would take. You can stay in the motel and wait. I'll pay. And visit." I took Lee out for a drive along the border and back to the motel where Money was waiting with tickets for an outdoor fair. I was not invited to go along, but watched her go off with Lee, anxiously. It was of course a set up because I wasn't alone five minutes before Temple appeared. I was not happy to see his face. He looked out of place in the west, even though he was wearing a string tie and a cowboy hat. He brought tequila and chips and salsa into my room and shook up margaritas while I sat under the bedspread, resisting both questions and alcohol. I thought he might have bad news, but he said don't worry, your kid is doing fine. Great. She'll get what she needs. In a matter of weeks I'm sure we can do the transplant. Drink. I took the glass and felt the heat of alcohol in my thighs and groin and upper arms, a toxin. Temple was as usual estranged from everything around him. He was present but indifferent. He stood by the television where he kept all the drink and chips and stared vacantly at the wall. He told me what he wanted me to do next. I felt my hair grow tight in my skull and heavy. I lifted it with my hands and laughed. No way! But he said I'm not kidding. Come on, Temple, I don't do that stuff, I told him and he said, I know, it's time you did. But what if I don't want to? I asked. That'll make it better for me, he answered.

—Please, said Tom, I don't want to hear this.

—I wouldn't do it, she told him. There are some things. You just don't do. I mean. I'm not going to tell you what, don't worry, because you're kind of innocent.

—So what did he do then?

—Well, obviously he didn't kill me. He left, for a short time. He still called me his slave.

—You're right. This is still a story I don't want to hear.

x

They sat up over the Avenidad Revolución, looking down on people's heads. They drank beer. The children had Cokes and hung over the stall-like balcony beside them. Tourists streamed by, pausing to examine the rugs and ceramics lined up on the sidewalks. The sun lay on Tom's face like a whitegloved hand, and he felt nauseous. Looking at her sideways, he couldn't stop wondering what Temple wanted her to do and what she finally didn't do. Stories can be stranger than experience. They can impart a sensation as heavy as morning breath. Sometimes women seemed profoundly impure to Tom—murky as an old lake. "When you swim in one, you don't know what you will brush against, what will bristle against your skin. At the same time, the cool and refreshing quality that the swim provides—there's nothing like it. Women are deeper and kinder than men, but I don't like the passage sometimes through those tender depths of theirs. It scares me. It can even sicken me." At that moment Felicity sickened him—or her story did, in a context of nihilism and commerce. He told her he wanted to walk back across the border before she could start up one of her stories again. The children had begun to warm up to him as he grew aware

378

of the subtle differences between them, and their potentials for intelligence and gifts of music, math, politics. They equally began to warm up to him—laughing, telling jokes, holding his hands. Someone thought they were a family and told Matty to get their father to buy them a ceramic Mickey Mouse. The sky was a high gray color. Ghost color.

Back in their room, the girls lay down on the floor to watch TV. Felicity meanwhile crawled under the bed to look for a shoe and stayed there plucking at the springs and talking so Tom couldn't see her. This time he placed himself against the drapes and stared out the window, the shadowy belly of a plane crossed over the room.

x

Temple came back and said he wanted to go for a drive. To show me hills I'd never seen the likes of before. I said I'd only go if he didn't make me do anything I didn't want to. He agreed but asked me one thing. What? To pretend to be his slave. Just for the duration of the day, the drive. Better a slave than your wife, I agreed, but he reminded me that in my own eyes they were nearly the same. He had a rent-a-car which was all white.

There's a panic in the noonday hour, in love's demise, no "controls." Over and over the wonder of wounds from human deceptions returns, the mind can't top off, or regulate its notions, and all emotions won't be stalled, but will roll and roll, backwards and forwards.

The car climbed over the mountain to see what it could see.

It shows you're not in love with me, if you could make me marry someone you're not in love with yourself.

He hates to think like this.

See that grass and the pretty bosom in it? I think that's strange.

A woman and her mother.

The highway's wet after yesterday's rain.

I can't recall who told me to be good to please myself, every time I make a bed.

And I'm not in love with her, not because she's a woman, but I don't want to marry anyone I don't really know.

Some people want to feel passion all the time, or do, and even dream about being adored, and adoring, in order to feel engorged.

Sunday is morning's obstruction.

I was mean to my child. Slapped her chest. She followed me once too often. The room, a kitchen, shuffled with shock absorbing sounds; the wings of heaven were palpitating at the cruelty of that act.

Such mad mornings when everyone is crying and furious, and no longer curious.

Green light on the colorless grass.

Flattened out, ironing cloud.

Trees, no leaves, pulled up by the wires.

He doesn't really want to make her get married to someone she doesn't know, but deep down only just wants to get rid of her.

The wrath of a man like this comes on as a muted whirl, west, or east, to another "girl."

Wedlock has no key; but matrimony is too often locked around matters of money.

I pitched my tent in a nest of thistles, by the side of Baja. The black asphalt, like the Nile, carried traffic to my left, easterly, and I sat in a field of scratched grass.

A car looks like the wind, if you could see it.

See the woman, and her master, there. One unstraps the other's bra. A comely bosom in the bushes. A prune-blue nipple points North.

I wonder who will vomit, from too much driving. This woman or that man.

He says it's never too late to mend a rip; but don't hang over the cloth, waiting. "Life is of good and evil woven."

He wants her to turn into a boy. He has a smashed quality, like there was a fist.

The car has settled, backwards, in a coppertone meadow, and the highway goes, mortal slope, down.

Turn round and round and seduce the first lady you see.

How can I convince you that the tapestry is full of holes, the earth's a carpet floating in space, and that hill, going up, is a loose thread?

Her master put her down in this field by the forest. He can't explain why he did such a thing, except he hints that he was really a good guy underneath it all.

She who has been given, says she has chosen, solitude.

We're near the head of the thread; bite it.

Let's have a picnic instead.

We'll never get home—up or down. It's the edge.

Say to him, me: "It reminds!" Say it.

We lay down on this bristly meadow that sloped down to the highway. Bracken like sea sponge. Tea-green stuff. Sucky stuff. Flowers like mouths and vaginas in the cactus. He was detached, and I was surprised to see his head flat on the ground, unmoving, almost placid. I kept thinking about him dying. He had seemed to die once, with me, when I was seventeen, and he was so drunk he didn't know what he was doing when he laid me, so to speak, under a hawthorne tree, using a slow hand and a lot of sweet talk to break me down. At the end he had let out a sigh which was like a rattle from a snake, a baby, and a dying man. All in one. I figured that this was a good time to tell Temple that he had definitely deteriorated over the years from being a reasonably screwed up individual, who was spoiled but troubled by things, to being that same individual without a conscience. I decided to tell him that he was, in a word, insane. He listened with an absorbing attitude, then took my hand and talked about body parts and how the human being is no greater than a machine with interchangeable parts. Livers, kidneys, hearts, tongues, penises, feet—he drew a picture of robotic reality, a take-apart toy, where the mind or the emotions were gaseous emissions from the machinery. He kept saying, If you could just understand, you'd see it my way.

—Never, I told him. I'm a mother. I just know I'm grateful to you for finding an organ for Matty. And it seems to me that this proves that there is such a thing as—well, unselfishness, or kindness—whatever you think of emotions.

—Now you do sound like a wife, he said. I like that.

And then he went on with an accounting of populations around the world and what this meant. Forty million people will live in the United

States by the turn of the century, most of them immigrants with too many children. I'm not being cold-blooded. Millions of children are starving already. Why have them? There must be a reason, there is a reason, he insisted.

—Come on, stop talking about children in terms of reason. Either you recognize yourself in the world, or you don't, said Felicity.

Agreeably, he changed the subject and entered instead into a paranoid and pornographic account of women he had known, their body parts, and the disgust he felt at any woman over twelve.

"Men are cleaner. More honest in their builds. No secrets there. When we were just buying blood, it was much easier to persuade mothers that the money we gave them was equal to the blood. They didn't then try to find out everything about the organization, or snoop into my business. But after that, they got dangerous, the way they do, and talked too much, and asked too many questions, and changed their minds a million times. I couldn't trust one of them. If only they had acted the way you have so far—with trust, silence, those qualities I associate with men, not women. But no. The female body is a manifestation of its meaning—secret, undisciplined, bloody."

—Stop it. I want to go now, I told him.

He reeled to his feet and down the mountain with me following, and a lizard running before us, delicate in its bones and feet. My eyes sparked, and I wanted to drink or get high to transcend the world I was in. We went to a place called Hart's Chicken Parts which was smoky and packed with rednecks and truckers and whores. We drank without speaking, and he introduced me as his wife to anyone who cared to be interested. Then we weaved back to the motel down a highway saddened by the evening shadows.

x

Tom left her lying under the bed and began to watch the news on TV. The girls were sleeping by then and he was not interested in any of them for that hour. She slipped out into the hall and onto the balcony and was gone long after he grew interested again. So he went and sought her out there. Planes rolled over them on air, and he yawned and groaned and caught scatterings of her news, while she dipped around like a shadow in the shadows.

x

I went out at night and whirled around in the light of the moon, a kind of dance in the marshes while the little continents between rushes of water squished underfoot and birds—dowitchers, plovers, godwits, curlews and one great blue heron—snoozed and cooed out of the dark. The watery sections were a dazzle of moonmud or sapphire and when the train rushed through I danced for the conductor to see and saw him in return trying to understand. One night I came upon a woman awake, with two children, pruning a silver pear tree in her garden near the highway. Her children sat on her shoulders like the angels that flanked Mary. She told me she could find me a bench in a church to sleep on. But I told her kindly, no. The infamous sun would be up soon enough and I back at work. I wanted to dance the devil's dance in the dark till the water blued and the sky pinked. Then I'd go back where I came from. She was nice. She accepted me. Later I found out she was creating a happy commune smack on the border. It was twined with geraniums and laughter rang off the adobe walls. She believed that America was corrupting and all a kid needed was freedom from it to break his or her bad habit, and she wanted to save kids. She had a theory that prisoners should be released from jail and airlifted to other countries, dropped there, in the wilderness, not the city, and left to survive. It was what saved her husband. The world is one, but there is no center. The state is a myth, she said as laughter scattered red petals onto the bone dry ground, both sides of the wall. It is not a coincidence that all the walls and buildings are held together with sand. I thought she was like a saint, but when she gave me a pear to eat it lay heavy, cold and mineral in my hand. The fruit had turned into silver, which for all its beauty, horrified me. I have never met a real saint.

Saving History

INFORMATION FELICITY GAVE TOM:

There is this man who does it by hand behind the supermarket.

The Nite Lite Motel is a good cheap motel, E-Z 8 another. Budget Beddy Bye stinks. The Mile of Cars is a nightmare.

She wanted to run away to Chula Vista, steal a horse and ride it to Coronado.

In El Centro there are fake farms, a desert atmosphere, and a detention camp for illegals; the broad margin includes them as they wait for immigration papers. To the west, at night, helicopters flash down floodlights and shoot into the underbrush; inside the helicopters are men whose people came to this country as immigrants.

In the maquiladoras are assembly lines operated at three dollars an hour by laboring Mexican people. These factories are US-owned and Mexico-based. Tarpaper shacks, the squatterdoms of the workers, and in town are banks for the wealthy and loan shops for the poor.

If internationalism was not working in favor of the rich and powerful, nationalism would continue.

"You have to crawl on your belly to get under fear. It's like a poison gas that floats at waist level. You can only subvert it by lying flat on your stomach and wiggling across the world like that."

When LA is north, you know you're really south. You drive north up the wall of the earth.

Don't ever turn your back to the water when you're in it.

In juvenile centers, the kids are all made to look alike, so no one will forget that they are as meaningless as numbers.

Okay, that's enough, said Tom. I know about juvenile centers. I am, after all, a lawyer. But you? How would you know anything like that?

Then she told him relentlessly about the place she had to stay while her children were in foster care. It was a halfway hell, a brick place where she was held in order to avoid a prison sentence for kidnapping her own children. While Tom listened, he gnawed at his cuticles and his knees jumped up and down nervously. Sometimes he even hummed so he wouldn't have to hear what she said, and he didn't hear, or if he did, he forgot.

x

I guess it was the next day we all crossed the border again on foot. She and the children with me. It was like leaving the end of the world and stepping into the beginning. I mean, for a few seconds, while you pass the beggars. Women with babies stuck to them. Clothes worn down like public carpeting. The faces were ancient as if cut from the turf. White people aren't so human, I think—so, in some sense—long-term. What do I mean by human? Imitations of Jesus? What do I mean by white? Individualists, loners. . . . Only inches, well, yards behind us, speeding freeways, pools behind motels, malls, gobs of food. It's all a cliché with nothing new to say.

We walked over a cement ramp stinking of piss and shit, past the first people in the world to the tourist strip where there were donkeys spray painted in zebra stripes, bars, taco stands, and lively full-faced humans. They were the citizens. The tourists had vacancy signs written in their flesh.

On sale: gold Rolexes, suede jogging shoes, leather vests, rainbow colored nylon hammocks, shiny urns, Disney ceramics, thick woven rugs and guayabera shirts. Everything seemed too expensive, even as a deal. As soon as an object has a lesser price than we would normally associate with it, it loses all its value. Then we start bartering greedily with the poor, asking them to lower their prices still further.

We went to a restaurant and talked, while Matty slept in a heap across her mother's knees, her wrists and ankles twitching and trembling as they sometimes did. Lee hoisted her little sister's feet onto her lap, and asked her mother what she did before she and Matty was born. I was a street person, Felicity said.

Yuck, said Lee.

Don't worry, it was okay, I learned a lot.

Did you love anyone then? she asked. Who was nice to you?

Felicity hid in her hair to reply.

Saving History

x

I never met a kinder man than the homeless alcoholic who introduced me to the father of my kids. He was my teacher through a period of my life which was both an actual and an allegorical journey. He was very thin, ruddy, and ratty in his orange beard and brown clothes. His eyes were either squinting or seeking. Sometimes he turned into a handsome young man and men and women grabbed his hand in passing—as long as they wore gloves! He never liked me to see that and always released the woman's hand if I happened to glance back and catch him at it.

We had hope. That he would one day be free of his addiction and be able to love someone in health. Now I know we could never love each other more than we did then. Can you understand? Because this is important. We were wrecks, but our relationship was complete. Sufficient. Why ask for more? He was much worse off than I. But I was a lost spirit clad in a dirty pile of threads and we had to stumble through the rocky streets of the city to find our way out to the green woods where white dogwood bloomed in the spring before there was acid rain. We went along with each other, never having sex or even dreaming of it, and he told stories with such velocity and verve that I vowed I too one day would tell stories like that. The voice in the Garden of Eden just walked around without any flesh on; that was like us.

We were so physically needy that we were freed from our bodies and lived intense spirit-lives. We were the extreme forms that certain human emotions express, but repress too. Extreme affliction frees you, finally, from desire, and so we sought the longest and most difficult route to the nirvana of a woodland setting, hand in hand, mind you, and imagining a prospect both physical and internal. A white tree is reflected as a white tree in brown water. No matter what you want to say about it, I saw a pure soul when I saw him.

x

Lee didn't enjoy the story one bit, and asked if they could please go now—back to the hotel, or to look for a real place to live. Tom agreed

386

with her—that they should leave and get serious about finding a home, and he carried Matty back through the hot streets to their car in a glittering lot. A mile of cars! He was feeling both claustrophobic and sad. Imagining his escape from this little afflicted clan made him suffer.

They went to the beach outside the hotel and swam. The salt water was a blessing, as sleep is, as breath and love are, and afterwards they lay on the sand, grateful for the wetness of the sea, Felicity hiding her face under a hotel towel while the girls dug in the brown sand.

—I have to get this out of my system, she told Tom. I mean, what's been happening.

—But why choose me to tell it to?

—You're a lawyer. I keep telling you.

—So? I don't know what that means.

—You might be able to help.

—I feel more like I'm receiving confession than seeing a client.

"Temple drove me to ranch to pick up Matty. The place was an oasis—all green and deciduous in the humpty-dumpty hills. The air stank of cows and manure—I saw them grazing udder by tail in pens that extended for about a mile. They looked to me like containers of spirits in transit: midway between one life and the next, they patiently attended their passage by slaughter. And I didn't really believe in reincarnation the way I did in perdition.

"Temple was dressed like a Wall Street broker. Smoked a joint which I refused to share, and babbled on and on about the evils of cigarette smoking, about the virtues of a vegetarian diet, about how the inherited rich were people who had done good in an earlier life. Money was their reward, he said. I said I didn't believe that God was really that involved with money and he shut me up by saying that it was money saving Matty's life, so I better believe something about money and power. I looked at him dumbfounded at the inconsistency of his thinking and remembered he was a sociopath and a madman because of the way he was smiling.

"And what, after all, was I? What was so consistent about me and my politics? All I was for that hour was a mother with one desire—to hold my child against me and hear her voice crying my name. I had been willing to do almost anything for that one event. The depths of my own murky ethics were never more known to me. My head throbbed and my throat dried and I thought of myself and Temple as two without faces. Once, when I was at the bottom of the pit as a drunk, I looked in the mirror and saw only glass and the image of the room behind me. There was no face there. I was gone. Now I felt the same horrifying absence of self-recognition. It would not go away and I leaned my head out the window for a breath of wind, as for the touch of the Lord.

"Instead, the stink of cow meat was so strong, I had to pull my head in. Ahead I saw the house, and a veranda. Two men sat there, with Money and Matty between them. One got up and came to the car and backed out of the way while I ran to hug and examine Matty. She looked a little pale, thin, but well. Her smile was as wide as ever, and this time she didn't push me away but clung around me, no matter how I turned. Money told me she was fine, the physician said it would be a 12-hour operation, and take her a while to heal, but the chances of survival (for a few years anyway) were good as long as she took medication to prevent the organ being rejected. The medication would be very expensive, but Temple pushed me towards the car, saying he would take care of it. He slammed me and Matty in the back seat and proceeded to laugh and fool around with the two big guys outside.

"Matty actually curled up around me and told me what had happened to her there. She called them all doctors, and she said they were nice, and did a lot of tests which didn't hurt. She said they X-rayed her insides after she drank something bitter, and that was the only bad part. She had watched endless videos and stayed in bed while Money hung around being nice."

—Were they hopeful? I asked Matty.

—They said the operation would make me all better.

—God, what bliss! I screamed and burst into tears.

"Matty wiggled on my lap all the way back to the motel. She really only wanted to get to her sister, and so did I. But we had to act patient and submissive in the car. Temple was colder than usual. Flies settled on his cheeks. I was scared of setting him off on some cruel line of thought, and stayed quiet, squeezing Matty against me.

"But even with the bad attitude coming off of Temple, for awhile I was really happy and filled with belief, and I rushed inside to tell Lee the good news as soon as we got back. Matty fell asleep. And Money sat outside with me in a patch of dull, desert-white sun, talking. She told me about Temple, about her own life, and about what she thought he wanted from me next."

—When was this? Tom asked.

—Only about a week ago.

—And what did you learn?

"He says you have class," Money told me. "He says some people are just born with it. It's the only kind of class he's interested in, he says, and you've got it. He wants you to work with him—"

—But at what?

—"I've been doing some of it, but I'm no good because I don't have class? Ho! I don't even have sex for that matter. He was going to pay for me to have a sex change, you know, and that's how I got tied up with him. But I backed off at the last minute. I make more money the way I do it now than if I was an ordinary prostitute. It's true. They get a thrill, straight guys sneaking off with me. They're so scared they're gay, they can only do it with a guy in a dress. It's sad. Lucky for me. The macho ones, the marines, love it too, I tell you. So why would I get a sex change? Besides, I sort of believe in fate. This is me, for better or for worse.

—Okay, I said, I get the picture. But fill me in on the so-called operation Temple has going here. The one he wants me for.

—Available organs. He gets them on one side of the border and sends them to the other side. At least this is my impression.

—What do you think he would do if I ran off, refused?

—Track you down, what else?

Money lay back on the bed and yawned. She wore a gaudy green nylon dress and her silicone breasts oozed partway out of the straps close to her armpit. Under the silk was the bulge of her genitals beside a pouch of money, and under her stockings, black hair. She closed her eyes and I was reminded—by her slack jaw, full lips, and sealed eyes—of an Incan statue made of rough gray stone staring through the leaves of a tropical forest. My throat thickened, she felt ill at the image of flesh becoming stone, and recognized it coming from a movie about the Amazon.

x

She climbed out from under her towel and got up abruptly off the sand. We were staring into the sunset, while the girls played on the shore outside the motel. She reminded me of the word CASBAH, with her pink glowing legs, back to the elements, an exhausted ocean, teeth chewing buckets of sand, the same doomed waters since Genesis, and a sky which was a theater for clouds and birds to perform in—swollen as if by a rainbow of emotions—and laying colors on every soft human face in sight. The children stood side by side while the foam tickled their ankle skin, squinting at the dolphins that sliced lines in the water. Creatures like black notes on water.

The girls were straight-limbed, their ribcages prominent, their thin arms long but muscular, their eyes large and luminous brown. I told Felicity I would stay with them while she returned to the motel. The dusk was gathering, reminding me that winter was not long past in the east. It wasn't late, and as the girls played with their hands in the languorous pink water, I turned off the ever-present mutter and grunt of traffic on the freeway and pretended we were off the coast of America, and somewhere safe. Safe from the life that Felicity was describing, and that was encroaching on every move we made. The coos and giggles of the girls seemed to stray in from an altogether different landscape. Matty backed up and sank into my lap, her bathing suit wet and cold on my legs. She twisted around and pulled open my mouth, looking inside.

—Just looking for your real face! she explained, and jumped away and was gone back to the sea before I could grab her.

Next day, without much ado, we found them a bungalow abandoned by students, phone and TV included. It was a wreck on a highway between freeways. It faced a marsh where the water seemed to have torn the chaparral apart, which fed egrets and gulls, and the ocean fed it through channels under asphalt. Cars and trucks belted by her front door, sending up dust and water from blocked drains. This strip of highway was in a no-man's land, belonging neither to San Diego County nor to the next town over. Only a sheriff patrolled the road, and then hardly ever. Trains tore over the marsh; a long, long series of boxcars passed by at 3:15 A.M. Ants infested the house—tiny ones, no bigger than the dust that produced them; they were orderly, moving in strict formation, discovering a crumb on a shelf only minutes after it had fallen there. Their prescience suggested that there are ways of knowing the future and the past and the present all at once. Daddy longlegs and woodspiders played in every corner and wanted nothing so much as to survive. When the night came, the darkness was a substance as thick as water, and the stars were winks and jokes tickling its surface. The ocean thrashed around in the background, becoming thunderous when the cars subsided and the air was silent otherwise outside.

She had a spidery room with a sagging double bed and pink bureau, and the children had a doubledecker bed on a glass porch in back. Tom slept on the couch, making elaborate plans out of dreams. They ate chicken, greens, and rice which she cooked with authority, throwing around garlic and onions and spices with her tiny efficient hands. A 12-inch television with poor reception could not dampen the joy of the children at having a place to call their own. During the day the military performed acrobatic aviation exercises in bat-shaped planes, riding out from the camp in the desert and over the sea where they disappeared mysteriously into the whiteness of far sky. Felicity and Tom were relaxing with each other, against his will. Their quarrels repeated history. He was revolted by her stories, which she insisted on telling, no matter what it did to him. And he began to become increasingly annoyed by her responses to people in authority.

—Why didn't you pursue medical care for Matty here? he asked in the kitchen. It seems like you gave up awfully fast.

"The American Medical Association has made the country a slaughterhouse of the poor for years," she said, then spat on the ground just short of Tom's shoe and hurried into the living room talking over her shoulder. "Fuck you," she continued. "I did not give up fast. You weren't there. Without insurance and without any job or real living situation, they, the doctors, didn't get too interested in helping us. The one place that was nice said it would take ages to find her the right-size liver. This has been going on for two years. We've been in and out of every hospital with any kind of program in pediatric liver problems. It costs hundreds of thousands of dollars, no kidding, to get one. And even then it might not work. I don't trust doctors, it's true, but I went as far as I could with them. If I had been rich or powerful, it would have been a different story. The lucky get luckier. And how are they so lucky? At the cost of their fucking souls."

—So okay, said Tom. Then what was wrong with Temple's deal? Why didn't you go through with it?

—You really want to know? And who says I didn't?

—It's not all over?

—No. Give me some wine.

—No.

—Please?

—No.

—I remind you of your family?

—Yes, right. You seem compelled to break even the laws you make for yourself. You subvert yourself!

—All right, I won't say anymore, except this. Between the United States and Latin America, there's a trade going on in body parts. This is the free market, get it? I thought you were political. I thought you cared about what's going on. I'm telling you, it isn't fair!

—Fair to who?

—People like me, and Matty.

—It never was fair to people like you.

Tom left the room and the house and stood on the edge of the highway with his hair closing over his ears each time a car passed. He felt contaminated, as if he had drunk insect repellent. The brown smog had settled on the rim of the sea and the air was dank and interior, like a vault rather than a greenhouse. The ocean was gray but its passionate salty smell was as pungent as ever and he inhaled the mist of it between jolts of exhaust. He felt the presence of his father in the air, but now as a mind and conscience, nothing physical. The conscience was instructing him to respond less bitterly and twistedly than he was. The conscience was telling him to be clear about what was happening. He tried. He surveyed the thicket of stories that lay in his memory behind him, the most recent unfelicitous stories. Temple worried him. He now believed Temple might even be behind his own presence there. He felt manipulated, and passive, and not without fear. These were his least favorite feelings, and produced a desire for revenge when he encountered them. To be a victim gave him no gratification; it did not prove to him that what he suspected about the world all along was at last being proved to him. No. To be a victim was hell for him.

x

On a warm May day when he was a boy of eight, Tom had to be taken to the hospital in an ambulance after a car hit him, while he was riding his bike. He lay bandaged and throbbing and passive and infantile in a ward at Children's Hospital for at least two weeks. His mother spent afternoons with him, his father evenings. He was wheeled around—his two broken legs raised before him and his broken arms splayed across his front—to witness children in worse condition than himself, though it was not always obvious. It was his mother who wanted to make sure he understood the meaning of luck.

On one of these trips, his mother, whistling, pushed him into a lounge and left him while she rushed off to buy some cigarettes. There was no one in the lounge, a television was playing soap operas, and outside the warm spring air had thickened into early summer. The limp and tender leaves of May—nearly yellow, weighted by spears of pollen— were already a darker green and he could just see the tip of a city tree looking robust, as if it were stretching with pleasure.

He waited for his mother impatiently and strained to see out the window to the world he longed to play in again. When she came back, though, she didn't pay any attention to his request to look outside, but wheeled him against a wall, sat down and began to talk to him about the years before his birth, to explain why she had never loved him and why he was now, obviously, the heir of her bad luck. He had seen children poke at wounded pigeons and insects to evoke a twitch from that small body with which they could feel not sympathy, but empathy. He had seen how they wanted that sense of extension and connection which the twitch of the little body confirmed. His mother's voice was the instrument which worked on him to make him twitch, as if to insist that only his response would confirm her sanity. He hardly breathed, though, as he listened to her ramble, and concealed all reaction in the white swaddling which held him. He felt as if he was all ears and little else, while the pains increased in his muscles and joints, over the hour that she spoke, until he was trying to commit suicide by holding his breath. Of course it didn't work, though his gasping gained him the high of a painkiller in the end. In that hour he acquired the desire for narcotics which returned to him later; he also acquired a dread of women who lamented, who whined, whose voices echoed with depression, who lost hope, who saw misery every way they turned. While he sat there, age eight, his mother told him that Pedro was a dangerous man. She said she didn't want Tom speaking to him at any time, or in any place. She said she was sure it was Pedro who had run him down with his car.

—Why? Where is he? he had asked his mother in a whisper.

—We don't know for sure! But this makes it clear that we have to make sure he never returns to Boston.

—But I don't think it was him, Tom sighed.

The heave of her breath was all he needed to hear to know that what he thought was beneath her contempt. She had made up her mind; Pedro had tried to run him over. That breath, like a gust of autumn wind, blew away his confidence that it was not Pedro who drove the car! But even though he went silent, and he set aside—for years—all thought about that accident, and who might have driven the car—some bruise

394

had malingered in his psyche, a sense of an injury that bound him to Pedro—a mutual injury.

Inside, Tom stood behind Felicity saying, "I'm leaving tomorrow to visit the prison and I don't know if I'll come back here."

—Thanks a lot.

—I'll come back under one condition. If you will go to the police and turn in Temple.

—I can't. Matty. Remember?

—I'm sure we can find someone else to do the transplant.

—We can't. I've tried. I know.

—It's hard for me to believe you've done all you can. Just knowing you this long makes me doubt you would know how to find help for her.

—Then leave. I don't need you.

—Okay, but you're making a fatal mistake over this.

—Maybe I am. I have a problem with authority.

—Not with Temple's authority you don't. There's no problem there.

—He's not the kind of authority I mean.

—I guess not. What kind do you mean?

—I'm scared of men with guns. I really hate them. Of judges. Of law in general.

—That's obvious. How soon do you have to see Temple again?

—Obviously, it could be at any moment. Whenever Matty can be done—or whenever he needs me to work for him.

—Then make up your mind. Grow up!

She slammed herself in the bathroom. Tom made sure the children were sleeping; it was night when he went out for a walk down the highway. It was pitch black, stars bristling or falling overhead, and coyotes shrieking from the canyons across the marsh. He believed he was in another country, the air was so sweet and clear, and he understood why every building here was like a temporary birdhouse and why lives were disposable as tissue. It had to do with the space and the sea, with the border and beyond. Here he could be a hobo in his own home, a tourist on his neighborhood street, a transient at work, and a derelict in his heart. His father was telling him—this something—was at his side talking and walking, bag in hand, and shoulders bent. "At night people are upside down," said the ghost, "by day upright. But in space there is no direction."

And this time Tom took notes from careful observation, to pass on to his brother Dan. "Daddy's ghost was shaped like a flagon," he wrote, "but it was the size of a cumulus cloud and the same consistency. Fluff from far off, a gray fog as I entered it. It rose up and up on any given edge, then vanished. Because of the appearance of this spirit, I can't help but think I've inherited Mum's insanity, and so please pray for the ghost to depart forever. I do, but I pray without faith, and so poor Daddy is stuck near earth with cloudloads of other ghosts whose children are equally faithless. The irony is this: if I were able to forgive him—which is what I think he wants me to do, in order to break loose from here— then I would have to forgive him, first, for failing to give me faith. And in order to forgive him for that failure, I would have to have faith!"

Back at the bungalow Felicity was lying in front of the television. Its image was a pile of wobbling iron bars, snow and blocks, but somewhere behind them was an erotic situation, running through a defective cable wire. Flashes of breast, nipple, buttocks and mouth cut through the snow and bars. The voices were adamant in their expression of excited contact.

—What are you watching? he asked her. There's nothing there.

—If you look carefully, you can see stuff.

—Any more popsicles?

—An orange and a grape.

—Can I have the grape? he asked.

—Why are you asking me?

—I don't know.

When he returned to the living room with the popsicle, she announced she was going crazy from lust and only making it worse by watching nearly invisible figures on television. Then she turned it off while he picked up a book and pretended to read. Actually he was twirling the icy popsicle between his lips and over his tongue and peering at Felicity who was herself nearly invisible under a blanket.

—Are you happy? he called out.

—For this house, yes, thank you.

—No, I mean are you happy in yourself, now?

—No.

—I didn't think so.

—Are you?

—No, I want to move on and finish what I came here for. You have introduced me to a level of corruption that I never wanted to encounter. Now that I have, I can't really relax.

—So what would make you relax?

—Reporting it to the police. If it's true.

—He'll kill me. Literally, she said.

—Chances are, he will anyway. If it's true.

—Thanks, Tom.

—I just want you to face the realities.

—I have. You're going to leave us here alone.

—You were alone before.

—True. So go.

—I'm going to call my brother.

—It's awfully late in New York.

—He never sleeps much.

—I hope he's nicer than you.

—It's just that he escaped. Home. Mother.

She twisted herself up in the battered armchair, with the blanket bent around her shoulders, and listened to his conversation with his brother. Tom told Dan everything—her whole story, where he was, and why, and what the phone number was; he told him Temple's name and asked what he should do. Then he listened for a long time, his expression registering change as fast as a television screen. His dark waves of hair looped around his ears, he kept twirling them in one finger. His face was gloomy with the shadow of a beard, his lips purple from the popsicle juice. He concluded his conversation with Dan by telling him he would be seeing his father, Pedro, the next day. It was evident to Felicity that Dan hung up in his face in response.

Tom put the phone down gently and she leaned over and said, "Let me look at your teeth," and she went over and pulled up his lip. "You had braces, didn't you, I can see the line of a band with a purple stain. They're really white and straight. Why do you tell your brother everything? You act like he's your conscience or your twin."

—He's my best friend.

—Gimme a bite, she said and snapped off the tip of the purple ice, smiling down at him.

He leaned away, and back, and looked at her feet. My brother says I should leave you. And never come back.

—That's really thoughtful, she said and sat down on his knees, facing him. Have you got a hairy chest like your legs?

Tom made no move, but sat still as if afraid she would fall. He addressed her neck when he spoke.

—Leave me alone, Felicity, get up. I don't like you that way.

—What way?

—Intimate.

—Why not?

—You just aren't my type.

—Can't we just fool around?

—No, not when my mind is full of images of sick children and surgeons and Temple getting away with it. Sorry, but my mind effects my body.

—How would sex interfere with that relationship?

—It's just impossible.

She pressed her chest against him, her arms across his shoulders, her cheek against his.

—Just so we know it's all still working.

—What all? The parts of the machine. Body parts?

—Come on, don't be so grumpy.

—Uh uh. Get off.

—Do I have to? I know you're leaving. I just feel lonely, scared, and why not. You're the sexiest man in the room.

—You think Temple knows I'm here, right?

398

—Obviously. He's coming to get me, don't you understand? Why do you think I'm scared? I don't want to do what he wants me to do, but because of Matty, I may have to.

—I'm sure you will do whatever he wants. You always have.

She pulled up and jumped off of him. And now he followed her into her bedroom and watched her slip into the closet to undress and change into a pair of boy's pajamas. She was ignoring him, or pretending to.

The effect of her indifference was powerful, now, far more powerful than her interest. Mesmerized by her distance, he felt the loops of pleasure binding him to the flesh between his navel and his crotch. Like most boys he became sexually aware, through his own manipulations, in early adolescence. For him, though, this activity was sufficient for his survival, and in fact it filled him with confidence to know that he could always go off alone and seek a rush from his vigorous imaginings. He needed no one's help. However, the longterm effect—because this activity did continue for years, even when he was in bed beside a woman—was to separate him from the world to the point where the material order of things was more of a representation than a reality. He observed life as others look in store windows, or up at movie screens. And when he looked in the mirror at himself, he was always greeted by the image of a stranger, someone much thinner, darker, more intense than he felt himself to be.

A woman for him was also a representation in his imagination, not an actual being, and in order to complete their collaboration, he had to become a representative of himself—a mutual invention, a double of the one doing the imagining. He had special places to which "I" would travel with the shadowy figure of a woman—to ramshackle mobile homes on the edge of a forest. And there he would suffer and enjoy at her mercy, a mercy which was experienced through his own hands, not "hers." She waited for "me."

In the world he moved around like one slightly dazzled, or defeated, unable to participate fully in any social gathering, because of his eagerness to get home to his appointment with "I" and "she" in his closet. Door shut. Yet the process, like all processes, was subject to entropy, and he had recently lost heart for it.

Only now when Felicity emerged from her closet in a torrent of hair did he feel his loneliness had a location on his body, and he recognized her as a candidate for his imagination, she being a pariah—a social enemy—an extra at the table of the world. The forgotten one. The place not set. The empty chair. The undesirable who only "I" discovered, and whose indifference made no difference.

At the threshold of her room he announced his resentment of her lack of interest in him. "You never show any interest in me," he said. "That is, in my trip to visit my brother's father. It's always you, and your problems."

She protested, requested more information about his plans, but suddenly he was not an articulate man. His throat stuck, his mouth was no avenue for his thoughts, no chute down.

He said "Oh never mind," and goodnight, and went to lie in the other room's darkness, where he could conjure up the familiar one, and not Felicity, to comfort him. At first, and this was unusual, he imagined a tunnel of semen sending up shouts, songs, laughter, whispers, cries—of unborn thousands—violinists, graphic designers, greenhouse builders, divorce professionals, pet groomers, clergy people, bus drivers, accountants, diamond importers, civil servants, sand blasters, models, cleaners, truckers, mountain climbers, athletes, addicts, divas, poets, politicians, saints, lovers—all those children trapped in his own groin.

And then he found his way to the forest. And the arcs of his two closed eyes formed twin smiles.

x

His true woman came in a season of thick fog—Indian summer—emerging like a peacock through falling cards. General outward moisture now brightened his aura of luminous gold. The gold of a loaf of bread held in the lap of a poor man.

For the time being there were people to be discarded. She was a protection by helping him deal with the tiresome ones. He could only take things as they came. When, later, he accepted her judgments, she was hurt by his corrections.

He didn't need one more advisor, and was always surrounded.

He directed this confusion like a captain, as out of a capsized boat, there's a rush.

Then into an excavation, not like Pompeii, but in the way the autumn day looked. Like a pack of cards. Large faces and colors. And she was sympathetic, not sarcastic, this time. The windup of their communion—a walk—put them as if in a boat together, pushed up and down a current.

After some trauma, he always took their trust for granted. The crouching kitten will, in time, kill the little gray bird. He wondered what she wanted.

She got inside his idea of himself, he didn't know when. She knew how good he looked, but this didn't help him adore her. Just her possession (entrance) into how he felt—always about himself—and he sensed her measuring and weighing his deeds as he'd do to himself, but more.

She was the spot concealed in his folds. The secret of her own life formed her protective entrance into his idea of himself. He fell short, but looked bigger. Better. He tossed their intimacy with intimations of defeat. Don't get the wrong idea. Passing cars assured his ears that sound was motion.

There are days when we have thought almost everything there is to think.

"I am, you say, a man of vision?" he asked her.

The end of your watching will lead to a view.

Recalls and results ran circles around them. She helped him to pass for a man like any other, but he was a bird of clipped, drawn wings. Into this egoistic gather, he relapsed, handsomely. Had another of his waits, while she watched.

Vertiginous orange air, a plummet and a yardstick on the void. The chill of a shock. Fog's catastrophic old fashioned fare.

She was almost old always. And medium-sorry for him. Scarce a corner of their October was orderly. Like fall in a valley of bankrupt branches, her poverty was BETTER than his failures.

No thought is sufficient to the day's bread, she knew about. An un-looked-for twist in the cavernous hours has possible rewards, was his style report.

She was washed by fog as if she was drawn in soft silver sand. She threatened the presence of trees by one desire—not to be seen. A sadness effective as a week of cool intervals. Visions as little as flame tips.

His was a cold light on something rained and orange, though she whom he couldn't t escape was part of the effect. Like the erotic hidings under some objective purpose, or a cat stayed kittenish, she was a deli-cate gray, serene as a dove.

The high flicker of her intelligent fires made the furniture of nature brighter. It was no costume weather, after all, not theater.

Walking with longing made consummation fall behind.

She'd shown him nothing but more rickety shacks he should know about, and an outer stiffness making things fall. A pencil on the path. A joy too much for consciousness to bear makes a bad balance, an imper-fect contract.

He and she had many more years of staying apart before they could really hurt each other.

Draped, soft, forlorn in her slimness. She was the wisecracking kind who clutches herself as stiff as the word I.

Two morsels of bread and bread, their appetites were still not nearly satisfied. Her hand kept him waiting. She turned the lights on.

Sprinklers twirled adjoining mists! She had something more to give him: the nothing that was something.

Even before you know a fact, it's true. In the most besotted impres-sion, there's coming information.

His gasp filled the air with more mood instilled as a hope and stroke in the limited atmosphere! Small chance. Even as, perhaps because, connection didn't come, his consequent passion was to possess. He would lose her for this, though there's no being sure.

She took up the hose and water met Rainbow's the spouse of fog. Eyes continued to be attached to her his, and occasional egoistic latching, as if he looked for a key to a clock so he'd be in control of the time that they touched.

She prays her stars will be invisible. Dipper and sprinkler, the fragrance moisture elicits and can be seen. Treading the earth, around and around, gravely. The OTHER side was what they didn't, couldn't, know. Mystification waded through the unbeaten paths.

The way truth welcomes, then rejects you. The way recognition of the really good feels like a blinding.

An anomaly of lack, abstention like abstraction—all NOT. She repeated and repeated, in fact to surprise him. He was.

Constancy shocks. But abrupt cessations did what they could in this case. Speculations love company. So she was grieving at his departure as soon as he was there. Graven tablets sprang out of the garden she tended. All engraved with their names in some captive cupidity.

Like a disconsolate, she roamed around with callouses, pencils and work to do.

The turn of her chin was superficially slight towards him, as to mean insufferable joy. He was, for that time, a maestro.

If the body is bread, his was a loaf she'd never eat, and she began to accept, too, the loss of silver, good luck, fame, in his and her days. So his postponement of possessing her was part of their scheme. It was to lead her where we allow the benefit of a doubt.

A smoking torch nonetheless still gathered her skills for human touch together inside her. He'd never want to know that her plans were always surprised by her approach into them. So she stayed hidden.

His intentions, meanwhile, were being met elsewhere, full of face and handling. He was addicted to orgasm. She had something else to give him which he didn't even consider. While he stoked the leaf tops mentally as if his thought was a responsible form.

She knew she'd pass from mood to move, as an exercise in giving up. Painting the sets. A door wasn't shut in any position of the steamy air. Buttery, light-colored leaves. And he could live a worthy life if she just knew how to tell him, so he'd understand, but she didn't.

He couldn't control or alter his inclinations, and his character was such that his sharp edges were gilding.

She didn't invent him, or the words he held on his lips. It only confirmed the authority he conferred on her that her presence made this particular wording possible. "I will do what is necessary to keep you safe."

A small branch snapped and fell into her hair.

The walk was a circle, shaped like a house, all edge and abutment, with whirling only in colors and gray. They kept two full bodies of air between them, not loafing, not rushing.

Having made his statement he washed his hands of all her questions, his curiosity was perfunctory. Now here, she did make another pause, which surprised him, as if she had abandoned her presence inside.

But he inhaled, and she was taken in, restored to his imagination, amusing as all expectations without.

He reached his door then and her anguish crossed the threshold. "Don't do anything to hurt me," she said. He winced as if the three or four things he most wanted to do would have to be put off, if they would ever by done at all. And much pain did it cause them, much, to step apart. He had a dreadful sense of standing before her for the last time.

A flight of chats. Let others be responsible for his guilt. He would attend to her needs, in spite of the consequences, and ask nothing in return. She sensed his concession and fell on her knees before him. "I," she whispered, "am he whom you know." He leaned to meet her, mouth and hands upraised. She was no shadow then.

x

The next morning Tom left to drive east, before anyone else was awake in the house. The terrain was flat, brown, baked. The social aura was venomous, redneck. He sensed it. He wrote on a large legal pad on the car seat beside him. His mind was alert and overcharged with language. He wrote to get rid of words. He tried to place Pedro in his past, and then to resurrect him from that ashy zone. Flying elements of thought and memory shot between his ears. His hand was tense on the pen, and shaking.

"The body is the first mask; what it does is only partial evidence of what is concealed inside. When the body is gone and the spirit is left naked and transparent, the essence of personality exists with a potency undreamed-of. It is easier to feel the presence of a bodiless spirit than any person you might sit and talk with—that is, if love is involved. I personally am much better at loving from a distance."

"To paraphrase an experience is a heresy, unless you can turn the paraphrase into an organic part of that experience. This is what confession does. This is what I will try to do, keeping in mind the terrors of earlier heresies, like Docetism, Marcionism, Adoptionism, Sabellianism, Nestorianism, Gnosticism, Pelagianism, Arianism. . . . If you paraphrase correctly, you must reproduce the original in its emotional and moral content. I mean, this is what I believe. I must reproduce the feeling of the original moments!"

"A ghost is the opposite of an angel. A ghost carries the residue or after-image—of its earthly existence. It's like a leaden emotion, laden with recollection. An angel has never experienced the earth as a sensual event, even though it may aspire to; a ghost yearns away from the object the angel envies. A ghost however still has a few last things to say. (What is the difference between the spirit and the soul, it might ask. The soul belongs to you personally, it might answer, and it is the accountant of your deeds. The spirit on the other hand is nothing personal. You live IN the spirit)."

The experience of throwing something ahead of me, as a child, and then running after it, was like the experience of aspiration and accomplishment in later years. The memory of my brother skipping stones across the top of the gray sea is like a painting of that experience. Utopian. I see his soft brown face squinting at a sulphurous sun and a smile wide on his lips as he jerks his elbows and the flat rock hops over the top again and again. That skipping action dazzled him and me, watching from a boulder. I never tried to do what he did well . . . I remember feeling the potential for heroism in Pedro's person, even way back, when he took Dan and me for walks in parks, especially the Arboretum. And the zoo. I remember he was tall, dark-skinned and fast-walking, with spectacles and a pair of enormous hands. He pulled us along, quickly, breathing hard from smoke and rattling off the names of the surrounding flowers and animals. Just as the shadow from a statue makes it seem alive, so the shadow from Pedro reminded me that he was not just bigger, but deeper, than me. In his presence I usually experienced a sense of largeness and power. It must have been the presence of the Hell from which he came and to which he was going.

The prison was on the desert, only a few miles from the border. On the way the language of the landscape was new to Tom: chaparral, sage, mesa, arroyo, mesquite. Hot as an oven, and as dry, the air might explode if he lit a match. If he hadn't had air conditioning he would've swooned in the car seat and crashed. His nerves were already boiling. Thirty-three years: this was the end of only imagining Pedro. He felt it strongly: each day is the end of a story, each day is an anniversary, but some have more magnitude than others. He had an erection and had to wait in the car till his thoughts could drive it down and away. How to deal with the coming hour, when he would finally see Pedro, again, he didn't know. He had to trust that the soul of the man would be unaltered and familiar to him; that it would not have changed in density or dimension or quality. "Technology is like an extra and artificial limb attached to the natural world," he mused. "How could the varied planet be viewed as insufficient? Why do we keep needing to add more? This drive to that building—has been almost Biblical—how could my parents have let this man rot in here and never reached out to him once?"

Tom parked in front of the yellow penitentiary where people who had committed crimes against society were cordoned off and guarded night and day. The building cast a long shadow.

Inside, there was a lounge and a booth where he checked in. He was frisked, thoroughly, stripped of extra articles, and sent through four heavy doors before he was told to sit down in another lounge area, this one containing several red vinyl seats with what looked like bite marks on them. A sad woman sat at one end of the room and he placed himself away from her and waited until he was led by a guard into a very small room. Foam rubber popped through the cracks in two green chairs; an ashtray wobbled on a steel stand. The walls were pea green, like the clothes on the guard.

Pedro was admitted in twenty minutes. He was a tall, bent-over man in his late sixties, white-haired, with a soft brown complexion. His eyes were long and papery, his lips thick and dry, and his teeth rotten. He had deep grooves in his cheeks which thickened when he greeted Tom. His eyes gleamed like garnet. He wore brown.

They sat across from each other and Pedro immediately lit a Camel, which he smoked with the intensity of someone chewing chocolate. His voice was gravelly when he asked Tom why he had come after so many years. When Tom began to respond, he stopped him, asking, And how's your father?

T: He passed away—recently.

P: And your mother?

T: Mum? She's still alive.

P: In the same place?

T: Yes.

P: And Danny?

T: He lives in New York.

P: Married?

T: No. He works like Daddy—as a printer—for a printer.

P: You're thinner than I imagined you. What?

T: Yes, I'm sure.

P: Why did you come here anyway?

T: I just want to know about you, do you mind? How much more time do you have to spend here?

P: My time will be up in five years, then I won't know where to go or how to live.

T: I'm sure you'll surprise yourself.

P: No chance of that. All the surprises have come from elsewhere. Not from myself. Your father was my best friend. Did you know that? What? He took me in, took care of me. Your mother was already my partner, though it was never legalized. Like all women she turned out to be deceiving and a whore.

T: I'm not so sure.

P: What? Women. They're much more complex than men. They have these bottomless desires. They want and want and want, and the more you give them, the more they want. Better to hold it all back from day one and let them learn discipline. Every story from every man in here repeats that statement. Women are driven by their bodies, their desires, your mother was no exception, not even with her mental problems which came from her intelligence. She was very smart, as you must know, but a victim of a deranged appetite—for the new, the unknown. When she couldn't satisfy her craving for the delicious new experience, she drank her way into oblivion.

T: I know about my mother.

P: What? You were fat as a boy. You had the personality of a fat boy too. Loud and needy. She must have destroyed you, too. I only recognize your eyes. What happened? I can guess what happened. And your father, did she ruin him too?

T: Probably.

P: Of course she did, not probably. He was easy prey. Decent but cowardly. He was the type who did more damage by his decency than he ever could have done by being a son of a bitch. Not that smart, but committed, which makes up for a lot. He let himself be used, picked apart by the people around him, so-called Fellow Travelers. His painting was only mediocre. That was the real tragedy of his life. He was second-rate, and he worked his ass off at it anyway, as if he didn't know it. He knew it. She knew it. There is nothing more unnecessary to the world than a bad artist.

T: I think she likes his work. Liked.

P: What? If he had put those energies of his into some worthwhile human work, his life would have been justified, but instead he scraped by with derivative oils on canvas.

T: I really just wanted to know about you.

P: What's to know? The story ended a long time ago. Since then it's just been thought. No story, no action. What? Your parents had me locked up. They threw away the key. And they went on with their own lives.

T: But after you left Boston—

P: What? Boston? I didn't leave voluntarily. I was driven out of Boston. They put out a warrant. Saying I tried to kill you. Why would I kill a little boy? For what? I had to go underground, change my identity. But they knew where I was. We belonged to the same party. We had the same contacts.

T: You really believe they put out a warrant?

P: I don't believe it, I know it. What? Your mother could always get her way, no matter what it took. She did it by erasing the connections between things. So she'd never feel responsible.

T: I guess you never remarried.

P: What? I never married in the first place. But I got another gal pregnant before I made the mistake of not shooting a man. You want to hear what happened? I was undertaking to raise funds for those witnesses who had been summoned before HUAC, I was assaulted from behind, and somebody shot him. Guess who got tagged for the crime? Correct. What? When I wrote for help to your father, he never even answered. So here I was put, and here I remain. . . . So what's your life story?

T: I practice law—it's a small legal-aid firm, we have an office on Tremont Street, remember that, in Roxbury? Mission Hill, across from the cathedral, basilica.

P: Run by the recidivists, or whatever that order is called.

T: Redemptorist. One of them is a healing priest. Mother goes there. To him.

P: She needs it. You can tell her from me that she comes up in my dreams, as a fiend, a devil figure, even now, so many years later. Why did you come see me instead of Dan? After all, he's my son, not you, you came from the loins of the harpy and the traitor.

T: He didn't want to.

P: Well, tell him he's making a mistake. Could be fatal. I've got emphysema.

T: Does anyone—from outside—?

P: Three women keep in touch with me. It's always women who have guts in the end. It's always women who act from the heart. It's women who cross boundaries. Not men. A lady lawyer, a hooker from Winnemucca, Nevada, and Dan's half sister, a gal you certainly don't know. They keep me going.

T: Where's the half sister?

P: Her name is Billie. She lives across the border, works at a hotel outside Ensenada, she's clean, about twenty-six.

T: What hotel?

P: You really want to know? The Mira Vista.

T: Billie what?

P: My name of course. You might like her. You and Dan. Have a family reunion down there on the beach. What? I remember you liked the water. The tub. Your mother didn't much like you, that's why she stuffed you with food. Every time you fell or got hurt, she'd pack you with cookies and go on directing her attention elsewhere. She was ashamed of what she did to me. She was ashamed of Dan's African features. She compensated by dumping on you. And the joke is, you were darker than Danny, your skin color, still is, I bet, Ha! Danny was high yellow, you're brown, like your father. She was the type of white woman who hooks into a black man to be validated politically, but really she despises him. I remember how shitty she treated you, just because of your brown skin, and there was lots of it! She probably turned Danny gay. What about it?

T: No.

P: Your father loved you though. I guess you know that.

T: He also loved my brother.

P: What? He stole Danny away from me. He better have loved him. Whatever that means. Action is all it means. You think the world is full of talk and no action? You know what it's really full of? Silence. . . . Well, go on now and build your own prison, boy, before others build one for you—one that doesn't fit any crime you know of.

Tom stood up obediently as Pedro began a fit of coughing. He went to the door and turned his back on the old man while he brushed his burning eyes. He knocked and almost at once the guard opened up to let him out. He didn't say goodbye or look back to wave to Pedro.

In his car, he drove without seeing, then got lost, totally insensible to the roads he was taking. This way he ended up beside the hills along the border, where rangers shoot smugglers who shoot and rob Mexicans who are illegally entering the country. There was litter everywhere down along the fence—parts of engines, car seats, styrofoam and the underwear off escaping people. High tall grass like bamboo shoots was strung with boxers and shirts and socks, and dust blew up from under the tires of raging American vans off to the west of him.

He recalled an image from a movie where the men throw an object in a white cloth ahead of them as they move through the gloaming towards an unknown goal. The object flies and falls, proving they can, also, pass through that zone. That was an image of the way human lives are lived: thoughts, plans, calendars thrown ahead into the void; he understood it. But something about time was skewed and he felt like one who has come to the end of his energies.

Other remarks, made by Pedro, returned to him now:

"You know what I learned, after all that shit and this miserable life? It'll surprise you. Any enterprise worth its salt is directed toward the relief of human suffering. This includes technology, science, art, politics, music, etcetera. What? Surprise you? Even a plain book—or painting— if it's any good, and your father's painting was not—makes suffering clear so the human reader can be relieved of pain. As far as I can tell we are here to seek cures to our rotten condition. I wonder why the whole world isn't as psychotic as your mother. It might as well be, it probably is. What? The United States Government is medieval if it isn't psychotic. The terms are laid down by science and technology, by systems of measurement. I'm writing a book about money. Marx is the only one in the last hundred years who has really taken it on as a subject, and now it's time for a new one. Science is the new narrative of our civilization, so soon it will absorb the old monetary values and we will begin to measure reality and social principles solely in terms of computer technology. Wait and see. You already see a praying mantis on TV dancing to Bach. You see brains being dissected to a background of Miles Davis. The circuits are crossed. A trap made of numbers. What? The world is a museum.

We have been colonized by our own government. The point is, with all this talk these days about culture, each person wants nothing more than to be liberated from the accoutrements of so-called culture. And what is culture? Kitsch. Who did I kill and why? No one. What? I was jumped by an informer at a meeting many years ago. And now I'm in for murder. The real killer went free, I was framed, but no one cares, even if they believe me. Science wins."

The words seemed to loop across the roof of the car, and to slide down the windshield, and Tom drove recklessly back the way he had come (a motion which contradicted his sense of termination). He let the wind whip at his arm and face and upper frame. Wind was the closest thing to water he could get for that hour. Water was what he was really after. Water to wash off every last residue of his time with Pedro. He felt he literally had time on his hands. A slick smear of it dotted with grime. Time, grime. Slick, illicit.

He had visited prisoners before. Prison always sickened him, but never so violently as this one. This time. The paradox of a place lost to the world being the very place most locked and sealed upon the face of the world—and in it Pedro—forgotten by the couple who were known to be activists—committed to the poor and displaced—his mother, his father. How did every citizen end up collaborating in the technique of silence?

"Maybe Pedro was lying. It's so hard to believe..."

Tom scanned the sky and the distant mountains thinking how good they were to the human eye. Why, he wondered, even in the thick of despair, does a person yearn, with a whole heart, for something good, something complete? Why, even on this brown sandpile, did his heart swing up to the places most linked to childhood—the snow on the windowpanes, or soft summer rain in the trees—to a face filled with the love bestowed on it by the very person dreaming of that face, his brother in this case? Why did he, stuck in the indulgence of time, and sad, still find himself driven forward automatically (platonically) towards the beautiful?

Am I responsible for creating tomorrow's objects and events out of my motions, or is it already waiting for me—a table set, a pair of hands producing food?

All he could really remember was the statement Pedro made about women. Not his mother, but others. And he wanted to see Felicity now. To tell Matty that the human spirit is the size of a bird, and that's why the holy spirit is always represented as a bird. To tell his brother that Pedro had the integrity of the stereotype and he should at least visit him. To tell Lee that she must learn to enjoy herself before it's too late. To tell the ghost of his father that he had in his life failed to live up to his words about brotherhood. To call his mother and tell her he would be staying longer than he planned.

When he got to the little house, Felicity and the girls were not there. No note told where they had gone, but there were tire marks in the doe-colored sand outside the house, not his own. He paced around, eating tortillas and cheese with his hands, and drinking Coke. He looked closely at the undeveloped land, so to speak, around the house. Jasmine, dichondra, poppies in the dust. Pepper trees tilted over a chainlink fence and a bamboo jungle struggled to break into the lot. In the background, where ravines were purple with ice plant, someone had hung a wind chime made of varnished seashells in the pepper trees. Shingles, tiles, tar and rusty hubcaps were tossed in a ditch. The walls inside the house were made of cork.

Roaming the empty house, he found odds and ends scattered as if they all left in a hurry. The clothes of the children moved him. He touched and folded little pairs of shorts and shirts and put them away. As he did, confused, he imagined saving Felicity and the children from Temple. But then he didn't dare interfere, because for the first time in many years he felt himself to be outside the law. Careless. Dislocated. He began to pack up everything he owned, and to stow it in his car. He decided he was at liberty to do whatever he wanted, and at once he began to know what he wanted as he disposed of his attachment to Felicity and the children. They, he decided, already had someone watching over them. No matter how vile Temple was, he was the master Felicity had chosen. And he had, after all, done his duty by finding them a place to live. No one had asked more from him than that, a fact for which he thanked God, as he took a long shower in lukewarm water.

x

And so, now clean again, Tom left and drove south through San Ysidro and National City, to the border and over. He drove through the abrasive hills, coastally, from Tijuana south to Ensenada and south some more. The great swells of mountain bracken and cliffs to the sea were lathered with the shampoo yellow light he had come to associate with the word California.

In a beach community he found the Mira Vista Hotel. There he rented a room for two nights and sat on the terrace to drink a Coke and sop up salsa with chips. His eyes were weeping though tears did not emerge. The lashes were damp. The sea glittered like Christmas as he imagined the girl, Billie, to be each one of the waitresses. Stocky, dark, serene, smiling? One cute one wore a cap to hold up all her hair and had American manners and attitudes. She was busy behind a small outdoor bar. The time was mid-afternoon. Citrus trees and roses were planted around. Crochet baskets hung full of geranium. The sun had an intense journey here—much more like an airplane on a trip under four hundred miles than a long distance ride. Up and down. But perplexedly, it stayed light longer, later, earlier. Old water where the fishing boats trailed beyond the laugh of the breakers.

—Which one is Billie? he finally asked. The cute waitress answered that Billie wouldn't be in to work till five; then she would be there all night. Tom gave a message, his room number, and walked between horses along the seashore, shoes in hand, and plotted and planned: if he was in charge of a country, would it be like this one and how. A place to disappear in, as Felicity had done. But he didn't linger over thoughts of her, he thought of a future which did not include her instead, and then went into a rickety seaside restaurant and called his brother in New York where it was night, the day over, events completed, people trying to forget this and that. He ordered Dan to join him and heard both temptation and hesitation on the line. Come on, come on, he whined and told his brother where to find him and how. Then he sat at a shaky table facing the sunset and drank juice. Lost colors sought form in the sky. An astronaut said that in outer space there are more colors than we have here.

In the night he dreamed he met Billie and between them there was a bond, instantaneous and pathetic. She turned when he came onto the terrace and saw he was the one she had always been waiting for. He was less aroused, or certain, until he was close up, beside her, and telling her his name and why he was there. Then he looked at her like a possession, because that was the way he felt, and he let her seat him, then sat beside him, while he blurted out specific hidden facts about himself: I was drug-addicted for a couple of years, I have never been able to love anyone wholeheartedly, I'm dying of loneliness. . . . All this was said quickly, and nearly at once. The experience was more primitive than romantic. There was no air between them that did not contain the spirit of the other. She didn't move much, except in lots of little ways, nervous motions of hands and eyelids and lips and shoulders, while she sat erect and perfected on the edge of her seat. She was breathing him in like a little animal composed of fear that twitches and sniffs each time it pauses.

She was smooth as honey, and its same color, with soft features, a full sloping mouth, and the garnet eyes of both Pedro and Dan. She was unadorned, unmade-up, dressed in a white middy blouse and blue uniform skirt, for her job. Her black hair was looped into a braid and a bun. At one angle she was sixteen, at another forty, no in-between. There were three ways she resembled Dan: her eyes, her lips and her delicate long hands. She was, even with all the above, not a striking beauty but a hidden one. He was sure she could pass through (had) all her days unnoticed, unloved, like a reddish stone under a stream. But now that he had found her, everyone would take notice of her—a fact he sat and regretted, one which made him hesitate, but not seriously, before moving forward.

x

While she worked he lay on his bed and listened to the radio. Most of the stations played Mexican pop, except for one where he heard Motown. It reminded him of his little office, his clients in that cold mean climate, the troubling disorder of black urban life, he felt his blood race.

Saving History

The frontier was a fortress. Every dog loves a daddy. His whole body was suffering there like the artwork described by Pedro. His hands were clasped and aching under his head, his bare feet clawed at each other, he listened and waited for her to knock on his door.

When she did she looked almost exactly like the woman in the dream. He proceeded to blurt out specific hidden facts about himself, to tell her why he was there. Just to see. A family member. I think I'm a primitive. I need a tribe. Help me, I'm dying of loneliness. They talked until the sky whitened into the film of a new day and then she, promiscuous and incapable of commitment, joined him under his blankets and they played with each other's bodies. This went on all the day into the afternoon, she was an expert at anything involving her hands, and then he got a call from the desk that his brother was on his way down from San Diego. Tom sang with a chest drawn tight as a drum as she showered, his throat knotted and cracked. He washed her long hair. She, behind his back, stuck her fingers in around his tongue, massaging his gums, and resting her own mouth against his ear, called him her brother.

x

Fog rolled in overnight from the sea. It moved around the canyons, swallowing greens and browns and turning the earth as white as the sky. It was restless, as if an army of ghosts were seeking out guerrilla activity on the lowest coast of California. This fog stretched way down into Baja drawing with it a smell of deep seas. Whiteness and more whiteness. Helicopters rested. The airport shut down. It was a field day for human coyotes sneaking people over the border. That same army of ghosts was for this day protecting illegal entry into America. Dan had been rerouted to Los Angeles and drove a rented car south from there; it took about five hours to get to Ensenada, where the whiteness screened and softened his first views of Mexico.

He found his brother with a woman on his knees. Her name was Billie, she looked familiar, so the fact that she was his half sister seemed to work on the surface of things. He watched them from the entrance to the terrace at the motel. The fog had made Tom's kinky curls go haywire. The woman was dealing with this, tying his hair into a tail with a thick elastic, her elbows on his shoulders. Dan called Tom.

The woman jumped off his lap as Tom leaped to his feet and rushed to greet his brother with an embrace. Dan's reaction was to recoil. He was not an enthusiastic man, but sensitive and uncertain. He was very thin and moved as if he couldn't see. His skin was caramel, his mouth red and wide, his hair nappy, and he gave the immediate impression of being repelled. Tom clumsily handed him a chair and danced around him, worshipping and worrying. Dan wore a lopsided smile; he always smiled on one half of his face only. But he accepted the offer of a Coke and a plate of food. He asked no questions but appraised his brother and the half sister. Her complexion was sallow, her features conventionally pretty, her eyes round and brown. Her arms were straight, thin, streaked with dark hair, and her hands were small and unusually shapely. The hands alone were similar to his own, and he took one of them and then held them together, appraising the likeness of bone structure, color of the palm and its shape, back to the wrist where it changed and each was alien to the other. He chalked up the familiarity of her face to its conventionality and watched her watch Tom.

x

They were moist, enclosed by the wall of fog, the only ones out on the terrace, it seemed like a snow, and was exciting as snow can be. They remembered mornings of snow they awoke to in the South End of Boston, pigeons cooing in the eaves, the way the white stuck to the brick and melted for the traffic outside. But they were here encircled by wild geranium, fuchsia, ficus and pepper and palm trees. They sat at the round table and spoke to each other in soft voices. She told Dan her story, as she had told it to Tom already, and Dan told them what he had been doing, and Tom didn't mention Felicity or the girls but only his days looking at San Diego. "It's really still part Mexico as far as Oceanside where the last border patrol is. You're not really back in America until you're about an hour north of the border."

Billie did not like her father and told Dan that. The way she didn't like him was firm, like a decision she had made for which she felt proud. But then she said she would never abandon him. She was sunny, a warm soul, as they say, with complexities postponed or swallowed. She lived in the moment, moaning with pleasure over every bite of food and sip of wine, swearing she feared nothing and no one, had no regrets, rarely thought of the future, and she spoke of her lust for Tom openly, and only obliquely referred to the time she spent blissed out, in ecstasy, numb, crystallized, stoned. For that experience she spent some time in prison where she was rehabilitated. Dan meantime loved his wine. As the fog blued and blurred with the setting sun, they ate and drank and expressed their intense pleasure at being all together there—a little tribe —a long-term team—a lost army unit—a disrupted happening—a genetic pool—a cross-pollinated forest—a family. Candles dripped in the fog, their butter yellow tips slipping into jars. Billie sprawled against Tom, her hand locked between his folded thighs, warm, and at an angle so Dan could see the old tracks in her arms. She said it was intensely exciting to commit incest with someone who wasn't her brother.

X

Late that night Jesus came to visit Tom. He tracked him down where he stood in the motel hall outside his brother's door. Tom had just said good-night to Dan and went to the outer door to check the fog. He stepped out. The moon was smoking. The fog was thinning. A fountain rolled with water and there Tom gazed at an image which he saw rising as from the spring of a spirit. It was hardly bigger than a bubble, but it was Jesus dressed in white, with brown skin, more modern than Tom ever imagined him, because he was so immediately recognizable with his easy attitude, and a sweet smile on his lips. Tom felt all his desire pour into the lightness of the water which sustained this image, and he realized that the water was actually light. He knew if he should reach out and touch it, it would ripple and vanish, and so he stood like one petrified, pouring all his desire out on the sweet-smiling form who slowly backed into the nothingness he came from.

x

Tom returned to his room, where Billie was on the phone. She slapped it down fast. An unnatural smile twisted her lips. Her knees were up, tenting the sheets, she threw them back to expose her naked body as if it were a surprise, small and neatly wrapped. He stripped, remembering how she felt, but his heart was like a red plum floating in pain outside in the fog while his mouth was sealed. The name Jesus was an imprint tight on his tongue, something he wanted to swallow and incorporate into himself.

He pressed his face into the curve of her neck, seeking ordinariness, her hair on his lips and eyes, and he nearly gagged on the emptiness he felt. It was the next thing to bliss. She stared across, then hoisted him up. Asking, Want a little something for the pain? He raised up:

—What?

—A little something, she repeated, like coke or even heroin.

—But you know I don't do that anymore.

—Just a tad now you're so sad? It rhymes!

—I thought you didn't do it anymore either.

—I don't or only on rare occasions. Like now. Come on. She rolled onto the floor and under the bed, clawing around under there as a child will do when looking for a stuffed animal. He lay flat on his back, but pulled a cover over himself, his smooth skin was covered now with goose bumps.

—I remember how good it felt, it's true, he murmured, but I don't live in a culture where it can be done without harm. If I lived in far and foreign mountains, alone.

—Come on, she begged from under the mattress. You know you're free of it, you've changed from those old days when Jay would deliver it to you. You're totally different. A lawyer! A man, not a boy.

He sat up then on his elbows, eyes staring at her words in the air. He leaped off the bed and fell on his knees on the floor, as if to pray, but hauled her out from under by the feet. She bumped her head and whacked him on the shoulder.

"Hey, man, why did you do that?" she screamed.

—Sorry, he said, gaping at her pained expression, which was the same one she had under pleasure too. And then he decided to say nothing more, he became inwardly official, child of the law and its many doubts and amendments. If she knew about Jay, his friend and former dealer, and never said so before, everything she said was a lie and a danger to him. While her sunniness returned, swelling her face into a smile, she twined her limbs around his on the floor.

"Forget it, little brother," she said. "You don't need it. I'm sorry."

—You smell like a lace cookie my mother used to bake, he told her. A lace cookie, it was called, Ha. Lace, laced? You could be laced with some ingredient which makes you as sweet as you are, and as potent, and I don't know it.

"I'm not taking anything, just wine," she murmured onto his mouth. "I told you, I'm clean."

He dragged his brother out of bed early and said they must leave at once. Billie was in a deep sleep with the pillow over her face. Dan kept hesitating and inquiring and wanting to hold back, stay longer, postpone their motions, slow down, but Tom almost brutally shoved him around. They had two cars between them, both rentals, and Dan followed Tom back up the coast highway, north around the green ravines and the cluttered chaos of Tijuana to the border.

x

Meantime Money drove Felicity and the children to a flat land where she said tiles supported the surface of the earth so it wouldn't sink into the sea. Dry chaparral and avocado groves. Money gave Felicity no choice in going, but told her that Temple required her presence at once. You are, remember, his slave. Felicity was not exactly afraid but did hold tight to her children, squeezing a knee, a hand, a lump of hair, whatever she was allowed from the back seat. Then Money told Felicity about white guys who ride around in trucks, with Soldier of Fortune magazine and beer, and shoot at people—even at each other—randomly, for the hell of it. They hate anyone with a shadow in their skin, she said, and this includes Jews. And even Catholics, especially when they're brown. Never saw a woman among them, she added. She was snapping and popping her gum to punctuate her emotions.

Felicity felt like Tom would about this story. She didn't want to know any more, but already felt sick. She hummed and curled over the seat to play with a stuffed animal. She bounced the bunny up and down on her daughter's knee, saying squeak, squeak, squeak, every bunny loves her mummy.

Temple had a bottle of Rafael and a couple of plastic glasses on the motel table when she walked in. Money took the children to a movie and Felicity, without them, felt naked. But it was Temple who was only in shorts and an open shirt. He was staring like a blind man at the floor. Sitting in the one armchair, while she took to the edge of the bed. She poured herself a drink and waited. Cars pushed through heat outside, one after the other, the curtains were drawn across the sun, and the smell of green deodorizer stank up the air. There was a black revolver on the round table. She could feel its weight just by looking at it, as if it was an erect penis. Temple was unaware of her, stoned, she supposed, but now she saw him stick his thumb in his mouth, and suck like a small child, steadily, rhythmically, an expression of docility covering his closing eyes. Mortified at being a witness to this, and disgusted at the pity it lifted in her, she lay back and dozed across a level of nausea induced by Money and the rest. She realized she could kill him then, there, and now. COULD, because the gun was available and he was all but a corpse already. COULD because his insanity, she knew now, probably didn't end in privacy, but was part of a political program. Money didn't mention those guys in trucks for nothing. Over politics Felicity might be able to kill, being the child of a violated history. Dozing is the poor person's meditation.

x

She met God and walked with Her around the edges of a garden. The snow had recently melted there—there were patches of white around, and jars containing fireflies on the planks that marked the edges of the garden. They walked around and around a wrought iron fence, looking for access so the old lady could sit in a safe place. When God was seated, Felicity raised herself up on her elbows and didn't know where she was in the world, but she yearned for her mother, father, aunt, uncle, the snow, and her children, all spirits who fell out of reach of her own. Temple was still stoned, even in the garden she saw the gun, and the curve in the back of his big nodding head, shaped like a canoe. Then he whirled around, the ground rocked, and he jumped on her, pinning her shoulders back. He accused her of spying on him, of seeing him in a moment of weakness. The mattress slipped, she struggled but all her limbs were weighted with the paralysis of her pity. Briefly she recognized the fact that it was a dream. She felt his weight across her own numb bones and wanted him to have sex with her.

—Go on, she told him. But he handed her the gun, saying, Kill me, I hate the world.

The gun fell out of the motel and she chased it down the street at full speed. Her head grew into a cookhouse down in back of a plantation mansion, and there was lots of commotion around. It was in her system as it had never been before: the cookhouse, that one. She was woman to woman. They could all be mean. Even the missus was mean to the maid. She who wanted to be the ambassador of the poor, of the children, of the anonymous, of the neglected, of the injured, of the women mauled and mistreated, of the hijos de la chingada, of the exploited before they are ruined, corrupted and poisoned as she had been, she was now a bad one too.

That's when she woke up on the motel floor with Temple watching her from his place in the chair and drying his thumb on his shirt.

Bad dream? he murmured.

x

And then he spoke: Look at me talk on TV. I recorded it so you could see it.

422

Then he set the images in motion through a VCR and sat smiling at himself on the screen. He was addressing a white female interviewer in a cheap studio setting.

"Hitler was a prophet, you've got to understand. Like Muhammad. Like Jesus. He had a vision. He didn't mean harm to the Jews. He simply saw the obvious. Races should not mix. Louis Farrakhan says the same thing. We agree. You stay on your side of the line. We'll stay on ours. It makes sense. This way each race develops its own abilities. Whites are the most intelligent. We should be allowed to stay clear of social chaos to pursue the life of the mind. As for all that holocaust business, no such thing ever happened. The Jews are always manipulating, interfering, they're very smart. But don't trust them. And the Papists are planning to take over the world far more than Hitler ever dreamed of. The Pope wants to rule mankind. The Catholics are confusers. They like to spawn mongrels. They talk gibberish. But they're dangerous because they lack racial principles. They want world domination the same way the Commies do. You can't school people in social etiquette in a place where violence rules. You know that, but you probably just don't dare admit it. There's a criminal ring that surrounds us all. It's like a border we don't know is there. It's the beginning of the end of all actions. You can say, 'Wow, those people are evil out there,' meaning the execs, the corporations, the banks, the pols, the etceteras, but you're evil too because you're inside their circle, being protected by them. This is the big circle. Call it a ring. You can do wrong inside the ring. Say you know a guy who works for a corrupt boss. The boss steals, say, computer equipment from his own company. So the employee says, hey, I'm going to do that too. He gets caught and has to serve time. He is destroyed in all ways. And why? Because he thought he could play like the boss. No way. The more inside the ring you are, the more you are required to obey the laws of the power boys. The winners. To do their thing. You think I like it that way? No, I don't like it but I at least know what I know. You can't confuse things inside the ring. You gotta keep whites here, blacks there, Chicanos there, Orientals over there. I'm sure most of them would agree. Most people of all races are against integration."

The interviewer with a glazed expression turned to the camera, and smiled, with her blue silk dress wobbling against her skin, just in time for Temple to switch it off. Now he turned to Felicity with a question in his eyes. Did I look okay? I thought I looked pretty good.

—Temple, if you believe all that shit, what are you doing with me? ME! she shrieked and threw loose her black hair.

—Who says I believe it?

—How can you go on public TV and say those things?

—I like to see myself in lights.

—I want to throw up, I don't want to live in this world any more.

—Oh stop the drama. . . . Now remember who sent you to the hairy lawyer's house to stay a few months ago? When you were down and out? Remember it was a girl named Billie? She was a friend of his former dealer, our friend Jay, and they set up the living situation in Boston. Billie is one of my slaves. She was supplying the boy with drugs years ago, not that he ever got hooked for too long, but he doesn't know anything about her. He's pretty dull-witted, I guess you know. Into sex and emotion. He's down there in Ensenada right now, and she's down there working for me. Get the picture? Now I have a job for you so wipe that killer look off your face. It will entail some traveling and some danger, but not of the physical kind. I'll supply you with a car. It's about body parts, this job, not auto body parts, but ones like your little girl will be given. Kidneys, livers, hearts, that kind. You're going to be responsible for collecting and carrying them over the border. In a Playmate Cooler made by Igloo, the kind you take to the beach on a picnic with your kids. All you have to do is pick them up and deliver them to a doctor here. I have all the directions written down. It won't take long, and you're the perfect foil, traveling with two little girls and a picnic cooler.

—Shit on your head. You never said this was part of the deal.

—I said you were my slave.

—I'm not good at slaving.

—So what's left to be good at. Woman.

—Moving. I want to go now.

—You just take what you want and go, right?

—In this case.

—How do you think that makes me feel?

—Like someone who did someone a favor.

—I don't do favors, said Temple.

—You already promised, you always keep your promises.

—I don't want to have to hurt you.

—Why not? Go ahead.

—How do I know you and the hairy one, Esau, won't talk?

—His name is Tom. You don't know.

—That's right.

—He has nothing to do with anything.

—Look, Felicity it's just a matter of grace and attitude. I made you a promise and you made me one.

—I hate you. I hope I'm there when they catch you and hang you. Rat bastard. Slime of the earth. Satan. I'll do it but don't hurt anyone but me. Get it?

—That sounds slavish. I could refuse the liver to your daughter.

—Come on.

—Why not. That would do it.

—Take my kidney instead. How's that?

—Sounds good.

—Take my body parts and sell them.

—What'll be left?

—Whatever you don't need.

—I might need your heart. We're looking for one.

—Okay. Take it.

—It's worth about 30,000 bucks.

—I'd rather live without a kidney.

—Of course you would.

—How much is that worth?

—About 3,500 as you know.

—So what are you gonna do?

—Take your kidney and something else.

—What.

—Your eyes.

Felicity rubbed her eyes. Then she said,

—Okay, but I hope you die in a fire so no one can use any part of you. Evil thing!

Her curse, so passionately made, disturbed him, and he grabbed her by the arm and held her against him as they walked outside to the car. He talked tight and quick.

—I am not evil, Felicity. Believe me. You have to think realistically and not in those primitive terms. We live in a waste economy. We produce waste. Kids who have, and kids who don't have, they're all part of it. You're right about luck and money, but it's an old story, a boring story. Look at the military instead. For what? It's thousands of dollars, hundreds of thousands, each time they send out a boy to exercise a piece of metal in the sky. The taxpayers don't bitch about that, they bitch about poor people and prisoners. Practice for what war? War is no longer the issue. Government is no longer the issue. Business is. Business runs the world. Not government. Street kids? There are trillions of them, all like living abortions unwanted by anyone. I'm in the business of recycling the organs. The lucky ones win. In this case, for once, you're one of the lucky ones. Now, here's the address—directions—of the place you're going to. Here's the car. Your girls are already waiting, with the cooler on the back seat. Go on now. Just go to the place, walk inside, they'll take the cooler, fill it up, you turn around, and drive right back across the border the way you came. How can that be hard? We're talking about saving your daughter's life. This is materialism, this is the new world order.

x

Blasting the radio on a jazz station, Felicity drove with the children in an old rattletrap south towards the border, and paused there before crossing over. She hesitated because she was tempted to tell the men in uniform about Temple, about her assignment, and the reason for the empty cooler on the seat in back. But she couldn't bring herself to do it—for reasons as old and polluted as the rivers which lived near people. Fish

washed up belly up. Birds teetered and keeled to the side. Their feathers blew like dandelion fluff across the top of such a river. Lazy morality,
slow water, the motion of her own history, and its attachment, hers, to
the child on the seat beside her.

So she drove on down, following the directions given to the clinic
where he wanted her to collect the organs and drive them directly north
again. Not just one. Not just the one for Matty, but many. The girls
were playing with a mix of soldiers and dolls, the soldiers being so much
smaller than the dolls that their shaven heads reached only to the un-
marked and empty female crotches waving over them. The girls had no
idea why they were making this trip, but Lee was uneasy, squinting her
eyes into razor-like slits as she glanced out at the passing landscape.

The clinic was near a stagnant lake in a desert landscape where a
highway—or was it an airstrip—came to a halt, and up and off in the
brown hills there was this little building with the kind of chimney she
had only seen in crematoriums. Two new cars were parked in front, and
Felicity pulled up the old Ford she had been given and stared at the
building. Lee asked what was wrong. She told her nothing. Matty said
the place reminded her of a chicken coop and went on playing. Felicity
finally climbed out, telling the girls she would only be a few minutes.
Lee handed her the cooler, asking, not for the first time, what she was
picking up.

—I told you, said Felicity. Something disgusting.

—Poo poo? asked Matty, grinning.

—Yes. A sample of cow poo. Don't look at it when I bring it back. It
stinks.

—Who wants it? asked Lee.

—Temple. And Money. They're doing an experiment.

Felicity left the car and walked to the door, but stopped again. Her
breathing was quick and dry. She felt faint. She walked around to the
back of the barracks-like structure, and tore at her face and scalp. She
made the twisting motions of a mime performing AGONY. Beside her
was a window and she lifted herself to peer inside, one knee bowed up
against her belly, the foot on the other leg stretched to a point. Inside

she saw two corpses, half covered with sheets. Flat-chested girls. The room's white walls seemed to bulge from the weight of the ceiling. She saw an open door at the end of the room, no one was there. And she saw arched brows, light smiles, and hanks of black hair swirled back from the two young faces. But what she focused on was their eyelashes dipped at the base of their long eyelids. Black lashes, longer than any she had ever seen, perhaps because of the profundity of their repose. Each tiny hair might have been doubled by its own shadow, she figured, and that was what made them seem so long and so silky. Or maybe it was just the word "lash" for such a little thing that made them into such a strong thing? But she was stunned by the image of those drooping eyes. No longer in service to the female bodies that were only half-developed. Undeveloped. Pinocchios. Boys with girls inside. Incomplete works. Lashed down. Christ's back lashed in the stations, lashed to royal stripes, the cross lashed to his back, and the donkey following.

She stumbled downwards and landed on one knee in the dust, then plunged along forwards, gasping, back to the car. Already the front door was open and a woman waiting there for her, but she ignored the cries from this woman, and banged inside the sanctuary of her car, driving off at top speed in a whorl of brown sand. The two girls clamored with questions, demands for answers, which she didn't give, but rocked instead, side to side, in the car seat, humming like a fly.

If she looked at Matty, she yelped and cried. So she didn't look at Matty. Instead she blocked out all their queries, and drove like a cokehead past silver olive groves and pepper trees.

x

The soul is a space and cries out to Jah who is the rest of it. But the mind tries to remember what the ancestors said. Because it's all there, stuck up inside the DNA—the cells of the baby mind contain and continue all history. Fragments of a united front—blocks of split text from an original Logos. I know it.

Saving History

Those queer night sounds and the speed at which the stars machined their way through the sky or was it earth moving? I never remember Abba's attempts at capturing me. But when God is a metaphor for d--th, then I cry out: Rescue me from Yahweh my enemy, and from unjust people and their decisions. Why should I care? Why has the enemy thrown me this far from home? Why is my enemy my only hiding place where I feel safe in the world?

She assumed the enlightened one would forgive her, who cast her eyes towards the earth where flowers doll up the plod through dust. And she sensed that humans are a race of elves. It made her laugh.

She wants only to get close to Alpha & Omega so there will be no more fear of the world. High fertility rates among the Latino and black communities make others hate them. Today the surf will be six feet, a green ray like lime pie on a watery table will follow the sunset. Caused by transport smog, white caterpillars finger up the Interstate.

To accept the duality of Jah is an impossibility; it is a contradiction in terms and must not enter the head of any individual. Technology's cunning turns halos into auras. It makes morbid men who only like snow-women with berries for lips. But I say that snow's white powder should knock down the high price of software and crystal.

For one thing, my loneliness was intense. It became my condition by a process of elimination made without logic or choice. She lost three pints of semen over the long run, each one was a wee child. Meanwhile my emerald did not change, but stayed as solid as a frozen ocean, a bottle chip, a chameleon on a leaf.

I lacked a community beyond my family, and had but two friends with whom I could discuss sacred texts. A truant child was hidden in myself on the way to church, and a playing card with a duck painted on it, the kind you kill. I thought I'd like to be children again in an illustration, mallard-colored.

The rest of the time she labored in front of strangers. When a black hole swallows matter, it's light-years away from earth and millions of times as far away as Pluto. We're really lucky. Out of it comes a stream of X-rays and green prayers.

Saving History

When I lay in blankets in the dark and empty house I heard sounds which made me cringe. Fuck you, someone shouted at a child but on my flying carpet, I could go as high as cloud-seeding experiments in the Sierra Nevada. It was there that I felt like a surrogate mother raising the question, Who owns the individual?

Night sounds were neither animal nor technological and the stars moved abnormally fast. I felt that Abba was demanding my attention, then yearning for it (here I say "I" and" my" but always mean "human") out of its spatial isolation. Another Santa Ana was moving in, peaking air pollution, and sea swell. From Point Pinos to Point Conception, hazardous seas and escapees. The sea under the rising sun was like an oriental rug for lying and flying on.

She lives with an oppressive sense of eternity and its presence in her, and is truly impatient of people who say, "You're lucky. Your faith must make you very happy. " How is she supposed to be happy with eternity? Can you tell me that? You must be crazy. What exists is named specifically, and there is no specific name for God. In the mountains are snow guns and enough high-tech gear to pilot a Lear jet. The wild cats leap down a hill called Sheep Dip. In lace tulle and millinery flowers stands the bride of snowmen.

I only want you to know that the bread of heaven feeds the poor human soul, begging only to be nourished in peace. Waste water is recycled into drinking water. There are lots of wonderful Americans out there whose self-hatred takes the form of rejecting immigrants. The sky is teeming with hidden blue machinery. And each act is the signature of thought, especially the sign of the cross.

I knew it was unpopular to think there was a city in the sky, one that scientists and satellites couldn't see yet, and even as I tormented myself with the idiocy of such a thought, I counted its turrets.

A command came out of the river: Mistreat the dark man, woman, and child. She felt weary and grave, a pilgrim bewitched by drugs and shades. Like a horse wearing a veil, the man at the border patrol, asking for IDs.

Everything is structured and complete. There is no physical matter that does not contain its precedent. Yet we are given lies and clamber up the facts like old hippos. At the zoo the animals are hardly more alive than photographs, yet people stand and snap pictures of these images. I think we all want to get back to the beginning to see what happened next. Physicists, as hardheaded as peanuts, want this as much as anyone. They talk about eddying water and how the ripples all come together in patterns of patterns. I've heard them. They are desperate to understand what happened first.

With a ring in his earlobe, sandy hair and red fuzz on his white upper lip, the patrolman acted like her boss. Two whites hovered over some fossils, and pink pajamas were hot and excited at the end of the motel. Oranges hung on trees and in the eyes of the orangutan was the whole world.

Down the river in rubber the alien was a kind of mud wall with eyes. Grass swayed where the hunters puffed. She spoke of the material body. Who belonged where and to whom. In Balboa Park one immigrant's mouth full of mud made her spit. She remembered a floating head, water full of dogs and wooden noses. Empty yourself to God, she said.

The earth trembles here and the orange rocks are heaved up at an angle in the deep canyons. This is a place where you can wash in the wind, but can never return to the heavy city.

My enemy is often my leader, especially when I have everything I need. He takes me where there are landmines, then, and where there is fresh water. I have less fear when my enemy is my guide because he draws me into meandering areas where I feel protected from the long shadows of evening. He comforts me. He knows where the dangers are that he himself planted. So how could I feel safer than when I am with him?

She has a terror of marriage because it takes a promise she can't keep. She really doesn't give her secrets away to many people. Like a gnome who fell from the sky in a bag and flopped around screaming on the ground, she's at the mercy of her birthweight and nothing else. The fact is, humanity has an adversarial relationship to that space which threatens the material body. In the desire to appease the wrath or appetite of this space, we develop many forms of behavior, most of them in postures of terror. We wish God was d--d so we could take care of our own prison.

Saving History

The Saint Augustine Bingo Program and the price of cement in Mexico are linked by a convent. There they paid her to laugh and brought the price of cement down at the border every time she did. By this time the sight of a uniformed police officer was almost a comfort. Back at Pleasanton Federal Prison people wondered which of the twin cities was the most important one.

Little fishes go in and out of a net and don't even know they're all wet. Diabolus simius Dei.

Stimulate ovulation in a dragon and you need to collect semen preserved in an old kimono. But who owns the seed? Confusions mark the end of an era. However negative, it's necessary to press on.

I think airplanes need eyeglasses as much as their pilots do. Technology has run ahead of ethics. Blustery weather in San Diego Bay and northeast is a dreamscape on the berm of Sunrise Highway. Bright-colored sleds, a rolling fog. In a materialist world the body is the ultimate possession of value. You feel like someone left in a refrigerator for years. Geographics are as cozy as nurseries or weddings smothered in headpieces, tulle, favors, bouquets, corsages, and ribbons by the bolt.

At the Rosarito Beach Hotel, a blue tiled bathroom and a blue tiled pool, white wicker chairs, and the sea, and horses. They had travelled on foot over black sand with rippling lines like shells to the mountains. Olive trees and jars of condiments at roadside stands. Is desperation truer than joy? Green seahorses on the tiled floor were nearly worn away by the vomit of American marines.

If ideology can be a substitute for action, then so can questions be clues. The muff and stick were in bed pretending to be illegal aliens. So ideas suffer humiliations you never even dreamed about.

Twin dogs in matching plaid sweaters stopped in the back of a truck at the border. One ran after a bugger, another after a beggar. I didn't know which was which only that this was that.

She was working at the orphanage. Her excitement was prodigious. A bad mother sat on the beach. For her all too human cruelty I would still call her pathetic. She trailed across the sand like some alcoholic tenant at a resort. The father arrived, smaller by a fart, and like a spider, rubbed his elbows and knees together saying, My sexual energy is high. He was laughing so I laughed and got paid again. The children wondered who owned the eggs on the stoves, while they starved.

I had in my possession a band of foundlings, with round faces, brown as flan, and the smell of chickens in their feathery skin. My joy sang in my fingertips at both the saw and the stove. I could hold, in this fifty-five inch frame, a tribe of free souls. I had forgotten though that I was south when I was and north when I was. Every bountiful place seemed to be an interval in a directionless galaxy.

I've caused you so much trouble, darling, darkling, chica and chico. Bite something rotten and you've got the essence of dreams, she told them. Do you apologize to cats when you push them off a chair? I bet you do. The borderland is no fairy place, so don't be afraid when the barns thunder with trampling and strangling, when the wooden infant grows a nose as long as Pinocchio's. I value nothing more than your voices, she continued saying. Like a flight of birds from an empty brown hood outside a little hermitage, a deluge of candles wobbles in your breath.

Twelve little faces turned to hear her. She wanted only to take care of them, to unfold them joint by joint until they could rise each day, eyes dark with joy knowing the hand of love would return and never forget them.

That was, however, never to be her vocation. Or mine. An error on the part of my compass, or an act of predestiny? We will never know. Hands are still the physical parts which give me the most delight. Look at them some time.

I personally was given the charge of a mad man, instead of children, and a bunch of white people, of which I was part one, crawling here and there useless as mushrooms or ushers in a dark theater. I kept a dollhouse instead of a photograph in my cell, later, in order to give me a remembrance of all the mansions in eternity. D--th, of course, is the winner, since we have to pass through it to escape it. But being alive, instead of never-here, still excites me, I'm happy to say.

x

Back in the world of commerce and voice, they stopped at a border town to breathe. She had driven so fast that she herself felt defeated. Now she was pasted in an outdoor cafe, with her girls sticking on either side of her. She was watching the crowds, traffic, individuals, most of whom she didn't like, except for the children begging and playing. She kept her head averted, wouldn't look at Matty, and only flashingly at Lee. "If something bad happens, blame it on me," she told them softly.

—You're scaring me, Ma, said Lee.

—Don't be scared. We're fine.

—But you didn't do what Temple said.

—I'm not his slave.

—Won't he get mad?

—Probably.

—Will he still fix Matty?

—Oh I'll probably look somewhere else for help.

—Maybe Tom can help?

—He's smart, maybe he can.

—What will we do with the car?

—Leave it and take the bus home.

—Ma, they're going to get mad.

—Just try to be happy right now.

—Happy?

—Can't you be?

Lee looked perplexed, and troubled, thinking, but Matty threw her head back, and began to chant and jerk her knees up and down in time to her litany.

—I'm happy in my bottom.

—Happy on my left side.

—Happy on my right side.

—Happy in front of me.

—Happy behind me.

—Happy on my back.

—Happy in my hands.

—Happy under my feet.

—Happy in my mouth.

—Happy in my ears.

—Happy on my head.

—Happy in my stomach.

—Happy in my spit.

—Happy in my pee-pee.

—Happy in my hair.

—Happy nowhere!

—Okay, Matty, we got your point, said Lee.

—Happy in the air, the little girl added quietly.

Felicity said, I could work in an orphanage again, and we'd all be safe. We could go back to the Ciudad de los Ninos de Infantile Mariana.

She glanced at Matty who was as yellow as a sunflower, and whose eyelids drooped in spite of all efforts at liveliness. Felicity swung away and stared into the street, her eyes burning.

—I want to go back to our house, said Lee. Ma!

—I do too, said her sister.

—But don't you like it here? All these kids? People?

—No.

—No.

—Life is easier here. No rush and tension. No shelters. No competition. What do you say? We might be able to find good medication for Matty. We might!

—No.

—No. I want to go home.

—But why?

—We want you to settle down.

—Get a job.

—Marry Tom.

—Be normal.

—A real mother.

—Please.

—What?

—Please, Ma?

—Let's go home.

—A real mother? Sensible. You know. Stop smoking. And drinking beer. Clean the house. Go to work every day. Get me to school on time. Me too. Nothing much. We love you. I do.

—Sensible? She doesn't have to be sensible. Okay. Just normal. Please, Ma. If you do, then you'll be happy.

—We know it.

—I am happy.

—You don't seem it.

—You seem sad.

—You're always running away.

—Please, Ma.

—Go to AA.

Matty uttered this instruction in a soft slurred voice. Her face was seriously jaundiced, as were her corneas, and she was slumped back in her chair with her wrist resting on a trembling hand.

—Ma, Matty looks horrible.

—Go on talking, said Felicity, her expression set in stone.

—We love you.

—You'll get sick if you don't.

—Take care of yourself.

—Maybe Tom loves you.

—No, he doesn't. He just likes her.

—Okay, but he'll be a help.

—She's gotta do this alone.

—Be a grown-up?

—No.

—What do you mean then?

—She's gotta live a regular life.

—That's a grown-up. I hate grown-ups.

—So what should she do?

—Take care of stuff, us.

—And still have fun?

—She can still have her beer.

—No cigarettes then. Right, yuk.

—But I doubt if she'll give them up.

—Or get a job.

—No, she's had jobs, she can.

—Please, Ma, I promise I'll get better at home.

—Or if we go to the seashells, said Matty and again her voice slurred and her hand trembled.

—Better? Felicity inquired. Better? You are the best. And the illness is just part of the perfect you, that's all. You're perfect. What is this "better"?

You know what she means, said Lee.

I feel better already, Matty said.

—I know what she means, but I know what I mean too.

Felicity stole a look at Matty arched lightly back in a wrought iron chair. Lee stood up and stretched, saying, "Let's go, you guys," in a motherly voice.

Matty climbed up on Lee's back and Felicity walked behind, holding her up with her hand. She was not conscious of her hair turning silver under the sun.

x

Tom and Dan walked along the sand which was blackish and flecked with gold. High reddish cliffs walled them. The water shoveled at itself—white and green shavings, clarities of light slipping through the shaft of a wave as it broke. The beach wound towards La Jolla, crouched in the sea like another Monte Carlo. They tiptoed over rocks and shells, watched a seal and moved on, till they came to a beach where bronzed men played badminton, jogged, lay flat, had sex, or waved to them, all naked except for hats. There they turned back. Dan did much of the talking, still walking with the halting steps of a blind person, his knees bumping, his feet crossing, his hands gesticulating.

—It sounds like Felicity is a pathological liar, Tom, and you've been taken in. I mean, let me go and meet her and judge for myself. Of course if she's not lying, then you'll have to report the story to the police. Won't you?

—I don't know, said Tom.

—Well, why not?

—I'm leaving. I want to go back home.

—What's wrong with you?

Tom lifted his hands and dropped them again, and told his brother he should stay, even without him, and enjoy the fine weather. There's nothing wrong with me, he said.

—She sounds like one of those people who are completely unable to learn from experience, said Dan. Know what I mean? I mean, most people have trouble with it, but she's taken it to the limit? Or she's got racing brain disease, like the lonely do, just can't stop free-associating and telling stories.

—She's learned some things. But experience seems very feeble to me at the moment, said Tom. Like the law, I don't find it satisfying as a way to respond to certain problems.

—I could've told you that years ago, said Dan, but you wouldn't have had the experience to understand my meaning!

x

Tom looked up at the sky where clouds were as thin as frost on a window-pane, and remembered a visionary dream: thin jets of milk issued from Felicity's breasts and filled a row of twelve white cups. Again, the same Jesus, brown as wood, stood with her. She would lean on him and he would feel nothing. Then she asked, Milk with your tea? And sliced a hard loaf of brown bread with a silver cleaver. And now the room filled up with children who drank her milk greedily and ate her bread and she still leaned the weight of her body on Jesus who said, To each a Lord according to her need.

x

—Are you in love with her, Dan asked.

—With Felicity? I'm not in love with anyone.

—Well, something is strange. I think you are. In love. With her.

—I wouldn't leave if I was, would I, said Tom.

—Yes, it's exactly what you would do.

—No, it's more that I feel like I'm caught in a tide pool, too many walls, connections, the same whirling faces again and again. Temple is probably pulling my strings, for all I know. I feel like I'm in a purgatory of people.

x

So I took the plane home before Felicity and the children came back again, and left Dan in my place. The transaction was, on the surface, a matter of the following: I believed she would be safer with him there, since he had no connection to any of the people involved. And I wanted him to have an extension of his vacation. He looked tired, a little shaky, ready for a break. I knew that Felicity would let him stay there with her, because it was in her nature to share what she had with anyone. I also had an instinct about the two of them—that they would connect in deep, quick ways. It would not be the first time that I gave to Dan a treasure or a secret I could have kept for myself.

Above all else, I was relieved I would not have to say goodbye to her and the children. If dying was distancing oneself from the things of the world—and the evidence of the world is conclusive on this score—then saying goodbye was too much for me to handle right then. Especially to Matty whose nervous gestures and luminous eyes would not leave my mind.

As I bounced through the clouds, the flight seemed to be a metaphor for my own helpless condition. I couldn't, and I hadn't, really helped anyone on that trip. Not even myself!

I had seen the red sea and sky melt into one horizon: the borders were as feeble and as vulnerable as my own forays into relationships.

The verdict so far showed that a response was always missing from my actions. All I ever did was listen. While it made me a useful companion up to a point, in the end I could see myself becoming nothing but an anecdotal old man, someone who told other people's stories. The law bored me, before I had hardly begun my career, and the thought of day after day of paperwork, and night after night of solitude, was horrifying. It was especially horrifying because I knew I lacked the will to transform myself. I wished I could take Matty's illness into myself, and be the dying one that I really was, instead of her. I wished this with my whole heart.

But my whole heart, in those days, was only half the usual human heart. When it was full, it was only half a heart-full.

X

The story of Matty came back to him later, in bits and pieces, there and here. Felicity and the girls arrived by buses exhausting in the dusk, the day after Tom left. They had bounced from one bus terminal to the next, sat among purgatorial crowds waiting, strapped to luggage and TVs and each other's hands. Homeless people hovered outside every terminal, begging, raving, sleeping. The children became increasingly sorrowful at everything they saw, but Felicity bucked up their spirits with stories about her childhood in Maine, stories which provided them with images of water and trees. They told her some stories, too. And they dozed all over each other like a family of cats. Hot and cold kept switching. Bus to air to terminal and back again. When they finally saw the shiny graph of buildings which meant the sea was coming close, they rejoiced and began grooming themselves. At the terminal they had one more ride up the coast on a regular bus to a stop near their house. They saw lights on in their house, a car. The girls thought it was Tom, but Felicity was filled with the bile of dread.

She found Dan, a stranger, listening to her radio and lying flat out on the sofa. She was wild with suspicion, but he proved his identity with a license and a picture of Tom which he carried everywhere in his wallet.

So now she relaxed and the children were exuberant at being home. Felicity headed for a beer at once, and slammed around her rooms, while the girls took a long bath. Dan explained what had happened to him and Tom, telling her about Pedro too, and about Mexico, when she asked. She guzzled her beer and stood looking down, her face suffused with varying emotions.

She put the children to bed, showered and returned to where Dan still sat, erect and formal, a bit embarrassed, on her sofa. Her hair was soaked into strings on her shoulders and back, she wore a white terry-cloth robe, and her bony feet were bare. She told him she was afraid for her life, but she wanted him to go out and buy some food. She gave him a list and he left, agreeably.

At the mall he did all the shopping quickly, under a feeling of pressure he couldn't identify. He was hot and trembling in a confusion of appetites and hungers. He hurried back to the little house and together they unloaded the groceries. She asked: How long will you stay?

—Can I spend the night? Then I'll leave.

—Stay here!

She cooked some pasta for them with rapid, almost spastic gestures, as if she shared his deranged appetite. They sat at the card table in the kitchen, gulping down their food in silence, when they heard a car outside. Felicity almost threw up. She jumped up and rolled her children out of their beds, and made them lie down under them. She told Dan to hide in the bathroom while she went to answer the knock on the door.

A young white guy was there, carrying a suitcase. He said he was trying to raise money for his education by competing in a door-to-door sales program. If she bought his product, he would get her money plus the same amount again. It was a blue cleanser which you diluted with water. She looked past him at the rotund moon. She told him she was sorry but had no money and slammed the door in his face. Then she ran back to her children and put them in bed again. In the room behind the kitchen, she found Dan and fell against him, gasping on her own breath, as if it were an obstacle to her survival.

—Let's walk around the house three times, he said.

Outside the moon was so bright, the whole world was alight. Bushes, trees, paths, houses. They could hear the cave-like roar of the ocean. The third time they came back to the front of the house, Temple was there.

—Go inside, she told Dan. Watch the kids.

She walked over to where Temple stood by the side of the road, next to a glittering puddle. No cars passed. His head was nodding more than usual and he wore a smile he had not worn for years. It was almost radiant.

—So, he said.

—So.

—Sleeping with the other brother now?

—No, neither.

—At least the other one is good and gone.

—Correct.

—Back to Boston.

—You know everything, why?

—You look scared.

—Money said you would kill me.

—Why would I do that?

—For failing to be your slave.

—She doesn't know me any more than you do. It's sad.

—I don't know you, it's true, any more.

—You still want that liver?

—No. Not the way you do it. I'm going to turn you in.

—That's tragic, childish. It makes me feel bad.

—So what are you doing here?

—To say goodbye.

—What?

—I'm leaving, for a long time, south, way south. To the Cape of Never Mind.

—Why?

—The people I work for were disturbed by the way you ran off. My fault for choosing you. But I've got to move on.

—And?

—I want you to do one last favor for me. Restore my reputation.

—What.

—Stop trembling, it doesn't suit you.

—What.

—Marry me.

She observed the moon to be a disk behind his head; how white he was—a Moby Dick of a man. He was wearing white too, a camelia pinned to his lapel and one, in pink paper, in his hand. The collar was tight on his throat, so a slip of flesh folded over it. His head nodded up and down instead of left to right, and he seemed to be saying yes for her. No, she replied, I never, and you know it.

He smiled with the condescending radiance of an imperial figurine, a look she hadn't observed on his face for years. There's a long story behind all this, he told her, but I'll make it short. You must at least give me a chance to explain. And as he explained, he pinned the camelia on her terry cloth robe, and gently nudged her to the side of the road.

"Many years ago, two representatives from the American Civil Liberties Union tried to raise funds for some witnesses who had been summoned before the House Un-American Activities Committee. They went to a Communist Party meeting in San Diego to do this. My father was one of them. He was a paid informer for the Committee, in fact. While he was at this meeting, he was shot by the father of your friend Dan, inside your house now. That was the end of my father. I was a young boy, it was before I met even you—but it ate at me, as they say, and I stayed interested in that man, Pedro. His family. He's been in prison for many years as you know. I have been working for our government, Dear, against groups who try to subvert our democratic system. This includes the marketeers in body parts. You were included in my plan to bust them. But that's okay. You didn't. You stayed clean which is the way I always liked you anyway. . . . Do you understand? I'm not the son of Satan you have imagined me to be. I work for the Government! Now I'm being sent to Latin America, and I'm certainly not asking you to come with me. I don't even want anything to do with you. Like that. But I want you to be my wife."

—Fat chance, said Felicity. He slipped away from her side and squinted down the street until a car dislodged itself from the oppression of shadows, turned on its beams, and swung up beside them. He pushed Felicity into the back seat and joined her there. The driver was the student with the cleanser for sale.

—Take us on down, Preacher, said Temple. He pulled from his pocket a marriage license, already sealed, with both her and his name on it. He flashed it in front of her with his white teeth gleaming a smile.

—It's done, without your consent, I know. But now you can perform the holy act of matrimony on the beach beside me. This man is a legitimate minister. He will do the honors.

—Why are your teeth so white? asked Felicity.

—I had them fixed—coated—this afternoon, he admitted.

—Why are you pretending to be good? You know I know you.

—It's not an act.

—So what about my children?

—Conveniently, you have someone there to watch them. I thought we'd have to bring them along, and that would have complicated matters. To put it mildly.

Felicity stared out the window at a cradle-shaped beach, black and white water tugged around by the moon above. Her eyes burned. She licked a tear from the crest of her lips. She wrung her hands and contemplated leaping from the vehicle. She palpitated in her throat and swooned. He put his hand between her legs and sighed with his head back and eyes closed. He looked so fine, anyone would believe he was a good man. He was colored so white in the night, a lot of people would think he was even a transparent man. She didn't, and at no point did she believe that he was the same one she loved before either; he was worse; he was a winner.

x

The man married them on the border between the United States and Mexico. Temple stood on the Mexican side of the beach, she on the U.S. side, the preacher between. She couldn't stand up for long and had to be married sitting down, in her robe, staring down at the sand as if it was a star in the sky: a phenomenon in which one could not genuinely believe. It was not just the mention of the Holy Name that sent her to the ground, but the terrible promise which she was making there and then; these were the usual wedding words and followed the ones she had sworn she would never utter (I do, I will) again and which still filled her with bile and grief. After it was over, she rolled on her side in the sand, and the young minister disappeared up the slope at the back of the beach and alongside Tijuana. Temple tapped her with his shoe, then, satisfied, followed the other up the slope and had him as his lover for the night. Felicity lay in the sand transfixed by the sky. Alone in the warm dawn she walked through a marsh to look at birds feeding. Already dune buggies with red and white American boys inside shot past them—it was Saturday—and a group of Mexican youths in American t-shirts charged into the bamboo-littered water, stripping, escaping. By now Temple had joined her and he smiled benignly at their moves; he was disheveled and roughjawed, and said, We let a few through the border every day, referring to the Mexicans.

Again he walked away from the beach to a parking area to see what the Reverend could do for him, while she watched four women running, babies bound to the chests of two of them. They wore raggy colors, pants under skirts; their hair was in braids as black as her own. They too plunged in a bunch through the reeds glutted with hubcaps and engine pans and cans, and hit the water with lighthearted shouts. It was murky water, brown as their skin; they seemed to become fluid and formless, she witnessed four women and two infants, on the run and splashing through the sloughs. Anonymous and red-faced, they were stripping as they fled north. She cheered them on, excited by the mirrorish vision of watery women breaking into parts. Then Temple returned like something hard and white that lives without sun, and she steered him away from the sight of the women back up the hill the way he came.

Soon he returned Felicity to her home the way he had brought her— the young minister yawning at the wheel—and said he would keep in touch with her, make sure she had a roof over her head, and would send

her regular support checks. He maintained his dignified and kind de-
meanor to the end, when she found herself standing in a mud puddle
by the side of the road with a wedding band on her left hand, and her
terrycloth robe scattering sand.

Inside the house Felicity woke Dan from his sleep on the couch and
told him the story in a detached voice. Actually he didn't know if it was
her voice that was detached, or if the sleep still folded around him was
making him detached. In any case he listened with gratitude at her safe
return. She had been on her knees and moved in over him, as if to reach
for something under his back or the cushion. Sand fell on him from her
hair. She smelled salty and the camelia rubbed off its pin onto his chest.
She climbed on top of him and lay with her cheek against his and in a
matter of seconds they were all over each other in the spirit of two who
don't care what they eat, they are so hungry. She was so small, most of
the time his chin was over her head, or he was hoisting her around. They
rolled to the floor and continued their feast down there. If God is wood,
she said, then club me with it. You, he kept repeating. Dreamtime was
a tool and they used it as best they could, then lurched apart, it was
his dream, Dan's dream, just another thing that never happened in the
world. But when he awoke, he felt as if it had.

Guilt and embarrassment burned in his face, which he kept hidden
over coffee and newspaper for a long time. It was after noon before he
had the nerve to open her bedroom door to check on her. Yellow sunlight—watery and evanescent—wobbled on the white wall above the
bed. They were all three together under the covers, arms thrown around
each other, and heads pressed close, black hair entwined with the shady
depth of sea-sponge. Their eyes were opened and he hesitated, waiting
for the black pupils to rotate in his direction, for smiles to de-center their
faces. But nothing of the sort occurred. Instead he noticed how weighted
they were, as if their flesh was burdened with liters of water, and they
were whiter too. He stepped closer, smiling, and only saw Matty smile
back; but her eyes were fixed on high. The other two reached up their
hands to him, Felicity pulled him down so hard he fell on the edge of
the child. He saw the water of their tears had soaked the edge of the

sheet. It had drenched the sides of their hair. She died in her sleep, said Felicity, last night, and I wasn't there to hold her.

Dan said he would call the police and left the room with the chill of the child's bones piercing his side.

x

None of the above ever happened according to Tom. Felicity and the girls were involved in a complicated scam, engineered by Temple and designed to throw Dan and him off the track. He came to this conclusion after Dan described Felicity's actions that day: she made him leave before the police arrived, she didn't act very upset, but reminded him, instead, of someone who has just lost her inner bearings. She had the vacuity of an angel. The house was as dim as a tomb but she was slipping around in boy's pajamas, smoking. He recounted his departure, a rush of actions aiming for a bus, and passing the police car on his way to the bus stop by the beach. Dan swore that Matty had died, but Tom refused to believe him. He kept seeing her in parks, on the subway, at the end of a super-market aisle, but he dared not approach too closely. He was ashamed to realize he wouldn't really recognize her outside the context of their time together. A few seasons after he returned to Boston, he was taken with a mysterious illness, a problem in the inner ear, which made him dizzy, nauseous, unable to work. He had to move in with his mother, and while she tried to sell his father's paintings, he stayed in his room day after day. A couple of the urban paintings—the ones depicting human misery in parks, and on subways—sold. But the rest—the ones that were self-consciously beautiful were rejected. These were ferns, and Tom sat with them, face to the wall. They were as useful as a bunch of keys to a huge demolished apartment building. Very little income was available to his mother and himself, while he was ill, and she finally made plans to move into a residence for the elderly. His company did her no good. It was clear to him that she preferred the company of her own generation by then.

One day, when his dizziness was lighter than usual, he went for a walk in a snowstorm and realized he couldn't go on with the life he was living. His face was fiery when he went into his room, shut the door, entered his closet and sat in a pile of sneakers and laces. Now he remembered Matty in full detail: one image especially, when she stood at the edge of evening water, bony and straight, and the water extended into the sky beyond her. He remembered having an insight, sometime around then, that at the moment of creation the body was made of light, and that form was solidified atmosphere, and that the auras around the flesh were proof of the indivisibility of matter from air. But he couldn't remember why, or when he had such an insight, or if it was even true, or, finally, if it mattered either way. His closet smelled like a thrift shop. Thrift shops smelled like churches. . . . Old wood, wet wool, used shoes. . . . And it was this simple, sensual link that changed the direction of his days; in the closet he made preparations to enter a novitiate in preparation for the priesthood.

x

When Felicity left the house with Lee, she only took a knapsack containing a few toys, her four books, a change of underwear, sweaters, toothbrushes and combs. She left all of their clothes, sheets and blankets behind. Anything belonging to Matty she left behind, except for a barette that always fell out of her hair, and one yellow seashell.

She didn't speak for a week. Then she had to, when she left Lee in the orphanage where she had worked, south of the border, with the nuns. She gave them the address of her one remaining relative—an aunt way up in Maine, on the Canadian border.

"If she will have her, and you want to send her, or if she wants to go . . . Until I come get her" was how Felicity explained her wishes, giving them the paper with the Maine address on it. The nuns spoke little English but nodded their assent, with their eyes fixed on the face before them. Lee was between them, almost as tall as her mother, and crying into her sleeve.

Then Felicity began walking. She walked back over the border, and up the wide freeways, along the edges of cars and condos and malls, heading north.

Saving History

x

I lived right up next to God in those days; it was as big and bristling as the Southern California hills, the rump of Tijuana, the desert and the ice blue sea all together. I talked to G-d in a watery babble for several mònths. It was great to watch the mystery unveil itself as fact. I had never wanted more than that.

I was a slave to kindness because it was so unpredictable. Unhappiness you know, it surrounds your hours, it moves ahead and behind you, but kindness—the kindness of people, or the kindness of events—is always a surprise.

In those days kindness took the form of food, blankets and a little floor space to sleep on—there was nothing abstract in it. I liked people who gave grudgingly the best, they turned out to be the most trustworthy and consistent, asking nothing from me in return. The ones who did it as an act of contrition or martyrdom always wanted something back from me.

For many months I hitched rides north, but only got to the edge of Colorado. I cleaned houses in a new development. Rows of pink stucco condos—all identical—clustered on the poor sore back of the earth. I cleaned laundry rooms and spas, then some people's houses while they were at work. I got the money in cash and slept with it in a canyon overlooking a highway. I liked it during the day when I could lounge in the houses, on sofas, on the edges of beds, they were all like motels, hundreds of units as they called their living spaces, the realization of socialism as much as of democracy, egalitarian cages, motelitarian resting places for the havers and doers, ideal in their anonymity, their lack of chaos.

The dollhouse-maker came alive in me, exploring these interiors, thinking of how the littlest, and the ugliest, and the most movable—the motel—had become the model for the biggest, and the most vulgar, and the most entrenched—the condominium—somebody's no-home!

I moved on, trying to avoid winters, but finally having to hitch a long-distance ride with a trucker who was claustrophobic and needed someone to take over when she got stuck in traffic or had to cross a bridge or pass through a tunnel. She understood right off that I was on a mission, but she never asked me what it was or where I was coming from. If we talked at all, and neither of us talked much, it was only about the weather, or the diner, or the cost of something or other. Mostly we listened to music.

When she left me in New York State, south of Albany, I started walking again, this time I sludged through the January thaw, and through unnatural warm days pushing on into the middle of February. By now I was talking again, to myself, and to God, and laughing aloud, and imagining the torch I would swing through the air around Temple's windows. I met a great woman named Cloda who had ridden a bike around the world, she said, with a Peace placard taped to her back. She had rosy cheeks and black teeth.

We had the exact same sense of humor and laughed and laughed until it was morning and she had to go.

I still remember the wind in the scudding clouds and wet red twigs against yellow: a yellow hill too, and a sealed door in a stone gray shack by the river, where I ran. Solid wires were pulled against the long cemented windows. A dog ran after a duck and looked into a cubby in a rock.

I stayed in a place where patients were not allowed bats or balls. Like horse heads inside human heads, we tried to decipher each other. My madness had been discovered without much difficulty. I stayed by the inferno to the end, and until my face was burning as the face of Moses might have burned when he came down from the mountain. People looked away, even as they dragged me to the wagon and far from Temple's charred mansion. Black charcoal bricquets were all that was left of his family estate, and Halloween trees.

I'm not a piece of wood you can burn, by the way, but I am a piece of human who can make wood burn.

After that act of violence, I continued to be subject to spontaneous gestures. I know how the spirit suffers from the interference of the flesh.

It was a smelly, gaseous place with soapstone basins for our shaved heads. Skin on bone since the food was mush. Often it was tubed through a nostril into the bellies of those of us who resisted, as if to say:

"If you suffered this long, you can suffer longer." Across the northern plains it's partly cloudy, though here the bricks and two thirds of each twig are gleaming. Patients tiptoe like fairies over spots of ice.

Temperatures will not return to normal. In this case, fat red gums and fallen arches will be your lot. Granular slopes covered by snowmaking machines yellow in the setting sun, kilowatts above red.

Accept agony's invitation to a hospital and you won't return the same.

It's like walking backwards through a storm of lines and circles in a comic strip, you try turning and your scarf goes gray.

On Christmas Day, white dots float across each closed window.

Stars mean flurries, and stripes mean sleet. Hail comes from above, Sister told me, but the Lord can't get rid of it.

Speaking of ecstasy, half an hour is a long time. In this state of ravishment, a body both dies and rises fresh and new.

At the forbidden green line, you are capable of anything.

Like young girls riding wooden saddles, the pink buds bounce on leafless boughs. A violent number looks like fun, they seem to insist.

A starfish detonation in the heavens, ground stations and aircraft go on alert, people shudder and hide. A polar electro-jet casts a shadow over the land like a little plaid pantsuit.

Whatever you know, know freely. It's hard to express afternoons as well as vacuum cleaners do.

What would have happened to a slave like me before technology? My parents' depression was sucked in and swallowed. While they were proud, they were never demeaning of me. Fixated onto my father and staying alive, I tried to avoid violation with all the intensity of one tramping.

In my dream boots I dreamed of a sensuous Puss in Boots, lounging under a tree. But all I saw was fluid and acrobatic figures blooming in the clear night sky; they were me, they were SHE. Weak, long rays grew like whiskers out of my flesh. I loved to be alone because then I didn't exist.

My aunt the philosopher asked questions like: What is more important—a diamond, or an almond?

Between shots of medication, I confessed I would rather have a dog-sled carry me to the cold than sleep all day. On those times the heavens sit on my thick head and between myself and God there is something like cotton in snowballs; they tell me it's the shot but I prefer to pretend it's angel hair.

Only Santa Claus, like a librarian, turned everything red and color-coordinated. In red and green. Grown-ups were buildings with apartments and staircases running up and down inside of them. I used to call my littlest child The Good Finder. Now I can never find her again, because she isn't here to hunt for herself.

Depression is a sunset emotion which comes with the regularity of the color orange. While US airplanes headed for Hanoi, we were eating lamb chops beside a highway in Mount Desert. I remember the day, and the Bay of Pigs. It's like sleeping with a loaded gun under your pillow and you dream of some dim war enacted in a snowstorm.

In hell you are forbidden work, so you can't even buy the food you want. Resistance takes the form of starvation, and then of a face averted, then of religion.

Despair and increased medication do damage to each femur and larynx. Skeletons strain against their ropes of arteries.

My pulse was my weakest act of protest . . . about as effective as water wearing down rock.

Where are the joys, and what, my aunt had once asked me, and her answers followed: children around a table, fresh fruit, women, a glimpse into well-known eyes, the eucharist, fishing in winter, music, a smoke, a lake.

Clean up the inpatient beds and you will soon see hills of misery growing again in each one.

I remember one veteran of pain. You'd need three doctors for that patient. They cleaned out the inside of his eyes and rolled his body away. I was proud of his determination. He found the inside out escape.

A charred black house on a windy hill.

Shadows lashing its roof, the shadows of branches battling the invisible rushes, clouds gaping open, and in the air the smell of the sea—all for Satan to roam and ramble now. I am glad my friend the veteran will never have to go there, will never have to travel on the other side of the high walls.

Now I tell myself, Take a quarter hour for prayer, then return to active life over and over again repeating this system.

The body must serve the spirit, obediently, though not slavishly. The body must be dignified and always at liberty. Outside the body there is no room for tyranny.

Growing old is growing wild. Going mad is growing old too fast.

The doctor's ashes fell into a plastic bowl of warm milk. He didn't notice. Everyone had bat's teeth, and a white dollop of spittle on a lip, and flat bare feet that smacked on stone.

What's brown on a wall? Humpty's dump.

Even when we laughed, the sounds in that place were all trucklike and flushing. No birds, but high walls and a watchtower. Whenever someone called Jesus there was a blur in the air, a cloud from a thicket of clichés, and in came a church man with unguents and golden toys in his hands.

Veterans of war, of school, of family, veterans of neighborhoods, hospitals, accidents and prisons, veterans of the power bloc, and of the weak bloc, of food, hell and water, this is your conscience, a tapestry of shadows, a screen on which the shades of the living live again, trapped, without sensation. Put your knife to the grindstone, stupid.

Put your shoulder to the wheel, fool. (My chocolate milk was stuck to the bottom of my cup.) I wanted to be free of these objects.

One day fifteen sweater people drowned off the coast of Newfoundland, and there was a Palm Sunday massacre farther south. A week later I heard about a man who drove a truck into a cafe and shot as many women as he could. The forbidden green line rippled in the water like a crease in marble. Auroral substorms were said to be the cause of fluorescence in the altitudes.

Let those who dare, go free, said the physician who hauled up dismembered weeds and made the water clear. No illusions ever came from one patient who commented, "We will never however be loved again as long as we are still in hell, free or not. Change our history, if you can, Doctor." Or save us, I suggested, instead. He was a kind doctor and set me free.

Saving History

X

One day Felicity saw her aunt. She was the size of a blackbird from where Felicity was standing. She was way out at the center of a frozen lake, fishing into a hole, and balanced on a red steel office stool. Felicity stared for a long time because the sky as was yellow as parchment ready to spill the alphabet of its snow. The ice was perilous, gleaming. Timorous, she began to walk on it. One foot after the other, her long black coat crowlike as it winged off her tiny frame. She dotted the icecap with her boot-toes, inch by inch; the ice creaked or moaned; flakes began to fall. Her eyes simultaneously stung and watered. She was terrified of expanse.

The particulars of the materials around her feet engaged and held her full attention. If she could focus on the fatty white ice, its knots and gnarls, pebbles and stuck leaves, she would be okay. My aunt loves me, she loves me, she litanized about the old lady she hadn't seen much of.

Her aunt sensed the ice rejecting another weight, turned, and, under her blue cap, blinked an acknowledgement that Felicity couldn't see. Beside the red stool was a bucket of cold water on one side, and a bucket of fire on the other. Between her two feet was a bottle of Southern Comfort. The closer these details came to Felicity, the more daring she became, and now, hurrying, she lifted her eyes up into the whiteness, and saw the snow was falling in larger flakes and faster. Not so far away, she could see the thin flying figure of a young girl skating towards her. A green cap was pulled almost over the child's eyes, her lips were pouring streamers of steam, she was smiling so enthusiastically. It was Lee. She whirred over the ruts and bumps gracefully—in tights and a ski jacket—towards her mother who opened her arms to her. And they both sank down on the ice beside the old lady. The black water rocked inside the ring of ice, where the fishing line hung loose.

The old lady lit a cigarette and handed it to Felicity, followed by the bottle of alcohol for a swig freely offered.

That's how we do it down here, she said to Felicity.

Felicity's shoulders loosened, she rested in Lee's arms, her cheeks flushing from the heat and the snow. She looked at her aunt intently, saying, I know what you mean. But the bewilderment in her eyes lasted far longer than the sound of her words, rushing through the winter air.

Indivisible

In the White Winter Sun

1-1

I locked my husband in a closet one fine winter morning. It was not a large modern closet, but a little stuffy one in a century old brick building. Inside that space with him were two pairs of shoes, a warm coat, a chamber pot, a bottle of water, peanut butter and a box of crackers. The lock was strong but the keyhole was the kind you can both peek through and pick. We had already looked simultaneously, our eyes darkening to the point of blindness as they fastened on each other, separated by only two inches of wood. Now I would not want to try peeking again. My eyes meeting his eyes was more disturbing than the naked encounter of our two whole faces in the light of day. It reminded me that no one knew what I had done except for the person I had done it with. And you God.

A gold and oily sun lay on the city three days later. Remember how coldly it shone on the faces of the blind children. They stayed on that stoop where the beam was the warmest. I wasn't alone. My religious friend came up behind me and put his arm across my shoulder.

"We have to say goodbye," he murmured. I meant to say, "Now?" but said, "No."

I had seen "I'm nobody" written on my ceiling only that morning.

Brick extended on either side. The river lay at the end. Its opposite bank showed a trail of leafless trees. My friend was curly haired, bewildered in his gestures—that is, without greed. He said the holy spirit was everywhere if you paid attention. Not as a rewarded prayer but as an atmosphere that threw your body wide open. I said I hoped this was true. He was very intelligent and well-read. He had sacrificed intimacy and replaced it with intuition.

I wanted badly to believe like him that the air is a conscious spirit. But my paranoia was suffusing the atmosphere, and each passing person wore a steely aura. "Please God don't let it snow when I have to fly," he said and slipped away. My womanly body, heavy, once productive, and the van for the children, gunning its engine, seemed to be pounded into one object. It was Dublin and it wasn't. That is, the Irish were all around in shops and restaurants, their voices too soft for the raw American air and a haunt to me. "Come on. Let's walk and say goodbye," he insisted. We walked towards St. John the Evangelist.

"I've got to make a confession," I told him. "Can't I just make it to you? I mean, you're almost a monk, for God's sake."

"No," said Tom. "The priest will hear you. Go on." Obediently I went inside. The old priest was not a Catholic. He was as white as a lightbulb and as smooth. His fingers tapered to pointed tips as if he wore a lizard's lacy gloves. It was cold inside his room. Outside—the river brown and slow. A draft came under the door.

I think he knew that a dread of Catholicism was one reason I was there. He kept muttering about Rome, and how it wouldn't tolerate what he would as an Anglican.

Personally I think pride is a sin. But I said "a failure of charity" was my reason for being there. This was not an honest confession, but close enough. The priest told me to pray for people who bothered me, using their given name when I did. He said a name was assigned to a person before birth, and therefore the human name was sacred. Then he blessed me. Walking out, I felt I was dragging my skeleton like a pack of branches. After all, a skeleton doesn't clack inside the skin, but is more like wood torn from a tree and wrapped in cloth.

Outside Tom was waiting and we walked over the snow. "I missed that flute of flame that burns between Arjuna and Krishna—the golden faces of Buddha, and Yogananda, Ramakrishna, Milarepa, and the dark eyes of Edith Stein and Saint Teresa. Are all Americans Protestant? The church was cold, austere. I'm a bad Catholic."

He nodded vaguely and said: "But you're a good atheist. Catholicism has an enflamed vocabulary, don't worry. You can transform each day into a sacrament by taking the eucharist. You just don't want to bother."

Even the will to raise and move a collection of bones can seem heroic. Only an object on one side or a person—can draw it forwards—or on another side an imagined object or person. Maybe the will responds to nearby objects and thoughts the way a clam opens when it's tapped. "Mechanistic . . . We really should put more trust in the plain surface of our actions," I said.

"Do we have to say goodbye? And leave each other in such a state?"

"We do."

"But first, Tom—I have one favor to ask you."

1-2

Exactly ten years before, during a premature blizzard, I left all my children at home and went to meet my best friends in the Hotel Commander. I did so carrying the weight of my husband like a tree on my back. This was a meeting I couldn't miss, no matter how low I stooped.

The walk from the subway to the hotel was bitter, wet and shiny. Traffic lights moved slowly on my right, while the brick walls and cold gray trees sopped up the gathering snow. I kept my eyes fixed on the left where dark areas behind shrubs and gates could conceal a man, and stepped up my pace. Lewis and Libby were already seated in a booth in a downstairs lounge. I shook off my coat and sat beside Libby and we all ordered stiff drinks, recalling drunker meetings from earlier youth. I leaned back and kept my eyes on the door, in case my husband appeared and caught me off-guard.

"Relax, Henny," Lewis reproved me.

"I've never met him," Libby cried. "It's unbelievable."

"He's unbelievable," said Lewis.

"He can't be that bad."

"He is. He should be eliminated. He won't let her out of the house, without her lying. She probably said she had a neighborhood meeting tonight. Right?"

"Henny's not a coward."

"She likes to keep the peace though. That's not good."

"I'm going to be back in the spring. I'll meet him then," Libby said. "And if he's all that bad, I will do something to him."

"Henny has a mercenary army of children around her, protecting her against him," Lewis explained. "They aren't even her own."

"Hen, tell me the truth. Do you wish he would die? I'll make him leave you if you want me to," said Libby.

A renunciatory rush went down my spine when I saw, out in the lobby, the back of a man in a pea-jacket and woolen cap. Gathered over, I left the table for the rest room, and Libby followed breathless. She was wringing her hands, smelling of musk rose, and dancing on her pin-thin legs in high heel boots that had rings of wet fur around the tops while I sat in the sink, "Was it him? Was it him?" she implored.

We never found out.

That was the same night we climbed out the hotel kitchen window and walked up a slippery hill, one on each side of Lewis, hugging to his arms, while the snow whipped against our cheeks and lips, and we talked about group suicide.

"Phenobarbital, vodka and applesauce, I think."

"No, Kool-aid, anything sweet."

"For some reason."

"Jam a little smear of strawberry on the tongue."

"Or honey."

"Catbirds and the smell of jasmine and we all lie in a line under the stars."

"With great dignity."

"Despite the shitting." "And die." "Die out." "I can dig it," said Lewis. "I can dig it."

"But we have to do it all together," Libby concluded.

1-3

There is a kind of story, God, that glides along under everything else that is happening, and this kind of story only jumps out into the light like a silver fish when it wants to see where it lives in relation to everything else.

Snow is a pattern in this particular story. It was snowing the day of my first visit to the Federal Penitentiary. The ground was strung with pearly bulbs of ice. I had visited many social service offices in my day, but never a prison. I associated prison with sequence and looked around for a way to break out. As a first-time visitor, and in the early moments, I remembered nervously standing with a crowd of strangers waiting for someone familiar to emerge from behind a green door with a big light over it. For each one of us, the familiar person would be a different person, but our experience would be the same. I already know that some conflicts in life have no resolution and have to be treated in a different way from common problems.

But prison seemed to relate to issues of privacy in ways that were unimaginable to those who had never been forcibly hidden. Simplistically I was scared of being in a jail because it was a space that was unsafe from itself, the way a mind is. But I forced myself, as I sometimes do, to go to the place I dreaded the most—to the place that was so repugnant, it could only change me. Maybe the sacred grove of our time is either the prison or the grave site of a massacre. I have always believed I must visit those sacred groves, and not the woodlands, if I want to know the truth. In this case, I only wanted to see someone I loved and to comfort her by my coming. And surely enough, I did undergo a kind of conversion through my encounters with the persons there. When you visit someone in prison, this paranoid question comes up: Do I exist only in fear? The spirit hates cowards. It broods heavily in the presence of fear. I only felt as safe as a baby when I was holding a baby or a child and so, sitting empty-armed, in a roomful of strangers, watching the light over the heavy door, was a test of will.

Then I saw a child—a little boy in the room with me—he was like a leaf blowing across an indoor floor. And while waiting for my friend to come out the door, I moved near him.

I asked him what book he had brought with him. He kept his face down and said, "Gnomes."

"Do you read it yourself, honey?" "No, I can't. Tom reads it to me." "Do you want me to read some?" "Sure," he said and lifted his smile. His eyelids were brown and deeply circled and closed, as long as the eyelids of the dead whose lashes are strangely punctuated by shadows longer than when they were alive and batting. He wore a limpid smile that inscribed a pretty dimple in his right cheek.

"I'm getting obsessed," he said, "with books about gnomes, goblins, elves, hobbits."

"How do you mean obsessed?"

"1 want to know everything about them . . . And sometimes I'm sure they really exist and run around my feet."

"How can you tell?"

"My shoelaces come untied sometimes, and I think I feel them on my shoes."

"I don't know, honey. I've never seen one. Let's go read about gnomes."

When I took his hot little hand in mine, I felt the material charge of will and spirit return to me. I had an instinctual feeling that the room held me fast by my fate. To be here was to be physically "inside" but the way a ghost is inside the world when it returns to haunt someone and still can depart at will. The ghost is confused, paralyzed by its guilt at being present without paying the price for it. Punishment is easily confused with safety.

1-4

There are sequences of sounds that musicians arrange by twelves, repeating the same twelve notes but in alternating and random sequences. They themselves don't know which three or four notes will come out close, in relation to each other.

It is sort of as if someone I loved indicated that he loved me too, but in unexpected moments and ways. And the three words "I love you" only popped into place once, by mistake, and after he had died, as in "too late." There were no witnesses to our relationship, and this created a credibility gap. I didn't trust that the experience that he and I had had had actually taken place because there were no witnesses; the verb tense was queer. No conventions stuck. I was the missing person at the graveside ceremony, an eyeball behind a bush. The person I loved would say, "Me. . . too. . . you," and this would be months after he died. Would anyone believe that I just heard him say it, no?

1-5

It was in that prison that I met a religious man for the second time in my life. Almost every time I visited there the small boy was there too with his beautiful ringed eyes, serious long face, and this man beside him. The child often wore a strange sidelong smile, the way the blind do. I could tell that his guardian was weirdly unlike a blood father. He always brought along a book that the boy ran his hand over. This man was either distracted or brooding when he talked to the boy's mother, a prisoner who was tiny and wild-haired and dressed in a green uniform which was fitted to say, "Not my own." She looked Italian.

They talked about the boy, eyeing him simultaneously. The mother's expression was sad and inverted. Her eyes pulled their surroundings inside, and then didn't let them out again. This was a common expres-

sion on many prisoners' faces here. Many of the women were locked up
for drug crimes. Either they were users or else they lived with a dealer
and took the rap for him. I found out all about this in upcoming visits.
My friend, who had been framed, told me the stories of the prisoners
around us. Often the guy was free while his girlfriend and/or the mother
of his child was locked up for her unwillingness to speak his name to the
Feds. Already I knew from experience how quickly a woman's children
could end up in foster care if there was no functioning family person.
I assumed that this was the case with those three. The man might be
a foster father, or a friend. Or was he her boyfriend? I was pretty sure
maybe the woman was one of those people who were political prisoners
left over from the sixties and seventies. In any case, I concluded there
should be a whole separate set of laws for women and watched the boy
back onto his mother's lap. Her name was Gemma. One day before jail
the man told me about Gemma the prisoner and how he knew her. We
stood in puddles that looked like mirrors of shadows around our feet.

"I used to work for a small legal aid firm in Boston," he told me. "I
hated law already by then. But a friend called me asking me to defend
this woman. She had been part of a bank heist with the Weather Underground. I told him I'd never been in court before, but he persuaded me,
and I did it. And failed. Lost. She got forty years. Life, basically."

"And her child?" I asked him.

"She was pregnant with him when she went in. It was before they
had any maternity programs in prison. She and the kid never really
bonded. I have watched out for him ever since. You know. Made sure
he had a home."

"What about the father?" was the natural question I asked.

"Never mind, nothing. He couldn't."

"Why? Why not? Was he in hiding too?"

"Right, but they are friends. Sort of."

I pressed him: "Why is the child blind? How?"

"She tried to kill herself. With some poison."

"After the trial?"

"During."

We walked from the parking lot towards the prison. I then had a vision of this man having huge lies inside of him, lies like helium that swelled up his spirit until it almost exploded.

I was sure now that he was the father. "What's your name?" I asked with a squint as if I had only forgotten it.

"Tom," he said pleasantly. "I'm in preparation for entering a monastery. What's yours?"

The sun seemed to be setting at 2 p.m. It shriveled and paled like a coin dropped into still yellow milk.

Inside the checking area I handed over my wallet and keys and found my tongue loosened. I am known for my silence, and liked for it, but with Tom I could talk. "I'm used to seeing the children, not the mothers, when they are lost, separated," I told him.

"I see the beginnings of their lives, not the conclusions, as in this case," I said.

"What do you mean?"

"I'm a foster mother—or was—I took children home."

"That's interesting. Want to go for a walk later?"

Outside again, Tom and I went for our first walk. It was early spring when the forsythia branches were yellowing up for the arrival of their flowers. The reservoir was scalloped behind a chain-link fence. The air was between black and oyster. He told me he was going back to Canada ultimately. He was going to live as a monastic in a Benedictine community. "Why wait?" I asked.

"To get the boy settled. I can't leave until he has a home."

"That could take awhile, because of his age, and affliction."

"Maybe, maybe not . . . and I would love to be somewhere warmer than this."

"Me too." There was a tolerant if melancholy quality to him that eased me. My breathing slowed, I believed I could express myself well in words, and nothing bad would happen. He seemed desireless, without being cold and ironic. I already dreaded saying goodbye although that word was planted and fated, because of his stated plans. On many of our walks, no words in fact passed between us. As soon as I had no fear of speaking to him, I had nothing much to say. It was in this silence that we grew familiar enough to travel side by side.

1-6

In a matter of weeks we agreed to go to the border of Mexico. The boy stayed behind with his foster family. It was late April, 1997. We went there because this border represented the most repulsive cut on the continent. A festering trench. By mutual agreement we decided to plant ourselves in that alien landscape; to carry a mystifying revulsion to its limits. This was a test of faith for both of us. He was still uncertain about entering a religious community. In retrospect I see that he had several months of exclaustrated wandering ahead of him. He wanted to know how much isolation he could stand. I wanted to learn about pressure without interference. He wanted to persuade me to become the caretaker of the blind child; I wanted to show him how much my freedom meant to me. So we had paused, together, there in an abandoned household on a canyon where it only rained after Christmas. Sand, dust, small stones, loose canyons emitting the gas of past massacres. The huts were wooden, open to spiders, snakes, lizards, birds and illegal aliens who fled like deer at our approach. Now when a fog dulled the difference between mother earth and air, we both remembered snow, our natural northern habitat. Tom said that Southern California was like a body without a head. "One of those bodies they plan to grow for body parts, to harvest, so to speak." Not far from our desert retreat lay miles and miles of condominium settlements splashed with blue pools. I was sewing curtains. The windowpanes held thick wadded spider webs and the bodies of flies and bees dried in them as if the webs were silver hammocks. At home I heard it was snowing again—large wet cloud-shavings.

1-7

Home for me then was on the edge of Boston in a town abutting Roxbury and Franklin Park. The pit and the puddingstone. Old Victorian mansions were shaded by spectacular trees which were pollinated by Olmsted's landscaping ventures around town. The streets had a secretive drift. Cardinals, bluejays, sparrows, swallows, crickets, robins and crows shivered the leaves with their singing. Almost every person was poor or about to be. You had to leave if you were getting money, because the neighborhood could not tolerate inequalities. Old families, all of them Irish, Puerto Rican or Black clung to their two and-three families while the newly arrived (soon to leave) dwelled in single family houses they renovated and converted into apartments before departure. My old house had not been renovated, but needed a new roof and a coat of paint, not much to make its butter yellow facade look permanent where it hid its flaws behind a mound of granite and five varieties of evergreen. It was occupied as usual by transients who sent me the rent for their rooms. McCool, my husband, was not allowed, by the courts, to pass the gate and enter, but when I was away the tenants called him anyway if a rat was swimming in the toilet bowl or a bat was sleeping in the shower. He would then enter our house proudly with his toolbox, look slowly around the premises he once occupied, deal with the problem and then postpone leaving over a cup of tea and chit-chat.

McCool said his dark hair and complexion were a result of the wreck of the Spanish Armada on the west coast of Ireland. The word "wreck" clung to his features then, like weeds on stones. McCool was not his given name, but his singing name. He played Celtic tunes with a small band who toured during March, and he played solo in Boston pubs the rest of the time. McCool and I had some qualities in common. We were both what they call the working poor. We were unrewarded artists—he on his fiddle played since boyhood, and me in my films which were obscure meditations on seven themes:

I. geographic cures as religious acts; 2. parental betrayals and lies; 3. the nearly unsupportable weight of the world's beauty (God); 4. how to stay uncorrupted; 5. a political act as a gesture of existential discomfort; 6. childhood for children; 7. race in America

These themes found their forms in my dreams and I committed them first to paper in the dark morning hours where eastern clouds were inscribed on our greasy kitchen windows. I wanted to find the unifying idea behind these themes, one sequence of lights that would illuminate the situation. Meanwhile McCool's music was never recorded but he moved from one shabby venue to the next, playing melodies that were both traditional and new ones he had composed. He was too early and too late for the Irish music scene. He was good at it, but got lost carrying it somewhere. He told stories. He lied. He had no conscience but compensated for this lack with a dogged survivalist creed. He would stay around, no matter what, and be difficult for everyone. To be a problem, he said, was the credo of his revolution. He needed someone to copy, rather than someone to love, and he was as faithful as a wolf in his way, never ceasing to pursue his family or stay near, no matter what the law said. Everyone knows someone like him.

A total of twelve children passed through our house. Nine of them were temporary; two returned twice, then left again; three were siblings; two were sexually abused, four were beaten; three had ammunition and drugs in their homes; one was abandoned on a church step; two had been left to stepfathers who didn't want them; one was autistic. Three children arrived as toddlers and stayed for life. These were the twins, and little Dorothy who helped me. She was motherly but became a nun in Yogananda's Self-Realization Fellowship after doing foreign missionary work. The twins also traveled far, separately. Then they returned and settled near their childhood home, my house. They both have done well in the world. I didn't adopt any of them and they could call me whatever they wanted. I didn't want to pretend they were my natural-born children but to use the slave model: a situation where abandoned children were simply taken in. They called their caretakers Aunt or cousin. This way no one tampered with the actual source of their existence, or set up a potentially disappointing arrangement. Strangely my three did call me Ma, Mummy and Mom, though they referred to me as Henny. They always called McCool McCool because it was cool. These three became used to an adult man being an outsider. They were street-wise kids who went through the national busing crisis siding with the black students or staying involved with race from kindergarten on because they were black.

Indivisible

Later I guess they chose to be permanently engaged with that most absurd social issue (race) because its very absurdity liberated them from all other delusions. These children were my soldiers. They liked to have fun. They grew up in that old house, watching other babies come and go, and left when they were eighteen. They themselves arrived as inert beings, barely able to whine or lift their heads, so neglected they made solitude into a luxury. Contact gradually restored them.

But when their training was over, and they left home, I could barely remember a single act of parenting. Instead I manned the everyday hassles without the bending over, but weeping out of the same personal problem. It was in my misty maternalist past that the life of the spirit developed into its present form. Material flotilla floated away, even the thoughts I had about children, and became transparencies. The passages, acts, encounters, always in transit and irritating made me move as a mother crab back and forth, sideways through the rooms, tipping and lifting whole tiny faces up to mine. And these faces changed continually becoming new faces and all of them were attached to the hands they would identify as their own for life. Home tried to stay stationary, to keep them tied, returning to their rooms and views of the moon, but once they were gone, they were really gone, and I was just a mourner at a vast immaterial site.

Through the Eyes of the Other

2-1

It is now many months after that first prison visit—again snow dots the night sky. A blue moon in late February will follow these white nights, there will be a thaw, a gush, this chunk of earth cutting up into cascades of fluid and sex. It is the copper light that I see on the water that saves me.

A net is like a honeycomb with its ridges and holes. But a net is not sticky, its weaving is made of string and air. I believe there are many similar geometries making up the physical world, but we can't see them.

Something is wrong because there are emotions between people a few miles apart. You would think that the dead had just traveled somewhere else material.

The details of streets along and near the river emerge sometimes and often against the meow of an ambulance rushing to a hospital nearby. This building is called Terminal Arms by laughing residents. Many of the tenants are elderly on a one-way corridor to the cemetery. The pale green louvered doors beside each entrance to each apartment, and the small wooden polished elevator make it feel like the Paris of my imagination. I hear from two walls in my bedroom and the ceiling the sound of tenants peeing and flushing their old age.

If you make a negative out of the popular image of Jesus' face, you see a set of heart-shaped stains where his skin should be lighted. The sacred heart, flat on his chest, pink with gold sticks coming out of its circumference, looks as if it has fallen from an area of his face where there is usually the beard.

"My guru is within my heart, he is the viveka within my heart," wrote Jnaneshwari. This means to me that our hearts are our whole bodies and our wounds are visible.

There are factories that produce the faces of Jesus and Mary out of one mold and press the beard onto only one of them. Snow clings to the rough brick walls and interferes with my view of the street and the river. People walking dogs, heads bowed, pass, and even in this weather there are joggers who in their spanking suits look like silhouettes from old children's books—the Pied Piper, say, leaping and stretching evilly along the page's border. Almost everywhere I look my eyes are straining against my guilt, rising and leaving the shadows. Silence is incorruptible as long as its owner is not possessed by anyone else.

The minute the owner of silence becomes property, its silence itself seems rooted in treachery.

I was fascinated by her—by them—as I waited there in the prison each day. It was as if I could read them into my future, like hills on a horizon towards which I was inexorably moving. The man was dark and handsome in a warm tormented way. But I wondered if he was half-blind. He never looked at the woman but always down while his hand on the boy's shoulder was heavy. The blind boy would lead him around the chairs and tables while the woman watched. She was like a small animal that might have padded feet and claws, her eyes wary under long lids, her cheekbones high, her body quickly gesturing, and withdrawing. I could tell that all access to happiness was closed off in her.

2-2

In the apartment the heat goes on as soon as the sun is gone. The pipes bang and chirp as if a family of crickets is dancing up a storm. The view to the river covers about one hundred yards. There is a well-used road between, a riverbank, the river, another riverbank, another road, and more roads beyond that one, but also hills and tops of buildings. The window is facing northwest. To the left the river is sucked in to the sea or disgorged. Still I do get a sunset and a sunrise along those lines of bank and river and the bricks turn into gold. My husband remains locked in the closet where he makes a racket. I don't want to tell anyone that he is there, least of all the monkish Tom, because everyone believes that a person is obligated by witnessing an event to report it. But if you're just standing peacefully by, then are you responsible for a glance to the side at something you knew would happen sooner or later. I mean, if you dreamed the thing would happen and then you are there finally, watching, when it does happen, are you responsible? Are you in a way the instigator? The most confusing situation is to be a ghost who sees terrible things and can't report it. Sometimes I think that God witnesses events sideways and doesn't stop because it all goes by so fast, and God can't believe what God just saw. So it is important to tell you everything, God.

2-3

Lewis became a solid man, thick with some belly not really fat because it was tight like a drum-skin girdling him. Burly is a better word. He had long eyes with soft eyelids and very thin eyebrows. His phenomenal strength was in his upper torso because of turning those wheels by hand. He didn't laugh now.

"Do you know someone who died, I mean well?"

"Yes, my father," I barely audibly said.

"Wait a minute. How did he die?"

"In Korea."

"Oh right. Poor bastard."

"I'm still waiting for him to come home."

"I believe it. I believe it."

"Believe what?"

"That you're waiting like that," he remarked. "You've always acted like someone who had to be somewhere else, just in case. Where to be when he comes, is the question."

"Do you think that a person can use intimacy as a form of resistance? I mean, since you melt into the shape of your enemy . . ." I asked him.

"Who knows? You mean all your children?" he asked. "All I know is that if there's a God, he eats everything in sight, and women like you keep producing food for him, in the form of children. Why?"

"Our babies? Our selves? Him? You must mean It."

"Okay. It," Lewis conceded. "You keep producing bodies for It. Why?"

"I am studying resistance now, Lewis," I said. "Not God."

"Okay, Henrietta, okay."

He rarely listened to me because I spoke so softly. He would hear and vaguely respond, but really his attention was always elsewhere. Today, war. He told me now that the practice of sacrifice went way back to creation stories where the universe was seen as a giant human—the Purusha with human attributes. Sacrificing people was a way of offering bodies to the big body of the cosmos itself. Spring was butter to its lips and its lips were butter. Earth goddesses were appeased by the sacrifice of young males because they wanted their seed for more young males and crops. Pentheus, a killjoy who wanted to stop his mother from having fun at night, was ripped apart by his mother herself. She held up his penis triumphantly for everyone to see, even as he screamed Mother it's me! And he listed the legendary wicked women—Cybele, Ma, Dindymene, Hecate, Artemis, Nemesis,

Demeter, Baubo, Medusa, Persephone, Isis. Aphrodite, Kali, Durga, Nana, Ishtar, Astarte, Nina of Ninevah, Parvati and the Great Mother never pausing to wonder what their points of view might be.

"Sacrifice," he concluded, "was the most developed form of materialism—way beyond the ones we know now—it was seeing and being food simultaneously. I think that's why so many women were involved." Loops of tempura glistened on his fork.

"What?" I asked.

We had many dinners together. Usually in the Tokyo Restaurant on a thoroughfare outside the city. Easy for Lewis to park there and undo his chair on the street. We rolled to the same table in a back room almost every time. The impersonal manners of the waiters pleased us both; they never acknowledged having seen us before. He liked one bottle of Kirin beer. I once had a glass of white wine that tasted like water in a graveyard and sent a chill down my spine. Afterwards I only drank sake. Then he had his chicken tempura and I ate a California roll.

We were always at ease together there. It was like being in bed being anywhere with him. The world outside grew cold. We had nothing we wanted but the time that we had.

I could see in his thick aging features the boy I once knew. He could see in mine the girl he met when I was seventeen.

2-4

I had met Lewis at the house of my best friend Libby in April, 1967. He was sprawled on a staircase with some friends, the first black American youth and the most brilliant man almost anyone there had met. It was the North. He was very smooth and hairless and the color of caramel. He never lacked confidence but dared to laugh with his eyes closed. He was twenty two, from the Midwest, a recent Freedom Rider. They had all come up from Mississippi. I listened to him talk about it.

"At one point I was speeding—I mean speeding—in this car with two Northern lawyers, from Oxford to Jackson, Miss., they were drafting documents in long-hand, going to try a case, get some so-called Negroes out of jail, and we got shot at and all of us couldn't believe it, laughed, these mangy dogs running away from the blast while our car shot up dust. That's when I decided to go to law school. That's when it happened."

I hated being so sure so fast but I knew that he was the one I was assigned to cherish.

He talked to white people without wanting to know them. I loved his attitude because I was scared of white grownups.

Seventeen, a virgin, a novice in issues of race and sex, I had already been told by one white man, the school principal, that he wouldn't recommend me for any colleges, and I had been kicked out of a courtroom in Downtown Boston where state officials were accusing other white men of being communist. The white firemen shot me down the outside steps with their hoses, only enraging me further, but Lewis held me back. I was a communist sympathizer, as was Lewis who nonetheless believed that the battle between rich and poor had been lost and the poor would always be with us. From the beginning he held the tragic position that the only revolution was the eternal revolution—an inexhaustible struggle for something already lost.

"Is it correct, the way people do, to depend on history to be the judge?" he might ask, and answer: "The idea is that history sorts things out later, in favor of the good and the just. History is the future glutted with recollected facts. It crosses back and forth, making swift but morally astute decisions about who deserves to be famous and who doesn't or didn't. History like God has an ethical bent so people should be nervous about its judgment later on, although to be remembered badly is better than to be forgotten entirely if you are someone who wants to be famous as opposed to saved."

2-5

I never sat on Lewis's lap. Once he pinned me down across him and I said I would call the police, it was a joke, but he was definitely manhandling me. Gracefulness of gesture had gone from him since he was shot overseas. What radiated out now was not so physical but more like a force-field, it was still attractive. To me. It was not easy loving someone both rejecting and kind. His suffering was so great it rolled up everything else he was feeling like jam inside a sponge cake. He, like so many injured people, seemed to have been chosen to be wounded as a sacrifice for the rest of us. To some his condition indicated bad karma. To others, it was moral ecology that someone had to pay for everyone else's fun and freedom. Besides, he had been cocky. And to still others, it was just an accident made of causes and contingencies. That big power-shouldered man, with light brown skin and a beard to his ears, was often seen laughing at things, papers, people, all by himself; in company he was grumpy.

He could make that wheelchair tip and spin and climb up steps; he moved it as if it was part of his body. But no one with eyes could fail to see what it cost him. Likewise the Hasidic men inside their beards and hats also seemed to be living compensations for the furious freedom of others. And like people who know that they have made choices their faces are hard, not curious or perplexed. Jesus with his curly black beard and prayer shawl might have been like one of them.

"Rabbi, teacher."

"What? What do you want?" Jesus asked.

"Rabbi," they said to him. "Where are you staying?"

"Come and see."

It was about four in the afternoon.

Already it is growing dark. The clouds pour up from the horizon to gorge on the sun going down. Yellow is the first night-cloud warning for snow but it also is the first sign of morning. "Give me what you know, my Lord. Give me that water."

A Crackle of Static

3-1

Originally the New England native inhabitant was described as outnosed, black-haired, small-waisted, lank-bellied, with small feet. They were called Brownettoes. Their backs were erect. They ate strawberry, raspberry, cherry, blueberry and elderberry breads, Boiled chestnuts.

Crushed butternuts and beechnuts for the bread. They would pound the corn fine, sift it, water it into a dough and pat it into little cakes and bake it on the hot ashes. Raccoon fat for butter or sometimes bear oil. Libby's father was a scholar of life in New England before the Puritans and Pilgrims arrived. He knew everything about weaving, arrowheads, sweat lodges and pottery, long before it was fashionable in the academic world. He worked for a museum instead of a university and felt bitterness all his life. His daughters were supposed to go to an Ivy League college and they did.

I was the well-read daughter of Libby's family maid. Often I had to be hidden with the intensity of our friendship concealed from others. Libby's older sister Eugenia didn't think it was a good idea for Libby to be so close to someone from a lower class. By a stroke of fortune, I was able to attend the same school as them. But I didn't go to the school dances in order to avoid being rejected by anyone, especially Libby who might be embarrassed by me. From our earliest days together, I felt that she had arrived first at every place we visited, that every situation belonged to her, and therefore that she deserved to have whatever she wanted at any given place. This is how deeply the feeling of being second sinks in. I had such a fear of taking exams and doing better than Libby could, I failed them all.

However, it was at Libby's house, before we graduated from high school, that I met the love of my life and could put my failure to good use. I was invited to a party, which included Eugenia and lots of her older friends, in order to celebrate Libby's admission to a top college. It was a day just warm enough to allow the party to spill out and over into their garden. My mother had left the house clean and another maid was there doing the food. I was humiliated at being the only girl we knew in school who was not going to college. But I believe I knew I would get my revenge later, through reading and bold living. Like Dorothea in Middlemarch I would learn the price of everything.

3-2

There are very few trustworthy men, many fewer trustworthy teachers, and even fewer holy people in this world. I've never met one outside of a baby or someone about to die. Why are some people born always wanting to be loved when it is so clear that few dare be wholehearted in love. The indifference of others, as well as oneself, should liberate every person to do as he or she pleases all the time. If I could really decide to make this my best year ever, would I know what choices to make—about my job first, since it determines my ability to live at all? No, because I have too much fear or too little desire. "We should all just try to be happy, which is very hard to do," Libby told me.

"Humans by now hate themselves," I murmured.

She looked at me with her eyebrows raised, lips pursed and then shot forward into an imitation of a laughing Buddha. Her narrow back was always held straight as if she had been trained as a dancer, and she folded her thin cold arms across her stomach pretending to be round and raucous. She was in that final saint-stage. She was bald. Her shirt was saffron colored to match her soul. She was a somewhat indigenous girl—Shawmut from Boston, you could place her in feathers on a green mountain facing the west, one leg resting on a stone. From the movies we learned that white outlaws ruled and exploited the Indians. There was however a happy twist to being a loser that qualified as a form of resistance. Otherwise, why did we side with them every time?

"Desiring true freedom, I surrender, I take refuge," is written in the Svetasvatara Upanishad. Libby Camp was my first friend and sister. Psychics have told me I was her mother in earlier lives. They have also told me I have been a mother enough times in earlier lives and now can move on to a new form . . . perhaps to become a nun in an ashram. Libby was the child of two white people. Her father's family, however, began in the New England forests. He interfered with Libby when she was prepubescent. I didn't know how bad it was because my intuitions about his evil kept me out of their house while my mother worked inside.

Libby had a horrible life. Alcohol, drugs, unhappy love affairs and an unrelenting quest for God who seemed to elude her even when she was dying because she was good enough to lack certainty. She had meditated dutifully for years. This discipline made it possible for her to receive without screams all the medieval torments of modern medicine—catheters, bags, chest and brain shunts, tubes down the nose and throat and IVs taped to bruised blood sites, hemorrhoids, enemas, etc. She sat tiny and brown and nutty in her face-making mood, the hospital comedian. Her resistance was always like this—a splitting and scattering of attributes. Together we pretended we were everyone else. For years she had talked solemnly about God but it was a dope-dream and now she admitted that she didn't ever know if God was "just an illusion." As you career into the void of your own being, you are bound to be scared, no matter how well you've prepared. Nietzsche was assigned the job of living this horror out for us all. "I love you, I love you" were the words Libby Camp uttered the most in her last weeks.

If a person arrives on earth for no reason at all, and no one really cares if she continues or not, then that person's adaptation to her body's irrelevence gives her courage. I think the creatures who are the least adapted to their own extinction are the ones who are most full of soul and beauty. Fear is their loveliest feature. Yes, I am sure that it was weakness, not fitness, that won the physical race to survive in this world. "You sound like an atheist," Tom said. I told him there was an atheist idea in me, alive and well, but you can't really be any kind of "ist" unless you are living out the terms of this idea in your daily life. Marxist, Thomist, feminist, existentialist, Christian or physicist . . . those are generally just thoughts parading as effective gestures.

Libby like Julian the Hospitaller had spent many dissolute years acting out the lamentable influences of her childhood. She drank till she was slumped. Got into weed, cocaine, heroin. After she gave much of her money to her dealer, she became a healer. Then she worked towards a degree in alternative medicine. The dainty dab of oil (rose, jasmine, honeysuckle) and her flare with clothes—deep colors in soft textiles, elfin pants and shoes, and only a ring on one thin finger and two little studs in her ears—drew people to her. Squeamish by nature, she learned to wash the shit off the butts of the elderly and give shots to AIDs patients, to massage the ugly and to stick acupuncture needles into the faces of the beautiful. Aquinas said that a person reflecting on certain choices is never closer to acting on a choice than he was before reflecting on them. Libby and I both knew that we had rarely made a choice in our lives; this may account for the forced lack of style in my prose, the absence of personality that I aspire to. I believe that Aquinas also implied that mental reflection is the ability to see what is not out there in relation to what is not in here. Nescience. No one is there.

Libby was a potentially plain and potentially good-looking person whose face and figure were mesmerizing because of the quick shifts in interpretation the observer was forced to make. Was she or was she not as pretty as she seemed to believe she was? She wasn't plain or pretty. She was plain and pretty. But why did it worry the observer? Her strong jaw, small straight teeth, smooth upper lip, hook nose, bright black eyes, short brow and small ears, the laugh-lines around her eyes and cheeks, could have added up to a classic witch's face. But they didn't. Instead, a volatility in her face made her adorable.

3-3

In the hall outside the apartment at 6 p.m. every evening there is a strong smell of cooking coming from one door: chicken, potatoes, never anything sweet, yet the smell is childish and comforting. Once I saw the elderly couple who live there entering with Christmas packages and they smiled kindly at me. They were exactly what I had hoped would live behind that door because they loved each other when they cooked for each other. If I eat anything, it is small and requires no chopping or grating. An oatmeal cookie and a cup of tea. Cheese on a thumb and a glass of wine. The occasional frozen dinner half-heated. I eat while I work and gaze to my left onto the river and the lights on it. I sometimes watch the news on television and a video I can rent in Central Square. Sometimes I see a show about Nature that treats animals like myths in the making; the programmers are getting us ready for this metamorphosis. The bumping in the closet is rhythmic at times, almost sexual, except for the humming that goes with it.

I listen from my bed while everything outside the bed grows cold. My children and I used to practically live in bed. We read and ate there on trays. Now I write in bed alone and read in bed but it is not my own writing but the writings by others that keep me from going insane.

3-4

Libby To Me:

Dear Henpecker:

When Oy found out that Oy had this thing, Oy vey! Oy was scared because it meant horse-piddles (hospitals). Our idea of hell? The woyst. And Oy wanted to go to altoynative medicine men asap. But the dox wouldn't let me. Said they were quax. Fux. Don't think I'm just trying to blame (bleem) boys again for everything bad, but Oy am still scared of them! (Remember when they whipped our legs?) Especially the official ones! I hate them. When are you coming (doyty woyd)? Hurry. Ach du lieber, Libby

Dear Heady Hopper:

You wouldnaw believe how bepressed I am to be so beset that everyone thinks I be de-dying The nice woman dr is the only one who gives me hope (ie continues to torture me). Where are you and why. You should know what sic people like. Someone they love sittin in a chair nearby, not sayin much. A gentle touch on the ravaged brow. Kind woyds. Some music but not too much. Gregorian or Gordian. Flowers, flowahs. They make me feel better. I never realized why they gave them to sick people. Now I do and will use them in my practice as soon as I am up and running. Except I am such a reck, rocked, racked, ruined, complete and total. (White flowers especially, roses and tulips.)
    Love, Libby

Dear Hen:

I did everything wrong in my life. Face it. I do. I screwed everything up. There are laws. Why didn't I obey them? There is such a thing as wisdom. I now realize, and it's too late. I screwed up out of pride. Now my children are lost and I have no one to take care of them, and I am alone. How did I screw up so badly? Why didn't my parents read the Bible to me? Moses was right! So was Jesus! Mohammed! Buddha! There are only three big things that count. Living with God, not judging other people and leaving something good behind. I didn't do any of those things. And now I'm scared. And when they said don't divorce or sleep around or steal or kill or commit adultery with a friend's husband, they were right too. I'm scared shitless. Literally, I can't shit. Dots come out. They're agony like torpedoes but dots. I fucked up. They're like burning coals. Royally. But I want another chance, God, help, come back. You've been gone six hours already. I'm in pain.

Dear H, I love you I love you I love you Dearest Darlingest Best First and Last

People dont believe it when someone is dying no matter how much they want to. They dont believe it any more than they really believe in God. I can see it so dearly because it's me not believing too. People come to see me and try to cheer me up, it's hoddible, they cant, because they hate themselves so much. People hate themselves. So then I make the pigeon face and the brisk walk nostril face and they laugh. I think maybe Jesus really believed that little girl was dying, and so he said Get up, Girl, and she did. If someone would just believe I was dying, and tell me what to do about it, the way he did, with practicality and love, I would get up and walk like that cripple in the cartoon who threw down his crutches when he saw the walk sign in traffic. Maybe if they just put signs around instead of coming to see me. Like "Jesus is coming instead today." Help. Sometimes I hate them all visiting and am BORED. I have to make conversation while they test their nerves by staring at the tubes coming out of my chest and butt. Pathetic. And now you're in the hospital too and cant come to see me. I hope you die on the same day I do and we can be buried together in Mount Auburn Cemetery under the willow tree. No, I dont. Live, live. Did you get the white flowers I sent you?

3-5

Libby who once loved reading Gandhi lay stark naked on her bed except for an orange half-slip in an apartment we shared. The doors were open and so were her eyes. She never knew how she got home that night. She was ashamed later and so I didn't tell her.

Kept silent from her that she had been dropped on the floor inside our door, had crawled stripping to her bed and when I looked out to see who had done that, it was her father the curator climbing into a waiting cab. Maybe she remembered and didn't want to tell me what had happened and she pretended she had blacked out and I pretended I had been sleeping when she got home. I lived out the rest of our friendship not knowing what she knew about that night. Her uncertainty about herself in the world was legitimized by my silence so I will be judged not by history but by God for that.

If you still desire a thing, its time has not yet come. And when you have what you desired, you will have no more desire, instead you will have time. Weak desires protect you from disappointment. But nothing keeps you safer than being a visible ruin.

3-6

Midwinter in New England makes me recoil, especially on those nights between Christmas and Epiphany when darkness is extended like a snake's shadow. In the building there is hardly any activity, except down in the boiler room where the superintendent spends his time. He is lean, white and around forty with a welcoming but anxious expression as if pride in his job and irritation at the existence of the people he is working for are engaged in parallel play.

He eagerly offered to fix things which he never fixed. He knew I came from people like his, because be was cousinly with me. When I left the building by turning left off the elevator and heading to the back streets, he was always in that little room with the radio on. The tenants were still away for Christmas and New Years, and only a few grandchildren came and went, using their grandparents' apartment for wild unsupervised parties. Grandparents often suffer from a morbid preoccupation with the safety of their grandchildren, then spoil them dangerously.

One day just before New Years there was an electrical shortage in the building and the superintendent had to take a flashlight and lead people in and out of their apartments. I arrived while he was busy with someone else, saw the elevator was out of order, and mounted the ever-darkening stairs to my floor. When I got there I had to take two turns which made the little light behind me weak then useless in the blackness that stretched ahead and over me. I wanted to persist, went forward wondering if this was what perishing felt like. The blackness became infused with its own form of gravity. I turned back. If all us people only had to adjust to a blackness like that, I suppose we would. Blindness for blind people is actually grayness. I held the wall until I saw the pale light at the top of the stairs. Having lived on the periphery of several wars and urban riots and having been the focus of personal violence, I feel that a devil is always just around the bend even while I am speeding up images of Jerusalem.

3-7

"Everyone has one idea of freedom that allows no one else to have another." When Libby sat across from me, her children rolling their heads to and fro on each knee, she was advocating a religious group with a guru whom she adored.

I could tell she had already smoked weed today because her rational faculties were not good. She couldn't even make a face or a joke. She droned and this was so unlike her, I believed she had fled her own body and been replaced by an alien. My kitchen was a mess. Neighborhood children were all over the house. My musical husband had gone to New Orleans. She needed shelter while she and her kids looked for a place to live.

My house was teeming with people. Two Africans, a West Indian and a white woman who smiled as if she had wind. And countless children. The house was built alongside Franklin Park at the end of the

19th century, purchased for twelve thousand dollars during the Deconstruction period when lots of us were renovating old wrecks.

We learned how to caulk, nail, paint, sand, shine with polyurethane, how to balance at the top of a ladder and clean up after ourselves. Libby was still carefully avoiding this kind of labor. Somehow she found her way into ready made living quarters with thick buffered carpets and shining bathrooms. While I grew sloppy and thick, she remained streamlined perfumed and light-fingered in her gestures. She made her living spaces into colorful new age lolling spaces with huge bright pillows flopped here and there and healthy plants in every corner and window. These were the leftover effects of her flying dreams, when she spread her arms and soared atop green mountains. The father of her children wanted to be rich and famous without working. He even tried movie-making and ended up running his father's billion-dollar real estate business. He was handsome and clever. He manipulated Libby and their kids in such a way that they believed they owed him something. Imagine if you were born a dollar bill the life you would have. Imagine if you were the thing that got the other thing, the thing equal only to the thing it got, the thing both held onto and quickly discarded.

Usually a person feels like the one who wants or the one who is wanted. One forgets to notice that one also feels like the thing that gets the thing that others want forgetting that one wanted that thing too.

After her stay with me, Libby's children's father gave them the apartment in New York, plus a new man to take care of them. None of them minded anything. They were all individuals, all free for that time, and imagined their liberty would last into infinity because their religion supported the notion of justification by fate alone. If you were born rich, you deserved it. He went away to make his fortune while she stayed behind with the new man, and was the casual caretaker of their children whom she loved. The new man was a drug dealer. We know our parts well, all of them individually, it is the whole we can't see or how our parts form an integrated contradiction. "The supreme Self is attained through the act of hankering. . . . This requires praying for its consummation before everything else." She gushed this to me and we both cracked up over the word hankering, laughing ourselves across the floors onto stacked pillows.

Libby was like a woman who wears skirts and no underpants because she lived in a state of protest that nobody noticed. She would on the one hand steal a little, he a little, and then she would also sneak away to meditate, her heart hankering.

3-8

Lewis on the sunbeam in late afternoon at age twenty was smiling widely. He was dressed in jeans, a tee-shirt, and a jeans jacket with some hippy embroidery sewed into the back. That sewing was another thing women did for their boyfriends then. I pretended to be a nice girl and learned how to sew too, in case it would make him love me later. ("There is," according to Lukacs, "no longer any spontaneous totality of being.") "What is that thing on your back?" I asked with a fake smile.

"A mandala but I know it looks like a flat tire."

"But you like to wear it. Why?"

"I have to wear it, or else."

"She would have a fit, if you didn't?"

"Almost. Almost."

"Is she here? Are you going to marry her?"

"In the kitchen," Lewis said, stretched and stood and pulled me by the hand like a sister. "There she is," he said pointing at a small wiry-haired girl with huge clothes and glasses and the giveaway slanting shoulder from carrying a book-bag to classes. In that arm she now held a motorcycle helmet. It was, I would later discover, his. He had ridden his bike east from his hometown in Missouri.

This girl would be the first in dozens I met over the years, all of them pointed out to me by a questioning Lewis. "Is she good enough? Am I?" She was a type that repeated though there were two other types too. All of them had skinniness in common, expensive shoes and dark hair. (Weight and shoes are the two giveaway signs for money.) But some were black, some Latino, some Jewish, a couple were Irish, and one was

Libby. Lewis never married. He grew decisive, influential, wealthy, instead marrying his work and remaining faithful to it. Girlfriends always stayed in touch long after they broke up with him.

The first time we met, Lewis drew me out the back door of the kitchen into the garden and asked me what I thought of his girl. Not much, I said sternly. Given the fact that I was a narrow stick, it was a pathetic response. The buds were pulsing in me from the cool wooden branches that spurted pink. A spray of forsythia gilded the picket fence at the end of the lawn and crocuses broke melting ice clusters dimpled and dirty. The grass crackled and squished. "Where are you from?" I asked.

"Post-Bellum, Missouri."

"What? Po Belly what?"

"No, no. Missouri. Not misery," he said. "Sort of. Everywhere is beautiful in spring. Everywhere."

And he began jumping as high as he could to bat at a dogwood branch that was dangling as if under weighty ice. He jumped and jumped while I watched like a fan. "My family came up there after the Civil War," he said, "and settled on a small farm." He had a gravelly voice with hard R's from living out there.

"How many?"

"Well, now I have my parents, an aunt and my brother. They're still there."

"Do they miss you?"

"Of course, but my father has his work."

"What kind?"

"Intellectual. We're middle class, in case you're wondering. Not poor. Do you live here?"

"I live nearby, in an apartment."

"Going to Radcliffe like your friend Libby?"

"No, I'm not going to any college. All I want to do is go to the movies."

"Seriously?"

"Until I can make them myself. I love movies."

"Well, you better start learning now. Soon, before you get too old to learn anything new, the way people do."

"I wonder how to begin."

"I know someone who might be good," he said and called back on his way inside. "I'll introduce you. I'll help you. I'll help you." I didn't follow in case he might guess that I was going to dog him for the rest of my life.

3-13

The Lewis-and-Libby love affair was a secret from me while it was happening but I received a full account soon after and realized that I was making a study of the anatomy of a cemetery while they were making out. Mount Auburn Cemetery was founded in 1831, the first in the Rural Cemetery Movement in America. Here the idea of a flowery and manicured graveyard (a garden) led to the reinvention of American parks. The act of creating little Edens in the midst of industry and commerce was in fact an act of lyrical resistance. As with all long-lasting resistance movements, it began in love. In this case, love of flowers. It was autumn when I was there and all that was left in bloom was Chinese sumac, a few old chrysanthemums and witch hazel. But never did a place look more like a 19th century engraving with dots of descending tints and a distant view of hills and a city. The landscape consists of a series of hillocks and ponds, ups and downs, showering shrubbery and clean-cut grass. In October I was studying the Northwest corner, from the Asa Gray Garden down Spruce Street to Crocus, Vesper, Western, and Mayflower Path. Bigelow Chapel including the crematorium was very busy all year. I remember that day there was a large party of bereaved African Americans outside, milling around the statue of the Sphinx—a statue built to commemorate the preservation of the Union after the Civil War and the destruction of African slavery. Everyone there, I could see, was unaware of the existence of this statue and stood around examining it in astonishment.

Meanwhile in New York Libby and Lewis were strolling around Central Park, near the museum, not yet touching but bumping against each other excitedly. Fewer leaves had fallen there. The day was gold and warm and crowds speeded around them on a variety of wheels and even horses. Jogging had not yet been discovered by the public. The Cold War was over. All four assassinations had recently been accomplished and the country was, unknown to its citizens, moving towards a rightwing takeover, which would climax in a violation of the Constitution, bombings of other countries, and the establishment of military alliances with dictators.

For me that day—marble, bronze, slate and Roxbury pudding-stone—sculptures that epitomized the late Romantic idealism that we associate with nationalism and a sentimental view of Christianity—and for Libby and Lewis—pulsing glands, quickened heartbeat, heat in groin and palm, the ache to reach each other's breath and find the taste of existence, etcetera.

The city's business banged on around them and from what I was told, they tried to ignore the magnetic pull between their bodies. They tried because of me. My presence between them was an embarrassment. It must have been like the Triumph of Chastity where veils are whirled from the two hands of an innocent woman through shadows warding off lust. Or as if Lewis and I had had years of humiliatingly great sex together, sex that had brought each other as low and as high as you can go and the spirit of these contacts hung over the two of them. In any case there was a brief resistance and then they rushed back to Libby's place. Later she reported that he was "not that good" and offered to describe it all to me in detail but I said no. They had several more encounters in upcoming weeks trying to justify the first one until finally they stopped, blaming their sexual failure on the ghost of my interest looming between them. But I knew that they simply lacked the lapping fire that one cannot arouse for just anyone.

I was writing my essay on the cemetery and having a romantic friendship with a much-older man. He was famous and so was his wife. I was his secret though not his lover and Libby told me about her affair with Lewis only when she believed that I was safely involved otherwise. She always confused fame with security. "You won't mind if I slept with Lewis?"

"No. You deserve him. You were there first."

A pittance is a meal that a monk eats. I lost my appetite and a decision was made. I would give away everything I loved after that.

Sewing Wings for Swans

4-1

Tom is reading theology in the bathroom at the border place we call the hermitage, the compound, the pile of sticks, the ashram, etc. Palm leaves like overturned baskets hide us from the daylight The fire is up, the rain is guttering down the windows, there is a crackerish smell of binding and old carpeting. I am tidying up happy to be a servant to objects. Outside there is the garden sunk in California's winter rains. We are not far from the border where helicopters buzz over the canyons snooping out aliens. Sometimes the officers think they see UFO's after midnight when they look up from their spotlights in the canyons. Tom knows about life in the canyons around us—from the prisoner he visits at the jail lounge: Gemma with the beautiful son—and we often bring food and clothing to those hiding out close to the border.

Today there is no buzzing or hunting, so the rain brings emotional relief. Each part of the compound is raised on stilts to avoid succumbing to mudslides. It consists of five small houses and one larger communal house, and one toilet, all connected by wooden hallways raised up from the sand.

"Where were you during the riots in Attica?" Tom asks me over flushing water.

"Not far from here actually."

"Were you aware politically?" he asked me. "Yes, I'd say I was."

"So what did the riots mean to you?" he wondered.

"Criminals are potential revolutionaries."

"Were you upset to learn this?" he asks stupidly.

"I was happy to learn it."

"You must have been really young." "Around twenty. When George Jackson was murdered." "Why weren't you in college?" he wanted to know.

"I didn't get into any. I was a bad student. I acted up. Joked around. They wouldn't recommend me to anywhere and all my friends went to good places."

"I was twenty two when Bobby was shot," he tells me.

"Where?"

"Boston, of course. All those murders helped drive me to law school."

Tom continues reading then while I continue dusting the bookshelves. His curls are dust-colored, tight, grayish and his large brown eyes are marked by thick almost demonically pointing eyebrows. He has a soft sensual mouth that stiffens when he reads, and his face is swarthy in complexion. He is quite hairy. He hates his body and his looks though he is very handsome to me.

Now he reads to me from Novalis with a question in his voice: "Destiny and the soul are twin names for a single concept. Do you think that's true?"

"No," I say, "although both are equally blind."

What is between us is nothing. There is nothing between us. Nothing is love, because if you add anything to zero, it becomes a word. The air is thin for us but it is as if we each had two little darts lodged in our flesh in exactly the same spot and they moved in relation to each other like charged needles that seek a thread.

Gold is not here to be used as a color because it is in every color already. In fact Florensky wrote, "Gold is pointless . . . It is not a color but a tone." I think everything is always an open secret the way the gold on objects is constant and unremarked. Light manifests what is alive in the dark. Some people in the world believe that they can manifest new forms out of their imagination; but there are no new forms where all the materials are the same.

Meditate on the difference between the Important and the Essential, I have heard, and you will learn something secret.

A form cannot be recognized unless its image already exists in the body that discovers it. This is an idea as old as bodies themselves.

Indivisible

The musician Messaien said, "It's extraordinary to think that the Hindus were the first to point out and use, rhythmically and musically, this principle of nonretrogradation that is so frequently encountered around us. . . . We carry these rhythms in ourselves: our face with its two symmetrical eyes, two symmetrical ears, and nose in the middle; our opposite hands with their opposed thumbs; our two arms, and the thorax in the middle; the tree of our nervous system with all its symmetrical branchings. These are nonretrogradable rhythms."

Other musicians like birds break off from the goal-oriented sounds of traditional music, and eliminate the usual structures, creating a sound pattern made out of parameters and crossings, rather than predictable sequences.

4-2

Some people use the word affliction when they mean infliction. They think that making other people suffer is painful to them because someone else made them suffer first. Libby never blamed her life on her father interfering with her but she wished she was not the drunk that her mother was. She experienced her addictions not as afflictions but as weeds that grow in certain gardens wild. No matter how you tugged and pulled, you couldn't ever get them all out of the ground. We wandered the streets together looking for Lewis to feed my passion with glances and surmising. Sometimes we found him and he talked to us. He was debonair even when he was selling encyclopedias door to door. Spring enveloped those last weeks of high school making studies impossible. Our desires were not yet as sexual as they were emotional, like reverse orgasms or what we called Melancholia which was really a pre-coital whine.

Libby necked with a variety of boys but didn't love anyone the way I did Lewis, until the romance was over. She, like Lewis, always believed that someone better than the person she had would come along.

"Why should you want to be a single individual once you have realized that you are everything already?" wondered the Hindu mystic Sankara.

4-3

A tree with pretty rubbery leaves is planted outside the kitchen that Tom calls the refectory. The rain is pulling at its thick roots. The rain is almost without air. Solid water flooding ground that is usually as smooth as a plastic cover. Now erosion produces layers of miniscule particles of earth, claylike that mush apart in the contact with water. He is playing Hildegaard's Canticles, the women sing over the rain.

"Hey, do we have anything to eat? We won't be able to get into town," he worries.

"I'll look but I think I can do something with some rice that's there."

Now he will ask if I need help and I will say no I'm fine. We are like birds with our words; they come out as calls rather than conversation.

The kitchen we painted is a plywood box on cement blocks. Here is a big wooden table, there some shelves and chairs. A fridge, stove, sink, and crockery that looks rustic but is store-bought, in other words cheap. The windowpanes seem to be melting against the rain. I watch him hurry back to the library in his slicker—a slippery gray figure like a dolphin, and the silence without him in it is whitish. I find rice, canned tomatoes, spices, limp greens that will wash awake, red wine, green cheese. The light outside seems to dilate and contract, the way I imagine the whole cosmos does, the way the lights in movies do before they go dark. I keep thinking the night part is weakening to let more light through but no. The rain will not stop before the night. We eat in silence after he says a perfunctory grace which changes the nature of eating anyway. I feel grateful for the food and the hour. I keep my eyes on the rushing water on the window panes, his eyes are facing his plate, one hairy hand up to his temple where a vein pulses like the throat of a small bird. I wonder why I got old before I was able to love a stranger and if I would have the courage to convert before I died. Then I wonder if he has had enough to eat and tell him there is more. He gets more and begins to talk now in a rush the way people on airplanes burst out of silence with the arrival of their plastic trays. There is nothing I think sadder than the clink of forks and knives on cheap crockery coming from unseen people eating.

We have often had this particular exchange about climate and land-scape and why we both feel so lonely here uprooted. It was what each of us had wanted of course.

Besides wanting to experience a place we hated, we wanted to be in-somniacs and loners, losers and drop-outs. To know the sky was the only location of meaning and joy left to us. Also I wanted to decide if I should assume the care of the blind child or not, when what I really desired was a life of seclusion. I was gladdened by the exit out the backside of the brick building onto small snowy streets when it came time for me to be in the present.

4-4

My mother, the maid, called herself a "Roosevelt man" until Truman dropped the H-bomb. Then it was clear to her that even liberals can do wrong. She was smart but split. She had the pretensions and airs of a 19th century European procurer, pandering to her employers, then de-spising them as soon as she was out the door. It's already hard enough to love and judge a person simultaneously, without pretending to love and to judge them.

I asked her: "Mother, how do we prove ourselves worthy of love?"

The daylight on whiteness was a mother's slap to me. It jolted my eyes into their sockets, my limbs lurched forward and a snap hit my skin, my cheeks. Little wooden houses huddled away from the brick. Now I was nearly in the commercial zone. A deli came first then an expensive wooden furniture designer. Dread leveled what little happiness had not already drained away after a few paces.

This was an automatic response to entering a public space that was also the site of childhood. Soon people would see me. I don't guess why no one else I know seems to carry this burden of embarrassment. My friends have always hidden me away respectfully. They have helped me to live obscurely as if they could, in doing so, preserve a secret reserve in themselves. Lewis told me to do one thing in the world which was good for other people and which had nothing to do with making money or friendship. He admired philanthropists for instance. He wanted me to sacrifice myself and not wait for someone else to do it for me. Lewis was someone who believed that artists know exactly what they are doing while they are doing it and we fought about this. All artists—painters, poets, playwrights, musicians—were discussed by him in terms of an idea they were trying to express, not in terms of a physical problem they were working through. "I think artists are like blind children on a new campus . . . More than most people, they trust what they don't know," I told him in the dark of the car and got no answer.

A white sofa, shined wooden floor, a white counter top, wooden stools, a white table shoved against the wall beside a window looking out to the river. When the sun is high and wavy these brick wings can be gloomy. The shade between them is like a hat's shadow creating a sense of selfhood and mystery. When I look out around two I feel like a child who has to go to school and hates it. Every gesture is directed at the air: "Please bring me happiness!"

4-5

In this dream Libby was like someone who had been stretched on a rack, her bones broken and folded. Thin and brown and dressed in orange, she was still making her way around on her own. A chimpanzee was doing the same, long-armed and easy, he entered and departed the small ancient spaces of this dream. A mailman wouldn't give me the large envelope addressed to both of us, green and winking its joke: "You've Won A Million Dollars" until I was near tears from wanting that money. It looked as if she had left me something. Some mark, after all, of our being best friends. A joint bank account in the afterlife. If this was India, they didn't say so but I felt Home at last!

When we were children we wanted to swing through trees so we went on our way home from school to the cemetery down near the plot where Mary Baker Eddy was buried. We took turns hurling ourselves forward on a willow branch, hanging on tight over a tepid froggy pond where the waters of the dead flowed up from under.

And now a chimp sat with us even on my lap eating stonewheat crackers but saying nothing. I wanted to ask him if he had been the cause of AIDS. They all said it began with monkeys in Africa. But they always exoticized diseases. The chimp was as wiggly as a toddler and Libby was sorting out her clothes with her last energies. She had lots of clothes. Salted porridge with brown sugar or maple syrup, and a cup of tea with cream and honey in it. Buddha gurgling or was it the fountain and the impatiens adding color but no life to the flower beds. On film the snow came down in wet cottony lumps and stuck. It was about the night we three walked up a hill outside my house, and the stars fell around us in a cone, and although Lewis was invisible, he was the only one we could really see. And he in turn saw into the future. He called out: "We thought we were invisible, but ah, oh no, they will find us out!"

4-6

I had begun to structure myself piece by piece in my father's form. To stay close to his image, to keep myself sane by emulating him. I pretended I was him—a man of poetry, war and honor. I was only five when he died and I had photos on top of the early memories. He had sent me seven little notes about the trees and birds in Korea, about beauty and revolution. He seemed to know he would die and wanted to teach me something of his mind. Sometimes it occurred to me that he might have gone AWOL, and not died at all, because he wanted to be rid of my mother who was a job. All jobs are tests and he brooded over me, year to year, like an angel with an inkless pen.

Lewis, like my mother, was a lapsed Catholic. She said proudly that she had even refused to baptize me. Lewis had left his interest in law behind as soon as he had a degree in it. He was now, like my father, a journalist committed to undermining almost all governments and famous people.

The sun begins in the night and ends in the middle of my head. It sets down my spine. As for the moon it always seems to float unscientifically wherever it wishes like a paper plate on water, upside down is so flat and

495

light it drifts without law. When the Anchorites in the first centuries after Christ went to the desert, they went looking for a father who had become pneumetaphoros. When they found him they all lived together. In such a community a person could study human behavior; contemplate God and learn scholarly matters in a peaceful and fruitful environment. Community, rule and abbot were and remain the three consistent features of such a life. The rules are: obedience, conversion of life and stability.

I told Lewis about Tom and he showed a brief interest in ashrams and skeets and spent a half hour lecturing me on the moral dimensions of a life spent in retreat. Mad or bad, busy or lazy. He in his wheelchair and me on the edge of my seat, pressed across my elbows on the table on alert for any sign from him—that he might after all admire me in return. But Lewis was someone who couldn't even utter the word "love" instead emitting subtle signs of affection through his eyes which didn't know what they were shining. Chicken, sushi, beer and Saki, hailstones ticking on the cars and tar outside. "Look, if you want to find the meaning of life, all you have to do is read the 4th chapter of Bambi, the 12th chapter of the Gita, and go see La Strada again. . . . Bambi, The Baghavadgita, La Strada." That was it. The mention of a movie set us off, our shared passion, what we had seen, what we wanted to see, what we thought of this actor and the way a thing was filmed. "Take the trees, the way John Ford films them, out in the west . . ." I was speechless in his presence although I was speaking, always pretending to be a bundle of joy but stuttering the way it was with teachers when they asked me for an answer. Articulation, reserved for my children and rages against my husband, failed face to face with others.

This way he could talk freely about himself and project and interject a few observations about and at me. My silence gave him the liberty to say all he needed to about the difficulties of his life as a tyrant. As if I didn't know it! The gunshot, people said, had taken away his desire along with his mobility. Still he continued to write articles and produce films and do much of his work stark naked in bed with a woman wishing around the edges. These women believed he couldn't have sex at all and they said they didn't mind.

Indivisible

"What a laugh," said Lewis. "When you have phony relationships, you watch the misunderstandings develop and you get bored with them, indifferent and fucking up visually, for the fun of it. Not the fun. Not the fun. The interest. To have some. I can see the girls around me getting incredibly agitated, as if I was a dog on a bed. Each one thinks she is going to be the one to turn me back into a man, or to find out, once and for all, if I am impotent. It brings out the sadist in me. I like to watch them flounder. That girl Irene's friend Susanna I think is her name . . ."

What his purpose was, in telling me all this—I now understand—was his mother's absolution. He had always had the feeling that I was a stand-in for her, and could praise him back to sanity just because I never did. And his now round face swelled into a grimace intended to be a grin. Lewis had grabbed and held me many times, stuck his hand inside my safety belt and squeezed, jammed me against the car door while standing to fall inside and had held me there breathing into my hair. The night trees flashed past a figure going forward at the same rate that they moved backwards. Transmigration of souls is about leaving one form of being behind for another while reincarnation means renewing a former state. Enforced transmigration follows a spinal injury, among other kinds, when a person is smashed into a new form. Or maybe it was still him but more. A bigger boss than ever, a smarter thinker, and a deeper feeler. He gave presents to those whose time he had abused. Little things like boxes and pins. To keep me in his pocket for life, he paid no attention to me or anything I did. His hand would idly twirl me around and then drop apart and reenter the world at large. The laughing boy had become a detached man. "All that is personal soon rots; it must be packed in ice or salt," are the words Yeats gave to it.

Before the shot Lewis had been bold, traveling the globe's trouble-spots as a front-line journalist, hanging from the masts of oil tankers in the middle east, squatting in tunnels with terrorists, starving with revolutionary armies in Africa, being shot at and missed. He had no interest in the west, only in developing countries, and sometimes as one of the few black American journalists he was asked to negotiate with political leaders. America made use of his America-hatred whenever necessary.

To describe him as far-left would not do the complexity of his thinking justice. Ingenuity, synthesis, amorality and conscience.

He had a fatal awareness of contingencies.

The Hindu Orange of the Fruit

5-1

The ground is brown but I am seeing it grow green under the heavy rain. There is the smell of Darjeeling. Large-grained brown sugar in a dish, cereal, syrup, candy, a few shriveled tangerines. We can't drive down the muddy road again to get food. The floods might wash us right into a canyon. Mud gluts our shoes when we trudge to the refectory. The snakes must be buttoning up their bellies at the speed of the mud. It is spring and they are babies. We stand together at the same window wondering. Tom has been ignoring the violence of the weather as if by dispelling it from his consciousness, it would depart the world. But now I see why. He is afraid that the unexpected will shake his belief in the power of the spirit. My loneliness breaks out of me like a beak inside a shell—it cracks and fills me while he bites his nails and his throat grows tight. "What's going to happen?" one of my children used to ask again and again when we went out walking. This question is written all over Tom facing the window.

Ramakrishna said: "I used to perform sadhanas in the Panchavati. A tulsi tree grove grew up there. I used to sit in it and meditate. Sometimes I would become very anxious and cry, Ma! Ma! or I would cry, Rama! Rama! When I used to cry, Rama! Rama! I would wear a tail and sit down in the attitude of Hanuman. I was crazy. At that time, while I performed the worship I would wear silk garments and would experience bliss."

"Why don't you meditate and think about Ramakrishna under the tulsi tree?" I suggest to Tom like a mother. Obediently he sits in the armchair, hands on knees, eyes closed, while I stay at the window watching the moving coat of water on the windowpane. A shimmering silver jelly. But the sky is lighter now.

Indivisible

One of the secret vocations—to be a monk. I wonder why so many know so little about this calling and so lose the chance of a lifetime. To be an old-fashioned closeted gay would be in so many cases the vital ingredients for this life of retreat, ritual, art and prayer. (Was Tom gay? I didn't dare ask!) Or to be Blake instead for whom self-annihilation without celibacy was the goal. His work was his obscurity. You can actually work in opposition to fame. Between the seer and the seen—a blinding stillness. A light cold white line on salt water is the world's resting point.

Recollection is for those incapable of meditation. It is the gathering up of all loose bits of memories and compressing them into an image the size of an eye.

5-2

Seen from inside my camera a young woman sleeping forms a slovenly image. The lights have gone out after an earthquake downstairs. The bed has rolled away from the wall and her dog has returned home, unfed, for cold manicotti, shivering. However it is not my foster daughter but a stranger sleeping there. To wake her is only to feel a terrible rage at this intrusion even after a natural disaster. I push her physically out the door to her car that has been in an accident. I can't bear to watch her drive away, run inside to plug in the electric phone upstairs to see how my twin son is and a woman on the line is wanting me to edit her natural daughter's film for her application to film school. She has been impressed by one review of my work, the only one. Again I am furious saying yes but how difficult this will be and hang up in her face, two of my short-term foster children watching me over their books. The lights are still shining on my script.

Upstairs in my old big house, there was lots of dust on top of useless mementoes including clothes from Nepal, Greece, stones from Patmos and Dublin, religious kitsch from Libby and Tom and the children. Bay shells from Rosarito and South Beaches, all undusted all unlooked-at, all given to me as the one who never gets to go away. Dust is pure—a snow that doesn't melt.

The strange girl is so slow to wake, sunk so deep into her waiting that it is a numbness. Shaking her doesn't help. She is pretty-lipped but not the Libby I want to see. If she had just had no hair on her head and a wider mouth, glinting eyes and a hook nose, she would have been the person my camera was expecting. Raising other people's children can make all people seem interchangeable as companions and you will take anyone who comes along to fill in the scene, the time. You see a floppy head of hair coming and think It's him! but it's someone who is almost him and for a flash you think I don't mind. I'll go with this one instead. This is detachment. Once I was surprised to realize that all individuals contain the same ingredients: "whoever this is."

Finally the day came, ten years after the promise was made, when Lewis introduced me to the person who would help me work with film. Irene was fat and famous among serious filmwatchers, a middle-aged beauty with creamy skin and huge hippy clothes slipping from her soft shoulders. Her fatness was delicious but few wanted to face the fact that heaps of skin can often be divine and seductive, torrents of loose and lickable substance bundling up the bones. I am always a mother but she was always a mother to me. She let me sit in while she edited for several weeks and then I could do it myself, and did. I edited for money and spent twenty years making one film and twenty five dream-videos for love. I want to see. To see so clearly that personality is of no account. Gestures that glide upward—where is their gravity. A child's spit viewed through a child's microscope was my inspiration. It led directly to the smearglass of galaxies and the most perfect sentence of all: "My soul magnifies the Lord."

5-3

Down in the boiler room the superintendent is listening to Senate Hearings and eating a gourmet sandwich from Darwin's Deli. The sandwich—brown bread, avocado, cheese and bean sprouts is the best he has ever had in his life, and happily he asks if he can help me. I wonder if there is a laundry room in the building. He directs me to the basement, picks his teeth and asks me how long we plan to stay. We have a year's lease, I tell him. Uh huh. How many people? Just two. He makes a lot of noise. Which number are you? 405. Mm. If he asks my last name, he will think I am a Catholic. I am so aware of people hating Catholics as much as Charlotte Brontë did that I want to be one even more. The same people who practice Buddhism and admire Tibetan monks make fun of a Catholic's habits. Many Protestants have become other religions these days and have brought to their practice much of the Puritan mentality of their forebears. They fuss over details and believe that clear accounts will add up to a better life. Antinomian, empirical, intelligent, self-sacrificing and rule-bound. I admire their discipline but I prefer the way Catholicism is a load of contradictions. Now the rain is letting up and a soft blue light is sifting through the flannely clouds. Gullies of water gurgle down the canyons and birds sing. I feel dread. The opening up of light and sky, the return of the responsibility that the empty air brings, horrifies me. Since God has abandoned the world, it is time who is left watching over us. Time is the spirit who breathes into the world. When it was raining, water was like an apology. The super doesn't ask me anything more.

5-4

The way the arms of the oak bounce reminds me of Siva beckoning and laughing. I think maybe Hinduism will guide us through the dead wood of Christianity and into fresh new greens. I was an existentialist, then I noticed how words could make things happy again. Many of the most lost people used the loveliest language in order to laugh. No hospitals but deranged and homeless movement from house to house, city to city, phone booth to public toilet. No college for them! This was how Mc-Cool found me watching him himself more insane, more poor, more lost than some others. All of these qualities mashed my worries. Rolled them aside like trash. McCool was all feeling and fast-talking. He combined several of the aspects of God that we dread (i.e. Satan's), the ones that allow children to compete, produce wars, massacres, infidelities, that allow sea-elephants to stop evolving and insects to remain machines. We met in a pub at a sing-along. Nobody cared I was there. They thought I was just a 21 year old hat check girl with a needle and thread, and I was. Some beings see the world as a palace. Some see it as a marketplace. Some see the future as a malign region. Others wait for something wonderful to arrive before they die. I always carried a sewing basket to work.

If you think you need to fly into outer space for a surprise, just go and look at some spider monkeys, a hippopotamus, an aquarium where there are fish with eyes in their spines, four mouths and no way in. They are like a secret code that unlocks a public event. My body continues to puke and yearn, withdraw, hesitate and jump out of danger. Is resting the goal of lusting? Virginia Woolf had wanted a steel body to clasp all the fluttery parts of her mind in an embrace. This became her butterfly aesthetic.

I have to keep moving my bones through hardship and ignore the obstacles. It is a kind of machete approach to the day. If I can recollect happiness, and I can, it is usually thanks to artists like God who made nature and Rossellini. Buddhists on the contrary are calm and don't cry for succor (Ravish me, God, please don't leave me alone.) Between a Buddha and a Buddha there is a bowing couple. An economy that proves equality. My kind of prayer is the prayer of a sucker who pleads for one smile from a face that is turned away from her.

McCool always looked me right in the eye accusingly.

Parents usually name a baby before it is born in order to reserve it a space in the angelic tablets. When you pray for a person the man said you must use their name, just as panelists on television must address each other by name so the camera will know where to turn. Wanting only one person to turn in my direction or to call me by my name or to see my films with my name written at the end, I would take a fake name cheerfully and hide the real one.

We married each other in an eccentric living room ceremony wanting to be saved by the words that the Unitarian read from Scripture. They were traditional wedding words. McCool wrote music and called me by his real name, when we got married, it began with a Q my favorite letter. Question, Quest, Quidam and Queer. It felt good having a Q there. It compressed my fragmented alphabet of a name into one letter. Put a magnet in the center and sucked the others in. Like the child of a drunk, I listened too acutely to the shifts in McCool's enunciation, not looking for a slur, but for an Irishness that would make me quiver with pleasure. His Irish accent came and went in strength. It was like losing signals from my father in outer space. When the accent was weak, I felt less safe. After all, he was infertile, so I was too. I had the foster babies instead—twins in one year, then one more one year after. Ruled them and played with them. "You have attained existence through my body" was never to be my experience. A Buddha can have thousands of eyes but God has arranged things so that eyes are dispersed equally among ordinary creatures.

Children's eyes followed me trustfully everywhere while McCool's were filled with suspicion and hate. "Who left this magazine here?" he might ask threateningly.

"I don't know."

"Yes you do. Who?"

"Oh it might have been Father Julio."

"Liar," he laughed.

"He came here for you too."

"I bet. I'll go look for him."

Julio Dumas was a parish priest who practiced Yoga and read Hindu scripture. We knew him very briefly, a small man with a starving face—that is, a face that seemed to be fleeing starvation, he rushed through our lives like a coke-head, at full speed.

McCool liked him and considered him a true revolutionary—that is, someone who lived out his beliefs. Ironically he was sure that a priest wouldn't sleep with a woman especially me. He went to find and have a drink with him but soon he was suspicious of something else.

My husband hated most people, including me. Strangely, he didn't realize it was his hatred that hated me. He thought it was all kinds of other things that were the problem with me. He was handsome for one thing, and couldn't understand how he could be married to one ordinary person.

He was gifted, a musician, and charming, and very smart, and so how could he only have one person at home to listen to him. I was an awkward woman so why was he bothering to be jealous of me unless there was something I was really doing bad to him. Julio politely said, "He just doesn't appreciate you." This priest was reticent and miserable, having come from the Seychelles into our drab slum parish. He had an international perspective, my husband would say. He was shocked that poor people in America said they were poor, himself having been in Tanzania and Bangladesh. When he left he didn't even say goodbye, only one more sign of his detachment. I felt a mission in him that was inspired by interfaith. He was one of the old school of heroic tormented priests who live in poor communities; who are tolerant, ironic and solitary. His father had been a priest too, and his brother Hugo had emigrated to this country and disappeared.

He might have said: "Beings are numberless, I vow to save them. Desires are inexhaustible, I vow to end them."

Years later—when we were friends—I told Tom about Julio Dumas as if trying to shame him by the example of this perfect priest.

He cried out: "Julio Dumas? But he was the father of Gemma's child." We both fell against the wall simultaneously.

Buddhism says, "In all things there is neither male nor female." And Jesus too said sex was meaningless in the kingdom of heaven. You can build around a space, but not build the space itself. A black hole is a spiral that rotates and drags stuff into it, it may be the home of ghosts, the goblet that drinks the drinker or the cone where God changes its mind and pulls everything back in again. If the universe is swelling and contracting, it sounds like a woman to me.

Gray winter branches scratch glass till it sings. My husband meantime played guitar and penny whistle and sang traditional songs. He had once been close to the Clancy Brothers and their friends in New York. Blue eyed and black haired, he spoke in rushes of free association linking local politics with Dante, a city sewage system with Pilgrim's Progress, and Weil with Virgil. He had managed to create a new identity for himself and a new passport and with the US Savings bonds I inherited from my father at age twenty one, we bought our cheap house.

He got along well with everyone who had a particular political take on the international situation; he was paranoid and idealistic at the same time which is a difficulty. There was lots of sitting around yelling. News items cited and columns and men. Theirs was a closed masculine system which grasped contradiction but never found a way to transform it into paradox because that would have been too complete a solution. To solve a world problem was frightening to them, for resolution had something of death in it, the death of their own perplexity and excuses. He said he was orphaned in County Carlow and raised by brutal and intelligent Brothers of the Holy Cross. He was distraught at his own infertility and often insisted it was my fault, and swore if he was just with someone else. . . . He wanted the children raised Catholic in order that they establish an identity with him, even though he called himself lapsed. He wanted to make tons of money fast, yet he had contempt for the new rich. Instead he appreciated the sagacity of the longtime wealthy. He was verbally violent towards most corrupt politicians except those corrupt politicians who had his interests at heart. If only he had known what his interests were! His confusion was his downfall. It was 1968 and the students were rioting. My husband was no fool but he was a coward. He got things wrong almost every time in order to steer clear of commitments. Yet simultaneously he was almost always right about other people's weaknesses and temptations. He was a great supporter of women's liberation and especially of women having children, taking care of them and working to support everyone all at the same time. He pinched the children's cheeks, gave me my orders for the day and left the house with a bang. My relief at his departure was the key to the paradox: I would do any amount of slave-work in order to be free.

5-5

The superintendent says: "I knew a family with your name in Dorchester. Any relation?"

"I don't know, there are so many."

"The Irish in Boston are pigs," he said. "I'm Italian. They kill you if you go in one of their Shamrock bars and shit. Gotta be Irish to be safe going inside one of them."

"I know."

"I know you know. The ones in Ireland I hear are different."

"You mean the Irish?"

"What happens to people when they cross the water?" he asked me.

"They become American. Half of them think America is an empire, the other half think it's a republic. But since all are American, there is no unity."

He threw a brown bag in the wastebasket and remarked: "Though I have to say, the Italians stayed pretty much the same low-life fools they always were. With the exception of Martin Scorsese . . . Imagine if you were black what people would do to you in this city."

I walked along the riverside, cars beating by, and reflections like fish in dresses were sequined on the water top. Dusk, lights, more colors than seemed possible were dotted on the screen, de-iced since sun had returned. I strolled over the walkbridge to the other side of the water and paralleled my path back northwest. The brick building did not reflect, but held its shape into itself. Some crows' raw cries split the air inside the trees. Not far ahead was the cemetery settling down for the night. An oblate is buried in a cowl but my mother was cremated in a cardboard box. Sometimes I thought I heard her banging to get out, but it was probably the Bumper (as Julio dubbed him) inside the apartment with me.

5-6

I can't explain myself God. It is as if my camera, my film and even a screen are reeling me in to my story and no one is operating them. A horse gallops down an oncoming road that is severed by a river. Oncoming into my head, that is. The road is white and bony like the streets in Antonioni's The Passenger. No leaves blow in the holy land but the horse's hooves turn up sheets of dust and a thick nearly creamy substance like the arms and bosom of my film teacher, Irene. I decide to stay paralyzed and accept the arrival of the horse's rider who will seize me without love. I forgot: Never any erotic love as long as I seek God. But it pounds past and I am dusted into a soft substance aghast at nearly dying when the body is everything and everything is a body.

Lewis helped me make my big film that I called The Mansion of Fun based on some writings by Ramakrishna. It was an orange film that used a variety of devices for voice-over to quote his teachings. Our actor had once acted as a child for Sarajayit Ray but was now an aging man. He sat at a table in a circle of small orange bonfires, flowers, fruit and smoke, reading into a series of voice machines, then playing them back. He was a very disciplined man, but he believed that the text was written for him. About two thirds of the way through the film, he danced off the set and wasn't seen again. Luckily Lewis with his camcorder captured the whole affair backstage and followed the man weaving off down the snowy streets. We couldn't have had a more appropriate conclusion to the bewildering messages of the film. Ramakrishna was a saint who liked to dress up as a woman or pretend to be Hanuman the monkey. He laughed at his own jokes and experienced raptures that others witnessed. Boys loved him.

They say when you wake up to Brahman, you wake up with the revelation that you are already blessed and the way you know this is that you don't need a witness to know it.

The film gave me more time alone with Lewis than I had ever had or ever would again.

"That which cannot be seen by the eye, that is the Self indeed. This Self is not someone other than you." Someone invisible is more emotional than someone who can be seen. A camera has its own eyes too that are borrowed from a self who lights its way through the lens, and what it has seen is turned around on the screen, and looks back at the eyes that saw it first, but as if it is looking for its origins.

You can write you are a Catholic and look in the mirror and really it is a Jew who looks back at you. These experiences are hard to manifest in images.

A man named Kosta helped us with the editing of my film. He was critical of every decision I made. He was an unknown filmmaker and his bitterness was a trouble to me.

First he was very good at editing. Second he was interfering in the way that only certain small men can be. Third he asked: "What the hell does this mean?" when Ramakrishna said, "The sacred tulsi tree and the stem of the horse-radish are the same thing!"

On the table among the voice machines was a wind-up monkey. The actor played with it while he read his lines and then listened to them. The monkey clanged a tambourine and marched up and down with his tail twitching. Ramakrishna chuckled up the back of his throat. I focused my camera on his mouth, his hands, the monkey, while Lewis took the long view of the stage and the orange fires.

From there Lewis used Naugasound while I used Walkman sound and stayed close to the actor. In the end sixty pounds of sound alone were collected along with footage and driven through a blizzard to an editing room. "A filmmaker has to take a quantity of pictures to create a single movement, and still the picture trembles when it appears," wrote Strindberg. We worked on synchronicity for three days and through two late nights. We moved whole sections of the performance around, slashing and rearranging and we even added new sound from a different source altogether (the chatter of monkeys and birds at the zoo) and then drove the reels to a mixing room in the suburbs and saw our film projected full-scale on the wall for the first time. I sat in the mixing room with its twenty three mixers that could have been part of a space station, taking notes while Lewis sat in a dark room next door. I could hear him being critical and so I insisted that we take it all back for one last editing marathon. I was crying. Lewis cheered me on and said he would send it to a festival in Rotterdam. He quoted Tolstoi who in 1921 saw a movie for the first time and remarked, "Now we don't have to invent stories anymore. The cinema can show Russian life as it is, instead of chasing after fabricated subjects."

"You can make more!" Lewis encouraged me. "You can. We can make another."

It is when a movie is full-square on the wall that there is nothing more in life to chase after. There is no future. You have reached bliss.

The film went nowhere afterwards. The guys were too busy and tired to fight for its showing and I was a domestic servant who could not sell her wares in the world. Lewis was always running and Kosta needed to move on to another job.

So either it was the world's fault or mine that it never was shown. Or Kosta was right all along and the subject had no commercial value.

I told Kosta that it was my intention that the actor should be its only audience. The world is a mansion of fun. I eat, drink and roll around having fun. He said, "Don't worry, it's a jewel, they survive in the dark." Kosta, a tough little man with a well-carved face, suddenly seemed to understand me and to feel sorry he had not done so before. But this was because I was now a failure like him, he could actually see and hear me. He organized a small showing for a few friends. Then he and his family went to California to seek their fortune.

Two Sides of a Crib

6-1

The birds are delirious at the ending of the rain. Perfectly straight strings of water gully from the gutters onto the ground and shine. Sun up and yellow. Colors never brighter than after a gush of water. A lyric of chirrups to fatten the buds, February spring on the border. You know that consciousness is fed by all things living, just the way the eye retains the white of an object.

The day the rain stops a boy about twelve years old comes out of the rain and canyon. White teeshirt, jeans, no sneakers no socks. He is brown with shaved black hair, a frightened face but one as transparent and pretty as that of a young Yogi. Lost, not well. Not wanting to be found or moved along, he is skittish with us. Asthmatic breathing or something, the steam is rising off the warming leaves and Tom leads him into the refectory for some oatmeal, maple syrup, butter, a hot drink. The boy is shaking, unable to eat or not to eat, and nodding and shaking his head jerkily to the remarks we make in Spanish. Then water as clear as from a sacred brook spills from his lips in threads. The veil around Mary is watery and the veil she spins around the world is water too. Babies break the water and spit it out on entering the air. But where does the water of the spirit come from? How did he have pure water running inside of him? For that moment, as I wipe his lips, I am looking forward to a day when there are no more possibilities.

Tom murmurs, "Another child in need of a home."

No, no, not me, I think. I have done enough for the world. "There are desperate and needy children everywhere, and I'm too old."

"He reminds me of Julio," he says.

"So? Just step down into the canyon and you'll see they're everywhere. People and children, who are homeless."

"Do you think he has family down there?"

"Well, let's go see."

6-2

Slipping over the ice, striped like bacon fat along the pavement, I waved goodbye to the superintendent as he bashed garbage pails around, and hurried to the movies. The theater was in a small brick building that also housed an Algerian cafe and bar.

I was going to see A Touch of Evil for the fifth time because I only liked things that reminded me of themselves. In the theater, I was almost the only person there. I found my favorite seat—left side aisle ten rows up—and waited for the fade-out of the lights. The old battered seats felt like a pile of rods under me. I knew that I would have to move if someone ate popcorn near me and looked nervously around at the few others plumped back into their chairs. I was safe from eaters.

To me, making a film—that is, editing in a dark room for days—was the only thing better than watching someone else's movie. It was like being a miner who polishes jewels before extracting them from their stony base. There is no enormity in this process. Erasure of self is its goal. Give me a little screen and a lot of reels or even digital action carried in, and I will say with Bambi's mother, "Oh, how kind last year's dead leaves are." What did she mean about the leaves being kind? And she added: "They do their duty so well and are so alert and watchful. Even in midsummer there are a lot of them hidden beneath the undergrowth. And they give warning in advance of every danger."

Do leaves have eyes? Does film?

Henry Adams wrote when he was in Egypt, "One's instinct abhors time." Catholics abhor calendars. Poised and pointed towards an altar instead, they prefer to have feast days with wooden dolls, colored glass, candles, goblets and a gold plate like Akhmaton's disk swept and dusted of the divine in front of their eyes. A different calendar from the rest of us—Advent, Easter, Salvation History and Ordinary Time. Henry Adams was "a Darwinian for fun." He was an atheist but in the spirit of one who wants to protect God from himself. He was disappointed in himself and everyone else. But he remained fascinated by great constructs.

Whittaker Chambers, who translated Bambi from the German with careful poetic attention, was a moralist and a snitch. Some bogs have their own lamps. My husband was fascinated by Chambers, by his genius and his treachery, his secrecy and unacknowledged homosexuality.

McCool's thoughts were tickled with the rage of a hangover after a night of cheap red wine. Hangovers can create entire belief systems along with hot sweats headaches terror. God would always be born in a place of such demoralized flesh. "The existence of evil here below, far from disproving the reality of God is the very thing which reveals him in his truth," wrote Simone Weil. My husband was a true believer when he was having the DTs.

Is it possible that excess bliss is the producer of evil? My husband hated himself, then saw nothing but wickedness and ruin in everything around him, sometimes even the children, calling the twins The Mutants. He didn't like two of them being identical when he had a hangover. Once Libby told him about yoga and he tried to discipline himself without luck. "La Fontaine and other fabulists maintained that the wolf, even in morals, stood higher than man," said Henry Adams, sick with disillusion. But my husband fascinated me, because he was so extreme:

too bad and too good to keep him steady. Goodness should have no force behind it.

6-3

Libby ate in order not to be hungry later while I ate because I was hungry. The difference is obvious. She ate without gluttony, with dainty concentration and pleasure. I gorged and picked with my fingers at leftovers like a ravenous dog who tastes little. She and I broke apart for seven years. She went off with an old friend from our elementary school days, a thin blond girl named Honey Figgis. They headed west together to follow the guru they shared and had what they called experimental sex together. They kept coming back to it. Libby sent me letters from time to time and I always wrote back but her affair with Lewis was a haunt between us. Every metaphor is a description of the world as it is. We raised our children separately and she began her classes in Spiritual Exercises not of the Ignatian kind. They were yoga-based and involved inhaling the colors of the world and saying ah.

There was a mandala in front of her. Under the altar in any Catholic Church is a huge hole that travels to the center of the earth, into hell itself. This altar is the stone rolled across this tomblike space. To get to the other side of the altar you must fall like Alice down into the hole and spin in hell. There is no hole under a mandala but nonetheless some who have these signs die young. I don't want to die. That gravity of the gods is irresistible, and its timing too.

I loved Quincy Bay in the summers where the descendants of starfish, polyps and trilobites rolled in the tides. But the water became polluted before I was a teen and the beaches were only for playing in the sand. Libby came to stay with us—seven years had passed—when she was desperate, her children at her side. We went to Quincy Bay to let them play. She talked non-stop about her religion. She was no longer taking hard drugs and had begun the slow struggle for liberation that almost every addict makes. It was a winter day and one of the children wandered into the sea in her snowsuit.

Libby would soon be herself again. I could tell because she was trying to remember things.

"What do you think of our lives?" she asked.

"We come out of a weirdly restless generation, children of the Cold
War," I said to her.

"Remind me. Who were they? We?"

"Our generation? Honey went off with that beautiful woman Valerie,
to run a hotel in Belize, they are happily partnered since then. And Mary
Casement went to Poland to go back to her roots. She married someone
old, like Josephine March, and runs an orphanage."

"God. My Honey. Who else?"

"My friend from later, Roisin, she and her son moved to Ireland. Her
partner left her for another woman, and never made a movie again. I
think Roisin ended up back with her first husband or whatever he was.
That's why she's in Ireland. Her mother-in-law made the news by going
to die on a nuclear stockpile out in the west. As a protest. Remember
that? They found her half-decomposed, there were photos . . . ."

"Sort of I do. And who else?" Libby asked.

"That handsome guy—Tonio?"

"Yuck. Fascist. Playboy. Moves around everywhere. He went
through wives, the last being a soap opera actress. I do remember him
because I slept with him."

"The most rebellious of all ended up in jails and mental hospitals.
Or on drugs . . ."

"Let's not talk about me," Libby said.

Mornings I went to my job while Libby had sex with my husband. The
twins were in day care in a concrete slab that abutted an old people's
home down by the subway tracks. Her children were in a Montessori
nursery. She and McCool were alone at home too long and he was a fa-
mously good lover, though I never warmed up to him.

She knew that I didn't, it freed her as she also worried about my lack
of joy, my general poverty. She could see that McCool's and my mutual
misery was our only intimacy. We made each other suffer so deeply from

our lack of love for the other, we were collaborators in a condition that rips two people open until they only know themselves through the eyes of the other. I saw at once he was in love with Libby now and didn't blame him. I wanted her to take him away from me before he murdered me, and she did.

Wolves are faithful and love each other throughout their lives. He and Libby went at it like that. The forest of empty rooms, everyone at work or school, concealed the play of motives between them. Their leaves were my bed. Leaves do have eyes. "The goal of the Unmanifested is hard for the embodied to attain," but sometimes love between two people can get very close to that source. The closer they got, the more they were in a protracted state of sore nerves and yearning for emptiness. I felt sorry for them, and I wanted to be rid of them, the way a mother feels towards sullen teens. My husband begged me, "Don't leave me. Just let me see this through." But I said, "No way. You don't love me. I'm getting out of here" and I bundled up the twins and the little one and laid them out to sleep in the back of our cheap little Opel station wagon and headed west. West is the end for mystics and East is the resurrection. About ten miles into my ride, I was elated at what had happened. I was free and he was guilty I had heard that Lewis was in San Francisco. Henry Vaughan the disagreeable and great Welsh poet wrote: "Though when we travel Westward, though we embrace thornes and swet for thistles, yet the businese of a Pilgrim is to seek his country."

My country was Lewis from whom I was in exile—or was I his devotee seeking a future through him as others seek samadhi? Were we congressional, unselfish, empathetic or out of sync when we were together? I don't remember. Nectar of friendship between Rumi and Shams could have been ours.

Three bowls of ice cream were downed by my children who rolled around in the car, having fun, released from day care and a drafty house. Otherwise we had the ideal food for deportees: a pound of brown bread, hard boiled eggs and salt, oranges, bananas and chocolate.

It was the February spring when we arrived in Oakland and there were fruit trees in bloom, the waxy blossoms flat face up already. Smears and gashes of broken sun across the branches and views of the Bay at sudden turns. Who could not admit that this little portion of the globe shone like that bulb Jerusalem?

Its civic pride, good works and resistance to war were epic. Sickle cells under a microscope are watery and various and insects seen up close are enormous, but the suffering of the people here is swallowed by white light. "I am in jail," Lewis wrote back to me, "just for awhile, but please don't forget me. Letters, cuttings, books, whatever. You are precious to me."

He had participated in a sit-in at Livermore and was doing shut-in time with two Catholic priests and a bunch of other protesters. My foster children were my allies. The liberation of children from grown-ups was my plan. All my children could dress themselves for school and this small achievement was part of our strategy.

I went and surprised Lewis behind some bullet-like holes in glass. He was wearing khaki colored prison garb. He was really elated at seeing me and saw me as physical for once. "You look good enough to eat," he said, "to eat, I tell you." I stared at his full lips, the rays of pinkness that lined them inside, and pressed my mouth to the plexiglass. He met mine with his. We laughed, and drew back.

Within a week a crazed McCool—ditched by Libby—arrived out of the northeast and drove us east again. He said, "I don't care what you did, but don't ever let me see you with him."

"Why is seeing so important?" I asked.

"Because I see all these half-breed kids you bring home, and I see some of them look like Lewis and could be his. I see only too clearly. You say you have chosen them, but believe me, I see this word 'chosen' could mean something else."

Soon we were stopping on the edge of California and Arizona at the border canyon compound. McCool announced that Libby wanted me to have it.

"This land is your land," he told me. "Atonement."

"For what?" I asked.

"For our sins, hers and mine, stupid. Libby thinks that we did you wrong. She wants you to have this place. I don't know why. I mean, considering." I saw from the way his face turned to view the property that he loved it. The face of a heart is a face.

I slipped postcards secretly into boxes, addressed to Lewis, all the way home.

6-4

"We have to deal with this child, find his home. I'll go down into the canyons and look," I tell Tom, pulling on my dungaree jacket. "No, we will come too," he says and gently gestures to the child whose face is luminous with fever. He seems to have eyes in all of his cells, there is a diamond fuzz in the moisture covering his cheeks, like the smashing atomic sunshine fuzz that California light is said to have. He follows Tom, lifting his feet up as if they dragged seaweed. The wet is evaporating with supernatural speed. A steaminess coats the trees that still are dimpled with bright bubbles. A rainbow crosses the sky, its colors sharply marked. At night coyotes bay from these canyons and there are fat rattlesnakes lounging on the paths. I have on boots and carry a big stick and sing a song I once loved called "Together Again." Tom follows with one arm loosely reaching back towards the sick boy.

Ninety eight steps up the canyon wall little stones are rough and puddled, a palm paddles the side of a eucalyptus tree. Women have laid out plywood to dry like linen on rocks. Clothing and bedding and trash bags stuffed with food are bundled and rolled neatly into the arms of a wet tree. The women's mouths are ajar like clay pots. They see me coming and murmur to each other, never averting their eyes from mine. It's a scene that reminds me of a neo-realist film made in Italy during the war. I am the camera that makes others self-conscious. There are no men here, only four women and one baby and one little girl with straight black hair squatting in overlarge sneakers among the women's legs. "Is one of you missing a child?" I ask.

"No, Mama went to Ensenada," I am told.

Indivisible

A really enlightened person only sees colors floating in air where there is an animal in hair with its mouth open. There must be a variety of ugly approaches to the hole yawning under the altar. To be hung, head first, into that pit, would be truly a time to call for help from the outside. I feel that all of us women are in that position, right there, walled by the muddy sludge and in the arms of the angel of defecation and poverty.

I remember Libby and other well-to-do people and wonder: Where is the profit in making money when having it already is the point? Libby was born with an income already. Expensive vitamin pills, herb teas, grainy breads and fresh grown fruit. She jumped from pillow to pillow, with a cigarette, an acrobat of jokes trying to make everyone laugh. Sat like a yogi and asked about Lewis. "Does he have a girlfriend? He's so famous."

She always forgot that I was low-life myself, a penurious and anxious head of household.

Even if I was almost able to report on Lewis, almost had seen him recently, it was almost always me who called him and found him happy enough to hear from me to relieve my embarrassment. "He is almost in Jordan now, with his hand-held camera. And he has a girlfriend as always, a woman who throws tantrums, is wildly jealous, has sex with screams, takes a shower before and after, is half English and half Indian, tiny, pretty, intelligent, well-read, classy, and making lots of money as an editor."

"God. I feel like a complete failure."

Libby dying was surrounded by everyone she ever knew. They drifted around her house smoking dope, drinking, laughing, playing music, praying, lighting candles, eating and whispering, carrying her between them and sitting on the side of her bed while she slept. They loved her. The last day they passed a bottle of iced lemony vodka around and around in a circle while she in her white silk pajamas had nightmares induced by morphine and death. She said she was afraid to open a door before she stopped saying anything. I wasn't there but in a hospital half-dead from a ruptured artery. My body wanted to die—had actually planned it that way—on the day that Libby died, but the doctors wouldn't let it. I noticed that the white roses she sent me had frayed yellow hems, but I had no needle. The color cream spreading at its fat part next to the stem was the color of my mother's throat and the ticking along the hems of her dresses.

That day the canyon smells of human shit and a rooster lies clobbered on a rock, its head a red stain shaped like a big beak. One candle burns in a blue glass. Dispassion was the biggest passion ever between McCool and me. One of the women was moving towards the boy, and he was moving in her direction too. It was—when I came out of the movies—dark and white, snow pee-colored under the streetlights and a touch of evil on all cold things. The clouds from the canyon are sand-gold and tumultuous from all the rain. When they lived beside the canyon Libby was overwhelmed by my husband's certainty and let him do whatever extra he wanted with her. My near-monk friend is interested in Tantric sex and actually asks me to purchase a book for him on the subject. Orgasm is not in itself sinful since it exists.

"In the first state there is form, in the second state there is the formless, and, after that, there is the state beyond the form and the formless."

"He look like Jesus," says the woman moving towards the boy. "But not Jesus, my friend's boy. He's this Juan. Maybe. His mother down there."

"He's sick," I tell her and make a throw-up gesture and face. "Well, bring him to mother. I bring," she says.

We all slide down ninety eight steps through the basin of the canyon littered with lots of paper and cans and up the slippery but not so sheer a slope on the other side. They are silent, even the children, and we all fall on our knees a few times. We are all wearing jeans and sneakers and arrive filthy at another encampment. "Shouldn't we call a doctor?" Tom calls out to me.

"Are you crazy? The INS, you know. They'd all be hauled away."

The soil has begun to resemble a clay and cucumber face wash that Libby used to give me. I tip down towards it.

"He should be examined," Tom insists and, next to last in line, turns back.

"He should be with his mother. Trust me."

"But what if he dies?"

"It's just the flu, or food poisoning. Let's go."

"But where is he?" Tom calls.

All of us turn together. The boy is gone. A stream of water slides off a palm branch onto the ground. The smell of eucalyptus is as acidic as tomatoes and sage, the light-color blue. Birds twirt and rattle. The rest is all green and still.

The Supreme Contemplated ones were of the female gender according to Ibn Arabi who had an angel cosmology, where women appeared and disappeared as manifestations of divine wisdom. Mary herself floats over the world, a see-through figure begging for peace but leaving no trace or effect on what men do. Mary holds her baby through all time crying, "You can't kill him, because he has been made out of nothing!"

God, we looked for the boy for an hour, remember, and returned, speechless, home. He was gone as swiftly as he had come. None of the people could explain, but the women didn't seem surprised or alarmed. "It goes!" one cried, lifting her hands to a laugh.

6-5

Libby when ill loved being cradled warmly in the arms of her friends who were grateful to her for letting them behave well at last. Her bones were palpable, her skin dotted with lesions that sometimes seeped out drops of blood spontaneously. She wore a shunt in the dent in her skull. She also had worn one for drippings in her chest. Once a male nurse punctured her lung looking for a place to dig in the needle. All this time she did not want to die or escape her torturers. She had the discipline that Krishna recommends in the Gita. Morphine and love to burn. Her features turned Tibetan as well as Native American, her face swimming through multiple migrations of meaning. Her sex dried up and disappeared. She kept wearing orange against her cinnamon skin and its lights played tricks.

"What if!" she cried. Wrinkles cover an elephant's hide; piggy creatures have wet upturned snouts and walk like penguins, there are even terrified bugs and rabbits who have survived.

Indivisible

Her children hung at her bedside like two sides of a crib.

There are mutations following nuclear explosions and germ warfare and birds with oil glued to their wings and beaks. Libby turned into a saint before she died. She might have chanted: "When I say I am God, God, I don't mean that I AM God. I mean that I am God."

Gobblers are turkeys that people gobble up. Evolution from lower to higher, the aggregation of the atom in the mass, the concentration of variety inside of unity and the way chaos is embedded in order—(there were anarchists who were Catholics and Marxists who were anarchists) these were the concepts that governed generations from the mid-nineteenth to the end of the twentieth century.

My husband bragged that he had been one of the men behind the wire in Ireland, after getting caught during some minor IRA scrimmage and released after a couple of years. Now he said he was American, thanks to marrying me. But he renewed his Irish passport dutifully. My husband didn't care for me but for his foster children he usually did. We stayed married although we could have divorced at once. Ireland, too, chose to remain neutral during the war, when it could have supported Britain during World War Two, made a deal ending partition and this way have avoided fifty more years of slaughter.

6-6

To Ibn Arabi the human creature is both pre-eternal and post-eternal and manifests itself in its earthly body (the middle) in multiple and simultaneous forms. There are no sequences but vibrant occurrences and conditions all over the place. For instance when Mimi Jones and I met, she was walking in the opposite direction from me but on the same street near Downtown Crossing. She was coming from the Department of Motor Vehicles where she had paid off her son's parking tickets and I was on my way to the zoo with four temporary children from one family. I asked her if it was too far to walk as we both paused at a bus stop.

"It's far but you can do it," she said casting an accountant's glance at the children. "Wow," she said, "they're all the same age."

"It's okay," I told her. "Not quite."

"Really? Looks to me like you've got your hands full. I'll walk with you."

I thought her kindness might be a sign of insanity, but she was trimly dressed, tidily coiffed, lightly made up. Her complexion was a lovely tea tone, her face round and smooth but serious as if she contained innumerable bruises and soft spots in her feelings. She moseyed along at my side pushing the bars of the three-person contraption with her hands beside mine. She told me about her son who was a Black Panther working a Free Breakfast program and about her other son who went all the way through law school, then dumped all that work to become a journalist.

"I know someone like that," I told her.

"It must be a trend then. I suppose you can use law for everything. He's not a hippy but he likes white people. Enough. His hero is Malcolm X. Heard of him?"

"Yes he sounds exactly like my friend," I said.

"My son? Well, it's generational. To want to break down artificial barriers. Your age group has done a great job already, beginning in the south. Now try the north."

We started up Blue Hill Avenue. It was autumn and the wind blew sticky papers and brown leaves around our legs. I wrapped my kids' faces in their scarves. "My name is Mimi. Mimi Jones."

"Jones. My friend's name is Jones," I said with a happy smile.

"There are millions of us."

"Lewis Jones," I said swelling like tunnel vision at the utterance of his name.

"Lewis? That's my son," said Mimi.

We both stopped, gaping and clutching our faces, then nothing was spoken for many seconds until she hastily embraced me, hooked her arm through mine and we walked, stuck to each other, pushing the kids, and didn't stop talking for hours. Goats, chicks, hamsters, piglets and a pony later, we were seated on a bench with cigarettes and cokes making plans to meet there the next Saturday. Gravity was more like it. The pull down and into, against and onto, the thick leafy body of relationship. Children toddled, squabbled, giggled, petted animals, ate, drank and rolled around while we told each other everything about ourselves but always returned to the heart, like hands grabbing a hot water bottle under the sheets, Lewis.

"When I am dead . . . they shall find your picture in my heart," John Donne raved to his beloved. I think Mimi understood that there was an agonic line between me and Lewis. It was an imaginary line connecting us though our declination was zero. Magnetics work at zero point. Magnetics can be gods or multiple gulps from the whole Logos.

Mimi understood power like this. She had warm dry hands and a tight grip. She had raised her boys in Lawrence, Kansas, then following Lewis, came to Boston in the eighties. The father's sister Ruby was already living there. They were all except the father quite young. The father was a fat old man, a reverend genius, who had followers rather than a congregation. He had saved Mimi from the streets when she was fifteen, implanted his ancient seed in her twice, then became flaccid and celibate and a bookaholic with a mystical twist. All he did was read. She was only fifty to his seventy when I met her and glamorous in a surreptitious way, certainly immaculate like Libby. Those low-key sweet perfumes, fitted muted and soft clothes. She worked at the post office in Post Office Square and brought home the bacon to the old man hibernating in their basement apartment on Warren Street.

She never talked when she was at home. Her mouth clamped shut. She became cattish, slinking around taking care of cleaning and feeding and the younger son when he came home at night. The old man retained everything. He had a following by day, men and women who came to learn Sanskrit and Indian history that included Jesus as a wandering avatar. He especially loved Muktananda.

At the zoo she and I talked about God through the Upanishads. The Bhagavadgita, Plotinus, Dionysus, Weil, Dostoevsky, Tolstoi, etcetera, it was a full time preoccupation for those of us who had no childhood training.

Boston had called to the old man although he rarely walked down her streets but ordered others instead to bring him the books that rocked on steep stacks around his sagging sofa. You might have guessed he was gay because of the high timbre of his voice and his dramatic gestures, but Mimi said he had been her greatest lover and even his corpulence could not make her stop wishing he would do it again.

The Light Over the Heavy Door

7-1

The apartment when I am up alone at night is lighted the way 1930's movies used to be when they showed dark rooms illuminated by a big white light from a tiny source. I can't make physical sense of this whiteness in the night room that faces the river. Only a distant streetlight. Other apartments gently shine behind drawn curtains. I think everyone else in the world except me is happy and in company. I know it. The enormous giant who inhabits this space with us we have dubbed The Bumper, and his head touches the ceiling, his shoulders slope. He would if he could burst into the space that divides heaven from earth, gush upwards dripping, naked and triumphant, the Purusha, an utterly enlightened embodiment of a fully realized human being, a feminine man luxuriant in hair and muscle, nearly red, both breasted and erect. The Bumper, however, is crushed and sad in the rooms we inhabit. Like so many losers and maniacs, his poor posture has always given him away.

7-2

There is a color that really has no name. I think also that there is one composed of a mix of silver and gold that can't be analyzed or faced because of its dazzle. Some heavy silver is where you see it sometimes. It is the color of Mimi's silence. Mabarosi, the Japanese call it when the silver sea-light sucks you back into itself. She said once: "I thought you were speaking of me." A strange sentence that made "I" into a reserved and watchful authority over "me" who was someone else entirely. She might as well have said, "I thought you were speaking of Mimi." She worked for society and was rewarded with a cell. In jail it is stupid to say that the cells are monkish because they are crowded. Three persons in one, each desiring freedom from the other. Mimi missed her husband who never once came to visit, but wrote her magnificent letters that the guards jeered at first. They were unsealed when Mimi finally received them and stained with coffee and the tear stains of laughter.

The Trinity in Greek and Latin has a feminine root.

Mimi said, "I knew that God was taking me seriously when he wouldn't let me have what I deserved. After all my work. This was the mark, the turning point. Others were being well rewarded for doing less. Including Lewis, my own son. There had to be a reason, and luckily I figured out what it was. I was being taken seriously."

During the early times with Mimi, there were assassinations and riots, and the city was cordoned off. At night it was like crawling across an anonymous floor in a pitch black room looking for a pine of light. Police cars and sirens playing "Break Up to Make Up." You expected the city to kill itself. I waited for Lewis out in my car on many nights during the riots. Why was I there and what did he need me for? To drive him here and there where he interviewed people and took pictures of things. My white face felt like something I had foolishly chosen to wear to the wrong place. Lewis was paranoid about being trailed so a white face helped. Sometimes he lay on the floor in the back seat. His parents' phone was bugged and tapped and the Feds were already following his brother while Mimi and the old man tried to keep him at home. We went from Connolly's to Bob the Chef to Joyce Chen's and the Heath Street projects. To Mission Hill and Fort Hill, Centre Street and Mattapan . . .

I lied to my husband telling him I was going to meetings down at the health clinic where I was on the board. He appreciated the lie. It meant I was scared. He would have been mad if I had told him I was helping Lewis because it would have meant I had no fear. He always said, "Just don't let me see you with him"—an order that had more to do with Lewis's looks than with mine. Sometimes I lay across the front seat in the car, listening to Motown play low, while Lewis was inside some build-

ing. I knew my maker, God, during those hours. Something that killed
and was not killable. When I heard a door shut and Lewis's footsteps, I
leaped up not wanting him to see me being a coward. How fat and ugly
I felt goes without saying. All I did was take up space.

Every footmark that closed the space between us, that put him
warmly in the closed car beside me, seemed to demonstrate a question
of physics. I didn't believe in acts coming to meet my hopes yet there I
lay waiting for his body to arrive, and it did. And I didn't believe in rela-
tivity yet there I lay counting the scuffs in time to my heartbeats.

7-3

Tom dresses sloppily and works in the garden without gloves. He has
a potential beard even after he has shaved, is hairy, thick and clumsy. He
will never tell me about his sexuality, but says he doesn't like "too much
man" in one place and this is his main problem with living in a monastery,
and at the same time "gay is here to stay" as if he knows why. He wants
to find a reason to condemn homosexuality but can't because it exists and
always has. My feelings are hurt if I sense that he prefers men to women.
He will only say that he would rather prefer women to men. God, I am sick
of him. He makes me hate myself. His cool is unending even though he
looks wild and passionate like an 18th century Russian ikon.

Some whites are secret blacks and some Jews are hidden Christians
and some blacks are secret whites and some Christians are hidden Jews.
Some children are old at heart and some old people are young. Lewis
was like a hidden Jew who was black all the way through. He was like
the missing page where the Old Testament meets the New. He had two
sides to him—one being a fiery activist, the other a prophet of tragedy.
When he first heard of my coincidental encounter with his mother, he
just said "fuck" and went on doing his push-ups. But then he, being
crooked like me, immediately took advantage of the situation and ordered me to accompany Mimi to Mass and to visit her every Sunday
when he couldn't be there. As a sign of the times, we were a negative, a
minus, and a below zero.

He told me to do things I would have done anyway and then took credit for me doing them. We had many disagreements about politics, people, books, music, art but not movies. It was hard to figure out the essential ingredient that made a situation good for him. In the end I realized that it came down to him being a Catholic. Nothing to him that was extra was good. Only necessities and the givens were uncorrupted. Vanity to him was the motive behind almost every act and production, and so it was only the spontaneous or heart-driven that got past his suspicion. Then he would smile knowingly and nod his head, arms folded against his expansive chest. He wasn't my brother, son, husband, father or lover, but being present at his pleasure made me happy. It is out of such weakness that the warlike male is created.

Bricks frame my view from this seat and I think the water wants to be saturated like a cloth dragged through water the way it runs so lamely. But it's a dark and frigid day, all gold disgorged onto the tops of things, the rain has turned to snow and the river is fast and brown sticks are rigid against the ripple effect.

Mimi asked: "Which would you rather be when you die—the air or the earth?"

"Please, the water," I told her. "And you?"

"We will never be either," is what I think I heard her say. And then she remarked, looking away: "Henrietta, why are you the way you are?"

THE MIDDLE

When Henrietta was seven, and her father dead, she was brought before Judge Bumpers, a left-handed comedian who had worked in the court system for decades. He declared her mother incompetent to care for her and sent her to live with two old people who had prayed for a girl to be sent to them. They were vegetarian pacifists and had her sleep between them in their double bed. They were white from the tops of their heads to the tops of their feet. They ate a surplus of raw vegetables, lots of chocolates and rice and this became her preferred diet for life.

At seven Henny was cheeky and cute and liked adults to like her even as she wanted to be free of them. She simply wanted to be near to every person without being seen, and that was why so many of them said, "I don't remember her." She was as thin as a kitten with pointy features, black curls and soulful blue eyes. She wore big shoes and socks and knee-length dresses, her legs like stems too weak for their fronds and always some peculiar piece of clothing, or an accessory was added on to give her a certain feeling about herself. Candy necklaces, tiny pins shaped like animals, fake pink pearls, and oversized hand-knitted sweaters with parades of elephants or flowers woven into the chest, which she chose from piles at the Salvation Army with the old lady beside her.

She didn't miss her mother who was incarcerated both in a state mental hospital and inside her psyche. The one grandparent (her father's mother) she had was living in Ireland up near the border. Eckhart said of the soul, "In the desert of herself she is robbed of her own form, and in God's desert leading out of hers, she is bereft of name." This child believed her soul was alive inside her. "I see for something else. I eat for something else." She played with her soul instead of dolls. The old couple were kind to her, they paid for her to to go a private school nearby, and they watched her skittishness with affection. She didn't like them to touch her so deep was her sleep-hell wedged between those two decaying but live bodies that tossed and snorted like sea monsters.

She was fascinating to her more privileged schoolmates at the Mystic School. Her tragic history, her eccentric clothes, and the fact that she was silly all alone made her interesting. She didn't seem to care what anyone thought of her as she jump-roped in her enormous shoes. She even sucked her thumb in public with a blissful look in her blue eyes. Soon others discovered she could be fun, which is a great human trait.

Once Judge Bumpers came to her in a dream, his body filling the view she had of an ocean shining like the moonlight of the soul. And his shadowy form laughing shouted: "Aren't people awful? A complete disappointment. And I made them!" He laughed warmly and engulfed her inner eye with his shadow so she had to wake up. She had a high fever and had to stay home from school. It turned out she had polio and the old couple had to drive her to a children's hospital. Once the nurses had to puncture her spine for fluid and they all held her down talking baby-talk and she learned irony from this arrangement—that those who cause the greatest pain, speak the kindest. The agony was incommunicable so she never mentioned it.

She learned to walk again with the other afflicted children but her legs were thinner than ever and she had an awkward posture for life. When she left the hospital and others in iron lungs and wheelchairs, she gulped down her grief at her good luck. Why live in such an unjust world if not to try to make things fair? For a year she had physical therapy with a woman who also massaged the muscles in her legs and leaned around her enveloping her in breath that was supernaturally light murmuring "angel" and "cookie" at her. Then she would go home to the old couple but now the man was hacking sick and dying. And soon she was left alone with the old woman who clung to her in bed so hard no one would believe it, not a social worker or a teacher at school, so she didn't try to tell them.

Only the physical therapist, who was also a nun, listened to something in her bones and assured her that she was not alone and that she would visit her once a week at home to make sure everything was all right. Sister John helped her to walk almost normally though she would never be exactly straight, her butt would stick out and her spine would curve in more than it should. She was still very thin and cheerfully played through her days at school, but at the center of her mind was Sister John who kept her promise about visiting her.

It wasn't long before Henrietta met Libby Camp at last. Libby was on the playground tar with her dress pulled tight by her little hands over her knees, its hems tugged down to her ankles so it looked like the plaid might rip around her knees. Libby had brown bangs lying over her eyebrows and a wide smile across tiny sharp teeth. She was bossy and riotously funny. From their first encounter on a May day in the playground, they were inseparable, their giggles preceding and receding around them. Or like two people performing the same religious rite, they seemed to move in unison.

Now the old lady grew ill from missing the old man and no matter how hard she squeezed the little girl she couldn't reinvigorate her own spirit. She began to decline. Sister John, who always had coffee in the kitchen with the old lady, noticed this and began arrangements for the child to be moved to a healthier foster family in a nearby town. The child howled, heaving her thin shoulders, her face between her skinned knees, saying she couldn't leave Libby.

Then Sister John taught her to pray and in the bathroom, they kneeled at the bathtub side by side, Sister's pink rosary beads clattering against the porcelain and they said the Our Father and Hail Mary nine times and begged Jesus to find a way for her to stay in her school with Libby.

Jesus did. Her mother was released from hospital and moved into a little brick flat near her school and the child was allowed to leave the old lady and go home. She was flooded with gratitude at being able to stay with Libby in school, and she never forgot the kindness of Sister John who went to Africa to teach, or the old lady who died in her sleep leaving her enough money to complete a private education through age twenty one. And Sister John didn't forget her, but sent her postcards for three years, and once told her about an English girl who became a nun but lived like an Indian, a boy named Julio and about a wounded gazelle. She lost and forgot these cards as the years passed.

"You may have settled your destiny with that one prayer beside the bathtub," Sister said.

Henrietta worried about her mother who changed her dread every minute. She was like a person you had to keep an eye on. Her mother had a worry M stitched into her brow, which she covered with black bangs, and her lips were circled with dark red lipstick. She called herself Creole and knew a few French words. She cleaned houses and offices for a living and listened to the radio. She was terribly tidy, but moved things back and forth a lot too. She had a special order for washing dishes (glasses first, cups next, cutlery last) and a special method for cleaning your bottom in the bathroom. She was in a perpetual state of insatiable desire which she fomented with alcohol. This way her eroticism was self-made but also required fuel which Henny was supposed to provide during the sober hours. Henny was asked to regale her with school stories, especially ones that showed how awful all her friends' parents were.

At home the child felt as if she was in a clay palace where she was deciphering shapes by touch. Her mother didn't seem to hear her or get her jokes.

Henny sucked her thumb until she was nine when Libby made fun of her, and she stopped. "Speak to my mouth if you want to talk to me but are afraid," a blind person might say, on being ignored. Henny often covered her mouth for fear of the effect her words might have, and how ugly her laugh might be. Burned toast was her favorite food. She left the bread in the toaster until it was smoking, then scraped off the black dust with a knife and ran her fingertips through the char, licking it off with the butter-grease. She also talked to Jesus for years even when she got smacked on the mouth for "nonsense" the day her mother heard her praying by accident.

She always wanted her mother to be happy but it was a futile business and soon her silence set in, the silence she was known for.

If a girl could develop her own ideas on the mysteries of the Torah, she might possibly have to be secretive about it and she would definitely have to be an obscure person.

There once was a shoemaker who stitched together the upper and lower worlds with his thread. He was an ordinary working man in a little shop in the Middle Ages. Sewing had a mystical edge to it, like arranging flowers and making tea.

Aristotle said that "woman has an extremely humid body, as can be known from her smooth and glossy skin, and especially from her regular purgations which rid the body of superfluous humors. So when wine is drunk and merged with female humidity, it loses its power and does not easily strike the seat of her brain when its strength is extinguished." The mother was without defenses and only confident when she had a drink in her hand when she jovially explained that she had a hollow leg, so the child once pretended she was an alligator crawling on the floor under her mother to see if her leg looked like a barber pole. But she saw a garter belt, skin, buckles and big salmon pink underdrawers.

On those happy nights her mother played music and took giant-steps. The wet sexual implications of her excitement did not go un-experienced by her daughter, who felt herself to be a dangerous stimulus. But she was always put in a scared mood the next day which made gin the cause of her mother's outbursts of bile and grief regarding human happiness, that same happiness that had been hers the night before. She hid in her closet and cried to God. She beat at the child's face and neck, it felt monkey-like, she pleaded, repented, swilled vodka and went back to work. A couple of her best jobs she got through her daughter's school—and one of which involved cleaning Libby's house twice a week. Henny always feared her mother would be caught by the law and imprisoned again for being insane. Women come in several forms like the ten names of the Sefiroth, and for each form there is its opposite—wisdom becoming stupidity, intelligence becoming intolerance, good humor turning to hate, fun turning to fury; etcetera.

Meantime the two girls were constantly switching forms between themselves, until graduation, and for them the search for truth was not active or passive but nervous.

The maid's daughter was aware that good things had unfolded for her out of trouble! She had a good school, and a best friends, neither of which would have occurred if it hadn't been for her mother's breakdown, the old lady's kindness and her sickness leading to the nun's attention. Likewise she never could drain from her cells the scent of Sister John's gentle breath, the stench of the old lady, her mother's liquorish laugh which all all combined later into the fragrance of Libby's bitter weed.

She grew into a slightly bow-backed hard-assed woman on two pin legs. Her walk was a bit stiff as if she had ridden a horse for the first time every day of her life!

Her expression was farouche, her mouth sensuous and small until it opened into a huge smile that creased her cheeks. A rare bird, weird. The best thing about her was two large eyes which held the luminous wonder of a baby. She and Libby spent some afternoons at Libby's house, the intensity of their friendship was a secret from their classmates, and sometimes her mother moved around them vacuuming and blasting Edith Piaf or Tchaikovsky on the record player. Like many women, Henny would never surpass her mother economically or socially, though her mind would travel to much farther, and worldlier places.

Adolescence has its own literature which will not be represented in these pages, but the history of a head is unavoidable being everywhere.

The snaky gray brain that doctors and scientists dump and slice and slap their hands around, chop, dice and analyse outside and inside its hard shell case, is not much to look at it. And you can't look into it, in the normal sense of seeing more. You only see less than enough, every time. Where are all those pictures being made? And why cry out of such a day? Ephraim, a Syrian father, said that until you have cried, you do not know God. And some holy men wanted tears to be a sacrament. The body, Ayurvedic healers tell us, contains its own cures. We have what we need. Incredulous are those who figure out that the Interior Life is simply the activity of human cells.

Having a relationship that begins with the ownership of a body and ends with the owner wondering who the owner is who is owning whatever it is that can't be owned, is peculiar enough. But having another body under your moving hands, crying "My turn!" or "Do whatever you want with me!" is even more peculiar.

However, knowing that it is peculiar is the really peculiar thing, because that knowledge indicates an awareness of a perfect being somewhere—perhaps even a good being against whom we measure all our qualities.

THE END OF THE MIDDLE

A Vault with a Red Stain

8-1

Some doctors inspect the brain as if each melody were a malady. They want to find the origin of song as if gray matter were a day reed that would play without breath. But the doctor who lived in the little border town near the compound was not reductive or materialist. We went to ask her about the boy we had lost in the canyon. Had a sick child come in? Where might he have gone? We were all standing in the parking lot outside her adobe office.

She was a woman with a plain long-lipped face in yellowish hair, she looked like a broken harp. Yet there was an intensity of compassion in her that was fruitful under the circumstances.

Her name was Kerry and she came from the forthright if eccentric Berkshires. She said, "Don't be surprised by anything you find out about children here. They get lost, they get raped, they get cut up for body parts, they get picked up by the INS. . . . He probably just wandered back to his campsite. These heavy rains always turn up ugly things," she said. "It's as if they wash off the top and what's underneath—well, you wish you didn't know it was there."

It was like finding meteor pebbles in the sole of your sneaker. Tom and I both felt sick and kicked at the tar. The doctor's drabness was a function of her selflessness, how I admired her! She had no time for herself and didn't even eye a cookie in a nearby window.

In The Revelation of the Veiled, Hujwiri says, "There are three forms of culture: worldly culture, which is the mere acquisition of information; religious culture, which means following rules; and elite culture which focuses on self-development."

There are also veils over nationalism, no one speaks of them, especially the ways in which the elite in their drive for individual power are feeding the military dogs they despise. Personal ego is the most precious bullet in the nation's arsenal!

The doctor said, "The sale of, well, the commodification of the human body, is as old as prostitution and slavery. I've got to go, but I'll tell you if I hear anything about where this poor kid came from. The other thing is, there is a place that takes battered kids and places them in foster care. I mean, you might locate him there."

"But something more humane? Are there nuns—orphanages?" Tom asked.

"There are," said the doctor, "on the other side of the border. But first take a look at this other place, way east. Desert! I mean, if you want to bother. But really I suggest just letting it go. He's probably fine."

"I hope so," said Tom and glanced at my silence.

"I had a really confused childhood," the doctor suddenly announced as she moved to her car, "in upper state Massachusetts. I never thought I'd be a doctor—just a nurse, a caretaker. But the men made me mad. So I went to med school."

Tom's head went inside her car window. "It's great you can do so much good."

"Good? You're a priest, right?"

"No, I'm between things, you might say"

"Oh, one of those," she said bitterly. "So why are you here?" Tom looked as if he had been hit, but replied evenly: "Well, Henny and I came here together. The place belongs to her, and we just wanted to see, you know, uh, take a break."

She stared clear-eyed at his morose expression, obviously wondering if we were having sex together there. "A break from what?"

"From, we have some things, to think about," he said.

"Why not turn that place into a sanctuary?" the doctor inquired.

"For?"

"You don't know?" she asked and gunned her engine.

"Women? Kids? Illegals?"

"All of those and more . . . Why not?" And then she roared away in her car, when she was ready to do so. No hovering or polite goodbyes. Tom had never looked more wounded by words.

8-2

"You can tell if a blind person is really blind if he can't smell a freshly baked cookie under his nose, someone told me," the superintendent said. "But I don't understand which he is—the one who can or the one who cannot smell." He wanted me to tell him about blindness, but I wouldn't.

Indivisible

He had fixed the lights in the building but now the elevator didn't work. An old lady was almost in tears, not knowing how to get to the fourth floor where her apartment was. It was around eight p.m. I asked her if she could climb a few stairs at a time, then rest, etcetera, and I told her I would go with her. She said she supposed she must and took my arm thinly. We climbed the back stairs in silence except for gasps. The usual question that arises in such conditions came into my mind: "Why live for this long?" The old lady was a frail wheezing dependent being, unwanted by anyone in the world (she told me this on the third floor) except a nephew who was impatiently waiting for her to die and leave him her money. "I don't know why I go on," she squeaked and stood still, clinging to me and the bannister, all but keeling over. "Well, yes, I do . . . To make that boy wait until it's too late for him to enjoy my money."

"Why not just leave it to some charity instead?"

"I don't trust charity. And he's adopted. I dislike giving him the family money. He can have it when I don't know. Why should he have it anyway, just because my sister took him in? Our society has lost its direction, I tell you, too many people. We should celebrate every time there is an earthquake and a war that kills more people. My nephew has no class, no taste, no matter how much my sister did for him. It's in his blood. I know you aren't supposed to say it but breeding makes all the difference."

She then began her final ascent up the metaphor of stairs. "There's an awful racket in the pipes here. Banging night and day like Samuel Whiskers. Have you heard it? Think it's a rat? Should we report it?" I didn't respond. At her apartment door I waited while she fumbled for her key, let herself in, fumbled for the light, and banged shut the door without a backward glance or thank you. The Japanese are said to have tossed a load of Vietnamese boat people back into the sea when they didn't thank them for picking them up. But certain Buddhist teachers advise you to use all negative encounters as lucky lessons.

Down below in my white room I remember Mimi while listening to a tape of Mozart's Quintet in G in my chair tilted to the left to point out at the straw-gold lines over the river. There is no sound from the closet down the hall—not a bump or a snore or a child's humming.

I think Plotinus noticed that enlightened people don't need to remember the past. Re-configuring days or minutes is of course impossible but, God, I remember Proust had rats delivered to his room so he could torture them. I don't believe in the unconscious, because whatever it is, it is not un-anything. That watery junk that floats through and around my bones is alive and well and near the tops of things, by no means under or reactionary. Why, dreams luxuriate in sheets and pillows and night all around them as if the head is a bed. If I am lucky Libby will swim by today, waving from a day that does not dwell in my unconscious but in the most wakeful part of my cerebellum.

8-3

The Gita Chapter 12: "Concentration is better than mere practice, and meditation is better than concentration; but higher than meditation is surrender in the love of the fruit of one's action, for on surrender follows peace."

Jesus is said to be a fisher of men and his hook and line fly into time and draw you to him. The hook digs in but only after you make the choice to bite.

The Gita wants the best for the reader. You can tell because of the many choices it offers unlike some cruel and dogmatic systems. It is written without judgment. If you can't meditate, concentrate. Or as Teresa says, "If you can't contemplate, recollect." Some people say it is enough to live seriously or to become "Zero at the Bone." But Keats wrote in a letter that our lives have a transcendent value that we can't apprehend. I think the way they talk about God as "love" is a heresy unless the word "love" has no meaning but then all words about God have to have less meaning than the word God itself which, because it already has no meaning at all, places all words in a difficult situation.

So why do they blow God into a word that is stuffed with meaning if it makes us all feel sick?

8-4

Through heavy drug-use, through child-bearing and rearing in a half-hearted reckless way, through sex with strangers and on, Libby continued meditating. Her stare then was like a beetle seated at the edge of a forest, and if a stone flew past, the beetle didn't see it. One true gaze into such an empty pair of eyes and your life is changed. . . "Whose sin was it that caused his blindness?" someone asked Jesus about a poor blind man. His answer was a reproof: "If you were blind there would be nothing wrong with your failure to see what's going on. But you do see and still you don't get what's happening."

What is a tea-person? Is it a person who meditates over the tea ceremony? When Libby was having her tea in my house and sleeping with McCool, I was given by fate the consolation prize of my friendship with Mimi.

McCool and Libby had each other and I had Lewis's mother and prematurely snow white hair.

My friendship with Mimi lasted many years that included the development of four to six children into their teen years, and her youngest son Walk into manhood. As planned, she never saw me and Lewis at the same time.

Mimi's apartment was lit electrically all day. Table lamps with weary shades gave the place a nearly occult glow. Books on the floor, the tables, beside the john, at the kitchen table. Some photographs of old family members were hung lopsidedly, the furniture was thrift shop but comfortable. It always held the lovely childhood smell of toast throughout its rooms. It was a floor-through with a big bed for Mimi and Pop and in the other room twin beds for the boys though Lewis hadn't ever slept there. He was the household hero. Mimi collected all clippings of his writings.

Walk was the one Mimi suffered over. He was born much later than Lewis—one of those children who should be a grandchild—but he was the son she loved like a mother. He went AWOL in the army. In high school, he ended up in a Columbian jail for carrying marijuana, all before the age of twenty. He was a guitarist, gifted, good at languages, in these he was his father's son. Walk was not as good-looking as Lewis, but he had more friends, was kinder, funnier, more artistic, and better to his mother. He practiced yoga and had an intense but eccentric religious intention that kept switching allegiances.

With Walk and Mimi the deep needle began its in-and-out movements through the tapestries pricking and drawing spouts of blood.

Walk came and went daily. He was stocky with a slight speech defect (a twist to his lips) that made him appear amused by all he observed and gave others the impression that he was always joking. So no matter what he said people laughed. It was as if he had been labeled a comedian after making one good joke. The punishment was, it was hard to take him seriously. He wore pleated workpants and a blue workshirt and a khaki army jacket. His friend Jimmy was a big frightened boy who married very young and let himself be bossed around. Heaven was his other friend, a tall mixed race boy who had traveled from somewhere south of New York City; who played bass, read a lot, and seemed dreamy like his name but in fact he was sharp, alert, and full of plans. Pop thought Heaven was gay and Heaven thought Pop was gay and called Mimi Ma.

Once I arrived home too quickly and too early for my husband and Libby to pretend they were just friends and be prepared. I sort of planned it like that. What I saw was the same as what I would get watching a blocked television channel where sex is coming through the wobbling ruptures, cheap music playing like bars. I hovered beside the door. My most beloved friend, a slip of a woman, was being fed on by McCool with his black hair torn at the roots by her two brown hands and two of them sounding as if they were in hell. Downstairs boiling tea my shoulders shook, but I felt nothing. The steam from the kettle rinsed my face and I let it whistle and left the house to pick up the children. When I came home, Libby and my husband were drinking Lipton fully clothed at the kitchen table. They each smiled wearily at me as if I was a victor who might extend kindnesses to them, my prisoners. This was not far from the truth since they only wanted my happiness to come through theirs.

Luckily I understood that Libby meant well in the sense of needing to justify herself by trying to take my husband away so I could focus on Lewis in peace. McCool, on the other hand, was possessed and had no ulterior motives. He adored Libby. He was out of his mind with love. And now he encouraged my contacts with Lewis (once he had threatened to kill him) in an ingratiating self-serving way. McCool might ask: "Where's your old friend Lewis? Still living at home? Is that why you go over there all the time? Well, go, go, go. Enjoy yourself."

He himself was a handsome man with bright blue eyes, fierce lines in his cheeks, red lips, black hair and a seething smile. He was charm itself, jumping up to fix a drink for you, kissing the children suddenly, telling hilarious stories when he wasn't ranting on about corruption in everyone but himself. He read a lot, remembered and quoted it, loved to hang out and not work except at his music. It took someone quite astute in human personality to notice the paranoia behind the kindness and the murder in his hysterical laughter. Libby certainly didn't notice these or need to. He was in love and wanted her only to know him as good. And she must have drained off some of the agony that made him twist and burn. He was actually soothed into a kind of honesty with Libby. McCool talked about race as if it was a disease. "He's smart, but black," he might say about someone we knew.

Pop would not let the subject of race arise under his roof. "This is a race-free zone," he said of his home and told how he had seen households poisoned by this subject all his life. He said, "Words will let you know, faster than any gesture, when a social issue is a psychosis. Race is a national psychosis, and I know it, because they can't fix a name for it. What are we? Black? Colored? Negro? Non-white? Minority? Of color? That's the worst of the lot, a sentimental slipshod phrase -'of color' Think about it. When the word fails, the idea is dead."

He was genuinely upset and lay down turning his back on all of them. Sometimes he listened to tapes spoken in Sanskrit, because it gave him peace of mind. Lewis said his father was not so much misunderstood as unable to express his ideas clearly.

Lewis recalled: "When I asked Pop what he thought about love, he said 'Live Time' in a jive voice and laughed.

"You mean like Live Music? Saturday Night Live?" I asked him and he nodded, still laughing from the belly up."

"But I think it makes sense," I said in such a low voice, Lewis didn't hear me.

8-5

They put on a nightmare for me. My own waste was splashed across my lower body. It was so bad, the doctor said, "No more theater for you, young lady." And I was horrified because just now Tom had accepted me as I was and didn't want me to be a stiff socialite (or socialist?) after all. What if he saw me like this? I would want to die. So instead I rushed away from the nightmare into the fog. I used this as the first part of a 13-minute video called This Shit.

8-6

Libby and McCool were so generous, they always stopped the car to buy something for someone they were visiting. "Whenever you visit someone, one arm should be longer than the other," McCool would say in his fake Dublin accent. But Libby had to be stoned no matter where she was going. And so McCool was useful to her because he cheated, stole, knew crooks, never paid his debts and lied his way out of all his troubles.

On the other side, he gave everything he had away, threw money at anyone who asked for it, stopped to help people in trouble, and knew how to fix a car. He always justified his petty criminality with weak politics that were all about despair and opinion and nothing involving risk and sacrifice, yet his life was all about risk and sacrifice. His debts lay far and wide, cutting a swath through pub after pub and restaurant after restaurant and bookstore after bookstore across the city. He was able to sustain this situation by his own acts of generosity.

He had a recurrent suspicion that I had saved Lewis's illegitimate children through foster care. "Because they all look like resurrected half-breed slaves," he explained. "I just bet that hack writer of a friend of yours has reproduced plenty." Yet he cared for the children tenderly and well.

Libby took him away to the Mexican border where her early husband had left her that crippled lot of huts on a canyon gold with nasturtiums. It was a deserted compound that might have been inhabited at one time by hippies or a cult. Birds flew out of its windows as soon as they flew in.

To St. John of the Cross, memory is an obstacle to spiritual progress. To someone else serious, memory is the way God enters the brain. I was left with the children in a big stone house I couldn't afford on a small park in Roxbury. I was the only white person living there. Another one had been burned to death with gallons of kerosene. She was a young lesbian liberal who ran screaming for help. Who could forget this story? Especially not one living being hated. One after another people who were not white moved in with us—Jimmy and his wife, Heaven, then Mimi's husband's sister Ruby who helped with the children, and soon I had nothing to fear about being there. Not only were my foster children an indecipherable skin tone, I was white-haired and plain. I went to work part time as a photographer for the city's one black newspaper, and then moved into documentary and editing, making short films of an educational nature, about safety belts and drugs. Here I began a 20-year project, a film made out of the unused ends of others' reels. And I made little videos from my dreams.

Years passed other years, the children left home, and my family was made up of a circle of old friends.

At one point Walk was driving Mimi insane. She called to him: "You're a waste of time, just like my brother, a total loser, I can't look at you without crying . . ." And he responded, "Look at you, slaving day and night, all your life, at a dead-end job and living in a dump. What's to be proud of? Obeying the law?" And then he slammed out and I stayed behind. Mimi was trembling but close-mouthed. We went into the kitchen, a wood and linoleum affair, always immaculate, and put the kettle on. Mimi drank Maxwell's instant coffee with evaporated milk. I steamed on about the mystery of the words, "Lead us not into temptation" which sounded to me as if they were addressed to the devil rather than God.

8-7

"You are always welcome to use the chapel as a sanctuary for prayer. Please consult the schedule for the brothers' round of worship and prayer." Here where the brothers live under the Rule of Life are granite walls, undressed slate floors, Belgian marble walls and roof beams torn from the old Mystic River Bridge. I like the way they have Mary here holding the child and wearing a sapphire blue robe and a crescent moon is beneath her, golden spikes come from her person pointing up to the twelve stars that circle her head. Nearby angels swing their censers and sing. That's where I pray, under the Rose Window, to be a worker who can stir the heart of Mary to intervene and bring peace to the world.

If you say her name, she looks to God for a response. Is there irony in heaven? The Roman Centurions knew irony and so did the Greeks, but did the saints when they were performing extreme acts of penance? I think they wanted to be crushed into bars of pure God. Irony marks the end of the year. It wears the face of an accountant who is adding things up that were never meant to connect.

I learned to think as I went along reading, listening, dreaming, filming, sometimes auditing a lecture somewhere, then I rushed home to my children and the gravity of the kitchen sink.

Lewis was epiphanized in all these people, blood relatives and friends. What is suzerainty without a real body to fill its shoes? Hidden feelings yearn to be heard and so our heart-words called out to Lewis, through all of this, Love us! If Mimi formed the center of his world she now formed mine too, so there we met. However, the vulva-shape made by overlapping circles is no safer than a full shape floating on its own proportions: squares, ovals, rectangles. Everyone pretended they were safe. Since all dying is a kind of murder by this world, I would like to be able to declare, "I served another world." Just to have been true to one desire would have been enough for me, the rest of it all is so confusing.

In accordance with the wishes of friends, family and white racists, no one saw Lewis and me together, not even Libby, so we were like two living underground in separate rooms but calling. Now I can thank God we were never lovers or I would have lost him. Then I suffered because I believed we were victims of our times.

One time he told me: "I have one regret. . . . No child . . . I wish I had had a child. I even put some of my sperm on ice, in case I got too old, or ill—and look at me now. Lucky I did."

"But you'll have to find a surrogate mother, if that's what they're called."

"Suffragette. Ha ha. And what does it really mean?" he asked. "I think we are all genetically identical over the long haul. I mean, in one lifetime you have individual characteristics and tendencies, but all humans have the same ingredients generally—dementia, schizophrenia, bad eyesight, cancer, heart disease, rotten teeth—just a difference in quantity."

"So what you're saying ," I whispered.

"Is that I should have just adopted some needy kid years ago. It would've been the same as having my own."

"I know," I agreed.

"You would. You did. You took care of strangers but I bet you wish you'd had your own."

"Of course."

"Why didn't you just dump McCool, or come to me?"

"You didn't ask me, Lewis."

"McCool should feel really guilty."

"He thinks you have fathered scores of children."

"Why did you stay with him? I always wanted to ask."

"Because I, well, you, in a way."

"Don't blame me!"

"I can't explain it."

"There you go, swallowing your words."

"I felt sort of sorry for him." "So?"

"Well, we both got into the kids. And loved them. It seemed like fate."

"Bullshit." "What?" I asked.

"You didn't want them yourself." "I didn't? Why not?" I asked Lewis.

"You don't dare love. Your mother was insane, I don't know. But I think McCool was perfect because you don't love him and not having your own kids was perfect because you might love them too intensely if they were yours. You love people you can't have. Believe me. I understand that one. Only too well. Only too well."

"But you came from a stable adoring family," I reminded him.

"It made me arrogant. I thought I was immortal for way too long. Now I'm fucked up in a fucking wheelchair, childless, like a baby, useless."

"I'll take care of you."

"Push another infant around? Thanks but no thanks. Enjoy your freedom. You've paid your dues."

Crushed, I pushed at the arms of my seat, getting ready to go. "Where are you going?" he asked.

"Home." "Do you need taxi money?" "Nay."

Hot behind the eyes, I left him there. At a movie theater, parked in the middle of the aisle. We had just seen Forbidden Games, watched the credits through to the end, in the empty afternoon theater.

8-8

It wasn't much later when Lewis's father said: "Those born before the war believed in manners and forms, recognizable gestures that showed social differences between people to be as intractable as caste differences. . . . social as in having to do with education, generation, experience, and money. They were polite. Now our children judge us and are rude, but honest. They exploit and belittle their elders. And they justify all this by their infantile politics." Pop ranted while Walk yawned.

"The problem," Mimi said, "was never what we couldn't have, ourselves, but what we haven't done for each other. This is what we can't face. A communitarian failure."

Walk moaned a yawn and his father snarled, "Get on out of here."
So he left for the kitchen, leaving Mimi to return to her happy silence
while the old man snoozed over a copy of The Cloud of Unknowing. I
was there but the hour seemed insignificant. Retrospect is sequence.
Sometimes you would be in Mimi's house, lose her for a few minutes,
then find her sprawled across the belly of the old man breathing him in
as if he were her baby and him stroking her with his two soft hands, a
book slid to the floor; him humming to her some song.

Then you would back out of the room and leave by the kitchen
door. Ruby and I had this happen to us and we remembered it together because there was something in the shape they made circled
in the gloom and the stacks of books that reminded us of the way
certain paintings have oil so thick it is a smear off the natural, so unreadable close up and then so readable from afar, that it is like learning to see for the first time, figuring out the perspectives and spaces
between objects.

Ruby and I loved to go to the Museum with the teenage children on
its free afternoons and look at the Impressionists, the American Wing
and contemporary art, so we saw lots of actual postures as paintings
where we learned all we needed to know about color and content. Walk
came with us twice. Ruby wanted him to go back to school, a community
college would do. But he used the excuse of having no money to resist
her. "I can contribute," Ruby said.

"And I can find it," his mother insisted. Mimi didn't rest when Walk
was out of the house or when he was in it. She watched his every move,
wondered where he got the little money he had from working playground duty in an after-school program down the street.

"Where did you get that ten?" "I earned it, Ma. Remember?"

"You spent what you earned already."

"How do you know? You haven't got radar vision."

"I know what you earn and I have vision enough to see what you
spend . . . Son, you better not be involved. You don't want to end up
doing shut-in after all. It's hell in there."

"No, I know I don't, not ever."

545

"So watch it, son. Pop is not too well. You might need to go to the library for him."

"Don't worry. And I'll be going back to school soon too." "To study what?"

"Music."

Walk played his guitar in the kitchen and sang the blues. She cleaned up around him and began to prepare a macaroni cheese and spinach casserole they all liked.

One Sunday Mimi took me into her room to look inside her deep dark wooden closet stuffed with shoes and clothes. We sat on her double bed which was covered with a quilt handmade by a friend in Lawrence, Kansas, a woman whose grandfather had been white and a slave. The quilt was stiff, heavy and geometrical in design. Red and yellow patches were sewn together with thick yellow thread. There was a cane chair in the room and an oak desk and dresser, plain white cotton curtains shut out the brick view. Books all over the right side of the bed which sagged lower than the left. Water guttered over the window panes. Mimi wanted my advice about criminal behavior because I was white, and she perched on the sagging side of the bed with her face turned toward the window where reflecting shadows off the water then gathered onto her cheeks. At the same time I looked at a picture of the family still in Missouri, many years before, and yearningly scrutinized Lewis young and athletic in his country clothes.

Mimi explained: "I think Walk has hidden some stuff in my closet. But I don't dare look."

"Stuff?"

"I don't know, just something illegal. There's a box back there."

"For how long?" I asked.

"About six weeks, six times, don't tell."

"What are you going to do?"

"He wouldn't do that, would he? I mean, hide it in his mother's closet!"

"It seems like the perfect place to hide it—to me," I said.

Mimi rubbed her eyes and scrutinized me who in turn scrutinized the photograph of Lewis with my hand shading off the place where the reflection of rain suddenly blocked my view of him.

"I don't dare look. But I don't want to know. Will you look?"

The closet door increased its depth by yards as I stood up to face it. Square darkness, square air. Clothes hanging neatly in rows and shoes stacked behind against the wall.

A closet is a kind of hole, its walls are floors. You want to crawl or enter on tiptoe. The fact is, a closet is equivalent to a corner of the brain where you hide the day's self-images. No one goes fully inside a closet but stands back and gingerly picks out an article of clothing, as if it was a cluster of fruit hanging on a bee-buzzing vine. "It's way in back, on the left," Mimi said.

I turned wonderingly, because she was so complex, so surprising to me. A mother. She couldn't face what Walk was really doing, even while she was monitoring his every move. Simone Weil suggested that the escalation of violence occurs because the victim imitates the tactics of the victor. I think the escalation of passivity occurs when a person fears for another person so deeply she can't move.

I was literally scared of the closet and of putting my hand inside. If there was a box in there, containing packets of white stuff, or if there was a sack of weed, a fetus, or if there was a gun in the box, I could only anticipate an explosion, napalm, something that sticks. "Wouldn't it be better for you to be innocent and not know?" I asked Mimi.

"You couldn't—you wouldn't—want to take it—away for me?" she said in soft tones.

"But, we don't even know what it is."

"You're right. Better just leave it. Say nothing, know nothing."

My attention had drifted up from my chest to my face. "I mean. . . . Well . . ."

"What's that?" Mimi was beseeching. It was a kind of falling, my evasion of her urgency—a yawn, a nod and a swallowing down into space. In fact it was guilt being gulped. My own, it made a place for itself in my chest like a burning frying pan.

Mimi stared at me expectantly, then said: "I feel so sorry for him. He has this heroic brother. What's he to do. He can't live up. He suffers, he has talent, lots of it, abilities, but his ego is crushed by—well, you know who, and Pop too. They look down on him. I want to help him, that's all, fifteen hundred a semester, not a big deal."

"You mean if he can sell whatever is in there? Can't Ruby help instead?"

"Help? Yes, but he doesn't want that. He says she'll make him pay in some way. She's so judgmental."

"But it's safer." "No, I know."

Her collar lay red and open, a V across her chest, where I could see a pulse operating in the little impression at her throat. "I'm immobilized. I feel so sorry for him. What do you think?"

I was afraid to say that I sensed that the police were already in the room with us, that Walk was someone who had bad luck, that I should pull it out and flush it down the toilet that minute. "I feel sorry for him too. Let's just risk it," I said instead.

Afraid it might pop the bubble in our thinking, I made some joke, backed away from the closet, went home and heard by word of Lewis's mouth on a breezy May day that Mimi had been arrested and put in the Federal prison to await trial for drug-trafficking. She was fifty four years old.

Lewis called to tell me. "Did you know about this?" "Of course not," I lied.

"Motherfuckers came into the house and took her away in cuffs," he said, his voice shaking. "Why the fuck would she have dope? Was it my little asshole brother's fault? I just don't get it. Henny, I'm going crazy, but I'm going to do all I can, all I can. I'm going to do all I can to get her out. . . . Listen. Never let anyone you know—ever—go to prison. Promise? Promise."

There are studies on philosophies of subjectivity, using the example of a witness to an accident. In this example, the witness is passively involved in the accident by the mere fact of seeing it.

There are four attitudes a witness might take in regard to the event: one is to testify boldly in court to everything he or she saw; another is to avoid causing further chaos by saying "I don't really remember;" a third is to laugh with certain skeptics who have wondered, "Justice? Impossible in such a world!" and back away; and a fourth is a parody of the first. In this case the cynical witness testifies with embellishments, exaggerations, lies, just for the fun of it.

A fifth example is unmentioned but it is almost the same as the third. In this example, the witness finds a way to save the defendant from going to jail because she feels she caused the accident just by being there to observe it. She is so conscious of the causes and contingencies that brought her to that place, at that hour, she knows that she is responsible for its outcome. It is wonderful how nothing works.

Who said, "It is an odd domain, this 'inner' country, this invisible and silent place where revolutions take place before news of them gets out." I think the soul is a possession of the person and not a part of the person. It is like a baby you carry around and give to it whatever you can so it will know good. But does your soul have to love you in order to stay with you? And will it leave you if it stops loving you?

"Yes, yes, it will leave you. Definitely it will leave you," said Tom.

Wishing Around the Edges

9-1

Whenever I visited Mimi in prison. I found her dressed in a crisp greenish uniform just like the other women wore, but Mimi looked elegant in it, just because of her posture and gesture. She always wore earrings which she rubbed between her fingers nervously.

Or else, seated, she leaned forward and pressed her hands in mine for the entire two hour visit. She was very thin and her complexion had developed something like stains. She always said, "I made a terrible mistake. I couldn't face reality." And she never blamed me.

Once early on she introduced me to people around. She did so with a low voice that gave me the impression that she was participating in their bad luck. A morose man with a beautiful boy under his hand and a wild-haired woman at whom the man never once glanced. She even introduced me to the guard who was a pretty Puerto Rican woman.

I was understood to be an aging beatnik and over a month of Sundays we all got comfortable with each other. Mimi wanted to hear details about my collection of children and hers. She liked to know about the weather outside and the animals at the zoo where she missed the birds especially. Mimi said her idea of paradise now would be to sit in the birdhouse and look and listen.

Walk had left the country with his money. Lewis visited his mother whenever he could, the old man never did because he feared he would die if he saw her there.

And now the old man would not let me into the house. He abandoned his idea of his home as a race-free zone and became on the contrary obsessional about the betrayal by whites. Ruby, standing on one crutch with her neck thrust forward, and her eyeglasses flashing tinny circles, told me all about it. She said race was all anyone talked about in Pop's house as if Mimi, in fact, had been the one holding the subject at bay. One night stones shattered the windows in my house and this action seemed part of all the rest, Mimi in jail and the old man's rage and the city at large, and I knew I had to move my skin to another part of town. I was laughing when I left. There was lots to laugh about. My house was sold for six times the amount we bought it for. Reagan was President.

One winter day Lewis came to jail at the same time as me, and I waited in the lobby until he had finished with his visit. Outside he told me about the people there, as if I had never met them.

Lewis reported: "That fine woman Gemma is in for life. So soon there won't be anyone to take care of her kid. The guy really wants to get on with his monastic vows. You can imagine. It's not even his child. Or so he says."

As Lewis told me this I imagined him whirling himself around to look at the group collected around a sticky table because "That's one beautiful child," he said to me outside. "Blind or not." I groaned and moved away from Lewis, abruptly, and went to line up with the people entering. But he called after me: "Why the fuck didn't we just go and do it, Henny? Have a kid together, anything. I mean, fuck." I started to turn back but was pushed forward into the little chamber with the heavy locked doors.

Inside, breathless, I told Mimi what he had said to me. "I don't know why he never had a child," said Mimi. "It's what he needs, even this late. He needs a real home. Even that priest over there seems to have had a child."

"Priest?"

I found myself examining Tom. There was no scent but a kind of heat around his person that I suddenly wanted to partake of. I envied him for believing in God. I wanted to sit beside him for a long time. And I was still under the spell of Lewis, as if I had brushed under a rainy branch and the drops still glittered on my clothes, in my hair.

"I'm going to go talk to them," I told Mimi.

The boy's eyes were closed and his expression alert, and he had a small but eager smile on his lips. As ever his eyes were ringed with shadows, his lids heavy and his mouth was full and pink. "Gnomes again?" I asked. Gemma his mother moved back to make room for me, and I could see that she loved him objectively but without the swallowing attention that mothers who live with their children have.

Tom smiled at me, weakly, and murmured, "Gnomes." I had felt some tie between us already forming on visiting days, because we often eyed each other, then looked away quickly as if sickened. Now it was not strange for me to plant myself beside him even though we had had only a few conversations, mostly standing in line for our credential check, or while stuck in the little room waiting to be let into the prison area officially. He glanced sideways at me with a curt nod and read my mind. "We should talk outside of this place sometime," he said.

9-2

I see what's coming but I don't see where it's coming from. Every face and step is pitching forward only to be gone missing. The plaza showed it. Sky a bakery, each tree on the ledge. Libby and my husband left me that mildewed love nest on the border. The buildings they built plus the kitchen on legs that Tom and I painted. We went there together only months after Mimi left for Missouri. We stayed there longer than planned because we were happy that we hated it. Eat and run little birds, pink hibiscus orange and red nasturtium, a jacaranda that grows blue, bougainvillea like butterflies, neon pink or nearly brown and eucalyptus silver blue and bittersweet to smell. Everywhere the monkey-like idea of palm silhouettes, banana-skins and a coat over cream. Sitting outside at night was like passing around a razor to shave a zebra down to its first shape. The black sky is really a weight, can hurt, so heavy a dump of stars, some falling all turning together bare naked between them. God planted the glass that grew language.

"Sand, glass, they're the same thing," said Tom into the dark.

"Do you really think that your Julio Dumas is the same one as mine?"

"He has to be the same. There can't be two."

"It makes me think there really is a big plan, or pattern."

"Well, isn't that what you always think, as a priest, or monk, or whatever you want to be?"

"All I do is try to stay on the side of belief," he said. "My doubt is enormous."

"Apparently not as big as mine. Mine is the foundation of my hope that one day I might find God. If I didn't doubt so intensely, there would be no hope for me. . . . By the way, Blessed are they that mourn for they shall be comforted. What do you think that means?" I asked him.

"I think the deeper you go, the safer it gets. . . . Plus I think Jesus means that mourning helps you cross out of the world, unlike other emotions that really take you nowhere. . . . Lust, and so on."

Rain again gurgling and bubbling around my dreams and I swimming in the water around the hut, it turned corners and created former streets, deep green, dean water that boats began to use and pollute as I swam along calling for Libby to come on down, leave her parents alone, and swim with me. And when she did she was finally smiling and happy because she couldn't hear them fighting anymore. She was dead or something.

Indivisible

When McCool returned from the border in the eighties, he came right to the house to reclaim me and the children. "I was only joking," were his first words to me. By then he and Libby had satisfied their curiosity about each other—or at least she had—and we had moved to a new neighborhood with people of all colors. Ruby lived with us still, Mimi was at home, and Lewis was always away. Cards from him in Jordan, Pakistan, Northern Ireland, Capetown. McCool got furious when he found them in my brown jewelry box tied up in a pink ribbon. I wanted him to leave the house as a mouse, dead in a box. He stamped around raving about my obsession with Lewis and how women never wait for their men anymore but dream of others like troubadours. He compared me to a rabbit saying I would inherit the earth because I lived in a hole. All of us cried, the children and me, and begged him to leave. Then when he left, we sat down and ate a chicken pie voraciously.

With McCool there was no balance. When we met in the bar in 1970, I was sewing a dress for my mother who would only wear one style in a variety of patterns made by me. A line below the knees, belted waist, buttons up to the neck, and a little middy-like collar. Just as she wore this style every day of her adult life, so she wore her hair in the same stiff little black bob. You don't often see someone with a sewing basket in a pub, checking coats and hats, contented if disconnected from the business of the place. My mother was already bidding goodbye to life and she still loved Jacqueline Kennedy. The fabric was apple green. In a matter of weeks I would lean down and kiss her moist refrigerated head where a tear shone in the corner of one eye, before she was shoved into the fire, dressed in this very same dress. I like to believe that it was my vulnerability during the time of her illness that catapulted me towards McCool. But such logic isn't natural to me. In any case he leaned on the counter where I was hidden among wet coats and stared into my eyes with an expression of astonishment and lust. "You look like your father," he said, "an Irishman, I wager, from the west. Are you twenty one?" Being naturally quiet, I only nodded but when I returned his gaze

I saw my fate. Whether it would happen then and there, or years later, I could read that he was written in. I was revolted. This revulsion was a form of fear, but it was also a sign that we would become intimate before too long. Revulsion often signals the inevitable, it is a kind of symptom of obedience.

McCool was his singing name by which he was commonly known and I had hated him every time he took up the guitar and sang, he was so handsome. But the fact that he came from Ireland where my grandmother lived—that he was Irish—thrilled me. Now I had an excruciating pain in my groin where my ovaries were firing off, and I clutched my guts. I never got what I wanted. We couldn't take our eyes off each other. To look was to feel. We were, in this one stare, too attuned. If I was witty, snide, fond, full of fear or sadness, he reacted with the right glance, as in sympathetically. As two who had suffered through similar childhoods—fatherless, mad mothers, foster care—the blood of actual Ireland in his body made him seem more tragic than myself. He was like my mother in his frenzied propensities. My pain was mirrored on his face.

"What hurts?"

"My stomach," I told him.

"Mine too. We need children. Let's have them."

"I need a ring."

"Well, all right then, and let's find a priest."

It was this quick and that easy. His poverty and his intoxicated claims to being Irish reminded me of my mother's intelligence staggered by dread and paranoia. But I was really after my father. The inevitability of our marriage came with the force of an accident. All the contingencies slammed us into a bed trying to produce babies, but unable. We tried and tried. Such a failure was like a funnel that drags you whirling towards its smallest point. Because of it, I would afterwards be able to forgive everyone everything.

Just as Languedoc was a sublime intention realized on earth, Lewis remained my courtly love, the one where joy was untroubled by knowledge. McCool was horribly real. Antigone says, "The God of the Dead at least desires equality," and it certainly is the case that all deaths, no matter how little, are lovely levelers of people. But I was a sucker for him because of his diction.

9-4

On one of those wintery days Lewis got Mimi out of prison. Not on probation but out scot free. He had friends in legal places, people who owed him favors and he put them all to work for her. Lewis always kept his promises which is why he rarely made them. Mimi had been inside for one year and six months. Her family came to take her home and I didn't see her again; it was one thing after another.

That same week Ruby took all her things out of her room and left my household, saying she wanted to live with Mimi. She said: "At my age you just want to go home. It's basic. I like the way she cooks those eggs." The women in that family were under the sway of the old man who now insisted that they all return to their house in Missouri. He said he had learned enough in Boston. I lost them all as quickly as I had found them. I felt like a monster banned from society and never loved by you, God, who would never reward me for my troubles. No children, no success. Lewis was in Africa when his family decided to start west and he returned only to boss people around, then sweep away again like a US Senator. He was wonderful at teaching me how to trust and love no man, to live without sex or affection except from my poor children. I was grateful for his annihilating insouciance by the time I was forty. Invisibility by then was my favorite thing. The only time I burned was when people noticed I was white and hated me for it, because then it meant I came from somewhere physical in history.

I decided that Ruby never loved me. She moved in with me only out of perversity—to make her brother—Pop the father—mad. His racism reminded her of the way he had always been cruel to her about her plain looks. She nonetheless went to visit him, even when she hated him, and the day I dropped her there—to return for good—I saw him thinner at the door, his pants baggy and his skin grayish in color. He shouted at me: "What have you heard from my son?"

"He's in Jerusalem."

"Well, tell him to leave Jerusalem and help us move out of this hellish city."

"I will. He will."

"As for you, it was you who let this happen to Mimi," he yelled at me. "White people always fail in the end. No moral attention, only self-interest—"

Ruby pushed him out of her way and they went inside with a bang of the door.

Mansions are resting places, like inns, and God has many of them for people to stop in, on their way home. I don't know why I found such a mansion there, outside that door, that afternoon, but I was flooded with the sky and its lack of names.

9-5

The dialectic of the 20th century (determinism versus choice) is as old as the hills. But today I realized that a choice can be wrong. I used to think otherwise. Now I see that choices are so difficult because people know that they can make the wrong ones. But I think that if a choice is made against you to reject you, your work or your love, for instance—it can't be wrong. It can't be wrong because it would always come to that, anyway. Sooner or later, you would be rejected by that party. And you would suffer throughout the whole process. So in a way what happens to you is pre-determined, but what you do to yourself is a choice.

In the meantime, and in one's innocence, forward motion drags more and more collected material to the surface of your person. In an ideal situation, when the weight is only a mild hindrance, the person examines the dream-stuff and shucks away the pieces that are the heaviest. I think it might be an error to throw away the recollected things that make you suffer and better to convert them into works. By works I mean actions or objects of beauty or functional value. However, you have to believe that there is no unconscious in order to do this. You have to be committed to wakefulness as a continual and total state of being. Between Brahman and consciousness there is no border. Wakefulness like sleep provides a person with a kind of emotional release since you can swim into non-being with your eyes wide open. If you stop thinking of your psyche as a bank, containing hidden capital, you can finally begin to spend your time. Siva and Sakti, Arjuna and Krishna, Mary and the Infant Jesus—these are images of the actual and the open-to-all.

"Scoot closer," Ramakrishna said to his faithful followers. He was alert and affectionate. It is important to remain faithful to something—that is, to finish the same thing over and over. Libby and McCool parted without tears like two little friends who are sick of their stuffed animals and are now ready for school. She was worried about her children who were unruly and dirty and she turned her full attention on them while she lived with a bunch of rich friends in Hawaii. There she was loved and safe. After McCool handed me the deed to the land on the Mexican border, he drove me and the children east, and stalked us for several years. What was his problem? He was convinced that Lewis was sneaking in to see me.

Suspicion is a magician, making fantasies become real.

Lewis did sneak in one night, arriving at my bedside uninvited, drunk. Everyone in the big wooden house was sleeping. There was an autumn wind scratching at pavements and windows and walls. The stairs creaked with nobody on them. The door swung lonely on its hinges. The glass panes banged. Lewis was dressed in a three quarter length black leather coat, wore a black beret and a light beard.

"How did you get in?" I cried.

"The window slid right up."

"Why? Your voice is slurring, you might get caught."

"By who? You're the only authority figure here."

"You know."

"McCool is a fraud, a coward, he will never lay a hand on me. "So why are you here?"

"Pop wouldn't let me in. He's gone crazy."

"Well, am I the only one left?"

"Seems that way. Let me in."

"My bed?"

"Come on, don't worry."

Lewis dropped his coat, shoes, pants and sweater on the floor and slid in his boxers and tee shirt onto and then into the bed. We scrutinized each other in the light coming from the nodding streetlights outside. He smelled like a gingerbread man, smiled, his eyes heavy. Go to sleep, I told him, and don't worry. He turned on his side facing me and shut his eyes so I could watch his face dose up in repose. The nostrils shaped like teardrops, the nose itself small, round and firm, the ears like pink shells pressed against his head, his nappy hair cut close, his wide smooth mouth with crescent lines engraved about a quarter-inch from each corner, no other lines anywhere, his eyebrows light but a furrow just beginning to form almost like a new small delicate bone, his muscular neck disappearing into his shirt where he snored.

I slipped gingerly into the orange aura that wrapped him like swaddling and lay wide awake there. I was wearing a plaid flannel nightgown and he laid his sleeping hand on my hipbone. When I breathed, he snorted and flopped on his other side so now I had his back in my face. And this way I ruminated about sex and remembered it as something that must have been courageous to do. If all exercise requires a dash of courage, sex does especially.

There is no deliverance like no delivery. He had laid down his life beside mine at last.

This is not directly a story about maternalism, about the hours and years of care-taking, rushing to and from pickups and drop-offs, the homework, the dressing, the health care, the nursing, cleaning diapers, toilet training, teaching to walk, chasing, fearing, reading, rocking, singing, raging, begging, trudging, lugging, dressing, shoes, clothes, mending and finding, trips to the park and zoos and pushing swings and grocery shopping, comforting and punishing, allowing and bitching, the meals after meals after meals and washings-up and washings-down, broken equipment, lost bottles, toys to be fixed and dresses sewed, the comforting, drying and cleaning, the preaching, forgetting and ironing.

Indivisible

This fake mother was as much mother as motel and as much convent as commune.

Saint Teresa said that ministry and suffering were inseparable. She believed that contemplation involved the love of one's neighbor, detachment and humility—these being the three virtues of maternalism as well. She hated dour-faced nuns, those who looked at the faults of others and never at their own. On Trinity Sunday, June 2, 1576 she began to write The Interior Castle. The soul she says is like a transparent diamond. It is so beautiful and glittery that it can blind a person approaching it, and make her stop outside. It is blind itself. Entering the soul hurts because it doesn't know how magnificent it is or how it magnifies the face of its servant. Knowledge is a function of the working mind but the soul shines despite the body. If it knew how it shone, it might shrivel from shame and let any servant enter easily. Its blind resistance saves it of course from corruption but it makes the entering servant feel barbaric, the way a mother feels when she lets a nurse give her baby its first shot.

Strange to imagine a diamond with airy rooms inside. But there it is. The soul. I think Saint Theresa understood the dilemma of personhood as a problem with physics, each cell refractive and self-contained, the universe stuck in each one in different positions, and the difficulty in examining it from the outside, when the eyes are on the inside of it.

For instance, in The Fifth Dwelling Place, she writes that the soul experiences separation from the body where "its whole intellect wants to understand what it is actually feeling."

Total attention to one thing of beauty puts the rest of the brain to sleep like the whole castle in Sleeping Beauty. Seeing is selective blindness because the shock of the beautiful numbs the rest. Teresa says there is a sweet wine near the heart of a person that makes her feel drowsy when she has recollected deeply. It was during my child-rearing years that I drank that wine and my mind passed through the divine mansions resting and realizing.

I had taken five children dutifully through first communion, confirmation and to Sunday Mass, while I hung back and watched my revelations. Two of the children went home to their families, the other three stayed with me, and still others came and went on a short-term basis.

The place where Lewis found me that night was the above. Reading and writing manifestoes in my sleep. At five we whispered while the dawn pinked and tweeted and Lewis asked: "What happened to Libby? Is she okay?"

"Yes, she's in Hawaii."

"So why is McCool so jealous of you if he ran off with your best friend?"

"McCool's a hypocrite."

"Crazy sounds more like it. Doesn't he hold himself accountable?"

"He lacks a conscience, a super-ego."

"Did you ever love him?"

"Did you ever love anyone?"

He didn't answer but lay silent, breathing heavily. So now I could doze. He was awake and still and the light was up and Saturday had descended from the sky preserving many from a day of labor or school. My situation took form as a dream of leaves and loam and growing things. Movements of snake and roach and rooms that had branches in them and grass where there used to be rug. No clothes, no chairs, no people, but tables and papers and reels of film hanging on clotheslines blowing with the twigs and their shadows indoors. This was no home, more like a rayogram by Man Ray.

God led me into the arcade, an energy sepulcher, the station where you travel to the other world. Of course it was very dark with intervals of lights engraved in arcs across the black air. I was scared knowing I had no will left for myself, had become like a calf who can't decide when or how anything will happen. All my life people had referred to this condition as "obedience" or Zen. But I felt no virtue in standing abandoned at a black wall. If I was as lively as a spider, it was only my nerves, but probably I was more like a piece of flesh on a production line waiting for the plant to turn on and me to be rolled to dust.

Downstairs four large children were watching cartoons as Lewis and I stirred in my bed. His hand lay on my head without weight.

"I could never sleep with you because you're the last stop," he said gruffly.

"Stop? Thanks, me?"

"Yes, it would be the end of our friendship. The end of me having fun. I couldn't stand it. I seem to like women I don't love."

"Yawn. That's the oldest boring story"

"I mean, I have wanted to have sex with you but, you know, it would have been too demanding. Somehow."

"You, how."

"I would have to end up with you. That would be like dying young."

"Great."

"It's awful, I mean being one of those pathetic people who always think someone better is coming around the corner. In the end, it's me nobody loves. It's me."

"Your mother did."

"And you. A long time ago."

"You're like someone who sleeps with their hat on."

"Too talkative?"

He pulled up his tee shirt to show me his rounded midriff and slapped it with disgust, saying he was getting fat like his father. I asked: "Could you ever marry a white woman?"

"Probably not, seeing as it would damage my image, whatever that is. We could sneak around. I do that all the time. Anyway you'll never get a man again, with that husband crawling around in the bushes, foster kids, no money, over forty."

We dropped into a silence that was moist. I was hurt, even though I knew I could have stuck my hand down under the covers and inside his boxers and rolled against him. Could have excited him and held him and his lingam and played with it until he was locked into the act, both of us smiling and pretending we were smiling. I could have seen it through like a tank entering a forest. We could have done a lot without even being intimate, our eyes shut, diamonds on our inner lids, and roaring brains shutting off the clamor of cartoons. Once Libby told me that one tantra divides the vulva into ten parts that are made for each aspect of the Great Mother. All tantras have at their center five sacraments: wine, fish, meat, grain and sex. Every act is holy because every act is holy. Tantric sex should take place among flowers, incense, colorful rice, sandalwood, a vessel full of native rum, sweetmeats and little cakes, but it hardly ever does. The lotus and the color red are reminders of happy and mystical sex. On the slopes of some blue mountain there is a yoni-shaped hole in a rock and it weeps red tears and water that makes you high. Someone said that a drop of Christ's red blood contains the universe. For the rest of us, it is just the cells in our skins and brains. Later we ate fruit loops and drank orange juice in front of the TV with Ruby and the kids and then Lewis went away to South Africa and his fateful encounter with a gun.

While Lewis was gone I met a sailor who had tattoos on his arms, as blue as his eyes, a reddish mustache and a veiny face from drink. He was introduced as McCool's revolutionary cell mate and a sailor who had crossed the seven seas on rigs and tankers. He was funny and quiet and meticulous. When he stayed with us, he was always straightening and lining up the children's toys and stuffed animals, and placing them in interesting relations to each other, ones that the children shrieked with laughter over, when they came home. He cleaned and tidied my cupboards too, and swabbed out the grimy drawer where the flatware lay in rubbermaid containers.

He stayed in my house while McCool was playing music somewhere south. The sailor drank rum in his juice in the morning, his face fired up and he told me jokes.

Over the afternoons when the children were still in school and I was home from work we'd sit in the kitchen with tea and chocolate chip cookies that I was baking, and he would arrange everything in sight. One night he got into my bed and made love to me. He was strong, his hands slow, his approach tender but unremitting. He was making me laugh all the time. We had beside the bed rum, candies, a candle, incense and red rosary beads from India. The laughter lasted all night, then at daybreak he snuck back to his room and snored loudly, leaving that afternoon. On his way out he told me my husband was a pathological liar and not Irish at all.

"We met on the merchant marine near Indonesia," he said. "I hate to be the one to break it to you, but you ought to know the facts." He was a plain ruddy man, nothing to look at, and I thought at first he was joking. After all his jokes occurred in direct ratio to his withheld violence. A roar of laughter replaced gunfire. But this time he didn't smile. And I felt like a thorny tree that cannot spout a bud at its head, a long stiff stem with its conclusion in air. "You mean—his accent—is a fake?" He nodded and I thanked him as he went out the door, while the children pulled on his sleeves, begged him to stay and called him Popeye.

It struck me as a familiar experience that shock could be administered not in a cold voice but through a mist of hugs and kisses. McCool was a forgery.

9-6

Libby flew me and my children to Hawaii one year. She paid for everything. We took three different planes, the last being a miniature one out of Honolulu into Hilo. It was raining where she lived in a wooden house beside a waterfall. Geckos climbed the walls. Six people lived with her in the house, two of them being her children, and they all had expensive four-wheel-drive cars. One was a man as thick as a heifer who acted like Zeus. His girlfriend was the school friend named Honey. Then Libby's lover had slicked back hair and strong features that found their focus in his bad teeth. He looked as if he had dirt in his bones. He had been a maker of documentaries, got into drugs, joined the religious group, gave up drugs and was now selling real estate in Kona. The hour I arrived, I was spirited away by Libby who never liked me near her real friends. She had rented a house on black sand for us all and there we stayed with our children. Was she ashamed of me? Or was she proud and wanted me to herself? She told me how she left her purse open for those men in the past, and they took her money freely and spent it on drugs and housing. We tripped along the dark sea's edge with our children and wished we were lesbians. Libby also wished she was somewhere else, she always did, wanting to be in New York when she was in New Mexico or want-

ing to be California when she was in Hawaii, she believed she was missing something important.

I told her I hadn't yet used the deed to her property on the border
and she assured me that she really wanted me to go and fix it all up
because then we could hide away together there, when the time came,
when the Millennium and the Apocalypse came, and when we were
very old. "It should be a force for good. McCool was at his best there,
and so was I."

"What is real sex?" I asked her. "Lying in bed with the one you love,
or maybe screwing a stranger?"

"That's like asking what is the difference between celibacy and
chastity."

"There is a difference," I told her.

"What."

"Celibacy is the choice to be single, unsexual. Chastity is something
you don't choose, it's a condition—of incorruptibility. You can be raped
and still be chaste."

"Which would you rather be?" Libby asked me. We squinted across
black twinkly sand to a sea so bright, it rejected eyesight. "I'd rather the
one that isn't a choice," I told her.

The Glass that Grew

10-1

Three days a week I worked in a darkroom editing film, then video,
then learning how to correlate images with monitors, and how to use
an elaborate toaster for aftereffects and then having to learn digital editing. The company was financially solvent, run by a practical idealist
named Rye who believed in the power of the media to change public
opinion for the good. He was a perpetual Pan and a Catholic convert.
Later he moved to Honduras to educate people in technology. For the
years I worked for him I was happy in the dark. At home Ruby was there

for the kids, along with others who came, stayed and went away. Ruby, disabled in an accident when she fell down an elevator shaft at a poorly run charcoal briquet factory, moved stiffly giving orders. She was by nature tyrannical. Like Lewis her nephew. Some perverse streak in her resisted accomplishment and sought salvation in struggling with objects and other people's needs. She was a Catholic who did everything "for God" when she could have worked in a powerful secular organization as an executive producer. Rewards, flattery and any other form of attention sickened her. Yet she suffered when she was ignored and wanted to make sure she was appreciated. She was always mad at Lewis and she only saw us together once, that morning in front of television after nothing happened.

My feelings for her went, "Help, Mommy, don't leave me, please love me. I hate everyone and everyone hates me. But not you, please not you!"

Outside our house two tall swaying phone poles, pines and stone, cars nearly crashing at the intersection every fifteen minutes, and a stinkweed tree.

10-2

Tom and I leave our compound and drive to the desert the day the rain retreats and the day after the doctor's visit. We have decided to look for the center for abused children, just to see. You climb up to get down in this desert. You drive about 4000 feet above sea level on winding roads through monumental bodies of green-hard hills, buzzed with bracken and mustard and tearing up any shadows. Unusable glens and pastures all dry. Five black bears and a jaguar had been spotted by residents recently.

Campers have seen coyotes, gophers, lizards and snakes. California oak trees remind Tom of paintings by Corot and Millet. He feels as if he has exploded into one of their canvases when we drive through a thicket and a tunnel of these dotty oaks, because when we walk on them the leaves are tough curls that crackle underfoot like hardened oil paint. I don't know why the mountains look as if they are bent backs moving forward as we approach them. We are speechless for a half hour at being far from our grievous hideaway and the tropical drops of the canyons and the dripping trees. It is mid-February. It is Valentine's Day.

He tells me that Jesus thought of the heart as an organ of intellect and quoted: "Out of the hearts of men proceed evil thoughts."

"It sounds to me as if Jesus means that emotions precede ideas."

"We're dropping into the desert now."

"Did we bring that water?"

This desert begins as a pallid field speckled with round cactus, then some crown of thorns loops up and over, the ground beachy and shelly, quartz and granite bits embedded in the brokenness like dusty trash-heaps from the 19th century. Heaps not hills and down we roll onto the flat plain, almost badlands, dry-dry and dappled with a variety of cactus red-tipped, yellow-tipped or flat purple spatulas dimpling thorns. Still, the light of it all is blinding. I press at my eyes, try to shield them, squint, blink and water. My friend is dazzled in other ways. As we drive towards a little town corrupted by a country club, he confesses to liking a sense of anarchy that the desert gives off. It reminds him of Mary of Egypt who walked stark naked across the sand with only her hair to cover her, aroused by visions and penances.

"And who does Mary of Egypt remind you of?" I ask him and my tongue feels like my heart because I am scared of his feelings for people.

"No one. Why? Who?"

"Maybe Gemma?"

"Well, I guess," he surmised.

"Do you think you can, um, enter a monastery with this kind of interest in a woman?"

"What interest."

"I mean, can you live a celibate life?"

"Well, that's the point."

"Of?"

"Of all this."

"You mean, to learn to hate everything?"

"Not everything." He waved his hand vaguely towards the cloud-free sky.

"Not Gemma?"

"Not everything in the world," he said with a glowering glance at me.

"Well, anyway," I said. "I can't think symbolically."

"But you do all the time. Thought is symbolic. Language is too."

"Then I mean something else."

"Mythologically, mythically, maybe," he patiently suggested.

"Well, I can't think of an idea outside of experience."

"Thinking with your heart?"

"I'm a mother type."

"Ma they called you? Your foster kids?"

"Each one called me something different. Ma, Mummy, Mom. Henny."

"Well, I'm not called Dad, Daddy, Papa or Father, and never will be."

"You chose this," I tell him.

"Of course, I know, but I mean, Gemma's child, I love him."

"It would be hard not to."

"Won't you take care of him? He needs a home. His foster parents are not good."

"I know about foster parenting first hand," I remind him.

"It's all intended," he said.

"Don't you want to ask what was wrong? Why I couldn't have children?"

"Don't make me," Tom pleaded.

I wonder, then say, "Forget it."

"I just feel that it's intended, that you are meant to be his parent, because of the Julio connection, I guess, and well, other reasons too."

"You feel guilty about Gemma. But are you in love with her?"

"God no."

"I thought there had been someone—maybe her—"

"God no."

"Who then who."

"Forget it. It's another story."

It is impossible for me to ask the inevitable question: Are you gay? The image of Mimi's closet is not far off. Denial, embarrassment, not wanting to know, because it will so profoundly exclude me from the history of his future.

I squint now at the horizon where there is a metallic glitter poured across the dust. Huge khaki colored war planes are hunched on a vast spread of land, behind high fencing. We slow to look, from our closed car, now outside the town.

"You seem upset," he says to me.

"I am but I don't know why."

"Those planes."

"No, I was before."

"I think I know why," he says.

"Why," I ask.

"You don't like thinking I have—had—ordinary feelings."

"I do like it."

"No, all of you lay people hate it. It makes you anxious, and angry at me. You would rather imagine me as uncontaminated, pure, inno-cent, whatnot."

"I do like thinking that one person I know lived without violence," I admit.

"It's bigger than that," Tom says. "It's existential. It's a wish for God to be here, on earth, visible."

The war planes seem abandoned. The site they occupy is abso-lutely without a sign of human life. But the sound of one buzzing in the faraway cut the air like the shape of a dog. "Don't worry. I won't tell you anything personal," Tom says and speeds up the car. "Give me that water."

Soon we pull into a diner called Hart's Chicken Parts which is also deserted except for one red-cheeked waitress watching television. She brings us sandy-like slices of chicken and cole slaw and Coke. "Eckhart talks about the birth of God out of nothingness," Tom says with his nap-kin covering his mouth, "and the nothingness is swollen like a pregnant woman. That's the image he uses."

"I wonder why," I murmur.

"And so it's sort of like the universe as physicists describe it now."

"It is? I wish we were outdoors again." "Why did you marry your husband?" he asked me.

"I think, I guess, we had something awful in common. Class anxiety. We were both outsiders. Libby was our shared object of adoration. God, analysis is boring."

"You women just after the Beats? My generation and class? Your age group too? Well, you got an awful batch of men," said Tom. "Bastards. Still believed they were demi-gods, spoiled, but angry when you began to get independent. Awful. I feel for you. You got a raw deal. The new generation of boys is better. So why didn't you have children?"

"Let's go outside. Him. He couldn't. Weak sperm or something."

Through the plate glass window and across the black stripe of highway, the ground was all white now, and hard to locate. "You could have left him," said Tom. "I mean, that's a legitimate reason to."

"Tom, are you sure that boy is not your child?"

"I swear, Julio Dumas, gone far east, is the father. He hates America."

"Does he even know he has this child?" "No."

10-3

It is snowing and I am watching from the window as the ground silvers. The brick around me is almost uniformly dark except in three other windows three other solitary women are staring out towards the river that is screened by a curtain of snowdrops. Mimi in her cell complained of one thing only, and that was the difficulty of finding anything beautiful to look at. She told me that she had a magnifying glass, just a little round solid stone sized cheap thing, and she would turn it around and around in a shaft of light in order to be mesmerized by the multiple whirls it concocted across objects. "Dreams describe the world as it feels." I hear McCool bumping and wonder what it sounds like in the apartment below. Sex probably. Or someone building a city in a closet.

Indivisible

A movie moves in place like certain minds when they think of a piece of river. They gave me a dark cone that night in time, me alone on an institution lawn and lots of night poured from that vessel scarred by twinklers (only the ones I couldn't see). I asked a woman for a ride back to my place, she wasn't very nice but said yes. Then all the lights were out everywhere and I thought of sleeping on the little balcony but it might break and fall into all those citizens whispering out there. Then they sent me my guard and he was checking his arms in a thin-lipped red-cheeked jovial Nazi way. His arms were okay so he left for his own place somewhere in the dark. I called this film Magnificat.

Once, during an all-night vigil in 902 AD, at a church in Constantinople, Andrew, a holy fool and his friend Epiphanios, saw the Mother of God. She was high above them in the air, surrounded by saints. Her veil was like a vessel painted with sails that whirled out for miles protecting people who didn't want to die at sea. I bet her veil was dark blue and spangled with sequins and blinding.

Now I am being easily enchanted which makes me worry that I will not have the courage to go through with my plan. The falling snow across my line of vision is equivalent to music entering my ears. That is, it gives me the impression that I am only a machine built to observe it. Then nothing would be written on my ceiling soon, slashes of shadow from moving cars outside.

One by one the other women turn away, draw the shades, disappear. There is no bumping now and the boy is sleeping.

The camera stays turned on the water but only snow blown on air is shown. My mother returned conciliatory from my film her grave which was really her genre. She was young and kind walking with me to work through this snow.

I dared to say things. We were in Dublin and she replied as you would hope anyone would, with civility, affection, appreciation and concern because I had forgotten my lunch. I don't know where we were or where that park was situated or what city is both medieval and gray and also a seaside resort. That's why I chose Dublin. But maybe it was a city in the next generation, a purgatorial condo settlement on the way around, where the dead congregate in their best suits and spirits for the difficult treck towards annihilation. She was so motherly, it nearly killed me—she was all that I ever wanted! She said we have plenty of time. Let's go back home and get it. The sky was dawning inkily, clouds unzipping and letting out some blue and yellow puffs. It was cold in that snow but my mother encrypted in her dream being was good-natured about it even when she erred, and we turned the wrong way through the years, the hulls of the buildings as close as young breasts.

I wanted to save my mother's history from the eye of the holy spirit so l aspirated and dispirated, trying to fog up the air around her with my own breath. When in The Stranger Merseault's mother died, he was finally open to the "benign indifference of the universe." That's why I called that dream (film) Mother Hen.

10-4

"One day, as a young magpie flew over the meadow, something cold and white fell in her eye. Then it fell again and again. She felt as if a little veil were drawn across her eyes while the small, pale, blinding white flakes danced around her. The magpie hesitated in her flight, fluttered a little, and then soared straight up into the air. In vain. The cold white flakes were everywhere and got into her eyes again. She kept flying straight up, soaring higher." "Don't put yourself out so much, dearie," a crow who was flying above her in the same direction called down, "don't put yourself out so much. You can't fly high enough to get outside these flakes. This is snow."

Henny's mother liked to quote that crow in Bambi. "Don't put yourself out," she would say to her daughter loudly.

This practice had to do with her own breakdown and wanting her daughter to believe that she might die in a fire like Bambi's mother. She wanted this child to save her from despair and watched her with dog-like desire ("Is she putting on her shoes to take me for a walk?") and twisted her fingers together excitedly. Her daughter was unhappy with her, and unhappy leaving her because of her failure to provide her mother with her deepest satisfaction which might be death. In fact the mother got impatient with her daughter when she studied and did homework and wanted her to pay attention to her, so she chatted and taught her to cook and sew instead of study. Her mother had a brain that was deluged like sea-sponge in salty emotional waves. She talked about her own dying hopefully and hoarded belladonna in case she wanted to kill herself one day. Her daughter wanted to be the one to kill her if she needed it and the one to rescue her if she changed her mind. This was because she loved her mother or was attached to her; pitied her; and longed for her to say in a sane voice that she was the most wonderful child in the whole world.

When they were on good terms, her mother read to herself only— Dickens, Hardy, the Russians, the Brontës—and let her read quietly herself. Her mother once had a dream that she was Anne Brontë raised to the same status as her sisters. She was in love with Bramwell and the father whom she said was "quite a sexpot," being Irish and shooting his gun off at the parsonage walls.

Henny's mother loved Libby and so she prophesied the worst for her. And considering she was just a maid, Libby thought her mother was pretty smart and intuitive. But Libby was sometimes ashamed of being friends with a maid's daughter and cultivated other friendships at the Mystic school, ones among girls who were glamorous like Honey Figgis or brilliant and tragic like a schoolmate named Mary who disappeared.

Still, the two of them studied ventriloquism together and threw their voices through clenched teeth in front of any number of strangers. Libby continued to practice ventriloquism all her life, in her car or bathroom, when she was alone. It was a deflection of solitude and was related to her obsessive face-making. In New York in the late sixties and early seventies she was admired by a variety of intellectual and artistic men, despite her Charlie McCarthyisms. She was filmed and painted. She go-go danced on the stage in the East Village, was photographed in the nude and voted Slum Goddess of the East Village. She was skinny, drug-addicted, terrified, but never without dignity. Like a disciplined dancer who gets drunk, or an animal in a crowd of violent humans, she stood out as being complete. Still, she was dubbed The Broken Arrow by someone famous.

"Higher than that unmanifest state, there is another unmanifested eternal being who does not perish when all beings perish. This unmanifested (state) is called the Indestructible. They call that the highest goal from which, having been obtained, beings don't return."

It was the expression on the face of a fetus Libby aborted several weeks into her pregnancy that caused the moment of conversion for her. "Find yourself if you're going to lose me!" its face squeezed out to her.

"Once you become aware of yourself as seeker, you are lost," Thomas Merton wrote. Now the woodland in her was green and bending when she escaped for Big Sur. While Edie Sedgwick and her beautiful dark brothers Bobby and Minty with their warm full mouths and eyes would perish, Libby struggled to outlive that era. She had to leave behind the brown lines of Central Park, leaf-settled and wintery under the stones, in order to become disciplined.

So for years she was gone from me. While I sank a decade deep away from my former friends and acquaintances, becoming immersed in children and the time they required, McCool danced around the edges of our slum estate playing tricks on the kids. Streams of bullshit poured from his lips as he swayed on our broken steps forbidden by law to cross the threshold. Whenever he was down and out, he called them for consolation, always asking, "How's Ma?" But since the truth drove him mad, we all got good at lying, displacing the facts by a few inches, writing fiction.

Ramakrishna rolled in the dust crying "Ma! Ma! Ma!" for Kali.

Aurobindo said that wider Hinduism was not limited to India but had lots of scriptures, including the Veda, Vedanta, Gita, Upanishad, Darshana, Purana, Tantra, not to forget the Bible and the Koran.

"However," he continued, "its real, most authoritative scripture is in the heart in which the Eternal has His dwelling."

"Is there still an above and a below?" asked Nietzsche shocked at finding himself riding on a ball in the sky.

10-5

In the great blizzard, just as it was during the black-out in New York, there was no white and the other black, but behavior. Snow wouldn't stop graying and flying, filling, splitting, spinning, windblown, rising as it fell into itself. I loved my husband three times—once when I saw him giving a homeless man the coat he was wearing through snow.

Once when he almost got off the train too late, after saying goodbye to me and the children and tripped in the gap between the train and the platform. And once when he came out of the clinic knowing that it was his own infertility that was the problem. Sometimes we lay in the dark of our bed holding hands. Sometimes you hear a horse neigh in a movie with one of those painful squeals that old doors get. It can be a man crying. In February, out west, the robin is already fat. There is silver lichen hanging off trees. It reminds me of this snow and not of literature.

"If you'd weave seven locks of my head into the web and fasten it with the pin into the wall, then I'd weaken and be like any man," said Samson to Delilah, but then he was able to do it himself pulling the pin, the loom and the web off the wall. She believed he was belittling her with this trick and so avenged him. Three moments of true love are more like nails than pins. Compassion is the religious term for that grueling sting.

I am haunting the ghosts. You can after all get sick from a dream. Projectile vomit, or projective verse—they are interchangeable in a dream. In a nightmare you can develop the germ for your own death. You can cultivate it in your heart. Once I walked towards my mother's apartment, wearing her hat, and longing to lie on the sofa there beside her, while she said, "Rest, dear, rest." But then Mimi hurled herself over the hood of her Ford, climbed around inside looking for dirty laundry that had spilled, angrily sobbing Can't you help? to Lewis in the backseat beside his wheelchair. Because she felt so sorry for him.

Lewis told me this: "I was sent out with a bunch of foreign journalists across these ice-cracked fields. To follow families being chased from one country into another, where they were supposed to be kept in refugee camps. There were about three hundred of them, moving in rough formation, rag tag as they say. Rag tag. December bedouins. Our van stopped at the crest of a field striped brown, shining with patches of ice still. We saw troops coming towards the people, about a quarter mile away, and watched them gather, climbing out of their trucks, around the people. Men were being pulled from their screaming families and made to kneel, the way you always see it in the movies, hands behind head, and then there was shooting and all the bodies folded into their blood. I mean folded. We didn't know what to do, weirdly, we sat there, paralysed, paralysed, while a couple of the trucks drove up to where we sat. These burly guys got out and asked who was what. British? German? French? American? Turk? Everyone was nervously telling the truth and pulling out press cards and ID's and I don't know what came over me but I said Catholic, when they asked me, knowing they hated Catholics even more than Jews and Muslims. So then while all the others were fumbling around, smoking, laughing, cracking out jokes, my brain was thinking words to describe what I just saw carnage, massacre, incident, litter, atrocity—when one of them just shot me, blam, in the side."

10-6

With a miniature image of the beloved implanted in me, I think my body is both a garden and a factory. A habitat that is a factory. A factory empty of electricity, but a little productive. About like a desert which is no place for a couple. There the sage smells like silver at a table set for animals.

To tell someone that a person contains the blueprint of the cosmos can be misleading because the person can't just lean over and read it. The blueprint doesn't exist without someone beaming the light on it and I hate to say it, but this operation takes a lifetime of excruciating searching. I can't say that the description of this blueprint forms "another" level of reality because I would automatically be separating them with the word "another."

I am in this dream film making dough figures who exist in a state of attention. They are waiting to be eaten. This is not "another" way of describing what happened, as if what happened was a thick and settled thing—like a castle that one could stand and contemplate. Objects rest from their flight only when you look at them without seeing them. I was so invisible, even birds rested mid-flight when my camera arrived because they didn't sense my presence at all.

It is important not to pin ideas down because they can turn into false gods. "To let the real God remain free and clear sometimes requires atheism," Lewis said once. I don't remember what he was wearing on that given day so the words have to stand in for the details.

"The church is a boat so well built that it lets you sail into the horrifying darkness and mystery and allows you to drift, to explore, because it is fit for wind and stars, over centuries constructed to meet unexpected squalls and drops. It doesn't eliminate the horror or the mystery, it just helps you enter them," Tom tells his hands that are pulling at stones.

I would like to tell him that God has already crushed me into powder. Holy-talk has begun to calcify and bone into that powder too. Those refugees on the road, whose children, wives and husbands and friends were executed, know what it is to be left languishing in time. You can be buried alive in blue air and still walk around in a soft coat of gold. But will there be less of God or of me after It has pressed out its energy here? Will It expend Itself? The word holy needs to be eliminated. The Emperor Wu wondered how the word void could be used when everything is void. But "died" is even stranger than "void" because to have "died" is to no longer exist, so there can't be any word for it. At least, however, it is in the past tense. I don't like the word "worship" either, God, because it is idolatrous to separate yourself from God like that.

The divine wafer is baked light as is the cremated body. Swallow the sticky circles it is paste and reduces to the size of an orange seed and goes down with only a little residue stuck in the mouth. Saint Ignatius built a palace full of little rooms for each memory. He could this way wander in and out at will. To let the memories disperse and vaporize all over the mansion would be to lose them as the sleeping shepherd loses the sheep.

It is like the shape of a tall brooding mountain smeared with shadow and black bracken and how it seems to be the last shape the dream might build before it is covered by sun.

Indivisible

Until you see the desert behind the mountain what should be a luscious field is now a pile of bleached bones. The color of the desert is bone. It crumbles, scratches underfoot just like this snowy New England street. Not to become hard or cold is my goal.

We walked on snow leaving the car shining behind us and I was moved somehow to tell what I had done. "Now will you do me a favor?" I asked him . . . I hated his lack of response when he stopped walking and I crunched on alone into the white. The snow stops very suddenly as in all at once after midnight. Snow, which cooperates only with itself, is caused as if by consensus. The sky clears away clouds and lays open its sparking dogstars. The color of the ground is diluted ink, the river thick and iced. Only one light in the building is turned on and hidden behind a shade. As long as the desire to do something is in me, it is not time to do it.

In the third dynasty of Ur, in Sumer, three thousand years before Christ, a dreambook described a woman holding a gold stylus and studying a cold slab of stone on which the stars in the heavens were perfectly inscribed. She was Nidaba the goddess of writing. In fact, she was in this image a kind of architect advising people to build their temples according to the outlines of the heavens. She also says to me: Write in stone!

"Did you perhaps love your husband?" Tom asks.

"What do you mean?"

"Well, why didn't you leave him? Why are you protecting him?"

"Me? From what?"

A veridical dream is the 46th part of prophecy.

None Can Go Beyond

11-1

Lizards, two at once, speed past my feet to another shadow.

Tamar's father-in-law Judah met her in the desert and thought she was a prostitute, because she wore a veil in order to blind him from her true identity. He slept with her by the side of the road and obligingly gave her his seal, his cord and his staff as evidence that it was he who had screwed her. When she gave birth to twins, a scarlet thread was tied onto the hand of the first one out, but he withdrew his hand, back into the womb, and out came the second baby first. Birthrights and entitlements, since the beginning of recorded time, have been evidence of pride as the first human error. People dread equality. They want to establish disparity more than anything else.

First, they wondered, which child was the firstborn. Then: why had this woman been so determined to reinvigorate her husband that she slept with his father?

If scientists could revive the eggs or semen of the dead, then that would be something far sweeter than cloning. The desert produces a variety of tough sticky plants that you can cook and eat, and some sage and threadlike red flowers. All of these seem however to be leftovers rather than the foundation of new life on earth. The ghost of ocean hangs over them, days of wetness and lullabye motion.

When I climb to the crest of the bony hill and see official buildings out on the flatland beyond, wires sparkling like Christmas car antennae, and the usual configuration of drab clay-toned buildings with a panopticon at the center, I turn to call Tom to come and see. He is looking at something else in the other direction.

In the next twenty years surely that center for abused children will be replicated from coast to coast in the form of a prison, each one asking "What is the relationship of crime to crime?"

"I know," Tom says. "Believe me. I know."

"Shall we go down, closer, visit?" Not even the Sabbath exists in such transparency.

"When the embodied one is about to leave the body, When he frees himself from it, what is left here? That, just that! That is the Pure, that is Brahman, that is called The Immortal; in him all the worlds are established and none can go beyond."

"No," he says. "Let's not."

Indivisible

11-2

"Why have you rejected me, bitch?" McCool kept asking me. "Why have you thrown me out of my own home? I admit that I did wrong, but now I want to come home! You should see where I sleep. I want to be back with the children. I will be good and baby-sit, just let me come back."

He appeared at the door banging, shouting and had to be led away by police or friends. When he was raving like that, he always threatened Lewis whom he had never met. Racial skirmishes and marital squabbles crossed paths, the courts being packed with abuse cases, many of them dropped in the courtroom on the way to the bench, the women too afraid of the men to testify. McCool arrived drunk at his custody hearing which didn't help his case. The times he saw the children he was often drunk too, and playing in a pub, while a woman took care of them. He played traditional Celtic tunes alone and with others, and the children were proud of him like that. Once I saw him at a distance and didn't know it was him, and thought, that's a handsome man. He was walking along Centre Street with a woman behind carrying a guitar in a black case. She was talking animatedly to some other woman, I was in my car, and when I realized it was him, the children did too and called his name. He called back to them excitedly and said, Hi, Ma to me, as if he was one of them, but that wasn't one of the times that I loved him. Shouts, waves, recognition, scattering the bitter losses.

11-3

During the Reagan years, Libby returned, desperate, needing a place for herself and her children to stay, when she got the idea of going back to school to become an expert in health care. But it took her several years before the idea took form. This was when she also had the thought that she had to radically change her life in order to save herself and her children. Even while she dragged on pot, she remembered when it was time to meditate, because she had returned from her training in California. "I only get shocked by how big the universe is," she said, "when I am feeling big myself. . . . When I am feeling small, the universe seems tiny too. Because I can carry it around with me, even in the dark. Do you know what I mean, Hen?"

This is also the time when she saw my husband building a shed outside and asked me to tell her more about him, and soon they were having an affair. I was laughing over garlic. My nails were black from the winter-hard garden. Bulbs had been buried that morning, and I was strangely glad when I saw her slip out and embrace him hello and his look of wonder.

How could the dead return to you except through sleep? All encounters in dreams are indications that relationships travel without their people. In those days before holy-talk, but when I had many insights, I only inclined towards aridity in my spirit but my body's storms would not leave me alone. Moods and longings besieged my walls. Working in the dark with cameras, monitors and knobs and watching the images for mergers in design and color, spotting sudden moving gestures from the ghosts on screen, I was a sucker for film but at the mercy of my body. It suffered me while it struggled for a second of peace. Was a woman built to be solitary, thoughtful, maternal, hard-working, hateful and God-crazy all at the same time?

"Why don't you love him?" Libby asked me.

"I don't know."

"It's the Lewis obsession. You have got to forget Lewis and appreciate what you have."

She was blindly looking inside herself alone while I gazed out the window at McCool joking on the corner. He might have been a phenomenon the Indians call a Kesi, he looked so wild that day.

There is no world in which a Kesi belongs—free as the wind, thrilled beyond all feeling common to others, intoxicated like a beggar or a maniac; in India the Kesi supports himself on his own spirit. Solitude and silence, total nudity, no memory, no sign, drunk. He is, to some, a sage. Mother is one of his names.

"Ma! Mom! Mommy! Ma!" the children that day squawked around me and Libby, each one with a separate demand.

"I have to help you get free," said Libby. "You've become nothing but a mother to other people's children!"

Actually she and I were ignoring our children and watching McCool on the window-glass, where he was imprinted and sliding around like something pressed there.

He was tearing off his winter jacket and wrapping it over the shoulders of a hunched homeless man with a big chin. "He looks like Edie's father in On the Waterfront, that man," I said to Libby.

"What's McCool doing to him?"

"It looks like he's giving him his coat."

"To keep? Maybe he doesn't want it?"

The old man struggled to get his arms in the over-large sleeves while McCool jiggled the jacket around from behind, unconscious of our witnessing.

"Yes," I said. "He wants it. I mean, McCool does. But."

"That's so nice of him," Libby whispered reverently. McCool, arms akimbo, shivered and stamped like a horse.

11-4

You have to live an obscure life in the eyes of America in order to make a livelihood for five on part-time poorly paid work. Renting out rooms helped, so that the house from top to bottom was filled with people, the kitchen available to all of them. The house had mattresses scattered throughout and plastic boxes for clothes, books and toys. It was an odd habitat, a noisy place where conversions took place before even the revolutionaries knew it. My tenants included an enlightened idiot, a pauper, a poor villager, a former cowkeeper, a current bookkeeper, and a scholar.

For many years Lewis and I talked heatedly without a third person to tell us the secret of our relationship. But the meaning of such things is revealed only when both parties are separated and have no hope of seeing each other again. After our first meeting, when we were that young, he and I kept meeting accidentally. This went on for years. He behaved like one guarding the seen from the unseen. He never wanted me to know what he was really doing but invented stories about his private life and laughed at my belief. He jumped around excitedly, his brow furrowed and a smile at the clouds. Sometimes he took me into a coffee shop to show me what he was studying.

He was twenty five when he read this: "Within the sphere of circulation capital passes through the two antithetical phases C-M and M-C; it is immaterial in which order . . . Commodities to money and money to commodities. We are concerned here with only the general character of the costs of circulation which arise out of the metamorphosis of forms alone."

"I am a Marxist," he said.

"It is just as if somebody," wrote St. John of the Cross, "were to see something he has never seen before and the like of which he has never seen . . . Despite all efforts he would not be able to give it a name nor to say what it is, even though he perceived it with his senses. How much less will he then be able to speak about a thing he has not received with his senses?"

"I thought you were a Catholic," I said.

"They are compatible," Lewis assured me.

He was feeling cocky and youthful the day he volunteered to go out in that van with the other journalists. He had seduced a beautiful Lebanese woman the night before, and the other American journalist was sick, so he said he would go in his place. He was in his thirties.

Mimi cried and screamed in her Ford and they flew her to him in a hospital in Rome where he was given his first wheelchair and taught how to lift his lower torso from chair to bed to toilet to table. Mimi stayed with him until he could come home. All these spaces but no structures suggest an adaptation to promise. Or a preference for waiting. Or maybe a gift for lacking. His body grew bigger from sitting and more bitter. Jefferson said that people perish when there is no vision guiding them. Lewis said he could tell that everyone wanted to know if he could still have an erection. It was all they really wanted to know.

"Should I carry a card reading Still Functional?" he wondered.

"I don't know," I answered.

I wrote him letters everywhere he went though it is hard to remember how I always knew where he was. Once he actually cared, saying, "I was waiting for your letter. Why did you take so long?"

"Sorry. I'm raising several children," I wrote on my postcard back to him.

And I watched every day for the blue uniform slowly meandering between trees and garbage cans to deliver the mail. It always arrived late in the day, just before dark in the winter. Hardly ever did a letter come to me from Lewis though once a box was left on our steps, and I almost threw it away, it looked like junk. It was a box of dates, with a card reading "eat one for every date we never had."

Our voices became both acrid and tender over the wires. Our laughter lowered. A woman always feels sorrow towards her son. Soon each of us could identify the other by the ring of the phone's bell while in all other ways he lacked psychic abilities.

"It's Lewis," I would know. Would you rather be an angel or a nun? At least an angel can fly, even through the dead zone.

One day Lewis didn't recognize me for the first seconds when he saw me coming. It was definitely me, rounded around. Because my hair was white and my face had softened, he didn't see what he remembered. I was at the age where I felt like a driver who has turned into her car.

"Behold, the lady of the phone calls," he finally said. We went into a bar, he wheeling ahead of me, bald and heavy set. I could see that he would become his father's weight if it weren't for the work required of his upper torso. Swinging as so many children do back and forth in perdition between one parent's indulgence and another's repression, he would never settle between Mimi and Pop. "I'm only working on one issue now," he told me.

"Prisons?" I asked. "Right. Night and day. Have you ever been inside of one?"

"Doing time or visiting?" I almost shrieked. "You know I have visited your mother a million times. This is me you are talking to."

"Oh right."

"How's Pop?"

"He's fading out. Your husband?"

"He's still haunting even though all foster kids have grown and gone."

"God, you don't do that anymore?"

"I'm now alone."

"Well you did your job for the universe. Let's make a documentary."

"On?"

"Attica etcetera."

"Good title."

"I can get the money but I need an assistant, you."

"I would like to," I told him.

"Sake?" he offered. Soon the alcohol burned down our walls.

"Libby?" he asked. "Where is she?"

"Here, getting a degree in holistic medicine."

"Wow. Is she still beautiful?"

"Yes, no one on earth looks like her."

"That's the thing. That's the thing."

"Her children are doing well. She is devoting herself to them." I told him.

"Does she have a man?"

"No! She swears she is finished with all that."

"Great, great. Sometimes I think I should have married her."

"Because you love her or because she can pass as Wampanoag?"

"I'm not proud of that, but racism is all over the world. I've seen it literally everywhere. So in that sense, racism isn't about so-called race at all."

"So then what is it about?" I asked.

"Racism would not exist if no one could see." His own face blended into the shady contours of the bar while his eyes smiled and shone. "But everyone can."

"Then it's structural. Not everyone," I said.

"Let's talk about the documentary, my dear one." "Attica?" I asked.

11-5

In a prison waiting room you want to turn everyone into a ghost and slip through the walls all in a line floating out into the atmosphere. "I know. That would be grand," Tom said and folded his arms and turned in on himself as he did whenever he was there. He averted his face from me and Mimi and spoke in low tones to his wild-haired soul-mate in her green uniform. She had one of those beautiful hard-boned faces that grow better with age, the lines grooved to match the best of expressions—laughter and surprise. She could have been Algerian but she was white American. She would never speak to me though she was friends with Mimi.

"How is your prayer life?" I heard her ask him once when I was silent with Mimi. They both cracked up laughing, almost hysterically, bent over, head to head, rocking. I liked to eavesdrop on their conversations but he spoke in such hushed tones I couldn't catch a single word. I liked his misery at being there and the way it came out as hysteria. Between their bodies there was some electrical force that made them each buckle and shriek with laughter. It was out of character. But when she asked how her son had been behaving, the hidden image of God rose burning to the surface of his face. His was a stormy face anyway, one that both caught and revealed what was coming. He gazed at her with a shrug repeating. Her face turned coldly aside and then she fixed her stare on me accusingly.

The Brahmin of Great Pride in India was a very learned person who could juggle manifest and unmanifest and also could articulate questions belonging to the Western religious traditions. He rode around on a donkey but had an extra dose of pride which one day spilled out of him screaming. It dropped alive into hell. People saw that pride fall and the way the Brahmin immediately became like one of them at last.

Confucius thought nine times before speaking. Was each time identical to make up the nine? And the Duke of Chou held up his hair three times in his bath and spat the food out of his mouth three times during a meal. Everything that has form is also a mathematical secret and has to move very quickly to avoid being solved. I told my children that pride is the most dangerous quality of all. A little too much of it and you bring the house down.

A blind man whispered to me that people were afraid of him and he came to church only because the conscience of the people was roused enough to exchange words with him,. Otherwise everyone on earth would hurry by, addressing the ground. He said his parts didn't add up.

"People are body parts. Where is the whole body? Is sight a sensation? Can it be separated from the rest of the signs?"

I think nothing is either conscious or unconscious. If you want to be fully awake while you're asleep, wash both of your hands thoroughly before bed and anoint the left one with water of lilies. Write a prayer on this same hand and sleep on your right side. You will be like someone editing their own video in a dark room, during the dream.

"I want to try it, I want to try it!" cried Libby. "But what is water of lilies? Do you mash up the stems?"

Westerners fear what is out of sight and like to think that people know what they are doing even while they are not doing it. Darwin and Freud assumed that individuals and creatures at some level select the being that they become; they invent themselves.

"Otherwise, why does something bad feel so good?" Libby wonders.

In the good old days politicians either beheaded you or sent you into exile—they were considered equal forms of punishment.

Mimi loved me but didn't want to see me with Lewis whom she loved more. I loved Mimi, Libby, Lewis and three of my foster children. Libby didn't love Lewis but she slept with him. I loved Lewis and didn't. She did love McCool but I had his body. He loved her but felt guilty because he never loved me and never gave me children. I loved him three times but it wasn't enough for any of us. Lewis could have loved Libby if he had dared but he didn't. He sort of loved me but was afraid to be seen with me. Old story. We were trying to become something new.

11-7

Soon Libby in her learning wanted to practice Tantric sex. She was a healer by then and a good one, her fingers crossed skin like a bird on sand, not digging in but dotting the top with spots of energy.

She suffered over the existence of violence in the world, it made her ill. She believed that men wasted their energy in orgasms when they should have held it in and let that energy coil up the spinal cord instead. Too much released turned them dry and violent. Rape camps in wars used the same energy as that used in killing, maiming and hating, according to Libby. Like that Brahmin of Great Pride, their excess went straight into hell-hate.

In order to teach Tantric sex, she needed to practice it herself, but she had no boyfriend and wanted one less. She was therefore interested in starting with Lewis because of his condition and because they had already been through their affair. Paralysis of the lower body with the life continuing in his genitals and most of his spine. She asked my permission soon after he and I finished work on our film.

"Kundalini yoga uses posture, breathing and meditation to raise your energy, send it up the psychic centers of the spinal cord into your brain," she explained. "This is part of the Tantric practice. It would be really good for Lewis. Someone has been teaching me. It's called 'being poured into the moonglass of pure consciousness.' Isn't that beautiful? Breath control is very important. I'd have to train him in that. The trick is to have an orgasm backwards really, to preserve the semen, or female energy. It would be really good for him, I think. He has so much anger in him. It's an ancient practice, thousands of years old. There's nothing intimate about it, I promise."

"But it's not for me to give you permission," I said. "As long as you don't kill him, I don't care what you do to him."

"You're cross at me," she said.

I convinced us both that I was not.

Lewis agreed to give the experiment a try saying he felt like stone. The plan was for her to arrive bearing perfumed water, honey, ointments and enough liqueur for both of them for weeks. She had been taught by a master who had her sit astride him while he was in the lotus position. He would barely penetrate her and remain erect for one to two hours while she practiced working her vaginal muscles and breathing in unison. She spoke of it with some reverence between roars of laughter. She was like many thin women—without strong sexual content but with a big longing.

"I've noticed," she said, "that the rich who exercise self-denial walk a little stiffly and are dry. The poor who are thin from starvation are ready for anything."

Libby was apocalyptic in her approach to the news and her days, and she believed in signs and portents while being very well informed in an ordinary way about the news of the world. Her fear of endings was greater than her desire for anything. Her kindness was greater than that fear, however, and she believed she could help Lewis feel happy again. "Where there's life, there's hope," she said like the medical establishment. "His grumpy male energy has to have somewhere productive to go," she added. "Believe me, I don't find him attractive at all. I can feel how blocked he is. I know he can be tyrannical, and look at him—he's all messed up physically"

During the first days she only massaged him. They sipped on creme de menthe or Bailey's and reminisced. He asked her if I was jealous. She said no, and then, "McCool would be jealous though."

"Because of me or because of you?" he wanted to know.

"He's never met you."

"No, but he hates me."

"Because Henny loves you."

"Do you think I should run off with her in the end?" he asked.

"Have you ever thought of that?"

"I am thinking about it now. No one else would want me." "Not true," she assured him.

"Well, someone would-for my money or my fame. She's the only one who would love me."

"I don't believe that, but I think you should run off with her, whatever that means."

"We would go live together on an island somewhere."

"Why didn't you do it earlier?"

"She knows why," he said, as Libby reported to me later.

He lived in a luxury building. He was high up overlooking the harbor. This time Libby had bought hard pillows for them both and did some yoga exercises at the foot of his wheelchair before helping him onto the floor. Old Ironsides, she said and did a little ventriloquism for fun. He was laughing then. She said later that his heaviness was beyond measure and she felt dizzy after helping him get down. The whole time she feared getting him up again, or being unable to, and her breathing became spasmodic, she felt pains in her groin, she ignored them. He was more broken than she had imagined. They sat on the floor. His legs were awkwardly placed and she tried to lift them, was dizzy again. They were laughing together by then, the laughter that runs through a river of humiliation, and is a weeping from the mouth. The Egyptians called the iris of the eye a "mouth." Eye goddesses had suns in their mouths.

Istar was a big-eyed goddess like many others in the Canary Islands, Ireland, Malta, Greece, Crete, Cyprus, Anatolia and Syria.

They couldn't look each other in the eye while she kneaded between his outstretched legs and helped him slide back to the wall and then they rested. She unbuckled, unzipped and drew down his pants to give him freedom and took off her own pants. They both wore white underwear. She turned on some Indian music she had brought along but nothing soothed the pain in her groin. She loved the room they were in, the deep white wall to wall carpeting, the glass tables and big leather furniture, the framed awards, the paper flowers and other signs of fame and fortune. They convinced her she was safe. So she could attribute her dizziness to his weight and relax. He lacked kindness, though he was thoughtful from intelligence. He knew a person was as alive as he was, and just as feeling, but he felt no particular sympathy for their plight. He was hard. But behind the buddha-like bronze of his face, she saw more metal and then none, but a kind of opening, like a vault with a red stain at the base of it. He watched her with cold amusement. "What are you going to do with me next?" he asked. "I thought this was about sex."

"Don't worry, it is," she said blurring.

"So? Go for it."

She moved on her knees and placed herself across his lap, her face facing his, her breathing uneasy. "But you need the right attitude," she told him.

"Well, give it to me, that's your job."

This was despair they were both stinging with. They neither wanted this nor that. "You have to open up," she said dully. Then he pushed

her roughly into it, making fun of her tantric fantasy, despising her pity
for him. He forced her onto him, to raise him from his own humiliation.
It wasn't special, sustained or pleasurable, and she was miserable, increasingly in pain where he pressed himself up in her, laughing. Her
agony he took as joy, because she didn't tell him otherwise. Instead she
went home as soon as she could after leaving everything, including him
still half-dressed on the floor beside his wheelchair. At home in her own
bedroom, she collapsed and within days learned she had cervical cancer.

11-8

The house was long, the rooms were crowded. My father had visited
me in the last dream on the right—just before the back door out to the
porch, and he had moaned about his difficulty with traveling through
that space and how heavy his bags were. It was his way of explaining
why he had been gone so long and I assured him "no more trips to the
airport" which made him relax, smile and call I love you to my receding back. The dead grow in stature as time passes. Their personality
intensifies becoming a scent. They seep into the faces of passers-by and
emerge out of trees and restaurants in dreary new forms.

One evening Charlotte Brontë was wandering around Brussels in a
state of profound despair and loneliness. She heard the bell from Ste.
Gudule tolling vespers. And she, who despised Catholicism, though her
grandmother was Irish Catholic, dipped into the church and wandered
about watching old women saying their prayers. She stayed. She was
paralyzed by her depression. Then she noticed several people entering
the confessionals and she sat close by, watching.

Weirdly, as she wrote to her sister Emily, "I felt as if I did not care
what I did, provided it was not absolutely wrong, and that it served to
vary my life and yield a moment's interest. I took a fancy to change myself into a Catholic and go and make a real confession to see what it was
like." Amazingly, she did exactly that. She told the priest she was a Protestant, he hesitated, but then urged her to make her confession anyway.
And, she said, "I actually did confess a real confession." For some reason

she compared her feelings at that moment to being alone on the Thames at midnight. But when the priest invited her to come to see him the next day, she said she would, knowing she wouldn't. And, she warned Emily, "I think you had better not tell papa this."

11-9

Blindness is often considered a punishment for seeing, which is like knowing. The blind, people think, must know something to deserve such an obvious mark of punishment. For instance they might have looked too intensely at something. People fear having the same thing happen to them, and think blindness might somehow be catching, so they don't look blind people in the eye. On the other hand, they think blind people might be more gifted than sighted people because they live in a world of darkness but continue to function. So maybe they should be worshiped and touched because of the miracle of their knowing anything at all. Many emotions follow blind people, so maybe it's lucky they can't see. Blind people are like souls without bodies, I've heard it said. They seem to have seen enough and to be saying, "No more!"

"But of course that's ridiculous," Tom commented.

"How can so many bad things have happened to one little boy?" I asked him.

"One thing leads to another. They are indivisible. I mean, the way things happen is not in a random sequence full of gaps."

"Why can't a relative of hers take care of him?" "There's just a decrepit grandmother in Italy."

"But that doesn't make him my problem."

"You're right about that," said Tom, opening up his car and standing back to watch the boy approaching with his red-tipped stick in one hand and a book in the other.

Lewis was in his usual rush getting into his car. I looked away from them all at the wintery trees pressed on a pink slab of cloud. Then I called to Lewis, "Wait."

Lewis was crashing wheels, chairs and doors open and shut. "You gotta adopt that child," he told me. "I'll help you," he added, "I promise. I'll pay for help or whatever."

"Why?"

"Well, it will keep us close. Almost married." He beamed his smiling face at the sun to see my reaction.

"I don't believe in adoption," I told him.

"Well, foster, or whatever, but consider him ours. I'll pay for everything." "But why?" "I just said. We can pretend we had him. Say yes."

I refused to say yes, but my eyes must have said it because he called, "Settled" before driving away. I noticed he had not promised anything.

There are children just like the god of happiness who dance around and don't let you touch them and run away just as you grab, but there are adults too who leave people soon after they say the one thing you always wanted to hear and those are the people you remember, I don't know why. The gesture seemed like a sister to suicide. There was a wipeout imperative behind it that unnerved me.

11-10

This strange interruption in the scheme of things—this sudden journey to Ireland—is hard for me to explain. But one day Tom—in a little rented car—is driving me and Julio past the Slieve League to see my grandmother in Donegal. She lives in a cottage set apart from a V-shaped road, near cliffs. She can catch a glimmer of water from a window in each room facing west. Her view is in the kitchen and she sits there all day staring at the aluminum gleam on the salt water. She squints at it. She is big like me but bent like a stuffed animal and her white hair is as thin as cotton and her white features fallen into a set of lumps. She has whiskers. Weirdly she knows a lot about me, remembers the details, pours us some decent tea, and asks after my mother and is clearly glad she is dead. Tom is very tall in the little rooms that are smelly and warm. He moves Julio around protectively, and takes him everywhere with him. Now he crashes with his cup and saucer on the edge of a couch reading The Irish Times while Julio hangs out an open window listening to the birds.

My grandmother wonders why it took so long for me to visit her. She had written me months before telling me that she was leaving me a little cottage she owned. "I didn't believe you," I explain. She tells me that American women have no faith and are driven by greed and ambition and are not as intelligent, brave or gentle as Irish women. This reminds her that I am married to a supposed Irishman and she grumbles then asks where my husband is. "We live separately," I tell her and she responds with a story, narrated in a smoker's husky and intimate tones.

"I once knew a woman who grew up in Purgatory. She met and married an atheist, a man she thought was good despite his lack of faith. But he was always taunting her for being foolish, until one day an angel floated down and sat on his head. When he reached up to bat it off, he found a crown of thorns in his hair. Now this is the truth. When he turned around to look at his wife, he was a new person, he had changed his tune. She saw it right away in his features, which had been twisted and now were smooth . . . And after that, they had several children, each one of whom they baptized. You might think about their example, darling."

But example of what? Did he convert?" I asked. "I don't get the message."

"Yes, it was a conversion," she said.

I heard Tom laugh in the other room and wanted to explain him to her before I had to leave her gazing out at the distant tinny water. But really she seemed not to care about him or why I had come at all until she told me to open a drawer in a chest in the livingroom and to take out a packet of photographs.

There was an old orange paper that held together a few treasured papers, two birthday cards signed "John," one very old card signed "Mother," my baptismal certificate from a Catholic church in Donegal years before, and an old wedding photo of me and McCool. There was also an old photo of my father as a teenager outside a tumbledown cottage. He was skinny and nervously smiling under his shade of hair. The other one of him in an army uniform I had seen before. She stabbed at the picture of my young father and said, "That's the cottage. That's now yours. Please don't sell it." She looked at me through filmy eyes and I cried and promised and helped her sit down. Tom was watching all this with his over-sensitive expression, and said, "We must go there at once."

"Did I really get baptized, Granny?" I asked her.

"What do you mean 'really'? Of course you did. Right at St. Patrick's, the way it's written there on the certificate. Take it with you." And then she suddenly focused her face on Tom and Julio.

"Who are those people with you?" she asked me. "They don't look American."

"They are. Just friends, Granny. The little boy—well, I am taking care of him."

"Poor thing. Bring him for a blessing. To Knock. Bring him, darling." Her words rolled around like fog on the rocks. She tipped her head and lowered her eyes when she spoke. The room had a loamy turf smell that only then did I notice. I went down on my knees and kissed the insides of her hands. "There's no time for that," she said. I looked into her face and saw my fate behind it. A cluster of genetic traits. Madness, included.

Tom and I drove for hours along the coast down from Connemara through Galway, along the cliffs of Moher, to Ennis. Just below there, near the water and Bunratty Castle, we found the cottage, in need of repair. So she wasn't a liar. The house was packed out of gray stone and stood in unshepherded fields not far from the highway to the airport. "Isn't it great? My mother lied. I was baptized," I informed Tom so softly he didn't hear me.

Instead he followed me through the rooms talking: "Have you heard of such a thing as saving history, or salvation history? Don't laugh. It's the history of revelations—not just the famous ones like Isaiah and Moses—or like the women saints Cecilia, Agnes, Felicity, Anastasia, Lucy, Simone Weil at Solesmes—but ones that are unrecorded and obscure. A negative history in a way. I think these revelations are like gusts of wind that fill the sails or winds that hold up planes and birds—utterly invisible but buoyant and strong-fillers!—resting places—inns negative only in the sense of their being empty rather than written, or material—the history of these spaces glue together the narrative of the world and pass through certain people, unarticulated they save us all—they come from the other side of the cross—in fact from other cultures and countries, Tibet, the Philippines . . ."

"Why are you thinking about that now?"

"I don't know. Those cupboards need to be rebuilt."

"When I get back here. . . . Look. Julio loves it. I think in some way my granny was telling me that the resurrection is erotic. An erection bursting up out of the dirt. All red, fertile. I mean, in her story about the woman from Purgatory."

"You think so? Well, there might be something to that. Once Jesus has been through hell, his rising can only be associated with re-birth, sex, excitement of the flesh."

"The whole house needs rebuilding and repainting. Too bad McCool."

We stepped out the back door into a puffy wind, it is spring, Julio is standing under a large oak tree listening. The birds are rioting. "What will we do?" I ask Tom.

"Go see Dublin and then go home." "I wish we could stay," said Julio. "Listen!"

Tom has come all this way with Julio to see if I can really take care of him, be responsible for his safety, focus on all the issues that arise out of his not-seeing. I have almost committed myself to taking him home with me. His foster parents, like mine so many years ago, are very old and unable to care for him properly. This contributes to my feeling of inevitability about the arrangement. Coincidence, a likeness, producing a collapse of judgment.

Sometimes you walk up some stairs, or down a hall, and a person is standing there, as if waiting for you. They are at a desk, but on their feet; or next to a bookshelf, face down; or on a telephone, and they wave to you as you approach, they signal you in.

This sometimes seems like a supernatural encounter, like a coincidence—the person being there at the end of thousands of days of walking, seeking, slowing. I wonder if Julio feels that way about me. For instance, what if Mary and Jesus are the ones actually producing all those statues of themselves? What if they are reenacting the traumas of their own sorrows again and again through the hands of humans?

Julio is always between us like a given except when we are in our beds. That night, after driving across Ireland, Tom and I sneak away from him sleeping and meet alone in the comfy lobby of the Mount Herbert Hotel in Dublin where we are staying.

"Do you remember the actress in The Double Life of Veronique? I would run away with her in a minute," Tom says out of the blue.

"Irene Jacob. You're kidding. I thought you didn't fall for women."

"Celibacy wouldn't mean much if I didn't want sex," he says impatiently. We have now mentioned both celibacy and erections in one day. But I don't dare carry the conversation further. I am afraid to ask, directly, if he is gay. I already know that he hated his mother, had a half-brother, his father was a communist, and he had loved someone sort of.

"But who do you want it with, besides Irene Jacob?" I start to ask but begin to quarrel with him instead, as if I have to make small-talk to keep his attention off an absent object of desire.

The subject of politics is a perfect one for fueling an alternative excitement and there are Germans wandering around us, speaking loudly and looking out the windows at the grey evening light that lasts for hours in Dublin at this time of year.

But I have no words. At that hour Libby is still alive in America. Lewis is too. The children I raised have grown and gone. I stare out the window into the blackening silhouettes of trees. A gold-rimmed cloud floats by, illuminating leftover raindrops. The candescence of each spot of water turns one twig into a rhinestone chain. The birds are very strong of voice, their notes are strung with nearly robust pleasure. And I am there to face the fact that I will never be loved by anyone on earth but children.

11-11

"What is the course of the cosmos? Is it Brahman? From where do we come? What do we live by?" The Upanishads are good enough to ask out of the mystery of making choices.

Indivisible

What is a mother if not a body that has manufactured and produced another body? All the parts are literally parts broken off, one from the other, severed, ripped, removed by force. The day itself and the trees planted in space are broken off from other ones just like them, are scattered objects too.

The mother—and almost any woman can be one if she wants—has undergone the ordeal of being physically broken—has had a living part ripped off of her. The mother who lives somewhere separate from her child—is she still a mother—Is the everlasting fragmenting of nature into bits and pieces a motherly act? Are all women mothers-to-be, even the little ones who hate children and the old ones who never had them? Why do so many people hate their mothers? There are institutions that exist for battered and abused children. There are foster families like mine who take them in for money. These welfare buildings that are broken into spaces are like inns in the mind of God—way stations for wounded children, mansions in the brain of time. Words are interruptions in an eternal moan. When a deaf child speaks slowly, you know how slowly you yourself speak, breaking into the long note with stammers. I think Lewis is right. All of us carry the same genetic imprint, but in a specific individual, the imprint has specific exaggerated features. I think he is right, that every baby is like any baby. But I know, too, that there is some strange extra force that thaws you to one child and not to another—some recognition that is like a magnetic field. A fate. The feel, the smell, the weight of the child, these are properties that have great intrinsic power of their own, and make each child special, each one different, each one lovable to one person and not to another. Never to meet a child you love like that—this would be a real sorrow. Fortunately, as you know, God, you can meet a child who is as close to you as your own would be; fortunately, for both of you because it is unmistakable.

The word "mother" is meant to be associated with love and care-taking that follows giving birth to a child. But it also means the love and the care-taking as processes in themselves. Therefore a father can be a mother. At its best, the point of the word "mother" is that it is a quality, not a condition or a situation. So let's say "motherer" instead of mother.

These types are treated badly often, abandoned or exploited. For a while their children reward them with love and kisses, but then the children, like burdens, cause them pain. You have to learn to want nothing in return for anything you do, in order to be an ideal mother. Ideal as in irreproachable and independent. I think that a motherer could be a very positive role-model in our society if she or he really developed its qualities into revolutionary ones. But this person would still have to love—in a fatal way—someone else. Child, baby, or full-grown person.

Why? A motherer is willing to die for the other and she or he is more independent in her spirit than anyone who doesn't love. She has eliminated the desire for rewards by the time she is a real motherer. And of course this is the essence of liberation because it is the opposite of what society wants people to want. If you had a society of motherers who didn't care if they died, who had no interest in rewards, and who just wanted to play all day, what would happen to this world?

11-12

McCool roamed and returned and roamed and returned like a bird wired for my nest. Wherever I went, he was soon on the phone or following. His unrelenting presence was the only evidence I had in my life that there might be a karmic system at work after all.

He was down to wine and bread in the end and raving. I put a mattress for him on the front porch or grass wherever I lived when the ground was either wet or cold.

One night he told me his true childhood story through a crack in the raised livingroom window. "I grew up in Virginia. My mother was crazy and ran off with a black dude, an electrician, and somebody dumped me in a foster home where the only nice person was Irish. I got my Irish passport because my grandma was Irish but dead. I'm scared the black dude might have been my dad. I mean, who knows. I mean, it's obvious. I mean, I'm not."

I didn't tell him that I already knew he was a liar. I slammed down the window.

"I love you, I love you" was all Libby could say to anyone, her shadow ripped like road kill where she hung halfway out of her bed. "I don't want to die!" was written in her eyes. But you HAVE to. You CAN'T have what you want, her body replied. It was this same body's resistance to her desire to live that brought about the supernatural transformation in her final being. She couldn't even pretend she could have what she wanted. And so she turned into a saint, right in front of my eyes.

"At least you have done something with your life," she kept insisting.

"Making videos of dreams is a useless occupation," I swore to her. "Instead I wish I had known this earlier. When you run out of ideas, become an activist, take care of things, or be a prophet who has visions. Don't get depressed."

Now she wanted to travel though she was very ill. She wanted, in particular, to visit the compound on the canyon, and so I flew with her there to stay for three days. She had oxygen and morphine, two muu-muus to wear, a cap for her bald head, and she only consumed mangoes and tea during that time. She was scared of anything physical coming close and damaging her skin. Insects, splinters, torn leaves and thorns in the bougainvillea. I had to take walks alone while she sat in sunlight wrapped in a black and orange muu-muu, rocking on a walkway between bedroom and kitchen. We tested our memories; identified things like stars and flowers; and reminisced. She slept early, breathing badly, on a twin bed beside mine. During that time she told me about McCool and she cried at her cruelty to him.

She showed me the strength of his building, the thick stilts, the strong carved cupboards, the varnished floors and walls, the details around the windows. How hard he had labored hammering, measuring, lifting, sanding, all with belief that they would live there for good. "He was even nice to my kids—took them to school and picked them up on time. Did a lot of the cooking. Oy vey! Och! Ach du lieber Augustine! Mein Gott! How could I have been so cruel?"

I walked the planks and inspected walls and rooftops and admitted that this was a good job indeed that he had done, the rough look of it was deceiving. "He grew up on a farm, building with his dad, he told me," Libby explained. "He said they were starving poor, black Irish."

"Right. Well, he must have been happy here with you."

"Then why do I feel guilty?"

"You always do," I told her.

"No, it was bad. I got bored. But he was so good in bed, you know, being infertile made him seem like an angel. Literally. I could be completely free. But he wasn't famous. He was a loser, let's face it, and all I ever wanted was a famous man. You know that. It's why I'll go to hell!" She bawled in tiny meek gasps, and I felt a sensation in my left temple that had come and gone for decades. It was the kind of pain that lets you know what it is to be a piece of wood being sawed. That is, it was not exactly pain in the usual human sense, more of a final sensation—a rush of too much energy. I pressed it, staggered, dizzied, then sat beside her. She didn't notice any of this but pressed her mouth into the flesh of an open mango I held out to her. The Hindu orange of the fruit against her face restored her soul's transcendence, and we smiled. She now made a monkey face, then shut her mouth and threw the word, "Yum" into the palm trees overhead. I had no impulse to say the perfunctory: "Don't feel guilty." Because I realized that remorse was what had made her a saint.

I have learned that people often get very ill or even die when someone they love is dying, but they don't connect the one thing with the other. They just get mad at themselves for being sick at such an important time. The blood vessel burst in my left temple when Libby was in her last days. I was hospitalized, became comatose, was operated on, survived, just in time to receive the white flowers Libby sent me two days before she died. I only heard, then, about her sublime exit, her words as she slipped away: "Henny, you would not believe it," and her cremation on a snowy Massachusetts day.

Tense

The present tense is depressed because it pretends that it can extend out to either side; that it can catch a fact as a series of words lined up in the same sentence. The past tense is calm since everything it expresses is already over. The past tense soothes its words into inertia until squalor becomes the past's natural habitat. That's why the past is the future of religion. Religions are fertile like garbage coming alive too. The over-now of the past haunts religion; mourning makes all the people stand up and sing.

The sweeping gloom of a church's interior hides the dead in the galleys while the people who pray are on deck and lighted. The dead in religion are its foundation, its energy base.

Monastic life is orderly and thoughtful but many people think it is a lazy, useless way of life. Every person has the potential to be a monk or solitary but only a few tend to develop it because it is so difficult and despised. Repetitious days, prayers, no results. What for? I think the imitation of the clock is a useful practice for all humanity to learn from, and the seed of revelation is buried in the monastery as is the salvation of the contemporary church.

As for the rest, the tenses should be graphically written in columns with the past on the left column, the future on the right, and the present across from the writer's throat where the heart pulses out of and into the past simultaneously. Out of, or in to? How can these be the same action? The dead inhabit the bodies of the living coming and going at will. The will is synonymous with the spirit and the spirit with time. The heart belongs to gurus. And God is as absolutely elusive as memory. It is fleet. It is elusive as in allusive. It is a carrier and an evaporator. Memory is God.

The dead have abandoned the bodies of the living to the world like mothers who leave their children. The dead have taken off in search of deep time. They have no feelings left for the living, or they refuse to tell the living what they really felt for them while they were all alive. This mystery is almost too much to bear for those left languishing on the top of the ground.

You must try to replace the dead who dropped you with someone else who will at least tell you how they feel about you before it is too late.

What is death but something related to faith?

Faith has experience but doesn't want to stop there. Faith knows that getting what you desire is disappointing. Faith converts that realization into a big angry shove against the facts. To have nothing in the way is the prayer of the truly faithful. Faith sounds optimistic but its roots are angry, its stem is impatient, its flower furious. Faith becomes a ghost-shape of the thing it once was, when it lived in a baby. Old faith turns a cold shoulder to new people.

I don't trust faith but I don't trust hope even more. I can't stop hope any more than I can quiet my mind. Meditation is the end of hoping and I can't meditate because I can't sit still and stop hoping. God hates me. I am someone who failed to be whole-hearted at loving God or others. I should have died for something by now. I know this is true but I hope that I am asking too much of myself. I know that I am a failure in this world. I should have been discovered to be worthy otherwise. I still hope I will be. The only thing I have in common with God is that I don't ex-ist. Nobody sees my films or my body.

If they say God is love, I don't know what they mean by love, though I know what they mean by God. I have seen terrible things that a loving and powerful God, who was like a parent, would simply not allow to hap-pen. I hate it when they give God attributes. God is not love or memory.

God is as plain as its meaningless name.

I don't admire haters, though I know some, and I do know what hate is myself, and God is not hate, but may have hate. God is not love unless it is everything else too. People admire haters and want to follow them wherever they go. A hater can be a great leader. Hate seems as honest as it isn't.

To believe in something means to understand it. I wonder if the rea-son haters can be great artists is that they put so much good into their work that the extra goes to making hell for everyone else. Why not do that after all if there is no Christ to be the best critic. Why worry about people's feelings unless you are either superstitious, or nationalistic.

History is not a help, the way knocking wood is. It is not fair. We all share one God in our imagination and it makes our one mind.

Most people are not famous or nation-conscious but live little diffi-cult lives kissing other people in case they are left alone like old moth-ers. The stones that people raised into buildings are beautiful. Anonymously lifted in a communal enterprise that the dead who plied them can be proud of. They aren't. They died and walked away, bored. How do I know this. The dead are disgusting and the dead are divine.

They carry attributes for a while with them and then become slime and/or sky! I don't understand them. I don't believe in them. I hate them. They are often mean-spirited when they return, glueing their eyes to you. They whine about their problems with travel. Yet, in spite of this, I don't mind dying and joining them. Not that there is a choice. But the world and living can be at odds. Only religion, while I am alive, can span the two conditions. Ask God. The sanctuary is the space that opens into death.

You dream of releasing a pack of aging, mangy dogs and cats from a pound and then not wanting them. This is what the sanctuary does not do. It does not release into your care the mouldering and miserable travelers from the next world. Their greeds and hesitations are not your business here. The sanctuary is like the back room of an alchemist's shop where the powdering and polishing go on. It wants to make things shine so the dead won't be able to see their way in. Rock crystal, citrine, copper, sapphire, ruby, violet, pale yellow amethyst, moonstone, opal, garnet, black and gold. I always come back to movies, paintings, ikons and music and how much hangs on them. A lot hangs on me and my never getting what I want, too. Withholding is holding. I withhold too much. Now I know nothing but the sentence of St. Bridget interests me. She blinded herself rather than get married. If she was the man I think she was, she promised herself nothing in order that others might live. This is not a joke. I too fear my happiness would destroy the world. If I allowed myself to desire and to fulfill my desire, the fragile alliances between people I love would falter and fail. They would grow ill, get hurt, lost. God keeps me from demanding anything strongly enough to get it. Why is it only me who has to make this path, you might ask in disgust at my whining. There are plenty of others who do too, believe me. We don't talk about it because people would laugh at us. In parks you see many of the people who have what they want because it isn't much. There, ducks honk like children's toys when the batteries are weak. I think the most admirable people on earth are the activists who take care of the poor. What I don't like about the dead is the size of their secret. It covers them completely. They turn inside out is what I don't like. We are always dying but we are never dead. The dead don't believe they are dead because a word like "dead" means non-existent and words only apply to what exists. That's why they don't understand what has been said when you use that word and they keep talking about being late and missing trains. One of them just looked at me from his youth unhappily as if to present his majesty in the role of tragedy. Never has one I knew returned radiant as in resurrected. Mary returns because she can't get over what the world did to her child. She is like one of those traumatized ghosts who still believe they are alive and completing a task.

Mary knows that people have made images of her suffering in a terrible world. She knows that some of us understand her. Nothing can comfort her as a mother. She comes again and again, saying "This didn't happen!" holding her baby up. She carries that baby everywhere.

Sometimes you see with the dead that it is all inside out. The sheet that is drawn over the secret inner body of the person is stripped away and you see what was buried but living all along. These are the recent dead. Some of the dead just evaporate. But the dead of God are like fiery beings, who can adapt to the freezing skies, happy bodies of transparent light, balls of colors you can see through.

They dance. They are joy. They don't take up space like balloons although they resemble them. They don't waste time. They have been ground to a powder, then a color. Annihilated. They swirl in front of and over you. They don't get cold, don't worry. They only want to assure you that they are fine. Their message is: have no fear. There are no secrets among the dead of God because they are God. Except God does not exist any more than Dead does. This is why there are no names for it or them when they have gone to God. God's inexistence is so deep, black and big, there is no way to see or name it. God is inert. Why bother with it then. What does it have to do with anything that does exist. In fact it is your own business if you want to bother with it or not. God doesn't care if you understand it or not, or talk to it or not. God stays quiet. That is all you can say. In the end, that's what you like about it. But you can choose to try to understand God in the meantime for your own sake. Just be realistic. When you can't enter and describe something, it is called unrealistic and fantastic. Unrealistic is confused with "not real." It is much easier to predict what will happen to people who choose evil than to predict what will happen to good people who suffer unjustly.

When I say God wants me to do something I don't mean that God is saying Do it, do it from somewhere. I don't hear voices or see angels.

I mean God is God and the godness of all being in all time gods that godness gods to God God greets God because it is already God, the rest is colorless.

I am a crackle of static between God and God . . . motion without color. The dead of God, who are they? How do we know which ones turned into worms and which ones into the sky tolerating the quiet in their house, the blindness in their eyes, the losing of their senses, the cold and absence of gravity? Who dares to not fear? Who dares to not land somewhere?

Who dares to ride between all things forever like the chirp from a bird's beak before it finds an ear? I don't know who they are. I don't know who God is, godding inside of me. Therefore I don't know who I am because I don't know where it will go when it comes out in the air.

Of what already happened I remember little though the parts remain dismembered in my godcells. God lives like a dream you forget. God are babies. God are beauty and ugliness. I remember God best when I feel worst. Explain this. Or my mother will because she was always complaining. When you break a real person, you break a little piece of God. The light whitens the pores of the person's skin, colding it, then it dies. I love you is the favorite message of the dying who have a chance to say it. The Beatitudes are great. They and the Upanishads are greater than any words except I love you. The Beatitudes understand the people and their suffering. They say how there are feelings that we all have in common, no matter where we come from and it reassures us for having feelings of hate, grief and littleness, for being remorseful and dry all in a mass.

At Mass they don't say that mourning for someone you loved is a happy thing because they wouldn't say "mourning" unless they really meant that you are intensely unhappy. But comforted how?

What he might mean is that mourning teaches you to love without an object.

Loved means pressed between God and God. Blessed means pressed there too. To not-know where the dead have gone and where, or if you will find them. It brings a discovery that all beauty is a geometry that is marked in relationship.

A blind singer said he couldn't describe blindness any more than you could describe color.

God-talk is nonsense since God is outside existence, so why can't we help it? Why can't we stop talking about it unless God is broken into words and God is not memory and God is not like memory. The Gospels are told in the past tense but after Isaiah who in some way made them. The year then ends with Christmas where it begins in retrospect and it begins at Easter where it ends in retrospect. Krishna, Moses, Ruth, Naomi and the Marys are great but Jesus is the only one we ever hear about who really died. All the others might have just disappeared, gone elsewhere, even Socrates, and we will hook up with them later at some station or other. But you know that Jesus died because he returned and not with his usual face looking sad or angry but as a cheerful stranger walking down the road. Easter is when the earth is reborn and so is Jesus who really died as in "was changed."

The Gospels look back at resurrection from the vantage point of already knowing the Passion at the end of the year and knowing the whole story beginning with the end.

If they didn't know the whole story already, they would not know what tense to use. Most human stories end before death. The people die to life. But they had the past all wrapped up together in a book. They could have left it carved on a stone, but wanted to turn pages, to show how it feels to see things multiplying and speeding by very fast, then also being preserved and contained between covers. Words carved on top of a stone would not convey the way God is always in the present because God is always present so you can be confident of speaking of God as something that speeds past and gets lost simultaneously or vice versa. What is sad to discover is that events in this world are both pre-determined and whipped up at the moment they are occurring. People are bewildered by this paradox unless they can grasp the difference between time and timing. It is like the way they write out their calendar, make predictions and watch events unfold according to plan. . . . and then it all goes wrong and a choice becomes necessary.

The choice seems to exist outside of the layout of time; there seem to be no precedents for what they have to decide. Has the result already happened? Is the choice going to affect all of history?

This is what is shocking about the story of Jesus whose life was prophesied down to its end and who nonetheless confused everyone when the prophecy was coming true. Peter had to make a big decision already knowing what the result of his decision would be. He failed three times anyway. He acted as if his life would be saved by remaining silent. This might have been the first time that determinism and free will came into slam-conflict, setting off earthquakes, an eclipse and a resurrection. Too confusing even for the heavens.

This must be why everything depends on how you place yourself in a book. The crucifixion is a kind of Christmas if the narrators already knew that he would be walking around on the next page. However, if they started with the resurrection, and left out his crucifixion, then you would not be sure he really died. Only having the resurrection directly follow the crucifixion proves that he died. I just wish it all could have begun with the resurrection and none of that suffering of mother and son had to happen at all.

Still, I better be glad that he really died because then I know something about one person that makes sense. You don't know that the others died because they never came back. Something else must have happened to make them stay away so long.

Jesus went into hell for three days and discovered death for the first time. He had to die of course in order to discover where the dead went and report back to us. Virgil and Dante did this too but they weren't tortured getting there so it was fiction.

It was the discovery of the world. In the museum there is a picture of Jesus lying under a flat stone with a light on.

Indivisible

Our ancestors believed that the dead took a journey and they left them food and flowers and had ceremonies to urge them on out. To Dis, Hades, the Elysian Fields, the Great Spirit, etc. They didn't expect to see them again. Meantime their gods were always elsewhere but on earth which may be why they didn't look at the sky for their metaphors. There was an underground god of geography to manage the arrangements for the after-life. The material fact is that we are already in heaven, every minute inside the sky. No wonder the Vatican has a telescope!

The resurrection threw all of us off because it proved that a person didn't necessarily go up on a trip but actually died down, the way it looks. There was an agony following a betrayal and torture, total loss of consciousness and a stone tomb. These happened to be death for Jesus because there he was three days later standing beside the same tomb they put him in. And he didn't look the same but was his soul. In the East there is a returning as someone else, too, after a long whirl through troubling eternities. But this returning isn't usually as fast or as site-specific as the resurrection though Milarepa did return soon to his devotees. It's more of a guess and a speculation by those avenging injustice. I myself believe that there is a system for sorting out the soul-cells according to quality and color and smell. This is why the eucharist is colorless, odorless, tasteless. It is trying to be nothing.

Sneak Away to Meditate

12-1

The moments seem to be what they are—a monument, a shrub, a ring, a hand, a foot—and to have no larger resting point, no gentle bounce in time. I am in Mount Auburn cemetery, on the peak of a small grassy knoll, where there is a sculptural semi-circle of marble, engraved with many names. Libby's will be chiseled there soon. But now there is a large crowd of friends assembled to say hello to her memory, and no officiating religious. Not even a saffron robed man is there. We all watch her children, now adults, place a black box in the ground, then back up. Gravediggers, two cheerful men in a truck, lounge and smoke at a distance. Crematorium, if it were the name of a color, would describe the sky that day. The people sniff, pray, giggle, cough, whisper and gulp. But they are not articulate or boasting people, and have no ritual language for their New Age grief. Some start to lurch forwards, recitation on their lips, but back-step, shame-faced, and this superb failure of words, like an experience of mass cowardice, makes us enemies for a flash.

Even Lewis is there, but set apart at the intersection of Anemone Path and Orange Path. He has lifted himself out of his car and leans there where a stone says Roland 0. His expression is unusually hard, the way eyes get when they stop in the middle-distance and see a reverie take shape. I, too, stand at a distance where I can see him and the hole in the ground through the legs of Libby's children's father. There are no leaves on the grass, though the trees are bare and crowing. The branches seem to speak through the black birds, to use them as emissaries for their mute wishes.

The sun is the color of a perfume in a transparent bottle. No one seems to know what to do, or when to turn to leave. I nod at Lewis whose smile lives alone in the air while I love it from afar. And in that moment I see the old silver car that belongs to my husband shooting like a bullet at the bunch of us. No, not a bullet. In retrospect a face made of steel, the silver teeth exposed and grinning. There is no noise.

Transparency of air has never been clearer and sound's dependency on no-sound for travel. Then screams and thumping, and then the car veers down Mound Ave. and off to the right, spins sideways for a few seconds, and continues away.

Lewis is hit. Wheels spinning like Gandhi's vision of productive village life. The people shrieking and shouting.

A coward's way of killing always resembles an accident. No one knows how to give the last rites, to say any words of consequence to him, but me, I have "I love you" on my lips and him held, though he's not there anymore. Soon I am speechless, clogged and swallowed, while the crows articulate the air's distress.

Indivisible

Some tepid green waters frogged at the bottom of a black and leafy hill. Many were born from Mother Sion, foreigners from Tyre and Ethiopia, among others who thought they had nothing in common. For half an hour we were strangers embracing and moving in a pack stinking of love and fear. Then this concentration thinned and the body was driven away in a van, Lewis was driven off into eternity.

Nobody but me knew what had happened and who had been driving the Honda. Everyone saw silver but each person thought it was a different model-a Mazda, a Saab, a Toyota, a Ford . . . so the police had unobservant witnesses that day. I didn't follow the body to the hospital but gave the police his family's name, though they were all the way off in Missouri. Then I went back to the little apartment in the brick building, where Julio and I lived alone together. Old ice as gray as cobble stones was welded to the edging and knotted up in patches on the cement.

Maybe when humans arrived on earth their wings tore from their backs, the wind too strong for them. Sometimes I thought I heard the ghost of feathers dragging behind Lewis when he moved that contraption. I wonder why he was always held back from ordinary action and cold like armor, even before anything bad happened. He didn't say anything to explain it to me.

Instead a thin layer of pain swished around his skin, and I could sense it, when he turned and wiped his face, but I acted as if what I was perceiving was a white lighted feather between his fingers and not a handkerchief. Likewise he always left me in the folds of the building's shadows and only pretended to care about me and Julio.

Once, I remember, Lewis's knee kept jumping up and down and up and down in front of the white light. He couldn't get the right angle on the film that was reeling around the knobs. What to cut and what to keep, it was very late at night. No one else was in the studio but us. He would then stand here and stand there, behind my chair and beside my chair, back at the wall or hunched over the little screen where the image was projected. I began to experience the air as a kind of toxin, the way it feels inside an MRI or some medical machine that is scoping out your interior.

Charged particles are black on the outside with light inside. Spit on a glass under a microscope will wobble like kaleidoscopic pebbles. Semen too swims at high speed, poliwogs on alert. We liked what we saw. Striped pajamas, a grey bar motel. Lewis liked it so much, he reacted as he always would to a woman at his side. He ran the side of his hand down the slide of my spine, until his palm flattened down and pressed my buttocks. We weren't in jail after all. So I pressed back into him at last and lay upright on the air, leaning, he might have been my bed. We were still young, my children were at home, while his hands moved around and onto my breasts, his face in my neck and my laughing. Then we couldn't stop hugging and kissing until we were down on the floor and our knees, necking. And up again, he was as agile as a lamb, with me saying I love you and him saying, "Me. . .too . . .you." And then it was over as fast as it started, and without more of an acknowledgment than a smile, we were soberly commenting on the cuts we must make. This would be our most intimate hour, in retrospect a black speck, a shell with a lighted interior, some atomic center, potential and immanent, transcendent and hot.

Augustine says that when you love, you are what you love, and so you love nothing, since you are nothing. When, therefore, the one you love dies, you don't physically die too, but you remain as you were in your love-state, before, when the person lived. You are incorporated into nothinglove.

Now anyone might think that McCool would finally vanish from my life after the hit-and-run. I certainly didn't turn him in, just in case I was wrong, let's say. But then I moved very quickly, because I really had nothing much left to say to anyone, not even Tom. I had already left my house and rented an apartment for me and Julio beside the river and nearer to the school for the blind. Tom formulated some plans for when to head north to the monastery and visited me infrequently, perhaps afraid of a mourning state that was outside of language. But McCool had no such fear, as I should have known, and found me.

12-2

He arrived, wet-coated and cold and stinking of gin. He might as well have been wearing handcuffs on his outstretched red hands. After all, what is repentance in solitude?

I let him in, and led him, obediently, to the bathroom first, so he could vomit and shit, and then to his closet. I made sure he had a chamber pot, a bottle of water, peanut butter and a box of crackers. The closet was plumped up with old coats and shoes, boxes of tools, paint, and a flashlight he could use. He slipped right in and sat down, sobbing, and we said the Lord's Prayer together before I shut and locked the door. Soon enough McCool was dubbed the Bumper by the boy because of the noises he made. For three days he banged around that closet, without any method I could interpret from the sounds. He was, in a sense, a musician without an instrument. The closet was a sound studio maybe, as well as an orgone box, a confessional booth, and a safe-house. Whatever he did in there, he didn't try to break free when I changed his water or emptied his chamber pot. Instead he stayed meekly crouched in the dark still praying and shaking.

The superintendent complained of the banging. The old lady upstairs complained too. But it was only when Julio began to seem frightened that I left the door open so McCool could come out. He didn't. Instead he formed himself into a mound in the back corner where he repeated the Jesus Prayer, the Hail Mary, and even a prayer to Hamlet and to Libby.

I stood and watched him. Tinny bells were ringing from St. John the Evangelist, down the street, because it was noon. And I had to meet Tom.

A gold and oily sun lay on the city that day. The children were going on a field trip and stood around on the steps of a library, huddling where the sun felt warmest. Tom had brought them apples and cookies. "I've got a plane ticket to Montreal . . . We're going to have to say goodbye," he told me when the van drove away. We walked in the shade of bricks and ended up on the steps of St. John the Evangelist where I wanted to make a confession. "Can't I just make it to you, Tom? I mean, you're almost a monk, for God's sake."

He wouldn't let me. And laughing pushed me in through the door. The old priest with a lizard's lacy fingers was perfectly nice to me, but even after the blessing, I knew I was lost.

Indivisible

Tom and I dragged down the street together, with me poised to tell him about McCool, what he had done, and where he was hiding. Instead I asked him if he would do me a favor, later, without telling him what it was, and he nodded, perplexed, then went on his way as fast as he could.

Alone, I walked for blocks, noting the whiteness of a winter light on stones. A whiteness that was really a kind of thin gold, a just tone across the tops of things. I crossed the bridge and ran to catch lights, and hurried to a building I had only casually noticed from the car before. It was a dreary fifties-style Catholic church. And because it was Wednesday, confessions were going on there, too. Down a long hall, and not in a booth, I saw the priest standing by a bookshelf in a wooden room, and he turned and smiled and waved me in. He looked like Jonathan Winters, jolly and neurotic at the same time. His heart's face was flat, red and kind. Un-probing, he helped me through my first confession sitting in front of me like a psychiatrist with his hands splayed on his wide knees, his plump fingers drumming on a book he held there. He listened, and prompted me, my mouth was dry, then read to me about how when you are young you put on your own belt but later someone puts it on you and drags you somewhere you don't want to go. In fact, it was what Jesus once said to Peter: "I tell you most solemnly, when you were young you put on your own belt and walked where you liked; but when you grow old, you will stretch out your hands, and somebody else will put a belt around you and take you where you would rather not go."

After I had told the priest as much horrible stuff about myself as I could, he asked me if there was some valuable penance I myself could imagine for myself. I told him, "Not to talk holy-talk ever again."

"That's a good one!" he roared and laughed, patting his hands together. "A true conversion." Then he blessed me.

Rushing and puffing through the yellow air, all the way home, I pulled my hands through the air, as if it was strung with theories I was pulling down. This dream was called The Holy Secular.

At the little apartment I ran into my room and squatted on the threshold of the closet and looked inside. McCool was still there. He might have been the Hunchback of Notre Dame, and me Esmeralda when she offered him a little sip of water and some kindness, up in the belfry. The bell-gongs seemed to come from inside the closet with him. I reached around him and took out the flashlight, and turned it on.

The closet had been transformed from a pitch dark and neglected site into a holy cave—gold iconic images were painted on the walls, faces of the Theotokos, the mother of God and her Son stared back at me, and angels spread white and red wings around them. INRI was written in red like graffiti across the back wall. The space had a poisonous metallic smell from the paint. "That's beautiful, McCool," I told him. "That's beautiful. But come on out now or you'll get sick." I moved back to the window to hear the rain wheeling upwards from the tires of passing cars outdoors, as if Ezekiel was sighing while his Merkabah visions hit the ground. Moans, regrets like the residual hiss of enormous winds billowing around the globe and making bells ring in all the steeples. McCool was full of regret. But he had made a closet into a sacred space. Into the place of his sobs and paintings were sucked the caws of crows, cars rushing, ice squeaking on the river, children's voices and dogs. He came out, saying "I didn't mean to, it was an accident."

I left the room and lost control of myself without using one sentence from a religious thinker. He might, after all, be telling the truth.

12-3

Julio, on the way home, asked, as he had asked many times before: "What happened to Lewis?"

"He was in a crash. You know that."

"I still don't get it. What does that mean?"

"A car hit him. Out of the blue."

The dusk was furry on the sycamores along the river. The brick arms of the building extended darkly out to us. "It's scary," said Julio. "Something comes and kills you."

"It's really scary," I agreed.

Indivisible

My hand lay lightly on his shoulder, we didn't have far to go, and he liked to walk remembering and counting and noting new effects. The cars sped by on our left. I told him, "The Bumper is out of the closet." "Who is it?"

"Just a man. You don't need to worry."

"What kind of man?"

"Good question."

When we entered the apartment, McCool was showering which struck me as obscene, and I stole his passport out of his bag. When I called Tom and told him that I needed him to do that favor now, he agreed to come over. He had been living in the Paulist Center and working with the homeless. Now he was aiming to go north at last.

The sound of McCool's voice speaking to the child made me gag.

"What does it feel like, being like you?" my husband was asking. "Blind."

"Well, I can always tell when Ma is coming, even when she is still outside," Julio answered. "It's not like hearing something special. I can't even say what it is exactly that lets me know. She does everything exactly on time, and maybe that's it."

"Undoubtedly. . . . She took you to Ireland?"

"Once and she gave me the names for things over there because she says she loves words."

"She does indeed."

"Leeks, pignuts, marjoram, mustard, a cuckoo, a bee, a chafter, wild goose, ducks, a wren and a woodpecker, a heathpoult and-um—heather, apples, raspberries and juniper, a lick of honey, a drop of rain and honeysuckle."

"Very pretty," said McCool in his Irish accent and punctuated it with a sob.

"We are going to design a garden for the blind in our new house."

"And I'm going to Ireland," said McCool.

The boy said softly: "You'll see. The birds are sharper and clearer and their songs have longer notes in Ireland."

"Is that so."

"They seem more awake than any birds I ever heard before."

"Really."

"I thought you were Irish," the boy remarked.

"Not any more. . . . I mean, I will be soon. Again."

"Can you stop?"

The radiators banged. I only heard feet and breathing while I prepared their food, and my feelings were heavy as if there were blackloads of new blood dragging on the red. I went to the door hearing a moan, a sob, and the boy asking him—to cheer him up.

"Where does a bird keep its ears? You don't know? I only know now. Don't worry . . . I've made big mistakes too. I used to think that dogs had only two legs and a person's head was attached to its arms, extending out of the neck and the eyes were holes. I have never held a bird so I don't know where its ears would be. Ma says a tulip has four lives and in the last one it might as well be called a poppy. She tells me stories, folk ones and new,—about sewing wings for swans and eating poison things, hiding fairies inside bottles and saving a forest, about The Odyssey and The Iliad. And she reads Bambi, Pinocchio, The Wizard of Oz. . . . aloud over supper. Do you like stories?"

No answer from McCool who had sunk into a chair, his hand over his eyes.

The boy slipped over and whispered in my ear: "I might not get what is happening. The Bumper doesn't seem like a man exactly. He seems to be a baby too. Is he? Maybe there are little people the size of porcupines that I can't touch. This is the main part that I don't get."

"Well, no wonder," I told him. "I will explain later, after Tom gets here." I saw on his small smooth face a look of perplexity approaching fear.

"Everything will be fine soon."

The boy turned his face wonderingly towards McCool whose head was now between his knees. I could tell he wanted to reach out and touch that head to see what it was made of, but he politely resisted the impulse.

"Have you been to an airport before?" he asked McCool.

No answer.

Then McCool blew his nose and muttered, "Huh?" And suddenly

he lunged out, his whole body lurching forward, to grab Julio's belt and slam him down. My body buckled, close to fainting, but in an instant Julio was laughing hysterically, while McCool wrestled him around, tickling and shouting, "Hit me!" and Julio pounded him and pulled his face, put his hand inside his mouth, felt his teeth, yanked it out, ran his hand over McCool's eyes roughly, feeling the bones, then his temples, his ears, which he pulled out and down roughly the way a baby might, and thrashed around with McCool now on his back, passive, allowing himself to be pummeled and explored, arms out and eyes shut.

This was an old familiar scene. I stood back and waited till it was done.

12-6

Tom arrived soon after the game was over, unshaven and wet, and Julio fell forward, burying his face in his overcoat, and wrapping his arms around him, asked him to stay. Tom—astonished—distracted—didn't lift his hands from his pockets but stared at McCool on his back on the floor.

A few speckles of gold paint still shone in his hair. He hoisted himself to his feet, asking, "Who the hell is this?"

"He's a monk," I said, "so be good."

I drew Tom into the kitchen and said, "I want you to get rid of him."

"Who?"

"McCool, that man, the Bumper."

"How?" asked Tom, his face drawn back in horror.

"Put him on a plane, Southwest, to the border. Let him have that place down there, just get him away."

"Do I have to go with him?"

"No, just put him on the plane at ten. A red-eye. It stops in Phoenix. I have the ticket."

"Oh, just take him to the airport?"

"Right, in a cab."

From the door Julio said, "I'm going too."

"What, why? You have to stay with me," I said. I grabbed and held a wet kitchen towel over my face to cool my eyes and whispered into

Julio's hair: "Okay, go with them, honey. But Tom will bring you back here after the airport. You have school tomorrow." For the first time ever, Tom put his hand on me, telling me to calm down, he would bring Julio home. I know that there were actions blind and rushed then, through bags and pockets and drawers, but they all seemed to bounce out of sequence like something solid spilling into parts.! called a cab and they all wore coats and carried keys. McCool had a backpack.

"What will I do down there on the border?" he roared. "It's the middle of fucking nowhere."

"Fix it up and watch your language. A child, a monk. . . . Fix it up. Make it into something. You love that place so go!"

"I want to go to Ireland!"

"Too bad. Ireland doesn't want you."

He jumped towards me, and Tom hauled him by the back of his coat out the door, with Julio still clinging to his coat. "You'll never see me again," were McCool's parting words called back to me from the elevator.

I ran to the window to watch. When I opened it up, icy rain floated across my face, and I leaned out so far the sill bit into my waist.

I saw the three of them, climbing inside a yellow cab, but McCool looked up at me, his face contorted like a tight fist. "Ma!" he called. "Don't make me go! Ma?"

12-7

For at least an hour I lay flat on my back waiting. Once I inspected the closet again, to see the wonder of McCool's creations, those figures and faces painted so meticulously according to some iconographic rules he must have learned somewhere. There was a figure, dark, with arms outstretched, who had silver and gold lines in his clothes and cheeks. Mc-Cool might say that this was his farewell and I would never see him again, but I didn't believe it. Instead I began to plan a move for myself and Julio—somewhere where we would live without him knowing, somewhere utopian, humane and gentle. But a great underlying sluggishness pulled at my ideas dragging them down as if they had too much water in them. I was afraid of McCool who had done the worst that could be done. Afraid of him at the airport, afraid of him at the border, afraid of him returning to find me, afraid of him coming for me when I was once again alone.

Exactly ten years before, during a premature blizzard, I left all my children at home and went to meet my best friends in the Hotel Commander. I did so carrying the weight of my husband like a tree on my back. This was a meeting I couldn't miss, no matter how low I stooped. The walk from the subway to the hotel was bitter, wet and shiny, just like this night. Traffic lights moved slowly on my right, while the brick walls and cold gray trees sopped up the gathering snow. I kept my eyes fixed on the left where dark areas behind shrubs and gates could conceal a man, and stepped up my pace. Lewis and Libby were already seated in a booth in a downstairs lounge, and later that night we would take a drunken walk up a white suburban hill, talking of group suicide and friendship. We made a deal. Then the two of them moved slightly off to the side, away from me, and their faces bluish from the snow-light never looked more radiant to me. Lewis said, "Poor Henny. She knows when she is happy." "Maybe that's why she's so quiet."

Now it was nearly nine when I heard someone coming down the hall and opening the door. I was lying on my bed and closed my eyes, waiting for the worst. But Julio called me: "Ma." I called back and he moved feelingly towards the bed and lay down there beside me, his cheeks rosy and cold.

Tom stood at the door and said, "Well, it's done. He's gone. Meek as a lamb once you were out of sight."

"Thank God for that," I said.

"So now," Tom announced, "I'll go."

Julio asked: "Till when? When will you come back?"

"Tomorrow—briefly—I'll see you off to school."

"Then why don't you sleep here? On the couch?" Julio asked.

"Scared the Bumper will come back?" Tom laughed. His face was bewildered, nervous, as he glanced around himself.

"No."

"Then what?"

I pulled off Julio's shoes and socks and got him his pajamas to put on, while Tom reluctantly unpeeled his coat and muttered that he might as well sleep over, if he was coming back anyway. I slapped out some sheets and laid out a quilt on the sofa, invented a pillow and sat on top of them all to test them. Tom stood awkwardly watching, his coat on his arm.

"Now what's wrong?" I asked him. "You've changed your mind?"

"No, no."

"So make yourself at home . . . Thank you . . . And goodnight."

I jumped to my feet, Tom took my hand as if to shake it formally, but instead he held it in both of his, and said, "I have changed my mind actually."

"Typical. You want to go home, then leave for Canada tomorrow, right?"

"No. None of that. I think I've decided. It's better. For me, for him, for Julio, for me to stay with you. For us to just keep on going. Together, I mean. Don't you think? I mean, what's the point in seeking meaning, so to speak, when this is what we have here? This child? I mean, something has to have meaning. And it would be a corporal act of mercy like visiting prisoners, or the sick."

"Really?"

"That's what I think, I mean."

"Or think you mean."

"Right."

"Tom, don't worry. You continue the way you were going. We'll be fine."

"I thought you'd be glad!" he protested.

"I'm glad you thought of it, and meant it. But no, go, or sleep, then go."

"The Buddhist Dogen once told a story about a monk asking his old master what to do when hundreds of myriad objects come all at once. And the master answered, just don't try to control them," Tom said to me with a knowing smile. But I had plugged my ears with my fingers while he was talking and could barely hear the words. "Did you hear me? What do you think it means? No answer?" A long pause and then "Okay, I'll sleep, then go," he assented, his face morose and shaded with a kind of apprehension that involved leaving me. "You sleep too, you've been through a lot."

"You go first."

"Don't worry. I won't look. Good night."

"Good night, Henny."

I went into my room, fell on the bed hard and rolled up beside Julio under the covers. Our feet were as cold as charity. He asked what was wrong. "Nothing, just tired."

He felt my face with the palm of his hand and brushed my hair back from my forehead. Then he rested his hand in the nape of my neck, as he always did when I told him a goodnight story. "You feel okay," he said. "Will you tell me a story?"

"Well. Now, okay. . . . This is an old, old one. Native American. I remember it was an old woman who told it to me when I was just a little girl. I slept in her bed for a few months and she told me stories, and strangely this is the one I remember from then."

"Go on, Ma."

"Once upon a time the sun was cheerfully burning in the sky and lighting up the world for everybody as usual. In those days the sun shone all the time, and there was no night. But suddenly the poor sun started to fall, spinning in flames, down, down onto the earth. It burned harder and harder but got smaller and smaller—until it became a tiny little human, a boy who was both weak and blind. He was like a little spark stuck inside of a person's bones. But he could no longer make everyone else see, the way he did when he was the sun. This upset him. Everything was scorched and brown around him, and the light was very dim.

"Meantime, nearby in a small village a big important chief was testing all the young warriors to discover one who would be a suitable husband for his beloved daughter. The warriors were all failures, one after the other. Either one was too greedy, or one was too drunk, or one was too funny, or one was too melancholy and one too mean—but whatever each one did, it ruined his chance at getting the girl to marry him. And at the same time the sky was everdarkening, and the world seemed to be closing down for a very long and cold night. The people were scared, and the chief's daughter was especially upset because she couldn't see anyone she could love.

"At that moment the weak boy—the spark—wandered across the sand and out of the desert not knowing anything about the contests going on. He stood and watched, with his mouth open, just the way you do. And I bet you can guess what happened. Yes. He—the poor sun, who had fallen to the ground—entered the contest and proved himself worthy! He really did. So of course the happy chief handed his even happier daughter to him right away.

"And at that moment the boy immediately grew huge and fiery and flared back into the sun in front of everyone's eyes and she, enflamed with love for him, became one with his fire and they melted and rose up into the sky together, filling the world with light and color again."

I watched the boy smile while he mused on the story, and then he said: "But you forgot something, Ma. What did he do to prove himself worthy?"

FANNY HOWE is the author of more than thirty award-winning works of poetry and prose, including *Night Philosophy, Love and I, The Needle's Eye, Come and See, The Winter Sun, The Lives of the Spirit/Glasstown: Where Something Got Broken*, and *Selected Poems*. Her fiction has been honored as a finalist for the Man Booker International Prize. She lives in New England.

Nightboat Books, a nonprofit organization, seeks to develop audiences for writers whose work resists convention and transcends boundaries by publishing books rich with poignancy, intelligence, and risk.

The following individuals have supported the publication of this book. We thank them for their generosity and commitment to the mission of Nightboat Books:

Heidi Arnold
Jennifer Chapis
Nick and Suzanne Chapis
Sarah Heller
James Muldoon
Rebecca Newth
James and Carolyn Patterson
Beverly Rogers
Anonymous (4)

In addition, this book has been made possible, in parts, by a grant from the New York State Council on the Arts Literature Program.